Aedifex:
the creator, designer, builder...

the *Aedifex*:
Building the
Pont du Gard

Thomas Hessler

This is a work of fiction. Persons named in the story may be real or fictitious. Incidents in this story may be actual or a creation of the author's imagination.

First Printing: August 2013
Second Printing: October 2013
Third Printing January 2014

the *Aedifex*: Building the Pont du Gard

ISBN-13 978-1492186038
ISBN-10: 1492186031

Printed by CreateSpace, an Amazon.com Company

Available on Kindle and other devices

DEDICATION

This work is dedicated to my father, Fred C. Hessler, to whom the world of numbers was fascinating. I must have inherited some of that penchant.

ACKNOWLEDGEMENTS

Once again I am indebted to my critique group, members of the Sacramento Suburban Writers Club, for their 17-month endurance run while reviewing this work. Those who contributed mightily to the story's sense of time, grammar, believability, descriptions, sensitivity, brevity, mathematical sensibilities and jargon are MaryLou Anderson (Edson), Westley Turner, Ron Smith and Mort Rumberg, all authors and insightful readers. On a parallel path, my friend, Jaqueline Conway, made sure that I paid attention to the human elements of the characters, letting me know when I had not presented one or another's viewpoint correctly, or slighted them when they should be observed or heard from. Also, once again, I thank MaryLou Anderson for accepting and accomplishing the supreme challenge of the final edit.

I consulted Linda Glazier about horses, their gaits and riding speeds. Noel Gregorian helped me on several French phrases. Larry Pagendarm and Mary Gorden provided a close review of the proof copy, performed nobly under duress of time. Jim Siler, former president and CEO of Underground Construction Company, Inc. reviewed the work for construction details. All are members of the Hangtown Hiker's Club, Placerville, California.

My appreciation to Elfrena Foord for providing the circumstance in which I was introduced to the Pont du Gard.

I appreciate and acknowledge those who will read this book, perhaps also fascinated, as I am, by what mankind has accomplished in the past. I hope they are as enriched in the reading as I was enriched in researching and investigating the territory, the people, the history, and the accomplishments.

The reader may be interested in viewing the list of "Suggested Reading" at the back of this book, works from which I gleaned interesting and valuable information about customs, Roman.

FOREWORD

One is overwhelmed in the research, struggling to discover and understand Roman architecture, engineering, building techniques, food, clothing, customs, nomenclature, and history. But the struggle is nevertheless dwarfed by this glimpse of Roman accomplishment—building the aqueduct of which the Pont du Gard is but one structure.

I've been involved in the building of many large projects, understand their complexity and am awed by the process—the original concepts, the intelligent consideration and consolidation of ideas, the detail engineering so needed in order to create order out of chaos, the gathering of materials and fashioning into superior products, the use of equipment, tools, devices, and the incremental drip of manpower expended, day-by-day, all focused on the eventual result. You might think that building a large project was less complex, more primitive, two-thousand years ago, soldiers with whips behind slaves, directing them to move this rock to that location.

No! They had to deal with the complexities and exert no small amount of sophistication to create their works. However, there is very little information on the building of this project—not much, really on the building of any of the colossal Roman projects. Yes, we can see the remains, we can study Vitruvius's *Ten Books of Architecture*, created during our time of interest, we can glimpse sketches of devices presumed to be used. But, for the actual process—a description of their methods—very little. There are no documentaries, Nova programs, or colossal movies that portray these dramatic, monumental, and significant efforts. One is left to imagine how the project would be built. I relied on my engineering and construction background, imagining the execution of the project, one step, then the next, keeping in mind the total effort. I think you will be surprised at the sophistication required of these ancient builders, yet, it all had to happen and somebody, many, actually, were involved.

As you read, if you are not already immersed in the building of large projects, you will understand how this project and many large projects are executed. The processes that are required today were required in the past, or should I say —the reverse is true. Those who *are* immersed—already understand the building of large projects—may be surprised to see parallels with modern methods and processes; that thought will surely occur to anyone.

This story is meant to entertain those who are familiar with the world of engineering and those who are not. Therefore, at times some will think the work, in spots, is too technical, while others will think explanations too simplified. I ask for your patience in my attempt to shine a light on the activity of the engineer so that those not involved will grasp the nature of the work.

I found that various assumptions have been made involving the means the Romans used to build this project. Some of these would not have been reasonable. Descriptions of many of the processes or procedures used are not available in our literature; therefore, I had to imagine the ways, reasonable ways, available to the Romans, to get the task done. It was great fun.

As I walk the paths along the remains of the aqueduct, as I view the Pont du Gard, I have the feeling– for me more than on any other ancient structure– that there were real people, with lives of their own, involved in the building of the project. As I wove the story, those people became real to me and it would be difficult to convince me, at this time, that those actually involved were not the people I created and did not take the paths that must have occurred.

It was my privilege to be so intimate with the building of a monument, so significant of our past. My fondest hope is that I am able to transmit some of that understanding and awe to the reader.

It is my intent that locations, dates, timing, customs, history and descriptions be as accurate as possible so that the reader can rely on such for a solid understanding. Nevertheless, some of these were imagined. However, I would be surprised to find that this story would be far from the truth.

Oh, yes, the engineering mind. Since we are exploring the world of engineering and because there is little literature written on the activity of engineers, we will spend a little time discussing the ways of engineers, heretofore enjoying only scant coverage. It is my hope that the reader will be left with a better understanding of engineering and the folks that prowl those avenues.

Thomas Hessler

LIST OF CHARACTERS
Characters (appearing more than once)

<u>Time, Roman</u>
Appius Petronius—tasked to find a water source
Antonia Petronius—wife of Appius
Claudius, Emperor of the Roman Empire,
    41-54 A.D.
General Artius Crassius—general with troops
    in region
Flavius Darius—the centurion
Vernius Portius—quarryman of Nemausus
Quantus Tarius—low bidder on quarry work
Bernius Caelius—the *architectus* and friend of
    Appius
Vibius—designer of underground aqueducts
    and tunnels
Gaius—designer of arches—the bridge
Numerius—designer of foundations and
    aboveground structures
Tarus Lartius—carpenter in Nemausus
Servius Arrius—the killer
Sergius Petronius—son of Appius and Antonia
Juliena—sister of Antonia
Publius Acilius—contractor for the bridge
Nemus Amatius—Leader of the *Aqua Corporata*,
    aedile
Marcus Atius—Member of *Aqua Corporata*,
    Appius interface, *aedile*
Julius Sergius—Member of *Aqua Corporata*,
    aedile
Aulius Acilius—Member of *Aqua Corporata*,
    aedile
Titus Domitius—Member of *Aqua Corporata*,
    aedile, partner of Quantus Tarius
Lucius—Young man from Ucetia
Tinius—associate worker with Appius
Decimus Nautius—employee watching quarry
    operations
Pentius and Marius—two woodsmen employed to
    assist on the survey

LIST OF CHARACTERS (cont.)

Twentieth Century

Warner—Engineer, constructor, researching the PdG
    in modern times

Renat—Retired engineer; worked in U.S. with
    Warner

Maurice—a French engineer interested in the
    Pont du Gard, friend of Warner

Laurie—Assisting Warner in his research; Ha!

Lisele—A friend of Maurice, mother of Laurie

Dr. Durand—Professor of Archeology, Marseille

M. Grambeaux—Chairman, Nimes Antiquity
    Committee

TERMS AND PHRASES

Roman term/phrase	Meaning
aedifex	Architect, builder, creator
aediles	Those responsible for the maintenance of public works
Alzon	A river in southern France; joined by the *Fountaine Eure*
amphora	Ceramic wine container with handles and tapered bottom
aquarius	Water carrier person (as used here)
architectus	Architect
basilica	Town hall, city hall
Castellum	The terminus of the aqueduct in Roman *Nemausus*
centurion	A Roman professional officer commanding 80-100 soldiers
chorobate	A device used to establish level; 20 foot beam on legs
cognomen	A third name: nickname, identifier, family differentiation
corporata	A commercial operation (*Aqua Corporata*) a water company
corn factor	A dealer in grain commodities
decanus	A military leader of a squad (eight men); a sergeant
equestrian class	A rank below senator, often involved in commerce
fontis	The source (or spring as used in this work)
Gard	River in southern France; sometimes called *Gardon*
Gardon	River in southern France, sometimes called *Gard*
hortulanus	Gardener
imperator	Emperor of the Roman Empire
lectica	A portable couch carried on poles by four men
lictor	Officer of the Imperial Roman court
Lugdunum	A town in southern France, now called Lyon
Nemausus	A town in southern France, now called Nimes
nomen	The second Roman name, often identifying family

<u>Terms and Phrases</u>, Continued

Roman

Ostia Antica	The port city of ancient Rome
palatium	Palace of Roman emperor
praenomen	First or given Roman name
Palatine	One of the seven Roman hills, above the Forum
Pannonia	Province of Roman Empire; current Austria, Hungary, Croatia
peristyle	A columned porch or open colonnade
petasus	Hat
petit dejeuner	Breakfast
pontis	Bridge
Pontis Vardo	Bridge over the river Vardo (now the river Gard)
quastor	An appointed public official
Rossello	A city in southern France known for ochre: now Roussillon
sestertii	Brass Roman coins; one buys 2 loaves of bread; buys one liter of wine
stola	Female version of toga
toga	A long wool garment (20 feet) wrapped around body; men
Tour Magne	A corner tower in the wall of ancient Nimausus
tri-nomen	The three names of Romans (*praenomen, nomen, cognomen*)
tunica	Tunic: worn by women and men; shoulder to knees or ankles
Ucetia	Town in southern France, now Uzes (source for Nimes aqueduct)
Versus Pontis	Toward the bridge: now village of Vers in southern France

<u>Months (Roman era)</u>

lanurarius	January
Februarius	February
Martius	March
Aprilis	April
Maius	May
lunius	June
Quintilis	July
Sextilis	August
Septembris	September
Octobris	October
Novembris	November
Decembris	December

<u>**Terms and Phrases**</u>, continued
French Terms and Phrases

café American	Coffee made by adding hot water to shots of espresso
combes	A fold of rock
Fountaine Eure	The spring, near ancient *Ucetia*, source of the water for the aqueduct
garrigues	A low lying scrubland; thick brush
La Fountaine	Springs in ancient Nemausus (Nimes) the original water source for the city
Maison Carree	A temple in Nimes (ancient Nemausus) dedicated to the sons of Agrippa
Nimes	A city in southern France: ancient Nemausus
petit dejeuner	Breakfast
Orange	A city in southern France: location of the Theater of Orange (Roman)
Uzes	A city in southern France: ancient Ucetia

English Terms and Phrases

constructor	A professional involved in the building of structures: often an engineer
windrow	A lengthy, triangular profile pile of excavated earth
falsework	Temporary supports for concrete structures or arches

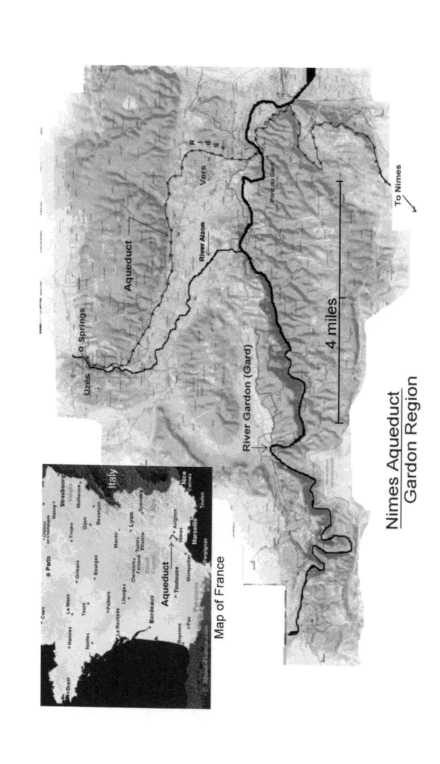

Map of France

Nimes Aqueduct
Gardon Region

Aqueduct Routing
Current Nomenclature

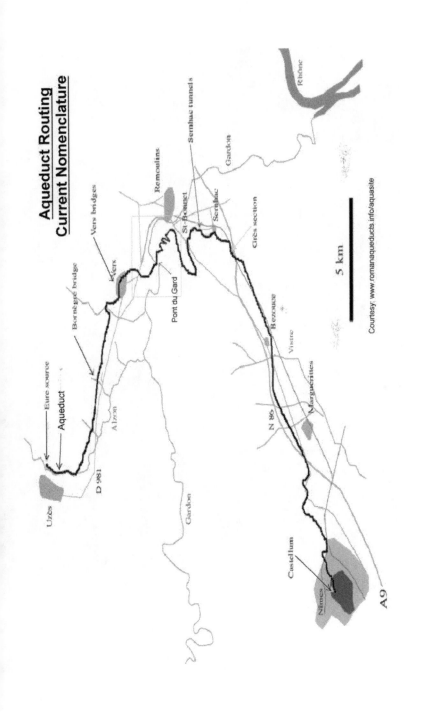

Courtesy: www.romanaqueducts.info/aquasite

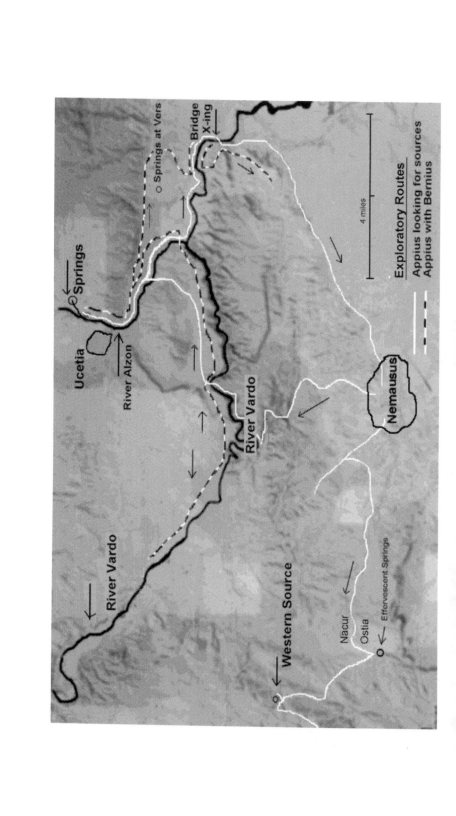

Springs

Ucetia

River Alzon

Springs at Vers

Bridge X-ing

River Vardo

River Vardo

River Vardo

Nemausus

Western Source

Nacur

Ostia

Effervescent Springs

4 miles

Exploratory Routes

Appius looking for sources

Appius with Bernius

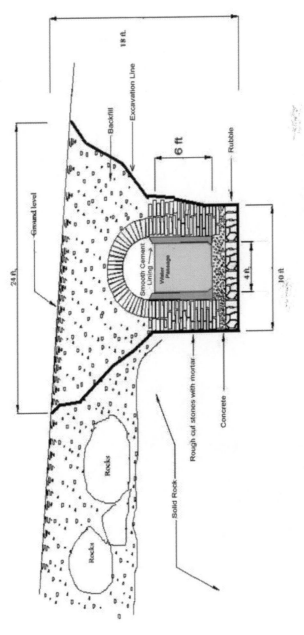

Section view-Underground Conduit Construction

18 ft.

Excavation Line

Backfill

6 ft

Rubble

Ground level

Smooth Cement
Lining

Water
Passage

24 ft.

4 ft.

10 ft

Rough cut stones with mortar

Concrete

Solid Rock

Rocks

Rocks

CHAPTER 1

Southern France, near the end of the Twentieth Century

Renat drove the twisting road through the canyon, a French challenge aggressively met, of course. I didn't know our destination. Renat had driven me to several remarkable ancient sites built in the Roman era—surviving, still functional. We had visited the Coliseum in Nimes and the Theater in Orange, both outstanding works. A tennis match would be played the next day in the Nimes Coliseum. Because I had spent my career in building, constructing and engineering, I had great appreciation for the structures man had wrought two thousand years ago.

I was chatting with Renat as he was driving. I'm sure he'd told me where we were going, what we were about to see, but due to his accent, my limited understanding of French, and my ignorance of ancient Roman structures, I was along for the ride, anticipating nothing. We cleared a turn in the canyon. Into my view, filling the entire scope of the windshield, lofting over us, surviving from two millennia in the past was an imposing three-tiered arched structure. It was as if the Roman era had suddenly sprung into my existence. I yelled at Renat, "What is that? Stop!"

Renat displayed a forced calmness, a slight smile on his lips as he dutifully responded to my request and steered the car to the side of the road. His response implied ownership, pride, and an understanding of the expected impact on me. "Warner, my friend, that is the Pont du Gard."

The car stopped, and I got out and gawked. I pointed to the structure, 160 feet above the river, not a crumbled ruin, but nearly intact. I demanded, "What is this?"

Renat responded in subdued tones, speaking reverently. "The Pont du Gard is part of an aqueduct supplying water to Nimes—or did so in ancient times. The aqueduct is over 50 kilometers long, bringing water from the *Fontaine Eure*. At this location, the water must cross over the River Gard... so, *Pont... bridge*, in French, over the River Gard. It was built by the Romans, two-thousand years ago."

"But...?" I had been transformed; I was now living in the era of the Romans. I would not have been shocked to see a legion

1

march or large-wheeled carts drawn by horses traverse the roadway at the lower level of the three-tiered arches. I don't remember ever having had this experience, the ancient past coming alive as I viewed the ruins. I could look at the Nimes Coliseum or the Theater at Orange and not have this feeling of presence. I said nothing for a while as I stared and unconsciously absorbed the significance of the structure.

I eventually looked back at Renat to register my appreciation and awe. He was pleased. He must have known the impact the structure would have on me. I said, now achieving a grip on my thoughts, "Can you tell me more about this?"

"Yes, of course. You can see the actual aqueduct on top, supported by the highest of the three tiers of arches. The aqueduct was covered... is still covered, as you can see... with flat stonework. It is possible for you to walk along the top. Would you like to do that?"

I was gradually taking account of the structure. "Yes, I would. I absolutely would," I answered. Looking at the structure, I noticed protruding blocks of stone just beneath the arches, obviously arranged to support the falsework used to hold up the arch before the keystone was set and the arch filled in. I've never seen an ancient structure where the construction details were so obvious.

"There is no cement in this structure." Renat pointed. "Every stone is fitted one against the other—no mortar."

I shook my head. The thought came to me that all these stones had to be lifted into place, 160 feet above the land... above the river in many instances. *What were the Romans thinking? They had to believe they would be around for a long time to have put this much effort into a facility this far from home.* "You say that the total aqueduct is 50 kilometers?"

"Yes, 50 kilometers. And, in that distance the source of the water is only 12 meters above the terminus in Nimes. You would understand this more than I, but to have engineered—surveyed— for this little of a difference in elevation is supposed to be of some difficulty." It was clear Renat was proud of every aspect of the project. He didn't need to say that his heritage to the ancient world substantially eclipsed anything we could offer in the New World, that the ancient civilization that existed here was of great importance in the history of the world and, for all of America's accomplishments, that history could not be trumped.

2

the *Aedifex*: Building the Pont du Gard

I had to agree.

"Let's go up," he said.

I nodded, but stood gazing for a while before I walked to the car. I wanted to burn the image into my memory, to be able to always recall the way I had seen the magnificent structure at my first viewing.

In the car, before he started the engine, Renat handed me a typewritten sheet. The heading said, *Henry James, 1884,* followed by....

> *The hugeness, the solidity, the unexpectedness, the monumental rectitude of the whole thing leave you nothing to say — at the time — and make you stand gazing. You simply feel that it is noble and perfect, that it has the quality of greatness... When the vague twilight began to gather, the lonely valley seemed to fill itself with the shadow of the Roman name, as if the mighty empire were still as erect as the supports of the aqueduct; and it was open to a solitary tourist, sitting there sentimental, to believe that no people has ever been, or will ever be, as great as that, measured, as we measure the greatness of an individual, by the push they gave to what they undertook. The Pont du Gard is one of the three or four deepest impressions they have left; it speaks of them in a manner with which they might have been satisfied.*

Almost... my thoughts. I chuckled to think that Renat had anticipated my reaction, to have prepared the Henry James passage for me. I looked sideways at him. He was smiling as he started the engine. I reached over the seat, retrieved my attaché on the back seat and carefully stored the sheet, but only after re-reading it.

We drove to the abutments and climbed the riverbank to the top of the structure at the level of the water conduit. There was a stair upon which one could climb to the slabs covering the conduit. You could also observe the width and depth of the aqueduct water passage and see the deposit of limestone on the sides, evidence of use for many years—as vast quantities of water were transported to grow crops, to bathe and to quench the thirst of the ancient civilization. I couldn't help but feel awed by what they had accomplished—with primitive gear. Now I understood the tasks occupying man in the ancient world. Energy and time was spent building things—the hard way.

As we walked across the slabs on the narrow top of the aqueduct to a location over the river, I was wary. Although I had, in my career, been atop a number of tall structures with little to keep me from taking a plunge, I still had a great respect for taking care, always mindful that I was somewhat clumsy. Renat led the way and turned to smile at me, but I noticed that as he turned he made a very tight circle with his feet. I was exhilarated—not just from the height, but to be a part of this colossal structure, bathed in the euphoria of being intimate with a feature, significant in the growth of civilization.

After we climbed down from the structure, I was able to buy photographs and a book in order to quench some of my curiosity and help me remember what I had seen. I dallied, still transfixed, as I tried to imagine the construction, imagine what it was like... two thousand years ago. Reluctantly, I strolled with Renat to his car. We drove to a café where we would have our dinner. An exceptional day.

"So what do you think of our sites?" Renat, now smug, wanted me to unload, wanted to hear me exude my appreciation, enthusiasm and pleasure. He exalted in a triumphant smile. "I'll order some wine first," he said, "a bottle—to commemorate your day."

I was still somewhat worked up, sitting erect in my chair, fists on the table. But, at his words, I leaned back, consciously relaxed and gave him the compliment he deserved. "Renat. I couldn't be more fascinated. I can't think of anything that would have been more exciting for me to see. I'll have to tell you I was ignorant—I didn't know what the Romans had built here—really don't know much about the Romans, at all. But, you've started me on a path, and I want you to know that you've added measurably to my life." It was a little flowery, but I felt expansive and magnificent, a mood to match the structure. The wine arrived and our allotment poured. I tipped my glass to Renat, and we performed the ceremonial clink. "To you, Renat, I'll be forever thankful."

Renat took the obligatory sip. "Perhaps, if you are so intrigued, you'll come back, take more time to investigate the aqueduct, drink more wine, eat more of our French cooking and pastries."

Quite some time ago, Renat worked in the U.S. on a hydroelectric project on which I had also worked. He was related to the owners of a French construction company, owners having a social relationship with the principals of the people who owned the company I worked for. An arrangement was made for him to work on our project. He enjoyed the six months, a single, young French engineer, charming the locals, male and female alike. I had befriended him, taking him here and there, invited him to my house, drank beers with him after work.

We kept in touch these thirty years, and he had continually invited me to visit his French home. Finally, I found the time and the gumption to do so. He had returned the favors and more, driving me from Paris through the Bordeaux region, to the Cote d'Azur, Monte Carlo and now, on my last day, had introduced me to an intrigue I could not ignore.

I replied, "Renat, I'll be retiring in three months. I'll take your offer and your challenge. I *will* be back. I'll read and research what I can about the Pont du Gard and Roman structures. Then I'll be here, touching the structure, walking the length of the aqueduct. I'll make my investigation the highest priority of my post-retirement life. I'm on my own; I have enough money to get by, and it's time I did something that really excites me. I have you to thank." I tipped my glass again.

Renat was pleased. "You'll really be back? No lady friends that will miss you? No obligatory home projects? No dog to take care of?"

"None of those... well... maybe a couple... here and there... nothing that can't wait. I've been divorced for ten years now, and I'm beginning to think single life is a prevailing condition. As to house projects, they will always be there. No dog. I'm going to do it. In my village, I'll be the most informed person about Roman structures. Worthwhile... yes?"

Renat laughed. "It's amusing to see you so excited. I hope that lasts. I hope you *will* return... soon. And I'll be the beneficiary of the information that you discover. Then *I'll* be the most informed in my village. Ha ha!" He tipped his glass to me. "To your return."

I nodded to acknowledge. I quoted MacArthur, not sure that Renat would be familiar with the saying. "I shall return."

He smiled.

CHAPTER 2

Transalpine Gaul, fourteen   years into the reign of Augustus Caesar

Caesar, the former Gaius Octavius, now Augustus, Imperator of the Roman Empire, sat astride his horse at the summit of Mont Cavalier above Nemausus. Behind him, the Tour Magne, a tower of 112 feet, was being completed. The Praetorian Guard waited at a distance that allowed Caesar private conversation with Marcus Vipsanius Agrippa but near enough to provide protection for their *Imperator*. Nemausus was lush, a response to the energies and vision of the locals who had developed a robust water system.   Nemausus was further flourishing under Roman rule and protection. The growth was not an accident.

Augustus spoke, nodding toward the town. "Nemausus is a jewel in our empire. You were right. It is well situated on the Via Domitia, a useful waypoint on the road from Italy to Spain. The weather is agreeable for living and food production. Under our supervision, we are constructing strong fortifications and providing adequate defense. Already, many in the province have opted to move to the city, to take advantage of the established markets, to drink the good water, to gain exposure of the knowledge that is available there—experienced men, books, art. It is my desire that we continue to nurture Nemausus, provide resources, provide direction, and continually be aware of its progress and problems. I'll continue living in the province, acting as proconsul, for a while. I'll see that the best possible direction is practiced."

Agrippa nodded. "Yes, Nemausus has a good start. I'm pleased that you agree with my thoughts. I would like to remain and be a part of its growth, but I do understand why you have invested me to take time in Pannonia. I, as you, see Pannonia as a valuable extension, as important to the Empire as any location... not to be neglected. I am ready for that challenge and anxious to be on my way. One thing to be aware of, Nemausus has an excellent water supply. However, growth as we imagine might outstrip that supply. It would be worthwhile to explore possibilities

7

for other sources. Compromising the water will promote ill health. The very growth that we seek could cripple the entire town."

"Yes, I agree." Augustus turned to face Agrippa whose forces were also waiting, 100 paces away. "I wish you well on your expedition. Please keep me informed. I will also send messages regarding *our* progress. And, yes, I will investigate and direct interest in acquiring additional good water sources. Go well, my friend."

"Go well, my friend and *Imperator*." Agrippa saluted and slowly rode his horse toward his cohorts.

Augustus Caesar presided over a gathering of Nemausus town leaders. He had been proconsul of the region for over a year, and the town leaders were accustomed to meeting with him from time to time. They understood they would be asked to provide information to Caesar, knowing that he often already had knowledge of the information asked. One had to be careful. They would also hear what was expected of *them*. This they dreaded as Caesar's instructions often curtailed their own interests in favor of the 'glory of the Empire' and, they reasoned, for the purse of the *Imperator*. Still, Nemausus and the surroundings had thrived under Roman protection, had received substantial contribution of energy and benevolence from the Empire. Countless sestertii had been introduced into their province, and most of the citizens now lived better and were more secure as a result. Still, one had to protect one's personal empire, lest it be whittled by assertive proconsuls.

Quintus Amatius Dives sat amongst the *aediles*. He was the ostensible leader of the locals, not formally, but due to his wealth in money and property and, not insignificantly, due to his force of character. As they sat, Gnaeus received deferential whispers from the other aediles surrounding him, whispers in response to questions or from the occasional directions from Caesar. The whispers annoyed Caesar, but he was accustomed to this practice, it being tolerated in the Senate, not sanctioned, but understood to be somewhat efficient in generating consensus of opinion.

Today Caesar was calling their attention to the accomplishments of the past year, the year starting from his installment as proconsul. Gnaeus Amatius silently wondered why they had been so fortunate to have been chosen... well, not *they*, really... why their *province* had been chosen by Caesar to receive the benefits of his benevolence and attention. It was sometimes difficult to make your way under such benevolent attention. It was not only *difficult* it could also be life-threatening if Augustus determined you were dealing at cross-purposes. If not life-threatening, ill intent on one's part could easily result in loss of property. Yes, one had to be careful. One had to maneuver in concert with only those one could trust and only then with leverage, meaning that Q. Amatius could extract revenge if his cohorts were not circumspect. Caesar continued cataloging the evident progress in case the town leaders had not been paying attention.

The cataloging, now having wandered into *works in progress*, appeared to be coming to an end. The leaders nodded in acknowledgment as Caesar revealed his list, conveying an understanding that they knew that the works were being done for their benefit, for the benefit of the citizens and only incidentally for the glory of the Empire. They had heard such before but remained attentive because direction involving further benevolence was sure to follow. Often, most of the time, actually, new directions influenced their lives and well-being. It was not always obvious to the individual that this well-being was truly to their *individual* benefit.

Q. Amatius, sensing that Caesar had reached the end of his list and correctly sensing that Caesar was expecting a display of adulation, obliged. "Caesar, our *Imperator*, you favor us with much indulgence. I know that I speak for all here and for the citizens of our region in expressing gratitude. You can be assured that we will continue to educate the population as to the gifts you have just spoken."

The group exclaimed as if from one, "Yes!"

Caesar nodded to acknowledge the accolade, a tribute he had expected. He then stood and began pacing in front of the group as was his habit when he was revealing new requirements, requirements he expected would be adopted, agreed-to, and carried out without exception and with enthusiasm.

The listeners braced.

"I am here, devoting valuable time and energy, time spent away from Rome, because we believe the region to be important to the empire. You were made citizens of Rome thirteen years ago. We intend that the region match the glory of Rome itself, and thus you have observed that benefit abounds. Nemausus will surely

9

grow, and if we are prudent men, we will continue to plan for its growth. Now, we have ten thousand citizens, thriving, but also depending on the lifeline of public works they have been provided—roads, a government, a judicial system, and clean water for the growing of foods, for drinking, for cooking, for baths. It is this clean water that I would like to talk about. At present, the system is good. Water—healthy water—is available from your local springs—the Fontis—and there are a number of good wells within the city walls. We have done a remarkable job in planning and installing water distribution systems, and the system is well maintained. Some of you men in this room, owning much of the water system, benefit personally from its existence." He looked at the men who benefited.

They nodded.

Caesar continued. "However, one does not have to visit the seers to know that with the success of Nemausus, more people will come to share in the wealth, to have a better life. And, we want this to happen. However, our own success may cripple us if we do not have vision.

We must plan for acquisition of additional, healthy water for the citizens. It may be more difficult to provide such water, and it may be at great cost. I am talking to you because I expect you, as the town leaders and as the operators of the water systems, to plan and to provide the means to expand the system. Of course, I know you will do this because it is in your own interest, and I am sure you know that if lacking a plan of your own and intent to proceed, the resources of the Empire, the distant empire, I might add, will be utilized if you are short on resources. To this end, I ask that you spend a year in contemplation of the requirements and consideration of possible water sources and means of conveyance. In a year, I will have Marcus Vipsanius Agrippa visit and hear of your thoughts. Agrippa understands large works and the considerable effort that must occur to build them. He also has a liking for Nemausus and anticipates its glorious future." Caesar paused, touching his forehead. "Do you understand what I am suggesting?"

Most in the group nodded their heads. No one voiced a response. They understood the direction and the implications.

"Good," Caesar said. "That is all I have for now. I would be pleased if you would join me at banquet to celebrate our good circumstance and our generous vision of the future."

After the dinner, five of the aediles, those involved with the water works, reclined on lounges, sipping red wine from fine Egyptian cups at the residence of Q. Amatius.

Publius Atius remarked, "Quintus, I've always admired your house, quite functional with its atrium, mosaic floors, several dining rooms—arranged to match the time of year, commanding view of the city, and this very impressive peristyle. Yes, quite functional."

"Publius," Quintus sat up from a supine position on his dining couch. "Nemausus has been good to me. I've constructed what I consider to be the finest that art has to offer as a tribute to the city, the region from which my wealth has sprung. As a town leader, I am obliged to hold many civic meetings here, and I wish to honor my fellow citizens with the art and splendor they deserve and crave."

"Yes, you've done very well at that," said Gaius Sergius.

The five took another sip of wine, enjoying the view, sheltered from the horizon-bound sun, intent on its hidden journey, underneath the Earth—the daily cycle.

Quintus spoke. "I would like to discuss our *Imperator's* 'suggestion' with the four of you. As in the past, I implore you to keep our conversations discreet. Even a casual remark could result in loss of station, property, or life for the individual—for all of us. So, if you enjoy your present circumstance, you will heed my thought."

They all nodded, solemnly.

Quintus continued. "Augustus speaks of our water system. We can be proud of what we've accomplished, mostly with our own energies and funds, although I'll admit, with the urgings of the Empire. The five of us all derive income from the present system, and that income does very well for us, indeed. The Fontaine, supplemented by the city wells, will be an adequate source for years to come. And, it is good water as witnessed by the robust health of our citizens and of the abundant crops nearby grown. Augustus may be right. At a time in the future, thirst may outstrip our present supply. But, I do not trust that the Empire's interest is purely concern that we do not suffer from a calamity of thirst. Delivering water from new sources may prove expensive and difficult. It is probable that such a project would be beyond the reasonable grasp of our little group. I'm afraid that under that

11

circumstance, the Empire would graciously provide the funds and the design. If *they* provide a larger, robust system, our present system may be absorbed within those works, the revenue going to the Empire. We may be compensated fairly, but we are not seeking fairness. We have our investment to protect, an investment that provides us with fine residences and the good wine we drink."

Gaius Sergius raised his wine cup. "I do not speak for all of us, but surely we all agree with you. However, the *Imperator* has told us we must report in one year, to Marcus Agrippa, of our plans for the future. What would you suggest we do?"

"Yes, we must make a report." Quintus paused. However, I am sure we will find that our supply is adequate for many years to come, and our water sources are of much higher quality than any other that are in our close province. We will note that there may be fine sources that are somewhat distant but agree that we cannot be assured that it will be possible to transport those sources to our fine city. We will admit that more study needs to be done and we will commit our own funds to continue a search for sources, survey the routes, and conceive of a design that will be worthy of our *Imperator*'s attention. In that way, we will be complying with the request of Augustus, will appear to accept his admonition as justified and beneficial, yet will maintain control and craft the timing more to our purposes. Do you all think that what I have said is a reasonable approach?"

The others, Publius, Manius, Lucius, and Gaius nodded, although somewhat slowly. Publius spoke, "Yes, Quintus, I think your plan is safe. We can show progress, yet address the magnitude of a project, one sure to require lengthy consideration and adequate design. But, several of us are younger than you, and look forward to and depend on revenue from our works for years to come. What do you really think will happen? Will such a supply eventually be built? If Augustus is persistent and if he continues to rule, the project will surely go forward. What is your vision?"

"Yes, Augustus may persist, but as we can all perceive, it will be years before the first rock is moved, the first shovel and pick wielded. As you have all witnessed, even the youngest of you, the Empire does not continue for long without challenge from those who have been conquered, without new costly adventures in lands far from the seat at Rome. Even now, Marcus Vipsanius Agrippa rides to Pannonia to exert the Empire's overwhelming influence.

the *Aedifex*: Building the Pont du Gard

What I am saying—close associates—is that given years of study before any large project is initiated, it is likely the *Imperator*, the Empire, will turn its attention to other matters. In the meantime, we will have uncovered knowledge of additional water sources in the vicinity. If we find sources and routes that make sense, I suggest that we pursue them, on our own time, at a pace that will enable funding from our own coffers—not some grand project that the Empire, in all its glory, will use as a showpiece, outpacing our own resources. What say you?"

Gaius Sergius, the youngest of the associates, sat up on his couch, feet on the ground, to emphasize his comment. He punctuated his words with thrusts from his wine cup. "You are right, Quintus. Even I, the youngest, have seen the Empire take one direction, then the other. We have heard grand plans from Augustus before, plans that have yet to yield substance. And, Augustus has many such plans to oversee, a vast empire to consider. Our province could easily be forgotten in less than a year, a mere glimmer in the imagination of Augustus, cast aside with many others to the scrap pile of grand plans. Yet, Augustus mentioned that our next audience would be with Agrippa. If that happens, we must truly present a work of substance. Agrippa is not a man who is easily fooled. He is also not a man who would treat us kindly if he thought our report was only a vapor." He gave a sharp nod to emphasize his comment.

Publius, Manius and Lucius, settled further into their couches, not because they felt assurance, but more to retreat from the implications of the consequences expressed by Gaius. Quintus waited for several moments, had more wine poured for all then grasped his wine cup with both hands as he spoke. "Gaius speaks with wisdom. Agrippa is not a man to be dealt with lightly. And, it would be my intention to display a reasonable product to him. I haven't had much time to think about what we must do, but let's do more thinking and gather again in several weeks. Publius, you have the best knowledge of our existing works. Expanding the water system within our city would be a necessary part of our report. I ask that you speak to us about the works, its current capacity, and what would have to be done to accommodate... no, let me restate... what we would have to *study* to understand what would have to be done. Agreed, Publius?"

"Yes," Publius nodded.

"And, Lucius, you, living outside the city, know well the countryside. I suggest that you investigate water sources existing at a reasonable distance from the city and tell us what must be done to determine whether they *are* viable future sources—or not. Do you accept that responsibility?"

"Yes, Quintus, and as it might involve considerable exploration of the countryside, I ask that either Manius or Gaius assist me with their resources, if need be." He looked at Manius and Gaius and then at Quintus.

Manius and Gaius both gave nodding assents.

Quintus added, "Yes, of course, and from me too if I can provide a resource or influence that is reasonable. Publius, the same is true for you. If you should need other resources, you must let us know."

"Yes, Quintus Amatius. I will do that."

"And... I should remark about this. We must be discrete, even amongst our own city dwellers. Any hint, any rumor, any discussion about possible grand projects always promotes intense speculation. Landowners maneuver to establish interest and make other moves that may or may not be in *our* best interest. To proceed without revealing the grand purpose will take your best guile and require you to be most clever. That consideration should be used from this time forward."

"I think your caution is well worth heed. I will proceed with great care as will the others, if I can speak for them." Publius looked at his associates.

"Good. Then let us enjoy the wine and the evening. I think we can feel comfort that we have a plan."

The others raised their wine glasses, as did Q. Amatius.

CHAPTER 3

At Nemausus, nearly one year after Caesar Augustus introduced the concept of a water source

Publius, Manius, Lucius and Gaius were reclining comfortably on couches, again at the residence of Quantus Amatius.

Quantus, after making sure his guests were well situated, perhaps saturated, with wine, cheese and bread, set aside his wine cup and crossed his hands above an indulgent belly. "We are soon to be visited by Marcus Vipsanius Agrippa. I expect we will see him and his cohorts within the next two months. Although this group has met from time to time to discuss the good work we have accomplished, we must now look at the whole of it and decide what we should reveal—and what we shouldn't. I feel foolish in cautioning you again to keep our discussions to yourselves, but I, nevertheless, would feel amiss if I did not say so, and I want that thought to be burned into your memory."

"Your have our assurances," Lucius said. "We understand, too well, the consequences of deception should it be discovered by those more powerful than us."

The others nodded.

"Good, then, we will go forward. Publius, you have investigated our existing works with an eye to what would be required if the town would be much more populous than now and if we were receiving water from new sources. What say you?"

"Yes, Qauntus. As we mentioned before, our existing distribution system works well, considering that it has grown with the town, was added-to piece-by-piece, area-by-area rather than having been planned from the start. Yes, there are improvements that could be made and should be made if we are to build a new system. In some ways Augustus has helped us, pushed us along, encouraged us to plan for any new system that we might build, in whatever manner as the town grows."

"We will, of course, acknowledge Caesar's vision when we make the report," Quantus noted.

"Yes, that should be done. I have also looked closely at our wells and our other existing sources of good water. There are, it seems, wells that struggle to now keep up with their requirements. They are a handful of the many but are possibly an example of other deterioration that will occur as we require more capacity. These wells are still producing good water, but they are slow to refill the cisterns under the increased use. In truth, we must be diligent to find new sources, but surely a new, immense project is not required to keep up with the pace."

"Certainly that is something we can do under our own control and with our own resources," Gaius said.

"Yes, but we need not make that point," Quantus blurted, a smile easing onto the lush landscape of his face. "It will seem that we are more interested in our own coffers." He laughed.

As did the others.

Publius continued. "As to new facilities, if we remain in control, we must use our influence to see that the town grows in areas where it is not difficult to provide the water. I think we can do that, considering new residences *require* water, and they would be fools to locate in areas where we cannot provide."

Quantus pontificated. "Unless, of course, these same fools are aggressive and clever enough to provide their own sources— out of our control—or the Empire is able to use that very circumstance to champion their cause, to assert their control, bring water from afar. The observation that otherwise attractive locations might have water difficulties should not be mentioned in our report. I would suggest, rather, we say that it seems that expansion of the town will not be inhibited by meager water supplies, but that we have to spend more time in the study of such. Does anybody disagree?"

No one did; however, several more acutely understood the nature of their deception.

"Publius?"

"Yes."

"I assume, Publius, that you have recorded information from your activity—your investigation. As we said, before, Agrippa is no fool, understands public facilities—knows the workings of water supply systems, considering he built aqueducts and extensive fountains and baths in Rome. I suggest you ready your investigations—our prior conversation an exception, of course—to show to Agrippa. And, you must be ready to provide detail of your examinations."

"I can do that."

the *Aedifex*: Building the Pont du Gard

"Good." Quantus pointed at Lucius. "Then, Lucius, what can you tell us of water sources not yet tapped and not yet considered?"

"I can tell you," Lucius looked at each in turn, "that new water sources of quality water, easily transportable to Nemausus, have not been found in my investigation. I was helped by Gaius and Manius—help gratefully appreciated. There are some bountiful sources with good water, such as the River Vardo, but it is at the bottom of a chasm and is 6 miles distant. Water could be brought to our level only with the contrivance of extreme mechanical devices and with huge expenditure of either human or animal power to lift great quantities of the water. I do not believe that these sources would be considered reasonable, even to an Empire that imagines facilities on a grand scale."

"Have you found other sources that do not have the lifting problem, but of perhaps less robust bounty—several sources that could be combined? Or sources of water which are not as sweet, but could be treated in a way to become acceptable?" Quantus put his hand to his ear, signaling that he was interested in the answer.

"I have found other sources of ground water at or near our elevation, but they are meager or not of good quality. Yes, they could be combined or treated to provide additional supply, but I don't think that concept is imagined by our grand leaders as an example of the glory of the Roman Empire in Gaul."

"Good. I think you can make your report, just as it is—not mentioning the remark about the grand empire, of course." Quantus swirled the wine in his cup then looked up, eyes confirming his satisfaction. "Yes, make your report as is. The obvious implication is that much more investigation is needed, in far-ranging, expanding circles. You should also mention that any source found will require a great commitment. My fellow water merchants, I feel we can be comfortable there is no certain approach to building a new robust water supply, no obvious adventure by the Empire. We may be offered help, but even lackeys from Rome will discover that a project cannot yet be conceived."

The others nodded.

"Then, prepare your reports as we have discussed—Lucius—with the same detail of which I spoke with Publius. I feel confident that Agrippa, seeing our investigations, will not be taken to vast ideas. Not yet, that is. And with some help from the gods, the men that rule the world will get on with other things. So now, let's drink more wine, and you can make a project of finding your way home. There is much wine to be drunk."

Two months later.

Qauntus approached Gaius in the town square, tapping him on the shoulder to get his attention. "Have you heard about Agrippa?"

Gaius reacted with a start, thinking—*Yes, while they were ready to report, there were concerns of whether their scheming would go well—or not.* "Agrippa is coming?"

Quantus shook his head. "No, Agrippa is *not* coming. Agrippa died of a sickness on his way back from Pannonia."

Gaius was stunned. "If that is true, the gods have favored us. Augustus will surely have more to concern him than progress of the Nemausus water supply."

"Yes, like preservation of his empire. Agrippa was a brilliant military power, and Caesar will be at a loss."

"Truly. I feel much relieved."

"Indeed. Have a good day, Gaius, and please tell the others."

CHAPTER 4
United States, near the end of the Twentieth Century

Retirement was glorious. Yes, at the end of my career I was still enjoying my work. My monthly compensation was a grand reward for my past effort. But, work certainly got in the way of other interesting pursuits. Before I decided to retire, I'd spent many hours calculating, devising spread-sheets, making lists, projecting expenses and cost-of-living increases. I looked at paying off the mortgage and fantasized trips to far-flung places. All of that. The answer to 'retire or not,' my decision, was 'yes,' propelled by my own will, of course.

I exalted in not having to get up early, get ready, drive to work, be there, be attentive, be accommodating, be direct, and be forceful. I, instead, got up, made my coffee, read the paper, and contemplated whether I should first do my walk or work on any number of favored projects. From this side of my retirement milestone, I can't imagine that I ever worried about being retired.

The euphoria lasted for a week and a half. I mentally flipped the switch, pulled the lever, and opened the door. I did some limited reading about ancient Rome, studied the book I had bought describing the Pont du Gard, imagined living in Roman times and, more vividly, imagined how the great aqueduct was built, or, since there was not much information available, how *I* would have built it.

When I had made the commitment to Renat—to return—I meant it, at the time. Yet, in the three months following my trip, before retirement, I wavered—thought about other adventures I might take, considered whether Pont du Gard was really that important to me—really worth the effort, the time, the money. However, as I read, as I contemplated, I became ever more intrigued. The capstone of that chain of thinking amounted to— *what the hell could be wrong with spending time in southern France pursuing a mystery that—oh by the way—involved my life's work, the career that I had the great fortune to experience?*

I had been single for ten years. The marriage ended because we found out we had evolved into creatures only slightly resembling the persons comprising the young couple. We had different interests. Yes, that can be an advantage; you can grow from sharing in the other's experiences, and that did happen. But, as we slogged along, after the children were out and surviving by their efforts, we fell into discomfort and were only being polite to one another. I credit us both for having the wisdom to pursue new lives. Tazi remarried and is reveling in a life of—what I might consider pretentious—social functions. I wish her well.

In the ten years, I had the freedom to travel to lands that I thought interesting—southern France to see Renat, for example— go to Forty-Niner's games, hike myself silly on the weekends and fall asleep in the chair watching a spy movie on the T.V. Oh, yes, there have been some women, some wonderful women, actually. Maybe they would have married me; the thought was only discussed casually and never made it to prime time. It's not that I didn't think about it. But, when I did, I asked myself—would my life be better married to this person, in constant contact, or do I like my life the way it is? The answer to that question was never ambivalent. I did not make pro and con lists. I charted my single life with few compromises.

I hadn't really intended that outcome. In the early years after the divorce, I more or less thought that life involved living as a couple—let's invite the Chatfields over for dinner; it's been a long time since we've seen the Brewsters; let's find a couple to go with us to the concert. Then, at some time, it occurred to me that I could exist as an entity—myself. To picture my situation, I would think of a well-to-do English gentleman who, by himself, existed as an institution, going to town, taking a trip, chatting with his friends at a function. I won't elaborate on the dynamics of how you are perceived as a single man, how couples then have a problem—or not even a thought—of inviting you, by yourself. However, there is a sea of single people out there, and you share the concept of... *entity*. Enough of that.

I made the arrangements. The house and the yard would be taken care of and checked occasionally by friends. Money would be accessible. I cancelled the paper and made arrangements for a neighbor to pick up the mail and to forward envelopes that looked important. Bills would be paid. I was ready.

I notified Renat of my intent. He was pleased and promised to ease my way into temporary living in the Nimes region. I hadn't decided where I would live. Perhaps Nimes was too cosmopolitan. I felt like I should live 'out,' in a village near the Pont du Gard. Wouldn't the actual project manager have lived there, somewhat central to the aqueduct and at the site of the most complex structure? Yes, I would look for a rental in that vicinity. How long would I stay? But even more important, what did I intend to accomplish? I wasn't sure.

Scant reading and research had upgraded my understanding of Roman times—the region, the project. I read that the aqueduct was built during the reign of Augustus Caesar. Caesar's right-hand man, childhood friend, military genius and civic builder, Agrippa, was tagged as responsible for building the great structure. I read more about Agrippa and found him fascinating. He was credited by many scholars for having been the force behind the expansion of Augustus's empire. He was a military genius, an expansive builder. He received many tributes and authority from the Roman Senate, tributes and authority that were almost equal to that of the revered and powerful Augustus. He surely would have succeeded Augustus if he had outlasted him. Unfortunately, Agrippa died before the end of Caesar's 41-year reign.

Agrippa's diary is lost to us, but there is *some* information on him. He appears in literature and accounts, but detail is sparse. Therefore, it was up to me to fill in the details. Was Agrippa closely involved in the structures to which he is given credit, or did he just *make it happen*? He constructed many facilities in Rome—the Virgo and Julian Aqueducts, the Pantheon, and baths and fountains, all with his own money as expected of those who had benefited from the Empire. There was only fleeting mention of his time in Gaul, attention paid to Nemausus. Was it possible to learn more?

Yes, that's where history left us. We don't have any accounts as to genesis of the Nime aqueduct's concept, the manner of its design, the identity of the designer or the construction supervisor. Was it done with slave labor or were the locals paid?

As Renat had mentioned, the difference in elevation from the water source to the reservoir in Nimes was scant. How could they have surveyed or calculated the difference in elevation in the first place and how did they lay out the great aqueduct with primitive instruments? The builders had to excavate several tunnels, construct miles of underground conduit. Precision would be important. It wouldn't be easy even with today's technology. I marveled at the colossus they had accomplished. Also, the entire aqueduct was built without the use of cranes, explosives, heavy transportation, structural engineers, plan-check and building department inspectors.

My career involved engineering and construction of expansive civil works—dams, powerhouses, bridges, waterways, harbors. In my career, I had to understand the engineering upon which the structures were based, devise a means of constructing them—always encountering obstacles that seemed impossible— then construct them dealing with the many difficulties involving labor, material availability, improper engineering, difficult weather—the vagaries of construction as it is called. Oh yes, and get all this done, spending less than the contract amount so we can survive to do another one.

I bent to look out the window of the airliner as we circled to make the approach to the Côte d'Azur airport at Nice. During our descent, we had a lavish view of the harbor at Monte Carlo, a display—a considerable display—of ancient but still elegant means of basic transportation—sailboats. They were of breathtaking beauty, a means of travel surviving in splendor from our distant past. I wondered if the harbor at Monte Carlo had been coveted so highly in the days of the Caesars. This trip would be enriching. How could I have ever had any doubts?

Renat, devoted friend that he was, pulled up to the curb, jumped out and embraced me as I stood next to my luggage, a considerable pile reflecting my commitment to a lengthy stay. He put both hands on my shoulders and pushed away, giving me a look that expressed his enthusiasm. "You did it; you really did come back. Our aqueduct must have been a strong allure, not that we don't have even more to offer. Welcome to my world, Warner."

"Renat, you take such care of me. I feel richly rewarded for anything I did for you thirty years ago—when we were both young."

"Yes, both young and enjoying life. But now, we get to continue the adventure. Having you around will enhance my own life, my own enjoyment. On we go."

the *Aedifex*: Building the Pont du Gard

Although Renat picked me up at the Nice airport, I would rent a car in Nimes. Said another way, I could have rented a car in Nice, but Renat *insisted* on picking me up. I was buoyed by his hospitality and his interest in my project. He was intent to show me and immerse me into all that southern France had to offer. He took advantage of our trip from Nice, driving through Cannes and Antibes with a stop at the Picasso museum at Antibes. Although Picasso was Spanish, Renat was quick to tell me that Picasso had spent time in nearby Barcelona before he was inevitably attracted to the locus of the early twentieth century world of art—France and Paris. I couldn't help but be impressed by the art treasures available—a great start to my adventure. We had lunch at an open-air seaside restaurant in Antibes. I was not yet used to having the *pescado* stare back at me as I consumed it.

Renat lived in Nimes, and I found temporary quarters there. I turned down his offer to stay at his home. I wanted more freedom to come and go—no compromises. My plan to rent a place—a villa seemed appropriate to Med living—nearer the Pont du Gard, in a smaller, less cosmopolitan setting, remained attractive to me. Of course, while in Nimes, I visited the terminus of the aqueduct, the *Castellum*, a surviving aqueduct structure, and one that easily allowed one's imagination to create the ancient scene.

I now had a plan. Of course I did. After many years of managing projects, I was compelled. As they say in the industry, when a project didn't have a plan—it just *happened*. But, my plan was just a start. I would inspect all the existing structures—the great structure itself, the tunnels, the above-ground conduits, the source at Uzes, the quarry. I suspected there would be scholars in the area, probably associated with universities—and, perhaps, local experts—people like me who were curious and made it their hobby to gather information and to speculate about the structure and its construction. I would find them. There must be a considerable amount of written material on ancient construction methods, yet I had not uncovered much.

I had read the *Ten Books of Architecture* by Vitruvius, written in the first century A.D. His account was helpful in presenting some understanding on what was available, what was known around the time that the aqueduct was built. But, of the aqueduct itself, almost nothing—nothing telling us how Agrippa was involved. I had brought several other books to read, filling the time that would not be spent walking the route, inspecting the structure, drinking wine at the bistro.

I would ask questions. Would I need an interpreter? I guessed that I would. Renat, I supposed, would be more than willing. I would find sources of information. Investigation would lead me to other sources. At some time, I would get a feeling for the project, and if I could not find a detailed account, I would plan the project in my mind, as if I were here, two thousand years ago, charged with the awesome responsibility of bringing water to Nemausus. So much for getting away from my work. Well, at least I didn't have to get up and drive to the office.

One beautiful summer morning, I drove from Nimes to the site of the Pont du Gard to renew my awe and to spend more time with the structure. However, my prime intent was to find a more permanent residence. There were several small towns in the area of the Pont du Gard—Vers Pont-du-Gard, Remoulins, or Uzes. Remoulins was a fair size town but seemed too far from the structure. I wanted to be closer.

I settled on Vers Pont-du-Gard because the village was on the route of the aqueduct, was quaint, and not overwhelming. Without the benefit of an interpreter, I stumbled my way around, trying to find a residence to rent. I spoke English where there was some understanding and fractured French of which I had absorbed a smattering. Those involved in commercial rentals were accommodating enough, but it was a struggle. Perhaps I should fetch Renat. I was sure he'd enjoy helping me get settled.

However, at one agency, I encountered a young lady, a whiz at English and quite helpful. Her agency did not have what I was looking for—either too large or too shabby—but she said she would use her resources to help me, including reading of the newspapers to find listings by individuals. Laurie would not let me pay her for this, but we settled on lunch at a café of her choice. I was more than happy to buy the lunch, for several reasons.

She helped me find quarters that somehow matched what I had imagined. You reached the villa by walking up the hill from town. It had a worthy view from a deck in the rear of the house and was surrounded by a garden that might be grateful for my attention. I imagined myself on the deck, reading, writing, napping in the warm climate, strolling the road, drinking the good wine, and talking—in a limited way—to the neighbors. Yes, pretty much as I had imagined.

I also was delighted to be in the company of Mademoiselle Laurie, an effervescent and attractive young lady, matching everyman's vision of the saucy, energetic French female. After making the arrangement for the villa, we relaxed over a glass— well, several glasses—of wine at the sidewalk cafe, overlooking a square lushly appointed with primped greenery and beckoning benches for the folk.

Laurie tipped her wine glass to me, "I am hoping that your stay with us will be most delightful. It is my honor to have you among us."

I grinned and took a sip. "Laurie, it's *my* good fortune to have found you. Look what my adventure has already produced— a fine villa from which to operate and the company of the fairest that inhabit the land." Well, I thought it was a bit flowery, too, but Laurie took it well.

"Oh, yes, Monsieur Warner, you told me what you intend to do here, something to do with the Pont du Gard, but I really did not pay enough attention. Can you tell me more?"

I told her about my initial sighting of the Pont, how I was struck—that I was an engineer, a builder, and now an adventurer. I was diving in, immersing myself in the culture, so to speak, and I would do what was possible to do in retirement, pursue an interest that before would be impossible, given the grinding requirements of making a living.

Laurie smiled. "You know that we who have lived here take the great Roman structures for granted. I am tickled—is that right—*tickled*, to think that you have been overwhelmed by something that we think so ordinary. But then, maybe I will learn something about the ancient structures existing in front of me all my life—that is, if you will share. Maybe I will buy *you* lunch if you are willing to educate me."

"Of course, I'm willing. I'd treasure any opportunity to share what I learn. I can't wait until I have something worthy to tell you."

"Oh yes," Laurie said, "I hope that you will share first with me so that I can be the local expert, for just a little while, anyway."

"A while ago, you mentioned 'tickled.' That makes me ask, how did you learn to speak English? You speak it very well?"

"Oh! Thank you. At one time my mother owned a shop in Lyon. We had many customers who spoke English. That is how."

I nodded and smiled. I next said, probably without good judgment, "And, perhaps you will let me buy you lunch at some time or another, even though I have nothing to report. It's very exhilarating to be in the presence of such a charming, stylish, and attractive lady."

"I hoped you'd say that," she said.

I was puzzled by her remark but I plowed on, nevertheless. "It occurs to me that you might help me more than you might imagine. In just a short while I have convinced myself that I will not get on well without knowing the language. Might I be able to persuade you, from time to time, to come with me to help me converse—be my interpreter? I would pay you."

"Why, yes. Absolutely. I have much flexible time in my position with the real-estate company. I am sure that you can arrange—whatever outing you might be thinking of—to allow me to go with you. I would be most delighted—and, to think that I would be getting paid and getting an education at the same time. Life can be wonderful. I am at your service."

Of course, Renat would have been delighted to be involved, to provide *free* interpreter service, just to be a part of the investigation. That arrangement would surely have sidestepped some difficulties. But, we often don't take the most reasonable path. I was smug and excited about my arrangement and progress.

CHAPTER 5

Nemausus—21 years after the death of Augustus Caesar

Nemus Amatius poured wine for his guests, Marcus Atius, Julius Sergius, Titus Domitius, and Aulus Acilius. Of the town aediles owning and operating the Nemausus water system, these were the inheritors or, in the case of Aulus, purchases of interest in the Nemausus water works—the *Aqua Corporata*.

As they lay on their couches, Nemus spoke. "I have gathered you to talk about the impending visit of Claudius, who now shares the *Imperator* with Caligua. As you know, Claudius was born and raised in Lugdunum, only 100 miles from Nemausus. He is touring the area to assess the status of our township, the health of the citizens, and the strength of our economy. He will certainly talk to us about water. We must be prepared to answer questions."

Julius laughed. "It is beyond my understanding—why did the Senate elect a sickly, feeble, lame person as *Imperator*, even though he shares that position with Caligua?"

Nemus nodded. "Of course, we do not know for sure. But, you must remember, Claudius is the last of the Julian line, and family ties are powerful. It does not matter. We must deal with the situation, his station and our own circumstances. Even though he is weak and a cripple, he has the power to weaken and cripple us. We must be careful."

"We have not had much Roman attention or supervision for a long time." Marco said. "Our fathers spoke of the direction by Augustus when he was proconsul and living here. He was pressing, at the time, for us to consider a more robust water system. Agrippa was to hear our plan, perhaps command a project to build such a system. Fortunately, Agrippa died. We were not required to provide water under the thumb of the Empire. They have left us alone."

"Until now?" Julius asked with raised eyebrow.

Nemus nodded. "Yes. As I said, we really do not know. But we have to be prepared, speak as one mind, convince Claudius, if he should ask, that our system is sufficient and does not need the assistance of Rome."

Marcus asked, "Do you think Claudius knows about the requirement that Caesar imposed upon our fathers—to consider other sources, other means of transportation of the water?"

Nemus, with palms upraised, said, "We do not know, but we must assume that he does. We must be prepared to tell him why we have not complied with the wishes of the Empire, even though no particular direction was given. We must convince Claudius that we have done a thorough job of managing and planning for the town's water and that our future will be equally successful." Nemus continued. "Now, Marcus, tell us what you know. Tell us how our water system is working. You are the one who considers our status and plans for the future. Yes, tell us."

Marcus raised himself from the lounge, supported by his elbows, to face the others, grasping his wine cup in his left hand. "In the time since Augustus, the town has grown from ten thousand people to two times that. We have had to find additional sources and build additional distribution in the city. We have been successful in ponding small streams to make reservoirs and have managed those sources to store water, easing our situations in the dry seasons. And, the Fontaine springs are a steady source, normally. We have upgraded our system to take better advantage of this bountiful supply. I think we have been adept at our service, so far. We do have occasional problems when the seasonal rains are of low incidence even though we implore Jupiter to treat us kindly. Yes, I think we can be proud of our system."

Nemus, thumbs locked under his wine cup, said, "Yes, Marcus, but what about the future? We think our town will continue to grow. What do we do next?"

"Our situation becomes more difficult with more population." Marcus shifted his wine to the other hand. "I do not have an answer to the questions about where we will easily get more water. We have managed to provide a reliable supply for the town, but the town is hungry, requiring more water to grow crops in nearby areas. The crops are competing with the people. We must either stop our population increase or eat less or find new sources of water. And, we are constantly thinking about this. There remain other streams to pond and sources farther from our town. We must develop these new sources if it is obvious that the population will continue to grow."

the *Aedifex*: Building the Pont du Gard

Nemus reacted, "But we can do this. We do not need the power of the Empire. We have made our own way in the past. We are men of substantial means and can pay for our building efforts with increased water sales. Do you agree?"

The others nodded.

Marcus looked thoughtful. "I do agree, Nemus. However, as I mentioned, our task gets more difficult. I have not yet balanced my estimate of increased demand with increased sources. The water required for crops sometimes confounds me."

"Yes, I understand. You are not certain. However, we must not display this uncertainty to Claudius. To him, we must present that we are fully capable of continuing as we have. Are we agreed?

All nodded. Marcus nodded more slowly and later than the others.

"Then we will greet Claudius and treat him with great respect. We will show confidence that we are good husbands of the water system. He will go on to other concerns, of which the Empire has many."

Nemausus treated Claudius with the attention befitting a co-*Imperator* of the Empire. He entered the town on a *lectica*, surrounded by members of the Praetorian Guard. Young girls in white attire spread flower petals before him. Trumpets blared in no particular style, precision, or method. Nemausus folk lined the road and streets to get a glimpse of the *Imperator* and to confirm their understanding that Claudius was sickly and known to be lame, yet ironically one of the most powerful men in civilization. However, he looked more ordinary than they imagined, confirming neither sickly nor powerful.

Nemus Amatius and the other co-owners of the water supply, the *Corporata*, met with Claudius as Nemus had predicted. Claudius surprised them by reading from information provided to him—population of Nemausus, population growth, water usage, crop requirements versus residential city requirements, water sources and an assessment of the quality of the water provided. Nemus, Marcus, Julius and Sergius, and Quintis were stunned, somewhat fearful that it might be difficult to create an impression that would appear realistic.

Claudius looked at Nemus. "Nemus Amatius, you are an able town leader, and to this point, to this meeting, the representative and owner of Nemausus water interests. Do you agree with the information that I have detailed?"

"I am impressed, Tiberius Claudius, that you have taken such interest in our town, that you have considerable knowledge of our activity." Nemus paused. "But, to answer your question, yes, your information is thorough and accurate. We may have slightly different numbers, but the information you have serves you well as a glimpse of our situation."

Claudius nodded, "Then, Nemus and you other water ministers, can you tell me how you will proceed in the future? What do you imagine in the manner of population growth? How will the water requirements for crops match your requirements for food for your population? If you need additional water, where will you get it, or are your supplies adequate?"

Nemus was constrained. Did Claudius know about the admonition that Augustus had argued, fifty years ago? Nemus was nearly convinced that Claudius had been at their recent meeting or had someone listen to their discussion. He must be careful. "Tiberius Claudius, you are very perceptive. We are constantly looking to our future, mindful of the suggestion of our dear Augustus when he was proconsul—mindful to look to the future. As you can observe, we have provided additional sources, have extended the system and continue to provide quality water for the inhabitants and for the crops. We have recently met to again consider the future but have no precise information as yet. You have, no doubt, observed that we have used our resources to pond the running streams, to conserve water for seasons, which would otherwise leave us in short supply. My thoughts, our thoughts, at this time, are that we will do much that is similar to provide additional supply."

"And, if that is not enough...?"

"Then, of course we will look further." Nemus looked at the others for confirmation.

They nodded, looking somewhat uncomfortable.

Claudius looked at each in turn. "I understand that the flow of your primary source, the spring, **is** highly variable, depending on the season. I note that you have means of making it through the dry seasons, using wells, rainwater and reservoirs, but that this condition stresses the town mightily. Is it not so?"

the *Aedifex*: Building the Pont du Gard

Nemus, edgy because Claudius seemed to have penetrated layers of history and understanding, said, "It is so."

Claudius stood up, favoring his weak leg they noticed, "Here is my suggestion. I *suggest* that you appoint someone able, someone who has worked in and with your water systems. This person will be charged solely with finding new sources, ponding streams, fountains, and identifying a water transportation system sufficient for a doubling of Nemausus population in twenty years. You shall—I *suggest*—include the amount of water to be used to grow crops to support your population. It is true that you get some foodstuffs from other localities, but you also must be able to trade these other localities with your crops, so perhaps you should use total support from your area as a target. Do you like my suggestions?"

Nemus, glancing first at his compatriots, also rose. "Claudius, our *Imperator*, you have great vision, perhaps even more than we who are close at hand. Of course, we will take your suggestions. We will appoint a capable person with the sole responsibility to investigate our future. You have inspired us to take on this task, and we will all provide the resources to enable the man selected. You can be assured that we will do this."

"Yes, I would like to be assured. I would like to hear from you from time to time on your progress. If you should need help from our vast sources of knowledge and treasury, you will let me know. The first report I would like to hear from you will identify the able person you have selected, his attributes, experience and his—or your—plans for investigation."

They all nodded. Nemus, eager to stem the 'suggestions,' did not question nor amplify the concept. "We will begin immediately, Tiberius Claudius. You may ask for your report in only a month's time. And we are pleased you have taken such interest."

Claudius nodded and walked outside to his waiting guard.

CHAPTER 6

Appius Petronius, a young man of 19 years, watched as Claudius entered Nemausus. With Appius Petronius was his wife of two years, Antonia. Appius was curious, as were the others lining the street, as to how the Empire would be displayed, curious also about Claudius, whose full name was Tiberius Claudius Nero Germanicus; 'Claudius' indicated his family line. As they observed the trumpets and banners, soon to be upon them, Antonia pulled at the arm of Appius, asking, "Why are he and Caligua both Imperator? How did that happen?"

Appius regarded his wife. She was bright and pleasing and had a natural bent, wanting to understand how the world worked. "You must have heard the history of Claudius. He was sickly in his youth, thin and pale, and walked with a limp. He was shunned even by his mother. She humorously referred to his ineptness as the standard for stupidity. He was passed from his mother to grandmother to an uncle—a mule trainer. Yet, he finally shook off some of the frailty of his youth and showed that he had promise. Tiberius, when *Imperator*, however, would not let Claudius pursue the path to public office. Yet, when Tiberius was assassinated and Caligua, the nephew of Claudius, became ruler, he saw value in Claudius and nominated him co-Imperator. With such a cloudy history, we really do not know what to expect of this ruler."

Antonia nodded, "He was born and raised in Lugdunum. I marvel that a leader of the Empire was raised so near, and the first man outside Rome to become *Imperator*. Look, there he is upon his *lectica*."

The trumpets and the banners passed them. The guards, fore and aft of the *lectica*, strutted by, lances at battle rest; some guards were to the sides of the *palanquin*. Claudius gazed from side to side, acknowledging his subjects but giving nothing away. To his subjects, he appeared assured and confident, not warped and retiring from the infirmity of his youth. It was notable that the perception of what they might expect from Claudius was changed within a few moments.

Appius nodded. "I wonder if he will bring any changes to our town. He is to remain here for several days. This display is not just ceremonial."

Antonia looked up at him. "The Empire seems to favor Nemausus, has built temples and the city wall. Surely we can expect that attitude to continue. And, Claudius is of the region. Perhaps we will now have a coliseum, a forum, a theater, or fine public baths."

"Oh, yes. Fine public baths. If they are any finer, I will never see you, the house abandoned for the sake of bathing like a royal. Now, if they were to build a coliseum, an arena for games and public entertainment—that would truly be an improvement."

Antonia looked down, pouting, then turned her head sideways, looking at him, displaying a slight grin. "Do you not favor a wife that hints of jasmine and sandalwood? Or would you rather I reeked of a week of strenuous housework?"

Appius smiled also but said nothing.

Nemus Amatius, after the initial meeting with Claudius, again assembled his companions at his *peristyle* house. The fountains in the middle of the courtyard gurgled, a fitting backdrop for discussion involving city water supply.

Nemus began. "We have told Claudius that we will nominate a person to be wholly charged with investigating sources and methods for providing the town—a town twice the present size—with water. I do not wish to have Claudius, or one of his enforcers, remind us that we have failed to do so. Therefore, I ask that you consider and offer some possibilities. How about you Marcus? You know more than all of us about the functioning of our systems. Could you be our nominee?"

"No, Nemus Amatius, no. If you think about the requirements, you will understand that our person will have to roam the valleys, follow the rivers, tour the regions, and talk to the locals. I could not spend one-tenth the time required for this chore. However, I do have a person in mind. This fellow has been working on our water system for over five years—since he was a young lad. He is a bright fellow and over the years has learned how to solve our problems, conceive of our system upgrades, and to do the calculations necessary to provide adequacy in the work. I do not like to lose his services, but he will not make us appear as fools.

33

This young fellow is named Appius Petronius. I would offer his background for your consideration."

Julius Sergius rotated his shoulders, then stretched his neck, a routine he often practiced before making what he considered an astute observation. "My dear Marcus, perhaps Claudius is looking for a man of some education. Is this... Appius Petronius... of an educated background?"

Marcus shook his head. "No, Julius, this fellow has not had the opportunity of formal study. His capability would be superior if he had. No, Appius has discovered what maths are required for him to understand our water system and the nature of water. From what others have told him, he has been able to go beyond, to apply his own thinking. I think you would be much impressed."

Julius nodded, "But what if Claudius is expecting us to engage a learned man, even if we must go outside our region, even to Rome to find such a person."

"We have not been told that by Claudius," Nemus offered. "We said we would advise Claudius soon, advise him that we have selected someone. I suggest we report to Claudius that we have selected a person. If Claudius wants a man of education, I suppose he will tell us so. We will detail the attributes of.... "

"Appius"

"Yes, of Appius, expressed in words that are complimentary to our candidate, of course."

Marcus smiled. "Yes, we are practiced in doing that, it seems."

Julius said, "If Claudius should talk to our candidate, do you think Appius would represent us well?"

"Yes. One attribute of Appius that I have not mentioned is his loyalty. I have absolute trust that he will... "

"Do as he is told?" Julius looked down his nose.

Marcus nodded. "Yes, Appius will represent our interests. He has always understood and promoted the circumstances of our water company in his dealing with customers."

Nemus crossed his hands over his stomach. "Marcus, you should talk with your candidate... you have not done so yet, have you?"

"No, I wanted to talk amongst ourselves, first."

"Good. Then talk to him and determine his attitude. We will continue his pay as is, I assume."

Marcus nodded. "I was thinking that we might give him an incentive so that he is more inclined to think of his task in terms of *our* requirements—with the approval of this group of course."

Nemus said, "I agree. I would hate to have his enthusiasm for a grand project overtake our interests. You have my support to offer an attractive payment, 75 sestertii per month perhaps. Will you talk to... Appius... and report to us?"

"Yes. Within the week."

A co-worker, Tinius, found Appius knee-deep in the drinking water channel, lifting then dropping a sluice gate as he adjusted pegs in the ways. Appius stood back, gauged the resulting water flow, then climbed out of the channel and slipped back into his sandals.

"Appius. What have you done wrong? Fouled the water system again?"

"What do you mean, Tinius?"

"I do not know what I mean," he laughed. "Marcus Atius wants to see you at the works building. He did not say why. I only imagined that is was something you did wrong." He smiled and flicked a rock with his sandal.

Appius grinned and straightened his wet tunic. "You would have a great laugh if I was in some trouble, would you not? Probably because it would not be your turn for once."

"Yes, well we can discuss our fortune, or lack of it, sometime. But for now, you had better get up there. If you did do something wrong, there is no need to put Marcus in any worse mood."

"He is in a bad mood?"

"No, I just said that. You will have to be the measure of his mood. Tell me later."

"I will, Tinius."

Appius entered the works building. There were tables for spreading diagrams and a desk arranged for customers to meet with the principals in transactions. The room had good lighting so that planning and payments were not performed in the dark. Marcus Atius occupied a separate room, surrounded by an interior wall, constructed in a corner within the larger room. Appius walked in, and Marcus Atius looked up, beckoning Appius to a stool in front of his desk.

"Marcus Atius, Tinius told me you wished to see me," Appius said, somewhat tentatively.

"Yes, yes. How are you Appius? Is the work going well? Have we managed to fix the leak in the pipe supplying water to the Regents District?"

"Yes, Marcus. That is taken care of. The road is now drying and almost everybody is happy."

"How is your wife... Antonia... is that right? She is a delight to look upon."

"Antonia is in good health. She has a wide interest and is always asking questions I am not able to answer. She prefers that I would drink less, but is a good wife."

"She is not with child?"

"Not yet, but... "

"But... "

"But we are thinking that one day soon... " Appius felt some anxiety. Why all these questions? Why would Marcus Atius want to know about his family life? Although he had dealt with Marcus a number of times in the past, almost daily, really, he was not sure if it was Marcus' nature to show interest, softening the blow that might follow. Appius had scooted to the edge of the stool. He smiled.

"That's good. That's good." Marcus leaned forward, his elbows on the desk. "Appius, I want to thank you for your hard work... and your good work."

A cold wave of worry ran through Appius. Here it was. What had gone wrong? "I hope that I have pleased the owners. I do like the work. It energizes me. Is there something more I could be or should be doing?"

"Perhaps, Appius, perhaps. The owners have a requirement, one suggested... if you know what I mean... by our dear Claudius who has just recently bestowed his benevolence and attention on our town. He has... suggested... that we investigate and plan for a water system for a town twice this size. We must calculate the requirements, consider our existing sources then find additional sources that will suit us—good water with abundant, regular flows. We need to employ a person who has some understanding of water systems, who is able to do calculations, and who has a sense of what resources it would take to transport the water to Nemausus, considering that the additional sources might be at considerable distance. I have suggested to the owners that

36

you would be the ideal person for that responsibility. What say you?"

Appius sat, stunned. His thoughts had swung from a possible dismissal to consideration of employment that he could only dream about. "I... I do think that... I would hope that... I really do not know what to say."

A slight grin twitched the corner of Marcus's mouth. "What I want to know is if you want to do the work. I asked about Antonia because the appearance of children could be a distraction. You will have to wander the region, spending a substantial amount of time away from your home. I will ask the question. Do you want to do this work?"

"Oh, yes, Marcus. I have not thought about what the work will involve, but I am thinking that I could not have crafted a better opportunity if I were allowed to think of such myself. But, how are you convinced that I could do what is required? You have to report to Claudius... the result of my investigations?"

"Appius, I recommended you because I have had the opportunity to watch you attain considerable skill while you have been employed by us. You take to calculations naturally. After you were shown how to calculate volumes and flows by our experienced surveyors and designers, you mastered those calculations and improved upon them. Now, we go to *you* when we want to know what will be required. You have a sense of the nature of... water systems. I think that you will not embarrass us in front of Claudius. We will have robust information, a good recommendation resulting from your search and your design instinct."

"Thank your for your kind words and your confidence. I must say that I am very excited."

"Antonia?"

"Well, she may not have the same passion for the opportunity that I have, but I am sure I can convince her that it will be good for our future." Appius fidgeted.

"Yes, she does appear bright enough to understand that."

"Marcus, sir, do the owners think that we can find abundant, clean water at a location that can be easily transported to Nemausus?"

Marcus sat back. "It is quite likely that we will *not* find such a source. If that should be the situation, we must be absolutely certain. We must have investigated all possibilities. If we neglect an important source, that clever Claudius is likely to skewer us for our sloppy work. He could take the works away from us, operating it for the town's benevolence and for the good of the Empire. That would not be a happy day."

"I cringe with the weight of that responsibility. I must be very thorough. Perhaps, though, I will find abundance. We will then show Claudius that we have done a good job."

"That is possible. But, if such a supply is found, it will, of course, be very expensive to construct a transportation system... so expensive that the owners could not possibly be expected to construct it... to pay for it... and too expensive even for the Empire to construct. I am sure you will be helpful in determining such grand expense. You are adept at conceiving costs and are influential in persuading those who must provide the resources."

Appius was not sure he had heard an opinion or an instruction. He merely nodded. "What will happen next, Marcus?"

"I am feeling that you are enthusiastic about doing the work and that you have the interests of the owners as your first thought. I have told the *Corporata* that I would talk to you and then report to them your reaction and interests. I intend to tell them that you are a fit and willing candidate within the next few days. If they are satisfied, and I think they will be, we will advise Claudius that we have made a selection. Unless Claudius insists that we have a more learned man at this task, and that is possible, we will be underway. It is my belief, however, that while an educated man might be capable of besting you in the calculations, he will not know this region nor have the sense of water system characteristics for which you are known, especially if the educated man is from Rome. They do not have the best of all things in Rome, even though it is the center of the universe." He smiled.

"I will hear from you soon?"

"Yes, probably within several weeks. Claudius is still nearby, visiting his birth city of Lugdunum. We will be able to get messages to and from him easily. We will travel there to meet with him if necessary."

"Is there anything else I should know, Marcus?"

"Yes. We are assigning you an important responsibility. To underscore this responsibility, the owners have agreed to pay you 75 sestertii per month. That I believe is somewhat more than we are paying you now. Yes?"

the *Aedifex*: Building the Pont du Gard

"Yes, Marcus. I am dizzy with thoughts of the opportunity you have presented. I can promise you I will do exceptional work for you. In the meantime, it will be hard for me to concentrate on my work. I hope that the business with Claudius is soon determined. I am most anxious to start. Thank you for your confidence."

"You have earned it, Appius. I hope that we are able to get you started soon, although we will miss your experience in our day-to-day operations. Go well."

"Thank you." Appius backed out of the doorway.

Marcus Atius leaned back to the wall, clasped his hands behind his head and looked at the ceiling. It seemed to him that he had pressed the clay into the mold. Appius would do as he was told.

Appius completed his work on the channel. He had increased the flow of water in order to wash sediment, branches and other waste from the waterway. He then adjusted the flow, returning it to that required for a normal day's supply to the villas of the rich and to the public baths and fountains in the area. As was his custom, at the end of his work day he met Antonia at the public fountain to help carry water to their home, for drinking, for cooking, and cleaning. They bathed in the public baths as there was no running water to the homes of those with modest means. Antonia brought the empty clay jugs and they both carried the water. They could not afford an *aquarius*, one who carried water for those who could pay.

Appius found Antonia amongst the several *aquarii* with their jugs on poles and amongst others of the public who were at the fountain with their jugs, filling them for their same purpose. He kissed Antoinia lightly on the cheek as she straightened up from filling a jug. "Antonia. Has the day treated you well? You look tired. Let me help you with the filling."

Antonia, hands on hips, said, "My husband, Appius." She leaned forward to emphasize her gaze. "I must say—you do not look tired. You look energized. What must I expect when we get to our home? I see a light in your eyes. What is it?"

"My dear, Antonia, I do not think I can have a thought without you knowing. I sometimes think you know before me. Yes, I do have a delicious thought, and it has nothing to do with

39

what we might do at our home. Let us fill these jugs and be on our way. I will tell you while we walk. I would rather our conversation be between us, not that I do not trust our neighbors." He glanced at those nearby.

Antonia, now feigning wide eyed amazement, said, "Appius, what could it be? Now you have got me wondering. I must admit that I do not know what is glowing under that curly hair. You must tell me."

They walked past the bricked area at the fountain nodding to those they knew, smiling at comments made to evoke humor. When they were on the dirt road leading to their home, Antonia gave Appius a nudge to his ribs. "Appius, not a moment longer."

Appius turned and grinned, his eyes burning in a peculiar way. "Antonia, Marcus Atius has today offered me a great opportunity. I am pleased that he has said that it is because of my hard work and interest in the water systems and my own efforts in trying to improve our system and its understanding. My work will change radically, and because it will have some effect on you, I told him I would first talk to you before I accept."

"You are not going off to fight in a legion, in some far land?"

"No, no. It's not that. I will be close—somewhat close."

Antonia eyed him sharply but said nothing. She would let him explain in his own words. If there were something amiss, a weakness to his explanation, she would immediately be able to deduce it and ask questions of him.

Appius drew a deep breath and went on. "Marcus Atius has asked me to engage in calculations and do investiage to determine the requirements for the future supply of water to Nemausus—it will be as if Nemausus were twice the size that now exists."

"Oh, that sounds interesting. Certainly Marcus must have much admiration for you to entrust you with such an important task."

"Yes, he said as much. But the requirement has come from a... suggestion... by Claudius upon his recent visit. What I am saying is that my work will be most important as the *Corporata* are to detail the requirements, the result, to Claudius."

Antonia now walked closer to Appius. "See, there is a reward for your hard work. You should be proud. How long do you think such a... calculation... and investigation will last—several months, I should say? You will then be an authority, probably consulted by Claudius himself. But, Claudius must have something in mind. He is not just curious. Will he then ask the water operators to provide such service?"

Appius grimaced, awed that Antonia could so swiftly understand the implications of the situation and drive him so quickly to explain the remainder of his task, the part that he suspected would be difficult. He decided to jump in rather than wade. "There is more to my task. Once I have determined the requirement, I am charged to find a source that is adequate, or sources if that is necessary." Appius held his breath.

Antonia said nothing for a few moments then nodded. "I see."

Appius was afraid that she did. He decided, rather, to dip his toe in the water. "What do you think? A great opportunity, yes?"

"I think it's a great opportunity for you to wander the region, having who-knows-what adventures, while I toil here at home, hauling my own water, depending on the neighbors and my family for protection. I suppose it will only last for several years though."

Appius knew that no answer or explanation would smooth the waters. "I am not able to determine how long it will take me. Perhaps I will find a source, a spring perhaps that is close. I will come home, report my findings and the *Aqua Corporata* will go on from there."

"You are responsible just to find a source?"

"In truth, Marcus did say that he would expect me to determine how we would transport the water to Nemausus."

Antonia glared at him. They had reached the entry to their small courtyard. They entered and set the water under a pitched roof attached to the house. Antonia went inside and gathered food stores and went back out to the courtyard to prepare their meal. Cooking, using fire, was done in the courtyard as it was too dangerous in the house. Appius found chores to do—cleaning his sandals, changing his tunic, sharpening his knife while Antonia prepared the vegetables and braised a small cut of lamb. Antonia, at length, yelled, "Appius."

Appius wryly noted that he had gone from lighthearted enthusiasm to the dread of now dealing with the issue at home. He knew that he would face resistance, but... he had hoped it would be otherwise. He sat on the stool, plate in his hand, clay water goblet on a bench to his side, across from Antonia, staring at her. She was not returning his gaze.

He began, "So, Antonia, I do not think you are looking at my assignment with the same enthusiasm that I am. Yes, you will have to spend some time alone, but you must know that I will not be too far away, nor away for too long. It would not be reasonable to find water far from the town. It will not be as if you are the wife of a soldier, not to see her man for years."

Antonia looked up. "But, Appius, we are very happy now, and you are home every night. What advantage will this new responsibility bring?"

"I do not know if my future will be more advantaged because of newly acquired experience, but one would surely think so. A better life for both of us?"

"The *Aqua Corporata* will make more money, and you will still be a lackey. That is what we can be most assured of. Can you see it differently?"

"You are right. One cannot be sure. However, life offers few opportunities. They are fleeting and one either takes the chance or submits to a more ordinary life. What do you say?"

Antonia said nothing. She shook her head picking deliberately at her vegetables.

Appius had not yet told Antonia the total arrangement. Would it make a difference? "Marcus did say that while I was on the assignment, my pay would be increased to 75 sestertii a month." He held his breath awaiting her response.

Antonia's head snapped up. "We could have an *aquarius* haul our water." She realized she had blurted an accommodation. "At least I would not have to do that by myself." She went back to inspecting her food. "Yes, Appius, you must accept. You would be very intolerable having missed the opportunity and the challenge of the work and the possible next promotions. I would be living with an unhappy man, full time. At least, with the assignment, you will be around and presumed happy for some of the time."

"Thank you, Antonia. And will I be living with a wife who is constantly unhappy with me?"

"No, Appius, I will do my best to do my best. Perhaps you will entertain me with stories from your travels."

the *Aedifex*: Building the Pont du Gard

"Thank you, Antonia. I would not expect less from a woman such as you." Appius slumped in relaxation. How would he have told Marcus had Antonia strongly resisted?

"Thank you, Antonia. I would not expect less from a woman such as you." Appius slumped in relaxation. How would he have told Marcus had Antonia strongly resisted?

43

CHAPTER 7

Vers-Pont du Gard

I relaxed on the eastward-facing deck of my villa, sipping wine, tearing chunks of bread, slicing cheese. Omar Khayyam would be smiling, although there was no 'thou.' I should have been thankful for that.

During the day, I'd arranged my somewhat meager belongings after doing a first echelon, cursory—very cursory—cleaning of my new residence. I'd done a practice walk into town, bought groceries and wine. At the local wine shop, with many gestures, fractured French and fractured English, I and the shopkeeper were able to come to an understanding of what local wine I must drink. I think I paid way too much for what I needed for solo sipping. It was red wine of course. White is for those of meager appreciation.

I had long ago understood that I thrive on accomplishment. I was, at this time, able to convince myself that my late accomplishments justified my current enjoyment. In addition to situating myself, I had done it—the larger 'it.' I had made the commitment and the arrangements to do this thing. Here I was, basking in the warm Mediterranean evening on the threshold of a new adventure. Life was good.

I heard knocking at the door. I'd left the doors from the deck open to the house. Somewhat regretfully, I abandoned my relaxed posture and thoughts and made my way through the villa to the front door and opened it, somewhat curious as to who should come calling. It was Laurie with a bottle of wine under her arm.

She thrust the bottle toward me then stepped in and gave me a hug. "Welcome, Monsieur Warner. I thought that perhaps you should like some celebratory wine on your first night. And, since you have no accompanying celebratory woman, I will provide both." She laughed.

I accepted her hug, gratefully. "Come in, please come in," I gestured a sweeping hand through the door. "But, as you will see, I'm somewhat ahead of you. The celebratory wine bottle is open, and I'm enjoying the view and the warm evening. Won't you join me?" I fumbled a glass from the cupboard.

"Oh, oh, I'm proud of you," she cooed. "I see you are already enjoying the atmosphere without my prompting. Perhaps you'd rather enjoy this party on your own?"

"No, no," I rushed to assure her. "Having you join me is delightful. Come out on the deck, and I'll let you catch up with me."

"Catch up, catch up—isn't that the disgusting... excuse me... the traditional American tomato blend, sold in a bottle?"

"I'm sorry. I didn't say ketchup. 'Catch up' means that you'll have a glass of wine to match the one I'm working on. Here you go."

"Ha, ha. I'm not always quick to understand American... English... phrases. One of the most difficult for me is to hear the difference between 'festival' and 'first of all.'" Laurie, still standing, accepted the wine, tipped the glass and took a sip. "Salut— welcome."

"I wouldn't have imagined a problem between 'festival' and 'first of all.' I certainly understand 'catch up.' Interesting. But who am I to comment, a one-trick pony as far as languages are concerned?"

"A one-trick pony." She laughed and sat down.

I admired Laurie from across the table as she took an impish sip. Laurie wasn't a striking woman in a classic beauty way, but her high cheekbones were attractive and somehow provided additional propulsion to the energy she exuded. Yes, it was the energy. You couldn't help but be absorbed by her energy and enthusiasm, punctuated by her engaging smile, accentuated by the cheekbones. Good observation on my part, I thought. She took you along for the ride, although you felt it was headlong. You became a part of her and it was somewhat sensuous. "I'm very happy you dropped by. Your clients must be very appreciative of you."

"Well, you are making the assumption that I view all my clients through the same lens as I do you. What if I think you are special—an adventure?"

"I can't imagine being anyone's adventure, especially of a very attractive, full-of-life, fandango dancing, single female that is thirty years younger."

"I don't dance the fandango."

"I just threw that in."

She laughed. "But, I like it. Maybe 'fandango' is a secret, maybe intimate, name by which you may call me, something whispered on the dance floor or in a passionate embrace."

What was happening here? Was this typical flirtation, French style? My turn to laugh—I didn't know how else to respond. "Are we going dancing, Laurie?"

"Maybe. Sometime. You didn't ask about the passionate embrace"

"I thought you just threw that in."

She only smiled.

If this *was* typical French flirtation, I was reveling in it. No wonder the French have a reputation for passion. I was still sane enough, sober enough, and had not yet been convinced she was sincere. I put the brakes on my enthusiasm, overwhelming as it was. What a great gift for my housewarming. I wondered what *really* was going on in her head. "Laurie, have another glass of wine."

We talked. We enjoyed the warm evening. We drank the remainder of the wine. There was no more talk of passionate embraces or secret, intimate names. As Laurie was leaving, she gave me a long hug and smiled before she kissed me.

Oh my!

CHAPTER 8

I walked from my villa to the Pont du Gard.   The Pont du Gard is only one feature of the entire 30-mile length of the aqueduct.   It is the aqueduct's bridge over the River Gard—sometimes called the Gardon.   So, yes, in this instance I'm talking about the bridge, the most impressive and best-known feature of the aqueduct. It was a good walk—enough to get my system going but not enough to require rest and great quantities of water to quench a thirst.   I enjoyed walking the neighborhood, enjoyed seeing the Med-style housing, most of plaster, but some of wood.

This was my first real day of investigation.   Yes, I'd read more about the Pont du Gard, knew more than when I originally encountered the structure. Today, I would focus on the bridge foundations, especially the three piers at river level.   Since no cement was used in the structure, I wanted to see how the stones were fit to the underlying foundation, rock which I assumed was natural.   The ancients may have chosen the crossing location because of the convenience of existing rock in the river. Otherwise they would have an arch span that was too wide, more susceptible to erosion, earthquakes and the like, or they would have to scour the riverbed, find bedrock and build the structure from that point. I imagine they would have to detour the river to do this, not an easy task if you're in a canyon. Of course, they would also want to pick a location where the gap between the hillsides, on either side, was narrow, to minimize the total length of the bridge structure. As it is, the top, the very top, of the bridge is 900 feet long.

So, the rock on which they set the piers must be robust, not likely to erode, and situated conveniently to allow a reasonable arch span. The other item I would investigate was evidence of high water marks for the Gardon in the vicinity of the bridge. Did the builders have to allow for rising water levels at some time or other of the year? I hadn't checked any data on river-level variation. There was no mention, so far, that the builders had to be concerned with fluctuation. But, I must say, there wasn't much information on most aspects of the construction. Perhaps there was more, or perhaps there were people who had made a study of this, but I hadn't yet become aware of them. If and when I did,

Laurie would be my help in enabling a decent exchange, considering the language barriers. My thoughts were still enhanced by her remarks.

I worked my way down the bank, through the brush, and approached a foundation on a rock attached to the shore but around which the water flowed on one side. It looked like the rock had been chiseled to some depth below its horizontal surface, the outline slightly larger than the blocks that were set in the depression. That made sense. The builders could carve a flat surface for the pier blocks to sit upon. Modern day construction would have us clean the rock then pour concrete to provide a level base for supporting the structure above. We would drill holes into the rock and insert steel stobs, which would project into the concrete, providing strength to resist the force of the river during high flow.

As I was looking at the stones, I saw inscriptions—ancient or more recent? Some were carved with letters and numbers. Others were more like graffiti, with images and whole words. I wondered if anyone had made sense out of these.

I couldn't get to the pier across the river. To do so would require a swim or a superhuman leap. From what I could see, the arrangement of the foundation looked similar to the one against which I rested my foot.

I had a measuring tape with me. I measured the height of one of the stones then counted the number of stones from the rock foundation to the top of the arch. The cut stones looked very uniform in thickness, so I thought that I'd be fairly accurate. My calculations showed that the arches at this level were about 72 feet tall. You would think that this height would provide more than adequate clearance for any rise of the river. Yes, the height was impressive. The falsework structure required to build the arch would not have been insignificant in itself.

That reminded me to investigate for signs of variation on river level. I looked at the stones of the pier. Surely the stone faces, carved and placed nearly two thousand years ago were more recent than the natural stone on the riverbank. The cut stones above the foundation rock showed water marks well up on the piers, which, if climate and waterways existed similar to when the structure was built, would indicate that the builders had to make sure they got the piers completed to a safe height in the dry times of year. However, climate and the river situation could likely be different. I would have to check information that might be or *might not* be available. If any dams or levees or diversions had been constructed, at any intervening time, conditions would be changed. Knowing that I could easily run into dead-ends made me realize that this investigation would not be easy; this project, self-assigned, might involve more time, energy and persistence than I had imagined.

Although the cut stones of the piers would more likely show the history of water-level changes after being incorporated in the structure, more so than the rocks that lined the canyon, I walked to nearby canyon rocks, anyway. No doubt that the canyon rocks would record a history of hundreds of thousands, maybe millions of years. A cursory glance indicated that at some time, probably many times, the water had flowed at a considerable depth through the canyon well above the foundations.

As I stared at the rock, I spotted a man walking down the slope through the brush toward me. As he neared, he waved. I returned his wave. I didn't think that I was trespassing or violating a restricted area. If there were signs posted in French, it was certain that I wouldn't have comprehended. But, from his attire, I didn't get the idea that he was an official of some kind.

He nodded, "Bonjour, monsieur, que faites-vous là ?"

"Bonjour," I replied, nearly stretching my limit of French communication skills. I added, "Je ne parle pas Français."

He stiffened. "American?"

"Yes, American." I suppose I could have offended any given Frenchman in any number of ways.

"Hello, American. What are you doing?"

"You *do* speak English."

"Yes." He continued to approach. "In my career I was required to speak with and correspond to the English, the Australians, and the Americans. I can understand you, but barely." He laughed. "Please go on. What are you doing?"

"Oh. Well, I'm looking at this magnificent structure. Is it yours?" I smiled.

He laughed, now standing in front of me, "You like my bridge?"

"I like your bridge very much. I've just retired, and I'm over here, living for a while, to find out more about the aqueduct and how it was built—an adventure of sorts."

49

"Oh, Welcome, American. I too am retired, but have lived here for several years. I wander the aqueduct, kick the stones and try to imagine what it was like."

"What it was like—building it?"

"Yes. Quite an accomplishment, don't you think?"

"Yes—and that it's still standing is a testament to their good work."

The Frenchman stretched his arm to shake my hand. "My name is Maurice."

"Hello, Maurice. My name is Warner—and thank you for speaking English."

Maurice smiled. "It makes life more interesting if you can speak languages of others. So, what have you discovered about our project?"

"I've read some, but not much. Most of what I *have* found repeats the same information—you know—height, length, and how many stones. There do seem to be a lot of mysteries, though. A few of the more detailed descriptions question how the builders were able to deal with the limited difference in elevation between Fontaine Euro and Nimes—how they were able to survey it—lay it out. Also, there is only scant information on who built the structure. They say Agrippa was responsible, under Augustus Caesar, but I can find very little in literature that mentions this. And, Maurice, I am just starting. Today, in fact, is my first opportunity to spend time with the structure."

"Yes well, you've managed to uncover some of the mystery in just a short time. I've had more luxury to be able to live nearby. I've let the sense of the project seep into my thoughts and understanding. You can look and see what is there now, but uncovering how it was done—that is not so easy."

I appreciated the meaning of his slight smile. "You said that you were required to speak English in your career—the British, Australians, and Americans. What did you do?"

Maurice nodded toward the northeast. I worked out of Grenoble for a firm that built hydraulic turbines. We sold and helped install them in many parts of the globe—some in the United States—on your rivers."

"I was involved in some hydro work. My career involved construction and installation of large gear. What projects did you do in the U.S.?"

the *Aedifex*: Building the Pont du Gard

"Have you ever heard of run-of-the-river turbine installation? I was involved in installation of several of our units on your Mississippi River."

"I do know about those. We bid on them. Actually we bid on them to a French firm from Grenoble. But, you didn't award us the work."

"Yes. As you know, you have to be low bidder."

I laughed. "Yes, that could've been the problem. How did the project go?"

He displayed an ironic smile. "Like all projects it had its problems—like a high-water year on the Mississippi while we were involved in installation. We finally were able to get it done, though."

I pointed toward the foundation of the bridge. "I was wondering if the builders had to worry about high water when they built this. I was looking for evidence of water levels on the pier—and then on the canyon wall. What do you know about that?"

"I do know something about that. The builders would have had to be very worried about what the river might do to them. If the seasons were somewhat similar to what we experience now, they would have very little time to prepare the rock and get enough stones in place so that the river wouldn't ravage the work. I have records that I will show you, that is, if you are going to remain here for a while."

I smiled. I had a collaborator, maybe a friend. "Certainly, I'll be here for a while, and I'm thinking that you might be a great source of information for me."

"Not only a source but an aqueduct of information."

I only smiled. I wanted to show him I appreciated his— humor. "I've got another question while we're down here—the inscriptions—the carvings on the stones. Are they from the time of the building or are we seeing more modern inspiration?"

Maurice led me to the base of the pier, nimbly managing the slope and the rocks. "Come, take a look." At the base he pointed to one block of stone, then several others. "You see these?

I noticed he was pointing to stones that had letters and numbers. "Yes," I said.

"These blocks were specially cut at the quarry. The inscriptions identify where they are to be placed. If you notice, and if you were able to use your tape measure, you would find that most of the other stones are identically cut. The builders made an effort to make it simple to eliminate the need for *fitting* every stone.

"You mean that Henry Ford wasn't the first to imagine mass production?"

"*Exactement.*"

I waved in the direction of the stones Maurice had indicated. "So, there must have been a design, a layout, maybe drawings. But, someone had to have a representation of the location of the block in the structure if they carved it in one place, and it had to be installed in a specific spot in the structure."

"Yes."

"Speaking of that," I shrugged, "what did they use for drawings? I mean they weren't still chiseling cuneiform in stone or clay. Did they have paper?"

"They used parchment and probably used oiled parchment. From that era, it seems likely that is what they used for documents that were expected to last the handling and the duration."

"Nothing survived, I imagine."

"No, nothing has been found that I know of."

Maurice wiped his brow. It wasn't really moist. It was just a gesture, as I found out. "Warner, would you like to have a beer with me in town, and perhaps something to eat? It's nearly noon and my thinking and talking is always enhanced by a good brew."

I brightened. "Yes. Surely. But I must insist on paying for the beer as *quid pro quo* for your tutorial."

"Oh, *quid pro quo*. Who is the Roman, now? Let's go. Are you walking?"

"Yes."

"Me, too."

I love sidewalk cafés. One can sit with a nice beer and watch the village in motion, many lives involved in a scurry that coincide. We were only getting a glimpse, almost a snapshot of activity-of-the-moment. That was the fun part. From the villager's expressions, determination and gear, we were able to draft mini-sketches of their mission while simultaneously witnessing the swarm... so much better than being inside, only viewing the restaurant interior. The weather was perfect. Life was good.

Yes, and I had easily discovered a compatriot, someone also interested in the aqueduct and someone with similar background, able to imagine some of the installation. I'd already done plenty of that. In the ancient Roman Empire and in our so-called modern era, you must first build it in your mind.

I tipped my beer to Maurice, after he waved to a grizzled gentleman, slowly ambling the distance to his destination, the tobacco shop. "Your health, Maurice. How do you say in French?"

"Ciao. I'm sure you've heard of it."

"Yes, Ciao, but isn't that Italian?"

"You don't like Italians? They get things right—sometimes." Maurice laughed.

"I have no problems with Italians." I took a swallow. Sometimes beer is just the right thing. Our walk to the village from the canyon had created a thirst.

Maurice set down his glass. "We French don't like Americans, you know."

I nearly choked, but noticed he was smiling. "Yes? Then what am I doing at your table—by invitation?"

He laughed. "I was wondering what you would say about that. It seems we have a reputation. What do you think?"

I thought for a moment before I answered. "I've encountered a few rude French, but I've also been charmed by some that are very accommodating and pleasant." I was thinking about Laurie. I added, "I have a French friend that lives in Nimes. He's, in large part, responsible for my interest in the Pont du Gard. He was my host and guide when I visited four months ago. So, to answer your question, I've had a range of experiences. Isn't that the situation with any culture—you find the good and the bad?"

"Yes, that is true. But, somehow we French have managed to create a stronger impression. I will say that some of my countrymen are aggressive in their dislike. My personal opinion is that they do this because looking down on others elevates their own perceived status—and, what better target than the Americans? If one can look down on the Americans—well, then." He held up his mug as if toasting.

I smiled. "Hmmm. When I think of arrogant Frenchmen, I think of Le Grande Charles. Is he the model?"

"Not so much a model. But Charles de Gaul created an image of French pride at a time we needed it. I think there is justification to saying that he had a strong influence."

I sat back. "Well, Maurice, can we be friends? I promise to behave and not talk about all the great things America has done. I'll even pay for the beer."

"Yes, American, yes. I only brought this up to clear the air and perhaps because I have a whimsical, maybe ironic, side to me." He tipped his glass, "To France and America. May we always be friends."

I laughed and tipped my glass. "An interesting match, don't you think? Perhaps we can keep each other from being too stuffy."

We reflected a moment in silence, but I wanted to know more about the aqueduct. "Maurice, I mentioned a mystery. Perhaps you can tell me what you know. When was the thing built? Everything I have read mentions Agrippa, which means that building was going on around 16 BC, just before his death. What do you know?"

"Several scholars have attributed the aqueduct construction to Agrippa because he did build some structures in ancient Nemausus. He was a champion of Nemausus and this area. From there, it gets murky. Other academics think it was built much later."

"Agrippa didn't build it or have it built—in their opinion?"

"No."

"Why do they think—*later*—carbon dating or some such technical device? Someone must have cared enough to investigate."

Maurice nodded and took another swallow of beer, wiping the froth from his lips. "I'm not really sure where the argument lies, or what has been determined. There is a professor at the Marseille University that has studied the structure—the aqueduct—in some detail. I think you should talk to him."

"Do you know him? Would he talk to me?"

"One can't be certain, but you might try. His name is Marcel Durand. He is a professor of archeology but has adopted the Pont du Gard as his special study. You can't really say you've done your investigation without talking to him—or trying to, anyway."

"Does he speak English?"

"I don't know. If he does not, I could go along. It would be interesting for me, also."

I laughed. "I think I've already hired an interpreter."

"Why do you laugh?"

I smirked, "Because this interpreter may be more than I can handle. Her name is Laurie, a young lady. Do you know her? She is from this village."

"Hahhh!" Maurice barked. "Laurie—not Laurie! Hahh! She is a wild one, that girl. And she's your interpreter? How did *that* happen?"

I told him. "Am I in trouble?"

"That remains to be seen. Oh well, you're here for an adventure. Laurie's a good place to start." He paused, "You will take Laurie to the professor?"

I was imagining a catastrophe: Laurie using her charm on the professor to get more information and the professor shooing us out, not in a good humor for farces. I shook my head then nodded. "I suppose so. I agree that you'd be a better choice, but I'd be afraid to tell her that she'd been replaced. Perhaps I could give her the assignment of getting me an appointment. If she is not successful at that, I will tell her that I am going to try something else."

"Excellent. You must tell me what happens. An adventure. Yes, I'm sure of it."

I took a deep breath, then two quick gulps of beer.

I called Laurie and told her we needed to talk. She insisted on coming by for coffee. I heard the knock on the door. I hoped she'd eat the croissants I bought, along with drinking the coffee. I opened the door.

"Bonjour, Monsieur Warner. I'm so delighted to see you again, so soon."

"Come in, come in. Let's go out to the deck. I'll bring the coffee out. Will you have a croissant?"

"You have a croissant for me? How nice. Well, I've already had my *petite dejeuner*, but I will share half of a croissant with you. Merci."

After we were seated with coffee and pastry, I said, "Laurie, I have a task for you—maybe two tasks. Are you still willing to help me?"

"Yes, of course I am willing. Do I not look willing?" She smiled—a coquettish smile. "What is it—or what are they?"

"I'm glad you'll help. Yesterday I met one of your neighbors, Maurice. He says he knows you. Do you know who I'm talking about?"

"Of course. Maurice. What did he say about me? But, I know there is only *good* to report."

I was circumspect. "He said you were very attractive and vivacious. He also said my association with you would be an adventure."

"Ha, ha. I like it all. I'll have to give Maurice a kiss. Yes. I am your adventure as you are mine. Now, how may I help you?"

"Maurice told me about a professor at Marseille University who has studied the aqueduct and the Pont du Gard. He suggests I talk to him. I would like you to set up an appointment. And, if he doesn't speak English, then I would want you to accompany me to the University—as my translator. How does that sound?"

Laurie nodded. "I will do it, of course. Give me the professor's name, and I will do the rest. We will have a lovely time taking a journey together. I will show you the French countryside." Her eyes somehow imparted a more playful emphasis than the words.

"Excellent. Here you are." I handed her a slip of paper showing the name of the professor. "Let's enjoy our coffee."

"*Certainement*. And enjoy each other too, of course."

"Of course." I suppose there was no question in Laurie's mind that she would be successful in getting a session with the professor and that he would not speak English. How did I know this?

CHAPTER 9

Appius struggled through another week of work awaiting word. Marcus told the *Aqua Corporata* that Appius would be willing to do the work and was enthusiastic to do so. Nemus sent a message to Claudius, a grand description of the attributes of Appius. It is very possible that Appius would not have recognized his own description and achievements from the document. Although the *Aqua Corporata* were waiting for a return message, an approval from Claudius, it was up to them, actually. They could hire Appius without the approval of Claudius, but they did not want to hear a rant from the *Imperator* later, should they not come up with a solution that pleased Claudius. Strewing the path with rose petals was always useful.

When Marcus summoned Appius to the water works office, he looked at the young man, tunic hemmed in mud, for several moments before he spoke. "Appius, your *Imperator* has smiled upon you. He has given his blessing, indicating you should lead us across the abyss, plot the future, and chart the success of our fair Nemausus. You may start immediately."

Appius knew that Marcus had received an answer from Claudius—word about whether he would proceed, or not and had fretted with mixed emotions. He was eager to grapple with the work, solve the problems, and devise the means of watering an expanded Nemausus. On the other hand, he felt the responsibility—the eyes of the *Aqua Corporata* upon him, not to mention Claudius. And then he must deal with Antonia. "Marcus, I accept gratefully, and I will start immediately. Your statement, though, is much too flowery for a task that will amount to hard work."

"Yes, it will be hard work, Appius. And, I am pleased to tell you, that as of this moment, your wages will increase to the seventy-five sestertii I mentioned. Also, you will encounter other expenses, perhaps. If you must travel, you will surely have to pay for meals or lodging away from Nemausus. Or, you may need an assistant to help you determine the routing of the water. For the expenses, please keep a record. If you require additional help or devices, please ask us first."

"Yes, Marcus. How would you have me keep you informed? Do you want to know what I have done or accomplished on a regular basis or only when I have something significant to report?"

Marcus leaned back. "While you are calculating the future town requirements, you will be nearby, of course, and we can talk casually from time to time. When you are away from town, communication will be difficult, so I would expect you to advise me of your findings when you return. That should be suitable unless, of course, *I* have a question for *you*. In that case, I will find you and ask. When you are gone, shall I deliver your wages to Antonia?"

"Yes, that will be good. She manages our money. Having it pass through my hands is only ceremonial, and I thank you for thinking of that arrangement."

"My pleasure. And, one more thing, Appius, have you reviewed the nature of your prior duties with Tinius? He will struggle to perform your responsibilities, I am sure, but do you think he will be able to learn, in time, to provide the service as you have provided it?"

"Yes. I have reviewed my work with Tinius. I must admit that he does not have the same passion for the work as I, so it may take him longer to handle the requirements. Yet, I will often be in Nemausus. I have told him to come to me if he is puzzled by a problem. I think Tinius will do well."

"Then go, Appius. Start your work. I do not have any thoughts on how you should proceed. That is up to you. That is why we are giving you the work. And, I hope you find the work enjoyable and that it bears abundant fruit."

"Thank you, Marcus. I am anxious to start."

Appius had been giving his task much thought—the initial requirement to determine the future water needs of Nemausus. It seemed clear that he must first determine how much water was being used, how many people were supported by this use, how it was being used, and where it came from. To determine the future requirement for a town twice the size, it would not be as simple as merely doubling the current amount of usage. With additional water, with more abundant water, especially at first, new and broader uses would appear. And how about water used for crop production? How would he imagine those requirements? Well, he would have to use his best judgment. If he were wrong, who, twenty years from now could pin the error on him? Also, he would show his calculations to the *Aqua Corporata*—even Claudius. If they did not agree with his projections, they could make changes. This chain of reasoning gave him some comfort, reduced the dread of responsibility weighing heavily on his shoulders. He could not wait.

But, he was puzzled. Yes, he could observe water from the springs flowing in a channel of a measured size; that was a good start. But the size of the channel only partly described the amount of water. The quantity of water was also determined by how swiftly the water flowed. How could he assess the speed? He could throw a wood chip in the water and count how long it took to travel a measured difference. But, what good was that? If he told someone that the water in a 4-foot by 6-foot channel flowed one-hundred feet while he counted to forty—it would tell them nothing. His count could be faster or slower than that of someone else. There were no devices and no observations that could be made to provide a standard unit of time. Well, maybe there *was* one.

"What will you be doing? How will you go about this work?" Antonia questioned Appius while spooning vegetables onto his dinner plate. Appius had told Antonia about his meeting with Marcus and had bought a jug of wine, a fairly good wine, to celebrate the occasion and to, perhaps, soften Antonia's perspective of what she considered the dark side of his task—his absence. He acknowledged he was being profligate before having received even one additional sestertii.

Appius accepted his plate after pouring wine into Antonia's cup and his. He set his plate aside and waited until Antonia shoveled vegetables to her plate, then raised his cup. "Antonia, please take this wine as a symbol of new beginnings for us. As the wine is good, as the winemaker did his best to make the wine good, we will, together, do our best to make our new venture good. Will you drink to that?" Appius realized he was being more flowery, more philosophical than was his nature, but he was buoyed by his enthusiasm.

"I will drink to that, my husband. As a dependable wife, you can expect me to help you in your task." Antonia took a sip, almost as if she were testing it for bitterness.

Appius was hoping for more joy—a more inspired response. "Antonia, my hope, my fondest hope, is that you will have the same passion for this as I, not just bowing to some requirement to be *dependable*. Can you not imagine our future in more happy terms?" Perhaps when she had taken more wine....

"Yes, Appius, I am sorry. My statement was cold. I promise I will do my best to be enthused about your work and to share in your progress, if not your adventure." She smiled and gathered corn on her plate. "Now, back to my question—how will you go about your work? You see, I do show interest. Tell me, please."

Appius took a long sip of wine, eyeing her thoughtfully. "Yes, Antonia, what is my plan? I must first determine the amount of water we get from the *fontis*. We also draw water from many wells in the city, capture water from streams and creeks in reservoirs we have built, and many citizens capture rainwater in their cisterns. I must know how much water we get from these sources. That will be the basis on which I determine our future requirements."

"But will the future—additional—citizens also capture rainwater? Will the additional citizenry consist of wealthy water patrons with baths in their homes and gardens to water? Are you such a visionary that you can tell us what will become?" Antonia took a sip of wine, not so measured as the first.

"No, Antonia. I am not a visionary. I can only imagine or assume our future uses—who will be using water and for what. I must make a reasonable guess. The alternative is to shrug my shoulders and say, 'I do not know.' So, in addition to listing our *sources*, I must also determine the present *uses* for our water, by whom, for what, and in what quantity. That will help me determine—or guess—our future uses. As you can see, there is much work to be done, here in Nemausus, before I go wandering in the hills. You will tire of me being at home so much. You will welcome my occasional absence." Appius smiled and boldly forked a cucumber slice into his mouth.

"It sounds like your work in Nemausus will take you to many doors. In investigating for your water information, you will find out much about our town, our people, our problems, fantasies, dramas, and intrigue. You must, of course, share that with me." Antonia looked up coyly from her wine cup as she sipped.

"Yes, dear Antonia, yes. Not only will I share, but I expect that you will help me imagine the future. Between the two of us, if either is a visionary, it is you, bright star that you are." Appius thought the statement would be useful—to entrain Antonia in his work.

"Oh, Appius. You know that understanding your work is way beyond me. I will be happy with only sharing knowledge of the town folk. Of course, you may tell me of your thoughts from time to time. I am sure that just the telling of them will help you make you form clear ideas. Yes, I will be glad to listen."

"You see, Antonia, we can be partners in this. May I refill your wine cup?"

Antonia held out her cup. "Yes. And, do not drink too much. The meal and the wine is only part of our celebration."

Appius had to quantify the output of the *fontis*. How could one tell how much water the spring provided? Just observing the flow was not useful. He had to know how much water flowed and was used in... let us say... a day's time. How did this quantity change over the seasons? He needed this quantity for means of comparison. If he found other sources, he must compare their flow to that of the *fontis*. Would they provide more or less and by how much? He needed a number, but what would be meaningful?

The problem was with time. The only measurement of time available was the length of a day—from sunrise to sunrise. No means of measuring part of a day existed—to him. Yes, he could run the flow of the springs into a large reservoir for a day and measure that quantity, but no such means existed. The problem was baffling, and he spent much of his time thinking about it.

The spring water had been captured and led into a stone channel by works that had been constructed well before his time. The channel was rectangular, so it was easy to measure the width and depth of the flow. To do this, he had to wade into the channel to measure the depth, ignoring the lines inscribed on the side of the channel by past water managers. Appius wanted to make sure the markings were correct. He made his own marks on the side of the channel but knew he would have to wade in again when the depth changed.

He could calculate a volume of water. He imagined the water as one piece, a slug—100 feet long, 6 feet wide and 2 foot high. His measured piece of water was equal to 1200 cubic feet. All good, but so what? How many of these slugs would flow past a given point in a day? That was the solution, he reasoned. One means of determining this would be to drop a chip, allow it to glide the 100 feet and immediately drop another chip at the starting point; he would need to do this for a day—sunrise to sunrise and count the number of trips. That number of trips times the 1200 cubic feet would tell him how much water flowed in a day. He shuddered to think of the tedium of doing so. Yet, it would be a start, something to work with. But, if he wanted to quantify any other sources, he would have to repeat the same tedious procedure. He needed to establish a means of measuring a shorter period of time—like the time it took for the water to flow 100 feet.

At the beginning of the water run, he tossed in a wood chip and was able to count to 393 in a measured cadence during its 100 foot travel. He performed the measurement again, in fact several times, getting counts ranging from 385 to 426. He reasoned that the difference resulted in his variation in counting speed and not the flow of the water. He scratched his head. *I think I must do better than that.*

He had an idea. He had heard of water clocks. They identified shorter periods of time—parts of a day—using water dripping from one vessel into another. The depth of water in the second vessel could be compared. He gouged a small hole in the bottom of a tall cup, filled it, and counted until the water had run completely out. He was able to count to 880 or 895 or 900 in several attempts, using his prior counting cadence. *It seems like the cup will be large enough to accommodate any flows that might be slower and take more time at another season.* The amount of water that flowed from the cup would represent time and not suffer the variation in his counting speed. Now he must be able measure the amount of water that would flow from the cup. He found a larger cup. He would let the water from the first cup drain into it then scribe a level on the inside of the cup. Now he could release his chip and note the level of water that had accumulated in the second cup when the chip had travelled the 100 feet.

To do this he needed help; someone would have to tell him when the wood chip crossed the finish line after he dropped it in the channel. When he dropped the chip, he would simultaneously start the release of the water from the one cup to the other and stop it when the chip had made the 100-foot trip. He found Tinius who was happy to help, taking the opportunity to ask questions of

Appius, questions that had already befuddled Tinius in trying to perform the duties he had acquired.

They performed the measurement several times; the level of water in the second cup obtained the same level repeatedly; Appius scribed a line at the water level in the second cup.

However, he had noticed when experimenting that the water ran out faster if the water in the cup with the hole was deeper. He must make provision for this. Therefore, he filled the cup nearly to the top and scribed a line at this level. Then he measured the amount of water in the second cup as the chip flowed for 50 feet, 100 feet, 150 feet, and 200 feet. He scribed lines in the measuring cup in accord, noting that the spacing between the marks decreased from the lower, upwards, as the length of the runs increased. He reasoned that he now had a means of measuring the variation in time.

He walked to Tinius. "Thank you, Tinius. I could not have performed this by myself. I may ask you to help me from time to time. Our managers would surely approve."

"Yes, Appius. It will probably occur that I seek *you* more often than the reverse. I wish I had been more attentive. But, perhaps you will tell me what you are doing, and I will learn even more."

"Yes, Tinius, and thank you."

Appius still did not have a means of determining how much water flowed in a day, only an accurate means of timing part of a day's flow. The water level in his cup represented only a segment of a day.

Using his thought about repeatedly dropping a chip in the water and counting the trips, he instead would let the water in his cup drain to the level in the second cup relating to the 100 foot flow—for one day. Yes, that was laborious too, but once done, he could calculate the amount of water represented. And, to evaluate another source, he could take his cups with him and make a similar time measurement. His accumulations would determine the amount of water that flowed in a day's time. He would not have to count how many times the chip travelled 100 feet in a day.

Over dinner that night, he explained his thought to Antonia. She asked him to describe his method and asked many questions. She finally nodded her head. To determine the amount of water that would flow in a day's time, the cup with the hole in the bottom would be filled to the scribed line. The water would flow and collect in the cup with the scratch mark representing the level to which the water had reached for the 100-foot run. He would quickly dump the water into the top cup and repeat the process. He would do this from sunup on one day to sunup the next day. He would then count the number of times he dumped the cup. He could then calculate that the 1200 cubic feet would have been able to run by that many times in one day. If he then accumulated the 1200 cubic feet that many times it would represent how much water flowed, the amount of water the spring supplied, running for a day. Other water flows could be compared using this same standard. He felt exhilaration, having come up with the method. He wondered what they did in Rome to make a similar determination.

Antonia asked, "Appius. Do I understand that you will fill and refill this cup for an entire day, with no sleep or break?"

"Yes, Antonia, that is what must be done. I can think of no other way."

"Then, my husband, I will assist you. Let me help you earn the additional sestertii. Knowing that I will spend them, I think it would be noble if I were to help you. I could surely empty the cups and keep track of the numbers while you sleep or eat. Yes, I shall do that."

Appius grinned. "I thank you, Antonia. That would be most useful. I like the idea of a team approach, and if I get some sleep, I am less likely to make a mistake. Perhaps, while I am emptying the cups, you could sing to me."

"Perhaps you should just be content with my help."

Appius rose well before sunrise, as did Antonia. She prepared olives, bread, and wine for her husband while he made preparations with water and the arrangement of the cups. Appius was careful to start precisely when he could see the leading edge of the sun's disk appear just at the horizon. He realized that the sun progressed to longer then shorter daylight during the seasons, but thought that an error between one day and the next would be slight.

Antonia stood, hands on hips, watching the operation. "I see you have positioned yourself so that you will be in the shade when the sun is at its highest."

the *Aedifex*: Building the Pont du Gard

Appius nodded. "Yes, Antonia, I am able to think that far ahead. You would think me a dunce if I were out in the mid-day sun. I have to keep ahead of you."

During the water-timing procedure, Appius had much time to think. *If I am to use these cups for other comparisons, perhaps taking them on journeys into rough terrain, I must be careful not to lose them or break them. If I used a different cup, it would be difficult for me to know whether the hole I have made in the new cup was the same as the one I am now using. It would be the same with the graduated cup. I must make duplicates—but I will not stop my procedure. I will duplicate my devices afterwards.*

The next morning he completed the procedure. He had Antonia tell him at the exact moment the disk of the sun appeared. Fortunately, no clouds obscured this view. Antonia had allowed him to sleep for a spell during the night, refilling the upper cup and dumping the lower cup, per his instructions. He was anxious to count the refills. There were 210 refills. He would accumulate the amount of water in 100 feet, the 1200 cubic feet, 210 times. That total amount would equal the flow from the *fontis* in a day's time. He did the laborious accumulation and arrived at his total. It was 252,000 cubic feet per day. That was the amount that the *fontis* provided in one day. He felt the glow of satisfaction.

After Appius made his calculations, Antonia was still sleeping, but Appius was too excited to do so. It was daytime, and he had work to do. He wanted to check his calculation, the amount of water in his 100-foot run. He thought he understood the concept but wanted more confidence. He had a way to do so.

The channel from the spring flowed into a large circular cistern from which it was distributed to various uses in the town—fountains, residential water supply and public baths. Appius thought that he could use the cistern for a further measurement device. There was a sluice-gate that could be used to stop the water just prior to its entry to the cistern. The water would be stopped from time to time to allow cleaning or other work on the cistern, and, in fact, he had stopped the water a number of times for just such an operation. Now, he would drain the cistern and temporarily close off the outlets. Then he would quickly open the sluice gate and let it run for the number for the time he had noted, equaling one hundred feet of flow. The gate would then be closed, and he would measure the amount of water in the cistern. Perhaps

65

he could try this several times, using multiple lengths of time—as measured in his cup, to see if the quantities could be scaled. *Marcus will think me mad.*

Marcus gave a nod to the scheme Appius had devised, although he did not completely understand. Marcus said it would provide an opportunity to do cleaning and flushing; Appius could work with Tinius to combine the efforts.

Appius looked for Tinius to make arrangements for running his water test that night. He found Tinius at the cistern adjusting gates in order to balance the flow to the baths, which at the moment were receiving too much water and were wasting some into the drainage.

He yelled from across the cistern, "Tinius."

Tinius looked up, inserted another board into the gate then approached Appius. "Appius, so good to see you. Are we dropping chips into the water again today?"

"No, Tinius, no. But, you are going to like this one. This evening, I would like to shut off the flow to the cistern. The water level will be drawn down a little by use for the baths and fountains but we will drain the remainder from the cistern using the flushing channels."

"Dear Appius, what do you have in mind? I can imagine someone having to do without water ready to poison me for this ill deed. How will you keep me from trouble?"

"Do not worry, Tinius. I have gone to Marcus and made it clear that this is my doing. You will not suffer. If we do this right, we will not cause any of our citizens a problem. But, you might want to take advantage of an empty cistern to clean sediment from the bottom. If we tell the citizens that we are cleaning the cistern for their own health, we will hear fewer complaints. And, it will be so."

Tinius nodded. "Yes, Appius, I will do that. I will have some of our workers help. Now, please tell me what you are doing."

Appius explained how he was comparing the flow in 100 feet to that which would be expected in a day's time.

Tinius nodded his head slowly. "Appius, I may not understand all that you are telling me, but I do get a sense of what you are doing. I will make preparations for this evening."

"And I will talk to Marcus then inform the 13 residents that receive water to their homes. If they want to bathe or accumulate water, they should do so before sundown. I will also pass the word to the *aquarius* folk to spread the word at the fountains and do the same with the bath managers. I will do all of this then find you in the late afternoon to make sure all is well."

All was well and the procedure worked as Appius had planned. He did an initial run, to the level indicated on his inscribed cup and noted the depth of the cistern after he shut off the flow. The cistern only filled to a fraction of its depth, so he made a flow run in which he ran the water to a depth four times indicated in his device, equaling a 400-foot run. He then again measured the depth of the cistern. He thought that making the larger run would reduce any errors he might be making from stopping and starting the water flow. Tinius was a great help and showed interest in the operation.

"What will you do now, Appius?" Tinius watched as Appius wrote notes on his wax tablet.

"I will calculate the amount of water for the 100-foot run and then the 400-foot run and see how they compare. If what I have done looks consistent, I will be confident that the method I used is good. And, I have told you that I will now know how much water our *fontis* can produce in a day's time."

"Why will that be useful?"

"I will then be able to compare that amount to any other flow from a source I find. Let's say that I found a source that has half the amount of the flow of our *fontis*. I would be able to calculate the amount of water that would be available in a day's time."

I am sure that will be valuable. What should we do next?"

"I think you should do your cleaning of the cistern then restore your water system. Continue to fill the cistern, refill any fountains that need so. The citizens having a water source piped to their home will know that they again will have water available. Next, I will determine additional sources of water used in Nemausus. That will include water that is drawn from wells, water that is available from rainwater, and water from our reservoirs."

"How will you determine the amount of water that is available from rainwater collection?"

"You are right. I will not be able to measure it. I will have to do a calculation to the best effort that I can."

"Sometimes I think that your calculations are mystical. I must say that I do not yet understand. Perhaps you will instruct me as you proceed with your work."

"I would be happy to do so, if you have the interest."

Appius confirmed his prior calculations using the cistern measurements. The town normally made use of all the *fontis* water, except in wet times of year when citizens were able to collect more rainwater for their needs, and when ponds and other reservoirs benefited from surface water flow and so were of robust accumulation. At such times, unneeded flow from the *fontis* was diverted to flush the drainage and waste systems and thence flowed to the river. Otherwise, flushing, although of less effect, was accomplished using the water from the public baths as the bathwater was replaced.

Appius proudly announced his calculation to Antonia. She blinked, deliberately, to indicate that she knew that Appius knew that the number was meaningless to her.

She smiled. "And now what will you do, Appius?"

They were having their dinner, their best time in the day for conversation.

Appius swallowed a hunk of bread. "Antonia, now I will determine how much water we get from other sources. I will try to find all the wells, talk to their owners, if not owned by the *Corporata*, to determine their draw. Then I will try to get an idea of how much rainwater is collected by the citizens. I will also survey the ponds we have constructed to see how much water is utilized from their supply."

"It sounds like the information you scour from these additional sources will be more difficult—I mean more difficult to be accurate."

"Yes, that is true. In many cases I will not be able to measure as I did the *fontis*, I will have to estimate the amounts."

Antonia stood up, adjusted her *timoca* then sat back down on the bench. "When you say 'estimate,' what do you mean?"

"I mean that I will have to use my best reasoning to come up with quantities and calculations. I will, perhaps, only be able to *sample* the available information. I will only be able to talk to *some* of the well owners about how much water they draw, rather than talk to all of them. I will use the best information from them to determine the total amount of use that is most likely. Also, I may not be able to find all the wells. Again, using my best information, I will estimate a total number of wells and calculate their supply. That is how I will arrive at my quantity of water drawn from all wells."

"What good will that be? It sounds like too much guesswork."

"Yes, my dear Antonia, there is some guesswork. However, a guess—or estimate—based on good data is better than having no idea at all, or just guessing at the total. Not all things in life are known to be exact."

"I will agree with you, but it seems like your estimate will be very much subject to your own notions. Does not that leave much room for error?"

Appius reached for his cup of wine and delayed his sip to say, "Yes, it does. But it has value in letting us reckon what we must deal with when we cannot deal in certainties."

"You could count all the wells. You could talk to all the owners."

"Perhaps. And, I could spend months doing it. Would my final amount be more useful after spending all that additional time?"

"Perhaps. I would be more apt to count them all. I do not know if your approach by means of estimate should be used."

"So, Antonia, what if I am to construct a plaza, paved with the marble from the quarry. I do not know for certain how many slabs of marble I will actually use but I can estimate the number and tell Denius, the quarry man, how many I think I will need. He will then make a plan to deliver that many slabs. The final number may be more or less, but our operation will proceed much more reasonably than if I tell him I do not know how many will be required and to just keep delivering slabs until I tell him to stop. With my estimate, he knows how many men he should hire to keep up with my requirements. He can tell me how many slabs he can deliver in a week. I can then determine how many men I must hire to place that many slabs in a week. Do you not see that it is better than if I tell him I do not know?"

Antonia was silent for a moment. "I am thinking. So, after you do your—estimate—on the wells and on the ponds and on the rainwater, what will you then do?"

Appius, somewhat content that Antonia's critical eye to his estimate was no longer an issue, savored his wine. "I will then...

calculate... the way we *use* our water. That will include our public baths, fountains, supplies to our wealthy citizens and to our farms where they have chosen to pay for city water and where they draw water from wells."

"Will you go to each property or facility and measure the amount or will you *estimate* these like you will do with the wells?"

"I do not know for certain. I anticipate that I will be able to measure most of the uses."

"You will talk to the wealthy citizens?"

"Yes."

"You will visit their villas?"

"Yes."

"Will you take me along?" Antonia smiled and sipped her wine.

Appius had no immediate response. He had not thought of this possibility but could think of no reason why he could not do it. It might render Antonia more favorably disposed to his task. "Yes, Antonia, I think I could take you with me. I might have to invent a reason to do so, but, really, I am on my own. I would not expect Marcus or his associates to object. The owners of the villas...?"

"Good. I will look forward to that. Perhaps I can get some useful ideas of design, ideas that we can use when we build our grand villa, possible because of the grand career you will have."

Appius looked at Antonia to see if she mocked him. Instead, he encountered an intense look, possibly to camouflage what could have appeared to be mockery.

She smiled.

CHAPTER 10

Appius talked to the private owners or operators of wells. There was no catalogue of wells within the city; there was no public role, no public inspection, just wells here and there. No, not really here and there as only *one* section of the town was suitable for wells: shallow water and clean. The expanding number of toilets, apart from the public toilets, feeding into the groundwater, had not yet been known to dirty the well waters—it seemed. Appius was able to discover the location of more and more wells as he talked to the owners; they knew other owners; they shared information and well-related experiences. They were suspicious of persons they thought were taking more than their share and happily identified those locations and owners. Appius knew he would not find all of the wells, but he thought his survey would be adequate. The private wells were in addition to those operated by the *Aqua Corporata*.

Plying quantity information on usage was more difficult. Well owners were apt to state usage on the low side when asked how much water they drew. It was reaction to the culture of suspicion, involving users drawing more than their share. Appius, not sure how to account for this, did his calculations to attempt a more accurate reckoning. One had to consider the uses for a well. After all, the town provided, really, all the drinking water you wanted, and you could use the public baths. Some wells allowed moderate wage earners to have their own baths, while not having to pay the fancier prices charged by the *Aqua Corporata*. Others, with wells, had gardens and raised their own vegetables, some for their own use and some to sell at the town market. Appius noted the private baths and the gardens. He asked for the owner's stated use. That number did not require fancy calculations, as did the flow from the *fontis*. Use from wells could be easily calculated from the number of buckets drawn. Appius was not surprised to find that many of the well operators did not know—could only guess how much they used. He asked them to count the number of pails drawn and keep a record. He would return to collect the totals.

He spent three weeks walking and talking to the people with wells at their residences. That done, he considered that he had substantial coverage. He worked with the data, fussed with the numbers, made calculations on the side, and was finally satisfied with the quantity of 17 cubic feet per day, summer use per well. This was expected to be a maximum use as winter baths would not be expected to be as frequent, and water for growing of vegetables would be minimal at cool times of the year. The garden was the heaviest requirement. If there was no garden, the use would be one-fourth. Yes, Appius was convinced, the use for gardens must be included. One would have to conclude that an expanded city would still have its private gardens.

Wells, even multiple wells, were used on properties with extensive farming. Appius spent nearly a day on each of such farms to determine water usage for crops—beans or cucumbers, for example. Such farms depended on well water for irrigation, but some used water from the Nemausus system to supplement their requirements. After a time, Appius calculated that water required for beans or cucumbers during hot weather was about 200 cubic feet per day for an acre. The farmers hand watered each plant, requiring them to often walk one hundred feet with a pail of water in each hand. Hard work, but the fruit on the plants was bountiful.

The farm water assessment had also taken several weeks. Appius wondered if it might be necessary to determine the amount of water collected from rainfall into cisterns or crude storage. He eventually reasoned, after remembering troubles in years of low rainfall, that if he were to determine water requirements, he should know if water supplied by a new source would be adequate in dry years. He took the time to make calculations for water stored from rainfall. Of course, this was the dry season, so no in-progress water collection could be observed. He visited over one hundred households, properties where they collected rainfall, understanding that this was only a fraction of those that did so. He asked the rainfall collectors how much they could store. In contrast to the well owners, who were guarded in disclosing the amount of water they drew, the rain water collectors were very forthright, often insisting that Appius see their system for collecting or see the scant stored rainwater that remained for use at this time of year. After ten days, Appius thought he had enough knowledge to calculate the amount stored by all the non-wealthy citizens of the town.

the *Aedifex*: Building the Pont du Gard

Since the time of Augustus, the *Aqua Corporata* diligently constructed a number of reservoirs to capture runoff from small streams. Appius had recently worked on or around these reservoirs as part of his prior water works tasks. He knew that in a fair rain year, the reservoirs would fill by the end of the wet season. At this time of year, some were still providing water for city use, but others had dwindled to merely a puddle. To assess the bounty of the reservoirs, he calculated their capacity and allocated that capacity, each day, over the higher usage, dry four months of the year.

He was now able to complete his sums, to make determinations of how much water was provided for the city. He arranged a table in his courtyard, in the shade, and labored at his calculations.

Antonia dutifully brought him a cup of water and grapes from time to time, hovering for a moment, looking over his shoulder as if to decipher the mystery, the meaning of his work. "When will you visit the villas of the wealthy patrons? Do you need to know how much water they are using?"

Appius looked up, nodded to the proffered cup of water, smiled, and said, "Yes, I do need to know how much they are using—but not now. I have finally collected enough information to determine how much water we receive from the various sources—the *fontis,* the wells, the reservoirs and rainwater. I will calculate an amount of water supplied to the town in one day by all of those sources. I am very excited to see that number. Now, Claudius has instructed the *Aqua Corporata* to consider water requirements for a town twice the size of Nemausus, or rather, Nemausus growing to twice the present size, which is not the same thing. To determine the *additional* amount required, I must know how we are now using our water. I can easily determine the amounts now used for the fountains and baths. I know how the wells are used and how much is supplied. What I have not seen is the water usage by our villa owners who are supplied city water. And, dear Antonia, to answer your indirect question—as soon as I finish these calculations I will visit the villas, and yes, I will take you with me."

"Is there anything I can do to assist you, my dear husband?"

Appius smiled. "Water and occasional food will be helpful, as you have been doing. I will soon be completed."

Antonia smiled and nodded, turned and walked the paved path to the house.

Several days later, mid-morning, Appius stood up at his desk, stretched his back, stared at what he had written, then looked at Antonia who was watering flowers in the courtyard.

Antonia noticed his movement and that he had gazed in her direction. "Appius, are you done?"

"Yes, Antonia, I am done—for now. I may later revise my numbers based on new information or from more wisdom I might acquire. But, yes, I am done for now. Are you ready to accompany me on my rounds to the villas?"

"Yes, Appius, I can be ready quickly. I must only change to the clean *tunica* I have been preserving for our task. Perhaps we will go after our meal, in the afternoon?"

"Yes. I am going to find Marcus and tell him of my progress. I will even tell him the numbers I have accumulated. He might find them interesting."

"You will tell them to me, also, Appius? And explain what they mean?"

"Yes, I will do that. I am pleased that you want to know. While I am with Marcus, I will also tell him that I am next going to assess the water usage by the wealthy. Of course, the principals of the *Aqua Corporata* will be included, and I will visit them first. My thinking is that if the other wealthy patrons hear that we have surveyed the homes of the *Aqua Corporata*, then we will have less trouble visiting the others. I will go now to find Marcus and will be back for our meal."

Appius sat in the office of Marcus. "Marcus, I have progress to report to you. I have surveyed our water sources and calculated the amount of water available to our citizens."

"Yes, Appius. I am pleased to hear that you have been able to accomplish this. I could not have done this. You have earned your additional twenty-five sestertii these several months. Tell me then, how much water are we supplying to Nemausus?"

Appius looked at his notes. "You must understand, Marcus, that I have calculated the entire amount of water available to the town. Some you are not providing—water from private wells and private rainwater cisterns. I do know how much we are

ing from the *fontis*, from our wells and from the reservoirs that we have constructed."

Marcus scowled. "Why is it useful to know what the town is using from other sources... oh, I see."

"Yes," Appius nodded, we must be ready to provide all of the water."

"So, Appius, will you then just double the amount of water the town is now using, to determine how much additional water we must find?"

Appius tilted his head to the side. "Yes, we could do that. However, for a town twice our size, will there be as many villas using water, will we have twice the number of public fountains and baths, and will we provide much of the water for the growing of vegetables? Will the individuals use more water if more water is available? I will investigate usage of these items. When we assemble to advise Claudius, we will use our best judgment to estimate future uses and perhaps consider additional wells and rainwater collection. We will have some confidence in what we are doing."

"What must you do to complete this task?"

Appius straightened. "Other than my calculations, I have one task remaining, and that will be to assess the amount of water used by our citizens who are supplied city water to their villas."

"You mean our wealthier citizens."

"Yes, and I am thinking that it would be beneficial to assess the homes of the *Aqua Corporata* first. In that way, others will be inclined to be more cooperative."

He hesitated. "Yes, perhaps that would be wise."

"I will have Antonia accompany me on these visits to assist me in making observations. Will it be possible that we visit your villa this afternoon?"

Marcus was somewhat startled. "Why, yes, or no—perhaps tomorrow morning would be better. You say Antonia will be with you?"

"Yes, sir. If that is agreeable, we will be at your door tomorrow morning, at some decent time after the meal."

"Yes, that is acceptable. I will welcome you and the lovely Antonia. I will also advise the other members of the *Aqua Corporata* that they can expect you though I think that it is proper that *you* consult them prior, before your visit."

"Yes, Marcus, I will do that."

75

Appius regarded Antonia on their way to Marcus's villa. She looked almost regal, yet wore only her unadorned *tunica*. Why did she give that impression? She was a beauty, brown hair flowing, lithe figure, and, yes, he was sure, bore a regal bearing. Appius looked down at his tunic. It was suitable, but, he was sure, it did not have the same effect. He was working, after all.

They walked the lane, arriving at an elaborate stone portico, entry to the property of Marcus Atuis. Turning in, they walked a lovely path, paved with broken marble, lined with shrubbery, some of which was not native to the region. Antonia admired the blossoms. Appius took note of the provisions for irrigation, the dikes built around the base of the shrubs, ponds for temporary storage of water so that each bucket need not be fetched from one remote source. The earth, he noted, was still moist from an early morning watering.

The couple walked up a wide marble stair to the entry. In front of the door, they were standing on a mosaic of many colors, depicting a heralding with men in white flowing beards and trumpets. Appius knocked at the colossal door. Antonia stood behind him, head slightly inclined. A servant, neatly clad in a tunic with decorative stitching at the hem, answered his knock.

Appius nodded. "I am here with my wife, Antonia, at the invitation of Marcus Atius, to assess the water use of this home." He hoped that his statement was sufficient to gain entry without further explanation.

The servant, without giving his name, stepped aside and gestured them inside with a sweep of his arm, head slightly bowed. Appius and Antonia entered a square atrium of which Appius thought to be about forty feet to each side. At the walls, plants in pots were abundantly placed, some, one could be assured, were there for their fragrance. Inset into the walls, between the plant arrangements, were mosaics of various depictions. In the center of the atrium were benches, inviting one to enjoy the sunny warmth on a cool day. Two fountains gurgled at either end of the benches. Appius was transformed. Left behind were ordinary pursuits and difficult labor. Life was to be enjoyed, art appreciated. One could quickly understand. He looked at Antonia who was trying to look unaffected, but nevertheless displayed a look of amazement. He caught her eye and smiled.

the *Aedifex*: Building the Pont du Gard

Marcus Atius stepped through a doorway, welcoming them with outstretched arms. "Appius Petronius, Antonia, I am pleased that you are here. Please join me in the peristyle. He turned and beckoned. They walked through an entry at the far end of the atrium. The peristyle was colonnaded on three sides. Ahead, a large opening, without columns led to a porch, semi-covered with a railing of framed marble dowels. The floor brightly flaunted several large mosaics, bordered with marble, irregularly spaced. The columns were of polished stucco, the walls adorned with giant frescoes. Entries to a number of apartments surrounded the peristyle.

Marcus Atius nodded to his guests, a gesture that was surely an invitation to marvel at his taste and accomplishment. His guests did not have to be encouraged to do so.

"Magnificent," Appius said, in nearly a whisper. Internally, he was discerning the wide gulf between ordinary styles of living and those of the wealthy. He again looked at Antonia to gauge her fascination. Antonia, it appeared, was struggling to absorb all that she was seeing.

"Perhaps you would enjoy a grand view of Nemausus." Marcus walked through open doors to the porch deck.

They gazed over the town. Appius could imagine lying on the couches, a wine cup in his hand, the expanse before him. For some, life was truly a grand journey.

Antonia eyed him.

After allowing Appius and Antonia sufficient time to marvel at the residence and grounds, Marcus summoned a servant, not so elegantly dressed as the one who had serviced their entry. "Appius—and Antonia—meet Paris Manlius, an able employee most knowledgeable of our water use. He will assist you in assessing the use of water on my property."

Appius and Antonia nodded, as did Paris. Antonia removed a wax tablet and a stylus from her *stolla*. The reason, after all, for her to accompany Appius, was as the dutiful recorder.

Marcus Atius smiled.

Paris showed them the lead pipe that brought the city water to the property, as well as the internal piping leading to the baths, the kitchen, and the fountains. Clay pipe led to the gardens. Appius quizzed Paris on the usage, asking Antonia to make notations that would later help him in his calculations. He thanked Paris and they left.

"Appius," Antonia took his hand as they walked the stone path to the road, "did you think such splendor was possible? Did you not think that the home of Marcus was beautiful, as much so as our public museum—all the marble and art—but more intimate, more personal? Can you imagine a life such as that?'

Appius nodded, squeezing Antonia's hand. "It is truly a wonder and beautiful to gaze upon. It makes me think that perhaps it is good that some have wealth to enable such beauty to be created. What did you like best?"

"I liked the view, of course, but the separate mosaics, laid in the floor—they look like individual rugs, overlapped—and they are so beautiful, so many colors. They must take a long time to create."

"Yes, beautiful and yes, a long time. I have marveled at the mosaics in the Museum of Agrippa. I have watched the masters working for over a year on the mosaics installed in villas of the wealthy—each piece selected, each piece cemented into place. I have viewed the work as they progressed, perhaps every two weeks. I am awed."

"Maybe we can have a mosaic, someday, in the middle of our marble floor, in our peristyle, once we become wealthy partners in a new water scheme."

Appius looked at Antonia to see if she was chiding him or serious. He could not tell from her slight grin. He thought his response, "Yes," was safe.

"Appius, what are you thinking?" Antonia said, not paying attention to his response.

Appius walked a few paces before replying. "Antonia, we have only a handful of villas to visit in order to accumulate the remainder of the information that I need. I am anxious to complete this part of my task."

"It is difficult for me to understand how you can be excited over such a mundane thing. I know you will not think that *I* will have such excitement. I will, though, help you celebrate with a cup of wine—or perhaps two cups of wine."

"Yes, Antonia, let us do that."

the *Aedifex*: Building the Pont du Gard

Appius, at the end of each day, transcribed the writing from the wax tablet to paper. Paper was not plentiful, therefore used sparingly. The wax tablet could be inscribed with the stylus, and used again, for other notes, by rubbing the wax smooth. He spent many days calculating, often leaning back, contemplating his results. Antonia eyed him quizzically, going about her watering, cleaning, tidying, and cooking during his labors.

"At last," he finally shouted, startling Antonia. She looked over to the makeshift desk he had created under an overhang. He was standing with arms crossed, a defiant look, pointing to his papers.

"What is 'at last,' Appius?"

"At last I have my information in a form that I can present to the *Aqua Corporata*."

"Will they understand what you have done?"

Appius shrugged. "In truth, they would not understand all. But, I will be able to make them understand the basics."

"Will you tell them that some of the information is from your... estimates? Will they understand that you have not seen all of the water sources and uses?"

"Yes, I will tell them. I think they will understand that I calculated some aspects rather than observed them. Also, I have calculated the error that might result if I have estimated incorrectly. They will understand that it is of little consequence. They will also be able to increase or decrease my numbers if they feel... safer... in doing so."

Antonia walked to his side. "What will you do next?"

"I will take my calculations to Marcus Atius and review them with him. He will tell me what to do after that."

"Review your calculations with the others of the *Aqua Corporata*?"

"Yes, that for sure. But will they want to present my calculations to Claudius? I do not know. I am sure they will want to tell Claudius that they have determined the quantities of the many sources and uses. Perhaps Claudius will then ask to see them."

"I am excited to think that something on which you have worked so diligently, and to which even I have contributed, may be gazed upon by the *Imperator* of the Empire. Not many citizens have that opportunity."

"Yes, Antonia. And now you may be able to understand why I have this excitement, and perhaps a little worry, also."

"Yes, my husband, I do understand and share your excitement. As to the worry, I do not think you need be afraid. Who amongst the *Corporata* could dispute you?"

"None could, in a manner of the *ability* to do so, but some may if it would, perhaps, collide with their interests."

"Oh! But is there anything in your calculations or your procedure which would collide?"

"I do not know, Antonia. I do not know. Claudius is no fool; he can also summon help from men who are wiser in calculations than I. But, what can I do? They selected me, and I have done my best. I will see Marcus Atius tomorrow."

Antonia said nothing but raised an eyebrow.

CHAPTER 11

Appius met with Marcus at the waterworks office. The afternoon was hot and dry. Marcus offered him a cup of water after Appius placed a stack of papers on the desk. The individual sheets of paper were of varying sizes, depending on the content of information presented and the scraps of paper that Appius had been able to find.

Appius took a sip of water, reached for a paper from the top of the stack and spoke. "Marcus Atius, I have spent three months measuring, investigating and calculating the use of water in this town. The numbers I have are my best calculation and have not been increased or decreased based on my concern for their accuracy. I think they are a good representation of what exists."

"You have worked hard at this, Appius. If your accuracy matches your efforts, it will be precise, indeed. Of course, I have no way to validate the accuracy—only by feel. So, proceed. Tell me what you have discovered."

"Marcus, the town uses water from several sources. If you include all the sources—the spring, rainwater collection, wells, and our reservoirs, we use 378,000 cubic feet in one day during the periods of highest usage... this time of year when we are watering crops and people are taking many baths. At this time of year, we use all that the spring can provide, use what we need from the wells, and are still able to use the remainder of the stored rainwater and the residual water in our reservoirs. I have calculated the amount of highest usage. That is what we must consider if the town size doubles. The amounts used from each source are listed on this." He handed the sheet to Marcus.

Marcus stared at the information for several moments. "So, of the total of 289,000 cubic feet, the water provided the citizens from *Aqua Corporata*, 274,000 cubic feet come from the spring and the reservoirs and some wells."

"Yes, Marcus."

"The amount provided by citizens from wells and rainwater collection is significant, especially the amount from wells."

"Yes, though most of that water is used for the growing of crops."

"Then, how will we determine the amount of water needed for the future? It is a mixture. We cannot determine the amount by merely doubling the amount we are now using."

"That is true, Marcus. I am happy that you see that. We must know how the water is now used, then imagine how the water *will be* used when the town size doubles."

"That is not so easy. But, you told me that you were also investigating how we use the water. Your visit to my house was for that quest. What have you found?"

Appius handed Marcus a second list. "This is how the water is used—fountains, baths, private residences, crops." He spoke the amounts from memory.

"I see." Marcus said nothing for a while. "The water for crops is substantial. I must assume some is from private wells and some we are supplying."

"Yes, 10,000 cubic feet from private wells and 12,000 from *Aqua Corporata*. It is shown on the paper."

"Oh, yes. That is this notation." He pointed to a spot on the paper. "So, now what must we do, imagine how the expanded town will use water?"

"Yes, Marcus, exactly right. I have used my imagination to arrive at these numbers." He handed Marcus a third sheet. "I made assumptions to arrive at the numbers. I can tell you what I have done. But, in my thinking, it is you—the *Aqua Corporata*—who must consider the numbers and verify that judgment."

"And then give that judgment, those numbers, to Claudius."

"Yes, if that is what you must do."

Marcus returned the papers to his desktop, thought for several moments then said, "Appius, you have performed your task in a remarkable manner. I am happy that I made a good choice in selecting you. I think your numbers are your honest evaluation of your observations. However, as you have explained to me before, you are not able to see every source or use of the water; estimation has been required. Prior to presenting the numbers to the *Corporata*, I would have you increase the total number of our usage by an additional one-tenth. In that manner we will be prudent in covering any errors that might exist, careful though you have been."

Appius reluctantly nodded. "I will do so. From what source would you want me to increase the numbers—all of them?"

"Let me think. If we show that we are providing more water, the price the citizens are paying will seem more reasonable."

"Yes, but will the citizens expect the additional water to be available at the same price?"

"No. Of course the new water will be more expensive. We must charge more. The new citizens must pay more."

"Then I will increase the amount from the spring, wells, and the reservoirs we have constructed. When would you like to present these numbers to the *Aqua Corporata*? It will not take me long to adjust the numbers."

"I will contact them and let you know."

"Yes, Marcus Atius."

Appius was disappointed as he walked back to his home. His numbers were a good representation of the water situation, yet his numbers had been increased with a wave of the hand, violating the care taken, sullying his good work. The numbers he had determined were a solid base, were much more useful than if the numbers were a mere guess. He had done good work, made diligent considerations, was careful in his assumptions. That would have to be his satisfaction.

The *Aqua Corporata* were again meeting at the home of Nemus Amatius. The other members, Marcus Atius, Julius Sergius, Aulus Acilius and Titus Domitius were joined by Appius. During his investigation, Appius and Antonia had toured Nemus's splendid house. However, Appius was feeling somewhat insecure in the presence of several of the town's wealthiest and most influential citizens. Three months ago, he would not have imagined that such a group would be assembled to hear something he had to say or consider anything of his involvement. He steeled himself not to show awe or deference. He must give them the impression that he was confident in his work. That is what Antonia had said, also.

Nemus did not have them arrayed on couches and served with wine, as had been done in prior meetings, probably because it would not be seemly to do so considering Appius's status. They sat on benches on Nemus's grand deck, under a colonnaded porch. Appius had his sheaf of papers including a new sheet with the recently inflated numbers.

83

Nemus spoke. "Marcus has advised me that Appius, whom we have selected to investigate our system, has spent the last three months doing so and is now prepared to tell us the results. Appius," he turned to face the young man, "Marcus speaks highly of your effort, and we have all experienced your investigation on a more personal basis when you visited our homes and assessed our water consumption. I imagine that we can be confident in your results. Please, tell us what you have discovered."

Appius felt he should stand and did so. He looked at the men. Marcus, Aulus, and Nemus were attentive, while Julius and Titus appeared to have other issues on their minds. He stated the information, much as he had to Marcus, only now with the higher numbers. They let him speak without interruption. At the end of his monologue, he said, "We must determine the additional quantity of water that we will need. I have presented the quantities we are using at this time. As Marcus has probably told you, it is not just a matter of doubling the amount of water now being used in order to determine the quantity needed from a new source. I will rely on your good judgment to imagine the requirements of this town twice the size."

Nemus asked, "Why is it not a just a matter of doubling the amount? Why does that not make sense, although I see a complexity in determining how much will be supplied by public service and how much by citizens' initiative—rainwater collection and wells."

Appius nodded. "Yes, Nemus Amatius, you are correct. One could assume that the additional town would be a mirror image of what now exists, but I do not think that will be true."

Titus Domitius waved as he spoke, "Why not just double the number? That will be as useful as any other number we might concoct."

Appius started to answer, but Nemus held up his hand. "I think, Titus, that Appius is correct. We cannot assume the additional population will be similar to the existing. We must be more diligent. Under the scrutiny of Claudius, we must explain the reasonableness of our numbers. It is best that we proceed in a rational process."

Titus shrugged. "As you like."

Marcus spoke, "Appius, let us take the usage, one function at a time. For example, if the town doubles in population, should we consider that we will have a similar number of public baths, serving a similar number of people?"

Appius was prepared to answer but Julius spoke. "One could assume the same as we have not limited the times a citizen may visit the baths in, for instance, a week's time, nor have we varied the amount of water used for each bath to refresh the water. Usage would be the same unless a demand was made for... fresher... water."

"For now, we will assume usage for baths will be the same. Would we take the same approach for fountains?" Nemus was practiced in the manner of settling issues.

Marcus started to answer but wanted to give the impression that the result would be from a group opinion. He gestured toward Titus.

Titus said, "Why wouldn't it be the same?" Are we creating a new class of citizen that drinks more or less?"

Julius asked, "Maybe we should discuss wells and perhaps rainwater collection first. It seems like fountain usage might depend on the nature of those sources as the town grows."

Nemus nodded, "I think you are right, Julius. What about the wells? It seems you might have an opinion on this, Appius, since you looked at most of the existing wells and noted their usage."

Appius had sat on his bench after presenting the initial quantities. He stood again, "Additional well usage may be different. Wells are easily dug in the southwest of Nemausus. As I have stated, some well water is used for private baths and some for uses that are also supplied by fountains, but those amounts are not significant. Much of the well water usage is for the growing of crops. If it is possible that wells may be easily dug in new areas of the city, then we might approach the total of new quantities in the same ratio. However, we don't know if the wells may be dug easily, if the ground water is abundant, and if it is suitable. A few wells have been dug in the east area, which have had to be dug much deeper, and the water is not as bountiful, although it appears to be good water."

Marcus held up his hand. "If we are to look at the highest possible usage—during the high use season—would we also want to assume that wells will not be available as they are now? If so, then we must include in our calculations for the growth, the additional water needed but not supplied by wells."

"If the well water is mostly used for the growing of crops," Nemus said, "must we consider that crops eaten by the larger city will be grown in or at the edges of the city, as they are now?"

Julius leaned forward. "In or at the edges of the city will be in new areas, probably to the **north**. Can we assume that these new areas will be suitable for growing of the crops?"

"Perhaps not as suitable," Marcus said. "The town location probably resulted from the existence of good crop land in an area where well water was easily had. If the new land is not as suitable, where will we get the additional crops?"

Nemus stood and paced, "They must be grown elsewhere and transported here."

"So what should we do? What should we calculate?" Julius looked at Nemus, then the others.

"This is what I think." Nemus was talking while pacing. "We should calculate the new requirement as if we have to provide the additional water and cannot rely on wells. If the crops are grown elsewhere, we may still have to provide that water. And, we should include the amount of water that well users now require for baths and fountain uses." He looked at the other members of *Aqua Corporata*. They gave no indication of acknowledgement. He continued, "I also think that we should then increase the resulting number by one tenth. That will be a relatively small margin to perhaps only partially cover any errors we may have made in our investigations," he stopped and looked at Appius, "and for what we cannot imagine, here, at this moment."

Appius looked at Marcus. The amount of estimated usage was inflating dramatically. Marcus saw his look and knew why Appius had registered alarm. He gazed directly at Appius and shook his head. Appius wondered why Marcus would not want the others to know the quantities had already been increased.

Titus stood up. "This is all nonsense. We might as well just guess at an amount. We employ an uneducated peasant to do our survey, deriving numbers that we can only accept as true, then attempt to make another guess at the future. Then, as if our guesses were not already wildly conceived, we increase that. We are mad men."

Nemus walked to Titus. "So, Titus, what are the consequences? Let's say we have overstated our requirement."

Titus bristled. "Do you not understand? Claudius will expect *us*, as the evident wealthy beneficiaries of water distribution, to provide the funds to construct and install a new system, one that I suspect will be magnificent and costly. Perhaps, though, you are not concerned with diminishing your vast fortunes on a project that may or may not supply one additional citizen. If our fortunes survive the initial requirement, we may not have the customers to pay back our investment."

Nemus, leaning forward to emphasize his remarks, said, "Yes, Titus, I understand. But the other thought is that a source for a large requirement will not easily be found, and as far as we know, is not near Nemausus. That situation should convince Claudius that the concept is too difficult. He will abandon his requirement and leave us to our own devices. The town will grow, only at that rate at which we can find and fund new sources near Nemausus."

Titus, not backing away, said, "I don't agree. If you wish to proceed in this manner, with these quantities, I vote to disagree."

Nemus turned to look at the other members of *Aqua Corporata*. "You have heard me and you have heard Titus. Which manner do you prefer?"

The remainder chorused, "With you, Nemus, with you."

Titus shook his head and walked from the porch.

Nemus said, "If we do end up financing a project, we will have a difficult time with Titus. He has not been careful with his inheritance and, even with the funds he receives from our operations, may be in difficult times."

Those remaining at the meeting looked from one to the other. It was difficult to determine what they were thinking.

Marcus dismissed Appius but told him to wait at the gate; he would join him shortly. Appius did not have to wait long until Marcus walked down the path and stood facing him.

Marcus, in soft tones, said, "Appius, please adjust the numbers in the manner you heard and give them to me. I will show these numbers to the *Corporata,* and they will then be given to Claudius. It may take a week or two for us to get a response. In the meantime, do not yet look for new large sources. We do not want the region to know that we have plans for any water they might covet. I suggest that you might look to find a location for the terminus of the additional water, should an aqueduct be built. To do that, you should consider in what direction the town will grow... or the direction we will influence it to go. Do you have any questions?"

Appius shook his head and answered, "No, Marcus, no."

CHAPTER 12

I drove to Nimes in the morning. Renat was meeting me at the *Castellum*, the terminus of the ancient aqueduct. Most of the *Castellum* still existed, and in photographs I could see that even the distribution system was still visible. I wanted to see all this close at hand. Because Renat lived in Nimes, he was a good source for information about the structure and, of course, I wanted to see my friend, feeling a little guilty that I'd made arrangements with Laurie to accompany me as my translator.

I thought as I drove—*Laurie, my... what a woman. Her spirit and energy are breathtaking. I wonder if she had been married. Well—I'll ask her. If she was, I can't imagine a man keeping up with her. Did a former husband shrug his shoulders and say, "You must go on without me." I'll ask her. Even if she doesn't tell me the truth, the story will be fascinating. I wonder if my adventure with her will end pleasantly.*

I navigated the streets of Nimes and found the parking area that Renat had suggested. He was already there in his red Peugeot 405, leaning against the car and smoking a cigarette.

He waved as I drove up. "Good morning, *monsieur* Warner," he said as I pulled into the slot next to his and jumped out.

"*Bonjour*, Renat. I'm so fortunate to have an experienced guide to help me in my research."

"Yes, well, I hope you're up for a little stroll," he said as he shook my hand and put his other hand on my shoulder, cigarette bobbing jauntily in his lips.

We walked to the surprisingly intact ruin. The *Castellum*, or water collector, was about 30 feet in diameter and about 5 feet deep. I could see the channel where the water from the aqueduct entered. Across from the entrance, in the walls of the pond, were ten apertures for the water distribution pipes each about 10 inches in diameter.

Renat pointed. "As you can see, the water entered through that square opening and was then distributed through pipes from the side of the structure. The pipes were lead, but they have been taken. I think that was done a long time ago. You cannot see, but there were three valves in the bottom of the structure so that water could be coursed through drainage channels."

"You mean to drain the structure?"

"Yes, and more. It seems that the town used water from the aqueduct to cleanse their drainage systems. They would open the valves and run a heavy flow of water to carry away what ordinary drainage flows would not."

I squinted at Renat, shading the sun with my hand. "You mean they *had* a drainage system?."

"Oh, yes, and one would think that it was somewhat sophisticated if they had arranged for flushing waters."

"Hmmm," I said. "I guess the workers would have had to wade into the pool to open or shut the valves. Sounds like a job I wouldn't like."

"Perhaps they had chains or another means of opening the valves without getting wet."

"Yes, as clever as these people were, you might think so. Renat, how was the water distributed? I mean, where did the water go from here?"

Renat nodded to acknowledge the question. "Did you say you read the *Ten Books of Architecture* by Vitruvius?"

"Yes."

"Do you remember he described a system used in the Empire in which there were a series of tanks at the location where the water entered the city? In other ancient distribution systems, the operators were able to control flows to areas they considered most important, a priority system. At the same time, sediment from the water supply was able to settle to the bottom of a tank, in the still water, while the cleaner water was drawn off from the top of the other side. Here there is *no* evidence of a tankage or reservoir system."

"Why do you think?"

"I don't know for sure. Perhaps the water was clean and the supply was abundant."

I looked at the distribution pipes. "What were the priorities?"

"The water system supplied many uses. There were public baths, public fountains, water supply to the houses of the wealthy, and there were some industrial uses like laundries or mills and the growing of crops. The public fountains were, of course, a high priority as were the pipes and channels leading to the houses of the wealthy. The wealthy were paying additional sums for the privilege. In fact, the water features at a given villa were significant in determining social class. The wealthiest had their own private baths, elaborately decorated with mosaics and statuary and their private, often extensive, gardens."

I laughed. "Makes me feel privileged with my private baths and garden. I don't have elaborate mosaics and statuary, though."

"Yes. Perhaps after this trip you will want to upgrade, to boast the best water features on your block—in your village."

"Renat," I said, "what did they do if they didn't have a big aqueduct to provide this robust system?"

"Before the Nimes Aqueduct, there was a substantial spring in the town, probably the reason for the town's existence in the first place. The spring, Le Fountaine, was also channeled and piped through the town, but rainwater collection supplemented the bounty of the spring. You can imagine that life was dire when the rains were only slight."

"So the aqueduct had the advantage of providing a more secure supply."

"Yes, the spring, the Fontaine, was fairly robust—a good supply, except in dry years. They also dug wells to trap phreatic water."

"What's phreatic water?"

"The term only means waters that run under the surface of the ground."

I took a look at the *Castellum*. It seemed smaller than I would have imagined. "Renat, how many people did the system supply?"

"It is thought that Nemausus, at its peak, was inhabited by fifty thousand people in the first century A.D. and was possibly an area of about 500 acres. The town was founded in the first century, B.C. Perhaps the aqueduct did not supply all the water, considering that there was the existing Fontaine, and many other wells existed."

"Where does the name Nemausus come from?"

"Nemausus was the goddess worshipped at the original spring. The town's name was taken from her. She is linked to Jupiter. There is an altar to her near the spring at the nympheum— also a temple built to honor Caesar Augustus in 25 B.C.

"What's a nympheum... surely not... "

Renat laughed. "A nympheum is a prestigious monument, with statues and mosaics built to impress. The *Castellum*, the structure you are looking at now, is utilitarian, not a showplace. However, when the *Castellum* was discovered in 1844, there were fragments of columns and capitols found. So, in this case, it is believed that the fancy architecture commemorated those responsible for bringing water to the city."

"The temple to Caesar. Is that why it is thought that Caesar had the aqueduct built?"

"It was once thought. The temple to Caesar is not here. But other temples built in the town, later, like the Maison Carrie, are thought to be more of an indication."

I relaxed and looked around. I tried to imagine the *Castellum*, flowing and in use. I turned to Renat. "Are they able to follow the course of the channel through the old town?"

"Somewhat. The route, as you can imagine is covered by more recent structures."

"Where did the aqueduct enter the town... the old town, I mean?"

"The aqueduct entered the town after the Croix-de-Fer tunnel.

"The aqueduct is buried conduit before and after the tunnel?"

"Yes."

"Why did they have to tunnel, or don't we know?"

"It is a bit curious. The tunnel is through an area of hard rock and is about 400 meters long. It is thought that they could have gone around the Mount Duplan, a distance of 1500 meters."

"It seems that would be easier than tunneling."

"Yes, one would think so. We can drive to the location of the tunnel, near the city wall. There is a nice restaurant there, and we can have our lunch."

"Great. Do I get to buy my guide a beer?"

"Most definitely."

We found a table—outdoor seating, of course. Did I say that I really enjoyed the outdoor, on the sidewalk, dining experience? I'm sure I did. After a brief tour through the menu and much help from Renat... at first I was mistakenly going to order fish heads... I tipped my beer glass to Renat and savored the cool

Italian brew. I'm not a fan of the French or Belgian beers... too sweet.

I watched the street scene, a documentary of Nimes daily life, in color and 3D. We could see the city wall, which I understood once encircled Nemausus at a length of 6 kilometers. I was getting used to kilometers by now and almost automatically made the conversion to 3.5 miles. No small task, that wall, and I said so. "Renat, that wall was a substantial amount of work in itself. Who was responsible for building it?"

"It was probably built at the direction of Augustus and perhaps with his money."

"It was built during the time of Augustus? That could have been any time between 27 B.C. and 14 A.D."

"Yes."

"Hmmm."

Renat motioned for the waiter to bring another beer. "So, Warner, how are things in Vers-Pont-du-Gard? Is your life enjoyable? Are you meeting the local villagers?"

"Oh, yes, Renat. I met a local gentleman—retired, who has lived in the area for some time. He is educating me, telling me what he knows about the aqueduct."

"He speaks English?"

"Yes. It turns out he was required to do so. He worked for Alsthom, in Grenoble. I'm sure you have heard of them."

"Oh, yes, they manufactured hydraulic turbines. Have you had him help you with translations? If not, or if he doesn't have the time, I would help you, of course. In fact I would enjoy doing so."

I shook my head. "Renat, sometimes it seems that we are not in charge of our own destiny. The lady that helped me find a villa has let me know that she will be helping me with translations. If fact, we are to visit a professor in Marseille who probably does not speak English. Laurie will go with me, translate, and has offered to plan a guided tour through the region, just in case I've missed something."

"Hmmmph. Is this Laurie attractive?"

"Yes."

He smiled and nodded. "Then I understand. Of course you are following your good instincts."

"No, Renat, no. This Laurie is way too young for me... a child. Also, she is so energetic I would have trouble keeping up with her. No. She is just part of the adventure, and I'm happy that she has taken an interest."

"You will keep me informed on this?" He laughed.

"Of course."

On the way back to Vers, I thought about what I had seen—the city wall. Built during the time of Augustus. I wondered when. If the aqueduct was built by Agrippa, it would have been built early in the rule of Augustus, as Agrippa died fifteen years into his forty-one year reign. I was curious about the construction of the Croix-de-Fer tunnel. Why did they decide upon such a difficult means of construction if they could have just gone around the hill? Well, they did save 1100 meters of length, but tunnels are tough. I decided that I needed to check out the topography. What if the city walls were in place before they completed the aqueduct? They would have had to tunnel under the existing city wall. The timing of the aqueduct construction would be much later than is supposed.

I returned to my villa then decided I would eat in the town of Uzes that evening. After changing clothes and driving the short distance, I ate at the Mousin de Fabre, outdoors, of course, consuming several glasses of wine. I paid the bill, got up, stretched and walked the sidewalk intending a village stroll before returning to Vers. While stepping off the curb, heading toward the other side of the street, a car, traveling at great speed braked to a stop in my path; the window was down.

"Monsieur Warner. What are you doing wandering around loose? You must get into my car." It was Laurie.

I bent so that I could see her as I spoke. "Oh, so it's you, Laurie. I'm glad you weren't a few seconds later. I would now be your hood ornament."

"Yes, yes. No, no. I am a good driver. Now, be an obedient tourist and please get into my car."

"But, Laurie, where are we going? And, won't I be inhibiting your notion to drive... aggressively?" The words, 'recklessly' and 'insanely' crossed my mind, but I tempered my comment.

"You will inhibit nothing. And, to answer your question, we are going dancing—in Nimes. They have a tango orchestra, and you will be the perfect partner. You dance the tango, yes?"

"I dance the tango, no! I'm club-footed, can't understand rhythm, and wouldn't recognize a Latin beat. I would be far from the perfect partner." I couldn't imagine what I'd be in for.

"Just please get in. You will be fine. I will teach you. The tango will be part of your experience."

I must have had too much wine. I opened the car door, got in, and bravely said, "Let's go."

Laurie put the car in gear and we launched. The tires screeched and off we went, Laurie with a smile on her face, intent on navigating the twists in the road, over the hill to Nimes. I can't adequately describe the trip. I'm not talking about the scenery; I had no idea of that. I was horrified. Laurie sped the auto to 140 km per hour when she was able, braking and downshifting for the turns, then accelerating again out of the curve. I had to admire her skill. When there were cars ahead of us, she would pull to within inches of the bumper of the car ahead, waiting until she had space—barely enough space as it turned out several times—to pass. I was so happy to step onto solid ground after we swerved into a parking space at a bistro in Nimes. The armrest was now imbedded with my fingerprints.

We got out. Laurie locked the car and beckoned me to follow. My nerves were in no condition to respond to tango manipulations, but on I plowed. We entered the bistro to sounds of what I would later recognize as a tango. Laurie exhibited me, introduced me to friends. They rapidly became aware that I was American, generating a field of raised eyebrows and polite nods.

Laurie found a table, looped the straps of her purse over a chair and pulled me toward the dance floor. For the second time in just a half-hour, I was terrified. "Come," she said, "I will teach you the steps at the side of the dance floor." She saw my expression. "You will do fine."

"Now," she said, "I am going to give you an easy way to first learn. Keep in mind the spelling of tango—t... a... n... g... o. The rhythm of the dance goes in the same way but you must spread out the 'g.' She demonstrated. Now, you walk forward starting with your left foot, three steps, then swing your right foot to the right when you are saying the 'g,' then join it with the left on 'o.' Easy, yes?" She reached for me.

I passed out.

Well... nearly.

The evening went on. Laurie instructed me in more complicated maneuvers. She got me to hold her while she leaned over backwards; she did flamboyant spins. She loved the drama of the tango, tilting her head back, giving rapid, intense looks over her shoulder, holding her arm out stiff, wrist bent. Actually, I rather enjoyed that part; she was entertainment, right there in my arms. We stopped only to drink water. On we went at a relentless pace. Finally, at what time I can't tell you, the band was packing up. It was time to go. I was soaked in perspiration. My legs were tired and beyond control. We said goodbye to Laurie's friends, and we were, once again, rocketing back along the road, only this time I was too tired to care.

Laurie screeched to a stop in Uzes where I would retrieve my car. As I climbed from the car, she said, "I would stay with you tonight, but I have an appointment early in the morning. We'll do that later. Thanks for going with me."

All I could do was wave. I should have been shocked at her offer... actually it wasn't an offer... but I just stood there as she pulled away and summoned the energy to walk to my door. If she had insisted on staying... I don't believe I could have, would have resisted... she would have been highly disappointed. *Oh my God!* I did manage a laugh. I remembered that while we were dancing, she whispered to me, 'fandango.' I'd forgotten about that.

CHAPTER 13

As Appius walked home, he kicked at rocks while trudging through the dust. *What use was it to be careful in your work if those who paid you waved their hands and changed the numbers?* First Marcus and arbitrarily increased them then Nemus. He would keep his original papers; perhaps one day he might be able to show that he was right—to his own satisfaction. What good would that do? Well, nothing as far as the *Corporata* cared. But, it would be good to determine if his approach had been correct.

He considered the events that were likely to take place over the next phase of his task. The information he had investigated and calculated would now go to Claudius. What if Claudius approved, scratched his mark on the paper, and told the *Corporata* to proceed? He would be away, looking for a source—a big source—soon. He felt better. Going forward on his task would be interesting, and he was earning higher wages. Could his situation be better? Oh, it could be if he did not have to discuss that subject with Antonia. It was possible that he would have to do that soon.

He entered his courtyard, conscious of the beauty they had created in that space. Because he was skilled in many of the building crafts, a requirement for his work, he had labored to enhance the area. He had built pot shelves and seating areas and even installed several mosaic insets, getting instruction and spare material from the masters who had crafted the striking mosaics in homes of the wealthy. He was no artist, but few of his status had art of any caliber in their courtyards. Antonia had marveled at it, added her own touch of flowers, greenery, and vases and proudly displayed her courtyard to her friends and family.

Antonia was preparing to bake bread. Appius loved the smell of baking bread, and sparring with the *Corporata* had made him hungry. He stood behind her, not saying anything.

Assured that all was well with the bread, Antonia stood and turned. "Yes, Appius, how did it go with the *Corporata*? Was the work you did of any use? Did you express yourself confidently?"

Appius kissed her lightly on the cheek. "All is well. I have to make some adjustments, at their suggestion, then the numbers... my work... will be sent on to your *imperator*."

"Claudius will be looking at your numbers? And, what will he do with them, have them chiseled in stone? Or, perhaps a bronze plaque would be more appropriate." She smiled. "If he inscribes something, I think your name should be there, not *Aqua Corporata*."

"I love your playfulness, my dear wife. But, I know you'll be proud, when... someday... new fountains and baths will be built. The town will be celebrating; all the important citizens will be there... and you and me, a garland of fresh flowers decorating your... *stola*... you shall wear a *stola*."

"My dear husband, I'm afraid your imagination has the same roots as your estimating means. Only fools would take it seriously."

"Only fools? I thought I had convinced you that my estimates were worthy. You are the same as... several... of the *Corporata*."

"Oh, so some of the *Corporata* looked at your method with the same critical eye as I. How did you explain it to them?"

"I didn't."

"So, they just accepted what you had done."

"Not exactly."

"What means—'not exactly'?"

"They... well Nemus instructed me to... increase the numbers in case there were errors and... "

"So, it is not just me who.... "

"And... for what they might not be able to imagine for the town that will be twice the present size."

Antonia smiled. "Would you like olives and wine? Surely you can take time and enjoy life after your effort. Yes?"

"Yes."

Antonia went to the house and brought the olives, in oil, wine and cheese. "Sit here, Appius, in the shade, and tell me what you will be doing next."

Appius looked thoughtful and speared an olive with a tapered pick. "I believe that my quest for a new water source will be simpler than I had imagined. The amount of new water they are seeking is of great quantity. There may be only a few possibilities."

"What would they be?"

"Right now, I do not know and neither do the *Corporata*, I think. They may, in fact, believe that no such source exists."

"Do we know what Claudius will think?"

"Of course not. He may shrug his shoulders—tell them to go home and keep on with their present means, doing the best they can."

"And you would go back to your old work. Would you like that?

Appius looked at Antonia, but said nothing.

While he was waiting for the response from Claudius, Appius used his skill at basic mathematics and estimating to help him understand the water situation. It was true, there was water of the quantity they needed in rivers, but unless Rome knew of a way to make water flow uphill, all the nearby rivers were below Nemausus, except for some small sources, most of which had already been captured and impounded in the reservoirs. What would it take to get the water uphill to a cistern in the town? He considered how much an ox could pull up a hill by cart. How many trips each day? How many oxen and carts? It was impossible, perhaps 10,000 loads per day, and Claudius would think it unfitting of a Roman entity resorting to such primitive manner. The Romans built *aqueducts* if Appius understood the cultural bent. He saved his calculations involving the oxen. Maybe the *Corporata* would ask. Would Claudius ask?

But, where would they go to find water for an aqueduct? Perhaps there was a spring or stream that was higher than Nemausus, something farther away, unfamiliar to him. Well, he knew in which direction to find *uphill*, and he didn't have to look downhill.

There were problems with rivers. Their flow varied widely requiring users to impound water during the heavy flows to assure adequate supply during times of low flow. Building a structure to impound a huge amount of water would be very difficult. Also, rivers were used as means to carry away the waste of a town or city. The Vistre flowing past Nemausus was an example. No person would drink from the river for several miles downstream from the town. And, even without waste-dumping, rivers often ran muddy, scouring material from their banks, heavily so during seasons of robust flow. A spring, at its source, with constant flow would be most ideal for ensuring pure water with little sediment.

Appius could also perform the investigation Marcus had suggested while the *Corporata* was waiting for word from Claudius. He could identify a location, the *terminus*, to which the new water would be brought. If the town should grow, in what direction would that be? They would want to bring the water to a location that was *above* the expanded town so that the water would be able to flow to the new residents.

He walked the existing town, keeping in mind the location of the existing *fontis* and the location of the present town in respect to that. Nemausus, within the city walls was only 550 acres, a square area with a width of less than a mile. He walked the north boundary of the town, beyond the wall, where the city elevation tended to be higher. It did not seem obvious that the city would grow to either the west or the east. His only conclusion was that it would be an advantage to bring the aqueduct to a high point, to the north, probably at a higher elevation than the existing city walls.

The *Corporata* received response from Claudius in a week. Marcus summoned Appius to his office. "Claudius sent a short note, complimenting the *Corporata* on its good work and made it clear that we should proceed. He did say that the required quantity, the source that should be considered, should have a third more capacity beyond that which had been calculated. This would allow for short-sighted estimates, leakage, thievery and buildup of water deposits on the inside of the channel." Marcus looked at Appius, knowing that the arbitrary increases were tough on someone who thought they had already done an adequate job of forecasting.

"I am not supposing that Claudius was told that the quantities had already been increased by 10% in each of two prior calculations." Appius was shaking his head.

"No, I do not believe he was aware of our prior increases. Now, I think you can see that the main concern of leaders is to provide cover for bad decisions. It is just misfortune that your results had to go through three levels of leaders."

"Yes, any more increases and the Mare Nostrum would not provide enough water to satisfy the requirement. I will try not to think about what has happened. My next task is to find this bountiful source in quantities that my leaders have concocted. I have spent some time considering the possibilities, and unless you know of a useful source, I will start my search. I do not know of a source that is useful. Do you or the *Corporata*?"

"No. I... or... we do not. We discussed the issue. If there were a nearby source, we would know about it. But, there is a significant amount of uninhabited land out there. Who knows what you might discover. My concern is that a source in distant lands will be difficult and costly to get to Nemausus."

"I suppose we must take one step at a time. I will start my search. I've been thinking that a horse would ease my task. You said that if I had expenses, needed equipment or help, I should talk to you. A horse is not either of the above but in a way is all of the above. Will the *Corporata* furnish a horse?"

Marcus tilted his head to the side. "I think your request is justified. I will talk to them. As for now, you are afoot. Please keep me informed about what you find. I will talk to the men about a horse. The next time you talk to me, I will have an answer."

Appius nodded and exited the office, starting his new venture..

"I will be starting on my search tomorrow," Appius said to Antonia, unusually silent at the evening meal. "I am looking for a source that will be higher than the town, therefore I will start my search to the north, in the hills."

"And how long will you be gone?"

"I am planning for three days. Although on this trip, I will walk through the lands that are north, there will surely be other locations to investigate, but I think it will be good for me to come back and gather my thoughts before going on again. I really don't know what I will find."

"I will prepare your food and wine. I think you will also want to take water. Just because you are looking for water does not mean you'll find water." She smiled. "What time will you leave?"

"I will leave at sun-up and walk as far as I can in the daylight. The weather is warm, so I should have an easy time keeping comfortable as I sleep. Antonia?"

She looked at him. "Yes."

"That is not so bad, is it?"

"No, Appius. That is not so bad. I will visit my sisters and my mother. I will bake bread. I will keep busy. But, really, I hoped your task, somehow, would not require you to be away. I am having a hard time being cheerful about what you are doing, and I am feeling sorry for myself."

"I know that. I will do my best not to let this task interfere with us. You are more important to me than the *Aqua Corporata* or even Claudius. Do you know that?"

"I know that."

"Then come here and let me hold you so that I can remember this when I am lying on a flat rock, somewhere."

Appius left at sun-up. Antonia had prepared food for him, more than he could eat, of course, and almost more than he could carry. He had spent time considering what he should bring—his wax tablet, papyrus and stylus, a blanket, hat, knife, and a 3-foot graduated stick to be used for measurement. He knew that if he found a source, he would have to return to take more measurements. He would probably have to take his measuring cups to gauge the amount of water flowing. He kissed Antonia heartily and trudged out the gate with a sack lashed to thongs over his shoulder. He went a few paces then looked back to see Antonia leaning into the jamb in the gateway. He raised his hand and walked on.

He walked out of the town, through a gate, into the hills to the north of the city, past the location he had considered for a terminus. He looked back to see smoke from early morning fires rise from the town; he saw the Maisson Carree and the Tour Magne, prominent in his view. Ahead of him, against a sky transforming from light gray to a deep blue, he could see a succession of hills. Mont Duplan was nearby, so he trudged to the top to view the terrain ahead of him, perhaps to spot likely territory. Several miles to his left he saw lower terrain; water would be flowing *to* that location. It was certain he wouldn't find a water supply at the *tops* of the hills, so he would walk in the direction of the lower terrain. When you don't know what you are looking for, any circumstance that makes sense is your guide.

He descended Mont Duplan and made his way in the direction of distant hills beyond to the lower terrain. He crossed the low area then walked between the hills, and eventually walked into a canyon: it really wasn't a canyon, more of a gully. There was water flowing. He noticed that the water flowed towards him— toward Nemausus—therefore was in the right direction to be useful. The flow was sparse, vastly insufficient for their purposes. He wondered though, if he continued to encounter hills of ever increasing height, what could be done if he found a source *beyond* the hills? Would they go to the expense of tunneling? Maybe not. His first priority would be to find water that could flow to Nemausus without having to build difficult structures.

After walking up the gully for less than a mile, the flow dwindled to nothing. Looking ahead, he saw that he would be continuing to climb. He walked on, between the hills, until he reached a high point from where he could spot, a little below his elevation, a narrow flat plain, which ran transverse to his path— from east to west. He walked down the slope and onto the plain and across. On the far side, the terrain descended to another flat area. Gullies drained the plain on which he stood, creating small water paths as they tumbled to the lower plain.

He stopped and pulled grapes from his pack. What was he to make of this? Water found beyond where he stood, at a lower elevation, would require that the water be lifted over the hills or tunneled through them. As a rough idea, he had climbed uphill and now down to this location in a distance of about 1-1/2 miles. A tunnel constructed for that distance would be difficult. But, maybe tunneling would not be required if he were to find water at an elevation higher than where he stood. Ahead of him was just such terrain.

On the lower plain he walked for less than a mile, to the west, noting, as he walked, that on the bluff to his south there were many gullies draining from above into the flat area. As he approached the west end of the flat area, he spotted a stream that had formed from the accumulated seepage down the gullies. It flowed away from him, to the north between two tall hills, sentinels guarding the stream's chasm. He followed the stream, and as it descended it was joined by other streams, becoming of reasonable size. Ahead, he could see that the stream pitched into a much steeper canyon. There was evidence that the water from the stream was, at times of the year, or at some time in the past, of powerful flow. However, Appius knew that the farther the drop in elevation, the less chance there would be of it being useful to the town. Also, considering the amount of land the stream had sculpted from the canyon, it must carry heavy sediment during the high flows.

Now, into the steep canyon, he made his way along its wall, sometimes having to climb higher to work around spots that were impassible because they were too steep. He held onto tree roots to prevent sliding into the canyon, and used rocks for footholds and handholds as he inched his way along. If one were to break a leg here, nobody would find them. There were no trails, no sign of humans or livestock. There was no village that he knew of, in this direction, this far out. Suddenly, he got the sense of loneliness—remote from help or comfort or wine. The effort was strenuous, causing him to sweat heavily in the warming day. A hawk wheeled overhead, screeching at him, mocking his slow progress. Perhaps he should have stayed higher, on the rim of the canyon.

After less than one-half mile, the stream veered to the west, flowing now in more of a narrow valley than in a canyon. Appius was glad to be through the canyon but felt hungry after his struggle. However, the sun was not yet at its zenith—too early to stop and eat. He walked on for another mile then looked again at the sun, satisfied that he could *now* justify a stop and his meal. He was ready to unstrap his pack, but before he did so he decided to climb to the ridge above him, on the north side of the valley. He would enjoy his lunch at that vantage point, a good view of the stream. He wanted to see where the stream would go, and to take a look at the terrain to the north. Perhaps he would continue his search in that direction abandoning the stream in this canyon. Although it was robust for this time of the year, it could never be tamed into a conduit back to Nemausus.

Appius crested the hill only to find he was on a knife ridge, at the rim of parallel canyon, containing a mighty river at a considerable distance below. He knew. It was the *Vardo*. He was awed by its size and by the canyon it had clawed through the wilderness. However, he realized that a river, in a canyon as deep as this, would create a northern boundary for his search. A water source beyond this river could not cross it. However, he would enjoy his meal, a reward for a difficult trek through unknown territory. He spotted a rock in a location that sported an excellent view of the river, walked to it and eased the pack from his back. Yes, he realized, *this was magnificent*—enjoying the grand view, the freshness of the wild region, the silence of the uninhabited. But as he munched on cheese and bit off chunks of bread, he knew that he had discovered nothing suitable that would serve their

the *Aedifex*: Building the Pont du Gard

purpose. He lay back on the rock, his pack under his head, and enjoyed the warmth of the sun. Would he find a source? This was his first sortie. It would be way too early to speculate that the task was overwhelming. It was good to relax his muscles. He dozed briefly, but in a short time he awoke and sprung upright, ready to go on.

He had traveled north and west, he figured, not straight north from Nemausus. If the *Vardo* was a northern boundary of what might be practical, perhaps he should follow the river, at the rim of the canyon, upstream to the east. From there, he might spot terrain to the south, landscape possibly having a useful water supply. He had no idea what this source might be, but, again, when you don't know where you are going, it doesn't take much to tip the balance one way or another.

The *Vardo* continued to run in a steep canyon, steep especially on the northern bank. Appius was nearly always over one hundred feet above the river as he walked the rim. He followed the river for nearly 7 miles, taking all of the afternoon. At this point, the river turned south from a course that had been northeast, a sharp bend seen from where he stood. As he had walked the rim, he had observed no promising features to the south, nothing that provoked his interest as a possible source.

He reasoned he had gone far enough for the day. Looking to the north, beyond the *Vardo*, he could see a wide valley, enclosed by steep hills angling to the northeast. In the valley, he could see sheep and a mile or so farther, slightly to the northwest, he spotted a village, probably the home, at times, for the sheepherders and their lot. He might have walked to the village; however, he would have had to cross the *Vardo* to do so. There was a flat area below him, adjacent to the river, and the slope was gentle. He walked down the hill. He would find a place to spend the night, hoping that the direction he should take tomorrow would become clear if he relaxed and had time to think about it.

On the gentle slope to the river, he walked to a solitary clump of trees on the expanse, unbridled his pack and set it against a tree. He wanted to drench his heated, abraded and swollen feet in the river, so he made his way to the bank and walked down it into the flow. Above him, on the bank, he could see evidence of higher water levels in times past although whether it was this year's or a millennium's past was not evident. At river level, he could not see the shepherds nor their sheep. The river was wide at this point and perhaps shallow. He could see blisters in the water, evidence of rocks underneath, and there were several rocks protruding from the surface. Could he wade across? It was not something he would try, owing to the circumstance that he could not swim. His pack would be a difficulty, also, if he should find himself in deep water. Yet, there was an allure to the other side. What was the land like in this direction? What about the people? He did note that another stream entered the river opposite and downstream of where he stood.

Appius spread his blanket under the trees. They didn't provide shade at this time of day as the sun was at a low angle, appearing to be descending into the canyon and sending rivers of rippling yellow in his direction along the water surface. The rays changed to orange and soon the sun was gone. He watched twilight ease its way onto the plain and the valleys to the north. He could no longer see the sheep although his vantage point was dozens of feet higher than the river.

He ate dried fish and olives along with his bread. Antonia had included a small jug of potent wine, one that could easily require dilution by water. His muscles ached. Yes, he had done hard work in his life, but a forced march of ten miles, holding on to the roots at the sides of canyons and ascending and descending steep inclines, was not part of his routine. The wine relaxed him, and as darkness spread across the plain, he lay back and dozed. Several hours later, he woke abruptly, not sure where he was, not comprehending, for a moment, his circumstance. It came to him. He sat up and looked across the river. He could see small fires, no doubt the evening refuges of the shepherds. He secured his pack against scurrying animals after he fetched another blanket. In the brief time before he fell asleep, he recounted that he had not allowed himself time to think of his next move.

The rising sun's rays grazed the unbroken plain, lighting and warming the sleeper. Appius awoke, again taking time to apprise himself of his surroundings and reason for being there. He sat up. If his muscles were sore last night, they were inflexible this morning. He could hardly stand, but by turning on his side and pushing against the ground with his arm, he was able to manage. He looked across the river. The sheep and herders were now much closer, almost at the edge of the river.

the *Aedifex*: Building the Pont du Gard

A shepherd was looking in his direction as Appius stood; apparently the shepherd was greatly surprised as he gazed at him for several moments. Appius waved and the shepherd waved back, then beckoned. Appius walked the 100 feet to the river, muscles protesting, head abuzz.

When he reached the river, the shepherd hailed him from the opposite shore. He thought the shepherd said, "Who are you?"

"Appius of Nemausus," was his reply.

The shepherd inclined his head and pointed to his ear. He hadn't heard or understood him.

Appius said his name again, but the shepherd shook his head. The rushing river was making conversation difficult. The shepherd beckoned again, pointed at the water, then pointed to his knees. Appius got it; he could wade across. He signaled the shepherd to wait and trudged back up the bank to retrieve his pack, reload his belongings, then reattach it to his shoulders. He approached the river's edge and entered the water wearing his sandals. He proceeded slowly. The river was about 100 feet wide and, as he had observed, had a rocky bottom. The rocks, their slick surfaces, and the force of the water made stability difficult; he could be upended swiftly. In the middle, while taking a step, he sank to his waist, startling him, losing his balance. He stumbled and drifted sideways until he could get both legs under him. He would kill the shepherd.

Hesitating, he now proved his footing lightly before taking another step. He encountered no more drop-offs. Instead, he started ascending to the edge, and finally exited the water. He shot malevolent looks at the shepherd while he rinsed pebbles out of his sandals.

The shepherd laughed. "I forgot about the sudden drop-off. I am not always reliable." He laughed again.

Appius found no amusement, owing that the humor was at his expense. He stood, hands on hips, waiting, but no apology was forthcoming.

"Now," the shepherd said, "now that we can hear each other, who are you?"

Appius considered. He could walk on and be smug, not acknowledging this peasant who ridiculed him, or he could talk to the fellow and perhaps learn something about this territory. He held out his hand. "Appius, from Nemausus."

The shepherd nodded and while clutching Appius's hand, said, "Ephrius, from that village you see, which has no name."

The two stared at each other for several moments before breaking the handclasp. Ephrius said, "What are you doing here, Appius of Nemausus?"

"I am looking for water."

"Search no more. You have found it."

Appius stepped back. "Yes, to be sure, there is plenty of water in this river which we call the *Vardo*—I think this is that river. Do you know it by that name or are your rivers like your villages and have no name?"

"Yes, the *Vardo*. We call it that too. But, if this water is not good, what nature of water are you looking for?"

Appius realized that it might be hard or even unwise to state his purposes. "I am looking for water that has not run for many miles in canyons, a *fontis*, if you will, and it must be of strong quantity and pure quality."

"For what reason do you need such water?" The shepherd looked puzzled.

Appius blurted the only reason his mind could contrive. "We believe that pure water from a spring is a cure for some illnesses. And, because Nemausus is a large town, we are looking for a bountiful source."

The shepherd leaned forward, perhaps not entirely understanding. Nevertheless, he waved his hand then turned and pointed to the northeast. "There is a very bountiful spring in that direction, near the town of Ucetia. Perhaps you should look there."

"How far is Ucetia? Is it less than a day's walk?"

"Oh, yes—less than a day's walk—much less than half a day." He pointed to the northeast. "See the hills at the far side of the plain? You must pass them and keep going in the direction that they point. You will come to a river that we call Seyne. Cross that river and keep going in the same direction as the hills. You will come to another river. If you follow that river upstream, it forks and if you follow the fork to the right you will come to the spring." He looked back at Appius.

Appius had no better plan or instinct of where to look or in which direction to strike. "Do you know of any other springs in the area—where you run your sheep?"

"Yes, small ones, but nothing as bountiful as at Ucetia. In fact, as you walk, you will find springs that are feeding this stream that empties into the Vardo. But, you should see the springs at Ucetia. You would enjoy them, even though they may not be useful. You will do it?"

"Yes, I will do it. And, thank you. I forgive your forgetfulness about the bottom of the river."

Ephrius laughed again. "Appius of Nemausus, I would offer you a meal and warm food, but our fires are out, and my thought is that you will be on your way."

Appius grinned. "Yes, I will be on my way but thank you for the offer, Ephruis of no name." He grinned and offered his hand again.

They walked together in the direction of the hills until Ephrius reached the vicinity of his sheep.

Ephrius shouted after Appius, "Go well. Perhaps we will meet again."

Appius waved and walked on, heading toward the steep bluffs, following the stream that emptied to the *Vardo*, that which Ephrius said came from the small springs. On his right were hills with many gullies. In a mile or so, he came to the succession of springs, which fed the stream. The flow was notable for this time of year. He would make a note of them although getting their flow out of this valley could not be easily done.

He remembered he had not eaten a morning meal. It also occurred to him that he had not made a record of his journey due to his rapid decline into slumber last night and the early morning encounter with Ephrius. He unshouldered his pack, extracted bread and grapes, papyrus, ink, and a pen. He would take the time, now, to record what he had seen. It wasn't that walking and seeing was the only part of his job, you know. He must be diligent in recording what he saw.

He made a crude sketch of his journey, drawing the hills, canyons, and valleys to the best of his recollection, including the present valley and the location of the springs at which he sat. Satisfied, he let the ink dry then carefully rolled the papyrus and stashed it in the sack. The spot was peaceful, and he was somewhat reluctant to get moving again, perhaps persuaded by his sore and stiff legs.

Yet, the shepherd's description of the bountiful spring fueled his curiosity. He stood, stretched, shouldered his pack, and continued his walk, soon arriving at the banks of the river Ephrius called the Seyne. A convenient means of crossing the river was not obvious, so Appius wandered to his left and right until he finally concluded that the terrain was flat and the river must be shallow. He waded, more carefully than on his entry into the *Vardo,* but *this* time he did not encounter water deeper than his knees. He smirked upon reaching the other side. *Nothing to this work.*

He looked to the steep hills to confirm the direction he must travel, then walked on. In about a mile he came to another stream. This must be the one that Ephrius described, the one that was fed by the springs near Ucetia. The flow was substantial; however, he remembered the stream forked and the springs were to the right.

He followed the stream up an incline and in a short distance entered a canyon, one side a steep bluff and the other more gradual. He walked up the stream, walking the side with the gradual bank. In another mile, he arrived at the fork and followed the right-hand steam to a pond, a point beyond which the water did not flow. The source—a spring. He gauged flow from the pond as adequate, perhaps as much as flowed from the *fontis* in Nemausus, or perhaps *more* as it was flowing somewhat faster. Still, the nagging question was—how would they ever get this water to Nemausus? It was a long way; there were hills in the direction he had traveled; the Vardo must be crossed, and he could not be sure that this location was higher than that of Nemausus.

He thought. *I cannot imagine that we would find this source useful, but perhaps I will note the location and try my skill at estimating a flow. At least it is at a higher elevation than the valley.*

Appius walked back downstream to a location prior to the fork. He waded in and measured the width of the stream using his stick, then measured and recorded what he considered to be the average depth. As he had done for the *fontis,* he laboriously measured a run of 100 feet, using his measured stick. He dropped a chip into the stream and counted in an even cadence for the time that the chip took to flow the 100 feet. He was able to keep pace with the chip, but it turned out that his cadence matched his stride, so he did his best to remember the pace. He could use his water cups to compare the time it took him to pace the 100 feet and then try to figure the amount of water that would be comparable.

He retrieved his papyrus from the sack and sketched the valley, streams, and hills he had passed since his last recorded entry in the early morning. At the location shown for the Ucetia springs, he recorded the dimensions of the stream and the pace relating to the 100 foot run. Satisfied, he stowed the writing material and hitched his pack. He was not ready for another meal and thought it would be useful to find and investigate Ucetia. He crossed the stream and found a shallow rise up the bank, climbed it and found that he was looking at the small village, about 300 paces ahead.

He walked in and saw women and children carrying water, a donkey towing a cart laden with barley stalks urged on by a boy of about 13, and people lingering in conversation mid-street. There were crude shops fronting a dusty lane, and a woman emerged from one holding a pair of sandals.

Appius did not see an inn or a structure where a traveler might rest. Public fountains were a town's natural meeting place, and he found Ucetia's by walking in the opposite direction to those carrying water. The villagers watched him and only nodded when he caught their eye. He was obviously not one of them.

Rather than possibly offending someone's wife, he walked to a young man filling his water jug and bid him "good morning." The young man looked at him and returned his greeting but said nothing more. Appius asked permission to refill his water jugs, and the young man nodded. Finally, Appius said, "You have a wonderful spring below the bluff, but my thought would be that this fountain water comes from somewhere else."

The man nodded his head. "Yes, the spring you saw is much below us. Higher up there is a spring from the same underground source that feeds the one that you saw. We have captured that water from the higher elevation and have run it to this fountain and to other reservoirs about town."

"It is good water?"

He nodded then grinned. "It is very good water. Look at our citizens. Do they not look healthy and thriving?"

"Yes. Yes they do. And the water is dependable—it does not dwindle in the dry season or in dry years?"

111

"No, the flow is steady. We do not... at least in my memory... have to ration the water. Are you going to stay in our village or perhaps move to the village?"

Appius shook his head. "No, I'm just a traveler, walking the land. I'm from the town of Nemausus, and I have been walking for several days, past the river Vardo and through the valley to your village. I work on our town's water system, so I'm always interested in the water that other towns and villages have captured and managed."

The young man regarded him, "And what will you do now?"

"I will return to Nemausus. I was to only be gone three days. In what direction should I head if I do not want to return on the same path that I took getting to Ucetia? Is there a route I might take that will not require me to cross the hills?" Appius was thinking that if water from this vicinity were to be useful, it would have to get to Nemausus without crossing the hills.

The young man thought. "Yes, I have been to Nemausus twice. Once, I took the route, crossing the Vardo and through the hills, much the route you must have taken. But, several times I traveled east, down the valley and beyond the location where the Vardo turns south. From there we walked to Nemausus, following a route that did not cross the hills. I was transporting barley by cart and could not travel rough terrain. You will find that there is a path that has been made. But, at some point you must cross the Vardo; there is a bridge where the river turns south."

"Thank you. Perhaps I will see you again. Is there a market where I might buy fruit?"

"Yes, the market is that way—two streets. Have a safe journey."

Appius nodded. "Thank you."

Appius filled his water container at the fountain, then walked to the market where he bought fruit, which, at this point, was much superior to that in his pack. He then sat on a rock wall and made notations on his papyrus.

He did not know how long it would take him to get back, especially by way of the route that the young man had described. A direct route, over the hills, would get him back to Nemausus by the end of the third day; however, it would be useful to investigate the land in the valley. While the water at Ucetia may be too far and too difficult to feed to Nemausus, perhaps there would be other sources he would spot along the way.

It was not yet noon, so he could still walk for a significant distance that day. He retraced his route back down the canyon from the springs, the canyon carved by the larger stream they joined. As he did so, he noticed that the stream ran fast as it descended from the springs and ran into the valley. He followed its course. As he followed its turn to the east, he looked north to a large formation of hills. To the south must be the *Vardo*. The stream he walked ran to the southeast for about 4 miles, gaining in strength from other runoffs, becoming more of a river, until it turned south and emptied into the canyon of the Vardo.

Appius stood on the bluffs above the rivers. He had stayed on the north side of the river from the springs so did not have to cross the stream before it gave itself up to the stronger flow of the Vardo. He remembered the young man said that he should cross the Vardo when it turned south, so he again walked the rim of the *Vardo* knowing he would eventually arrive at the crossing point. He had not spotted the path that the carters used in traveling to Nemausus, probably because he had been taking his own route, up to this point. In 2 miles he encountered a very hilly section through which the *Vardo* flowed. He had to make some steep climbs along the rim to stay within view of the river. It looked like hundreds of feet down to the water from where he stood. When he cleared the hilly area, he could see that the valley ran behind the hill. At last, after another 3 miles, the great Vardo turned south. He was down on the flats now and didn't have the vantage to see where the bridge might be. Nor did he see it when he was in the hilly area. However, he did see the path of which the Ucetia villager spoke, or at least he thought so. It was heading in the right direction.

It was well past noon, and he had not yet stopped to eat a midday meal, so he sat on the banks of the Vardo and did so. Perhaps he would travel this afternoon as far as the bridge, and spend the night there. There would be a good chance he would encounter other travelers. He could talk to them and see if they knew of any water sources. He laughed. He knew he would sound silly asking about a water source while astride the robust *Vardo*.

He thought maybe he had three more hours of daylight. Surely he would encounter the bridge in that time.

He arrived at the bridge in less than 2 miles. He was now walking in a very flat area, but ahead of him, across the bridge, there was a set of steep hills stretching to the southwest toward Nemausus, as far as he could see. It seemed reasonable that there may be water sources in those hills and that one of those sources could be brought lower and along the edge of the hills to Nemausus. Yes, this was looking more promising. He had abandoned the idea that water from the Ucetia springs could ever be channeled to Nemausus, but, somewhere in that long chain of high hills, there were many valleys collecting water, supplying underground pools, feeding springs from which to service the thirsty town. He had a vision of this water system in his mind.

There were other travelers, several with donkeys pulling carts and some walking without the accompaniment of beasts. The bridge was crude—timber stretched over rock piles in the shallow river. The bridge looked like it had been rebuilt in the center section, probably, Appius reasoned, because the Vardo swept it away during high runs. Who rebuilt it and why?

Before the bridge, there was an encampment area, and several travelers were stopped. It looked like they were making preparations to stay for the night. He walked to a cart tender, so engaged, and asked where he was going.

"I make this trip several times during the season to Nemausus. They pay me the best price for my corn, so it is worth my journey of two days to get there. Of course, I spend most of the payment before I ever leave the city, but I can bring many provisions back on my cart and sell to those in my village. That way, I have commerce in both directions." He laughed. "And you," he said, removing his cap and wiping his brow, "where have you been and where are you going?"

Appius had removed his pack and was carrying it in one hand, preparatory for establishing his night camp. He pointed back up the valley and said, "I walked directly from Nemausus to the north, finally arriving at the town of Ucetia, which I reached this morning. I am now heading for Nemausus, avoiding the hills, more or less. Do you think I can walk there in one day?"

"Oh, yes, I do think so. It will be a long day for me tomorrow, but even I will get to town before dark unless my cart breaks a wheel. You will be faster than I, so you should make it easily."

Appius had to ask, "I am looking for water that we might bring to Nemausus. As you walk this path, on that side near the hills, do you cross any streams that might be worthwhile for a water supply?" Appius cringed, expecting the obvious.

"Do you not know that we are on the banks of a considerable flow of water? This Vardo would supply many towns of Nemausus' size." He laughed.

Appius laughed. "I knew I was going to have to explain. You see, the Vardo, especially when it is flowing just after spring rains, carries much sediment with it making it difficult for our water system to handle. Also, in very dry years, a river like the Vardo would be undependable. And, it is not certain to me that the Vardo is higher in elevation than is Nemausus. Water may flow toward us, instead."

The carter nodded. "Yes, well, I do see that your requirements may be more difficult than dipping my jug into the river. But, to answer your question, I have seen some, but not many, small creeks that flow from the hills. Now that you mention it, I would think there would be more. Perhaps I missed them, but I do not think so. You will be more attentive, I am thinking."

"Yes, yes. I will. If you are staying here, I will offer you fruit that I bought this afternoon in Ucetia. Their fruits and vegetables were of good quality."

"Thank you. And, if you are staying the night, I have more than enough of a meal that we might share. Do you happen to have any wine?"

"Yes, I do. I have a fair amount, and it would be a tragedy to arrive in Nemausus not having it consumed. We will prepare for the night then drink our wine.... "

"And eat a fair meal besides. Life is good."

Appius spent the remainder of his wakeful time writing an account of his journey. He would complete most of his days at this practice.

In the morning, Appius crossed the bridge and walked the edge of the hills, following a path. The hills, with the exception of a few breaks, were on his right all the way to Nemausus. The carter was correct. There were only a few streams that crossed the path, mostly near to his destination. They did not look promising. Nevertheless, he recorded their locations on his charts along with the other elements of the landscape he had noted. Last evening, he used the remaining light to record his observations from Ucetia to the bridge. This effort had been done after the wine. He looked at the clumsy notation and shook his head.

He was starting to consider the nature of the report he would make as a result of his journey. He certainly had not found any source that would be worth considering. However, finding landscapes that were *not* promising was part of the task. But, where would he look next—a route that departed Nemausus more obliquely—toward the northwest, for example? He now knew though, that the Vardo might be the northern border to his search. His journey had been useful.

It was good to be back in Antonia's arms. But soon she pushed him away, looked him over and laughed. "I did not know you would have to fight wild animals. Are they responsible for your tattered clothing and many scratches?"

"No—no wild animals and not too many humans. Most of the tatters and scratches are self-inflicted, a result of making bad decisions about which way to go."

"I have a clean tunic for you, and you know the way to the public baths. And, hurry. I am anxious to hear where you have been. And, Marcus got word to me. You are to meet with him when you can arrange it. Claudius will be here in two weeks."

CHAPTER 14

Appius arranged for a meeting with Marcus. He had the look of a voyager—darkened skin and scratches after spending three days in the sun and wild terrain.

Marcus said, "It does look like you have been somewhere. Have you found our water?"

"No, Marcus. I do not think so. I walked north of Nemausus, through the hills to the Vardo. Yes, there is water here and there, but nothing that would have the flow that we need. There is much water in the Vardo, even for this time of year, but it is in a deep canyon along much of its length until downstream, to the east, it flows through the plain. However, a local told me of a spring at Ucetia, and I walked there."

"You walked to Ucetia... then back?"

"Yes. It was a natural outcome of the direction I took. But, although I walked over many hills going north of Nemausus, I did not go through the hills coming back. I walked from Ucetia, following the spring that surfaces there, through a valley to the Vardo, followed the Vardo downstream, then skirted the base of the hills back to Nemausus."

"What do you say about the springs at Ucetia?"

"The water is very good. The people of Ucetia drink from the water, and they appear healthy. I talked to a villager who confirmed my thoughts."

"And, how far is this spring from Nemausus?"

"It is only about 12 miles if you were to walk in a straight line, over the hills, but, you cannot bring the water straight, over the hills. From Ucetia, the water would have to flow through the valley, cross the Vardo then follow the hills to Nemausus. That route would be long, perhaps a distance of 23 miles on the map that I drafted."

"Hmmm—as I thought. What will you do now?" Marcus raised his eyebrows.

Appius pointed to the south. "The land to the south of Nemausus is lower. It would not be reasonable to expect the water to run uphill for us. We do not have to look there. To the north, it appears that all of the land between Nemausus and the

117

Vardo is very hilly. There may be some water in those hills that is worthwhile, although I walked the rim of the Vardo and did not see any streams of promise that emptied into it. But, even if we did find something in that region, we have the same problem with trying to get the water to flow over the hills. I also investigated the hills after I crossed the Vardo on my way back to Nemausus. I found a few streams but nothing of interest. So, all the area to the northeast of Nemausus does not seem to have a useable source... with the exception of Ucetia."

Marcus raised his hand to interrupt. "Perhaps that is what we will tell Claudius. He will be here in two weeks. However, I do not want to bypass a useful source. If he finds one and we missed it, he will cause difficulties for us. He may already suspect that we do not have the same interest as he in bringing great quantities of water to the town. I do not think we can report to him on the basis of one three-day trip."

Appius nodded. "Yes, I think the same. I have reasoned that I should walk to the west of Nemausus. I have heard that a number of streams and springs are in that area, although eventually they empty into the *Vistre,* the *Vidourle,* or the *Vardo.* I suggest that between now and the arrival of Claudius I investigate the land to the west. I think that will make our effort look more complete."

Marcus leaned forward. "Yes, please do that. And talk to me as soon as you return. I want to report to the *Corporata* so that we can determine what to tell Claudius. They have already asked me." He shrugged.

"I will leave in two days. Did you find a horse for me?" Appius tried a wry smile.

"I am still looking for your horse. I have not found it... yet." Marcus countered with his smile.

"Could it be that the *Corporata* does not want to fund a horse for me?"

"You cannot tell them that I told you, but they dismissed your request." Marcus stood up. "They do not have to do the walking. They think that walking is your natural state and that you feel more comfortable and able in doing so."

Appius looked up at Marcus. "In truth, I had to hold onto roots to make my way through some of the canyons. I could not have made my way through the canyons on a horse. But, I would choose another route, high up, on the canyon rim. I ask that you

118

look for another opportunity to discuss this with them. I do not have a good argument for you to use since they are not too interested in having me investigate much territory and truly find something that is worthwhile."

Marcus shook his head. "I am afraid that you speak the truth. Therefore, I wish you a good... walk."

Appius nodded and left the room.

"Yes, Antonia, I will spend another three days to walk the terrain to the west."

"What did Marcus say? Was he disappointed that you didn't find a good source or several sources to the north?" Antonia was slicing bread.

"No, he listened to my report calmly. He did not think that I would find a source, but he was somewhat surprised that I had walked all the way to Ucetia."

"Not surprised enough that he requisitioned a horse for you."

"No, no horse. To be honest, I do not know how useful a horse would be. But, I think I will keep asking. It is good to nurture guilt on their part. If I ask for something else, they will still be tender about the horse." Appius chanced an encounter with Antonia's knife to whisk away an early hunk of bread.

"When will you leave?" Antonia held up her knife then pointed it at Appius.

"I think I would like to stay at home another day or two. I can prepare for my trip then be on my way."

"If I understand you, when you complete this additional exploration, there are no more obvious territories to explore. If you don't find a reasonable source, your search and your task may be over." She emphasized 'over' by feigning a knife slice across her neck.

"That is true. My task may be only a week from ending. Will you be happy if I go back to the water works?" He smiled.

"I am torn." She shrugged. "I am somewhat caught up in the adventure of the search. Yet, I know if it happened that a project was started, I would often be alone. I can only visit my mother and sisters once in a while. They are tiresome in large doses, and I think they think the same of me. They also have children to look after."

"I am also torn. I do relish the adventure but do not look forward to being away."

"I think it would be much easier on you. You will be engrossed in your work. I will have not much more to do than wait for you to come back through our gate." Antonia nodded towards the gate.

"Let us see what I find when I travel west. I have been thinking about my overall task. Do you see that there is a chain of tasks that lead to an action or a decision? I was thinking about that on my trip to the north. Even though I was *not* finding a useful source, I was providing useful information, an answer that must be determined in the larger picture." He accentuated with a nod.

"I am not sure what you mean." Antonia looked up and over to Appius.

"I mean that we had to determine whether or not a source existed in one of several possible areas. I investigated one area and found little of use. We now have information we did not have before. We can draw a line around that territory, describe what is there, and go on until we can say that we know what possibilities exist or do not exist in other territories. That will lead to the next decision or point to the next requirement for information, which, in this overall concept, could be to find out whether a source is abundant, or higher than Nemausus, or whether the water can be delivered."

"I can see it is a path you must take. But I think it is important to determine what you must know."

"Yes, my dear Antonia. You are a bright girl. We must be aware of the information that needs to be gathered, the alternatives that must be considered. So far I am on my own. I have to collect information I think will get us to the next step."

"Are you sure you know what you should do?" Antonia set the bread plate down, beyond the reach of Appius.

"If I keep the final result in mind, I can think my way through as I did when I lay awake near the bridge that crosses the Vardo. I must admit the wine seemed to direct my thoughts to solutions that were much simpler than they really are. But, I'll keep thinking, with or without the help of the wine." He took a gulp of wine, emphasizing his remark.

the *Aedifex*: Building the Pont du Gard

"You are saying that if you can imagine the completed project, you can see the steps that need to be taken to get there?"

"Yes. I just imagine them, one at a time. Each new step builds on the old. I build the project in my mind. If I found five sources of water, I would know that the next step would be to determine which source would be best to utilize. I would establish those things that are important for a source and identify those things for each of the sources I am studying. From that information, I would conclude which I would use. Picking the favored source would consider the means I would use to get the water to Nemausus. So, I must now think about how to build an aqueduct: a design. I ask, what information do I need now? How will I use it to complete the design? So, you see, it is a constant process of finding more information."

"I am overwhelmed thinking about building an entire aqueduct. Do you not think it is a magnificent undertaking?"

"Yes. I do. And, I am exhilarated to think I might be part of it. I *must* find a source."

Appius departed after a sorrowful goodbye to Antonia. Again, he was well stocked with food, wine, and writing material and had his measuring stick. He considered the task at hand. He learned techniques during his prior trek, north of Nemausus. He now understood that he would have the best chance of finding a viable source if he could find one that, although eventually draining into a valley from higher elevations, might be led to Nemausus by capturing it at the higher elevations. It could then be led to gently descend along hills, avoiding a descent into a valley, only to have to climb a hill—as an example. When this thought occurred to him, he saw the spring at Ucetia as more of a possibility, although its distance and need to cross the Vardo still made that source a difficult proposition.

Any water source he encountered, be it stream or river emptying into a valley, might *not* be suitable at the point it entered the valley but upstream it might, having a greater elevation and being less subject to sedimentation during high flows or perhaps less subject to contamination by waste from a village. To the west, perhaps there was not too much concern from waste as there were few established towns. Yet, if he *did* encounter people, they could provide valuable input in finding a

121

source that would be useful for Nemausus. He remembered the shepherd telling him of the springs at Ucetia and the young man at Ucetia who had described the less hilly route back to Nemausus.

He walked directly west from Nemausus. On his prior exploration he had walked almost directly north, slightly to the west, so he was somewhat aware of the territory in that direction. If he walked 4 or 5 miles to the north, he would encounter the *Vardo*.

After walking west for several miles, he encountered a broad valley. He stood at the juncture where another drainage, originating in a northwesterly direction, joined the valley. Mindful that he could only search a little further north before he encountered the Vardo, he, nevertheless, followed the drainage uphill on a gradual slope. He trudged up the slope for over a mile then encountered a summit. The terrain would now be downhill if he continued. However, he might still find water at an elevation higher than Nemausus and remembered that Marcus was concerned that they did not miss finding a possibility.

He strode on and came to an intersecting stream draining into the canyon in which he was walking. The stream was not of high flow, so he did not track it to its source.

He encountered more streams, now joining the first but draining away from Nemausus, probably, he suspected, heading to the Vardo. Again, none of the streams was sufficient to warrant exploration to their source. He stopped for a drink and his mid-day snack. He was not very hungry so just munched on bread and cheese. He ate a few grapes relishing the cool and refreshing juice they provided.

Appius turned and retraced his steps. Back at the wide, grassy valley, he made his way westerly, veering slightly to the north. There was no water running in the valley as he made his way up the slight grade. But, there must have been at some time, he reasoned, water must have created the valley.

After a short walk, he stood on a high point beyond which the valley descended, away from Nemausus. Ahead of him he could see evidence of water flowing to the valley, although he couldn't see the water, *per se*; stands of trees and bushes indicated its presence. He continued walking, stopping at each creek or stream to consider the possibilities. All were of small flow. Even the stream that now scoured the valley was more of a brook.

However, after 6 miles, he encountered many streams, all headed north. In this vicinity was the village of Nacur. He made his way to the public fountain and was able to find an *aquarius* who had time to talk to him. The *aquarius* verified that the several streams in the vicinity eventually made their way to the Vardo, a little over a mile to the north. Appius asked if there were any sources that were plentiful, at a higher elevation. The *aquarius* told him to walk in a southwesterly direction, keeping the line of the higher terrain to his right, staying close to the foot of that terrain. He would encounter another village, Ostia, and he should ask residents for directions to find 'the spa.' 'The spa' used the waters from higher locations for the healthful benefits they were supposed to produce.

Appius walked the flat terrain in the direction of Ostia. Several brooks flowed into the wide expanse he walked, but the meager flows discouraged him from investigating their source. As he reached Ostia, daylight was nearly gone. He could find no lodging, so he again spread his blanket at a suitable refuge and ate a meal that was more robust than that at mid-day. As he lay on his blanket, swatting mosquitoes, watching the moon subdue the stars in its full light, he considered what he had found— nothing that looked promising. He did not think that he had bypassed any streams that he should have investigated. The wine—he drank it without dilution—smoothed any concern that he might have missed anything useful. That was his thought as he fell into slumber—perhaps, tomorrow—perhaps....

After waking and making a meal of olives, cheese and bread, he accosted several villagers. None knew about the spa. Finally, a man, looking more affluent, knew what Appius was seeking and gave him directions leading to a spring that would became a brook as he walked on. If he followed the brook, he would eventually spot the spa.

Appius did so and was able to find the spa after walking 2 to 3 miles along the edge of a range of hills. The spa's proprietor had situated the spa to take advantage of the natural pools in the brook, creating more useful pools by constructing stone walls and decks. Appius judged the flow to be too little but nevertheless searched for and found the proprietor. The fellow, lively, with a robust silhouette, turned out to be full of information, some of it

123

useful. The spa, he was eager to say, had remarkable qualities—could cure no end of common maladies. The evidence of all this, other than the well-being of his clientele, was the effervescence.

He gave Appius a cup from which to taste the waters. Appius liked the bubbly sensation and taste, although the water, charmed as it was, would never make a suitable source for Nemausus. Perhaps he could ask if the *Corporata* would be entertained in considering the possibility of a substantial aqueduct transporting effervescent water to Nemausus. He laughed but did not think *they* had much of a sense of humor.

Appius explained to the proprietor that he was looking for springs at their source, at higher elevations and of more flow than that of the spa. Did he know of any? The proprietor turned and pointed toward the north. "Two miles, up the canyons, in that direction are many springs. They join and eventually flow to a river in the west. But, if you are looking for waters at their source, you may find what you want. The terrain is very hilly so it will not be easy to get there."

Appius ate his midday meal at the spa, still in the windy exhalations of the proprietor. Appius thanked him kindly, took a deep breath, and headed for the canyon mouth.

The proprietor indicated, "Keep working your way north and a little to the west. In several miles you will encounter an area of many *fonts*."

It was rough going as he walked through the canyons. Appius was never sure where he was, and there was no sign of habitation or paths. Many times he had to backtrack to avoid obstacles to his progress. Near the end of the afternoon, he climbed the highest hill he could see. To his north, in less than a mile he spotted a steep canyon. He couldn't see the bottom but thought there might be fresh water there; he would make the canyon bottom his destination for the night's rest. He walked down the hill, across an intermediate valley, around another hill and soon found himself facing the steep canyon wall he had seen from the hill. Indeed, there was a tumultuous flow of cool, fresh water. He would find a place to sleep, have his meal, and drink a little wine; he would investigate in the morning.

The canyon was enchanting, the water noisy. Although the morning sunlight had not yet reached the canyon floor, it grazed the trees and brush above him, a promise of warmth and light.

the *Aedifex*: Building the Pont du Gard

The birds and a number of scurrying animals thought the same and so worked hard to get their early morning chores done, so they could enjoy the coming warmth at their leisure. Appius sat up on his blanket, enjoying the sights. He had his usual morning meal of olives, cheese, and bread then walked to the rushing water, found an eddy, and dipped his cup. This water was not effervescent but—was it his imagination—had a very refreshing taste.

He observed that the flow originated at the east end of the canyon and, in a series of rapids and cataracts, tumbled hurriedly to his location, then continued downstream. He walked upstream and found that beyond a point, no flow existed. As at Ucetia, multiple springs contributed to the flow. He walked back to his camp, retrieved his charting materials and made a rough sketch of the terrain and streams he had encountered the prior day and the location of this canyon.

He needed to know more. He gathered his gear and continued down the canyon to the west, finding other springs intersecting the stream, increasing the flow. In his judgment, the flow was sufficient and of interest, but he followed the stream until it was intersected by another stream from a canyon south but parallel to the canyon where he had spent the night. Although the water from the new stream also looked fresh, he did see some evidence of sediment on the banks. He measured the cross-section of the original stream before it was joined and did his traditional 100-foot measurement and time measurement using his cups. He retrieved his charts from his pack and noted the flow data that he had determined.

The flow from the intersecting stream was decent, so he thought he should investigate this canyon also. The slight evidence of sediment on the banks indicated, that the flow might be subject to more variation than that of the stream from the first canyon. He walked up the canyon for less than a mile and was able to determine that the water from this canyon came from springs but was subject to substantial runoff from the surrounding gullies. The flow through this canyon was steep, also, forming cataracts and roils against the rocks as the white water raced on. Appius walked back to the confluence, removed his charts, and made his notes.

He continued walking downstream less than a mile and encountered another stream that joined the already strong flow in the gorge. Farther downstream he could see that the canyon ended and the terrain flattened in that direction, effecting smooth flow of the stream rather than the crashing, hell-bent torrent that he had been tracking. He did not know what data would be important later, but he thought he should make some comparisons. He measured the cross section of the secondary and then the tertiary flows and again performed his customary walk-off, although all the streams were difficult to measure due to the rapids. He had certainly found a source to be considered, and he felt exhilarated at doing so. Could the water be transported to Nemausus? That was another question to be answered; he would do his best. There was no question that he was in higher elevations, but finding a route to Nemausus was not apparent. He would go on.

He followed the stream downward onto the flat area, where it was evident that the muddy joining waters of that terrain were not fresh and, it was possible that the terrain was not higher than Nemausus. Prospects were much better upstream. The 'stream' was now more of a river, having been joined by other water sources from the flat terrain. The spa proprietor had said that the waters from the springs joined an even larger river to the west. Appius followed the water until it joined the larger river near a village. He inquired as to a route he might travel to Nemausus. It was evident, as this was his third day, he would not be able to walk home in the remaining daylight. What would Antonia think? It could not be helped. Perhaps he should have not been so definite on his three-day plan—or—estimate. But, what could he do?

The village was in a low plain that sloped upward in the direction of Nemausus. Clearly a source for Nemausus must be taken from a higher elevation and not brought to this low point. Villagers indicated that the path to Nemausus was almost directly east, up the slope, through a relatively flat expanse between the gentle hills to either side.

The next morning Appius walked back upstream, towards the *fonts*, to the confluence of the first canyon with the second. Was there a route out of this hilly area that would flow gradually downhill? His plan was to, as best he could, walk at a constant elevation to the southeast out of the hilly area until he intersected the gentle hills above the valley that extended east towards Nemausus. Rather than telling the *Corporata*, and eventually Claudius—a route *might* be found—he would be able to provide more information. He was the one. None of the others had ever stood where he now stood. He was the person, at this time, to make the determination.

At the confluence, he started walking, following the hillsides, constantly looking forward and visualizing a target location at the same level, then walking to that spot and looking back to the location where he had stood. There were many gullies to skirt, several hills to walk around, but he was able to gradually make his way to the southeast. He shook his head trying to imagine an aqueduct with so many wiggles but perhaps they would—or could—span some of the gullies with small bridges. Yes, that is what they would do.

It occurred to him, after practicing his approach, the water should be flowing lower at this point—gradually descending—so he lowered his target slightly and carried on. It was nearly afternoon before he rounded a hill and spotted flat terrain substantially below his position. So, a route to this point *was* possible. He walked down into the valley and, looking to the east, was able to determine that he was at the foot of a range of hills that progressed to the east—toward Nemausus. He walked several miles along the flat area, now approaching a range of hills that ran north to south. The area looked familiar. Yes, he had traveled a circle and had ended back at the spa, tucked in the far corner of the intersecting hills. He laughed and felt contentment, realizing that he could now more accurately describe his trip.

He found the proprietor and, with a grin, described what he had found and what he had done. The proprietor, now possessing more information than only two days ago, was pleased and, therefore, invited Appius to share his meal and to spend the night. Appius was out of wine and dried fish so was happy to take the offer and to share the proprietor's wine and lamb. The proprietor, now that he had acquired background, questioned Appius more thoroughly on his task. Appius, somewhat aware that he should be circumspect, nevertheless told the proprietor that Nemausus needed an expanded water supply.

The proprietor's eyebrows arched. "It would be a long way to transport water. However, it seems that towns are always interested in resources in the region," the proprietor said, with suspicion.

Appius, ignoring the notion that he could not speak for the *Corporata*, said, "Nemausus has no interest in water that bubbles."

In the morning, Appius, feeling ever more guilty about extended time away from Antonia, got a more precise description of the path he should take to Nemausus. Hiking up the hills above the spa he saw that the aqueduct could travel above a wide, flat area that was at a higher elevation than the spa. After that, the aqueduct would still travel the hills but must now cross the flat area to the steeper hills on his right—running east, towards Nemausus. Walking the aqueduct's imagined path, he crossed the flat spot along the north-south hills until he encountered the range of hills that ran to the east. He continued traveling east, following a path. About 5 miles from the spa, the terrain descended towards Nemausus. Eventually his route would intersect the Via Domitia, the road to Spain on which Nemausus was perched.

It was possible, he thought with exhilaration, that the water could be routed to Nemausus. Would the *Corporata* or Claudius make it happen? That was something they must consider. His task was to provide information about possibilities. Well, he could not quarantine his responsibility to just that. He could also be a salesman. This he understood. Although regarded by the *Corporata* as a subordinate, his viewpoint would still have an impact. So, what was his viewpoint? He would discuss that with Antonia.

CHAPTER 15

Appius braced as he approached his home, not knowing what manner of onslaught he would face. Would Antonia be mostly concerned or mostly angry?

Antonia displayed both. She embraced Appius soon after he walked through the gate, crying and saying, via short phrases, how much she had worried. Then, after several moments, she chided him for putting her through the ordeal. His explanations—having to complete his work, not wanting to walk at night—did nothing to dilute the attack. He let the tirade reach its tiring end, nodding and looking at the ground during its fury, saying nothing when the storm abated.

Antonia glared, then again hugged him, took a deep breath and said, "What did you find?"

With relief, Appius described his trip, his morning in the canyon, the effervescent water and, somewhat to justify his later arrival, his extra effort of following the terrain to determine a route. "I do not know if the *Corporata* or Claudius will engage in such a substantial project, but I have done my job. I have looked for and found water that could be used. If the territory that surrounds us does not contain a viable source—that is not my fault. My contribution is to determine—what is."

"What will happen now?"

"I must complete my charts and display them in a more acceptable form than what I have scratched on the paper and written in a confetti of notes. As usual, I will first tell Marcus what I have discovered and what I think. He will then assemble the *Corporata*, and I imagine that I will talk to them. They will, of course, have questions and will probably have objections. I will be pressed to answer. I must say, I intend to show enthusiasm for the possibilities. They may not react to my viewpoints with the same enthusiasm. They may be hostile. Perhaps they will throw rocks at me." He flinched, as if to avoid the rocks.

"Rocks, no, but they may not be happy with you. But, *I* am curious about what you are thinking and feeling. It is becoming clear to me that you are generating your own enthusiasm for a project. You would like to have a part in what you consider a magnificent undertaking. Is that not true?"

"Yes, Antonia, I am not sure how my enthusiasm developed, or when, but, I have to admit, I would be sorely disappointed if nothing came of the venture or I was not involved. I find the idea grand and exciting—a challenge. And, it is better than wanting to fight a war."

Antonia only stared. Her thought was that she might become secondary to his obsession. She had witnessed this phenomenon before. What should she do? He would resent a negative outlook from her; she would not play that role. Perhaps she could make sure he was realistic, make sure he was not playing the fool. If his approach turned out to be more fantasy than reason, she would have done her best. She did realize that her challenge to his thoughts might be viewed negatively, even though they might be useful questions to consider and work through. She would have to be careful in her discussions. "My husband, will telling me your thoughts help you prepare for your report to the *Corporata*? If so, please do tell me. Your adventure interests me greatly." She smiled.

"Antonia, you shall be with me every step of the way." He put his hand on her shoulder. "I shall, indeed, be happy to tell you what I am doing. Your interest is helpful and encouraging to me. Your questions will help me prepare for those of others. And... it would be useful if I were to keep my enthusiasm in bounds, from time to time. Perhaps, though, you will also be entrained in my adventure."

"I am sure that will be, my husband, but, now, I will prepare a 'meal to remember' for my returning adventurer and after, perhaps a night to remember. Are you glad that you have me?"

"It is so, Antonia. It is so." He reached for her hand.

The next morning, Marcus sat drumming his fingers on the table. "How many days on your most recent quest?"

"Four. I took four days. I took an extra day to follow the terrain to find a possible route for the very excellent water source that I found."

Marcus stopped drumming his fingers and clasped his hands. "And, how did you do that?"

130

the *Aedifex*: Building the Pont du Gard

"If you imagine an aqueduct leading away from a source, it would conveniently follow the terrain in hilly area, gradually descending to a lower elevation. The architects would, no doubt, straighten the course I took using small bridges. But there *is* a way to the valley and once there, a reasonable chance of following the terrain to Nemausus."

"What would you recommend?"

"In truth, all I can do is state that there is a possible source; it appears to be water of good quality; it appears possible to transport the water to Nemausus. You principals, with loftier understanding of that which is required to sponsor a project, will have to decide if such a grand project is something that you will pursue."

Marcus leaned forward, across the desk, and spoke in low tones. "As long as we are speaking 'in truth,' a project employing a source that you have found is way beyond the capacity of this relatively small water company. However, if you are from Rome, you can have visions as grandiose as required by such a scheme."

"Claudius?"

"Yes. We do not see the project from his perspective. I can tell you now, the schemes involving either the water from Ucetia or the bountiful source you have discovered will not be embraced by the *Corporata*. It will not happen if it is up to us."

"And...?"

"That remains to be seen. Claudius will determine."

"Perhaps we could channel effervescent water to Nemausus and sell it at a premium, valuable for curing illness." Appius smiled.

"What are you talking about?" Marcus leaned back.

"I stumbled across a spa run by a fellow that makes use of such water. The water is naturally effervescent, flowing from a nearby spring."

"Ha. We should tell Claudius." He laughed. "He would think we have surely all drunk from the water, and it caused us to be crazed. Succumbing to strange waters would be more excusable in his world than an outright rejection of his plan to bring water."

"I'll leave that up to you. You will let me know if the *Corporata* wants to hear more about my search?"

"Yes, I will let you know. I must make sure, though—do you believe that we have done a serious effort of searching the surroundings for a source?"

"I do. I followed upstream every water flow that looked suitable. In addition, I talked to the locals. I think I would only have missed source that they did not wish me to know about."

"Which is possible."

"Which is possible." Appius nodded.

"Let us go with what we have. We should be able to get an indication from Claudius if we have to continue searching or if we are beyond that which he is thinking."

The *Corporata* reacted to the additional input from Marcus with silence. The western source, over 12 miles from Nemausus, through successions of hills, was not something they could grasp. It was beyond them.

After a while, Nemus spoke. "What can we say? We have now heard of two possible sources, both at an extreme distance from our town. Both require design, construction and financing that we cannot comprehend We must tell Claudius our results. In my thoughts, he could direct us to investigate further or conclude that the sources available are too difficult. I do not know the man well enough to predict what he *will* do. Should we arrange to tell him—I ask?"

Titus, never one to shade his meaning, said, "Yes, we should arrange to tell him, but we must make it clear that *we* cannot fund this. He must do this, must make the arrangements, bring on the designers if he will, for the glory of Rome."

Julius slowly shook his head. "My guess is that if he is interested in the least, he will direct us to continue, have us make a more thorough consideration of the two sources, perhaps prove a route. He will expect us to do this."

Titus reacted. "Yes, and if our additional effort goes for nothing, the funds we expend will be ours to shoulder."

Nemus nodded. "Yes, one of the advantages of belonging to the Empire." He paused. "They know what is best for us."

"They know what is best for their own glory." Titus raised a fist in mock salute. "But, there is one matter to consider. When asked to pursue this mad caper, Claudius had been appointed co-Imperator, at Caligua's request. Now, we hear, Caligua may decide to rule his kingdom alone. Claudius may fall from rank. Perhaps he will not have the power to demand so much from us."

"I think it will make no difference," Nemus offered. "He will probably be appointed proconsul of Gaul, a position often assumed by a prior *Imperator,* and likely for Claudius as he is from Gaul. Would you care to challenge him on the issue?" Nemus looked at Titus.

"No. I will not challenge him. I suppose I was thinking wishfully—a fantasy in which he would abandon his effort after having been diminished in power. But, if I am in my right mind, I understand that one *takes* the power on issues like this rather than it being bequeathed upon him. Claudius will build an aqueduct if he wishes."

Nemus settled back in his lounge. "I will contact Claudius and make the arrangement."

One week later, Nemus was speaking to Marcus. "Claudius will be here immediately before the equinox. He has requested that the person who did the investigation be present."

"Appius?"

"Yes. You will tell him?"

"Of course. I will also school him to understand that he is not to make light of the effort required. I will have him explain, in detail, the difficulties and reveal that that there is a considerable amount of unknown information."

"Yes. Appius must describe the rough terrain he encountered. Perhaps other large aqueduct systems that have been built were not nearly as difficult."

"I understand. We will be ready."

CHAPTER 16

Within a short time I'd accumulated a teetering stack of maps of the local area, those that were adjacent to the route of the aqueduct, of course. I hadn't found the aqueduct route detailed on a topographic map, so I'd transferred the route while comfortably seated on the deck of my villa, a beer—well, maybe beers—at close reach. When the work exhausted me, I took a little nap in the warm afternoon on a deck lounge, the twittering birds and the occasional noise of a car struggling up the hill the only background when my eyes were closed.

I had great interest in the land as the ups and downs of the topography surely dictated the eventual route of the aqueduct for the ancient builders. The route, when observed on a map, instead of heading directly south from the Fountaine Eure, the source, to Nimes, first heads southeast for about 7 miles, then in a very twisty manner directly south for another 7 miles, finally drawing a bead on Nimes in a southwesterly direction for 12 miles. In other words, a block 'C' mirror image. If the ancient builders had been able to make a straight shot to Nimes, the route would have been only about 12 miles. Of course, it probably occurred to them—but you can't easily make water flow uphill.

I was trying to imagine what the ancient builders encountered. From what they knew and observed, how did they lay out the route? To assist my abstract thoughts along this line, I planned to first visit Fountaine Eure, near the town of Uzes—called Ucetia in Roman Times—and see what I could determine from that vicinity. Would the route be obvious from observation? I was thinking that the Romans wouldn't have known whether they had a route that would work until a significant amount of information had been accumulated, calculations made, measurements taken, designs considered, and a number of alternate routes tried. Incredible when you think about it. It would be a significant chore today, even with 3D topography using fly-over cameras, our best and most accurate elevation measuring devices, and clever engineering. How did they do it? I was impressed.

While I was looking at the route, my tracking finger wandered to Nimes, the terminus. I was again curious about the tunnel that had been dug there, a construction method much more difficult and risky than cutting an open trench around the mountain to reach their destination, even though tunneling saved them about 1000 meters of trench digging. I highlighted the section of tunnel then traced the alternate route around the mountain. No explanation leaped from the map—no obvious topographic hurdle to jump. Perhaps it looked different back then but probably not *that* different unless rampant erosion had occurred or a large structure such as a dam somehow dramatically altered the landscape. Were they trying to avoid an obstacle that might have existed then, let's say in the path around the mountain? Did the obstacle exist now? If it did and was significant, it would be on the topo map. There was no indication.

I scratched my head. I remembered seeing the ancient city wall on my visit with Renat. The wall wasn't shown on the topo map, so I dug through my stack to find a map of the old city, which did show the wall. I then transferred the layout of the walls to the topo map, actually to another topo map, more detailed in the area around the city. Hmmm.

I leaned back and looked and took a swallow of beer, the heat of the day having evaporated the moisture from the outside of the glass. If the aqueduct had been built before the city wall, and if they took the route around the mountain, they would enter the city at a different location. Either way, the city wall would have had to be built over the aqueduct. Would that be a problem? Could invaders enter the city through such an opening in the wall, even if they had to wade some distance to pass through the wall line? That possible breach could be avoided if the aqueduct passed under the city wall in a tunnel, especially a 400-meter tunnel. I wasn't aware of any invader that could be ready for a fight after navigating a walk, possibly holding his breath through such a stretch of water. If the aqueduct was built before the city wall, did the builders even know that a wall was going to be built? If not, breaching the wall would probably not occur to them, probably not be a factor to explain the tunnel.

But, what if the city wall was already there when the aqueduct was built? Even the route around the mountain would require them to pass through the wall and perhaps would have required a tunnel to avoid the invader problem. If they knew they had to tunnel, why not just get on with it and head straight to their destination—*voila*, the tunnel that they built?

From what I remembered, the date attributed to the building of the wall was vague. It was called the wall of Augustus, but Augustus's reign covered 41 years, and the wall could have been dedicated to him or named for him following his death. That left a wide swath. Was it likely that the wall was built or started when Augustus, as *Imperator*, spent three years in the region—16-13 B.C.? If so, Agrippa was in Pannonia during that time and died in 12 B.C. upon his return. If the wall was built after Augustus was in the region—after Agrippa's death, and if the wall was already built when the aqueduct was tunneled beneath, then Agrippa had nothing to do with the building of the aqueduct. He was dead. And, if the aqueduct was *not* built during the time of Agrippa, then the aqueduct would have been built somewhat later than has been assumed. Information sources were admittedly vague on the time frame of the aqueduct building, but most stuck to the Agrippa attribution. Maybe the professor in Marseille would have thoughts on this. He surely would if he was a student of the aqueduct. Nevertheless, I would read some more, investigate some more, before I visited him. I was intrigued by the mystery.

I thought that it would be worthwhile to take Maurice with me to visit Fountaine Eure. I called him and he was enthusiastic. He had not considered looking at the landscape to try to imagine how the ancient builders had conceived of the aqueduct route. His visits and inspections were more focused on what now existed, not concerned with how the ancients selected one method or alternative over another. "That would be interesting," he said. "I wonder if it will look the same to us as it did to them."

The road from Vers to Uzes parallels the route of the ancient aqueduct. As I drove, I looked to the right, knowing that the aqueduct was in that direction. Several bridges had been built so the aqueduct could cross rivers, creeks, canyons, and low areas. Maurice balanced a coffee container on his knee as we passed through the Alzon River countryside and the outskirts of small villages.

We arrived at Uzes. Maurice was familiar with the roads and directed me through the streets and beyond the city. We drove to the Fountaine Eure. I had never been there, so we spent several hours looking at the site. The ancient water source still existed. I was fascinated by its persistence, meaningful to me as a distinct visage of the past. One could see the ponding from the springs and the stream that led nearby to the Alzon River. Between the pond and the Alzon, the Romans had intercepted the clear, cool spring water and channeled it into their aqueduct. A few hundred meters down the valley was a diversion structure, remarkably intact. Remains of the conduit walls and arches and the gate slots provided self-guided description displaying the construction method used for most of the aqueduct.

Continuing downstream, one could follow the remains of the structure's walls and floors as it continued down the valley of the Alzon. We were in a canyon, so I could not see a view of the terrain to the south that might be helpful. We would have to climb higher. I made notes and a few drawings and took a number of pictures. We got back in the car and drove north, searching for a road that climbed a hill. We found one, drove up and were able to park in a clearing allowing us to see over the trees. I got out of the car and looked to the south. I had the compass heading that would point toward Nimes, so I could visualize a straight run in that direction. I wondered if the ancient builders would have even had a means of determining the direction of Nimes. Not that it mattered. It was clear that the aqueduct after being routed down the canyon could not then be routed directly to Nimes. I looked in that direction using my field glasses. I saw canyons and hills—very rough territory. As I gazed, I wondered if the ancient builder, the engineer or the route surveyor stood, perhaps on this very hill, and determined that a direct line to Nimes... well... to Nemausus would be out of the question.

I wanted to start thinking like the person responsible for imagining and engineering this colossal project. I wondered what his name was.

We ate lunch in Uzes at another outdoor restaurant. I bought, of course. After we'd received our beer and were waiting for our gazpacho, we both took a celebratory swallow... well, not exactly celebratory. The beer tasted good after our explorations.

Maurice tabled his beer, leaned forward, made sure he engaged my eyes, and said, "I understand that you had a wild time in Nimes," he chuckled, "dancing the tango with our Mademoiselle Laurie." He didn't blink, wanting to make sure he didn't miss my reaction.

His remark jolted me—stunned that he would know. Then I remembered. I lived amongst a close-knit and loose-lipped band of villagers. Who knew what tortuous route the information took before it got to his ears. No doubt, Laurie helped the communication along.

"Oh, you know about that." I smiled to suppress any look of shock I felt. "Yes, it's true. I spent more hours than I can justify in the throes of the tango—a lot of work for one my age. What did you hear?"

He laughed heartily. "I heard that you danced nearly every dance and closed down the bistro. Yes, and I heard not just from Laurie. I understand that you are thought to have given last breath and available energy for the dance. You had better be careful. Hanging about with Laurie may be bad for your health—maybe fatal." This sent him into an uncontrollable bout of laughter.

I grimaced. I couldn't help it. He spoke too close to the truth. I laughed to appear to be going along with the fun. "That's not all, Maurice. She nearly killed me driving to and from Nimes—on that serpentine road. The woman is mad, out of control. I am at great risk in her hands and especially in her passenger seat."

Maurice continued laughing, my statement renewing his glee. At length, he was able to gain control. "Warner, my friend, what is going to happen? Is this wild French lass going to snare a retired American? Surely you can't help but be attracted to Laurie's very exciting lifestyle, her effervescent nature, and her bright good looks. I think that there is no hope for you to escape unless you somehow leave in the middle of the night, never to return. It is your only chance. Go now!" He laughed again.

I felt I needed to tell someone my thoughts on the issue. "Maurice, there's no way, no *damned* way, I might add, that I'm going to become tangled up with Laurie. She's thirty years my junior, and you're right—in a short time she'd kill me. So, for now, I'm along for the ride. She keeps referring to me as her 'adventure' and I'm doing the same. To be honest, though, it seems that this episode could spin way out of control. On the one hand, I've told myself to go along with all of this. Why not? On the other, I fear that at some time I'll have to call a halt, and when I do that, she will be upset. How do I keep from courting disaster?"

"My American friend, you are providing me way too much entertainment to want to give you advice. In fact, you are now a village legend. Several of my friends are curious—want to meet you. So, I have an idea. I've been looking for a reason to have a dinner, to invite some of my friends on a nice evening. You provide the perfect excuse to do so. You will meet some villagers—my friends—and they will be able to meet you. It will be the perfect chance to defend your actions. Will you attend if I make this arrangement?"

I scowled. "I don't know Maurice. I'm not sure that focusing on my situation will end up well. Your friends will be disappointed if I don't say or do something scandalous. I might be very uncomfortable. Will Laurie be there?"

"Yes, she'll be there. Oh, don't worry. You haven't even slept with her yet. You don't have to explain *anything*. You will dazzle them. They are already impressed that you have the interest to find out more about our Pont du Gard. And, you're from California—San Francisco; they will be star-struck."

I thought—*of course, the village knows whether I've slept with her or not. They might as well find out what the real Warner is all about.* "Maurice, Maurice. I hope you won't build me up to the 'star' category. I wouldn't want them to expect way more than I can deliver. I'm just a retired engineer and builder knowing only five words of French. They'll dismiss me in a heartbeat. But, to be honest, I *would* like to meet your friends. That *would* be an adventure. I'll close my eyes and say, 'yes.' I'll muddle through, somehow. "

"Excellent, my friend, Warner. You'll find that the dinner will be a delightful experience."

I wasn't so sure.

CHAPTER 17

Appius walked to the opulent residence of Nemus, a roll of charts under his arm. He was tense, perhaps because he would be *the* person explaining the nuances of a grand project, a project that would affect the lives of his employers and thousands of others—explaining the situation to the leader of the Roman Empire. He was aware that his own preferences ran counter to those of the *Corporata*. They would like to scuttle the project. He was frothing for the chance to play a major part in a significant undertaking, one he fancied highly suited to his interests and probably to his future well being. This fancy could cause him trouble if he was not careful. He took a deep breath as he turned into the entrance and walked the path to Nemus's home, ncountering an assembly of guards—oh, yes, the Praetorian Guards, for Claudius.

Appius was shown into the atrium. He spotted Claudius immediately, inducing a wave of fear that nearly paralyzed him. Claudius was seated at a table in front of the others. All the members of the *Corporata* were present, seated and wined. Appius stood rooted until Nemus bade him step forward, indicated a bench, and called his attention to Claudius. Appius had the presence of mind to bow to the Empire before he sat and to nod to the *Corporata*. He carefully arranged the charts across his lap.

Nemus was standing, apparently finishing a monologue that praised Claudius for having the insight to look to the future of Nemausus, praised the *Corporata* for pursuing the investigation without delay, having done so in a manner which, surely, was thorough and intense. He concluded by saying that it appeared that finding an obvious water source had proven difficult, although their representative—Nemus nodded to Appius—had scoured the hills and valleys, walked the canyons, and followed flowing waters to their sources.

Claudius nodded to Appius, thrilling Appius to think that he had been acknowledged and perhaps given a small tribute by the world leader.

the *Aedifex*: Building the Pont du Gard

"Perhaps, Claudius," Nemus extended his hand, "you would benefit from detail that we can provide. At your request," he executed a slight bow, "we have asked Appius Petronius to appear. He will describe more precisely the territory that he, under our direction and employ, has investigated and can explain to us the extreme remoteness of the possible sources he has found and the noted difficulties in transporting the water to Nemausus." Nemus nodded to Appius.

Appius was not sure what was expected of him. He was aware of the tone set by Nemus, no doubt a message more for his instruction than for Claudius. His instinctive thought—tell the story of his investigations in a straightforward manner. He stood up, laying the charts across the bench for the time being. Again he bowed to Claudius. "After I determined the quantity of water needed for a future Nemausus, and after a more robust quantity had been specified,"— he knew he was on a questionable tack now, a chancy way to start—"I was asked by the *Corporata*," he nodded in their direction, "to perform a detailed investigation of the surrounding territory to find a source that would be adequate—of sufficient flow, of satisfactory quality, one that would have a reasonable chance of being transported to Nemausus and would be located at an elevation that would allow a freely flowing source to... flow downhill.

"I searched north of Nemausus, encountering some small brooks—inadequate small flows—and eventually came to the steep canyon of the Vardo. Although the flow of the Vardo was impressive for this time of year, I realized that getting water out of the canyon would be impossible, and there was much evidence that the flow varied greatly and that much sediment was carried in the strong currents. I crossed the Vardo and, by talking to the locals, was able to find a very robust source, of good quality, near the village of Ucetia, many miles north of the Vardo. The source is at a higher elevation than the Vardo, but, flow toward Nemausus could not occur in a direct line, a conclusion of which I am sure even without having the tools of the architect. That source, in order to flow to Nemausus, would have to flow first to the east, cross the Vardo, then flow back towards the west, following the hills, a route two to three times the 12 miles I traveled on a direct route from Nemausus."

Claudius held up his hand, "And the reason for that, is...?"

141

Appius nodded, "Because, otherwise, the aqueduct would be required to rise over terrain which is much higher."

Claudius nodded.

The members of the *Corporata* looked satisfied. Several assumed postures that were more relaxed.

Claudius said, "Do your charts show the route that would have to be taken?"

"Yes."

"We will look at those later." Claudius waved his hand to continue. "What else?"

Appius took a breath. "Along my return to Nemausus, I investigated streams that entered into the valley, from the hills. It seemed reasonable to think that I would find one of sufficient flow—but I did not. Therefore, several days after I returned to Nemausus, I continued my search in the hills to the west. I followed many streams which might result in possibilities. Most of those were unsuitable and eventually flowed to the Vardo—to the north. Again, on the advice of a local, I was led first to a spa that utilized water from a spring—water that contained bubbles and was said to be of great therapeutic value. I judged that source not to be suitable—insufficient flow a major concern—however, the proprietor told me of a region of many springs in the hills to the north. I walked to and entered the canyon in the direction he noted and did find a region of many springs at a higher elevation—a land of rushing waters of good quality."

Those of the *Corporata* assumed a rigid stare—a warning.

Appius noted the expressions of the *Corporata* but continued. "I took measurements of the flow of these converging springs in several locations. I followed the stream into a valley and through the valley to a river—not the Vardo—but one that runs north and south. In the valley, it seemed that the river was at an elevation too low to be suitable, so I walked back into the hills, higher and closer to the springs. I then walked a route, as if I were an aqueduct, slowly dropping in elevation as I walked the terrain, around the hills, around the gullies. It was not easy to make my way through the brush and the rocks. But, finally, I approached a location from where I overlooked a broad valley, one that led toward Nemausus. If the source I found is suitable, it may be possible to follow the hills toward Nemausus."

Silence. Claudius appeared to be thinking. Some of the *Corporata* stared, not giving away their thoughts; others looked at Appius, even glared at him. They waited for Claudius to respond.

"It seems we have two possibilities." Claudius stood up and paced behind the desk. "Both are remote, and we do not know if it is possible to make the water flow from their source to Nemausus. Appius is right." He nodded to Appius, still standing. "We do not know if either of the possibilities will be useable. Perhaps the charts you have would provide more information?"

"Yes, your Excellency."

"May I please look at them?"

Appius gathered the charts, walked to the table behind which Claudius stood and unrolled them. The *Corporata* rose as one and arrayed themselves at the table, behind Appius. Only Marcus, of them, could understand the charts. Appius, without prompting from Claudius, used his finger to trace his route from Nemausus, north to the Vardo then indicated the location of Ucetia and the springs. The chart showed, in rough form, the hills between Nemausus and Ucetia and Appius's best understanding of the route of the Vardo.

"So, this is the location of the first spring you encountered." Claudius planted a manicured and gilded finger at a point on the chart.

"Yes, your Excellency."

"And the possible route to Nemausus would be down this valley, across the Vardo, and would follow the hills to Nemausus?

"Yes, your Excellency."

"And, where is the other source... to the west?"

Appius shuffled the charts, smoothed one then pointed to the location of the multiple springs. "There."

"Then this line is the route you took when you were pretending to be an aqueduct?" Claudius traced the line.

"Yes." Appius was impressed that Claudius had paid attention.

"And you were able to ride the route, through the hills until you came to the valley?"

"I did not ride. I was walking."

"Oh? What did you do with your horse? Was the terrain so rough that you had to lead it?"

"I had no horse."

"Why did you not have a horse?"

143

Appius hesitated. This was not going to be good.

The *Corporata* were studying their sandals.

Appius said, "I did not know if the terrain I would encounter would be suitable to travel with a horse. I walked instead."

Claudius eyed the *Corporata*. He nodded. "I am sure that your employers would have provided you a horse if you had thought it suitable."

Appius now studied his sandals. "Yes, I am sure of that, your Excellency."

"Of course." Claudius straightened up and looked at the *Corporata*.

They slowly lifted their heads to meet his gaze.

Claudius paced, hands behind his back, his limp noticeable. "Appius has given us a good start. However, we do not know if we have water sources that will be useful. Appius said the water is of good quality, and he is probably right. However, to determine whether the locations are higher than Nemausus and whether it is reasonable to build a structure that will transport water to Nemausus, is not easily done. Appius cannot tell by looking." He looked at each of the *Corporata* in turn. "Will you have Appius continue in this investigation? He has done an excellent job so far, and I would think you would want him to continue. However, I am not here to dictate your means of accomplishment. What say you to that?"

The *Corporata* were transfixed; none looked at the others.

Nemus spoke. "Yes, Appius has done a good job, and we would be fools to choose otherwise. He will continue."

Claudius smiled and turned toward Appius. "It is good. I will send help to you, Appius. I have an architect who has designed and worked several aqueducts in the past. He is a bright fellow and is very talented in the arts of architecture. He studied under Vitruvius and, I think, has eclipsed the skill of Vitruvius when aqueducts are considered. Bernius Caelius is a delightful fellow to be around although he requires some guidance in his approach to the drinking of wine. Yes, Bernius is rather fond of the grape, and it is possible that Nemausus may not be sufficiently stocked." Claudius laughed.

All of the *Corporata* appeared wide-eyed to hear Claudius talk of Bernius's excesses.

"I jest, of course," Claudius continued. "But what I said is nearly true. However, you will find Bernius of great help, and I trust him to determine if our sources are useful. I will send word and have him on his way. He is nearby, in Legudnum. He will have a horse. He will not be *walking*. One more thing," he looked at the *Corporata*, "I encourage you to find a way to reimburse the Empire for his use."

Nemus, forcing a faint smile, said, "Of course. We are delighted you can provide our town with such a resource, a benefit that is obviously a result of belonging to the Empire."

Claudius said, "Yes, there are worthy benefits but many worthy responsibilities, also. I will return when the studies have been made. The studies will surely take some time." Claudius reached into a leather bag and extracted a bound document. He handed it to Appius. "Appius, we thank you for your good work. And, although I am sure you are being fairly compensated, I give you a copy of the *Ten Books of Architecture* by Vitruvius. As I said before, Bernius will tell you much more than you will read in Vitruvius. However, this book is a treasure—one that you should be proud to have."

Appius was startled. He accepted the book and bowed. "Thank you, your Excellency. I *will* truly treasure this volume."

Claudius smiled.

The *Corporata* were not happy. They realized—although Appius was employed by them—their influence had dwindled. They barely masked their displeasure. Claudius nodded to one of his staff in the back of the atrium and was escorted from the room without a closing ceremony. Appius and the *Corporata* watched as he left the residence.

The *Corporata* swiveled in unison to look at Appius. He stood, book in hand, staring at it, then raised his gaze, realizing that he was the object of attention. He dared not say anything, understanding the delicate nature of his circumstance.

Nemus looked at the others. "Marcus, we had better find lodging for... Bernius... and... a horse for Appius." He did not look at Appius.

Marcus looked away from Appius and nodded.

Nemus spoke. "It appears that the process of determining whether the water sources can be transported to Nemausus will be lengthy. So, for the time being, we can go on to other matters that currently concern the *Corporata*." He turned to Appius. "We thank you for your effort and for presenting the information. Marcus will contact you if and when there is a matter in need of discussion. In the meantime, you can prepare for... Bernius. Perhaps information in the Vitruvius book will be helpful." He nodded in dismissal.

Titus, face contorted with contempt, said, "Take your time, Appius. We want to make sure that your conclusion is... right."

Appius looked at Marcus but could read nothing from his expression. He gathered his charts, turned, and walked from the atrium.

After Appius exited, Nemus said, "Well, Marcus, it seems we must find a horse for Appius."

Marcus said, "Yes, it would not be seemly to have Bernius riding, just able to stay on his horse, we presume, and have Appius walking along. Otherwise, Claudius may be more direct with us about this subject in his next meeting. Unfortunately," he looked at Titus, "our reluctance to provide Appius a horse has created an impression with Claudius. I will find Appius a suitable animal."

Titus smirked. "And, why did our dear Claudius favor Appius with a gift? What has he done that deserves special consideration?"

Nemus sat back and engaged the eyes of the others. "I understand that Claudius handed details of the Nemausus water use survey—those done by Appius—to trusted architects. They were impressed with his ability as one, not schooled in the sciences, to approach the investigation as he did. They advised Claudius that Appius had a mind that should be cultivated. Claudius, knowing from his background and experience that those with talent are often overlooked, decided to initiate some recognition. At least, that is the best that I can reason."

Titus said nothing but shook his head.

Appius stared at the book as he walked home, oblivious to the surroundings passing in his periphery. *What was the meaning of this? Why had Claudius given him the book? Antonia was already excited about his meeting with Claudius. What will she dare think of this?*

The gate creaked as he entered the courtyard. Antonia was out of the house in an instant. She halted, hands on hips, and said, "Well?"

Appius smiled, arranged the charts and the book into one hand as he gave Antonia a one-armed hug and said, "It was the experience of a lifetime."

Antonia looked up, puzzled. "What do you mean? What happened?"

Appius thought he should not quickly blurt his story about the book. He would lead to that surprise. "Let us sit here in the shade," he gestured toward stools beneath a tree, "and I will tell you what happened. But, we should drink a cup of wine for there is something to celebrate."

Antonia whirled, rushed into the house, and returned with a jug of wine and two cups. She carried them to a table between the stools. "There. We are ready. You must tell me before I strangle you." Her eyes glittered with excitement.

Appius sat, poured wine in the cups, and said, "Take a sip. I will tell you what happened." They each took a sip. He set down his cup and paused as if gathering his thoughts.

"Appius!"

"Yes, yes. The *Corporata* asked that I tell Claudius of my expedition. Claudius was seated at a table in front, elegantly dressed in his toga, as were the rest of the *Corporata*. I, of course, looked more common in my tunic, clean and neat as it was."

"Appius, I do not need to hear how everybody was dressed. Will you please get on with it? Were you nervous?"

"I thought you would be interested in the setting. Yes, I was nervous. So. I told them about my trip to the north and then to the west, describing the water I had found in those territories. The *Corporata* made sure that Claudius understood the extreme distances and the difficulty. They did not seem pleased when I explained that I had walked a course that might be taken by the aqueduct."

"What do you mean? Why were they not pleased?"

"I think they would rather I had left the impression that getting the water to Nemausus was impossible. But, Claudius was listening closely to what I was saying. It is apparent that he did not think 'impossible.'" Appius stared hard at Antonia.

"Why do you say that?" Antonia was anticipating the reason for 'celebration.'

"It was apparent because Claudius did not dismiss the situation as hopeless. Instead, he said that he would send technical help, a person... Bernius, I think... who has experience in the design of aqueducts."

"Is that the reason for our celebration—that the task will go on?"

"Only partly so. That was of great importance to me, of course, but that is not all."

"Will you be working with Bernius? What will you be doing? Oh, yes, I see. You will determine if the sources of water can actually be brought to Nemausus. Am I right?"

"You are right, my bright star. Bernius and I will determine if the sources are viable. I am sure I will learn much about architecture and aqueduct building. I am excited."

"Yes, Appius, I can see why you are excited. Your work has been fruitful, and you will be learning architecture. This is much to celebrate." She raised the wine cup, a signal for another celebratory sip.

Appius took a sip, also. "But, that is not all, my dear Antonia. I will be helping Bernius, astride a horse."

Antonia laughed. "I should have known—you and your horse. Why, I am already jealous. But, how did that happen? I thought the *Corporata* would not provide such."

"It is my thought that Claudius shamed them into it." Appius smiled. "It was one of my best moments, but not *the* best."

"If the horse was not the best moment, then...?"

Appius removed his charts from atop the Vitruvius book. "Claudius, with his own hands, gave this to me." He handed it to Antonia.

She looked puzzled. "What is it? "

"It is a book by Vitruvius—you have heard of him? He has written the accumulated knowledge of what is known in the Roman world of architecture. It is called, *The Ten Books of Architecture*."

"Claudius gave you a gift? I do not understand. Why did he do so? I am giddy to hear he would do this. Did he tell you why?"

"No, he did not say. I can tell you that the *Corporata* was stunned. I think it is meaningful, though. This," he pointed to the book, "is the reason for our celebration. You will have to assign what reason you will to its meaning."

Antonia picked up her wine cup, but before she sipped, took a long look at her husband. She took the sip but said nothing.

The next day Marcus met with Appius. "We are getting you a horse. The *Corporata* were somewhat appreciative that you did not tell Claudius that you had asked for a horse and we did not provide. It is clear, though, that Claudius knew what was going on."

Appius nodded. "Now that a horse is on the horizon, so to speak, I must find a way to stable it and acquire feed. The horse would make a mess of my courtyard."

We—the *Corporata*—will make those arrangements at the stable. You, though, must learn to ride the horse and to provide for it while you are in remote areas."

"Perhaps Bernius will help me with that."

"Yes, Bernius. He will be here in three days, by the way."

"Three days? I must get my thoughts and my charts in order." Appius raised his eyebrows.

"I am not sure that haste is required, and timing is a matter of which I would like to speak. It is clear that the *Corporata* has not impressed Claudius with our enthusiasm for the project. We will make sure that we are supporting you... and Bernius... with everything you might require. But, between you and me, this is to give an impression. It is rumored that Caligua will retire Claudius as co-*Imperator* and rule the Empire on his own. Caligua, it seems, is of great ego and now thinks he can administer power solo, in grand style. As such, we are mere subjects to the whim of our *imperator*. But, the *Corporata*... several of the *Corporata*... suggest that by the time an aqueduct route is determined... if one or both are possible... then Claudius may no longer share power. They think that the project might then be abandoned and we— the town of Nemausus—would be on to other things—under the influence of Caligua of course. Nevertheless—the *Corporata*— their message is that you are not to complete your work with Bernius too quickly. Look at the situation this way. We will increase your monthly wage to 100 sestertii and you now have a company horse. The longer you take for your investigation, the longer you remain employed with those benefits. If the sources turn out to be unworkable, then the project may go away. So— do you understand what I am saying?"

"Yes, Marcus, I do understand. At this moment, I do not know how long such an investigation will take, but, for several reasons, I will do my best to insist that we be thorough. You... and the *Corporata*... can depend on me for that."

"That is good. We will be talking in the next week, I am sure, after Bernius arrives, regarding provisions and your horse. Thank you. Go home and read your Vitruvius."

"Yes, Marcus."

Appius walked from the water works office. Prior to this time he had a notion that the *Corporata* did not wish to see the project take place. Marcus had now convinced him that it was so. Appius understood that he was to delay progress in the hope that the project would fall out of favor, along with Claudius. Appius clenched his teeth. Not if he could help it.

Appius was reading Vitruvius. He concluded the book did not contain much about the building of aqueducts—not enough information to build one. The span of the book was impressive though, a wonder of descriptions about music, history, houses, temples, machines, and astronomy. Appius was fascinated.

Antonia had been to the market and entered the courtyard with a sack of vegetables and a jug of water. "Appius—soon your Bernius will be at our gate. He arrived in town with his belongings on his horse and asked those at the fountain where you might be found. They pointed to me. He will find his room, store his belongings, and then follow the instructions I have given. What should we do?"

Appius stood up. "We should invite him to have his meal with us tonight. I will," he laughed, "go and buy some suitable wine to celebrate his arrival." He went inside to store the Vitruvius book in its revered space, then, as he prepared to leave, asked Antonia, "What else should I buy?"

"I will broil lamb. Perhaps he will like that. Lamb, get lamb, and more water."

"I will hurry."

"I think it will be some time before Bernius arrives. He was dusty from the ride, and his tunic was soiled. He should be spending some time attending to those matters."

Appius picked up two empty *amphora* for wine and water and started for the market and the shop of the wine merchant.

When he returned, there was a horse outside his gate. *It appears that Bernius has already arrived.* Appius walked through the gate to see a man, perhaps a few years older than he, engaged in conversation with Antonia. He must have only just arrived as they were standing. Bernius, obviously well fed, was laughing at something Antonia had said. They turned as he walked through the gate. Appius walked to Bernius and clasped his hand. "You must be Bernius. Welcome to Nemausus." Appius noted he still wore his dusty tunic.

"Appius. I am glad to have arrived. I have met your lovely Antonia," he nodded to her, "and she has told me I will be eating in your courtyard this evening."

"Yes. I am anxious to hear what we will be doing. Please sit in the shade, and I will pour you a cup of wine if you like." Appius held up the newly filled *amphora*—wine, the merchant swore, befitting a regal guest.

"I *would* like a cup of wine to relieve a throat dusty from three days of travel. Thank you."

Appius gathered three cups and the *amphora* and brought them to the table under the tree. He and Bernius sat. Antonia stored the lamb and the water then joined the small gathering.

After ceremoniously filling all three cups, Appius raised his, nodded to Bernius and said, "To you, Bernius, and to our future expedition. As you are widely traveled, you must tell us what you think of our local wine." Appius was wondering if Claudius's remark about Bernius was true.

They all drank. Bernius lowered his cup and said, "This wine will do fine, Appius. I am glad to know that I will not suffer from dismal rations while I am here."

Antonia raised her eyebrows. Appius did not know if it was because she liked the wine or because of Bernius's comment.

"Bernius, we hear that your experience with aqueducts is great. As we are to be a team, can you tell me what we will be doing?" Appius knew he should ask Bernius where he was from, about his family, and his education but that could be done later.

151

Bernius laughed. "I do not know much about your circumstance... here in Nemausus. The information passed to me by our dear Claudius was that there are two possible sources. I am to assist in determining the quality of those sources and whether the water can be transported to Nemausus."

"Yes, it seems that we must travel to the sources to determine their quality. But, I am curious. How do we determine whether they are at a higher elevation... higher than Nemausus... sufficiently higher?"

Bernius suspended a hand in mid-air while he took a drink of wine. He set down the cup. "Ahhh—contentment! You are right. We will first visit the two sources but, to determine the elevations—and the route—we must build a chorobate."

Appius nodded. "I read about the chorobate in the book by Vitruvius."

"Yes, then you know what it is."

"Yes, but there is much I do not know about its use. I have many questions."

Bernius settled back to relax. He looked at Antonia who appeared as eager to learn from him, an acknowledged expert, as was Appius. He looked at Appius. "The chorobate is made from a timber that is twenty feet long. We shall need to find one that is well seasoned so that it will not be subject to warpage when the weather warms or cools or becomes moist. Even a slight amount of warpage would render our measurements meaningless." He nodded. "You saw from the drawing made by Vitruvius that there are legs at each end."

Appius held up his hand. "I will get his book. That may help us to understand." He looked at Antonia. Appius walked into the house and retrieved the book. He returned and proudly opened the page to the chorobate drawing, showed it to Antonia, then presented it to Bernius. "Yes, I see the legs."

Bernius pointed to the drawing. "Once we have attached the legs, we will take the chorobate to a still, shallow body of water about 300 feet in length. To the top of the chorobate's horizontal timber, at each end, will be affixed short vertical rods of identical height. These will be what we call sights. We look across the top of the two rods to *sight* a straight line.

First, we will block and shim the legs at one end of the chorobate so that the bottom of the legs are just above the top of the water. We will measure the distance from the water surface to the top of the sight at that end of the chorobate. Then, we will cut a stick to that length. One person with the stick will walk to a convenient location from the chorobate—maybe at 60 feet—in the line of the sights. A stake will be driven into the bottom of the pond until its top is level with the top of the water. Then, we set our measured stick on top of the stake and look along the chorobate sights towards the stick. It will naturally happen that the sights do not line up with the top of the stick. We must now put blocks and shims under the chorobate legs at the other end from where we sighted, raising or lowering, until our line of sight just grazes the top of the stick. When this happens, the chorobate is level with the water. And, as still water is level to the surface of our land, we now have a leveling device."

Appius looked at Antonia to gauge her understanding. He knew that the description was a prelude to the nature of his work to come. She took a sip of wine and looked at him. He imagined that she was aware of the context.

Bernius took a gulp of wine, sat forward then continued. "We are not done with building the chorobate. Now that we are assured that it is level, we must have means of setting it level when we are not on a body of still water—when we are out in the rocks and the dirt. So. While still in the water, we attach strings with weights to the top of the legs on both sides of the timber. The strings and weights are arranged so that they hang freely, yet the string just grazes the vertical leg. Then, we will scribe a line on each leg, behind the string along its distance. Now you can see that when we are out in the rocks and dirt, we adjust the height under the legs until the strings exactly match the scribed lines. We have an instrument that we can use to determine level or, said another way, determine a surface along which water would not flow." Bernius seemed satisfied with himself. He took another drink of wine, leaned back on his bench and folded his arms.

Appius scratched his head. "I understand how the chorobate may be used to determine what is level, but what if the line is along the top of a hill and as we sight along the hill, the hill descends to a lower elevation? We are then trying to establish a line which is way above the ground we are standing on."

Bernius laughed. "Yes, yes. We will not establish one level line at the same elevation from start to finish. As the ground drops or rises beyond a height that is easy to measure, we will drop or raise the line accordingly. Of course we will keep track of the differences in elevation so that we can compare to the elevation at the start."

Appius shook his head. "I am having trouble imagining this. Perhaps in the morning you can show me how this works, using a series of drawings."

Bernius nodded. "Yes, of course."

Appius, index finger pointing upward, said, "I do have one question, though. If the ground is severely dropping, it seems that measurement will be difficult."

"Yes. In such circumstance there is much work. Work with the chorobate is tedious, yielding slow progress."

"Then let us have our dinner, and we can discuss chorobates tomorrow. I do not think my wine-soaked mind can comprehend at this time."

"Yes. Dinner and tomorrow. Is there more wine?" Bernius held out his cup.

CHAPTER 18

Bernius appeared, not exactly bright and early, at the home of Appius and Antonia the next morning. His late arrival was possibly excused by his long ride the prior three days and perhaps by the consumption of more wine than might be considered 'his share.' After he arrived, Antonia forced him to eat some provisions. He then arranged papers as he and Appius sat at a table. "We will continue our understanding of the chorobate," he announced.

Appius leaned his elbows on the table, eager to soak up more knowledge and expertise now that his mind had cleared. Bernius made several diagrams and explained how the chorobate would be used in the various applications. Appius, observing the situations suggested by Bernius, inquired about other possibilities, other measuring instances that might be encountered. Bernius nodded and demonstrated the solution. Finally, he spread his hands to indicate that they had traversed the understanding of the use of the chorobate.

"Now we must take our first steps," he said. "I understand that you have walked the terrain, ranging a fair distance from the town and have identified two sources to consider. Yes?" Bernius raised his eyebrows.

"Yes, and thank you for schooling me on the chorobate."

"We are not ready to use the chorobate. We will first ride to your sources and evaluate their suitability. I—or we—will want to know if the water is wholesome and if there is a reasonable manner in which to route the water to Nemausus. I have experience, having been involved in the early stages of several aqueducts. That is why I am here. Claudius wants my viewpoint. He has sent word that he will not exert pressure on the *Corporata* until I validate that there is a reasonable project. Therefore, I suggest that we ready our supplies in order to ride tomorrow morning. We will visit one site, then return to Nemausus to replenish our supplies, take a rest and make our notes, then visit the other site and return. Can you be available to do that?"

155

"Yes, yes, of course. That is my job. Can you suggest what provisions we will want to take? Antonia will help us gather and prepare them."

"Yes. We should carry enough provisions for—four days—let us say, and we should imagine consuming standard fare—olives, bread, cheese, dried meat, fruit—water—although I am thinking we will be able to make use of natural water sources. Oh yes, it would not hurt to take some wine. I think we will find it soothing after a rigorous day."

Appius nodded. "Yes, I thought to bring wine on the treks that I took. It is as you say."

"Then, let us go about our preparations. I understand you also need to get acquainted with your horse."

Appius grinned. "Indeed. I think I should do a test ride before our trip. It would not be suitable to find out that we do not get along in the midst of it. Do I need to bring anything for the horse?"

"I should think that we will find grazing for them. Our rest stops and nightly encampments will consider this."

Appius nodded. "I understand. If I have any questions, I will find you at your lodging."

"Yes, or not too far away. Perhaps it would be good if you found me at the end of the day, even if you have no questions. We can arrange to meet and our time to start for tomorrow."

"Yes, I will do that. In the meantime, Antonia and I will work on the provisions." Appius stood and stretched. *I will tell Antonia the plan.*

Bernius walked from the courtyard giving thought about what he would do during the day.

Appius, in his lifetime, had only a few occasions to sit astride a horse. He was not sure how satisfactory his new means of transportation would be, even though he had lobbied for it. At the stables, he was shown the horse and given a detailed description of the scrupulous care and feeding this very proficient stable was inclined to provide. He was given the appropriate tack for his trek. A quizzical look in the direction of the stable operator was enough to encourage his instruction, apparently a pastime the stable man treasured highly.

Appius watched with a focus only reserved for those who must display proficiency, in the near future, or be thought a rank novice by his peers. After watching, he thought he could handle the saddle arrangements, although he noticed that at certain critical steps—in tightening of the girth, for instance—cooperation was required from the horse, and cooperation was not always forthcoming. This horse had more experience than the rider. A somewhat gentle kick to the gut caused excess air to be expelled so that the girth could be tightened ensuring that the rider would not be toppled by a slipped saddle. When the stable operator completed his preparation, he extended his hand toward the horse in presentation—"Here you go."

Appius had watched others perform the mounting procedure. He grabbed the reins in his left hand, put his foot in the stirrup and fairly leaped up into the saddle, but leveraged himself way wide of the mount's center of gravity. This resulted in a scornful backwards look by the horse, an attitude not lost on Appius. Nevertheless, he flicked the reins and off they went.

Appius was able to get the creature to turn right, turn left, stop, and start without much difficulty. He did have trouble getting the horse to ignore locations where edible grass or free-flowing water would slake a hard working horse's hunger or thirst. At the end of the ride, his will versus the horse's was about equally shared. Satisfied, he returned the horse to the stable and removed the tack. The stable operator checked the horse for abrasions, scratches, and other possible abuse. The horse made the best of this inspection, wincing as suspicious spots were probed. Appius wished the horse a good day and advised the stable owner that he would arrive to take the horse just after sunrise the next day. Should he think of a name for the horse? Perhaps he should wait for a few days, not to be prejudiced by the animal's attitude displayed in their first encounter.

At home, after confirming a sunrise start with Bernius, Antonia asked Appius, "How did it go?"

"Not a problem," spoke Appius, shrugging. "You just have to show these beasts who is boss."

Antonia eyed Appius with a scornful look, similar to that that which he had endured from the horse.

At sunrise, Bernius was awakened, horses were retrieved and saddled, provisions stashed, and Antonia kissed. Bernius, not altogether talkative at this hour, nodded to Appius to indicate he should take the lead. Appius, not wanting to cause Bernius the

Thomas Hessler

discomfort of a reply, also nodded, and flicked the horse with the reins to get it moving, turning it deftly toward the east. They would travel the route Appius had taken on his return from Ucetia, not the shorter path over the hills.

As the day warmed, so did Bernius. They rode until after noon, reaching the location where the path crossed the Vardo, the spot where Appius had overnighted on his previous trip. After a light meal and water for both riders and horses, Bernius made notes involving the location of the river crossing, the quality and flow of the Vardo, and the nature of the terrain in their vicinity. Appius had brought the maps he made on his prior expedition. Bernius made additional notes and scratched relevant topography. Satisfied, he handed the maps back to Appius. "Let us continue," he said.

They rode up the valley to Ucetia. Before visiting the springs, they rode into town and found a room, where, for a very few sestertii, they could stay the night. Nearby, a tender would board and feed their horses. The room proprietor advised them that near the fountain they could pay for a hot meal if they wanted. A room, hot food, and quality water—Appius noted that his lot had improved since his first trip.

There was daylight remaining, so the duo once again mounted for a ride into the canyon to survey the springs Appius had discovered. They made their way down the same decline that Appius had ascended after finding the springs. Appius, leading the way, was excited to show Bernius what he had found, although he did not really understand the criteria by which Bernius would assess the value of the source.

They arrived at the pools—accumulation of the springs that created them. Bernius marched his horse to the terrain beyond the pools, turned to Appius and said, "I am looking to see whether the pools are fed from springs or some aboveground source at a higher elevation. We should continue uphill for some distance to ensure that a stream does not run then dive underground for a short distance. If that were so, we would *not* truly be considering true, spring-fed water."

They rode the gently ascending floor of the valley for nearly one-half mile. Along the distance, they spotted no signs of water nor indication that water had at one time or seasonally flowed the route.

158

the *Aedifex*: Building the Pont du Gard

Bernius explained, "We are not seeing any evidence of water flow here, probably because any flows upstream drain to the nearby river, Alzon. That is good. It appears that springs are solely responsible for the pools."

Back at the pools, Bernius dismounted and retrieved writing material from his saddle pack. "I will show the location of the pools and note that the water from the pools flows for nearly three hundred feet before it joins the river Alzon. If we are to use this source, we will have to capture it before it reaches the river, of course, at the highest elevation possible to ensure that the Alzon in flood stage does not mix with our source. I can see there is an elevation difference between the pools and the Alzon. I estimate it at 10 feet."

Appius got off his horse and walked to the bank of the river to make his own assessment. "I see the difference you are talking about. Must we measure it?"

"If we decide that we favor this source, we will return to measure elevations—with the chorobate. That is when the hard work begins."

From his pack, Bernius took a jug with vertical sides and no top. At a spot where the water from the pools tumbled through a rock channel, he filled the jug, set it next to a tree then covered its top. "We will let this settle overnight to see if there is any solid matter carried by the water. If there is some, but not too much, it would not eliminate the source. However, it would be better if we did not have to accommodate the issue. Settling ponds and such would be required before the water could be channeled."

Bernius turned to Appius. "You say that this water is healthful?"

Appius smiled. "A local said it was good water and claimed that the town fountain was fed by water from the same underground source. I am not sure how he knew, but he claimed that the citizens were of good health. Other than that testimony, I cannot say."

Bernius used a cup to scoop some of the water, held it to his nose and sniffed. "I do not detect any noxious odor. The water passes that test." He looked at Appius, "Have you drunk from this water?"

"Yes, on my prior visit."

"I have a suggestion. Fill one of our amphoras with this water. You drink this water and continue to do so on this trip. I will continue to drink the water from Nemausus, from the supply we have packed. If you survive or are not tormented with stomach problems, we will have some confidence that the water is safe."

Appius's eyes widened as he involuntarily looked at the water. "If I survive?"

Bernius laughed. "Forgive my jest. My style of humor often runs to exaggeration. I do not have real concern that the water is unhealthful. If I had not said anything, you would not have a concern, would you?"

"No, I would easily drink this water if I encountered it on a trip. Yes, of course I will drink the water. I will be an element in your test. Does it mean, if I am the test person, that I cannot have wine?"

Bernius, currently making notes, looked up and grinned. "I should consider that condition. It would leave more wine for me, possibly ensuring that I did not run the amphora dry, but, no, I would imagine that our test person, under normal conditions, would have his wine. Perhaps if we run out, we could buy more in Ucetia."

Appius did not reply, but smiled to himself. *I am thinking that he might run out of wine before he runs out of the stash of Nemausus water.*

Bernius stowed his writing materials and mounted his horse. "The evening is upon us. Food, wine, and a fine sleep are at hand. We will continue, tomorrow."

Bernius and Appius used water from the public fountain to scrub the grime accumulated from their ride. Bernius sniffed the fountain water and set some aside for settling, curious to see if any differences from the afternoon sample would appear. Refreshed, they purchased cooked vegetables and a stew from the vendor near their room, retrieved a wine amphora from their pack, and enjoyed their meal on the steps of the fountain, the incoming water background music for their enjoyment.

Appius paused between spoonfuls and asked, "Bernius, how do you like your vagabond life, working on aqueducts here, investigating new aqueducts there, in the Empire? What I am asking is, do you like moving from location to location? Do you have a family? Do you have a wife?"

Bernius took a sip of wine, a sip longer than usual. "My father was engaged in the works of aqueducts in the city—Rome, I mean. From an early age he schooled me in reading and in the mathematics and the mechanics of structures. I met Vitruvius, the architect who wrote the book Claudius gave you. What I am saying, as far as I can remember, I have continually been schooled in and involved in this work. As a boy, I would accompany my father to projects, staying for many months as he did his work. At the age of fifteen, I was able to provide valuable help in the planning and design of aqueducts due to my understanding of the mathematics and the mechanics. After that, I never gave a thought to the manner of life that I might have. It was exciting—as a young person—to be involved in projects that are the pride of the Empire. Traveling to and living in this location or another was an adventure—different terrain, vegetation, people, and cultures. I have enjoyed that part of it. I cannot imagine having lived in just one location the past fifteen years. Yes, I have had romantic episodes with women in the various locations, but I always said, 'goodbye,' never considering that I might want to take one of them with me. I have never given deep thought to my actions, but perhaps I did not want to curtail possibilities for a new adventure." Bernius stopped talking to take another sip of wine.

Appius shrugged, "If I understand you, if I may interpret what you are saying, you do not regret that you do not have a wife or a family. The adventure and the work have been enough."

Bernius nodded and leaned back to brace himself against the fountain steps. "Yes, although I have never had those same thoughts, I think what you say is accurate."

"Odd, is it not," Appius said, also leaning back, "I have never had a thought other than having a wife and forever living where I was born. There has always been the possibility of the military, but it does not have the allure for me, and I have not much considered it."

Bernius grinned. "Yet, here you are, a day ride from home, away from your wife, drinking wine with a vagabond architect, experiencing a different people and culture, and different terrain. What do you think about that portent for your future? If a project should result, this will be your life. You will spend much time away from your home."

Appius was silent for a moment. "Yes," he said, "perhaps like you, one finds that they are involved in such a life, never having planned or imagined such. I am thinking that my future will be a compromise, but, I do not want to give up the work. I would say that I thrive on it."

"That is my observation, also, but I am not a good person to give advice. You must work through this by yourself, and with your good wife, Antonia, too, that is."

"Yes—Antonia. I can see that my future is not going to be simple. I am willfully complicating my life."

Bernius nodded and stood, grabbed the wine amphora to stopper it, had a better thought—poured a half-cup of wine, swirled it in his cup and downed it with finality. He held out the amphora to Appius who shook his head.

"Time for a rest," Appius mumbled. "We have more exploring to do tomorrow." Appius stood, winced from saddle pain, and gathered accessories from their picnic.

They walked to their room.

After a meal shortly following sunrise Bernius and Appius walked to the springs and to the jug that had been left overnight. Bernius picked it up, walked to where the light was helpful, gave a long look, then dipped his finger in the water and traced a line across the white bottom. He looked at Appius. "No sign of any sediments. That is helpful." He poured that sample into a jug that could be stoppered. "We will take this back to Nemausus and pour it into a vessel in which it will evaporate. That will tell us how much *dissolved* material might be in the water."

Appius watched Bernius make the transfer. "What is the significance of dissolved material? What would it be?"

"You have seen dissolved material before, on the walls of the fountain in Nemausus for example. The dissolved material seems to be evident in most water. Our experience has shown that over time the dissolved material is deposited on the sides of the aqueduct and over a very long time may build to as much as 6 inches or more. This thickness will reduce flow in the aqueduct. We should get an idea of how much material is dissolved in our source. We will use that information in our design."

Appius nodded, aware that he was learning bit by bit.

When Bernius was finished with his water inspections, he consulted the maps that Appius had scratched. "You have made determinations of the amount of flow from the springs, and I was told of the methods you used to determine this and to compare it with the flow from your springs in Nemausus. From what I can see, your assessment seems reasonable. If we become more interested in this source, we will make another measurement to confirm what you have calculated. One more thing," Bernius pointed a finger at Appius.

Appius looked toward Bernius, "Yes?"

"I want to say that the means by which you reasoned and devised a flow measurement was quite inventive. You impressed several people—architects—in Rome with what you had done, especially considering that you had not had much prior exposure to those concepts nor instruction in the calculation. It is the reason that Claudius was moved to give you the book by Vitruvius."

Appius said nothing for a few moments, not having realized that what he had done might be considered impressive. "Thank you. I was not certain why Claudius gave me the book. I was too overwhelmed by the act to understand why it had happened."

Bernius nodded.

They headed back up the hill toward the village. "We should use the rest of today to investigate the possible routing of the aqueduct, should we choose this source. You have traveled some of the area on foot, and your knowledge should be useful. However, we will ride on horseback and use your maps to help us."

They retrieved and saddled the horses then rode back down to the springs. "As you can see, our water source is in a fairly deep canyon meaning that a routing would have to descend through the canyon until there are other options. We will try to find those other options."

They rode alongside the Alzon 6 miles until they could see its junction with the river Vardo.

Bernius pointed, "Of course, the aqueduct cannot be routed to this location—this low elevation. It must be maintained at a higher elevation to be able to flow to Nemausus. We must either cross the Alzon closer to Ucetia and route to the west or turn east from the Alzon and cross the Vardo somewhere to the south. Let us say that we cross the Alzon at some point upstream because we want to route the aqueduct to the west, assuming we could follow the hill line up the valley. You have walked from that direction, from Nemausus. What will we encounter?"

Appius dismounted. "I can best show you." He retrieved his maps from a leather satchel, found a flat rock in the sandy area near the confluence upon which he unrolled the maps. Using the map he had sketched while crossing the hills and before encountering the Vardo, he said, "If we were to route the aqueduct

163

to the west, we would encounter hills, steep ones, in the direction of Nemausus—that would be so if we were to consider the route that I took in getting here. On my other walk to the west of Nemausus, I also encountered a line of hills that are south of the Vardo. However, I cannot say that there is no means, no canyon nor valley in which we could get through. We would still have to cross the Vardo at some point."

"Yes, it looks like we have to make the crossing, no matter which direction we take. So, my young aqueduct explorer, here is my plan. Today, we will ride to the west, looking for a canyon, a way through the steep hills you have encountered, to see if there is a possibility. From what you have described, there is *not*. On our way back to Ucetia, starting from here, we will try to see where the aqueduct can depart from the Alzon riverbed to be routed, instead, in an *easterly* direction, crossing the Vardo at some point, then heading down the gentle slopes, taking the route that we took to get here. Does that make sense to you?"

Appius nodded while rolling up the maps, stretching to relieve stiffness from the prior day's riding. "Yes. We will ride for some time to get beyond the shallow water where I crossed the Vardo. I am happy to say that it will be much easier on a horse."

Bernius laughed, grabbed the reins of his horse and mounted. "Yes, I hope you enjoyed the walk. I am sure it was good for you."

"Other than nearly falling into a canyon and being left for the scavengers, I would think that the walk *was* good. It is a shame I am sacrificing that healthful practice for the sake of completing our task in a shorter time."

Bernius flicked the reins and started off. "Yes, it is true, I think swiftness is becoming the practice and preference in the advancement of society. I can tell you this. If investigating these aqueducts required walking the distance, your companion Bernius would be back at the office."

There was no breeze, and it was a warm day as they rode through the valley and around the springs Appius encountered after crossing the Vardo on his prior trip. Appius rode behind as they proceeded, without haste, noting the contours of the hills they were passing. He noticed the relaxed slouch of Bernius as they rode, a riding practice that closely resembled one that amounted to sleeping in the saddle. Then Appius realized, Bernius *was* asleep in the saddle. Appius pulled alongside and gently nudged him. Bernius woke easily, as if he was used to this occurrence.

"I suppose sleeping makes the time go faster," said Appius, grinning.

"Well, yes. You work me too hard. I have to have some means of restoring my vigor," said Bernius as he assumed a more firm posture.

Appius, worried that he might have to manage a situation in which Bernius fell on his head, decided to keep him talking. "Bernius—Vitruvius—he calls his book the *Ten Books of Architecture*. The book has information in many fields. Is an architect really thought to be involved in astronomy and music? Let me ask my question another way. What do architects do?"

Bernius rode on for a few more feet. Appius glanced to see if he had fallen asleep again. Then Bernius said, "The term *architectus* comes from the Greeks, clever souls that they are, from two sources—the '*archi*' part means chief while the '*tectus*' refers to mason or carpenter or builder. So, taking a loftier look, the practice—*architectura* involves the planning, design and construction of those objects that masons and carpenters and builders are involved in... structures."

"Structures—as in aqueducts and buildings."

"Yes, and baths, bridges, harbors, temples, palaces and amphitheaters."

Appius thought for a moment. "All of these... structures... involve the understanding of building practices and mathematics."

"Yes, and if you ask a leading *architectus*, he will also tell you that he is responsible for the art or that art that is part of the rendering of *architectura*. But, there is even more. The architect is also expected to consider the use of devices for getting a structure built—meaning ramps, hoists and such."

Appius reined his horse, causing Bernius to do likewise. "These *architectus* are knowledgeable in many practices. They are, indeed, talented men."

Bernius, not sure why they needed to stop to emphasize this statement, nodded. "The *architectus* is expected to know many things—hence Vitruvius."

Appius flicked his reins, starting his horse moving again. "If I had ambition, I would be one of those men."

Bernius grunted and also got his horse moving. "Is that what you want to do?"

"Yes. Can I do it? Am I too old? Will you help me?"

Bernius looked sideways. "I cannot predict whether you can become an *architectus* or not. There are many circumstances involved. You have to engage someone to teach you the practices. You have to encounter the opportunity to apply what you have been taught. You have been exposed to some mathematics, and you have shown that you have an aptitude for applying those principles and for innovation when solving problems. That is an excellent start. And, you have a mind that is interested in the subject matter. All this is extremely important. There may be an opportunity, the building of an aqueduct, in which you are already involved. All that remains for you to proceed is good fortune, politics, a huge quantity of sestertii, and that someone should favor you for the work." He laughed.

Appius rode on for a while, absorbing the implications of what Bernius had said. "Bernius, are you an architect?"

"Yes, Appius, I am. I tell you that all architects are not like Vitruvius—having a great universal knowledge. But, you have read his book. He thinks that the ideal architect would have background on all subjects. He makes a point, but there are certainly many architects who function at a lower level. If you are deeply involved with the planning, design, and construction of a structure, you may be considered by most to be an architect. If you are involved with public discourse, making laws, and enforcing them, you may be considered a statesman. It is like that. There is no public guild that stamps your forehead with a red filigree 'A' for Architect."

Appius reached with his reins and flicked Bernius on the wrist with them. "*If* I have the opportunity, and you are also involved, will you teach me?"

"I will, Appius. I will happily do so. In the teaching, one sharpens his skills. In the higher view, we advance our civilization by expanding the ability of the citizens. I am not a philosopher, but we are part of a process. At a time in my life, someone made the effort to teach me. I will balance the universe by teaching you."

Appius nodded exhilarated that he had charted an exciting future. Well, if it worked out, that is. He dug his heels in the horse's flanks and rode on ahead.

They rode west for four hours, keeping to the north side of the Vardo. Appius showed Bernius the location where he had crossed the river. He looked in vain for the shepherd. They rode well beyond that location, stopping only for a brief time to eat lightly from food they had packed. All the while, they scrutinized the landscape to the south, across the Vardo. There was no indication of a canyon or valley through which they might route the aqueduct.

Bernius stopped abruptly. "There is no need to go farther. At this distance we have discovered no possible routing, and I cannot even see a possibility from here. We will turn around."

Appius turned, happy to have the sun strike a different side of his head. However, he was somewhat deflated knowing that one alternative for his future was scratched; but, there were others. He unconsciously encouraged his horse to walk faster.

They returned to the junction of the Alzon and the Vardo.

Bernius explained. "We must consider that if we route the aqueduct down the Alzon valley, we must maintain the bottom of the aqueduct higher than the river, but we do not know how much higher. Now, as we ride back toward Ucetia, we will note low passages to the east leading out of the canyon. We will identify any such possibilities on your map, estimating their height above the Alzon. On the way back to Nemausus tomorrow, we will depart the Alzon canyon through one of these passages to determine which of the several possibilities might be the most useful and if such a routing is possible."

They rode up the valley to Ucetia noting several possibilities. "We will know more after tomorrow," said Bernius. "A routing from Ucetia is still possible unless we discover otherwise."

They arrived at the stables, tired, sunburned, dusty, and thirsty. As Bernius dismounted, he said, "Let us get our horses taken care of, stow our maps, then purchase our meal and eat again at the fountain. Perhaps we can even wash and remove some of our dust. I do not think this village has a public bath. Let us not forget the wine. I have much catching up to do to quench my thirst."

At the fountain, after a cursory wash, they arranged the food they had purchased, cups of wine at the ready. There were several villagers at the fountain, including children splashing water on each other, a game that provided entertainment and refreshment in the warm evening.

After some time, Appius noted three villagers, men, approaching the fountain, gazing at them. The man in front looked familiar. In the fading light, Appius was able to recognize the young man he had talked to on his prior trip. With a piece of bread in his hand, Appius waved in acknowledgment.

The young man, leading the group, nodded and spoke as the group came to a stop. "I see you have returned."

"Yes," Appius replied. He remembered his prior conversation and remembered he was careful not to mention his mission. "I am happy to return to your village and to see you again. I left without knowing your name. What is it?"

"It is Lucius," the young man said. "And, you are...?"

"Appius. My companion Bernius...." He nodded in the direction of Bernius who was assessing the villagers while sipping his wine.

Lucius said, without bothering to introduce his companions, "When you were here before, you said you were just a traveler. Now you have returned. We—the villagers—have noticed that you are taking much interest in our springs, taking samples and considering the flow. Some have suggested that you might want to take our water. We would like to know what you are about."

Lucius had been looking at Appius, but Appius did not want to respond. He then looked at Bernius who remained inanimate, not preparing to speak. Appius thought an *excuse* for their activities would be immediately detected as a diversion. He decided to aim nearer to the truth. He stood up. "Lucius, we are looking at several possible sources to provide additional water to Nemausus. The water from the springs is good, as you know. Of the possible sources we are looking at, we must determine if it is possible and practical to transport the water to Nemausus. Not all things are possible. For instance, this day we have determined that the water from Ucetia could not be transported to the west. It will not work. There is no route. Tomorrow we will ride to the west for the same purpose. We will do this also for other sources we have found. If one or more sources are useful and the water can be transported... that decision will be made by our governors... we are here at their direction. What I am trying to say is that the waters of

Ucetia may not be practical—or the most practical—for use in Nemausus."

Lucius looked at the two others and nodded. They did not appear pleased. Lucius looked back at Appius, then at Bernius. "You will not take our water."

Appius cringed. He had feared this response. "I do not believe we will be interested in the water that supplies this fountain and the other water of the village... just the water from the springs that is not being used." He knew that his response would be challenged.

Lucius pointed his finger at Appius. "The water belongs to this village. *We* may have use of it. I swear that we will not let you take it from us." Lucius turned, the others turned with him, and they walked away.

Bernius grinned and said to Appius. "I did not mention the political side of architecture. People are sometimes ungrateful if you take their water."

Appius took care to include lessons of the day in the log he wrote that night.

CHAPTER 19

After Maurice and I spent the morning at Uzes to make a full day of our investigations, we traveled to other sites in the area where ruins were accessible. At times we had to hike a distance over what I supposed was private property. Along the route of the aqueduct, there were a number of bridges and other structures before and after the Pont du Gard. Close to Vers were the Roc-Plan Bridge, the Coste-Belle Bridge, and the La Lone Arcades. I asked Maurice... what was the meaning of an arcade?

He said, "What is meant *here* is a series of single-story arches. It could be also called a bridge, but when the structure is of considerable length and not too high, they are called 'arcades.'"

Then, before the Pont du Gard, the aqueduct crossed a canyon on the two-tiered Font-Menestiere Bridge followed by the Pont-Rou Bridge and another arcade, the Valive, before arriving at the regulating basin and the breathtaking spectacle of the great bridge itself. After the Pont du Gard, in perhaps 2 miles if measured straight, the aqueduct contorted in a series of severe wiggles, a meandering to slow the water in its traverse of the many streams, creeks, gullies, and washes over a series of seven bridges. In comparison to the straight run of 2 miles, the aqueduct actually travelled a distance of nearly 5 miles. To build this much additional structure must have seemed overwhelming to the architects. And, how did they work out a route? Did they know that Fountaine Eure was higher than Nimes? If it was only 39 feet higher and they couldn't see Nimes from Uzes or the hills above Uzes, how did they know that they even had a drop? They would have had to be assured that they had a drop, a drop that would adequately transport the water. They had to determine that first. If they just started building the aqueduct without knowing, the situation would fall into a category often mocked in the admonition: "Don't start vast projects with half-vast ideas."

I'd read that the Romans used what is called a chorobate to determine level. I needed to know more about this device. I asked Maurice as we walked a lane back to the car. "Do you have any information about chorobates?"

the *Aedifex*: Building the Pont du Gard

"Are you wondering how the builders established the grade for the aqueduct?"

I shook my head. "Not just establishing the grade, Maurice, but to determine, before they ever started building, that Uzes was higher than Nimes. They needed to know *before* they expended huge sums to build this colossus. Once knowing they had a drop, they then needed to layout the slope with great accuracy in order to arrive at the correct elevation at the *Castellum* or at the Pont du Gard or any other required elevations along the way."

"Yes, I have thought of that also, but have not thought through the consequences if they were wrong. What do you think?" Maurice shrugged.

"Well, besides getting it totally wrong—like Uzes wasn't *really* higher than Nimes, let's say that they made their initial measurement and thought that they had an elevation drop along the whole run that was... three times the actual. They would have been convinced that they could go ahead, but then what?"

We were walking across a grassy field. Maurice stopped and turned to me. "If they just started at one end and went to the other, they would end up 100 feet below the ground at the end point in Nimes. Of course, we hope it would have occurred to them, long before that, that they had made a mistake."

"I don't know when it would have occurred to them. I assume they would be following the slopes of the hills, following the contours, gradually dropping in elevation. But you're right, at some point, if they were wrong, they would run out of hill, be down on the plain, and have to dig a very deep trench in order to continue at that slope." I started walking again.

"Here's one thing. About in the middle of the run, they would have to encounter the top of the canyon of the Gard River. They must have known at what height they wanted to build the bridge—not too high—more expensive, more risk in building a higher structure. And, if they were too low, they would obviously be tunneling until they daylighted into the canyon. It's nonsense. They had to do better than that."

I shook my finger. "Keep in mind that they probably built the aqueduct, not from one end to the other, but had crews spread out along the route, each building a section. Otherwise, it would have taken too much time. They must have done it that way."

Maurice wagged his head, "Which means...."

171

"Yes, they must have laid out the entire run before they started, establishing the elevations along the way, making a map, a profile to keep track of how deep to dig or how high to build a bridge at any given point."

Maurice shrugged. "Maybe they did it a number of times, an iterative process. Let's say they initially, incorrectly, laid out a drop of one inch for each 100 feet of aqueduct run. That would be almost three times the actual average fall rate of the aqueduct which you say is about 3/8 of an inch in 100 feet."

I said, "That isn't much, especially if you don't have precision equipment."

"It wouldn't be easy even with today's equipment. But, let's say they do their grade staking as far as the Pont du Gard and realize they are too low, so they do it again, realizing they have made a slope that's three times what they should have, so they adjust."

I held up my hand. "Yes, but what do they think about the errors they might have in their measurements or in their measuring equipment? Do they think that they have just assumed too much slope, or is their equipment doing that to them? They could have assumed the right slope, and their equipment is constantly giving them more slope than they want."

Maurice shrugged again; he liked to do that. "So... does it matter? Whatever it is, they just go back and adjust. This time, as they go along, their equipment is automatically cranking in part of the slope for them."

"Okay, as long as the equipment is always erring in the same direction. If it isn't, they might have some dipsy-do's." I looked at him.

Maurice laughed. "What the hell's a dipsy-do?"

I also laughed. "I mean that the aqueduct might have low spots and high spots, all of which would be a problem. The water would flow over the side of the aqueduct in the low spots and not make it over the high spots."

"So that's a dipsy-do. I like it."

I wagged my head. "Do you think the engineer would have thought the same things we're thinking, had the same discussions?"

Well, they—in this case I mean the Romans—had built other aqueducts."

the *Aedifex*: Building the Pont du Gard

I scratched my head. "So they knew they had to have some accuracy; they had to be able to depend on their equipment.'

"It seems like we're back to the chorobate."

I looked at him as we continued walking the lane. "Do you have any information on chorobates?"

"Yes. So do you. Vitruvius describes them in his *Ten Books of Architecture*."

"Oh, yes," I said, "I must go back and re-read that. What do you remember?"

"I remember it was twenty feet long, with legs on each end; it looked like a sawhorse. Plumb bobs were used to establish the level."

"Hmmm. How high do you think it stood?

"From the picture, I'd say it was about 4 feet."

"They adjust the beam until the plumb bob is alongside the scribed line. Does it seem like they could be... say 1/32 inch off?"

He looked at the sky as if the answer was there. "I'd say so. That's only half the width of a string."

"Okay, if they are 1/32 inch off in the vertical measured at 4 feet down, at the end of the 20 foot beam, they will be 5/32 inch off."

Maurice scratched his head, presumably to aid his thought process. "Yes. That calcs. So in 100 feet you'd be.... "

"Off five times that amount or about 3/4 inch."

"That's twice the amount of the slope of this aqueduct."

We reached the car. I opened the doors but stood with my hand on the roof. "Question: was the chorobate suitable to determine the slope of this aqueduct? Perhaps the other aqueducts they used it on were steeper—the error could be absorbed."

Maurice looked over the roof at me. "I see where you're going. What do you think is the answer?"

I shrugged. "I don't know. I'll do more thinking, but I'm going to ask the professor."

"Good idea. When are you going?" He climbed into his seat after knocking dirt off his boots.

I got in and started the car. "I believe it's in two weeks. In the meantime, if you get a bright idea, give me a call."

"If your phone rings at 3 am, it'll be me with a bright idea."

I turned and grinned. "I understand. If you were to wait until morning, you might forget."

173

"Yes. Wish I had my thirty-year-old memory."

"Keep in mind the Romans. You've got to go with what you got. How's that for a two-edged meaning."

"I'll drink to that one. Oh, and Warner.... "

"Yes?"

"I am thinking that I will have my party in three days, on Saturday night. You are available, I assume?"

"Oh! Yes, I'll be there."

"Very good." He grinned.

I wondered why he was getting so much amusement from the thought. As it turned out, he was apt in doing so.

On the party evening, I arrived at Villa Maurice, elegantly situated on a hill, as was my villa, but on the other side of Vers. I had to admit he had a nicer view.

He greeted me, took the bottle of wine, raised his eyebrows, and said, "Warner. You are my guest. I did not need you to bring wine."

"I want to show my appreciation for the opportunity to meet your friends and for the hospitality that you've shown me. The wine is but a small token of my appreciation. I hope it will be adequate."

"I think you are running off at the mouth." Maurice laughed. "The wine will be fine. Thank you. And, now I will introduce you to the guests who have already arrived." Maurice motioned me out to the deck, made a short speech in French, gesturing several times towards me.

They greeted me in a chorus of hellos and *bonjours*. The men shook my hand. The women acknowledged me with a nod and perhaps a raised eyebrow. I noticed that Laurie was not among this group. I was anticipating her arrival, but apprehensive, knowing I might suffer at her fine hand.

Maurice had scurried to get me a glass of wine. One of the men tipped my glass with his after I had been handed a Rhone varietal. He said, "I understand you are investigating our ancient history. I do think you'll find that we are very well preserved."

"Very well, indeed. And not just your fair bridge—but the folk about are keeping up with that tradition—well built and perseverant. And, sir, you speak very good English. How is that?"

"Thank you for the compliment—compliments, actually. My name is Antoine. I was required to know and speak English as a foreign-exchange banker employed in Marseille for Credit Leonaise. We financed and brokered many overseas shipments. I dealt with the English speaking when there was a requirement."

"And now you're...."

"Retired and living in Vers."

"Well built and perseverant." I smiled.

"Of course. And speaking of well built and perseverant, I believe the lady with whom you have been romping has just arrived." He grinned and nodded in the direction of the house.

I gulped. My apprehension peaked, and I was struck that a casual guest had already made note of my... romping. I turned to follow his gaze. Laurie was making her way towards the deck, gesturing wildly to Maurice and wearing a flowing, ethereal garment, not unlike those of a sultan or sultaness—or in this case a whirling dervish. She leaped out onto the deck, nearly pushing Antoine aside to give me a hug. This action was a crowd pleaser as it captured everyone's attention. How do I get myself into these situations?

Laurie gave my shoulder a public squeeze and said, "Warner, you have met all these people?"

"Yes, Laurie, yes. We're old friends, now. So good to see you." I made room to let Antoine back into our intimate circle. He had a smug look on his face as he nodded to Laurie. "Madamesoile Laurie, you are breathtaking tonight."

"Oh, thank you, Antoine, but just tonight, not just any night?"

"I'm not privileged to see you every night. Perhaps.... "

"Perhaps, perhaps, perhaps." She launched into a string of French phrases, the subject matter of which would never be known to me.

They looked back at me, and each of them said, "*Oui.*"

Others were joining us on the deck. Laurie took me by the arm and introduced me, first in French, then in English. I'm thinking the English version was tamer than the French, but I steeled myself not to care. After the new guests were accounted for, and Maurice found time to get them wine, Laurie excused herself, and mentioned something about real estate. She let go of my arm, walked to a man at the deck railing, and engaged him in conversation. I mumbled a few words to the newly arrived guests, but they answered in French. We all shrugged and laughed.

I wandered into the house to see if I could help Maurice with the wine distribution. He waved me off, "No, no, I am doing fine. Perhaps, when I have filled these two, you may take them to Monsieur and Madame Verdier."

As I patiently waited, a lovely creature arrived, walked to Maurice, gave him an affectionate kiss on the cheek, and cooed a greeting. She had walked right by me, I suppose because we hadn't been introduced. Maurice, fighting to conceal a grin, introduced Madame Chapeau to me—Lisele. She uttered a mild, "I'm so pleased to meet you," and manufactured a tight grin.

I, of course, was glad to meet her. There are some women whose eyes hold yours hard in a spell. Such was she. Such was she. I stood there, silly, for several moments.

Maurice was viewing this entertainment. He then said, "Warner, I'll give this glass of Chateauneuf du Pape—her favorite—to Madame Chapeau, and you can deliver these to the two Verdier. Lisele can point you in the right direction." He handed me the glasses.

Lisele and I walked out on to the deck. She waved to Laurie, now in the corner, rapidly engaged in real estate gesticulations. Lisele then steered me in the direction of a nervously thin couple, who were only too glad to have a wine glass in their hands before they self destructed. They nodded to me and each took a hurried sip, which seemed to relax them. I stood there as polite conversation ensued in French between Lisele and the Verdiers. I stole a sideways glance at Lisele—relaxed as she exerted effortless control of her cadence, punctuating her conversation with nearly imperceptible gestures.

I was looking nearly directly into the setting sun. Over Lisele's shoulder I saw a silhouette, recognizable as Laurie, detach from her conversation and glide in my direction. She kept her eyes on me as she made her way, semi-circled the Verdiers and Lisele and reattached herself to my arm.

Without looking at me, looking directly at Lisele, Laurie said, "I see that you have met my mother."

I nearly dropped my glass of wine. "You... your mother is...?"

"Hello, Mother dear," Laurie chirped then leaned and kissed Lisele on the cheek, and in a fluid motion, faced the Verdiers, and greeted them with sparse comments and smiles.

176

the *Aedifex*: Building the Pont du Gard

I was transfixed, barely able to comprehend my situation, one straight from the comic players' guild, the stuff of which great conundrums and farces are constructed. I supposed that I was expected to say something, after Laurie's remark. "Yes," I said, but that hardly carried the moment.

From Lisele, the thin smile reappeared. What must she be thinking? Laurie, her daughter, more than thirty years the younger, was hanging on my arm. If I could have dissolved Laurie on the spot, I would have. My world was focused on Lisele's impressions. How could I rise in her esteem? How could I, if ever, be a man she would admire? I took a deep breath and accepted my plight. To try to climb out of the pit would seem futile and juvenile. I reverted to humor. "So you're the mother of this wild child." I was under the impression that Lisele could speak English: not so the Verdiers.

"*Oui*, I am Laurie's mother. Do you find her wild?" No smile, not a trace escaped Lisele's bearing, no subterranean mirth, no waiting for the punch-line.

Now, I'd done it. No humor taken. I might as well have tried to explain my statement to the Verdiers. My situation had worsened. I went blindly on. "Do I find her wild? She nearly killed me on a drive to Nimes. Once there, she tortured me with the tango, using every trace of energy that I could summon. I am only here by the grace of a number of not so minor miracles."

"Wild child, wild child, wild child. I like the sound of it." Laurie, in this instance was aware of my buffoonery and had moved to belay it. "I do not think, Monsieur Warner, that I can give all the credit to my mother. If the truth were known, she would have me behave, although she is not above having men dance to their death. Yes, mother?"

Laurie's mother, only three sips into her Chateauneuf du Pape, looked at Laurie, not at me. "My Laurie, as you can see, has a vibrant gift. It is not from me... nor from her father, I think. No, Laurie has invented her own brand of life, her own stage, actors, and plot. And, it seems, Monsieur Warner, that she has plucked you from central casting to be one of her characters. The plot is, of course, unknown to the audience. In this case, the plot has probably not even been revealed to the actors. Do you not wonder how the play will end?"

I did, indeed.

CHAPTER 20

Bernius and Appius, after rising, rinsing, feeding the horses, and munching on stores they had brought, saddled the horses, paid the proprietor, and started their ride down the Alzon canyon. Bernius led the way, upsetting Appius's horse. He displayed his annoyance by constantly nudging Bernius's horse, trying to regain the lead.

Bernius held one of the maps in his hand as he rode. In less than a mile the canyon widened, revealing a meadow to the east. On the far side of the meadow, 1000 feet away, hills rose abruptly. They rode through the grass, noting that some wildflowers had survived the sun's heat through the intense summer.

Bernius said, "Let us ride across the meadow and up the hill to look at the terrain and beyond."

Higher, they could see that the hills sloped toward the southeast.

Bernius noted, "The aqueduct could head east at this meadow, but it is evident that there is no passage through the hills to lower elevations on the other side. We would have to excavate a deep trench or a tunnel to reach the correct elevation on the line of hills to the east—not that those practices are impossible—just more expensive. Let us go on.'

They returned to the banks of the Alzon. When they had traveled nearly 2 miles, Bernius again pointed to the east. "We will take a look at the terrain heading this direction." The steep hills that formed the Alzon canyon dwindled at this location, the end of their run.

They rode 1/2 mile traversing a hill at an elevation somewhat above the Alzon. As they looked back, it appeared that continuing a level or sloping route along the hill contours at this location and beyond could be done.

Bernius said, "We have intersected the line of hills that run east. I am fairly certain that we would have little trouble routing the aqueduct to this location and follow the contours. I do not intend to follow that hill line."

Appius pointed. "If the aqueduct were to be routed along these hills, or any run of hills, for that matter, would it have to snake in and out of the crevices between them? It seems like many sharp curves would be required. What is the practice?"

Bernius halted his horse and pointed to an example of two hill contours intersecting to form a gully. "We often cut the corners. We Romans are known for our tendency to straighten the conduit routing while the Greeks tend to be more faithful to the contours. To straighten the route, we would bridge the gullies or crevices. If it does not take much structure to do this, it is not more expensive, and you have a smoother flow condition. In other words, the water moves along faster, not being *confused* by the turns." He grinned.

Appius returned the grin. "So, when design is underway, how do they determine when they will go back into a crevice or cut across a crevice, building a small bridge?"

"That, my budding apprentice, is more art than science. Any two architects would, no doubt, come up with different approaches." Bernius encouraged his horse to get moving again. They headed back toward the Alzon.

Appius shrugged and nudged his horse. "How would I know when it is art and when I should do calculations?"

"There is no guide that I know of. It would be a matter of experience. Sometimes our work is based on judgment, a conclusion that could not be put on paper—or is not put on paper. However, know-it-all public officials might question such judgments from time to time."

Appius smiled. "I had not thought about public officials reviewing my work. You must include instruction on that situation when you are teaching me."

"I am the last one to ask on that issue. I am not patient with pompous officials who ask stupid questions. I am likely to give them an answer that is drivel just to illuminate their ignorance. I have been in trouble because of this more than once."

"I would like to be there when you did that, assuming, of course, that I knew that the answer was drivel. I can see that I must be confident of my understanding of the science before I can enjoy the nuances of public official baiting."

Bernius laughed. "I am happy that you have that viewpoint. It will make your work more enjoyable. But, my understanding of what you said is—you do not take yourself too seriously. I find those who do have a much more difficult time in life and are just fooling themselves. Do you get my meaning?"

"Yes, I do." Appius looked at him. "I can see that I have much to learn from you. Is our lesson on public officials complete?"

"I know you do not think that. Now you are baiting *me*." His grin broadened. "No, dealing with public officials is difficult, and even if we are jesting about it, one can encounter great difficulties. They do not have to be right, they just have to be the ones who have the power."

"Claudius?"

"Claudius is not so bad. He seems to have little tolerance for nonsense—yet, I get the idea that some of the projects on which he has had a part are somewhat of a monument to himself—in his mind anyway."

"I am wondering how he views this project, although he seems to have enthusiasm."

"Yes, he does. But, you realize that the situation may change. If the Empire goes warring or *imperator*s change or if political payments must be made, grand projects may disappear somewhat like the morning mists disappear as we ride."

"Hmmm. My dreams could become naught along with the mists, but, Bernius, I want to ask about our encounter with the villagers last night. I cannot help but think there would be trouble if we should take the water from Ucetia."

Bernius turned to look at Appius. "You are right. This has happened before. If the villagers become too belligerent, they might find that they have more trouble than they can handle."

"The might of the Empire?"

"Of course. Those that live in a small village, one that has not had much to do with the Empire, or much else in the modern world for that matter, can easily be mistaken as to the power that may be brought to bear. Most of the time they are good folks, just protecting their own as they have done for generations. They do not realize they may be harmed."

They continued to ride. Appius thought of the young man he had encountered on his first trip and who had challenged them the night prior. He fit the description just stated by Bernius. It was possible that the Ucetians could bring trouble to themselves, thinking that the strength of numbers in their village would be enough to carry the day. *Yes, my prior job—taking care of the*

Nemausus water system—had fewer difficult issues. Do I want to be involved in all of this? Strongly so. But—what of becoming an architect? What would it mean for me... and Antonia, of course? Where would such a career take me? Would I... we... be like Bernius—nomads—wandering from project to project, town to town, region to region? Or would I... we... end up in Rome, perhaps. What is it like... what would it be like to live there? Is such a life possible—for us? The horse had noticed a lack of attention. Appius nudged it.

They continued down the Alzon and investigated another location at which the route could be turned to the east. At this location, the low point appeared as a reasonable alternative for a turn; however, it was beyond the point where the route could intersect the hill line running east. The aqueduct would have to be routed back to the north to get to the hills, causing much irritation with the water, bringing about the difficulties of which Bernius spoke.

Bernius indicated to Appius that they should dismount and take advantage of shade provided by trees lining the Alzon. There was also a flat rock under the trees, suitable for setting their meal and, Appius discovered, ideal for looking at the map, which Bernius now spread.

Bernius traced the line indicating the canyon of the Vardo. "Let us say that I am correct, and we can route the aqueduct along the line of the hills extending east, from the location we investigated prior. If we do so, we will still have to cross the Vardo at some point. From what we have seen and from what you have described, the Vardo runs in a deep canyon until it leaves the hills and flows through the broader valley beyond the point where we crossed on the bridge. While it might be an advantage for the aqueduct to cross the Vardo where there is no canyon—near the bridge—we may find that we are too low at that point if we do so. In other words, it may not be downhill to Nemausus from there. I am suggesting that we now ride along the canyon of the Vardo to see if we can spot a location where it should be crossed to provide the best advantage. If there is such an apparent location, we know that once we head east beyond the ridge paralleling the Alzon," he looked to the east, "the aqueduct must be sloped to the top of the canyon where we cross the Vardo. Are you following me?"

"Yes, I am, but it is difficult to know if the route can be sloped from the springs to the point the Vardo is crossed or if the route to Nemausus could be sloped if the Vardo were crossed in the vicinity of the bridge."

"Yes, you are right. We will not know for certain until we do our level checks with the chorobate. And, although we might be able to slope the conduit to cross the Vardo, it must be suitable on the other side for a continuation. We will have to determine that also before we pick a useful crossing point or even consider that we have a route that is possible. On this trip, then, we are just considering possibilities." Bernius rolled the map and stuffed it back into the pouch. He took a handful of olives, tossed one into the air and caught it in his mouth. "Are you ready to go?"

Appius tried the same trick, missed and decided to eat his last olives routinely, after which he drank more of the water from the Ucetia springs. He pointed to the jug then his stomach, "No problems, so far."

Bernius, while gathering their food, said, "That is good. We cannot make much progress if you are constantly dismounting to eliminate, and there is no need to mark our trail in such a fashion."

Appius grimaced, not altogether happy at being the test person.

They rode south to the Vardo; its canyon was impressive. The riders stopped at the rim and gazed for some time. The steep walls focused one's sight on the roiling water below, diffused white as it dodged the rocks. Shrubbery, at their elevation, grew to the top edge of the canyon on both sides as if the earth had been split to reveal the river. After a while, Bernius turned his horse toward Appius and said, "What is wrong with crossing at this point?"

Appius turned his horse to look back in the direction they had ridden. "To get to this point from the hills, the conduit would have to take a path down into a depression and then back up this hill—which means a lengthy bridge would have to be built to avoid that."

"How about the other side of the Vardo?"

"I cannot see from here, although I did walk the other side on my prior trip. There are hills sloping toward the Vardo, but I do not know if there is a way in which we could route the aqueduct between the hills—downhill." Appius made a sideways sweep of the terrain on the opposite rim with his hand.

182

the *Aedifex*: Building the Pont du Gard

"Yes, I saw that on your map."

"I think you mentioned that we eventually need to follow the hills above the existing Vardo bridge on the way to Nemausus. Is that right?" Appius turned back to Bernius.

"Yes. For now, anyway, we will use that concept. Let us continue following the Vardo canyon to the east." Bernius nudged his horse.

They rode the rim of the canyon for several miles until Bernius stopped. He pointed back in the direction they had traveled. "As we have ridden the canyon rim, the ground has sloped away from it, into the depression you mentioned." He looked to the north. "However, you can see that at this point we see a ridge that is crossing that depression. It is possible that the conduit could depart the hill line it is following, after leaving the Alzon, and cross the depression on this ridge to the Vardo. We should ride to the north, along this ridge, to see if it is useful, to see if it continues to the hill line."

Appius nodded.

"But, before we ride the ridge, let us note this location on our map. We may need to be able to spot it from the other side." He looked up at Appius. "How far from this rim is the rim on the other side?"

Appius looked, squinted, and said, "I would say one-thousand feet, but it is difficult to measure against nothing."

Bernius made a notation on the map and said, "This would be an important dimension. If this crossing became a reality, if the aqueduct were built and it crossed the Vardo at this point, the distance we are discussing would determine the length of the bridge, a bridge that would have to be very tall." He looked into the canyon. "And, as long as we are discussing that, how deep do you think the canyon is?"

Appius got off his horse to get closer to the canyon rim on feet he could trust. He stood there for several moments, then said, "One-hundred-seventy feet."

Bernius scribbled a notation. "And—how did you get that?"

Appius turned, stepping away from the canyon rim. "For this measurement, I was not measuring against nothing. I saw a tree growing against the canyon wall and estimated it to be fifty feet tall. In my mind, I stacked three trees and added twenty feet, down to the water."

183

Bernius looked up. "This would be a very high structure, indeed, perhaps the tallest in the Empire."

Appius looked up at Bernius. "Could it be done?"

Bernius put the map away. "I do not know for sure. I do know that it would not be easy. But, for now, let us ride the ridge. We will record *what is* and leave what *might be* for future consideration." He turned the horse to the direction of the ridge.

Appius got on his horse and followed. The brush and trees were profuse to the point that they could not see beyond several hundred feet, at best, and much less most of the time. The ridge was not well behaved, in that there were depressions and high points, several changes in direction, and the ridge disappeared for several hundred feet because a gorge bisected its path. Appius and Bernius rode down into the gorge, then up the other side where the ridge continued. They followed the ridge until it intersected the line of hills that ran east-west from the Alzon valley.

Bernius stopped his horse and looked back at Appius. "This ridge would provide a means of reaching the Vardo without requiring a substantial bridge to cross the depression."

Appius took off his hat and scratched his head. "Yes, but there are many high and low spots on the ridge."

Bernius nodded. "No route is perfect. I am guessing that the conduit would be embedded in the ground when following the hillside, then as it headed to the Vardo—if we used this ridge— would at times be elevated, on low bridges." He looked at the sun, now on a collision course with the hills to the west. "We must take some time to make notations on our map—the crossing of the ridge from the Alzon, the line of hills, this ridge, the Vardo, and the depression that must be crossed. I have made estimates of the distances and noted them as we rode. I think we should find a place to spend the night, make camp, and do our map work."

Appius replaced his hat. "And tomorrow?"

"Tomorrow we will continue riding the rim of the Vardo, looking for other possible locations to cross. We will investigate them. If we have time, we will cross the Vardo. Perhaps it will not be possible until we get to the bridge. Then we will ride back on the other side and see if the crossing at this ridge—or other possibilities we have noted—can be routed after reaching the other side."

Appius smiled. "I like this work. It is like solving a puzzle except that nature has arranged the landscape for us to discover and resolve."

"I have to admit, I have not thought of it in that way."

They followed a decline parallel to the ridge. After nearly a mile, they encountered several small springs.

Bernius stopped, looked around and said, "This should be suitable for our camp. The horses will be happy at the springs, and we can work on our maps, though we must be careful not to get wine on them—the public officials might get the wrong idea."

"And what would that wrong idea be?" Appius dismounted his horse.

"They might think we were delirious from wine when making our maps. It would be a good excuse for them to throw doubt—if they wanted."

"I shall be careful."

The next morning they rode back to the rim of the Vardo canyon and continued to follow it to the east. No other ridge or geographical advantage appeared to encourage them to investigate. After a time, the hills that created the canyon disappeared, and the Vardo flowed into the valley, not too far upstream of the existing bridge.

Bernius inclined his head toward the bridge and said, "We will cross the bridge and ride back upstream on the other side until we get to the location where we would cross the Vardo. I think we should eat our meal at the bridge and take time to make notations on our maps."

Appius nodded. He was in familiar territory.

After their meal, they crossed the bridge and rode upstream until they recognized features they had noted from the opposite rim, where the ridge intersected the river.

Bernius looked across the canyon spotting the location where they had stopped the day prior. He was in front of a small hill. "I noticed this hill yesterday but did not know if it would be a problem. We will see if the aqueduct could be routed around, or if a tunnel would be required."

"If the Roman way is to obtain the straightest route possible, are tunnels used often to accomplish this?" Appius asked this as they made their way around the hill.

"Yes, tunnels are used, but they are more difficult to construct and additional provisions must be made for access. Often, a tunnel is used to avoid a long detour around the hills or if the route is blocked by the terrain."

"Why are tunnels more difficult to construct?

Bernius stopped to gesture with his hands. "Access to the work is very difficult. All of the material to be removed must be transported back through the tunnel. In other words, there is no access from the sides. You can imagine that on a trench, multiple locations can be worked. In a tunnel, the progress is linear. However, tunnels are often driven from both ends, allowing the final work to proceed in two directions at the same time. All this does not consider that lighting is a problem, as is insecure rock and soils, as is underground water, as is ensuring that the tunnel is heading in the right direction."

"Do tunnels sometimes head in the wrong direction?"

"Yes. When driving the tunnel from two headings, the excavations sometimes miss, especially if an underground curve is required."

Appius shrugged, "And why would that be—an underground curve—I mean?"

"They are to be avoided, that is true. However, a curve is sometimes required to avoid difficult rock or soil or substantial amounts of water flowing into the tunnel. Sometimes these conditions are not known until the tunnel is underway causing alteration of the route and abandoning work that has already been performed. We can avoid errors of this kind by first sinking shafts from the ground above to determine the nature of what would be encountered below. These shafts also help in establishing the alignment and serving as access points after the conduit has been put into use."

Appius thought—*it is interesting how I am learning the means of building an aqueduct. But, I do not think that knowing the technique just mentioned by Bernius, for example, will be sufficient. I must actually be involved in a real process.* To Bernius, he said, "Do you think that we would have to tunnel through this hill?"

"Perhaps so. Now that we are on the other side, we can see that the excavation would not be too lengthy. Yes, perhaps so."

Again they were in thick brush and trees on the other side of the hill, but they could see that they were in a location where the conduit could be sloped downwards on the side of the hill.

"Let us ride on," said Bernius, "but first I must begin a new map. Your prior map did not include this area."

After Bernius had made notations on the prior maps and transferred some of the information to a new map, they again mounted the horses and followed the contour of the hillside. Bernius noted several depressions where bridges would be required. After a half-mile, they approached the sides of a deep canyon.

Bernius, astride his horse, gazed across. "This crossing would require a substantial structure, probably one with multiple arches—I mean arches upon arches. I must note this. It looks like it is too steep for us to ride. We will have to lead the horses and maybe head up the canyon to cross where it will not be as steep."

Appius laughed. "Here I am, on foot again."

"You know," Bernius said while dismounting, "a horse walking is not much faster than a man. The advantage is that you can carry more gear and food."

"And wine...."

Bernius looked back. "Oh, yes, and wine. Your education is progressing. You are able to spot the priorities with very little prompting."

Appius laughed again. "It is true. You are a very good teacher."

They both laughed.

After crossing the canyon, they continued, maintaining a slightly downhill route. However, doing so required meandering along a number of severe switchbacks. At each turn, Bernius stopped and made notations of distance and direction—as best he could. Finally, beyond the switchbacks, they reached a wide depression.

Bernius made notes from what he could see. He noted a location on the other side of the depression appearing level with the ground on which they stood. He also sketched the outline of the depression, defining the route the conduit could take—a wide sweep in the shape of a 'C.' Bernius, on his horse, motioned Appius to come alongside.

"As part of your training, you must become skilled at estimating distances. How far is the hill on the other side, across from us at the same elevation as where we stand?"

Appius gazed for a while then said, "It would be hard to say. I could easily be fooled."

"Can you compare it to a distance you know?"

Appius looked again, "Well, it seems like it is much more than the straight run of the trough that contains the flow of our fountain, in Nemausus, which I know to be 600 feet."

"How much more? Is it two times or three times?"

"Perhaps four times."

"That is not a bad estimate. See, that estimate is much better than having no idea. Of course, better measurements can be made later, but at least we have a means of representing the distance on our map."

Appius grinned, "What was your guess... estimate?"

"I was going to show a half mile, but we will use your number of 2400 feet. I think we can get a better idea. There is no reason to follow the hill contour around to the same point. We can see it from here. We will ride straight across... rather, I will ride and you will pace the distance while I lead your horse. But first, we must measure your pace. So, if you dismount and walk... let us say... 30 paces on the flat ground behind us, we will measure your stride."

Appius dismounted, gave his reins to Bernius, walked around some rocks until he stood in front of unobstructed ground. He scratched a mark in the ground with his foot and strode off until he counted 30 strides. He scratched another line and returned to Bernius.

Bernius handed him a measuring stick he retrieved from his pack. "Now measure the distance."

Appius did so. "It is 70 feet."

Bernius noted this on the map. "Let us begin. If you count aloud, starting over each time you reach thirty, I will keep track of the number of times you reach thirty strides."

"Will my stride increase as I go downhill and decrease as I go uphill?"

"Yes, but because we are going down and then back up, we will say that it will balance. Off you go."

On the other side, Bernius noted that Appius had reached thirty strides fifty-one times. Bernius said, "If you had reached thirty strides 100 times, the distance would be 7000 feet. Since you did one-half of that, more or less, the distance is more like 3500 feet."

"Our estimate was short."

"Yes, one can easily be deceived. I will change the notations on my map." Bernius laid the map in front of him while astride the horse.

"Do you use similar means to get other distances?"

"Yes, I use what technique I might be able to devise. For instance, each time my horse, while walking, plants his right front foot we have traveled 6 feet.

"How long were each of the switchbacks we just maneuvered?"

"About 1500 feet; some more, some less."

"And you recorded that information?"

"Yes."

Appius was silent as he remounted his horse then turned to Bernius. "I can see that it is important to keep good notations if you are in this trade."

Bernius nodded while making entries on the map. "It is important. You made a good start though, by writing a daily log and bothering to make maps of the terrain and important features on your prior trip. You must have intuitively known."

"Hmmm."

They continued, now on the slope of the range of hills that stretched toward Nemausus.

Bernius, behind Appius, said, "From here to Nemausus, I believe a route can be taken along the hills. That is my judgment, for now. We can head toward Nemausus and note the terrain as we ride. Perhaps we will find something interesting to note. Otherwise, you should be sharing a meal with Antonia, tonight."

"I do like *that* thought." He unconsciously prodded the horse. "Bernius, what do you think of the terrain we have seen and measured. I mean, is there a reasonable means of getting the water from Ucetia to Nemausus? How would you compare it to other aqueducts?"

Bernius rode for a moment before answering. "The Ucetia routing is not an easy one. The crossing of the Vardo will require a massive structure, and, as you noted, on either side of the Vardo are depressions, some serious, that must be bridged. The route we have noted is two to three times the straight distance from the springs to Nemausus. Of course, we really do not know if the springs are higher than Nemausus. We will have to make sure of that before we submit the Ucetia possibility as a viable one."

"We will look at the western source first?"

"Yes. Let us take a few days in Nemausus—you can get reacquainted with Antonia and make friends with your dog, so he will not bite you."

"I do not have a dog."

Bernius chuckled.

Appius thought as he rode. *Did the difficult routing dampen the possibilities of a project? One supposed that it did. Perhaps the western source would turn out to be more useful—it seemed to be higher, allowing more slope to aid the flow. That was it. If the route from Ucetia did not work, the western route surely would.* He deliberately straightened out of the slump he had assumed. Nemausus was only a few hours away.

Antonia somehow knew he was coming and was waiting at their courtyard gate. Appius had left the horse with the stable proprietor but was carrying equipment and the remainder of the provisions on his shoulder.

He grinned as he approached. "The faithful wife awaits the husband's return." He hugged Antonia, shoulder cargo and all. "Are you glad to see me?"

"Of course I am glad to see you, but I tell you that on one of these ventures I am going along. Come inside, I have water so that you can wash. You must tell me about your trip before you go to the baths."

"Let me get rid of this." He unshouldered his gear then turned to Antonia. "So, you are telling me that you will ride with us?"

"No, I would not do that. Besides, the *Corporata* would not look kindly on a request for another horse. Which leads me to ask. Did you and the horse accommodate each other?"

"We did get along. Once the horse convinced me he was in charge, it all worked out. It turns out that the horse has more experience in these matters than do I."

"Funny. What did Bernius think of the water you found?"

Appius sat down. "He thinks that the water is a good source but the route difficult. There are still some tests to be finished."

"What would they be?"

"We brought water back with us. We will evaporate the water and see how much residue remains."

"What else?"

"Well... I am part of the test. I have been drinking the water from the springs to ensure that it does not, somehow, make one sick."

Antonia eyed Appius. "And how do you feel?"

"I feel good and I will soon give you proof of that." He smiled and pulled her to him.

"Hmmm. How was it to travel with Bernius? He seems likable." She looked up.

"He does like his wine—and good wine."

"What else?"

Appius looked at Antonia until she met his gaze. "Antonia, on my trip I questioned Bernius about the nature of the architect... he is an architect, you know. He told me of his background and experiences and what is generally expected of an architect."

"And *you* want to be one."

Appius nodded. "You know me too well. Yes, and Bernius said he will help me—school me. I learned much on the trip, and I must say, it appeals to me. I am much enthused. It seems like this path has been waiting for me."

"And for me?"

Appius, momentarily at a loss, said, "Oh, Antonia, of course you will go along with me. But, you know, you are the most important and exciting thing in *my* life."

"I was hoping you would say that." She wondered if it were true.

So did Appius.

CHAPTER 21

Appius briefed Marcus about the trip, downplaying the difficult aspects of the route. He told Marcus that after a few days, they would leave again to investigate the water source he had found to the west.

Bernius and Appius replenished their supplies. Bernius poured the sample of water from the Ucetia springs into a shallow pan, safely out of the way in the courtyard of Antonia/Appius. The water would evaporate while they were away.

After a few days they were on their horses heading for the springs to the west. As they rode over a slight rise, leaving the city, Bernius looked at the hills to the right and left. Could an aqueduct be constructed in the slopes?

Appius led them to the springs with the bubbles, thinking that Bernius would enjoy this diversion and probably the hospitality of the proprietor. Appius was correct in this assessment, and they decided to stay the night rather than sleep on the ground at the springs. The proprietor manufactured his own wine and was delighted with Bernius's attention and compliments to his skill.

They rode through the canyons the next morning, arriving at the springs about noon. Because they had stopped at the spa, Appius was not able to follow the path he had taken when imagining a route for the aqueduct on his prior trip.

Bernius went through the ceremony of taking samples, smelling the water, and riding uphill to determine the runoff situation. He consulted notations on the map made by Appius and acknowledged that the flow calculations were consistent with what he saw. They spent the remainder of the day at the site and, because there was no nearby village, made camp on the banks of the spring.

"What do you think?" asked Appius after they made their dinner from provisions they had packed. They had their backs against their saddles, cups of wine in hand.

"I think this is also a good source," Bernius said, "and the flow is in the range of what we would expect of one we would send to Nemausus. It does not appear, from water lines on the rocks, that there is a severe variation in output. However, in looking at the gulch from which the water appears, it would seem that the flow might be subject to runoff from the hills in heavy rains. There is no river to provide a cutoff for these flows as the Alzon does at Ucetia, but, as there is not much terrain above these springs, perhaps runoff would not be too severe."

"Are we... am I... going to drink of the water to test for stomach problems, as we did with Ucetia?"

Bernius laughed. "And, how are you doing with that? I have not noticed any activity on our travels to indicate you have a problem."

Appius, not experiencing the humor, said, "No, I have not experienced any problems. It must be good water."

Bernius, in a simmered chortle, said, "To demonstrate that I am fair minded, *I* will be the test on this trip. To be honest, it is not a matter of being fair. I will be the test person because if you were to do it, we could not be sure if any problems were from this water or that from Ucetia."

Appius scoffed. "I really did not have a concern. How many times have I drunk from springs and not given a thought about it? Oh—here is water from these springs for you to drink." He passed a jug of water to Bernius.

"Gladly." He took a drink. "Tomorrow, we will walk your route and consider whether these waters can be transported to Nemausus. But, for now, I think darkness and several glasses of wine have made my eyes tired. I think I will go to sleep if you will excuse me."

Appius, already with eyes closed, only murmured a response.

Appius easily remembered the route he had taken. The next morning he led Bernius along the intended decline, noting spots at which the aqueduct could bridge the switchbacks, demonstrating his appreciation of what Bernius had explained. At noon, they stood on the hill overlooking the valley, the one reached by Appius on his prior trip.

Bernius dismounted, leading his horse to shade and short grass. "Let us have our mid-day meal here. It would seem that the route to this point is reasonable—not too difficult. We should spend the remainder of the day doing our best to determine a route from this point."

Appius asked, "Have you been making a notation of the distance?"

Bernius, digging in his pack for meal provisions, said, "Yes. Why do you ask?"

Appius grinned. "I too have done this, but have not written notes of the distances, only accumulated them in my mind. I want to compare my numbers with yours."

Bernius walked to a rock on which to sit and view the valley. "That is a dangerous suggestion. What will we do if we have a vast difference?" He laughed.

Appius walked to join him and said, "We will use your numbers, of course. I am only the apprentice, here. Our difference can easily be explained as my error of execution and lack of experience."

"Let us compare then. What accumulation did you have?"

"I have 13,400 feet—and you?"

"I must add my separate notations. Give me a moment." He scratched numbers on the map. "There. If I have summed my numbers correctly, I have 14,200."

Appius said, between olives, "Then I must adjust my method?"

"Not so. At this point, your number is as good as mine. It would be easy for either of us to make errors even larger than our difference. The useful result from our means is that later, when our minds are clouded with other activities, we may refer to our notes and determine that it was more or less 14,000 feet rather than 5000 or 20,000. Such magnitudes become important when we are calculating costs. If we were doing so, I would be comfortable in using our 14,000 number. Am I making sense?"

"Yes," Appius nodded. "I think I am getting a feeling for the value in noting what we have observed. It is similar to what I did when I was determining the flow of the Nemausus springs. I needed to be able to refer to the work I had done on prior days. When I was able to describe the flow of the springs and the various usages by the inhabitants, using numbers, I was able to understand the entirety of the situation. Is that what you mean?"

"It is exactly what I mean. Numbers can be powerful in explaining a situation. Consideration of the numbers keeps us from making foolish decisions based on offhand remarks."

Appius stopped chewing bread he had dipped in flavored olive oil and swallowed. "I do understand what you mean, but can you give me another example?"

Bernius thought for a moment. "Suppose that the *Corporata* thought that building an aqueduct was nonsense—too costly. They decided instead to haul water from their river by means of oxen. Yes, they could start the project. A path would be cleared, oxen bought or contracted, water carts built, drivers obtained. They could get started on the project employing first, dozens of carts. Soon understanding that the number of carts would not be enough, they remain determined so then make arrangements for hundreds of carts. This folly could be done without anyone making calculations and could easily continue until some wise person finally said, 'Now using 200 carts, we are able to transport one twentieth of what we need in a day.' The *Corporata*, understanding that they did not want to increase their number of carts, oxen and drivers fivefold, abandon the project, use the carts for firewood, send the oxen back to the farms and the drivers home. But remember—you, spending perhaps only a day of calculation—based on the information, the numbers, you had already collected—were able to state that it would require in the nature of ten thousand trips per day to provide the flow. Thus, the carting alternative, one that might easily be considered, is eliminated, and rightfully so, because some person was able to suggest a number that represented a huge expense and effort, one that was unworkable in the long run. Do you like my story?"

"I like your story, somewhat so because I was in it. But, it is true, we have seen projects started, efforts made that would never have been started had someone applied mathematics."

Bernius nodded. "Yes, the ancients truly understood the magic of numbers, hence their phrase, 'Mathematics is the Key to the Universe.'"

"It is so and you are encouraging me to continue to apply that lesson. I learned much in studying the Nemausus water supply. And, if I think about it, what we know is based on numbers."

Bernius, while dipping bread in olive oil, said, "I think you will find that the world of the architect is one in which you will constantly be calculating, accumulating, checking, and recording numbers. You will use the numbers to understand the importance of whatever you are observing and to provide a basis and partial information for further consideration." He held up a finger, "And, you will use numbers to explain a situation to others... even to argue with others."

They repacked their provisions, stood, and re-attached the packs to the backs of the horses.

Bernius pointed to the valley and said, "Now we must get this aqueduct to Nemausus. Do you remember the rise in the valley we encountered when riding this direction?" He didn't wait for Appius to answer. "We must see if the conduit could be routed so that its elevation is higher than the rise at that point. From what I can see, it appears that we would follow the contours on this line of hills then cross the valley, perhaps utilizing bridges, and then follow the hill line on the other side of the valley.

Appius climbed upon his horse and nodded. "Yes, from here it does look that way. I think the more difficult routing is behind us. If so, this source would be easier to transport to Nemausus than the one from Ucetia." Appius was thinking that he would not have to tell the young man from Ucetia that the Roman Empire was going to take the town's water.

Bernius, now working his way along the hillside in a line that descended gradually, said, "Yes, it does appear so. I have to say, though, that for reasons I cannot identify, I favor the Ucetia location."

Appius was silent for a while then said, "Yes, I feel the same way. Perhaps the grandeur of the terrain, the dramatic gorge of the Vardo, makes the project seem more exciting."

Bernius turned in his saddle and looked back. "I think you are right. If one were to imagine a project in which you only routinely followed a hillside, we would not be so intrigued. On the other hand, as architects, it is our responsibility to recommend the most economic solution to the public... or the Empire."

Appius nodded, but said nothing to Bernius. He thought to himself. *It is interesting to note how one can be influenced by one option that is more exciting than another.*

They followed a descending contour of the hillsides, noting that it could be possible to descend more quickly or more gradually. The hills were very accommodating. At the end of the line of hills, as they had observed, it made sense to cross the valley. Bernius noted on the map that it was likely that an elevated structure would be required in order to do so, to maintain a sufficient elevation upon reaching the hills on the other side. They rode on, again following the hills, noting the distances, until they were opposite the high part of the valley, the rise, not too far west of Nemausus.

Bernius spread the map in his lap while on his horse, making notations and sketches that were useful at this important location. As Appius rode alongside, Bernius said without looking up, "It would seem that the aqueduct could be routed to arrive at an elevation higher than the rise. From here, the water should be easily routed to Nemausus." He completed his notations, then looked up at Appius.

"Yes. I think the same. Does that mean that we abandon the option from Ucetia and recommend this route?"

"We must complete our testing of the water before we make any recommendations. But we must surely make the *Corporata* aware of the circumstances involving each option... and Claudius too, I think. No doubt we will be given direction as to our future. The next phase of our work will involve more time and more expense. We must determine the elevations and what will be encountered. That will require our use of the chorobate and a crew of men to hack out the brush and trees so that we may sight through the landscape. This will involve many months. The *Corporata* must agree to pay for that additional expense."

Appius said, "As I have dealt with the *Corporata* and noticed their reluctance, I am not certain how they will react to this proposition."

Bernius put away the map. "Let us ride on. We should be in Nemausus in time for a leisurely evening meal."

Bernius checked the jug used for purposes of evaporating the water from the Ucetia springs. The water had disappeared in the warm weather. He ran a finger across the bottom of the jug and noticed a fine chalkish residue. *We must consider this*, he thought.

Appius met with Marcus in his office to brief him on the latest excursion. "We have investigated the two sources I discovered on my prior trips. The water from both is of good quality, unless it turns out that there is too much dissolved material in the sample from the west."

Marcus clasped his hands in front of him, as if to intensify his attention. "What did Bernius say about the difficulty of the terrain? Is it possible to get the water to Nemausus?"

"It seems that a conduit from the west could be built without much trouble." Appius held one hand higher than the other. "There is more elevation difference to work with, an agreeable line of hills in the right places, and no severe obstacles. The amount of structure that would be required to be built is not unreasonable."

"And for the water from Ucetia?"

"Ucetia is more difficult." Appius concentrated his gaze upon Marcus to determine his reaction to what he had to say. "We must cross the Vardo. There are a number of structures that would have to be built to maintain a constant elevation drop. The route is necessarily longer to avoid the hills between Nemausus and Ucetia, and we are not certain there *is* an elevation drop." Appius observed only that Marcus raised his eyebrows.

Marcus raised his hand, palm up. "It would appear the favored option would be to utilize the water from the west."

Appius hesitated, "Yes."

"What would be the next activity—what would you do next—design the aqueduct?"

Appius, elbows now on his knees, looked up at Marcus. "No. As I understand from Bernius—he apologizes for not being here—we must more accurately describe the route and the elevation along that route. That will allow us to determine if the aqueduct can be run as a trough—in the ground—or in an elevated structure or in a tunnel if there is a need."

"From that you can determine the cost?"

Appius nodded. "Although the design will not be done at that time, Bernius says that it is possible to estimate the costs of building the aqueduct."

Marcus settled back on his bench. "How long will it take to perfect the route and to establish the elevations—as you have described?"

"Bernius said it will take many months and that we will require some additional help to transport the chorobate and to remove brush and trees... it is necessary so that we may sight, using our instruments, along the way."

"What is a chorobate and how many men?"

"A chorobate is a device that will allow us to measure the elevation drop or rise. It is about twenty feet long and will require two men and a cart to move it. Bernius says two men can transport the chorobate and trim the brush and remove the trees. It is somewhat a slow process."

Marcus nodded, taking note of 'slow process.' "Why was Bernius not able to meet with us?"

Appius displayed a slight smile. "He said he was not feeling well. However, I do not think he likes meeting with public officials—no offense to you, I am sure."

"Hmmm. Well, yes. Tell Bernius I hope that he gets over his difficulty soon. This public official will meet with the *Corporata* to inform them and to secure their agreement to proceed to determine a route and to pay for additional men. Anything else?"

Appius wondered if he should mention the trio at Ucetia who had threatened—they would not allow their water to be taken by Nemausus. However, he did not say anything, reasoning that it seemed a scheme utilizing the water from Ucetia was unlikely—at least that was his first layer of consciousness.

Marcus reported to the assembled *Corporata*, the group casually and randomly strewn on lounges at Nemus's peristyle deck. Marcus repeated what Appius had told him and remarked, "What say you to funding the continuation of the work—those funds would provide for Appius, Bernius, the horses and the additional crew?"

Nemus raised a hand. "Thank you, Marcus. From your report I have learned something about the land that surrounds us. Now, if I understand, the route will be established and from that a cost may be determined. I am thinking that we would then advise Claudius and he would 'advise' us," here Nemus smiled wryly, "as to whether we should proceed with construction. Is that correct?"

Marcus shrugged. "I believe that if it were decided to proceed with the project, design would have to more accurately describe the actual work and structures. Then the construction."

Nemus nodded. "I see. Do I also understand—or misunderstand, as the case may be—that the one source appears to be useful—the west—while the other would be difficult? In other words, we should not waste our time trying to determine a route for the very difficult routing from Ucetia?"

Marcus nodded, as did Titus.

Nemus continued. "So, I am certain Claudius expects us to authorize the work to continue, as you have described it, Marcus, on the western source. Are we agreed?" Nemus looked at the others.

Titus sat up. "I have a further thought. Perhaps we should not depend on the efficacy of just one route. If we only consider and estimate the costs for the western route, we have nothing to compare and if that route does not work, for some reason, we might appear foolish. Would it not be prudent to have a second route for comparison and backup?"

The others looked at Titus with quizzical expressions. The additional effort and cost he was suggesting did not match his prior attitudes. To their questioning looks, he said nothing.

Then Julius said, "But, Titus, determining the Ucetia route would cost more sestertii and take much more additional time. Is that what you are suggesting?"

Again, Titus said nothing.

After a moment, Marcus said, "Oh—I understand. Think about the additional time required to map the Ucetia route, how long it would be before Claudius expected the *Corporata* to fund construction."

Titus inclined his head slightly. The others, after some thought, nodded theirs.

Nemus took their nods to signify approval. He sat up and said, "Then would you agree that we should direct our forces to survey both routes, to cause two estimates to be made and that we will tell Claudius we are—diligently and generously—considering two alternatives?"

The *Corporata* nodded. A few raised their hands. Marcus nodded slowly, more to indicate he understood the intention than to agree with its wisdom. Nemus continued. "Then, Marcus, please tell Appius... and Bernius... what we have decided, and that we will fund the additional crew and expenses. I will get word to Claudius. Yes?"

Marcus stood. "I will do so. It will be done today."

Appius sat with Bernius in his rented apartment. Appius had to move piles of clothing and gear to clear a place to sit. "Marcus has presented our findings to the *Corporata,* and they have given us direction."

the *Aedifex*: Building the Pont du Gard

Bernius smiled. "Our employers. And what have they decided in their comprehensive wisdom?"

"I think you will find that their direction is somewhat unusual... a surprise. They want us to survey both routes—the western and the one from Ucetia."

Bernius frowned. "Really? You are right. I expected them to immediately discard the Ucetia route. Even we—you and I—do not know if it will work, and the difficulties seem daunting—and expensive. Very puzzling—and unexpected."

Appius nodded, then said, "Marcus did not say this directly, but if I consider some of his other remarks and his facial expressions, the direction to survey both routes will result in a longer time passing before the *Corporata* has to decide whether or not to spend significant portions of their fortune on the construction."

"I am sure they did not consider the option of employing two crews, working at the same time to survey the routes." Bernius reached for his water glass but stood and retrieved the wine amphora instead, gesturing to Appius that he would pour a cup for him.

Appius waved off the wine offer. "I made that suggestion to Marcus—perhaps I am too anxious to see construction take place. He bade me not to pursue that option. He clearly did not want to give me a reason for this."

Bernius sipped. "Then, my good trail friend, we must get on with our work. We must build the chorobate and calibrate it. Then we will spend our time in the wilds, hacking a route through the brush and trees. I suggest that we survey the Ucetia route first. Our task will take us into the season when the weather is more difficult. I am thinking we should do as much as we can on the Ucetia route before the bad weather. Then, it is possible that we might, more easily, be able to continue to proceed on the western route."

Appius nodded. "Let me know what we must do to build the chorobate. I will make the arrangements."

"We will need a timber—perhaps 6 inches wide and 8 inches deep—20 feet long. The timber must not be recently cut—in other words, it will be well-seasoned so that we would not expect it to twist due to shrinkage that occurs upon drying. If you can find the timber, we will have an easy time with the remainder.

We will incorporate the talent of carpenters to assemble the device. I am sure you can arrange for that, also."

Appius stood. "Yes, I will arrange for all of that and come for you."

Appius and Bernius were standing in the carpenter shop of Tarus Lartius. Appius pointed to a hewn timber of approximate dimensions to that given him by Bernius. "This timber has been removed from the roof structure of a building that was recently razed. Tarus has inspected the beam and found it sound and without twists or warpage. Do you think it will be acceptable for our chorobate?"

Bernius sighted along the beam, walked its length, looked at the ends and kicked it several times. "It appears that it should be acceptable for our device. How long did you say it remained in the building?"

Tarus, standing behind the beam, said, "Over twenty years. My father installed this beam that many years ago."

Bernius nodded. "Here is what we must do." He handed a sketch to Tarus. "It is somewhat simple. The legs of our device should be built of oak and attached with pins to the beam. It is essential that the legs be very rigid and securely attached. No movement can be tolerated. Then, the sights are attached to the top of the beam as I have shown."

Tarus nodded and pointed to the sights. "The sights are made of metal?"

"Yes. Iron or copper can be used. They should protrude about 2 inches above the beam."

"And what is this line down the top of the beam?" Tarus traced the line on the paper with his finger.

Bernius stood back so that he could look at Appius *and* Tarus. "That line represents a trough on the top of the chorobate. Usually we level the chorobate by means of weighted vertical strings. However, if winds are present, the use of strings is difficult. We then put water in the trough and level the chorobate until the water intersects lines we have scribed at the ends of the trough. The depth and width are shown on my sketch." He turned back to Tarus. "When you have constructed our chorobate, we will transport it to the channel that is the overflow of the Nemausus fountain. We will cause that channel to be shallowly flooded so that we may do our calibration. The channel is over 200 hundred feet long and will allow us to achieve reasonable accuracy." He looked at Appius, then back at Tarus. "We will also need to construct a cart to transport the device. I suggest that the cart be constructed to transport the beam from its middle, but also able to allow the beam to be moved to either end in order to accommodate use over varying terrain. Also, please construct a number of small blocks of varying thickness. These will be used to support the legs on uneven ground. We will then use thin wedges—we call them shims—crafted to a small incline to make our final adjustments. Do you understand what we need, Tarus? Can you craft these for us?"

Tarus expanded his chest, pursed his lips, and reached for the sketches. "What you have asked is not difficult. I will easily build the device and the accessories. I may ask you to tell me more about how you intend to use the cart. I can benefit from your ideas."

Bernius nodded. "I will tell you more about the cart. How long should we wait for you to do the work?"

Tarus looked skyward for his answer. "I think my son and I should be complete on the third day. It is not difficult. How will I be paid?"

Appius said, "The *Aqua Corporata* will pay you. You must tell me what you are owed, and I will deal with Marcus... you know Marcus?"

Tarus wagged his head from side to side. "Yes, I know Marcus. I will proceed based on what you say. If he does not pay me the sestertii, I will burn your chorobate." He laughed.

Bernius looked at him and joined in on the laughter, once again kicking the timber.

Bernius, Appius, Tarus, and his son handled the chorobate into the channel, now filled with 2 inches of water, a pond arranged through the good offices of Appius's friend and prior workmate, Tinius, who also stood in the water, ready to assist.

Bernius said to Tarus, "The cart you have constructed is excellent. It was easy to maneuver and to attach the device. Do you have the blocks and shims?"

"Yes." From the cart Tarus retrieved two satchels and displayed them to Bernius.

Bernius nodded. "Let us calibrate the device." From a pouch, he extracted two lead weights, round and tapered like an extended cone in their length. He attached a string to a hook in the top of each and had Tarus attach them to hang alongside a leg at each end. He looked at Tarus. "Now, we need the two sticks that I sketched. We will use them to measure the distance from the top of the water to the top of our sights. We will use a process called *iteration* to do our calibration."

Bernius, with the help of those assembled, measured the distance from the water surface to the top of one of the sights and marked the measurement on the stick. Then, with the measuring stick at 100 feet from the chorobate, along the sight line, they blocked and shimmed the legs of the chorobate until Bernius was able to look along the two sights of the chorobate and intersect the mark on the stick. This required several sightings, blockings, shimmings and re-measuring to arrive at a condition that pleased Bernius. He said, "This is our iterative process." He then removed a stylus from his pouch and carefully scribed a line immediately in back of the strings attached to the lead weights. "Now," he said, "when we are on the terrain and we adjust the legs of the chorobate so that the strings are aligned with the scribes, we will be able to use the sights to determine a line that is level... assuming this water is level, that is." He looked around to see if any got his jest. Only Appius grinned at him.

Appius stood, hands on hips, looking first to the chorobate, then to Bernius. He imagined the next phase of their task and slowly nodded his head. "Bernius," he said, "how long do you think it will take to measure—the Ucetia route?"

Bernius turned from the chorobate. "I could merely make a guess, but let us use our math to do an estimate." He first turned back to Tarus and his crew and instructed them to transport the chorobate to the carpenter shop then turned back to Appius. "We have a rough idea of the length of the aqueduct—let us say that it is 30 miles long. Establishing our line through the brush and trees will be the difficult part, and it seems as if two-thirds of the route will be in that difficult terrain, the remainder in grasslands on the side of the hills before we reach Nemausus. Does that seem reasonable?"

Appius nodded. "Can we climb out of this channel?"

"Yes. Sorry. I get distracted when I am doing my numbers." They got out of the channel and stood on its edge. Bernius waved his hands. "Let us say that in the *difficult* 20 miles, our crew will be able to hack out 1000 feet in the time of one day and that during that same time we will be able to adjust our chorobate so that it is level. In each day we can progress 1000 feet."

Appius, not sure how to express his statement, said, "Unless we run into difficulties."

"Yes," Bernius nodded, "there will be troubles. We will provide for that, but let me go on. If we cover 1000 feet per day, we will complete the 20 miles in about 100 days."

"But, the grasslands will be easier."

"Yes. There, our progress will depend on the time it takes to level and transport the chorobate. What is your guess?"

"I think, once we have become skilled, we can transport the chorobate, adjust the blocks and shims and take our measurements in half the time needed to hack our way. We could measure 2000 feet in one day." Appius looked pleased.

"I will accept your estimate which means that it will take another 26 days to complete the 10 miles. If we add the two durations, it will equal 126 days.

Appius raised his hand. "And how about the difficulties?"

Bernius smiled. "For the unforeseen difficulties, time off for rest, lazy days, bad weather, crossing streams and big rivers, time off to replenish, re-doing our route because we have made a mistake, I would add a third of the time—say another 40 days. If we were able to work continuously, we could perhaps perform the work in 6 months."

Appius could not help but think of the increases the *Corporata* and Claudius had made to *his* estimates. However, the most crushing thought on his mind involved Antonia, thinking that it would be most difficult to be away that long. He said, "Did you say that we would have time off to replenish. What do you mean by that?"

Bernius grinned. "I used that word mischievously. Of course, we could replenish our supplies in Ucetia when we are working in that area. Other villages would be helpful along the way, in doing so, but my meaning also had to do with replenishing whatever needs replenishing between you and Antonia. I think Nemausus would be the perfect location to 'replenish,' yes?"

Appius smiled, somewhat relieved. "Then we will return to Nemausus from time to time?"

"Yes, of course we will. You must also make a report to the *Corporata*, I presume." Appius nodded although his smile had faded. He was still thinking that he faced difficult times with Antonia. His time away would now be measured in weeks, if not longer. "When shall we start, Bernius?"

"There is no reason we should not make an immediate start. We should use the fair weather while we can. You must arrange for our brush-cutters and their equipment. As soon as you have done that, we can start."

Appius nodded. "I will make the arrangements and let you know. Will you join me and Antonia for the evening meal?"

Bernius, having insight as to upcoming difficult discussions, knew that he would be the foil. "Yes, of course," he replied.

The two followed the chorobate, on its cart, back to the carpenter shop.

"I have invited Bernius to join us this evening." Appius stood behind Antonia as she was tending to flowers, glorious in the corner of their courtyard. He closed his eyes, not wanting to see Antonia's expression when she turned to face him.

Antonia turned and looked up at Appius. She said nothing.

Appius felt that he should say something rather than try to navigate their continuing communication by gestures, alone. He opened his eyes. "With your agreement, of course." He hoped that his statement would bring about a response, an indication of Antonia's frame of mind.

Antonia probably suspected that Appius intended to gently ease into a discussion of his upcoming absence. For her to wring maximum impact from the situation so that Appius could understand the depth of her distress, she could not 'ease' into such a conversation. She sensed that maximum impact could be dramatized by silence.

Appius could not accommodate silence. It would indicate that they both knew that they were entering into a difficult situation, and it would not be seemly to acknowledge that he understood the difficulty he was creating. Easing into the discussion would be more comfortable, as if the importance and difficulty were not that obvious. He tried, again. "Antonia, what are you thinking?"

Antonia brushed past him and walked into the house.

Appius *had* bothered to consider the line of reasoning he would use in the discussion. His primary element of reasoning involved a statement such as—"What would you have me do, go back to the waterworks?" He did not think Antonia could, with just cause, say yes. But, it would be best if Antonia would express *all* her objections before he resorted to use of this pinnacle of reasoning. In that way, it would be obvious that regardless of the difficulties, there was only one rational course of action. That would be the end of it.

Antonia was, no doubt, painfully aware of that very principle. She was unsure what she wanted to extract by making Appius uncomfortable, but by instinct she thought that she should. She would do this to emphasize her distress in the situation. That was it. Antonia did not calculate that she could bank this understanding for future leverage. She did not say so to herself in so many words, but that was part of it. The bigger part, also not directly expressed to herself—she wanted her husband, the person that meant the most to her, the most important element in her life, to understand that she would be deeply in sorrow at his prolonged absence. His expression of this understanding would be all-important—not that there was a powerful reason that the circumstance made sense.

Between the two of them, there was no shortcut to a mutual understanding.

Antonia appeared in the doorway and said to a flummoxed Appius, "I will prepare our meal to include Bernius."

Appius was sure that they would not be discussing his upcoming tasks, his painful absence, before Bernius arrived.

Bernius, lugging a wine amphora of a size larger than usual, appeared at their gate. Appius greeted him, slapped him on the back, and helped him to unshoulder the amphora. Antonia appeared from the house, a brilliant smile enveloping her face and her being, a manner that Bernius had not expected. From behind him, Bernius produced a clutch of flowers and handed them ceremoniously to Antonia.

Antonia bowed. "Thank you, sir. They are beautiful, and you are so thoughtful."

Did Appius notice a momentary glance from Antonia in his direction? Rather than give serious thought to the idea and to its implications, he retrieved a trio of cups and poured from the amphora.

Bernius, not oblivious, held his cup at shoulder height before sipping and said, "To monumental projects—may they bring persons of good quality together and, although bringing great trials—resulting in difficult experiences in the duration—they make us the better for it."

Appius looked at Antonia. Her smile had lost some of its brilliance, her lips were more compressed, but she still wore a smile in a noble display.

They sat to enjoy the wine before eating. Antonia, appearing to exhibit great control, said to Bernius, "Appius has told me that he intends to learn much from you. Would that include bringing flowers to a lady that he favors?"

They laughed, although Appius had to use more than the usual energy to do so.

Bernius replied, "Antonia, your husband has a good mind. He will learn much on his own, and his own curiosity and ability to think in the abstract will propel that learning. To the extent that I can fill in with my experiences and knowledge, I will be most proud to contribute." He looked skyward. "Whew—that was more flowery than I intended, but, I am sincere."

Antonia elevated her wine glass. "Yes, Bernius, thank you... I thank you for your observation. I may have thought the same, but in his latest tasks Appius has shown that he has the attributes you have mentioned. I salute my husband."

Appius felt like he was only an observer in this exchange, knowing that neither a protest nor an affirmation would be viewed with appreciation. Yet, the conversation was removed from reality, the comments at most superficial and a filler for other pressing questions. He accepted his secondary role and let the conversation proceed.

Antonia, practiced in the art of directing a conversation in the path she preferred, said to Bernius, "Yes, Bernius Caelius, I think that you have much to teach Appius. I am happy he has the opportunity. What will he be learning in the upcoming time?"

Bernius looked at Appius, now understanding that he had not discussed the immediate future with Antonia. "Antonia, now the real work begins. We will truly hack our way through the forests to determine a route—a possible route—for the aqueduct. Appius will learn the difference between understanding a principle—the physical and mathematical means of establishing elevation—and actually applying that principle in the real world. In other words, it may look easy on paper but is actually much more difficult to accomplish."

the *Aedifex*: Building the Pont du Gard

Antonia nodded, not looking at Appius. "It sounds like the task will be laborious and lengthy."

Appius did not miss the reference. Neither did Bernius.

"Yes, to both." Bernius wagged his head. "But, work is often lengthy, just as the time Appius spent with the water works." He looked at Antonia to see how his statement was reflected. She reflected interest. He continued. "Yes, we must look at our task as a year's assignment. It is often up to us to manage that task and that year as best we can."

Antonia frowned. "Yes, that would always be true, but what do you mean in this circumstance?"

"I mean that in this particular task there are expectations from us that are understood at the top of the Empire; they are not just our own aspirations. However, even if that *is* true, we must manage the work so that our own lives are not subservient to the task—or to the Empire. In this particular circumstance—as you say it—we must accomplish the work yet leave some time for our own lives."

Antonia looked at Appius, wondering how much he understood or had considered of this viewpoint and wondering to what extent it would matter to *their* lives.

Bernius continued. "I know, Antonia, that you regret the time Appius will be away, but he is also concerned. I have told him that we will regularly return to Nemausus. This will not be like a military assignment or career."

Appius looked hopeful.

Antonia looked resentful. "I will only have a part-time husband, and my part will be trivial, indeed. You cannot expect me to be joyful knowing that he will not *always* be away."

Bernius took a drink of wine. "No, of course not. As I say, we will try to make the best of it." Bernius knew when he had reached the limits of his persuasive charms.

They sat in silence for a while, breaking the tension only by sipping the wine.

Antonia, simmering in her difficulty, eased the group out of their unspoken yet congruent thoughts. "I think that it is time for me to prepare our meal. If you will excuse me."

Appius and Bernius nodded. After Antonia entered the house, Appius said to Bernius. "It will not be easy."

Bernius nodded, "As we are in the midst of great accomplishments in the wilds, we must be mindful of Antonia. It will be easy to be distracted."

"Yes. As much as I am looking forward to the work, I am aware of the difficulties."

CHAPTER 22

I drove to Uzes to enjoy their several restaurants with sidewalk tables. At my favorite cafe, as I approached the seating area, brightly shaded with umbrellas and an occasional elm, I spotted Lisele sitting alone at a table. I stopped for a moment before approaching her and gazed upon her looks and observed her manner. Captivating. I was taken by the woman. She had short hair, a piquant look... well, I couldn't see her eyes behind the sunglasses, but they must be striking. I'd meant to call Maurice and ask him about her but had not. His party was only two nights ago. Any thoughts of what could happen with her or what would be reasonable, given that I was just a visitor, did not get processing time. Why did she have to be Laurie's mother?

I couldn't walk in and sit somewhere without acknowledging her. That would be rude. I would merely walk to the table and say hello.

I stood at the table, opposite Lisele for a few seconds before she looked up. She was reading a magazine while waiting for her order. "*Bonjour, Mademoiselle* Lisele." I thought I sounded a bit stilted and knew my pronunciation was probably revolting.

She looked up, took off her sunglasses, blinked, perhaps deliberately, hesitated, then said, "*Bonjour...* Warner... *oui*? You are walking the town?"

"Yes, yes... no, I've driven here so that I might have a meal at what has become my favorite place, this café. Do you mind if I join you?"

She shrugged, but slightly. "Of course, you may join me, if you wish. I have already ordered, so I am ahead of you, perhaps...."

"Oh, that's fine, that's fine, I'll let you go when you are finished." I slid out the chair and sat, elbows on the table, hands clasped. "Did you enjoy the party, courtesy of our host—Maurice?"

"Yes, very much so. And, Laurie has talked much about you, so, of course, I wanted to meet you. A wonderful evening."

I, somewhat beyond my capacity to navigate my way, said, "Oh, yes, your comment about us all being actors on Laurie's stage.

211

That was classic... and perhaps, true. But, I have to ask, is her mother subjected to that same drama?" I thought I had turned the phrase somewhat skillfully.

"Yes, her mother, too. My comment was right at the fore, because I have long thought that."

The waiter noticed me, nodding in recognition, and brought water and a menu.

I paused, not knowing how to approach the subject of my relationship with Laurie. Perhaps Lisele's comment would be a lead in. "Lisele, your daughter... Laurie... I feel that I've been hijacked to participate in what she calls her adventure. I'm not comfortable with all that. Oh, she's a very attractive, energetic, fun girl... lady... but... what should I do?" I hoped, even with my rambling, Lisele would pick up my plight, my attitude toward the situation.

She would not ease my predicament. "I do not think I can help you much. You must make your own way. I can tell you that Laurie will not respond to a gentle hint. So, you will not be here forever. Just enjoy what you can. You have a good tour guide, as her companion."

The exchange wasn't going in the direction that I had hoped. I nodded. "Lisele, your English is very good. How did that happen?"

"Oh, I studied English in school and... did not Laurie tell you...? We had a shop in Lyon, one that catered to tourists, many English speaking tourists."

"Yes, yes, she did mention a shop, but didn't say that she and her mother were there. You lived in Lyon? Have you lived other places?"

"Oh, yes: Paris, Nice, Bordeaux and two years in London. I suppose London also explains my skill with English. When I was married, my husband... Laurie's father... was in commerce, on the banking side. We were posted to several locations, over time."

I had a feeling that Lisele anticipated my next question. "And what has become of Laurie's father... your... husband?"

"He has gone on to other things, at my request, actually."

"You're divorced."

"Yes." I anticipated her next question.

"And you, Warner. Why is it that you are having this grand tour without accompaniment? Where is your wife or lady friend? Do you not wish to have someone share this with you?"

I smiled. "No wife... and no lady friend at the moment. Yes, it would be nice to share, but that is not the circumstance. I'm just enjoying my... adventure... on a solo mission. My investigation, and an opportunity to live here for a while, has its rewards."

"Your investigation. You were... are... an engineer. You were engaged in building structures much like the Pont du Gard?"

I laughed, and rearranged the table settings to make room for Lisele's salad, which had arrived. "Engineer, yes. Structures like the Pont du Gard, no. But the Pont du Gard is great fodder for the engineering mind—mine anyway—trying to imagine how it was conceived and built without all of our more modern methods."

"Engineering mind... what is that? Do engineers have different minds than others? I know they are more difficult to talk to." She smiled.

I laughed and said, "Engineers are often cast in that frame... thinking about how the world is designed and built—or could be—not able, not adept at conversation and other people skills." I laughed again.

"Monsieur Warner, you are laughing at yourself. That is a good trait. That is a people skill." She smiled. "But, I am interested in... what is the engineering mind? Can you tell me more? Is your statement serious?"

"I'd have to think about that, some—to give you a good answer, if you would really like to know. Perhaps you will give me a little time, and I will try to explain." I saw Lisele's eyebrows rise over her sunglasses. The implications of a future meeting were not lost. "Briefly, I can say that engineers like to put numerical values on things. We make comparisons on that basis rather than on perhaps a more subjective basis."

"Can you explain?"

"I'll give you an example. You have two routes that you can drive to Paris. One is more scenic, with nice pastoral vistas, but slow driving through quaint towns. The other is more direct and takes less time. The engineer would say that the direct route is shorter by 98 kilometers, and if you drive at 120 kilometers per hour will get you there in 5 hours rather than 6-1/2, assuming an average 80 kilometers per hour on the more scenic route."

"Oh, I see what you mean. It is almost too much information, and the value of the scenery is dismissed."

"Yes, that would be an example of the popular perception of the engineer mind."

"Engineers are very boring people?"

I thought before I replied. *She responds to humor, especially self-deprecating humor. I'll try that.* "Of course. Is it not evident?" I laughed.

Lisele smiled but said nothing.

Nevertheless, I plowed on. "But, then, we do have our usefulness. Say, perhaps that you had to decide which route to take and you wondered if either route would get you to Paris by 5 pm so you could visit your friends before they went out. You would ask the engineer rather than just try to guess."

"Oh, yes, I do see. At times it is useful to have an engineer around."

Was her wry smile mocking? I thought this would be the best time to make a suggestion. "Lisele, may I call you sometime? I will take you to dinner and do a better job of explaining the engineering mind." I raised *my* eyebrows.

"I'm not sure it is a good idea to be associating with two women from the same family. There could be problems, and not just for you, but, I will let you make your own way on that matter."

I heard the warning, but noticed that I didn't get a direct no. I nodded.

I wanted to investigate the ruins downstream of the Pont du Gard, the section in which the aqueduct maneuvered through a number of switchbacks, five or six, down rough and steep terrain. I called Maurice to accompany me, but he couldn't go because he had a dentist appointment—nothing trivial, unfortunately. I asked, "Maurice, Lisele is an exceptional woman. Why didn't you warn me?"

Maurice laughed, a mannerism of his of which I was becoming familiar. "Oh... Lisele. I thought you might enjoy Lisele. I heard that you had lunch with her. I must say that you are working—perhaps overworking—that family to good advantage." He laughed.

I shook my head. Maurice couldn't have framed my dilemma better. "Yes, Maurice, and now I understand why you were having such a good time laughing about the encounter before it happened. You thought that I might like Lisele and relished the situation I'd be in. I think you have a very impish mind."

"I do relish some of life's ironies, not my only pleasure, but one I enjoy."

"And why, if I might ask, do *you* not seek the more intimate company of Lisele? It would seem she would enrich your life... bright, attractive, witty conversationalist... just your type of thing."

"Oh, yes... me and Lisele. Well, Warner, I did give the situation some thought and even some energy, but at the time, Lisele was not looking for a companion. She said it was too soon after she had gotten rid of her man. I backed off, maintained a friendship but nothing else. Since that time, the relationship has remained that way, more or less at a kind of equilibrium. Maybe I should have given her a little time then tried again. But you... "

"I'm in a different situation... surely. I am running around with her daughter and am only a temporary resident... not the stuff from which solid relationships are crafted."

"I know, Warner, but it is my duty to expose you to life's opportunities. What you do with them is up to you. If there is some difficulty, it is up to you to manage. Otherwise, you just catalog the opportunities, think about what might have been, like all the rest of us."

"That's a pretty savvy comment, and I must say that I didn't know it was your duty to expose me to life's opportunities, or did you just assume that role?"

"Warner, perhaps the lines between duty and interest are blurred. Guilty. And as to *savvy*, I have always been suspicious of the similarity between savvy and the French *savoir faire*."

"I like it. And, as to your duty or interest, I like that too. Just don't get me into too much trouble."

"That my friend, Warner, will depend much on you."

"That's what I'm afraid of. Sorry you can't go with me. I hope the dentist treats you kindly."

The aqueduct downstream from the Pont du Gard puzzled me. Of course, the terrain would have had to be accommodated, given that the river Gard was crossed in the location of the Pont du Gard. But, why did they choose to cross there? I had looked at the topographic maps, and it appeared that it might have been much easier to cross the Gard farther downstream by following the lines of hills, crossing the Gard where the structure would not have had to be so high and avoiding 5 miles of wiggles to cover a 2-mile straight shot.   Perhaps if I could *see* the landscape, I could understand.

The route of the ancient aqueduct ran right through Vers Pont du Gard. I used Vers as a starting point, not quarreling with the route taken upstream. From there I drove the road to the main highway, not following the route of the aqueduct but heading more directly in the direction of Roumelins. Possibly the aqueduct could have been routed in that general direction. Yes, there would be a number of small bridges and some wiggles, but compared to the difficulties downstream of the Pont du Gard, it seemed less of a challenge.

Today, my plan was to start at the Pont du Gard and walk the aqueduct's tortuous route downstream through the rough terrain to the vicinity of St. Bonnet, at which point the aqueduct careened through a large switchback then headed to the vicinity of the village of Sernhac. The aqueduct tunneled under Sernhac for a distance of over 1200 feet. It seemed like they had picked a difficult route considering the many switchbacks and the tunnel.

My walk would be at least 3 miles, and perhaps another 1-1/2 miles should I walk all the way to Sernhac. Maurice said that he would drive there and pick me up after his dentist appointment so that I would not have to walk back up to the Pont du Gard. I had not said absolutely "No" but relished the thought of a long walk of maybe 9 or 10 miles, a round trip. I parked and loaded my waist pack with water bottles, snacks, writing material, a map, compass, and a camera.

The terrain after the Pont du Gard was difficult.   To accommodate the switchbacks and many canyons, a number of bridges had been required. In the canyons, there were some bridge remains and piles of rubble. Following the route, I was able to spot ruins at the Valmale, Combe-Roussiere, la Sartonette and at the Joseph, Pradier and Gilles bridges.   The bridge at Combe-Roussiere had been impressive, at 88 feet high and 325 feet long, a two-tiered arch bridge built of quarried and hewn stone. At each of the ruins, I looked at the manner of construction and the rubble piles.   At several of the ruins, I noted inscriptions in the hewn stones, especially those attached to the abutments. Were these designations of their placement in the structure, ancient graffiti, or signatures of the builders? I had a general sense that I had seen some of the inscriptions before, probably at the Pont du Gard but maybe at the *Castellum*.   Perhaps, on another dedicated investigation, I would catalog the inscriptions. If they were designation for placement in the structure, that would be of interest. If graffiti, they would have the value of most graffiti. If the inscriptions were the signatures of the builders, perhaps they would provide a clue as to the *identity* of the builders, a mystery that has persisted, and, as I had discovered, often incorrectly assumed. Yes, one could spend a lot of time puzzling about what had been done, investigating what remained, reading the history. I could appreciate the interest of the professor in doing so.

As I waded through the piles of rubble, I would occasionally see a fragment of clay pipe. The Romans were profuse in their use of clay pipe. I had seen them at other Roman city sites, so it was not unusual in that regard, but here—what could they have used them for? Was it necessary that captured water from one of the gullies be routed around the structure? That seemed reasonable, but the clay pipes were only about 6 inches in diameter. I inspected several of the fragments, thinking from their appearance they had *broken* longitudinally. But, after looking at several pieces, the breaks would have to be uniform—too much of a coincidence. Inspecting the longitudinal *surface* of several, it appeared that the clay pipe had been cast as a half-circle rather than a full round pipe. They were more of a culvert than a pipe. Well, that could make sense, but I had not seen that before. Interesting note: I would ask the professor about the pipes and about the inscriptions. Was there a cataloguing of the inscriptions—a Rosetta Stone of meanings?

I continued my walk down the *garrigues*, being careful of my footing but not able to avoid my thoughts. *Am I nuts? Why do I want to try to develop a relationship with Lisele? I'll be out of here in a while, and any attachment formed would be shattered by my departure. Better to leave it alone. And, she must think something similar. She surely is not taken by me—an American— complicated by the fact that I've been running around with her daughter. Cool it! Well, I'll just be civil to her, make polite conversation. Maybe it wouldn't hurt to take her out to dinner—after all, it's only a dinner. And, I told her I'd tell her more about the engineering mind—not that she cares a whit about that. Yes, that's what I'll do—all on a friendship basis. After all, we both need to eat dinner, and the exposure will do us both some good.* Interesting how your mind can invent reasons to justify behavior that you had already intended.

At the end of the wiggles I could see the village of St. Bonnet and, from a map, see how the aqueduct followed a gentle course from where I stood, down the profile of the hills to the southwest, then turning east to head toward St. Bonnet. That made sense, as did the direction it took after St. Bonnet.

Rather than follow the longer half-circular route, I cut directly across to St. Bonnet, about 2/10 mile distant. Beyond St. Bonnet, though, I was curious, as to why the builders had chosen to tunnel under Sernhac, so I committed to walk the additional 1-1/2 miles to understand why. I knew I was going to do that before I started. It was a mental gymnastic of some kind.

CHAPTER 23

In three more days, Appius completed arrangements for two men to accompany them. The men, Pentius and Marius, had spent much time in the woods harvesting oak or poplar or pine for use in timbers or other objects made of wood. They were accustomed to living in the wild; their resourcefulness for doing so was thought to be an advantage.

Appius was anxious to get started yet dreaded the required parting from Antonia.

In two more days, they had gathered provisions and the necessary equipment to hack their way through the dense forests. Goodbyes were said, and in a short time they were on their way. For Appius, it did not take long to transform from the gloom which overlayed the parting with Antonia to the adventure of the task. They would start their work at Ucetia and navigate toward Nemausus.

Travel to Ucetia took two days. Pentius and Marius were able to manage the chorobate and cart over the paths without too much difficulty. Their provisions and additional gear were stacked on a shelf attached to the cart. Upon reaching Ucetia, the crew did not stay in the town but made camp near the springs because their provisions were fresh and water was—well—at hand.

Tomorrow would be a milestone; they would start the work of the *mensor* or surveyor.

Bernius had prepared new maps, or at least the layout for new maps. While daylight remained, he showed Appius how they would chart the route of the aqueduct, noting nearby elements of the terrain such as the river, bluffs, flat areas, or sightings to distant distinct landmarks. These notations would be as if one were looking down from above. The route would be shown as a line, traversing the landmarks; distances of straight lines would be noted. Changes in direction would be recorded as the angle represented by two sides of a triangle. At each setting of the chorobate, along the route, a symbol would be shown. Bernius went over the concept again. Appius nodded his head.

Then, Bernius said, pointing at the empty area on the map below the route, "We will make notations such as this." He drew a horizontal line. "This line is the same line as above, however this line is viewed from the side representing a *level* line as established by our chorobate." He then drew an undulating line along the horizontal line, gradually increasing the distance below the line. "The line I just drew represents the ground profile as measured from the level chorobate line to the ground. So, you can see, for every segment of the route that we can see from above, we have a corresponding view that shows that segment from the side."

Appius pondered the scheme. "Yes, but as we talked before, we will have to adjust the height of the level line up or down to accommodate the elevation change in the terrain."

Bernius nodded. "Every time we do that, we will show that change on this map. In that way, we will be able to tell the story of the entire run."

"We must be very careful not to lose this map nor allow it to be destroyed. All our work will be of little use."

"Very true. In fact, we will make other maps showing the same notations because it is so important not to lose the information. I will carry a set and so will you. Our chances of keeping the information safe will be much greater."

Appius saw Pentius and Marius near the chorobate, working with their hatchets. "What chore do you have them doing? They are not spending that much time fashioning firewood?"

Bernius laughed. "No, not firewood. As we make our way, we will drive a square stake into the ground, the top even with the ground, at the point we are measuring. The short, square stakes they are making with the point at one end are for that use. After we have driven those stakes, we will apply red paint to their tops to make them easier to spot. Then, at some distance from the square stake, let us say 5 feet, we will drive a taller stake into the ground and apply white paint to the upper surface. The tall stakes will make it easier to find the square stakes. We call the tall stakes 'witness stakes.'"

"How tall are the witness stakes?"

"About 3 feet. You can see why it would be easier to spot them from 100 feet rather then trying to find the square ones that are even with the top of the ground. Sometimes, when dirt or brush has covered the square stakes, they are still difficult to find, even if we know they are within 5 feet of the witness stake."

the *Aedifex*: Building the Pont du Gard

Appius looked at the waters from the spring as they tumbled toward the Alzon. "I am anxious to start."

Early next morning, they prepared their meal then began the setup for the mapping. Appius, while lashing provisions to the back of his horse, looked across the Alzon. Standing in the shadows were the Ucetians, the young man and the two others who had accosted them at the fountain on the prior trip. They said nothing, intently observing operations in which Bernius was directing Pentius and Marius in the placement of the chorobate. Appius did not wave. Communication did not seem appropriate.

Appius walked to Bernius, calling his attention to the men. Bernius said without turning, "I am not surprised. There is not much we can do. My thought is that no explanation would soothe their perception. Let us make the initial setting of the chorobate."

Appius and Bernius walked to the chorobate. Bernius said, "I have asked Marius and Pentius to set the chorobate near the channel of the spring so that we can measure the distance from the sights down to the water level. When we have leveled the chorobate, we will take that measurement. To level the chorobate, we will first make a rough alignment of the sights to a location about 100 feet away, a location chosen so that it will not be difficult to position the device and of course should be at nearly the same level as where it now stands. Appius, take my measured rope and find a spot, level with the one on which we are standing, about 100 feet away."

Appius walked downstream, unwinding the measured rope as he walked, counting the major markings until he had reached 100 feet. He looked at the ground around him, looked back at the chorobate, then stood on the spot. Bernius moved the downstream end of the chorobate until it pointed towards Appius.

Bernius then beckoned Appius. "So, let us begin by attaching the strings and weights at the legs."

After the strings were hung, Bernius said, "It is evident that the downstream end of the chorobate is low. Let us first try to raise it by using a medium size block."

Marius placed a block under each of the two downstream legs. Bernius looked at the strings, then nodded. "That is close, but a little too high. Exchange each block for a block the next smaller in thickness."

It was done.

"Good." He looked at the weighted string, which was nearly aligned with the mark he had scribed when they had calibrated the chorobate. "Now the downstream end is just barely lower. We may now use the tapered shims to adjust so that we are level. Marius, place the thin edge of a shim under each leg. I will ask you to tap it so that it becomes thicker at the point it supports the legs." He checked the alignment of the string against the scribed line. "Go ahead and give a small tap on each." It was done. "Closer—now once again." After several such iterations, Bernius knelt and squinted at the string, moving his head from side to side. "We are level," he said.

Bernius looked along the sight line in the direction the aqueduct would be constructed. "We will not have much trouble with brush interfering with our line of sight along this section. We have none to remove for our first sighting. But, let us measure from our line of sight down to the level of the spring surface." He moved to the other end of the chorobate. "Pentius, if you would, hold the measuring stick on the bank of the springs so that it rests nearly at the same height as the water surface." Pentius looked for a few moments then set the stick. Bernius looked along the sights. "Two inches to the left, please." Pentius complied. "Ahh, now we have it. I read 3 feet, 10 inches." Bernius retrieved a map, made notations on both the horizontal and vertical view, and marked the height measurement. "We will not drive a stake into the water," he said.

Pentius looked at Marius. "I think he is jesting with us."

Bernius walked to the end of the chorobate nearest the spring, sighting now in the opposite direction. He walked to his satchel and withdrew another weighted string. "Marius, please take this string and walk to where Appius picked the next location of our chorobate. Then suspend the weight, nearly touching the ground. I will move you right or left until the string is along the sight line. Then, lower the weight, gently. As it lays on its side, the pointed end will show you where to pound your square stake."

This was done and the stake driven into the ground. Pentius, as instructed, painted the top of the stake red. Bernius sighted along the chorobate to the measured stick that Pentius now supported on the top of the square stake, then made a notation on the map.

Appius looked at the map, nodding as he looked at the notations. "If we can see farther than 100 feet, should we do so? We would have to set up the chorobate less often."

Bernius beckoned Appius to look along the sights. "Pentius, please hold the measured stick on the stake again. Now, Appius, I think you can be fairly certain of the point at which our sight line intersects the stick. I will have Pentius move out another 50 feet. I think you will see that it becomes more difficult."

Appius tried this after Pentius moved the stick and it was aligned with the sights. "I see what you mean. It is difficult to see the measurement. Now I understand."

"There will be times that we will have to view at a distance more than 100 feet—across a river, across the Vardo for instance. We just have to do the best we can." He pointed to the chorobate. "We can now move the chorobate to just beyond the stake and set it level again. We must be able to look back along the sights to see the measured stick when set on the square stake."

Bernius looked downstream, pointing. "We must continue our mapping down the river canyon, picking a route that is level or dropping slightly. When we get to the low spot we investigated on our prior trip, we will exit the canyon." He looked at Pentius. "Drive a witness stake to the side of the square stake, then we will move on."

They continued the hop-scotch of measuring, moving, adjusting, and measuring for six days, down the canyon. Bernius directed their route on the east bank of the Alzon as it flowed south, staying well up on the bank, nearly to the bottom of the canyon wall as it intersected the bank. Not all the sightings were as easy as the first. Pentius and Marius were busy chopping brush and the occasional tree so that they could have a clear sighting. They often angled the path to go around a cluster of larger trees but tried to maintain continual relative position on the bank of the river.

In the evening, Bernius spread the map on a flat rock. He pointed east, to the edge of a hill, still ablaze in the late sun. "Tomorrow we will turn our route to the east. I have made calculations along our mapped route and find that we have dropped our level line 4 feet, which is somewhat less than the fall of the Alzon for the same distance. Yet, we are still on the bank of the Alzon. The aqueduct could fall less or more depending on what

223

must be done to get the water to Nemausus. I am using a fall of **1** inch per 100 feet. Vitruvius says 1/4 inch per 100 feet is a minimum to establish good flow, although most of our aqueducts have 2 to 4 inches. For now, we will assume a slope steeper than the minimum. Later, upon design, we can use our present line and modify it, should we require a slope greater or shallower than what we have assumed."

Pentius and Marius had gone to retrieve the cart and had returned. Rather than attach the chorobate to the cart for each movement, the chorobate was more easily carried. Bernius watched as they approached. They were not pulling the cart.

"Where is the cart?" Bernius asked.

Marius walked to Bernius and said, "It has been destroyed."

Bernius said nothing, nodding then shaking his head.

Marius continued. "They," he nodded in the direction of Ucetia, "have hacked it to pieces."

"We are not seriously crippled," said Bernius. "We carry the chorobate for each movement and do not need the cart. However, we will have to be wary as they will see that we continue. The cart destruction is intended to be a message. We do not know how much mischief they might create in addition."

Pentius, because he and Marius were tough and maintained scrapper personas, puffed his chest and said, "Should we go back to Ucetia, find them and make them understand that it will not be easy on them if they do more damage?" He held up a fist.

"No." Bernius shook his head. "But, they do not understand the difficulties they might bring upon themselves. Let us hope that they do not continue—for their own good and ours."

Pentius and Marius slumped their shoulders.

Appius said, "Perhaps we should go talk to them, although we did tell them before that we were doing our task at the direction of Claudius."

"Perhaps we should." Bernius walked back to his maps. "In a few days, we will need to freshen our provisions. We will try to talk to them at that time."

The others, standing around Bernius, imagined other mischief at the hands of the Ucetians.

CHAPTER 24

Bernius directed the crew on the transition from the Alzon River channel to a route that would head the aqueduct to the east. It was a matter of following a hill contour that led in that direction rather than continue down the canyon of the Alzon. It took several days for them to hack their way through the forest and to determine a route that would finally intersect the line of hills that ran east-west.

At the end of the day, Bernius said to Appius, "It is time we acquired fresh provisions. We should go to Ucetia for these and also talk to the angry men of the village who might cause trouble for their village and for us. Let us go this evening."

"What will you tell them?" Appius looked up from the map to gauge what Bernius was thinking.

"I will ask them to think about what the Empire might be able to do to them—not our small crew, but soldiers with armor and horses. I will also tell them that the Empire is often fair to its citizens. It does not often take without compensation. I, of course, cannot promise that they will receive revenue from the Empire nor Nemausus, but I can lead them to understand that that concept might be the best course of action for them to pursue."

Appius observed tension in the face of Bernius, a face that usually reflected tranquility. Appius said, "When we last talked to them, we—or I—told them that the Ucetia source was only one of several being considered. Now we know more about the sources and their paths back to Nemausus. Will we tell them that the chances for this course are less likely?"

"Yes. But there is a danger should this course actually be selected. They will feel they have been lied to. The situation could get worse."

"But it does seem obvious.... "

"Yes, I know. I am just considering the possibilities. Let us get our horses and go."

Upon entering the village, Bernius said, "I think we should confront the town leaders first. It is probably expected we will be upset because they have smashed our cart. Rather than causing trouble amongst the vendors as we acquire our supplies, let us first make our peace, if we can. We will ride to the fountain where I am sure the village will discover our presence. I would expect that responsible parties will be summoned."

They were not long at the fountain, still astride their horses, when the young man, Lucius, and now five others approached them. Other villagers were now gathering. Appius looked carefully to see if they carried implements that might be used as weapons. He saw none.

Lucius looked up at Appius. "So, you are back. We see that you are preparing to take our water. We are asking you to go—not to do this. We will not let you do this."

Appius nodded. "Lucius. We must talk to you. I am just a worker, but Bernius...," Appius turned to look at Bernius, "...is a representative of the Empire. He was sent here by Claudius... perhaps you have heard of Claudius."

Lucius grimaced. "Yes, of course we have heard of Claudius. We travel to town, your town, and we do pay attention to what is going on." He looked at Bernius, "So, Bernius, representative of Claudius, what do you have to say?"

Bernius dismounted and approached the group. "I want to let you know that the Empire is not tolerant of those that cause it trouble. Often, there is no talk from the Empire, only action. What I am saying, Lucius, and to the rest of your village," he swept the crowd with his gaze, "is that if you continue," he paused to let them consider the implications of the word, "to bring about trouble, you may see a mounted Centurion and his forces at this very fountain. You will not like this, and you will not be able to defend against them." He remained silent for a few moments to let his message be considered.

Lucius, defiant and propelled by the backing of the crowd, said, "What would you have us do, welcome the Empire, tell them we are grateful they are taking our water, invite them to take also our crops and animals and... women?"

Bernius shook his head, fixing his stare on Lucius. "No, I would not expect you to do that. But, I would like you to think about this. Although it is true I am a representative of Claudius, I cannot guarantee this, but... if the Empire should select the Ucetia springs as a source for Nemausus, I would expect that the Empire would not take without giving. I mean that the Empire would pay your village for the water from revenue collected from its sale. I will advise Claudius and the *Corporata* in Nemausus that you are upset. I will not mention the cart." He paused, but kept his eyes locked on those of Lucius. "I think you will find that method more reasonable than to receive the blows from an angry Empire."

Lucius said nothing but glanced around him to gauge the attitude of the crowd. They looked concerned.

Bernius continued. "I must also say this—although not with certainty. We are measuring two routes—considering two sources. The other source is to the west of Nemausus. It is a good source, and it would be much easier to transport the water to Nemausus. Appius and I," he nodded to Appius who had also dismounted, "both think that the other route will be chosen. I am suggesting you stand down before you cause yourself harm that, in the end, will gain you nothing. What do you have to say to me?"

Lucius looked around again, the villagers now looking to him for wisdom, perhaps expecting too much, given the circumstance. He was buoyed by the support from his people, his manner defiant. "Leave our village. You are not welcome here. Please tell that to Claudius and the people in Nemausus. We will do with your operation what we will." He pointed to the road that exited the town square.

Bernius gave a slow nod. "Please do not do anything foolish." With that he mounted his horse. Appius did the same.

Bernius rode his horse to a vegetable stall, not far from the fountain. The crowd turned to watch. Bernius dismounted and walked to the tables of vegetables. The proprietor eyed him, then, looking at the crowd, walked into his hovel and lowered the curtain.

Bernius turned to Appius. "Perhaps we should have secured our supplies first." He nodded towards the exit and they rode off.

After they had ridden down the bank to the river canyon, Bernius said, "I do not know what to expect. It is possible that Lucius and the rest of the villagers will act more reasonably, now that they are not facing us directly. But, there is not much more that we can do."

"Will you tell Claudius—and the *Corporata*?"

"No. I will let that dog lie. But, since we were not able to replenish our supplies, we must make a trip to Nemausus to do so. That should please you."

"Yes, I wondered what we would do. I do not know where else we might get fresh supplies. Perhaps at the bridge there will be some vendors camped—it seems a natural meeting place—but we could not depend on that and could not depend on having a variety to select from."

Bernius spoke from behind, "I think the same. Nemausus it is, but we must make better plans, knowing that Ucetia is not available. At some point it would be shorter to go to Nemausus, anyway. Let us get ready this evening to leave tomorrow."

Appius wrote a generous account of the conflict in his daily log.

Bernius and Appius, astride the horses, rode from the camp. Marius and Pentius stayed behind, as they were afoot and preferred to remain. They had provisions to last a sparse three or four days and said they would prowl the territory asking and looking for vendors who might have vegetables or meat for sale. The time in Nemausus would be short due to a need to get back to the task, but Appius was still excited to see Antonia.

The ride was uneventful, and they were able to hurry the horses and cover the distance by riding a long day. Appius secured the horse at the stables then trudged to his home. When he entered the courtyard, he saw no signs of Antonia, so he took the time to wash from water stored in the jugs. Presently, before it was altogether dark, he heard a shriek at the courtyard gate. It was Antonia. She rushed in and gave him a hug and looked quizzically into his face. "I thought you would be gone longer. Is anything wrong?"

Appius smiled and held her at arm's length. "No, nothing is wrong except that, due to inhospitable locals, we were not able to buy supplies. We are back for a short visit to replenish and then ride back out."

"I thank the villagers for their inhospitality. We shall make the best of it, and... Appius... I have an idea. I hope you will like it."

Appius, nearly overwhelmed by Antonia's buoyant mood, something he was not expecting, said, "Tell me, Antonia, tell me."

She remained at arm's length but looked at Appius intently because she wanted to gauge his reaction. "Appius, listen to my idea. It seems that you will be spending much time away and me with nothing to do—or not much, anyway. I think that I... we...

should have a child. That will certainly keep me busy, and we will be the better for it. Would you not like to have a child?" Her eyes were bright, eyebrows suggesting a positive answer.

Appius was shocked. He had not expected Antonia to be excited at his return but the idea of—a child—was a thought that had surfaced on occasion but not lately. "A child, why... I always thought we would, but... yes that is a great idea." He smiled. "Where can we get one?"

"Not *get* one, silly. We will make one. We will start on that task tonight."

Appius frowned. "But, Antonia, we have been together for three years, and a child has not appeared. Do you think it may not be possible for us?"

Antonia drew him tighter in the hug. "Appius, it has been because I have not tried hard enough, perhaps not done the things that should be done to make it more... possible. I have thought that it would be good for us to spend time with each other before we had to share our time with a child. You must trust me. Women know these things. It will happen."

"Of course. Of course. A child will be magnificent... I think. What must we... I... do?"

"Leave it to me, my husband. I will do my magic. In the meantime, you must tell me what you are doing... what you have done."

Appius disengaged from the hug, put his arm around Antonia's waist and led her to a seat in the shadows. "We got started... a good start. I am learning how to run a line through the rough country and how to keep track of the elevation of the ground as we go. We are making reasonable progress. Yet, we ran into trouble in Ucetia, more of what I mentioned to you before. Some thugs from the village broke up the cart... the transport cart for the chorobate. We went back to talk to them, but it seems that the village is in an ugly mood. The vendors would not sell us provisions. We—Bernius and I—had to return to Nemausus for fresh provisions while our woodcutters forage the land looking for other sources of food. I will be leaving the day after tomorrow."

"Only two nights here?" She paused. "Is it possible you will return in two weeks for, perhaps, a longer stay?"

"Is it important, Antonia?"

"It is important. It is all part of the magic I must do. I have learned much from my sisters, of which I have multitudes."

"The wisdom of the multitudes wins, then. I will press Bernius to keep the return of two weeks in mind."

"You can possibly persuade him of its importance. He is a reasonable man."

"I am depending on that... for many things."

"Speaking of reasonable, what do you expect from the villagers... at Ucetia. Will they continue to cause you problems? Is it possible that you are in danger of being harmed?"

Appius sat back, reflective. "We talked to them... Bernius did. He told them that they could incur the wrath of the Empire. They appeared... the ones we were dealing with... appeared not to be concerned. We do not know what they are really thinking. Bernius told them that it was likely that the water of Ucetia will not be used, will not be the source chosen because the routing is difficult and costly. If I were them, I would wait until a source has been chosen. That would be the reasonable plan. Yet... one does not know."

Antonia sat back also, tapped her fingers three times on the table. She looked at him. "You must promise to be careful."

He grasped her hand. "I will, Antonia, I will. I must make sure that our child will be brought up with a father."

She smiled.

Antonia suspected that it was due to Appius that they were childless. Her five sisters were fertile, dangerously so. It did not make sense to think she would not have shared the same physical makeup. She might use all the techniques she could muster and the outcome would be... as it had been. Yet, she was resourceful. Yes, she would do all within her ability to see that they created a child... or... several. Appius would be pleased.

Bernius sought vendors for the provisions he must buy. As he talked to the vegetable vendor, he thought of the reluctant vendor in Ucetia. He hoped that the village would be sensible, yet, out of 300 people, there were always a few hot-heads, those that thought that they must prove something, show that they are valued in the community—that having a cause made their life more dramatic, more to be envied. Yes, folks with a cause could create problems. He knew that it was more likely than not that such would be the case. Better take a good supply of wine.

Appius, with Bernius, started the return trip toward the valley of the Alzon on a morning that was cool even given the approaching cool season. The leaves had not yet begun to turn, but there was a chill in the air, a sign that change was possible. Appius was thoughtful as he rode, letting the horse make all the decisions. Appius did not really understand Antonia's disposition. She had been morose upon his prior departure, and rightfully so. It had been difficult. Yet, by the time he returned, she had managed to work through the situation, uplift her spirits and his... with hope and expectation... something to look forward to. Yes, Antonia was truly a remarkable woman. He could not have expected that *any* woman would have crafted a bright viewpoint and idea. Oh, that reminded him. He would have to talk to Bernius, ask him if they could return in two weeks, so Antonia could work her woman's magic, as she called it. He looked behind at Bernius. His horse, as was Appius's, was packed with a generous load of provisions. Bernius's eyes were fixed at a location on the horse's neck, unseeing. He was in deep thought.

After several hours of riding, Bernius urged his horse alongside Appius. "Appius, do you remember—not too many days ago—you asked me to tell you why numbers were important, and I told you the story about the ox carts and the water?"

Appius looked over. "Yes, Bernius, why? Did I make a mistake in my calculations? Should the *Corporata* really use oxen and carts rather than try to hack this foolish aqueduct through very rough land?"

"No, no," he laughed. "Your oxen numbers are a true vision of what would be required. No, I am talking about something else, something that you might consider as a part of your decision making as you meet life's challenges."

"I am interested, and we have the time." Appius adjusted his felt *petasus* to shade the glare as he looked in Bernius's direction.

"Yes, here we go. Suppose that you want to make a trip on a sailing vessel. You start to make arrangements but are warned that, due to weather at this time of the year, sometimes the ship does not sail. Disappointed, you find out that there are times of year when this does *not* occur, and so it seems you should arrange for passage at some other time, even though it is very much less favorable for you. But, if you have an inquiring mind and believe in the power of numbers, you ask, 'And how many times has the ship not sailed in the last five years?' Let us say that the answer you receive is that it has not sailed ten times in the five seasons. You calculate. The ship leaves twelve times in a season and in the last five years it has failed to sail ten times out of a possible sixty. Now what do you think? The chances are only one in six that you will not be able to sail—five sixths that you will. Are you willing to go based on those chances?"

"I see what you mean. Rather than just making my decision on the basis that something *might* happen, now, at least, I have a feeling for the possibilities. If I feel that the trip is valuable enough to be done at this time, I will take the chance."

"Yes. I have to say that your chances of going to a war and coming back are much less than five out of six. Yet, men... and boys... march off all the time even when it is their life on which they are taking to chance. You will find that life presents many such predicaments to ponder, of which the outcome is not certain. If you can use a numerical approach to resolve those predicaments, you will be much better in the long run even when the outcomes do not always follow the heavy side of the prediction."

"Is this a method which you devised?"

"I have done much thinking on the idea, but I originally was intrigued to do so by reading ideas presented by Cicero, bright boy that he was. Do you know who Cicero is... was?"

Appius scratched his head. "I have heard of Cicero. Was he a writer... an orator... a politician?"

"Yes, he was all of those. He was educated by the Greeks and repeated many of their ideas to us Romans. Many of his ideas are worthy of exploration. I have chosen just one of his many."

Appius smiled. "I am excited to try this manner of thinking. If we encounter such a situation, one in which we can apply numbers, will you tell me?"

Bernius nodded and urged his horse to pick up the pace. "Yes, Appius, but you may spot one as well as me... chances are." He grinned.

Appius grinned at Bernius, not so much at the comment he had made, but acknowledging that Bernius was most happy when he was able to see the humorous nature of a situation.

They continued cutting, slashing, and hacking the route along the hills now to the east of the valley of the Alzon. Pentius and Marius were ferocious in their attack on the insistent bushes, trees, and vines that blocked their line-of-sight. They imagined the woods to be a challenge, were happiest when they were wet with effort, muscles aching, and tired at the end of the day. "They are truly worth their weight in gold," said Bernius.

In the evenings, after the meal, while Pentius and Marius were fashioning more ground stakes and witness stakes, Bernius worked on his maps amid measured sips of wine. He explained to Appius as he entered notes, adjusted the elevations and scribed the lines, "I am gradually decreasing the elevation of the aqueduct to provide for the slope required for flow. I have been using a drop of one inch in 100 feet. If we use too steep a slope, especially on this run, it seems we would run out of hills. We will know more about this particular slope when we intercept the ridge that runs across the depression. I cannot tell, at this point, whether we have kept the aqueduct too high by using a shallow slope or have made too great a slope. If we have assumed too great a slope, then at the ridge we will be sighting our level below the ridge and will know that we have to adjust... if we can."

"It does not seem to be remarkable, but I am fascinated that we can do this. I suppose my fascination has to do with being able to craft a useful structure by the means of devices and a method, something that would not be possible by good judgment alone." Appius looked at Bernius to see if he had the same appreciation.

Bernius nodded. "Yes, I think that the same understanding captures me. Not all would have the same... fascination... as you have said. Now, let us copy my notations onto the maps that you carry. Then, we can sleep, wake, and start again. I think that at our present progress, we will reach the ridge in five days.

The next five days were more difficult than Bernius had imagined. The trees were thicker, the brush more unyielding, the footing for the chorobate uneven. The crew worked hard to maintain progress. While the woodsmen were removing trees required for a clear sighting to the next stake, Appius and Bernius investigated the woods ahead, walking around the brush and sometimes crawling under impenetrable hedges of hardwoods to establish the next sighting location. Looking back, they could never see the spot from which they would be sighting so had to do their best to determine a location, nearly at the same elevation as that at which the chorobate now sat, take a route which was close to the route they intended yet did not require the removal of so many trees.

At nearly the end of six days, they had reached the ridge they would follow across the low area. The ridge was above the spot where they last set the chorobate.

That night, Bernius worked on his maps. "Appius, you have noted that our level line is 26 feet lower than the top of the ridge."

"Yes, I have noticed. Does that mean that the slope we assumed is too steep, that our slope will have to be shallower?"

"You are correct. If our measurements are right, the bottom of our conduit will be too deep. However, we must run our line along the ridge and arrive at the edge of the Vardo canyon to be sure. If we need more slope than is available to this point, it is possible we could dig deeper at the beginning of this ridge, thus crossing at a lower elevation. But regardless of what we do on the ridge, at the edge of the canyon, all will be clear. If we choose the Ucetia source, the slope must be adjusted so that the bottom of the aqueduct is nearly equal to the top of the canyon. The moment of truth."

"I shall be excited to see how it turns out."

"Yes, me too. But, it seems like we are due to return to Nemausus for several reasons, not the least of which is for you to start the quite beautiful Antonia on her way to motherhood. We must also get provisions for more difficult weather—colder and perhaps with some rain. We may be driven from our task, on this route, at least."

"I will welcome my task with Antonia. How many days should we allow?"

"I would think one day each for the trip to and from and three full days in the town. Marius and Pentius will again stay in the area but will return with us after our next phase at which time we should have reached the canyon of the Vardo... I hope. After that time, we will see what elevation has done to us and decide if we want to continue on the other side of the Vardo at the time of year we can expect difficult weather. I say that we have done well, so far. Also, it seems that the hotheads at Ucetia have not interfered further. Perhaps they *did* hear what I had to say."

"I am grateful for that. I have been wary that I would see a small war party, ready to do us great harm while I have been at my tasks. I am relieved that it did not happen. I will now be thinking that there is no danger for the time, at least."

234

"Yes, they could easily overcome us. Let us make our camp at the springs we found on our prior trip. Pentius and Marius should find it comfortable there."

Appius and Bernius returned to the site five days later. Prior to leaving they had established a line of sightings along the ridge. Marius and Pentius, always challenging the woods with their powerful frames, cleared an additional 2000 feet and had hewn a substantial pile of stakes in the duration.

As the team swiftly moved the chorobate along the ridge, taking measurements, Bernius noted that the ridgeline had dropped. They followed the drop into a gorge and back up the other side, continuing as the ridge emerged again. In twenty days, although fighting two days of rain, they reached the rim of the Vardo. The ever-present energy of Marius and Pentius propelled Appius and Bernius. Bernius was only able to convince the woodcutters to take one day of rest during the time. On that day, they fashioned more stakes.

The canyon was, indeed, a milestone, but Appius felt the significance of progress more than expected. He was not sure what drove the exhilaration. He yelled and made great display, goading Pentius and Marius to join in. Bernius leaned against his horse and laughed. Pentius, pointing across the Vardo, said, "At least we will not have to clear trees across the canyon. Looks like you two will have a hard time setting the chorobate on the next few sightings, though." He laughed, turning and pointing to the gulf before them.

That evening, Bernius took a long time with his maps, wine cup at his side; Appius watched him in silence, refilling Bernius's cup when necessary. Finally, Bernius motioned Appius to sit alongside so he could explain. "I have calculated the drop in elevation from the surface of the spring at Ucetia to the edge of this canyon. We have measured only a 20 foot drop, which, in the 54,000 feet we have measured is a drop of less than 1/2 inch every 100 feet. This drop is much less than the 2 to 4 inches for the usual aqueduct, yet our level line is about 33 feet below the rim of the canyon. We have assumed a slope, 1 inch per 100 feet—much steeper than we can use.

Appius scowled. "Does that mean that the water would not flow from the springs to this point?"

Bernius looked up. "No, it would. Aqua Virgo, built by Agrippa, has a slope of about 1/4 inch per 100 feet. In his book,

Thomas Hessler

"The Ten Books on Architecture," Vitruvius recommends a minimum drop of 1/4 inch in 100 feet. But we must consider something else. We must consider the accuracy of the chorobate. Given that our outcome is about 20 feet of drop, it is probable that the actual drop is more or less, regardless of our lines on the paper or the calculations we have carefully made."

Appius scratched his head, looking puzzled. "What do you mean? We have been very careful. I do not understand why you would question our measurements."

Bernius had been stooping over the maps on his knees, the map spread on a rock in front of them. He sat back. "We have taken about 540 measurements of one hundred feet each. One assumption we could make is that we have been precise and the measurements we have taken are entirely useful. But, let us imagine that with each 100-foot measurement that our chorobate line is high or low by just one-quarter of an inch or that we can only judge the position of our sight line within 1/4 of an inch—it is too difficult to be more certain. If we were 1/4 inch off on *all* our 540 measurements, all the errors accumulating to either high or low, we would be in error, at this point, over 11 feet. So, it is possible that instead of 20 feet lower at this point, we are 31 feet or only 9 feet lower. My guess is that we are not able to be accurate to even 1/4 inch in 100 feet. We could easily be off 1/2 inch in every 100 feet. In that case, our actual measurement could be a drop of 42 feet or, instead of a drop, a *rise* of 2 feet. In using either of those numbers, the assumption would be that we always erred to one side or another. Of course, if we have a rise, we can be assured that the water will not flow."

"Is it likely that the errors would all be in the same direction? It seems not."

"It could be likely if there is a consistent flaw in our chorobate, for instance, or a consistent flaw in our eyesight. But, we do not know. At this time, we could not tell the public officials that the water would flow from the springs to the edge of the canyon."

"What must we do?"

"I think when we get back to Nemausus, we should do some tests in the channel where we originally set up the chorobate. We will get an idea of its accuracy by seeing if we can get the same results repeatedly. Beyond that, if greater accuracy is needed, I know of one other way, but it is cumbersome—the use of an A-frame. However, I also question its accuracy, and it would be a dreadful device to have to transport through the woods."

"And for now?"

"I think we should *not* continue this route, for now. The rains will make it difficult to manage the terrain on the other side of the Vardo, and we must determine the outcome of our chorobate measurements. It is reasonable that we should soon go to the source in the west and map a route from there. Marius and Pentius will return with us and bring the chorobate."

Appius nodded but was silent. He felt depressed thinking that the Ucetia source might not be possible. What if they encountered a similar problem to the west?

The entire team was back in Nemausus. Antonia was delighted to hear they would be in town for nearly a week. Marius and Pentius found their own entertainment, which included an opportunity to wrestle a bear that was making a tour of the region with its owners and challenging all comers.

Bernius, after several days, organized a test session at the channel, the one used prior to set up the chorobate. They waded in the channel, taking their measurements to determine the possible amount of error that might be expected in using the chorobate. Pentius and Marius, having no trees to chop, aided in the leveling of the device.

Bernius explained to Appius as they were setting up the chorobate. "Here, in this channel, we can measure level accurately. If the chorobate and our method were accurate, we would obtain the same measurement from the sights to the top of the water at the chorobate that we measure sighted one hundred feet from the chorobate. But, we cannot be totally accurate. Here, we can measure the differences to determine the extent of our sighting and set-up errors. To do our test, we take sightings as we do in the woods. You will sight and then I. We will measure any difference in what our eyes see versus the actual measurement. Then we will reset the chorobate in case lighting has an effect in the reverse direction and repeat the operation. We will, each of us, take a number of sightings to a graduated stick and see how much variation we get. From that we will see if we can determine how much inaccuracy, due to *sighting*, we are contributing to our process and perhaps find a way to improve."

Bernius also had Marius and Pentius participate in the sighting. After they had done the operation several times, Bernius called to Appius. "See, Appius, most of the time there is some error in determining the sight line of the chorobate against the measuring stick at one-hundred feet. We have been off as much as 1 ½ inches, but it looks like we are most often either low or high by ½ inch. Between us, there is no tendency for either you or me to read either high or low.

Appius said, looking at Bernius and shrugging his shoulders. "What do we do now?"

"I have noted that Marius does better, continually, than the rest of us. It could be that his eyes are better for sighting the stick at that distance. We could also reduce the distance so that we can all see the measurement better. That will mean more setting of the chorobate, more time spent."

Appius nodded. "More time spent, yes, but it seems to be important."

Bernius pointed toward the chorobate. "Our last test involved errors due to our inability to sight accurately. Another error may be involved due to imprecision in setting the chorobate. We will now set up the chorobate a number of times and see what differences result."

They went about this maneuver and again looked at the data they had recorded. Bernius pointed to the calculations on his sheet. "Our tests show that although we have been careful to make sure the string and the scribed line were parallel, we often had errors of 3/4 inch. The result of both our tests is that the chorobate is useful if the slope you are using has an elevation difference of over 2 inches in one hundred feet; however, if the elevation difference is less than that, the errors may be masking the actual direction of the elevation change."

"Should we use the chorobate in our work on the western source?" Appius looked discouraged.

Bernius nodded. "I think we can. We can improve the sighting part of our method by making shots of only 50 feet, perhaps substantially reducing any error that we might have had. Also, my judgment is that we have much more elevation difference to work with. But, we will see. Let us take three more days in Nemausus, gather our provisions then travel to the other source. Can you have the carpenter build us a new cart? Although Marius and Pentius did not complain when carrying the chorobate back to

Nemausus, I think they will need the cart if they carry their provisions also."

"I will talk to the carpenter. I think he will be able to build us a new cart in three days." Appius inclined his head in the direction of the carpenter shop. "I will go there now along with Marius and Pentius as they carry the chorobate."

Nemus addressed the *Corporata*. "I have received word. Caligua has determined that he will no longer share the Empire with Claudius; in other words, Claudius is no longer an *imperator* of the Empire."

"Ha," Julius snorted, "I knew that if we waited long enough the situation could change. What will Caligua say or do about building this aqueduct?"

Nemus turned to Julius. "Your happiness, I have to tell you, is short lived. Claudius, as one might suspect, *has* been named proconsul for this region. For us, nothing will change. However, I cannot tell you what Caligua thinks about our project—what he has told Claudius, if anything. I can tell you that we would have heard if Caligua intended to have it stopped."

Julius looked intently at Nemus and said, "I still think it is a better situation for us. It is likely that Caligua will imagine other monuments to build, other wars to fight, and lands to conquer. It could very easily happen that the aqueduct will suffer for attention and resources under the ambitious hand of Caligua."

Marcus nodded. "One hears that Caligua is impulsive and egotistic. Julius is right. Perhaps he dismissed Claudius so that he could have a freer hand to craft his ambitions. It would not be the first time the Empire served that purpose for the *Imperator*."

Nemus let them have their say, then spoke, "So, what would you have us do? Clearly we are not going to tell Claudius that we will wait for Caligua to smear the aqueduct from the list. I do not see us making changes at this time."

"You may be right," Julius shook his head, looking at Marcus, "but I understand our crew investigating the routing has found that perhaps the land does not slope in the direction from Ucetia to Nemausus. We must, when we have the opportunity, express our concern. It would be folly to build an aqueduct in which the water does not flow." He smiled.

239

Marcus nodded. "Appius has told me of such. Claudius's man, Bernius, is prudent, it seems, and will not recommend a route which he thinks is in doubt."

Titus spoke for the first time. "What are they doing now?" He looked at Marcus, then Nemus.

Marcus replied. "They will soon leave to investigate the route for the western source. Appius tells me that the western slope appears to have more slope than that from Ucetia. But, it will be many months before they can complete that routing, even without considering the weather they must encounter. And, after that, they intend to finish measuring the route from Ucetia, as, at this time, they have measured only as far as the Vardo. It will be more than a year before they are able to tell us what exists."

Julius scowled. "They will continue on the Ucetia route? If they are not sure of measurements to that point, how will they...?"

Marcus looked at Julius. "To answer your questions, Appius told me that they will find a way to improve the accuracy."

Nemus, with outreached arms, said, "Let us have them continue. All is proceeding in line with our notions. In the meantime we can collect revenue from our very worthwhile water system, as we have done in the past. Is there anything else to discuss?" He looked around.

Titus looked at Nemus. "How much are we paying Bernius?"

CHAPTER 25

Appius, Bernius, Pentius, Marius, horses, chorobate, cart, and provisions left Nemausus on a day markedly cooler than those they had experienced on previous departures. The ride and the carting of the chorobate were more pleasant under cool conditions, but all, without speaking of it, knew weather would now be a factor in their work. Predictably, practicing what was now becoming a routine, they stopped at the spa for the night, enjoying the bravado, the baths, and the excellent wine of the proprietor.

Pentius punched Marius's shoulder, "I think I could get used to this life." They both laughed heartily.

The next morning they were able to reach the springs of the western source, although lack of a path or road made the journey difficult. In the fall the flow of the springs seemed to have diminished only slightly.

Bernius stood, arms akimbo, looking at the flow. "I am enthused; this source should be excellent, perhaps only debased by winter rains. We may have the opportunity to witness such." He looked at the sky, now obscured, a contrast to the cloudless days of summer. He summoned Appius. "As we follow the contours, we must again assume a value for the slope of the aqueduct. I believe that this source is much higher than Ucetia based on our journey to this spot. I will use a slope of 2 inches in 100 feet; it will not be too much, and it will be beyond the error of the chorobate as we have recently measured. If our measurements show that the slope exceeds 2 inches, or it is even close to that, we can be assured that there is a useful drop from this source to Nemausus."

Appius nodded and stared at Bernius, not entirely sure of that what he heard.

Bernius, now adept at resolving Appius's looks, said, "If we use 2 inches per 100 feet, we know that we have a slope that is outside our worst situation of making errors, that of making all our errors in one direction. That we have demonstrated that we are *not* making errors, all in one direction, should make us even more confident. Does that help?"

Appius smiled. "Yes, it does help. I do see it. I am anxious to see how this will work out." He gestured to Pentius and Marius, who, for the moment, had no instructions so were foraging for wood from which to make stakes. Appius, remembering the beginning of their task at Ucetia, pointed to a spot on the ground from which they could backsight to the level of the water flowing from the springs. "Let us set the chorobate here."

Bernius, hands on hips again, smiled to no one in particular, except to his own appreciation of accomplishment—his teaching of Appius.

Over the following weeks they worked their way to the valley overlook, taking the opportunity to overnight at the spa; they were in the neighborhood and thought they would stop by. This time, baths in the bubbling water were much needed by all and especially by Marius and Pentius who had achieved a measurable amount of crust on their bodies, salt accumulation from a number of days of hard work, even given the cooler weather.

The proprietor commented. "I believe those two have tainted the water for many miles down the stream from the accumulation on their bodies." He laughed.

Marius and Pentius threatened him with clenched fists. Pentius yelled, "Anyone who drinks of this water will never drink of it again. We are your big mistake." He laughed, pounding Marius on the back. "You are way worse than I, you know."

Marius flexed his arms. "It is because I have done most of the work."

Bernius, in a less buoyant mood, said to Appius, "So, it seems that our use of 2 inches drop for one-hundred feet has been satisfactory, at least to the location we stopped, the overlook. I think that from there it is very possible that we will be able to reach Nemausus by following the line of hills. It should not be a question of whether the water will run downhill."

Appius, happy with that thought, raised his wine glass. "I have to say, Bernius, I was afraid that this route would somehow not be useful. We can surely present to the *Corporata* and to Claudius, when we are finished, a route that will work."

"Yes. Perhaps when we complete this measurement, we should ask the *Corporata* and Claudius if we should continue the task on the Ucetia route. They may favor us not to bother and to proceed with a design on this western source rather than waste our time and their sestertii only to have a vague understanding that Ucetia could be useful." Bernius took a long sip from the wine cup in contemplation.

The weather turned difficult. Apart from the discomfort of the cold and the rain, muddy slopes caused difficulty in walking and setting the chorobate. Rain, even light rain made sighting more difficult and, realizing that they needed to improve their sighting accuracy, they sometimes waited until the rain had stopped. The somber weather flattened the enthusiasm of even Marius and Pentius, who did not enjoy the work nearly as much as in the warm weather, grumbling on occasion as they fought the terrain. Although the hillsides they now worked had less foliage, progress was slow.

The task took the remainder of the fall, the sloggy winter, and on into the spring to complete. The crew took more trips back to Nemausus to warm their bodies that in the outdoor never quite recovered to a comfortable temperature as they slogged through the mud. They stayed longer in Nemausus, taking their time to replenish provisions, and taking care of nagging chores. As they made progress on the route, they, of course, worked nearer and nearer to Nemausus, making it easier and more... reasonable... to return home. There was no doubt that this combination of weather and attitudes extended the total time of the task.

On one such return trip, Antonia, greeting Appius with more than the usual enthusiasm and radiance, took him by the arm and led him inside their castle, asking, "Appius, do you think there will be enough room for three?"

Appius was mystified at the remark, his mind dulled somewhat by chill and the continual pounding of raindrops on his forehead over what seemed like a long period of time. "Your mother is coming to stay with us?"

"My mother is *not* coming to stay," Antonia pouted. "But a child will, at some time, come along, and he or she may want to stay here."

"Oh," said Appius, catching on but slowly, "when we have a child, we will need to provide whatever space they require. Are you saying that we should think about providing more room?"

"No, Appius," she put both hands on his shoulders. "It is not a question of someday. I am not hinting at a larger home. My mother is not coming to stay. I... we... will have a child in perhaps seven months." Her eyes sparkled with delight now that her ruse was over.

Appius, still slow to grasp Antonia's meaning, seemed to absorb the situation gradually. "You... we... are having a child?" His eyes widened in amazement.

"Yes, my husband. It has happened. I told you that it would be so. Are you happy?"

Appius put his hands around her waist. "Happy, yes I am... I am just... well, I did not really expect it. You truly have worked magic." He picked her up and held her above him in a hug, then said, "Oh, must I be more careful?"

"No, Appius," she said, laughing, "I and the baby are tough. You may give us all the hugs you want."

"I cannot wait," Appius said. "Will our lives be forever changed? I cannot help but think that while you will be busy with the child when I am away, I will be more tempted to be at home."

"Yes," Antonia said, "I have thought about that, too."

Within two months after the spring equinox, they completed the measurements of the western route. Bernius met with Appius in the courtyard, enjoying the sun, having been deprived of warmth so often during their recent cool adventure. Bernius led Appius through the calculations. "If we use the measurements we have observed and recorded, we could assume a drop in elevation from the western springs to Nemausus of 240 feet... that is if there were *no* measurement errors or if the measurements that were in error on the high side were balanced by errors made on the low side. I think we can be assured that there have been errors both ways but we cannot assume it was balanced. Let us say that we will take the middle ground. If all the errors were all in one direction, we would be off by 38 feet. We will split the difference between the maximum error and no error to arrive at an assumed error of 19 feet either too high or too low. So, the drop from the springs to Nemausus could be in the range of 221 feet to 259 feet. We will use that consideration for now. This means that over the entire route, the drop is 1-3/4 inches in 100 feet Water will flow to Nemausus."

"Is it time to talk to the *Corporata*? I have yet to tell even Marcus our results."

Bernius nodded. "Yes, tell Marcus of our situation. If we must, we will appear before the *Corporata* and explain what we have done and our results, in detail. I compel myself to understand that such an appearance before public officials is part of my work... not that they would understand what we are talking about. You will talk to Marcus?"

Appius reached for paper on which to make notes. "Yes, I will see Marcus as soon as he is available and let you know what he says."

As Antonia emerged from the house, Bernius smiled, speaking to Appius. "I see that Antonia must soon respond to the thought that will be apparent to all. When will your child be here?"

Appius sat upright, beckoning to Antonia. "Antonia tells me the child will appear in the early fall, after the equinox. I wonder what we will be doing at that time. If the *Corporata*—and Claudius—approve the western route, we could be designing the structure. I am excited by that thought."

Bernius shrugged as Antonia approached him holding her hands in front of her in greeting, distant early warning that a hug was imminent. "Yes, we should know soon."

Antonia hugged Bernius. "I see that you two are still at your task but doing so in our warm courtyard, with seating, good food, water, women, wine, and comfortable sleeping quarters close at hand. It is good, yes?"

"Yes, Antonia, it is good. Appius and I are now wondering what will be next. How will our lives be changed?"

Appius, looking at Antonia, said, "Yes. Indeed."

As Appius entered Marcus's office, Marcus appeared to be in intense concentration, studying a document. Marcus greeted Appius without looking up.

Appius sat down, waiting for Marcus to engage him, which he finally did. Appius said, "As I am sure you have heard, we have finished mapping and taking measurements for the route from the western springs. When we visited them in late summer, they had varied little in output. During several days of heavy rains, we made

245

a trip back and determined that, although the water quality suffered somewhat from runoff of the near hills, the amount was not substantial."

"The water source is good?"

"Yes."

"And the route... would we be able to get the water to Nemausus?" Marcus frowned.

"We determined a route that would be useful. The aqueduct will require bridging structures but nothing overwhelming. Some tunnels will be required."

Marcus spread his hands vertically. "And the drop, there is sufficient drop in elevation, not like the Ucetia source."

Appius nodded. "While the drop from Ucetia to the Vardo is only about twenty feet, the drop for the entire route of the western source is about 240 feet. Bernius says that it should be useable."

"Do you have more to do... more checking or measurements or calculations?"

"No. We will be waiting for direction by the *Corporata*. We were directed, at the end of summer, to investigate the routes for both sources. We have only investigated a third of the distance on the Ucetia route. We think that the *Corporata* should again consider their direction, based on the difficulty of the Ucetia route and what appears to be useable route from the western source. Spoken another way, does the *Corporata* want us to complete the investigation of the Ucetia route or go into the design phase of the western route? What will the *Corporata* say?"

Marcus shrugged. "I do not know what the *Corporata* will say." He actually thought he did know. "I will have them meet; we will get word to Claudius, if necessary. We will let you know when it has been decided. In the meantime, you can get used to living in the city again."

Appius straightened, grinning. "Do you know that Antonia is with child? I will be a father."

"Yes, I do know. Congratulations."

"Oh, that is right. You probably would know. Antonia thanks you for being prompt at delivering the payment of our wages. She must have told you."

"Yes, she did." Marcus, anxious to return to serious review of the document on his desk, said. "I will get word to you as soon as there is a decision."

"Thank you. It seems at that time there will be much to discuss."

"Oh, yes—much to discuss. Well, we will have to do that when the time comes." He waved as Appius stood up.

Appius gave thought to the meeting on his way home. Marcus was unusually distracted—did not engage him on the importance of the routing. What could be happening in Marcus's life that might cause him to act in that manner? His attitude could be temporary, just a bad mood due to household worries. Or, perhaps Marcus was pensive because the good results of the western route meant that an aqueduct could be built, a circumstance that—Marcus had told him—was not favored by the *Corporata*. Maybe that was it. But, before, Marcus had not seemed to be aligned with that concern. It was always the other members. Why was the situation changed? Perhaps he would know in good time.

Marcus got word to Appius that the *Corporata* had determined that the investigation of the Ucetia route should be completed. When questioned by Appius, Marcus acknowledged that the *Corporata* was aware of the small elevation drop *and* were aware that the instrument used for measurement was unreliable on such a slight slope, and that due to the imprecision of the procedure, there might not be a drop at all between Ucetia and the canyon of the Vardo. It did not matter. Marcus did not give Appius a reason.

Appius was not sure what to think. He guessed, correctly, that it amounted to the *Corporata* not wanting to proceed with the costly construction of the aqueduct, that continuing the investigation would extend the time. Yes, it did make sense from their viewpoint. It just did not make sense if one were trying to proceed in the most reasonable way. For Appius, it meant they would be out on the land again, whereas if they were to proceed with the design, one could presume it could be done in Nemausus. Would his child be born while he was away?

And what of the measurements they were taking along the Ucetia route? Were they useless because of the inaccuracy of the chorobate? He hated to think that their time would be folly, even though he was still getting paid and still in the company of his teacher, Bernius.

Thomas Hessler

He had been thinking about the chorobate, imagining ways to improve the readings. Perhaps there was a way. He would talk to Bernius.

CHAPTER 26

I was to meet with Professor Durand in Marseille in two days. I telephoned Laurie. "Bonjour, Mademoiselle Laurie, this is your friend, Warner."

"Oh, yes, Warner. I was going to call you. We must talk about our trip to Marseille. I have a perfect plan. We will follow the route of the Rhone, and you can enjoy that scenery. I know a wonderful spot to have our lunch by the edge of the water. Our discussion with Professor Durand is not until 5 p.m., after his classes, so we have additional time to spend in Marseille. It will be a wonderful day, and I will be most happy to be your tour guide and interpreter."

"Well, Laurie, it is gracious of you to spend a full day on my account. Are you sure that you'll not be involved in extraordinary real estate transactions, working your calculator, sending aides scurrying for information, checking with conspirators briefly by telephone?"

"Oh, is that what you think we are doing? Vers is much too sleepy for that much activity. It is more like—an American drops by the office to see if we know of anything to rent, and we jump up at the chance to do something. Who knows, maybe the encounter will lead to an adventure with a fascinating personality, someone with whom one can share capricious events."

"Yes, there is certainly that possibility. I hope that it happens to you, as you deserve the best... especially the capricious part."

"And, aren't you glad I will take you along with me?"

"Yes, 'capricious' has always been part of my plan."

"Now you are mocking me. Yes?"

"Of course not. What time are we leaving? I'll pick you up."

"Oh, no. I must drive. I'm too impatient to sit in your passenger seat. I'll pick you up at 10 a.m. *Oui*?"

After a large intake of breath, "Ten o'clock. *Oui*."

Thomas Hessler

I had a number of questions to ask the professor, based on my investigations and thoughts. Even if the professor could not answer all of my questions, he probably would know whether such information was known or conclusions had been reached. He would be a great help in letting me know how I should spend the rest of my time.

Laurie was in my driveway at 10:30 a.m, skidding to a stop in the gravel as was her usual maneuver, nearly abandoning the wheel before the car was through with its journey. As I opened my front door, she had her head tilted to one side, arms on her hips and a jaunty smile to match her cap. "Let's go, *Monsieur* Warner, let's go."

I found it hard to relax, subject to the skilled but fast and reckless hand of Laurie's driving. "Laurie, you have never mentioned your mother. I was surprised to meet her at Maurice's party. It's not difficult to understand where you get your good looks."

"Oh, you think my mother is good looking? I hear that you had lunch with her at the café. I hope you didn't quiz her about me. Anything she would have to say would be from a worrying mother's viewpoint."

"Surely you don't do anything to worry your mother. I'll bet she's proud to have such a bright and energetic offspring. But, no, we did not discuss you. Our time was brief because I walked into the café at a time she was part way through her meal. I think we talked about engineers."

"Good—better 'engineers' than my mother talking about me, but, I must say, I'm sure engineers can be fascinating, and there are many tales to tell. You must tell me some."

"Laurie, we're cast as a pretty boring lot. If your television is the same as ours, you know that we have TV series about doctors, lawyers, writers, cops, detectives, forensic medical examiners, psychologists, sewer workers, bartenders, and musicians. None about engineers. You can gauge how interesting our lives must be by what people are willing to watch."

"Hmmm, well, are there any interesting engineering stories—bridges in danger of collapse, skyscrapers to the sky, the drama of a runaway nuclear power plant?"

"I do have some stories, but I only tell them to other engineers."

"Oh, but you must try them on me. Do you promise?"

"Yes—okay—sometime today. But, you must tell me when you've had enough."

"Yes, Mr. Warner, I will certainly tell you when I've had enough."

At the university, we climbed broad, elegantly finished, marble steps to a less dignified entry to the hall in which Professor Durand had his offices. There was no reception, just a dim corridor and a sparse number of students entering doorways, or exiting the corridor, hitching their books for the ride—some invested in earnest conversation with a companion, heavily gestured by a waving of arms.

Laurie looked at her note and checked the numbers on the doors. "Here we are, Number 137."

We opened the door and walked in, not to a den of clutter, as I had pictured it, but to an all-in-order, display of neatness and sterility. The professor had one sheet of paper on his desk, pen in hand. His appearance, however, was somewhat as I had imagined—sparse curly hair, pointed beard, loose tie at his neck. He looked up as we entered, nodded, consulted a note stuck in the border of his desk protector and said, "Dr. Warner and Mademoiselle Laurie," in French.

Laurie then launched into French, mentioning the word 'doctor' at which the professor raised his eyebrows and gave a slight nod. He waved to the chairs and we sat down. Laurie gave me an impish sideways look. Apparently she had used 'doctor' to wheedle the invitation.

He spoke to Laurie for several moments then she turned to me and said, "The professor says he understands that you have a special interest in the Nimes aqueduct. He asks me to let you know that he is highly regarded as one of the most knowledgeable academics on that subject."

"Please tell him I am grateful that I am able to have this chance to... "

"Yes, yes." She launched into more explanation than I thought necessary to cover the subject.

He shook his head, uttered a short sentence then shrugged.

Thomas Hessler

Laurie said, "How may he help you?"

I said, looking at the professor, "I have several questions—mysteries I can't solve. I've not found answers in the material I have read, and some of the material suggests that several of the questions I ask have *not* been answered." I kept going because I knew Laurie could preface my questions with the preamble I'd just uttered. "One question I have is that most of what I have read indicates the aqueduct was built in the time of Caesar—Augustus—under the supervision of Agrippa. Yet, I can't find any descriptions directly referencing this. Might there be more information available as to the time frame in which the aqueduct was built and under whose direction?" I looked at Laurie, indicating she could take it from there.

Laurie looked at me while she repeated what I had said, as if I could advise her if she incorrectly interpreted a statement. I looked at the professor.

He adopted a smug grin, one I've seen before on those who are impressed that they have superior knowledge. He started speaking, stood up, took a few steps parallel to his desk, turned, gestured to the ceiling, shook his head, spread his hands and sat down. His smile persisted, and he nodded at Laurie.

Laurie turned to me. "The professor said that the popular conception is all wrong, mistakenly touted because of a *mis*conception made by a researcher many years ago. It had to do with structures that were constructed in Nimes, at the time of Augustus and that were related to Agrippa. They associated the aqueduct with that same effort and time frame. The professor has been concerned with your very question and will soon present a paper explaining that the aqueduct was built much later, had nothing to do with Agrippa, and most likely was built during the reign of Claudius, although that still is not clear.' He says, 'You must read my paper when it is published.'"

I asked, "Is there any evidence in existence which leads to that conclusion?"

I watched the professor as Laurie translated my question and as I listened to his reply.

The professor wagged his head. "I don't want to reveal the means of my determination. I have competitors in the field. I *will* say that artifacts have been found in the rubble to indicate the structure could not have been built in the time of Augustus." He smiled.

252

the *Aedifex*: Building the Pont du Gard

"Thank you. I think that may help clear up a mystery for me. Does the fact that they tunneled or had to tunnel under the city wall have any meaning in the determination?" I was able to watch the professor as Laurie asked him the question in French.

The professor leaned forward and glared at me. "I cannot say. And, where did you hear that?"

I shrugged. "From an engineering viewpoint and a construction viewpoint, it seems an odd choice had the wall not been there."

"You have had experience in construction?"

"Yes, my entire career. I find that when I consider how I would have engineered and constructed the work—the aqueduct— my construction background helps me imagine what went on."

The professor looked directly at me. "I was led to believe you had a more academic background." He looked at Laurie.

"No, I don't. However, my background does help me visualize some of the problems and alternatives that the builders encountered. In your studies, have you consulted any builders?"

"I haven't considered that to be necessary. Do you have any more questions?"

Laurie and the professor looked at me while I thumbed through my notes.

"Yes, professor. As I was looking at several piles of rubble, I spotted fragments of clay pipes, cast as only an invert. Is there any significance to these?"

The professor shook his head. "None that I know of. Not much attention has been given to them. They were probably used to channel troublesome water away from the excavations or in the building of the conduit liner." He nodded to emphasize the reasonableness of his statement.

"Also, Professor, I notice inscriptions chiseled into stone at many of the important structures. Has anyone catalogued those inscriptions or identified them as names of the participants, or are most of them graffiti?"

He settled back in his chair and steepled his fingers. "Much of the inscriptions are graffiti. We can determine this by expressions used that post-date the construction. However, there are a few which seem to have been made by the builders, references to the height of the arch, for instance that would have likely been inscribed by the builders. But, there are no catalogs of the inscriptions. It hasn't been deemed worthwhile to do so."

253

I nodded. "I've been puzzled by the route selected for the aqueduct. It seems like they picked a very difficult stretch to overcome, downstream of the Pont du Gard. Would it have been easier to follow the Gard downstream a ways farther, cross the Gard where the canyon is not deep, then follow the hill profiles to the vicinity of Sernhac?"

Again, I focused on the reaction of the professor. As Laurie repeated my question, the professor scowled and said, "They crossed the Gard where it was most convenient to cross the Gard."

I continued. "It seems to me there should be a question as to why my alternative was not considered; the Gard crossing and the route following would have been easier. If there was a reason that my alternative was not taken, it would seem that someone would have considered it—even in the academic world."

When Laurie finished that translation, the professor bristled at the last phrase, taking the barb that I, in my dwindling admiration, had intended. I knew it was a mistake.

The professor's response was to inform Laurie that he must soon leave, and his time with us was coming to an end.

I had one more issue on which I wanted a response. "I've been doing a lot of thinking about the slight elevation drop to which the aqueduct had to be constructed. Have you investigated any methods that might explain how they were able to initially determine the elevation difference, then how to construct the aqueduct to an even more precise requirement during the building?"

The professor shrugged. "They used the chorobate. You don't need to waste my time asking about that. It is even described in Vitruvius's *Books on Architecture*. That is how all the aqueduct elevations were determined."

I held up my hand. "Yes, I have read that," I punctuated 'that' with my finger, "but, for this aqueduct, it does not appear the chorobate is nearly precise enough to do the job."

"Not precise enough—what are you talking about?"

"It is an easy calculation to make. Even if they had calibrated the chorobate precisely, presumably on a smooth body of water, an error of just one-half of a string width—one thirty-second of an inch—less than one millimeter—in aligning the plumb-bob strings, would bring an error of twice the required slope of the channel."

the *Aedifex*: Building the Pont du Gard

The professor exploded and stood up. "I have no more time for this. If the Americans want to send a person with advanced degrees to discuss issues of which I am most familiar, in an academic manner, then let them do so. Now, builder and your conniving assistant," Laurie grimaced, "please get out of my office." He pointed to the door.

We stood up. I took another look at the flustered professor and shook my head. I turned, grabbed Laurie's hand and left the office. In the hallway, Laurie looked up at me with a look of surprise and puzzlement.

I said, "That went well."

She shook her head. "I don't know what to say. I am sorry. I admit that I may have puffed up your background, but the professor was hesitating when I was making the appointment."

"That's quite all right. That wasn't the problem. The professor got embarrassed because he couldn't answer questions that he, with his great interest in the subject, should have—at least—asked. He lashed out at what he perceived as my weakness—being a non-academic and a constructor. What has not dawned on him, as it has now dawned on me, is that background as an engineer or constructor is helpful, if not vital, to understanding what the Romans did. You see?"

"Yes. I see, perhaps, although I don't really know what you know and how it helps. I really don't know enough about building an aqueduct."

"That's okay, Laurie. I am thankful for your extra effort to get me an appointment, even if you had to apply some misconceptions, here and there. You probably did that skillfully, as you were skillful in the translation. Thank you for that. I'll buy you a wonderful dinner. Do you know where we are going?"

"Yes, Warner, yes. I did want to get you an appointment to see the professor, and you have to remember that I am in sales. I don't directly tell people the wrong thing, but let them make their own conclusions. Let us have our wonderful dinner, and yes, I know where we are going. I have made reservations."

At dinner, Laurie, in her free moments, smiled at me without provocation, indicating, to me, meaning of which I was not aware. We didn't talk about Marseille, or dissect the meeting with the professor.

255

Instead, she said, "Warner, do you notice that we get along very well together? I suppose it is because I admire your knowledge and your ability to solve a problem—not that you are so adept with people. But, what do you admire about me? If we are experiencing a closeness, the admiration must run in two directions. What is it, Warner?"

Now I had to come up with a statement that would appease Laurie and also make sense. I thought. Could it be done? I answered. "Laurie, you have been so helpful, how could I not admire someone who has gone to so much trouble for my benefit." From her look, it was easy to figure out that my statement was not what she was seeking. "And, to my delight, I am in the company of one of the best looking, delightful, and vivacious females that France has to offer."

"Oh, Warner, that is true? I mean—you think so?"

"Of course I do. How could I be so lucky? You are an unexpected adventure. Do you mind that you are an adventure?"

"No, Warner, I do not mind. I am happy to fill that very important facet of your experience. But there is more. You will see—and, soon."

I smiled.

I looked at my watch after paying the bill. "Well, Laurie, we've managed to enjoy a very civilized, relaxed but extended dinner. It's nearly nine o'clock. Best we start driving back to Vers before the driver falls asleep." I cringed thinking about Laurie's driving, in the dark, after drinking several glasses of wine, no doubt boosting confidence in her driving skills. Perhaps *I* should sleep.

We were in a booth, Laurie seated on the same side as me. She scooted over on the bench, linked her arm through mine and inclined her head to my neck. "Warner, we will not drive in the night. I have made reservations in a hotel that you will find remarkable—ocean view, stylish, not to mention clean sheets and a willing girl."

I was speechless, and she was waiting for my assent. Two weeks ago, I had convinced myself that I would go along with her adventures, a picadillo that would be a testament to my trip. But, since I had met Lisele, I had it in mind that I would disengage from Laurie's clutches and cultivate a relationship with... her mother. Sleeping with Laurie would be 'game over.' How could I tactfully refuse?

256

"Laurie, that is very thoughtful and intriguing. A night with you would be a night to remember, I'm sure. But, I must insist that we return to Vers tonight." I knew she was going to ask, 'Why on earth?'

"Why on earth? It makes no sense. I will not take 'no' for an answer. I have made the reservations. I will lose the money, and you have no reason to be back tonight. I will be embarrassed after telling my friends." She lifted her head from my neck, slid away, and regarded me sharply.

I steeled myself. "I must insist."

She said nothing, waiting.

I got up from the booth, waited for her to exit, and we walked to the door. She walked stiffly and looked straight ahead, even when I acknowledged the waiter as we passed. This was going to be difficult.

The drive back was my personal hell. She did not speak a word and drove very fast. I tried conversation but was met with headshakes and nods—or, nothing. The atmosphere was so negative that I did not react uncomfortably to the horn-honking from other drivers, to the needle at a radical angle on the speedometer, nor the abrupt lane changes. Nevertheless, even with the speed, it seemed an eternity before she braked to a skid in my driveway. I opened the door and got out.

She looked straight ahead.

I mumbled, "Thanks," but she did not respond. I closed the car door, softly, and stepped back so she could speed away, gravel flying. I could only wonder how this difficulty would affect the rest of my stay. My guess was that I would not have the favor of either Laurie or Lisele. What a dumb ass.

CHAPTER 27

"Bernius, I have talked to Marcus." Appius was sitting at a table in Bernius's apartment. "They have directed us to continue the mapping of the Ucetia route."

Bernius, joining Appius at the table, said, "Is that a surprise? Did they tell you why—after you explained the worthiness of the western source? No, I do not think it is a surprise. I wonder if Claudius knows of the details?"

Appius, hands on the table, looked around at the clutter, maps ascatter, leftover food, empty wine jugs, clothes at the ready. "I do not think Claudius knows. Marcus got back to me in three days. They could not have talked to Claudius, lest he was in town. I think not."

Bernius gestured, hand upraised. "I am concerned about what we will report on Ucetia. As we have discovered from our tests of the chorobate, we cannot really tell if we have a slope from Ucetia to the Vardo or whether we are subject to errors. You and I might understand the difficulty, but if we were to talk about the limits of errors to the *Corporata*, we would put them to sleep. Let us say I imagine that we are before them and explain to them we cannot tell whether there is a slope downwards or whether it is flat or whether it is uphill. They will shake their heads and demand to know what we have been doing if not determining just that. I will hear a comment about drinking too much wine. How we will proceed, I am not sure."

Appius was silent for a moment then said, "I have an idea, but because I am not familiar with the math and the natural sciences, I do not know if what I have to suggest will be useful."

"I have great confidence in your ability to imagine alternate means. What are you thinking?"

Appius sat back. "It was when I was at the river bank of the Vardo, down from the bridge where the slope on the banks is very shallow. I noticed that if the river rose one inch, it crept 12 inches up the shoreline. That gives me an idea, perhaps a way to improve the accuracy of the chorobate."

Bernius scowled. "I am not following you so far, but please go on."

Appius grinned. "Here is how I would use the river bank to give us a more accurate measurement. We determined that when we used the string on the chorobate to bring it level, a small error in judging the position of the string caused a great difference. Something barely noticeable at the string caused nearly an inch of error at 100 feet."

"Yes."

"And, although we have the trough on the top of the chorobate to use if the wind is bothering the string, we have never used it."

"That is true, but...."

Appius sat forward again, looking at Bernius, "What if we created a curve in the trough, as if the bottom of the trough were similar to a shoreline. I am thinking that a very small movement of the chorobate would result in the water traveling a much longer distance on the bottom of the trough. If we were off level a small amount, we could more easily spot it in the trough. In that way, we could more accurately set the level."

Bernius said nothing, maneuvering the images in his mind. His eyes were closed. In a few moments, they blinked open. "Oh. Well, I would have to perform some mathematics, but your idea is sound. It is worthwhile to consider."

"You will do it?"

"I will do the calculations. If there is a significant advantage, we can talk further."

"Can I watch you do the math?"

"I think I need to run these thoughts, scribble diagrams on paper, remember my trigonometry, start over again several times. I would rather I get the concept right, in my head, then go through the thought process with you. I will call for you."

"I am most excited to see what you determine."

Bernius nodded. "There is one more improvement we should make—to improve our sighting. Before I left Rome, one of the architects was showing me an improvement. I had forgotten until now. At the sighting end of our chorobate, they replaced the upright spike with a flat piece of copper through which a small— very small—hole had been made. The result was that you didn't have to try to focus the near sight, far sight, and the target at 100 feet at one time. If we recalibrate the chorobate using your trough method, we should also try the improved means of sighting."

Appius said, "It seems like we should try using the small hole for sighting even if we do not modify the trough. I will get the carpenter... or perhaps the metalsmith... to fashion what you have described."

"I will get busy with the calculations."

Bernius did not take long to work out the diagrams and mathematics. That evening, he walked to the home of Appius, a sheaf of papers clutched loosely in his hand. Appius greeted him, saw the papers, and beamed with excitement.

After he had seated Bernius, brought him wine and olives, he asked, "Bernius, you are here to talk about the chorobate?"

"Yes, and drink wine and eat olives."

"Wine and olives are important, but at the moment I am more interested in the scribbles you have on your papers." Appius sat across from Bernius.

Bernius pointed at him. "You, my friend, have a very good idea. My calculations show that if we were to craft such an improvement to the chorobate, we could dramatically improve our accuracy, at least when it involves getting the chorobate level. The accuracy related to the level of the chorobate is 13 times better, using water in the sloped trough. We also have a method to improve our accuracy somewhat in sighting and generally improved our lot because of that. These improvements will both be steps toward a more precise measurement. You can be proud... well, assuming we can make it work. No, you can be proud of thinking of the method. I will now show you what I have diagrammed and calculated."

Bernius unrolled his papers and led Appius through the principles and the calculations. In the end, Appius was not able to follow the concept; he was not adept in the mathematics of trigonometry. He did, however, understand that by the use of the mathematics they were able to determine what might be expected from trying the new method. Mathematics, a magical tool, indeed.

Bernius took a sip of wine, and set the papers on the table. "Have you also imagined how you will build the device? How can such a trough be cut in the surface of the chorobate?"

Appius smiled, also taking a drink of wine. He sat back. "Yes, Bernius, I have. We will lay the chorobate on its side, on supports. We will use a line, one that does not stretch easily, and we will install a stake in the ground some distance away, at the center line of the chorobate. With the line tied to the stake, we will swing it from side to side. If the string scribes a circle that is too deep, we will move the stake back until the part of the circle scribed on the chorobate, from end to end, is just right. We will then tell the carpenter to chisel the trough so that the string just traces the bottom surface. I think that will work."

Bernius thought. "I think it will too. Shall we visit the carpenter?"

"Yes. Tomorrow"

In the carpenter shop of Tarus Lartius, Appius stood with Bernius looking at the modified chorobate. The carpenter hovered nearby, anxious to show them that he had done an excellent job shaping the trough.

Appius pointed to the line and the stake. "Show us what you were able to do."

Tarus retrieved the line; he had attached a stylus to the end. He stretched the line to take out the slack, made a small adjustment, then demonstrated that the stylus made a continual scratching noise as it lightly grazed the bottom of the curved trough when swung from one side to the other. "See," he said, "it is perfect."

Appius ran his finger along the bottom of the trough. "Indeed it is. Fine job, Tarus." He turned to Bernius. "If the trough is satisfactory, I will have the carpenter install the new sight."

Bernius pointed in the direction of the channel. "We must now calibrate the trough and the new sighting means. We will arrange for the water in the channel, again, then, using several sightings, we will set the chorobate dead level. Then we will put water in the trough, enough to wet ten foot of the bottom, let us say then scribe the limits of the water onto the trough. We will add small amounts of water incrementally and scribe the limits of each until we get to the end of the trough. In that way, we will have a range of marks that will be useful for varying amounts of water. I am anxious to see the accuracy that results. We will test the accuracy once we have done our calibrations. Repeatable level measurements should be our indication."

They performed the calibration and did the tests for repeatability. Bernius stood in the ankle-deep water, hands on hips. "Appius, I think we have advanced the field of architecture. Clearly, better accuracy was needed for our particular situation, our slight slope, but I believe that your idea will be useful for many applicatons. I also find that the new sighting means is much easier. We should also have more confidence in marking our line of sight."

Appius smiled, elated because he had made a contribution in the field to which he aspired. "Are we ready to go back to Ucetia?" He nodded toward the north.

Bernius shook his head. "I am concerned about the Ucetians. They will interpret our return as continued or increased interest. I suggest that we begin our revised measurements at the location where the route turns away from the Alzon, 2 miles below Ucetia. My thought is that any error we might accumulate to that point is in the bounds of a foot, or so. We can easily adjust that, at some time. By starting at that location perhaps we can escape the suspicious gaze of the concerned citizens."

Appius nodded. "That is good; it reminds me to ask you about the accuracy we might now expect as we re-measure?"

Bernius fished into his tunic and extracted a tablet. "Yes. Our accuracy is much improved. I will be anxious to see if we really do have a slope—and if we do, how much."

"Will we be able to use the same path? If so, we should have less to chop away."

Bernius nodded and climbed out of the channel, shaking the water from his feet. "If it turns out that the path we cut results in too great a slope, then the actual route of the aqueduct will have to be built higher on the slope; we could not follow our path. I will calculate the differences as we go along. Once we leave the hills, having arrived at the ridge, we will make an adjustment as we did before. We are still following the top of the ridge, so our prior route will be useful. Again, the moment of truth will be at the top of the canyon, at the Vardo."

Appius was imagining the next phase. Would the work for the Ucetia route be a waste, considering the better conditions of the western source? Would it, in the end, be more likely that the western route would be chosen? It would not be long before they had an answer. His mind raced to embrace the design phase; he would learn much. But, for now, they would be 'out' again. At least the weather was favorable. The time in Nemausus had renewed his energy, and he had enjoyed the time spent with Antonia. They had spent many exciting hours talking about the child that would soon be part of their lives. But, for now, he strode purposely to his home. Time to get ready to travel.

Two days later, starting at the Alzon, they worked their way along the path that had been cleared on their prior run. They used the same red-topped stakes they had established before. Because there was only new growth to clear, Pentius and Marius did not have to spend much time clearing for a sighting. They helped set up the chorobate, becoming somewhat adept at doing so, now able to quickly select required blocking under the legs. They all worked as a team, making excellent progress.

There was an additional requirement. They must now carry water for use in the chorobate's trough. Because the trough ran nearly the entire length of the chorobate, it was not required to always have the same amount of water in the trough, so losing a little by spillage was not a problem. Marius and Pentius carried the chorobate carefully to avoid spilling the water. In the beginning, after they had executed a number of handling errors, they became more careful and the amount of water to be added was minimized.

Pentius remarked to Marius, "We are the best there is in the business, you know."

On a warm afternoon, they reached the Vardo. Bernius was as anxious as Appius to determine the results of their re-work, with Pentius and Marius nearly as interested. After taking care of his horse, Bernius found his flat rock, spread the documents, and began his calculations while kneeling. Appius kept busy—cleaning the equipment, looking over the rim of the canyon in order to imagine how they would measure to the bottom; he walked by Bernius on many occasions to check progress. Soon it was time to eat their evening meal, but Bernius worked on. Appius prepared the meal, set a portion and a cup of wine at Bernius's side. Bernius grunted what was probably a 'thanks' but did not look up, grasping the wine cup via his practiced peripheral vision.

Finally, ingestion of the food and the wine were completed and so were the calculations. Bernius looked up. "It appears we have a slope. In fact, we were not that far off before, meaning that the concept of errors in *both* directions *is* happening. As before, the slope is slight; it is at least 1/8" per 100 feet or could be as much as 7/8" per 100 feet. We have measured a drop of 23 feet from Ucetia to this point, which, if accurate, would be a slope of ½ inch per 100 feet. The architects in Rome were able to make the Aqua Virgo flow at ¼ inch per 100 feet. However, if our slope is really as low as 1/8, although it is not likely, I would not be able tell you if adequate flow would result.

Appius smiled, Pentius frowned, and Marius shrugged his shoulders. Appius said, "On to the other side?"

Bernius nodded, rolling up his charts. "Yes, on to the other side, tomorrow. What is behind us has been easy. Back to chopping wood again."

Marius and Pentius raised their fists and flexed their muscles, anticipating the effort.

Bernius said, looking at the canyon, "On second thought, we should make a rough measurement to the bottom of the canyon while we are here. And, we need to make a sighting across the river—our point to start when we get over there. Let us do both tomorrow morning, before traveling to the bridge and walking back the other side."

"Maybe we can find a way down into the canyon and up the other side while we are measuring the depth," said Pentius.

"Great idea, Pentius, and perhaps you can fall enough trees to build a bridge so we can get across the river." Bernius pointed to the river below.

"Oh," Pentius laughed. "I forgot that part. I guess we will be walking down to the bridge."

Marius punched him in the shoulder. "Good thinking, Pentius. Keep those ideas coming."

They laughed, Pentius along with them.

In the morning they made a rough measurement to the bottom of the canyon—to the present river level. They did not jostle the chorobate down the steep canyon wall but used a long measuring stick, offsetting the measurement by eye as they proceeded down the wall of the canyon. They used flat spots, protruding rocks, footholds, handholds, and tree roots to work their way down. Not surprisingly, Pentius and Marius took the lead, having great fun hanging by crooked elbows on the tree roots and supporting precariously on a toehold while thrusting the measuring stick into mid air for marking by the partner below. An observer would not have thought that monkeys could have a better time of it.

Bernius smiled after Marius and Pentius and Appius scratched and pulled their way back up the canyon wall and trotted to his side with the result. He recorded the distance—a drop, roughly measured, mind you, of 154 feet. He looked at Marius and Pentius, dirty, scratched, and sweaty and said, "Good enough for now. Well done."

Pentius, with a mock quizzical look, rested his hand on Marius's shoulder and said, "Do we get extra pay for hazardous duty?"

Bernius, picking up on the play-acting, said, "No. That was your rest and recreation. Now we must make a sighting to the other side of the canyon, then carry the chorobate to the bridge and trudge back up the other side. Get moving. You took way too much time on that easy walk into the canyon."

Marius and Pentius hooted. Pentius remarked as they turned and walked toward the chorobate, "I wonder who his slaves were last year."

They used extra care to set up the chorobate to make a sighting to the other side. The shot was over 400 feet and thus subject to increased error. Bernius identified a protruding rock at the sighted elevation on the other side, but asked all in the crew to make the observation until they agreed.

They then packed the gear and prepared to walk downriver to the bridge and back upstream to the other side.

Once they had reached the opposite side of the canyon, they resumed sighting from the point they had identified. Bernius had a vague notion that they were higher than Nemausus at this location, but he had difficulty imagining by how much. He would have preferred to work to a slope of 2 inches in 100 feet, but given his result on the run from Ucetia to the canyon of 1/2 inches in 100 feet, he instead used 1 inch.

Beyond the Vardo, after hacking, cutting and sighting their way through the dense growth, they made another long shot across the deep gulch they had encountered on the prior trip. Beyond the gulch, they found that they had to establish the route following the contours of many switchbacks as they descended to the great bowl where they had executed their measured-stride exercises. At this location, though, they escaped the tangles of the thick undergrowth; the hills were relatively barren. Instead of establishing their route straight across the depression they had crossed on their prior trip, this time they were required to route the conduit around the edges, making a large sweep.

Bernius, making notes on his wax tablet, looked back to where they had encountered the switchbacks. "It seems that this stretch has its own difficult nature. We must take the aqueduct on a wild ride, using many turns and eating up a lot of distance to keep the slope from becoming too steep."

Appius, also looking up into the hills, shuffled his feet, then said, "I would guess that we are just performing an exercise. From the viewpoint of our employers, we are only spending time. The results of our work on the Ucetia run, although interesting and useful under other circumstances, will surely amount to nothing."

Bernius nodded. "I have told myself to accept and enjoy the challenge, although knowing that our work will not be used is sometimes nagging and bothersome. We can be thankful we are getting paid."

Appius, now watching Bernius perform calculations, said, "Yes, and for me, I continue to learn. All is not lost."

Bernius finished his calculations. "We have once again assumed too much slope, but not by much. I am satisfied that we could easily make adjustments. It is also apparent that we have a drop to this point from the Vardo. The burning question remaining is whether there is adequate drop from here to Nemausus. It would be possible to establish the route, from the river to here, with less slope, if we need to. But, we will determine that after we have measured all the way to Nemausus. I will keep using the same slope and make adjustments as we go."

Completing the route to Nemausus took another 3 months. At Nemausus, as they finished the work, Marius and Pentius were morose, not knowing when there might be another tree to hack. For the time being, they were able to find work with the carpenter.

Bernius preferred to do his work in Appius's courtyard where it was light and pleasant rather than struggle amongst the dim and dismal walls in his one-window apartment. He checked his notes and made additional calculations, hovering over a table making endless scratchings on his papers from one end of the chart to the other. He would shake his head, explain the results of his calculations then start over again.

the *Aedifex*: Building the Pont du Gard

After several days executing this iterative process, he sat back, beckoned Appius to his side, and sighed. "Appius, I have calculated, adjusted, calculated, and adjusted many times. I think that we have an understanding of the drop that is available to us—from Ucetia to the Vardo and the Vardo to Nemausus. Within the limits of our accuracy, and making a reasonable guess as to the errors we have accumulated, there *is* a slope. The water will flow but, as we have discussed, the slope determines the speed of the flow and we do not have much slope. Our calculations show between 30 and 50 feet of drop in the entire route. That is about 1/3 inch per 100 feet—a little more than the 1/4 inch recommend by Vitruvius."

Appius sat back and looked at Bernius. "Then the Ucetia route *could* be used?"

"I still cannot say for certain, but it is highly likely. Although there is a slope, I am not able to know whether the water would flow fast enough to transport the full flow of the spring."

"I can understand that the water will flow faster when the slope is greater. It also seems that the water would flow even if the channel was flat, having no slope. Is that right?"

Bernius nodded. "Yes, that *is* right."

"How will we know if the flow will be fast enough—short of building a structure?"

Bernius scratched his head. "Our science is not yet developed to be able to make that calculation. We have only experience on the Aqua Virgo and opinions to guide us."

"What would you do if you had to decide on this route?" Appius thought he knew, but wished there were, somehow, a better means.

"I could go to Rome or wherever Vitruvius might be at this time and talk to him. The water manager of Rome could also be consulted. He perhaps has more experience in the matter."

Appius sat back. "Will you go?"

Bernius said, "The slight slope only exists on the run from Ucetia. I think the route from the western source, having a greater drop, should transport a sufficient flow of water. We could assume that the western source will be chosen and not have to fine-tune our understanding of water-flow characteristics."

"Will we present the results to the *Corporata* and Claudius now—let them give us direction?"

Bernius shook his head. "I think I would like to provide additional information, another comparison for them to consider. I would like to give them an estimate of the cost to construct each of the routes."

"But, how could we do that? There is no design. We do not know the quantities required or costs of quarrying stone, digging trenches, or placing the materials. It seems impossible. The bridge across the Vardo...?"

Bernius reached for an unused piece of paper. "Here is what we will do. The route will consist of several different means of construction. We will devise a rough scheme for each one of these types, then estimate the cost for performing one foot of each type. Finally we will accumulate the number of feet for each means of construction, multiply the footage by the cost of one foot. This will give us the total cost. Easy, yes?"

"I think you have made it sound *too* easy. What are the different types of construction?"

"Most of either aqueduct will be constructed by first digging a trench, providing a floor, walls, a cement lining, and an arch over the conduit; over the arch, earth will be backfilled. The conduit will be buried."

Appius nodded his head. "And...?"

"Where the ground level is too low, we will need structures on which the conduit will be supported. From our map, we are now able to determine this from the existing ground and conduit elevations I have shown. Where the conduit must be above ground level, in most instances we could provide support by a series of stone arches one arch high. Occasionally, when we cross a deep canyon, we will require additional tiers.

"And the bridge over the Vardo?"

Bernius laughed. "Yes, the bridge over the Vardo is a special circumstance. It would be a magnificent structure, and our 154-foot measurement would require it to be the tallest structure the Empire has built. We will have to spend time on that estimate."

"It seems overwhelming to me. I do not think we can know how much each type of construction would cost until the design is done. Do you feel comfortable presenting these numbers to those who will decide?"

Bernius nodded. "You are right. When we determine the cost for each type of construction, we will not be determining a precise cost. However, we will arrive at a relative cost of building the trench type, or single arches, or double arches. Because we use the same costs on either structure, the comparison will be useful even though not precise—not that any estimate ever made has been precise. Those that will make the decision will be able to make a comparison between the two routes and also gain an understanding of the magnitude of the cost to provide the water."

"Is there not more to what we must do? What of clearing the forest and providing food and shelter and transportation? Our cost will not be as simple as you have described."

Bernius laughed. "Yes. There are a number of other costs we must consider. I gave you a simplified method so that you would understand the principle. Have I done that?"

"Yes. I understand the simplicity of the method. What do we do now?"

"Let us get started."

Antonia was close to delivering. One sister or another would visit daily to check her condition, each sister offering her particular brand of advice. Some of this advice was useful.

Antonia watched Appius and Bernius from her doorway, leaning for comfort against the frame. She was grateful that Appius was home at this time. If he had still been working in the woods, it would be nearly impossible to summon him home in time to be present when his child was born.

She thought ahead, imagining their life with a child. Would Appius like the child or would he treat it as another fixture of the household—perhaps an important fixture—another 'something' which he must accommodate? Antonia hoped that he would have great feelings for the child, be captured by it, long to be with... an extension of himself.

As Bernius worked in the courtyard, Appius, interested in every scratch Bernius made on the paper, nevertheless glanced up at Antonia. She looked ready... and tired. Soon they would have a child. The child would provide interest to their lives. He had seen this happen before, seen it in the families of Antonia's sisters. The babies provided endless entertainment. It was a good thing that babies had this quality, the ability to draw affection. Otherwise they would be thrown out as a nuisance... too much trouble. He wondered how he would adjust.

Bernius was calling his attention to a sketch. "This is a drawing of a typical section of the aqueduct which will be constructed by first digging a trench—the underground sections. As you can see, once the trench is dug, stone is placed on the floor. On that base, a concrete floor is laid and walls of rough-hewn stone are built. A cement lining is then applied to the walls. After the lining, the conduit is completed by building an arch on top of the walls and construction completed by backfilling natural soils and stone over the arch. From the surface of the land you will see nothing."

Appius scratched his head. "When I see the construction drawn thus, it does not seem so overwhelming. Yet, there are many operations, and it seems we must imagine the work required for each of these."

"Yes."

"You have told me that you figure the cost of constructing just one foot of the type of aqueduct section we have been talking about. I think it is very difficult to imagine just constructing one foot. It is not really done like that."

"You are right. It is not. A crew of 20 men will arrive and dig a trench that is 100 feet long, let us say, in three days. There may be difficult operations that occur in the 100 feet that do not occur with every foot. Perhaps breaking and removal of a large boulder that only occurs in one spot. Yet, in many, if not most of the 100-foot sections, some difficulty will occur. We will include such difficulties. We will add the time of all the operations and calculate requirements for an average length of one foot. That rate will include a provision for difficult operations encountered."

"But, Bernius, though it is easier to imagine what is done at the site, what about the cut stones and cement? You said a facility would have to be built to produce the cement. Is it difficult to establish a cost for one-foot worth of these materials?"

"Yes, we must account for that. The cost of a facility will be included in the cost of the cement but spread out so that cost is included in each portion. If we add up all the costs that are incrementally included in each portion, we will pay for the cost of the facility."

"When we first started talking, it seemed like it would be easier. The more we talk, the more complicated it gets."

"Do not be overwhelmed. We will approach the cost on these items one at a time. We will use our best judgment. In some instances we will be wrong. However, when we finally total all the costs, an understanding will emerge. The magnitude of the cost will suggest, or could suggest, many things—that the project is too expensive for the resultant service, that citizens will have to be taxed 200 sestertii a year over ten years, that the cost of water will be something like 20 sestertii for 100 cubic feet or, in our case, the aqueduct from Ucetia is three times the cost of one constructed from the western source. It is a worthwhile exercise, and while it is not without faults, the benefits are substantial if not vital."

Appius paused. "It is hard not to be overwhelmed. I think I will be more comfortable after I have watched you calculate the cost of a few of the activities. How about the bridges, the arcades, the huge structure spanning the Vardo?"

"Ah, yes. We must build structures to cross depressions, valleys, canyons, and the like. Of course, due to the lower ground level, the aqueduct emerges from its underground journey and 'daylights' as we call it. That is where we have to build the aboveground structures. The simplest would involve a situation where we do not have to carry the aqueduct too high above the ground—let us say up to 6 feet. No arch is required. In that situation, we will excavate a foundation and then stack rocks, held in place by mortar until we have a structure as high as the floor level of the aqueduct."

"You do not need an arch?"

"No. The reason for the arch is to reduce the amount of stone that must be quarried, shaped, transported, and installed. If you imagine an arched structure, you can understand that all the area underneath the arch did not require the stones. It is economic. Stones are very costly; you will see."

"But are the arches needed to create open space, also, like in a building?"

"Yes." Bernius displayed an arched structure with his hands. "And, for aqueducts, they allow water to pass beneath the structure. Hail the arch. For our estimate, on the arched structures other than the great bridge, we will determine the amount of footage of the aqueduct built atop a simple foundation of piled rocks, the footage of single arch structures, and the quantity of structures in deep canyons where stacked arches will be required."

271

Appius scratched his head and picked up one of the map documents. "But how will we determine how much of each will be required?"

Bernius pointed to the lines on the map showing the side view. "This heavy solid line represents the floor of the aqueduct. I have reworked our measurements and calculations to establish the slope that we will use. The irregular line running either below or above the slope represents the ground level that we have measured at 100-foot intervals. When the ground level line is above the sloped line of the aqueduct floor, it means that the conduit will be buried. If the irregular line is below the floor of the aqueduct, we will have to provide an elevated structure. From our map, we can also calculate how far below the ground or how far above the ground the aqueduct floor would be, and that will determine what kind of structure we will use."

Appius felt a surge of excitement. "This is wonderous to me. Knowing that this can be done, can be planned beforehand with some confidence, is like getting a tool that greatly simplifies our work. I did not know that such practices existed. I am excited to be able to use the tools of the art."

Bernius smiled. "It is so. I have been at the practice for a long time, so it does not seem such a marvel. But I do remember my excitement as the procedures were first demonstrated to me."

"Can you show me some of the different requirements?"

"Yes." Bernius grabbed several of the map sheets. You can see that for most of the map, the floor of the conduit, the solid line, is underneath the ground line. That means, as I stated before, that most of our aqueduct would be buried. Now, see here," he pointed, "we can see that the sloped line is only a little above the ground. If our measurements are 100 feet apart, we can gauge the length of the simple structure—that of piled rocks—as about 125 feet. But here," he pointed to another section, "we are crossing that deep canyon beyond the Vardo, and several tiers of arches will be required to span about 300 feet. And, of course, just before that, the great canyon of the Vardo will require a magnificent structure of many tiered arches."

Appius contemplated the various examples for a moment then pointed to a section. "But, here, the floor line is many feet *below* the ground line. Will we excavate an enormous trench?"

"No. You have spotted a section in which it appears our best option is to excavate a tunnel. It will save us from having to build many feet of conduit to get around this inconvenient high spot. We did follow the contours around the hill when we staked the line, but from our map I have been able to consider that a tunnel would be best, as long as the earth is not too difficult and there are no substantial water problems. Note that I also show a tunnel under the city wall at Nemausus. That also saves us some distance but will allow the conduit to pass into the city without a breach in the wall."

"The tunnels will not be difficult?"

"They are not so bad, as long as you do not lose your way." Bernius laughed.

"What do we do now?"

"For a few weeks we will be imagining how much effort each of the tasks will take. Then we will apply the effort required for each to the amount of footage involved in the various structures on the route. And, behold, we will have our estimates. This should be enjoyable. How is your imagination?"

"I cannot think that I will be able to do this" Appius shook his head, "but I am excited to learn."

CHAPTER 28

It was Antonia's time. During the night she was fitful and not able to sleep. Appius considered the activity as a symptom of late pregnancy but was unable to understand that the event was about to happen. In his mind, the birth was always a far-off thing. He understood the concept but had not yet grasped its reality.

Before morning, after moaning for hours, Antonia tapped Appius on the shoulder. "It is time. The baby is coming."

Appius turned and blinked at her. *Baby? What? Now?*

"Go get my sister, Phylandria. She has promised she will help me, but you must hurry—I think. What day is it? Our baby will be born on September 8, a Saturday. Get going."

Appius drew his tunic over his head, sat on the edge of the bed, shook his head and reached for Antonia's hand. "The baby is really coming? Are you sure?"

"Appius, go get my sister. I am sure."

Appius, after rousing Phylandria, hurried home before Phylandria could ready herself, her birth equipment, and supplies. She awoke her eldest son and instructed him to run for her sister, Polynia. Phylandria, the eldest, had been present at the birth of each of her nieces and nephews. From the five women, including her, there were thirteen children, a seemingly endless production from the sisters. She lit a lamp, picked up the bundle she had prepared for the occasion plus a few other essentials for 'who-knows-for-how-long' vigil. In the dark, she stumbled her way down the rough streets, the birth kit swaying with each step. Appius met her at the courtyard gate, but Phylandria whisked by him as if he were part of the wall and darted in to take care of Antonia.

Before twenty minutes had passed, Polynia, Juliena, Appina, and Clothia, the remaining sisters—the multitude—had burst through the gate and barred Appius from his home. He sat on a bench, in the dark, feeling that while it was true—he would be no help at all—perhaps he should be a part of the scene. One more attempt after an Antonian yell got him nowhere. He poured drinking water from a jug and again sat on the bench eventually entertained by the rising sun. A good omen, he thought. The sun has chosen to rise again this day. What would it be like with a baby? He was bewildered.

The sun had lifted well above the horizon, and Appius poured three more drinks of water before Juliena appeared in the doorway waiting until he raised his gaze from the ground. She put her hands on her hips then beckoned.

Appius looked over his shoulder, pointed to himself, then said, "Me?"

Juliena nodded and beckoned again, standing aside to indicate he should enter. He walked to the door and gazed toward the bed. The birthing area was well lit, but he could not see Antonia because the multitude was standing about. He walked to the bedside, nudging a sister or two out of the way. There was Antonia holding... something wrapped in a blanket. Antonia turned the baby for Appius to see, smiling.

Appius froze. It had happened. He looked at the sisters to verify this was reality. They nodded. He said, "Antonia, what is this?"

"It is a baby my husband; were you not expecting a child?"

Appius shook his head. "No, no, what I mean is—what is it—I mean a boy or girl?"

Antonia smiled. "Say hello to your son, Appius. What shall we call him?"

"A boy? Oh. Certainly, he must have a name. I will think."

Antonia stretched her arms offering the bundle to him. "Would you like to hold your son?"

Appius again looked at the sisters. They were looking at him expectantly, but he detected a secondary attitude of disbelief—what a dolt. Nevertheless, he extended his arms and accepted his son, handling him carefully, fixing on his eyes. "He sees me," he blurted.

"Oh, yes, yes. He sees nothing, you fool. He will not be able to see for days." The response was from Polynia, a rather saucy and sarcastic woman, often known to skewer someone for a misstatement.

But Appius was oblivious, struck into stone. He watched as the baby went back to sleep, watched his breathing, touched his face.

Finally, Phylandria reached for the baby. "The baby and Antonia must get their rest, and we have things to do. There will be much time to see your son later. But for now...." She waved a hand toward the door.

Appius sat on the bench again, oblivious to the sunlight that now warmed him. He was a different man, sitting on this bench, than he had been just a few moments ago. He was now a father. He was part of the interminable lineage that was the human race, the culture. Someone would call him 'father' as he had spoken of his father. And, 'this is my son....' He shook his head. He must tell someone. Bernius. Yes, Bernius had been his closest confident for nearly two years. He stuck his head through the doorway, saying to no one in particular, "I am going to tell Bernius."

Several looked around but gave no response. He turned and walked quickly through the courtyard.

The next few weeks were cheerful as Antonia and Appius marveled at their child. Appius was experiencing an attachment for his son that overwhelmed him, flabbergasted that he could not have anticipated this. The baby could now see, and Appius was sure that his son was eager to learn from him, gurgling over thoughts of future activities they would do together. One had to admit, the baby did have a bright-eyed stare, one that seemed to indicate that he was fascinated with what he was seeing, anxious to absorb all that his new life promised.

Antonia thrived upon this scene.

They would call the boy Sergius Pollonius, after Appius's father.

The time since Sergius's birth had not been entirely occupied with entertainment by the infant. Bernius was a regular fixture in the new parents' courtyard, not merely to participate in the baby watch. In the courtyard, it was convenient for Bernius and Appius to craft aqueducts. It was a cheery spot; Bernius was close to food and drink, and Appius need never be too far from the nursing Antonia and the baby.

At a table, shaded by an elm tree with bounteous canopy, they sat, and Bernius explained to Appius. "As we have discussed, we will now tell the *Corporata* and Claudius about the two sources we have investigated. Besides just waving our hands and describing the *flora* and *fauna* and the quality of the springs, we must present the cost to build the structures, an aid in making a decision. The estimate of both routes will help them choose one route or the other. And, they will have to grapple with the magnitude of the cost of whichever route they choose."

Appius, his chin resting in the palm of one hand, said, "I do not know what cost we will generate, but, I think the *Corporata* will recoil as if stung by a wasp. I do not know what will happen if they refuse to contribute their fortunes to construct the project."

Bernius, understanding the ways of the Empire, said, "If Claudius wants the project to be built he will have his way. Perhaps he knows the *Corporata* will not go along and has his own strategy."

"But, why," Appius shrugged, "why should Claudius be so intent on this project? Can it be that he is so moved to provide for the region or to grow the Empire?"

"That, Appius, I do not know." Bernius stood, walked to his satchel of documents and retrieved maps and fresh paper. He walked back and unceremoniously dumped them all on the table. "We will now do the estimate." He sat down. "Appius, you now enter a new phase of your architectural training. Estimating will require distending your imagination. You, or we, must imagine how this project will be built. From these thoughts, we will further imagine the effort that it will take, leading us, in a more structured exercise, to the cost. Are you ready?"

Appius brightened. "I am ready. I am anxious. To be honest, I do not understand how this can be done. If I learn from you, it will be as if I have learned magic."

Bernius smiled. "If you learn to do this well, meaning that you have a good imagination, people will think that you *can* perform magic. This will be a necessary and important tool in your bag of architectural tricks. Let us begin."

Bernius spread the Ucetia route maps and organized them so that they proceeded from one end of the aqueduct route to the other. He fished through the remaining pile of documents and extracted a sheet displaying a list. He placed the sheet in front of Appius and explained, "While you have been occupied with this baby business, I have been at labor over our work. We have already discussed that there will be varying means of construction used—underground, structures supporting the aqueduct more or less at ground level, tunnels, and structures that will support the aqueduct at various levels above the ground. I have, at great expenditure of time and effort, accumulated the distances of each type of construction. You can see on the maps where I have coded various stretches as one type of construction or another." He pointed to several examples on the map. Then, holding the list, he said, "This list identifies the quantity of each type of construction. That was the easy part. Now we must imagine our way through the construction." He fished for several other sheets upon which he had drawn sketches. They were scattered through the documents, some upside down or sideways.

While Bernius was fishing and organizing, Appius flipped through the set of maps, pausing occasionally to note the coding of the various sections. "I do not know what your code means."

Bernius, grasping the sketches, said, "See the code 'A' on the maps. Those stretches on the map correspond with this sketch I have labeled 'A,' the most common construction for this route—an underground structure. As you can see from the list, the footage of this type of construction is very large compared to the others."

Appius nodded, then picked up the 'A' sketch.

"What you are looking at is a cross-section of the completed structure—as if you removed a section of the underground aqueduct and were able to look at the end of the slice." With his finger, he traced a line, a nearly horizontal slope, drawn across the top. "This is the original ground. Of course, we must clear the forest above and remove the tree stumps." He then traced the outline of a 'U' underneath the ground line. "This is the outline of the excavation that must be performed. In our estimate—for now—forget about the stones you can see and the arch and the cement—we will calculate how much earth must be removed for this excavation. I should note that the excavation is about 18 feet deep. The earth will not be removed in one operation. Our practice is to remove the top depth of 6 feet, proceed for a distance and continue but then start removing the second depth of 6 feet for a distance, then start on the bottom 6 feet. If you were to look at the operation as it is going along, it would be staggered, or stair-stepped."

Appius scowled. "Why is it done like that?"

"Because a man can only reach—with a pick—to just a little above his head. Can you picture a crew trying to hack out the entire 18 foot height?"

"The scene does seem difficult. I can better imagine the stepped means that you have described."

the *Aedifex*: Building the Pont du Gard

"Good. When you imagine it in the way it is being done, it is easier to imagine the effort required. Now, inside the excavation, you see walls and an arch made of stones and a cement floor. Of course, we must build from the bottom up—a layer of rough stones on the bottom of the trench, a course of smaller stones on top of that, tightly packed upon which a pad of concrete is poured. Upon this layer the walls of roughly-hewn stones are built. This will be the actual floor of the conduit, the surface against which the water will flow."

"Why do you say the walls are of roughly hewn stones?"

Bernius pointed to his sketch. "Because, as my sketch shows, there is mortar between the stones. They do not have to fit precisely, one against the other. The mortar fills in between the irregular faces. Some construction involves stones more precisely placed, without mortar. Those structures are stronger but the stones take more effort to be chiseled precisely, of course."

"So, for the floors, walls, and the arch of the underground conduit, stone must be found, and stone masons must still work them to an acceptable size and shape?"

"Yes. And, as with the other materials, they must be transported and placed, again using mortar mixed from the cement that was produced at the facility."

"What of the cement for the floor and the mortar?"

"We must manufacture cement and haul it to the site. To manufacture the cement, we will build a facility—no doubt several facilities along the route. We must crush limestone to make the cement, cook it, then transport it to the site, add the small stones, water, and sand in order to make the concrete."

"This seems to be an incredible amount of work, and we are just getting started."

Appius pointed. "What is this thin wall attached to the inside of the stone walls?"

"That is the conduit liner. The conduit is lined for at least two reasons. The lining provides a means of sealing the water inside the conduit. Even though you would think the walls would prevent leakage, they do not. We know from experience. The other reason is that the water will flow easier against a smooth surface. If we were to leave the water to flow against the stone wall, it would cause much turmoil in the water and slow its flow."

"Of what is the lining made?"

Bernius sat back. "It is made of cement, but in this case of a very pure white limestone, finely ground. The mixture also contains broken and smashed terra cotta tiles. In fact, it is called 'broken tile' mortar. Of that we make the lining water resistant and smooth. If we had to construct this aqueduct with only a slight slope, this treatment would help the situation."

"Then the arch is built on top of the walls?" Appius pointed.

"Yes. The arch would not be put in place until all of the interior work was completed so that the builders do not eliminate their access. After the arch is built, some of the excavated earth is returned to cover the arch, up to the original ground level. Excess earth will be used to build a road. Do you understand how the work will progress, the sequence?"

"Yes."

"Good. So far, we have *not* been required to stress our imagination. Now we will have our chance. Imagine that we are in process of removing the top 6 feet of earth. From my sketch, how wide is the excavation for that section?"

Appius compared the depth of 18 feet with the width at the top of the excavation. "It looks like about 20 feet wide at the top, but it narrows as you go deeper to perhaps 12 feet."

"Good. How many men, working with picks could reasonably work, side by side?"

"I would say four... no more."

"Yes. Now for the difficult part: how many feet, in length, can the four men hack in one day?"

"It will depend on how hard the rock is... and on the top layer, there is usually softer earth."

"That is correct. Make an assumption; we will note what you have assumed, so if we find it to be different later, we can make a correction. What is your assumption?"

Appius squinted. "I imagine there is a 2 foot depth of softer soil on top and the rest is limestone rocks or solid limestone that we often see about. It can be hacked apart by a pick without too much difficulty."

"I have the picture. Now, how far can these men hack in one day?"

"Someone else is taking away the hacked earth?"

"Yes."

the *Aedifex*: Building the Pont du Gard

Appius looked across the courtyard. This view was not helpful, so he went to the gate and peered out. "How long are these men working in one day?"

"You are asking very good questions—the right questions. These men are working 11 hours in a day.

"I think they would hack 30 feet in one day."

Bernie smiled. "Excellent. Now, if we know the quantity of the total footage of aqueduct to be excavated, you could tell me— give me an estimate—of the days required to excavate the top 6 feet."

Appius smiled, realizing the power of the process he had stepped through. "But, we must also account for the earth to be removed from the digging area."

"Yes. It is the practice to haul the earth in buckets to the far side of an area we have cleared for the route. By that means, we will allow carts to travel alongside the aqueduct, provide space for materials to be stored, and space to work on the structure. We will clear a path 80 feet wide. I am telling you this so you will imagine what the man hauling the earth will do. Now, how many men will keep up with removing the material from behind the four men with the picks?"

Appius picked up the sketch. "Well, it seems like one man behind each man with a pick would keep up."

"I agree. You can now calculate how long it would take to hack *and* remove the earth for the top 6 feet. Now, if we go down one level, what would you imagine?"

Appius tapped the sketch. "Now they are more likely to be hacking at more rock. They do not have the easy 2 feet of dirt. There is room to work only three men, and they will not gain footage as fast."

"If it was 30 feet in a day before, how many feet will these men hack?"

"I will say 20 feet, and, although the hauling people will have farther to climb out and climb back down, I still think that three men can keep up with removal of the earth."

"Yes. Even though they are climbing farther, the hackers are going slower. Would you use the same numbers for the lowest depth?"

Appius nodded. "I think I would."

Congratulations. You can now tell me your estimate for excavating the entire underground section of our aqueduct. We

281

must now use the same method to estimate a few more activities that will be required to get the aqueduct built."

"A few more? What would those be? It seems like...."

"Off the top of my head," Bernius patted his head, "I can think of the effort required to clear an 80 foot path for most of the distance, quarrying the rock and stone, shaping the stone and hauling it from the quarry location to installation, building a plant for the manufacture of cement, quarrying the limestone for the cement, grinding it and hauling it to the installation, and then, of course, placing all these materials in the excavation. Oh, yes, I should mention the backfill. I am sure I missed something."

"Do the arches have to be temporarily supported?"

"Yes. That. You see, more will occur to us. Are you ready to go on? We are still talking about the underground section and have not considered aboveground arcades and tallest-in-the-world bridges to cross roaring rivers."

"I am ready to go along, but already my imagination is reeling."

Bernius sat back and swilled his water as if it were wine. "I know; it is a lot of work. But, think of this. The work we do estimating the operations on the Ucetia route can be applied to the western route. We will just have different footages to apply."

Appius grimaced. "I am sure that will be a breeze."

Bernice gulped the rest of his water. "Have we earned a cup of wine?"

Appius and Bernius worked at the estimates for nearly a month. Finally, Bernius said, "I think we are there. I will add administrative items, and then we can review our work."

Appius shook his head. "My mind is swimming with numbers. I will be glad to take a break from imagining for a while. I even look forward to doing chores for Antonia."

Bernius said, "Maybe I will join you."

They both laughed.

Bernius shuffled the many pages of written documents. A close view showed many lines of activities, after which one would observe calculations. A typical line entry read:

Cut Rough Stones for Buried Conduit

the *Aedifex*: Building the Pont du Gard
153,000 feet of buried conduit x 41 stones per lineal
foot = 6,273,000 stones
Cut rough stones (prox. 8" x 18" x 12") (= 1.0 ft$^{3)}$)
1 man at 44 stones per day; therefore <u>142,568</u>
mandays required
Note: rate = 0.93 mandays per lineal foot

Appius stared at a summary of activities—the results, not the calculations.   Each route was summarized, showing an accumulation of the hours for each activity and finally, a conversion to sestertii. He looked at Bernius. "The Ucetia route is a lot more costly than the western route, and you can see why. The stone required for the bridge over the Vardo is a huge cost." He scanned the summary sheet.   This was the first time he had seen it. "Bernius, there are several items I do not understand. My architectural curiosity beckons me to have you explain." He moved to Bernius who gestured for him to sit at his side. Bernius arranged the summary so both could see.

The summary appeared as so:

SUMMARY OF COSTS
UCETIA ROUTE

Quantity	Unit	Task	Mandays
155,000	feet	Final Survey with improved chorobate	564
155,000	feet	Clay pipe level operation	1,240
Underground Section			
100,000	feet	Clear path of brush/trees (80 ft)	50,000
38,000	feet	Clear path of brush	3,800
17,000	feet	No clearing required	0
153,000	feet	Excavate for underground (first 6 feet)	106,057
100,000	feet	Stump removal	33,333
153,000	feet	Second 6 feet, Exc	125,182
153,000	feet	Third 6 feet	233,673
6,273,000	stones	Gather stones for rough cutting	47,523
6,273,000	stones	Rough-cut stones, for buried section	142,568
174,250	R/T	Haul rough-cut to site and return	31,682
1,273,000	stones	Handle and place rough-cut stones	57,027
153,000	feet	Install/remove temp support for arches	16,691
3,672,000	stones	Gather rubble for aqueduct first layer	4,173
51,000	R/T	Haul first layer rubble stones	9,273
3,672,000	stones	Place first layer rubble stones	7,418
918,000	cu ft	Gather aggregates for second layer	4,173
25,500	R/T	Haul aggregates	4,636
1,836,000	cu/ft	Quarry limestone for cement	27,818
68,000	R/T	Haul limestone to grinder	6,182
1,638,000	cu ft	Grind limestone for cement	3,338
68,000	R/T	Haul cement to site	24,727

Thomas Hessler

18,360	R/t	Haul water to site	6,676
918,000	cu ft	Mix and place cement	13,909
229,500	cu ft	Quarry fine limestone for liner	3,477
8,500	R/T	Haul fine limestone to faculty	773
229,500	cuft	Grind fine limestone and add broken tile	417
8500	R/T	Haul fine limestone mix to site	3,091
229,500	cu ft	Place liner on walls (Incl mix and haul)	13,909
155,000	feet	Backfill earth and build road	169,091
155,000	feet	Clean conduit interior	564
155,000	feet	Paint conduit interior	2,818

Total Underground section   **1,153,999** mandays

the *Aedifex*: Building the Pont du Gard

Raised Structures (other than bridge at Vardo; Single and Multiple tier arch structures)

Quantity	Unit	Task	Mandays
186	each	Layout foundations	271
186	each	Excavate for foundations	2,029
1	each	Mob & Prep quarry (below for bridge)	2,88064
800	stones	Quarry stones incl to chipping yard	1,473
64,800	stones	Cut stones to finish size	1,473
3,600	R/T	Haul stones to site	655
64,800	stones	Place stones for arches	5,89
166	each	Arch temp supp (fab, inst/rem)	5,332
166	each	Extract/haul rubble to arches	8,149
329,040	cu ft	Infill arches with rubble	1,449
166	each	Build conduit walls	543
8,100	cu ft	Quarry limestone, grind, haul (liner)	265
8100	cu ft	Install liner	1,105
900	each	Quarry, haul and shape slabs	1,145
900	each	Place slabs	982
5,400	feet	Clean conduit	20
		Total Raised Structures **33,660 mandays**	

Raised foundation only—(no arches)

Quantity	Unit	Task	Mandays
10,000	feet	Layout foundations	28
10,000	feet	Excavate for foundations	5,455
10,000	feet	Quarry stones	4,545
200,000	stones	Haul stones to site	2,273
2,000,000	stones	Place stones	4,545
10,000	feet	Extract/haul rubble to arches	7,636
7,000,000	cu ft	Infill arches w/rubble	4,242
10,000	feet	Build conduit walls	3,182
10,000	feet	Quarry limestone, grind, haul (liner)	491
10,000	feet	Install liner	606
10,000	feet	Quarry, haul and shape slabs	2,121
1,667	each	Place Slabs	1,818
10,000	feet	Clean conduit	55
		Total Raised Foundation Only **36,997 mandays**	

Misc Structure

Quantity	Unit	Task	Mandays
3	each	Build diversion structures (3)	1,636
545	each	Build intake structure at springs	546
1	each	Build castellum	909
1,000	feet	Tunnel section exc	750
1,000	feet	Tunnel section build wall	636
1,000	feet	Tunnel section install liner	121
		Total Misc Structures **4,598 mandays**	

Vardo Bridge

Quantity	Unit	Task	Mandays
11	each	Layout foundations	12
19	each	Prep native rock for foundations	290
1	each	Mob/prep quarry	2,880
80,000	cu ft	Extract, haul rubble to bridge	873
80,000	cu ft	Install rubble into bridge void	1,818
50,000	each	Free stones at face ; haul to storage	200,000
50,000	each	Chisel stones to precise size	109,091
50,000	each	Transport stones to site	18,182
18	each	Harvest wood for arch supp large	353
47	each	Harvest wood for arch supp small	273
18	each	Shape wood for arch supp large	1,964
47	each	Shape wood for arch supp small	1,709
18	each	Build/remove arch supp large	1,964
47	each	Build/remove arch supports small	1,709
18	each	Remove arch supports large	393
47	each	Remove arch supports small	154
50,000	each	Install stones	40,909
900	feet	Build conduit on bridge	573
50	each	Quarry, shape, haul slabs	273
50	each	Place slabs	41
1	each	Clean conduit	23
	Total Vardo bridge	**383,547 mandays**	

All Labor (mandays)   **1,614,605**

Hour and labor cost summary	ManDays	Sest/day	Sestertii
Quarry labor	244,894	11	2,705,929
Rough cut stone labor	144,507	16.5	2,384,363
Haul (incl ox time/cost)	149,936	22	3,298,588
Finish cut stone labor	109,091	22	2,400,000
Carpenter labor	30,541	22	671,921
Mason installation labor	100,818	22,	2,217,991
Clearing	53,823	11	592,053
General labor	778,052	11	8,558,576
Technical	1,843	33	60,807
Totals (mndays, sest)	**1,614,605**		2,2890,226
Contractor Profit & Overhead			4,578,045
Subtotal Costs			27,468,271
Supervision	37,440	22	823,680
Inspection	18,720	22	411,840
Military			180,000
Administration	1,872	220	411,840

Total costs   **29,295,631 Sestertii**

Bernius sat back.   "We have generated costs for both routes. The estimate for the Ucetia route is 29 million sestertii and

the *Aedifex*: Building the Pont du Gard

for the western route is 20 million sestertii. We are now ready to go to the *Corporata* and Claudius."

CHAPTER 29

It was a warm summer day in Vers. In mid-morning the temperature was already edging towards 90 degrees. There was a slight breeze, so I used it to advantage, letting it cool me while I read and made notes while sitting on my deck. I answered the knock at my door. It was Maurice. I invited him in and beckoned him to the deck. "Would you like coffee?"

Maurice seemed to be bristling with anticipation. "Yes," he said, "*Americano*, if you please."

I prepared two *café Americano* from the waiting pot in the kitchen and returned with them to the deck. I saw Maurice watching my moves as if he were scoring a gymnastic stunt. "Here you are."

He sipped, looked up then asked, "I am interested in hearing what you learned from the professor."

Ha! I wasn't fooled for a minute. He had already heard, but from Laurie's skewed prism. Nevertheless, it would be good to air my viewpoint of the session. I pretended that he hadn't heard anything. "The professor was useful on several questions that I had. Thank you for suggesting that I talk to him."

Maurice squirmed. He knew he was going to have to exert more effort to dig out the truly useful information. "You are welcome. I am happy that the professor was helpful. He is very knowledgeable about the aqueduct—yes?" Now, Maurice was pretending and goading.

"In truth, Maurice, he did provide useful information about the timing—about the time frame in which the aqueduct was built—much later than is stated, as I had suspected. He is submitting a paper, actually."

"Oh? That's very interesting. Did he help you on other questions? I know we discussed measurement of level and...."

I would now be telling him about the part of the session in which the professor came up short. Maurice knew this of course. "Yes, Maurice, I asked about level, about the route of the aqueduct and about inscriptions and about fragments of clay pipe—all mysteries to me. It seems the professor has not considered these questions. He also didn't think that the opinions of a constructor were of value in determining how the aqueduct was built. I think he only talks to academics. I won't say that he threw us out of the office, but nearly so."

Maurice's eyes widened. "Oh, my goodness! What did Laurie think? She must have been flabbergasted—even Laurie."

I was impressed with Maurice's great job of acting, however I answered as if the comment were routine. "She was a bit taken aback. However, I took her to dinner, and after a few glasses of wine, both of us were able to take a more tranquil view of the session."

"After the wine, how did she handle the auto on the return drive? I know that you are... terrified... of her driving, even without wine."

We were now arriving at the prime element of his interest in the conversation, the actual reason for his visit, I presumed. "The drive home was... uneventful. The wine seemed not to have improved nor hindered Laurie's maneuvering skills. I arrived without incident. Perhaps the wine dulled my sensation for fear."

Maurice was momentarily flummoxed. It was clear that he wasn't sure how to continue the conversation. "But... you drove home that night?"

"Yes." Perhaps I should have explained rather than make him reveal his sources.

"Pardon me, but I have heard from Laurie's mother, Lisele, that you spent the night with Laurie, at the Hotel Belle View—in Marseille." Maurice set down his coffee.

Maurice seemed oblivious to having revealed his subterfuge. "Maurice, it is not true." It was incredible—the story he had heard... others in the village, too, I imagined.

Maurice was dumbfounded. "But... I'm sure that Laurie has told her mother... her mother would not.... "

"Maurice, it didn't happen, no matter what Laurie has said. She left me at my door at eleven... in the evening." I did my best at a level stare.

"*Oui*?"

"*Oui*."

"I am puzzled. I don't know what to do."

" I know you are in a predicament here, but you may find out for yourself. Perhaps you could call the Hotel Belle View and check with them."

"Would I find out that there was a cancellation?"

289

"Perhaps, or maybe a no-show as we Americans say."

Maurice was looking down. "I don't need to call them, Warner. I believe you. I think I know what has happened."

I didn't challenge him to explain. I nodded. "I don't think I will do anything or say anything, Maurice. I regret that Lisele thinks that Laurie and I have spent the night. I'm sure she will have nothing to do with me."

Maurice nodded. His mission to interrogate me had not turned out to be the mirthful experience he had presumed. He looked up and smiled. "Warner, my guess is that Laurie is upset. I'll just see how events develop from this point. If I understand, you will not be 'seeing' Laurie from now on. This fact will be perplexing to our village folk."

I wondered how many in the village were waiting for Maurice's report and what he would say. "Yes, perhaps the village loves a mystery. I will be watching to catch their expressions as I encounter them in town." Their expressions might depend on what Maurice would now say. I imagined that he was considering that very thought.

"Yes, well, you will now walk about in a shroud of mystery. Not a bad aura, I would say, but, now, with regard to the aqueduct, you will be trying to investigate the mysteries that the professor was not able to solve. If you have lost your interpreter, I will be happy to volunteer, although I am not nearly as good looking as Mademoiselle Laurie."

"You're not so bad, Maurice. I'd be seen anywhere with you." I laughed. "And, I will surely have use of your offer."

He tipped his coffee cup toward me in salute. I wondered what he would say to Lisele.

I busied myself with matters of the aqueduct, the questions I had asked of the professor—the ones he couldn't answer. I had already done my calculations on the chorobate, and I still didn't understand how it was able to provide the accuracy needed for the Nimes aqueduct. I used many sheets of paper diagramming its use over differing terrain, calculating possible accumulations of errors, wondering whether the architects would have known about the accuracy and the errors. If they had, what did they do about it? I set that mystery aside. Perhaps my subconscious would work on an answer.

the *Aedifex*: Building the Pont du Gard

I then directed my focus to the *routing* of the aqueduct. In my travels I had crossed the Gard upstream, along the highway from Uzes to Nimes, and downstream of the Pont du Gard on the road near Roumelins. In both instances, the terrain near those locations would have provided easier crossing either because of a narrower canyon—upstream—or one that was not so high—downstream. I supposed that the route had depended on being at the right elevation with respect to elevation drop required at a given distance along the path. But, I remained puzzled as to why or how they chose the route that they did. After the aqueduct encountered Sernhac, though, it was fairly obvious that the route followed the hill topography to Nimes: not a puzzle.

I considered the routing from the source at the Eure Fountaine to Sernhac. I drove again to the Eure Fountaine valley and walked the aqueduct or its traces, downstream. You could not always see the aqueduct, but you could follow its route noting that the Romans had cut into the rock slope on the east side of the Alzon. This cut-rock face, on the uphill side of the slope, had braced one wall of the aqueduct structure, eliminating the need to dig a trench; it appeared that the Romans used this method to advantage where they could. The floor of the aqueduct was above the level of the Alzon, about 6 feet. My thought was that they needed to stay higher, both to maintain the gradual slope required and to keep well above the Alzon in flood stage. Otherwise, the Alzon could contaminate the waters of the aqueduct. This made me wonder if they had to build additional structure to protect the springs for the same reason. I didn't see any evidence of that.

The topo maps showed that a ridge followed the east side of the Alzon. On the far side of that ridge were hills that the aqueduct could follow, creating a gentle means of allowing elevation drop as the route followed the contours of the hills. I knew that the aqueduct actually did follow those hills, but I was trying to think through the situation as the Romans had. The aqueduct would need to cross the ridge to arrive at the hills. If the aqueduct went too far down the Alzon, it would have to backtrack to catch the hill contours at the right elevation. The builders needed to cut over at the earliest possibility to minimize the travel. Perhaps even a tunnel would have been justified.

As I walked along the aqueduct south from Eure Fountaine when following the traces of the aqueduct, I had to cross private property. On several instances I encountered the owners. They forgave my trespasses, but were rather curious as to my mission. I took a while to explain, elaborating on my stay in France for purposes of aqueduct sleuthing and commenting on the wonderful crop of tomatoes or onions or horses that the particular farmer was cultivating. Understand that we were conversing in half poor-French and half poor-English. Nevertheless, with hand waving and common words, we were able to achieve some understanding of what we were trying to say. All, after I explained, were *tres* helpful in showing me what ancient traces remained on their property, proudly displaying their 2000-year-old personal artifacts.

After nearly two miles of walking, I finally came to a location where it appeared the Roman architects could have made the run out of the river canyon. It was a location where the ridge had worn more rapidly. I supposed it looked similar in Roman times. Weathering of these rocks takes millions of years, doesn't it?

I walked around the end of the ridge. Even though they could now bypass the ridge, the builders were required to dig a deep trench to avoid going uphill. The excavation was still visible, and it looked like a considerable amount of work was performed However, it had to be done or else chase the Alzon River canyon for another mile, then backtrack to the hills. Building aqueducts is tough enough without having to build 2 extra miles. They were probably pleased that they could bypass the ridge with only about three months of work, using hand tools, of course. The requirement made it clear that there was very little that was done easily on this project.

From the point that the aqueduct joined the hill contours, I was less interested. It was clear what they had to do. The aqueduct continued for 6 miles until it reached Vers. At that point, the determined builders had to pull tricks from the engineer's hat. I would look at that part of the route later.

After following the aqueduct beyond the ridge, I retraced my steps to my Renault, parked at the Eure Valley. I could have walked to a road rather than through the farmers' property, but the aqueduct route was actually shorter, and I thought that I might see something that I had missed while walking downstream. On the way back, I re-encountered two of the farmers and told them what I had discovered. The farmers were interested in my reasoning and discovery, but of course, when revealed, they claimed to be aware of it all along. I bid them a cheerful goodbye and promised to return when I'd dug up more information (not literally).

I drove to Vers, parked at my house, made a lunch of tomatoes, cheese and basil, refilled my water bottles, changed topo maps, sharpened a few pencils, put on sun-block, and continued my quest. For this episode, I would not need my car. From the springs in Vers, I trudged up *Chemin des Crozes* then *Chemin des Vistiges Romains,* continuing when the way became a path rather than a street. I finally encountered the remains of the aqueduct as it crossed the path—or as the path crossed *it.* The aqueduct was there first. At this point, the aqueduct is at least partially embedded in the ground rather than being supported above ground by arches. I had discovered that over ninety percent of the aqueduct had been underground, the aqueduct structure built in the trench and then buried. Where some of the walls remain, you can see the conduit lining, red because of the rose-quartz sand used for the cement. At this location, the path turns and heads in the general downstream direction of the aqueduct; however, the aqueduct was buried through this stretch, and you don't see much of it. But, there was very interesting evidence of wild boars rooting for truffles. Do wild boars root for people? In one of the Vers cafes, I'd seen a picture of a wild boar that had been shot. It was large enough to fill the bed of a pickup truck. Yes, aqueduct strolling can be dangerous to your health, I supposed. I kept turning around to see if stealthy porcine pursuit might be in progress.

I made it safely through the truffle patch and lifted my gaze to the thick brush and trees covering the landscape—what the French call the *garrigues*, or 'wild area.' The growth here is very thick. I tried to imagine the Roman engineers, frustrated by the brush and trees while working to establish 'elevation.' There wasn't a twenty-foot clear sight—a surveyor's nightmare. As I was peering through the brush, I spotted an arch, ghostly, hidden from view on the path at this point, unless you were taking a hard look. I took a deep breath, adjusted the baseball cap on my head to dim the reflections, stood and gazed for a reverent moment. I decided "ghostly" was a good description of my impression. The structure was a vestige of the past and appeared to me unexpectedly. I was impressed. While the Pont du Gard is a standout, swarming with people, this structure remained, remote and obscure, out of place in the forest, speaking as much to the connection with the past as did the great structure.

I walked on. Soon the path led me to a series of five arches crossing the depression. Without realizing it, I had descended about ten feet as I wallowed through the truffle patch. The aqueduct, of course, had to accommodate this change to its earthly grasp. The conduit was now supported by the series of arched structures in the depression it now crossed. At one point the floor of the aqueduct channel was 20 feet above the ground level. I clambered on top the structure, of course, finding toeholds in the rubble and displaced masonry. On top, I looked forward and back, imagining the continuous structure that existed rather than the intermittent remains that survived. Imagine just the hauling of the rock required. That thought alone was staggering.

I clambered down from the top of the arches and continued along the path. After a while, the ground level rose and the aqueduct was, once again, embedded. Near this point, it turned and made a run in the general direction of the Pont du Gard. In doing so, the route crossed the highway, and I presumed that there had been an arched structure there, as the highway had been constructed in a gully much lower than the bluff where I stood, the same level as the floor of the aqueduct.

I crossed the highway, falling as I made my way down from the bluff. I skinned my elbows trying to abate my slide and had to take time out for first-echelon repairs. I then scrambled up the bank on the other side and continued on the path paralleling the aqueduct. There were several abrupt turns, evidenced by structures that accommodated the sideways thrust of the water and also served as a chamber to enter the conduit for the purposes of inspection and maintenance. I understood that these chambers also served as a safety valve. If a section of conduit becomes plugged downstream, the force of the water would blow the stone slabs off the top of the chambers, allowing the water to escape rather than wreck the conduit.

Continuing, the natural ground level once again sagged. I ran into more arched structures, a series of twenty-eight arches, called arcades, then on to another eight. I noticed that to either side of the routing, the ground sloped downward. I was on a ridge. The aqueduct, after leaving Vers, was aligned to run atop the ridge until it intercepted the Gard River. In doing so, the builders were able to minimize the height of the structures they must build to maintain the height of the conduit. The ridge continued to the vicinity of the river Gard, thus dictating the crossing point. I had discovered the reason for the routing and in doing so was experiencing a moment of epiphany, an illumination, something that I had reasoned, investigated and discovered. I smiled to myself. But, I realized that crossing the Gard at this point only resolved the requirement upstream of the Pont du Gard. What if, after crossing the Gard, they had encountered a series of impassable hills? Of course they didn't, but did they know that before?

Based on my prior walk on the downstream side of the Pont du Gard, I was aware that the aqueduct followed the contours of the hills descending across the deep Combe Roussiere canyon, maneuvered through a series of sharp hairpin turns above Remoulins, managed a severe detour around the hillside to follow the contours, then headed in the general direction of Sernhac. How fortunate that the hills were arranged thus, after the Pont du Gard, notwithstanding that they were not easily adaptable to the construction of great waterways. It did all work out, but then it had to. But, I realized, I was able to determine what they did from following the remains. The Roman engineers had to devise the best route from an array of alternatives. I could imagine their explanation—"Yes, we have to create a route through the persistent canyons, after the bridge, routing the aqueduct 6 miles to achieve 2, but we are able to run across the ridge using a minimum of structures." I could imagine the complex process that they went through, calculating the cost and determining the resources available for each alternative. I was overwhelmed.

Overwhelmed as I was, I retraced my steps and returned to Vers and my home, then found my way to the refrigerator and a cold beer. On my deck, I settled in my chair, relishing the 'discovery' I had made, enhanced by the refreshment of the cold brew. Life is good.

As I was basking in appreciation of the good life, my rosy outlook accommodated by the beer, I was able to imagine that other aspects of my life were simultaneously rosy—my possible relationship with Lisele, for example. She seemed to be a reasonable woman; she would believe my story about the night—or the lack of a night—with Laurie. What could I lose? I gave her a call.

"*Oui*?" In France, the answerer (in this case, Lisele) says 'oui.'

To discourage further conversation in French, the caller, knowing only a spare number of French words (in this case, me) says 'hello.' In fact, I said, "Hello, this is Warner."

A silence prevailed. Then, "Oh yes... Warner."

Suddenly, the glow I had been experiencing evaporated. Nevertheless, I plowed on. "Hi, Lisele. I'm not sure why I called, but I thought that I should."

More silence. This was not going well. She then said, "And why did you think that you should?"

I *should* have given my wording some thought before I called. Exactly what *was* my reason for calling? I could blurt that I understood that the village was of the opinion that I had spent the night with her daughter—and it wasn't true. Instead, I said, awkwardly, "Maurice was recently here. He discussed my trip to Marseille with Laurie. I'm wondering if he, by any chance, has talked to you—after the conversation with me—that is?" I was not displeased, having artfully escaped a more brutal discussion involving 'spending the night with....'

Lisele responded promptly, this time. "No, he has not."

I had to consider that her answer might not be accurate—more that she did not want to discuss the topic with me. "Well then, the purpose for my call has become clear. I would like to take you to dinner, to discuss—rather—to tell you what I have told Maurice."

"I'm sorry, I'm busy that night." There was finality in her tone. "And, to get to the point of your call, I'm guessing, Laurie was at my house, using my phone, in my presence, to arrange for the hotel room in Marseille—the Belle View, as I remember."

"But, Lisele, we never went there. We did not stay overnight."

"So you say. Is there anything else, Warner?"

I had the feeling that my bleatings would not be viewed with cold, hard logic. "No, Lisele, I thought that I should try. I won't bother you anymore. I wish you a good day."

"Thank you. Good day, Monsieur."

the *Aedifex*: Building the Pont du Gard

Hmmm. I held the telephone in my hands looking at it as if the instrument were responsible. From 'glow' to 'blue funk' in less than two minutes. Yes, that was quick. I regretted the outcome, but I would have had this call on my 'to do' list, nagging me until I had made the effort. That thought actually boosted my outlook. Perhaps I would keep busy on matters aqueduct. The second beer also helped.

CHAPTER 30

It was two weeks before Claudius could make arrangements to travel to Nemausus. Nemus accommodated Claudius at his home, praising Claudius in a political sense for activities he had promoted while sharing the title and responsibilities of *Imperator* with Caligua. In private conversation, Nemus asked Claudius his opinion about Caligua, about the character of the person who was now singular *Imperator* of the Roman Empire.

Claudius considered carefully before he answered. "Caligua asked that I be *co-imperator*, a responsibility I had not expected and especially not expected Caligua to offer. I do not know why he did this. The public statement does not tell the story. In my own thoughts, although Caligua is a... an impulsive person. I feel that he may have at first been uneasy in managing the reins of the total Empire. I was inexperienced in doing so myself, so I would not be considered able to provide the needed skills. However, he had someone else to burden with criticism, should such come about. After a year of trying on the *imperator*'s clothes, he became convinced he could rule solely... and he *wanted* to rule solely. Now I am proconsul to Gaul."

"Yes," Nemus said, "but what do you think about the man, the *nature* of the man, Caligua?"

Claudius had hoped that his prior answer had deflected the original question about character—had put the issue to rest, a tactic he had observed and developed in the political arena of Rome. He paused again before he answered. "Caligua is aggressive. Whether that is good for the Empire is debatable. As with many *imperators*, it is difficult to tell if his aspirations for the Empire are conflicted with his own aspirations. In his actions, there are clearly both."

"But, Tiberius Claudius," Nemus leaned forward from his seat on the couch, "we often hear that with Caligua it is more than aspiration. We hear that his actions are part madness. Is that true?"

"Nemus, that I do not know... but... sometimes he does give that impression as when he had his troops gather seashells after they refused to board ships on the attempt to invade Britain."

Nemus knew he would get nothing more from Claudius on that question. He pointed to the peristyle deck. "We meet tomorrow at midday to discuss the aqueduct. I think you will find that the team we have employed has done an excellent job in assessing two alternate sources and routes. They have even prepared an estimate of costs. You should find it quite interesting."

The *Corporata*—Nemus, Julius, Marcus, Titus and Aulus—met, dined, and wined with Claudius before Appius and Bernius arrived. Nemus had the remains of the meal removed from the portico before the duo arrived but did offer them wine, as wine would continue to be present for the more titled guests. Claudius made a strong show of greeting Bernius and Appius, passing on the remark that he understood that they had done excellent work.

Bernius, selected as the anointed architect by Claudius, made the presentation. Would this group understand or appreciate what he was saying?

He walked to Appius, who held an impressive array of charts, calculations, summaries, and sketches, and selected a large sketch, recently made, showing the region, its landmarks, and displaying heavy marking—the routes of the two aqueducts.

Bernius beckoned Appius to display the sketch. They walked to a table in front of the *Corporata* and Claudius. Bernius addressed the regal assembly, first taking a sip of wine, looking at the cup and smiling in admiration of the selection, a tasteful benefit of substantial means. "You were advised in our prior meeting, nearly one year ago, that two sources had been found and investigated—one near the village of Ucetia and the other to the west of Nemausus, near no village of note. We investigated further and found both sources to be of good quality and not subject to contamination by runoff from rainfall or even *heavy* rainfall. At that time, we did not know if it was possible to route the water to Nemausus nor even if the springs were higher than Nemausus. Our time since that meeting has been used to answer those questions."

Bernius instructed Appius to hold the sketch so that all could see. "The route from Ucetia was investigated and chosen...

perhaps this is the only route possible from this source... to take advantage of the natural topography. But, as you can see, it requires a distance of 30 miles to avoid hills, mountains, extensive valleys, and impossible fords. The straight-line distance from Ucetia to Nemausus is only 12 miles. However, the Ucetia route has only a small elevation difference between the spring and Nemausus. We had difficulty ensuring that it did, indeed, slope downward toward Nemausus. Also difficult is the crossing of the Vardo river canyon. To cross will require a magnificent structure, arches with many tiers, a structure taller than any structure the Empire has built."

Titus set down his wine glass; it was thus easier to make expressive gestures. "We understand that the method of measuring the elevation was so inaccurate that you could not tell that the slope of the route *was* downward." He intended that his statement be met with a reply. He looked at the other *Corporata*, then at Claudius.

Bernius nodded. "When we surveyed the route from Ucetia to the Vardo, we discovered that the drop was only slight... by our measurement. It is so. We could not be certain that our method would be of sufficient accuracy to accommodate such a small measurement. But," he nodded to Appius, "with ingenuity from my associate architect and by calculation, we were able to report that there *is* a slope. Of that we have some confidence."

Titus bristled. "I do not trust your method or your calculations."

Bernius looked at him expectantly, by way of inquiring whether Titus had more to say. Titus just shook his head. Bernius knew he could challenge Titus's assertions but nevertheless continued. "Yes, the slope is slight. That is the nature of the Ucetia route.

"Let me tell you about the western route. The route for the western source is somewhat shorter than the 30 miles for Ucetia. Also, there is no Vardo to cross, and there is a *substantial* slope. We have determined that there will be several tunnels to construct, but that is the nature of aqueducts. When we compare the two routes on the basis I have been describing, the western route is favorable. However, to assist you in making your decision, we have also estimated the costs of constructing each. Understand we did so without the benefit of a complete design. However, the costs are representative of the work that must be undertaken and give a picture of the relative costs between the two routes. The western route is estimated at 20 million sestertii while the Ucetia route is 29 million sestertii.

The *Corporata* were stunned. Although their fondest dream involved evaporation of the project, the magnitude of their presumed commitment numbed them.

Claudius spoke. "You say that the Ucetia route is only of slight slope. Is it sufficient to transport the water to Nemausus?"

Bernius scratched his shoulder and took another sip of wine before answering. "You are familiar with Aqua Virgo, supplying substantial water to Rome, built by the magnificent Agrippa?"

"Yes."

"Aqua Virgo has a slope as slight as the Ucetia route, although the Ucetia route is somewhat longer."

Claudius shrugged. "Then the Ucetia route could work."

Bernius was careful. "Yes, it... *should* work."

Nemus had recovered from the shock upon hearing the staggering costs of the projects. "Bernius, even if the less expensive western route was chosen, it appears to be of substantial cost, enough so to overwhelm," he looked at Claudius, "the ability of our local resources."

Claudius addressed him. "I am sure you mean that you are concerned that you could not fund the project. Let me say that the costs will be spread over a number of years. If that lower rate is still burdensome, then the Empire is able to assist in funding the project over a longer period of time."

"But," Titus said, "how can we even be assured that revenues we receive from the water will be sufficient to enable return payment to the Empire, notwithstanding that we might profit from its existence."

Several of the *Corporata* nodded.

Claudius smirked, "You should not worry about that. The building of the aqueduct will attract many people to the region... the builders and their families. The town will prosper. The Empire will prosper. You will prosper. Have you no vision?"

Titus, not altogether comfortable with challenging the proconsul, said, "But, your Excellency, this is an enormous commitment for us. We will have to expend many sestertii before a drop of water reaches Nemausus. It is fearful."

Claudius gave a measured look to Titus then splayed his hands. "It is like most investments. You must take a risk to reap the rewards. It seems like you have no stomach for that... a bunch of fat cats?"

Nemus was careful but knew he must ask the question they all harbored. "Claudius, if the *Corporata* felt like the burden was too great for us to shoulder, what then?"

Claudius took a deep breath. "The Empire would build the project. The Empire would own the project and receive revenues for the sale of water. The Empire would benefit from increased taxes on the increased population. The *Corporata* would continue to survive, if it could, on the system you now own and now control."

The *Corporata* was silent but not surprised by the statement. Nemus, looking at each of the other *Corporata* in turn, said, "The *Corporata*... cannot say at this time that we could finance the project. If we cannot commit at this time, then it would seem that the Empire, as represented by you, Claudius, would make the decision as to the route to be chosen. If you agree with that, which route would you choose?"

Claudius looked down, then stood, addressing the *Corporata*. "I do agree that if the *Corporata* will not commit, I will make the decision." He looked at Bernius and Appius. "The structure that will be needed to cross the Vardo will be substantial. How high?"

Bernius answered. "The height will be 155 feet. I estimate that the width of the canyon is 900 feet."

Claudius, while standing, looked beyond the decking, stretched his shoulders. "And what nature of structure will it be."

Bernius shrugged. "We have not done the design, but it is likely it will be at least three tiers of arches, a magnificent but costly structure."

Claudius gazed at the sky for a moment, turned and said, "We will build the Ucetia route."

Silence prevailed until it became stagnant. The *Corporata*, Appius and Bernius were all shocked. Nemus, finally reasoned that someone had to ask, said, "But, Claudius, your Excellency, at greater cost and taking on greater risk—the slope, the bridge at the Vardo?"

Claudius turned and swept the *Corporata* with a stern look. "I know you have difficulty understanding, but there are political

302

reasons. I could expect difficulty in dealing with magistrates overseeing the western area. I would not like to build an aqueduct that takes water from there and distribute it to Nemausus. The best situation is to bring the water from Ucetia, from within a region that I control."

Appius, eyes wide in surprise, turned to Bernius. Bernius indicated a like response. The *Corporata* looked at each other, then all of them focused on Nemus, who nodded to them.

Nemus stood, addressing Claudius. "Claudius, your Excellency, as much as we would like to participate in the new aqueduct, we think that the resources required would be far beyond our capabilities. I regret—and I speak for the *Corporata*—that we must leave the execution of this matter in your good hands." He sat down. The remainder of the *Corporata* were looking at the floor.

Claudius, still standing, put hands on hips. "I see. You would excuse yourself from the project, a responsibility one would expect would be undertaken from the men who have benefited from the existing water distribution, a project which, if one had foresight, would be the backbone of your Roman town for years... centuries... to come. Yet, you have not heard the nature of the arrangements which I have said could be made... to assist you... by the Empire. I can only conclude that you are *not* men of vision and would rather stand mired in the muck of stagnation." He paced in front of the table, in front of Appius and Bernius, shifting his gaze in their direction on one of his passes.

He addressed the *Corporata*. "I fear you may have made your decision too quickly. I will not accept the response. I will remain in Nemausus for two more days, and on the second day I will listen to either the affirmation of your prior statement or reconsideration, stating a forthright objective to find a means of participating in the project. Do you have any questions?"

Nemus wisely probed the circumstance. "Claudius, you have mentioned the offer to have the Empire assist in the resources—the financing. For us to consider such, it would be useful for us to understand the nature of a possible agreement. If, for instance, the *Corporata* could not make payments required as the project is being constructed, my thought is that the Empire would make those payments and that the amount of sestertii the *Corporata* owed the Empire would be paid over a substantial number of years. Is that your meaning?"

Claudius, still pacing with his chronic limp, stopped and addressed them. "I would expect the *Corporata* to make substantial payments during the progress of the construction. The Empire would finance the remainder. The *Corporata* would then return the payments of the Empire, from funds generated from water sales, over a period of, let us say, ten years. That should be sufficient. Does that answer your question?"

Nemus nodded, then shook his head. "And if the *Corporata* was unable to make progress payments of the amount stipulated or unable to make the repayments, then.... "

"Ownership of the facility would revert to the Empire. And, the existing works, those existing now, would be subject to seizure by the Empire as partial payment of the debt."

Nemus looked at the other members of the *Corporata*. "I see. I believe we have the information we need. We will respond two days hence."

Claudius nodded, turned to Appius and Bernius and, pointing to the maps, asked questions until the *Corporata* had abandoned the room. He nodded in the direction of their departure. "They are fools if they do not become willing partners with the Empire. I hope they know that." He addressed Bernius. "Regardless, I would like you to start on the design. I know the process will be lengthy, so it is best we begin and accomplish as much as possible while I remain proconsul for the region. I would like you, Bernius, to lead the design effort, but I know you will need assistance. I will recruit capable designers from Rome and arrange for them to reside here. Appius, of course I would like you to be involved in the design, and I would say," he looked at Bernius, "if there is other talent in the area that could be used in this effort, you should utilize them. Of all this, I will guarantee that payments will be made—the *Corporata* or the Empire."

Bernius looked at Appius and nodded.

Claudius continued. "Now, what are the immediate tasks you will undertake?"

Bernius took a deep breath. "From my experience, we should determine the project features that will take the longest time to design—and presumably to construct. We will begin their design. We must establish a more precise route so that we can be certain of the nature of the structures at each location of the route and so that we may possibly begin clearing for the route."

304

the *Aedifex*: Building the Pont du Gard

Appius was thinking about the villagers, the Ucetians, but he kept silent. Would Claudius be able to solve that problem—if Ucetia was in his region? He looked at Claudius.

Claudius nodded. "What you say is reasonable. I assume the structure over the Vardo will require the longest time frame. But, in the next two days, consider the resources that you will soon need, and advise me before I leave. Has the *Corporata* made payments to you to this time?"

Both nodded.

"Good. We shall find out from what source your next payments will come." Claudius turned and walked to the railing at the edge of the deck.

The members of the *Corporata* were in an ill mood. Nemus had assembled them, once again, making sure they had ample wine before leading them to serious discussion. The afternoon was otherwise relaxing. The temperature was warm, and a gentle breeze wafted in and out of the portico. The men appeared relaxed on the lounges on the deck belying the undercurrent mood.

Finally, Nemus cleared his throat and looked at the others. "We have had a day to consider what Claudius has suggested. Several of you have talked amongst yourselves. What have you to say?"

Marcus shrugged. "Claudius—our dear Claudius—was clear." He looked into the house making sure that Nemus's regal guest had not overheard. "We will incur the wrath of the Empire if we do not participate. The Empire might bring in the military to execute the project. Their line of supervision will be indifferent as to what is required to execute the work and what is required of Nemausus citizens and... leaders. I believe we must agree to participate, or at least... " he looked into the house again, "appear to cooperate."

Titus shifted quickly from appearing relaxed to appearing to be livid. "You cannot be serious. We will contribute to the funding of this project, possibly for several years, then fail at being able to continue. The sestertii we have paid will be lost as the Empire takes control and forgets and dismisses our participation. We might as well stop the pain now and accept the consequences. Perhaps we can save what we would have contributed, save enough to maintain our... lifestyle."

Nemus scowled. "But, Titus, did you not suggest that we should stay in, thinking that the project might somehow vanish? You suggested that we would somehow not be required to consider the very heavy funding that would eventually be required, that the Empire and *imperators*, especially the current one, being chaotic and fickle might find other interests? Is that not what you have argued, successfully, I say, in the past? Why is the situation, not now, reasonable?"

Julius nodded and looked at Titus. "Yes, Titus, we still have a time frame, perhaps two years of design, in which the costs will be small compared to the cost of the actual construction. Perhaps we... you... should consider that your original thought had merit, that we be patient, knowing that it is possible that the Empire may balk at spending... or at least guaranteeing funding of... 29 million sestertii."

Titus, fighting internal demons and overwrought by financial problems, said, "I was willing to participate in the funding of a few people, a few horses. Now, a force of designers, no doubt to be bolstered in the time hence, will keep eating into the revenues that we are presently able to spend on our own accord. Now, you would have us risk more of our sestertii. I say no."

Nemus took a deep breath and looked at Titus, speaking softly. "Titus, our partner, would it be best for you and for the *Corporata*, if we were to buy out your interests? In that way, you will have funds to pay off any debts you might have accumulated, and you would not have to risk the ownership that you now enjoy."

Titus shook his head. "No, I do not want to trade the sestertii that regularly come my way for a pile that would surely be absorbed by my creditors. I would certainly be on hard times. I must stay in."

"Then," Nemus said, lingering his gaze on Titus but then including the others, "if I can speak for the rest of us, we must find a way to participate, understanding that you object to our action."

Titus folded his arms, glared, but said nothing.

Quintius, not often heard to mutter an opinion but having a calculating mind, said, "Claudius has suggested an arrangement—that we pay some costs as the project progresses; the Empire will pay the remainder. We will return the funds to the Empire in ten years. What if we suggest a limit to our payments during progress, a limit that we find comfortable, then suggest a repayment period of a longer time? After all, Claudius said that the project should be viable for... centuries."

Julius nodded. "In that way we will not appear to have shut the door. If Claudius rejects the arrangement, we can argue that we tried to participate to the extent of our resources."

Marcus added, "For what good that would do."

Julius acknowledged with a shrug. "To that I agree."

Nemus took a long sip of wine from a cup made of glass, the first to appear in the region. He held it so the sun shown through, a gaudy display of light. "I think Quintius—and Julius—make the argument. If we propose an arrangement, what would we offer as a cap on... let us say monthly... expenditures and how long to pay back?"

Quintius, furthering *his* idea and demonstrating that he had given more thought to his concept, said, "I have looked at our revenues, expenditures, distribution to the partners and considered funds that might be required in the near future for upgrades and additions to our system. I believe that we can offer to pay up to 3000 sestertii per month for the next two years, and still receive a substantial monthly payment, as we now enjoy. In two years we would have risked 72000 sestertii, a large sum, it is true, but not crippling. After two years, when the construction is underway, we may be compelled to contribute more. At that time we decide to continue... or not. If we continue, I suggest that we pay off funding from the Empire in twenty years from new revenues we receive. We will have control over the amount being charged for the new water, so we may be able to repay with more ease than we might think. What say you?"

Julius looked at Quintius. "I am sure that the amount—3000 sestertii per month—will be dwarfed by the construction costs. We will be required to contribute substantially more, perhaps beyond our means."

"Yes," Quintius answered, "we must, at that time, be skillful in our discussions with the Empire. It is a risk. The Empire might force us out by demanding a monthly funding that we cannot sustain. But, what can we do, as members of the Empire, enjoying the fruits of that bounteous tree... they say? It *is* the Empire. They will do what they will do. We can try to influence the outcome, but they will have their say. We must do our best to position our interests."

The *Corporata* was silent. The weight of remarks made by Quintius forced their consternation. Eventually, Nemus spoke. "Do we favor the suggestion made by Quintius? Can most of you," he looked at Titus, "agree that we should make a proposal and include the numbers that Quintius has stated?"

Again the *Corporata* was not quick to react. Marcus answered first. "No other course seems prudent. I have no quarrel with the numbers Quintius has suggested."

Nemus looked at each of the others in turn. In turn, they nodded, except for Titus who glared and did not nod. "Then," Nemus said, "That is what we will tell Claudius."

Titus stood, smashed the new glass wine cup on the floor, and walked from the meeting.

"We may have to accommodate Titus's monthly contribution," Nemus said, scowling at the glass shards, the remains of an expensive cup, "Also, we must consider that Claudius may make a counter offer. I suggest that we go no higher than 4500 sestertii per month at this time, as a limit. Possibly we can be more flexible on the payoff time."

"Perhaps we can suggest a payoff time of 30 years, thinking that we can come back to twenty." Marcus shrugged and took a drink of wine.

Nemus glanced at the remaining members. "Yes. Then that is what we will do. We will meet tomorrow at noon. I will serve a meal. In the meantime, let us finish our wine."

The breeze on the portico deck continued wafting, unaffected by the malice it encountered, a characteristic of all breezes at all times.

Bernius held his pottery wine cup with both hands; he paused before he took a sip. Appius was holding Sergius as they sat under the shade tree. Antonia watched from the doorway. Bernius spoke. "We must now revise the route of our aqueduct to one that is more precise. The more precise route will give us an accurate picture of the structure that must be built at any particular location."

Appius looked up from Sergius. "Does that mean that we will go out again, spending months correcting the alignment? I thought we must be here to work with the designers."

Bernius tried to nod while he was taking a sip, causing a minor overflow at the brim of the cup. He wiped wine from his tunic. "Here is my plan. You will take Marius and Pentius back to the route and, with my maps, establish a new line. My map will show where a change to the route is required and will not apply to the entire route, only those places where it appears that we would have to dig too deep or that we would have to build a structure when we might be able to avoid by rerouting the conduit farther up the hill. I suppose your work would take one month—perhaps two. In the meantime, I will get the designers started."

Appius looked over at Antonia, then at Sergius. He would again have to explain to Antonia that he would have to be away— away from his new son and family life. That bothered him but so did the thought that he would not be present to further his own learning, the road to becoming an architect. He scowled. Maybe it was possible that he could get a substantial part of the rerouting done before the designers arrived. He spoke. "What you are saying seems reasonable. Is it possible that I might be here when you first address the designers, when you instruct them on how to proceed? I think that I would learn much from what you tell them and from their questions."

Bernius nodded, wine cup now at a safe distance. "Yes. You are right. We can surely make arrangements so that you are here at that time. After that, the design will proceed slowly. There will be questions and decisions, but I can note them and tell you of them when you return."

"And, Bernius.... "

"Yes?"

"I heard Claudius say that he does not want to take water from the western source, that it would be best if he dealt with his own region. Yet, I do not think ease of those arrangements was the motive that propelled his decision. I am surprised and I know you are, too. Do you have any thoughts...?"

Bernius set his cup on a table and clasped his hands. "I cannot be certain. I am only able to hear what he said and to watch his mannerisms, but... I think he relishes the idea of building a grand structure and that grand structure—across the Vardo—will be associated with his name."

"He would choose a more expensive, more difficult route for that reason?" Appius relaxed his support of Sergius, the infant's head now draped over his knee.

"As I said, I cannot be certain. As you remember, he wanted to know the dimensions of the bridge just before the moment he made his decision. Such are the vagaries of empires and *imperators*. Do not expect that all public works or actions will be decided on what you might think is a rational basis. This is not the first time that a leader promoted a project for his own glory."

Appius was silent for a moment but did reestablish support for Sergius's head. "We are just puppets for their glory. Yet, I favored the Ucetia route. I have to admit I am exhilarated imagining my involvement in building the structure across the Vardo. In this case, the whims of empire have worked to... my glory."

Bernius smiled and paused. "I have not mentioned this to the Corporata or Claudius. Because I did not think we would use the Ucetia water, I have not mentioned that there was a residue when the water we were testing evaporated. We will have to consider that in our design."

Appius asked, "What must we do?"

"We must design the aqueduct size somewhat larger to accommodate the buildup over time of the residue."

Appius continued. "But, the thought now intrudes—what is to be done with the villagers of Ucetia? We assumed that the Ucetia route would *not* be chosen and did not mention the situation to Claudius. What should be done?"

Bernius frowned. "Yes, I have been thinking about that too. I suppose that we should have spoken of that at the meeting, but it all happened quickly, and to our surprise. I am not sure what we should do and will have to think on it. My first thought is that we again talk to the Ucetians and encourage them to talk to the Empire about compensation. Perhaps we will see if Claudius really does have influence in what he calls—his region."

Appius managed a grim smile. He would soon be in the vicinity of the Ucetians, restaking the route. Talking to them would be his chore, no doubt. He shivered, involuntarily. Might they be hostile?

Claudius stood in front of the *Corporata*. The accommodating breeze was absent this afternoon, allowing flies to buzz without concern in and about the sumptuous luncheon provided by Nemus. Appius and Bernius were not required to be present.

the *Aedifex*: Building the Pont du Gard

Claudius raised his chin, an emporial affectation, and looked at Nemus. "Have you thought about the venture? Have you anything to tell me beyond capitulation? Have you been able to peer into the future and imagine that you might share a benefit of its glorious bounty?"

"We have given the venture serious thought. We have reviewed our present resources and struggled with our concerns about wanting to be a substantial partner with the Empire." Nemus stopped, somewhat mischievously, to give Claudius the impression that they could *not* manage to be involved. After a well-timed pause, he continued. "We are resolved to be part of the project. We have determined that we can support payments to the progress of—up to—3000 sestertii per month, understanding that we must provide from revenue that we presently receive. We realize that the costs will, at times, be substantially more than that but will accept your generous offer—that of the Empire providing the additional funds." He paused and looked at the *Corporata* members. Titus stared straight-ahead, arms locked. "We also understand that we must repay the Empire the funds they have advanced and request that the Empire allow us to return payment in 30 years. In the arrangement I have stated, you will find that we are a willing partner."

Titus shook his head. Claudius noted this, scowled, but said nothing. Claudius embarked on his accustomed erratic pacing, hands behind his back. The *Corporata* followed with their eyes, anticipating the moment when he would turn to them and respond. Finally, the moment arrived. "I am pleased that you have chosen to participate in your future, pleased that you would risk and forego your present compensation to provide for your city's needs. However, I feel that you suggest an arrangement that is too comfortable. Of course, the Empire could accommodate your proposal. As I have stated before," he made a wide sweep with his hands, "the Empire could finance the entire project. However, I would like you to be stronger participants, to know that you must work hard to protect your investment, that you cannot shrug your shoulders at a future moment and wash your hands of the matter if things do not go your way."

Members of the *Corporata* sat back, involuntarily anticipating a storm of requirements. Even Titus was rapt, but with a somewhat smug look.

311

Claudius paused looking at the *Corporata*. "I propose that you provide up to 5000 sestertii per month to fund the progress. That is the substantial difference. The time frame in which you repay is not of great concern, but I propose that you repay in 20 years, given that accounts with the Empire should be satisfied sooner, rather than later, and to give me more leverage, to present a tidier package when I talk to... Caligua."

The *Corporata* had not imagined or considered that one situated as high in the Empire as Claudius must also please his superiors even though Caligua, the *Imperator*, was his nephew. They remained silent.

Claudius shrugged. "What say you?"

Nemus felt he should stand to make his statement. "Your Excellency. I believe, knowing that *we* can establish the price for the additional water, that which will travel the aqueduct, we can accommodate your request for payoff in 20 years." He looked at his *Corporata* to see if there was dissent, as he had not polled them on this consideration. He saw assent, therefore continued. "As to the 5000 sestertii per month, we believe that to be burdensome, that at that amount it will drastically curtail our ability to best operate our water system and will substantially curtail our present lifestyle. Nevertheless, if it would help your Excellency to talk to... Caligua... we, in the spirit of cooperation would agree to provide 4000 sestertii per month during progress." He again looked at his partners, this time receiving fixed stares. Titus was slowly shaking his head. Nemus looked at Claudius and smiled.

Claudius returned the smile. "I accept your proposal to return payment to the Empire in 20 years. That is where I expected we would agree. However, I must insist on the 5000 sestertii per month. I have some understanding of the revenues you receive from your present operation and think you could well afford it. I want you to participate at that level. Further, it is likely that you will not be required to contribute at that amount for some time—during the design. You will be able to fund the project with ease. I must insist."

Nemus took a deep breath. "We... the *Corporata*... have not discussed the possibility of an obligation at 5000 sestertii per month. I cannot speak for the participants. I will say this. We understand you are leaving Nemausus tomorrow. You may assume we will accept your offer unless I advise you before you leave—after I talk to the members." He knew the *Corporata* was trapped.

Claudius, arms splayed, smiled and said, "I would presume, then, that we have an agreement." He was also aware that the *Corporata* must take his offer. "I anticipate that with the passage of a number of years, we will be celebrating our foresight and commitment." He reached for his glass goblet and raised it in toast. "I salute you, bold men of Nemausus."

CHAPTER 31

Appius, after prolonged good-byes to his son, and... yes... to Antonia, departed Nemausus with Pentius and Marius. The two woodcutters were happy to be on the road again, jocular and rambunctious as they pushed and pulled the improved chorobate along the path. They threw rocks at birds and at each other. Appius felt somewhat apprehensive not having Bernius at his side, Bernius calculating, using prior experience, and providing direction. However, Bernius had taken care to make sure that Appius understood the task and the means to overcome obstacles that might appear. He would re-route the aqueduct to allow for a shallower slope.

But, what bothered Appius more was a possible confrontation with the Ucetians. It was unfortunate that the *Corporata* and Claudius did not know about the hostile reaction from the village. Now, Appius and Bernius were reluctant to broach the subject for fear of scuttling the arrangement between the *Corporata* and Claudius.

Yes, he and Bernius had talked about the Ucetia villagers and discussed an approach in which Appius would go directly to the village and tell them that the Empire had chosen the springs of Ucetia to supply Nemausus. Appius would advise that he was only an employee, but, because he had been present at the discussions with Claudius, he would suggest that the villagers go to Nemausus and talk to the *Corporata* about compensation and favorable treatment for the village. The *Corporata*, if agreeable, would take their suggestion forward to Claudius who would be inclined to approve.

But, they discarded that approach. Perhaps Bernius knew that Appius was at risk in such an encounter. Bernius, instead, stated that the route from Ucetia down the Alzon was well behaved and not in need of re-routing. The crew would start their task again at the point the aqueduct departed the Alzon, thus possibly avoiding problems with the Ucetians. Regardless, the thought of possible savage encounters pressed upon Appius as he nudged his horse along, somewhat dreading that each step took him closer to possible confrontation.

They overnighted at the bridge and arrived at the Alzon in the late afternoon of the following day. Appius was able to convince Pentius and Marius that it might be prudent to curtail noisy enthusiasm in favor of a peaceful existence. Pentius and Marius tilted their heads, gesturing that they would surely have enjoyed the challenge of a fracas. Nevertheless, the anticipation of hard physical effort kept them from sliding into a funk.

That night, Appius slept fretfully. The thought of the Ucetians taking them by surprise nagged him, and he did not like the idea of proceeding by stealth. By morning he was convinced he should ride to the villagers and tell them the outcome—dictated by the Empire. He did not think they would harm him.

After they had their morning meal, he beckoned to Marius and Pentius just as they started to arrange the gear for the day's work. "There is something I think we should do before we start. I would like to talk to the people of Ucetia and tell them that the springs below their village will be used to supply water to Nemausus. There is a chance we could go about our work and they would not discover us, but we have to face this problem at some time. I would like you two to walk with me. In truth, you will aid in my protection, but I do not want you to appear threatening. When they see the might of the two of you, they will understand that any assault will be difficult."

Marius looked at Pentius, nodded solemnly and involuntarily flexed his shoulders.

"So, let us do that," Appius continued, "I hope that we are doing right."

The trio walked to the village and in the manner of the prior discussion with the villagers walked to the fountain, knowing that the villagers would summon those who should hear what he had to say. At the fountain, it was not long before Lucius appeared. He approached Appius, taking in Pentius and Marius, stopped, gave Appius a long look, and said, "So?"

Appius nodded. "Lucius, I need to talk to the leaders of your village. If you are the one, so be it, but I would like your council to hear what I have to say."

Lucius said nothing, turned and walked in the direction of the market. Ten minutes later, after the trio had taken the opportunity to drink of the fountain, Lucius returned with four men. Appius recognized two of them as those that had participated with Lucius in prior confrontations. Lucius led the four men to Appius, beckoning the two new faces to stand either side of him. He nodded right and left. "The senior members of the village council."

The council on the left spoke. "What do you have to tell us?"

Appius took a deep breath. "When we last talked to you, we told you that it was likely that another source would be chosen—a new source of water for Nemausus. We urged that you not jeopardize the village by creating trouble. Apparently you have chosen to rely on our statement. I must now tell you that the Empire has chosen to use the waters of Ucetia."

Lucius and the four men crossed their arms. The villagers surrounding Appius murmured as one.

Appius waited for a moment, holding his hand up to stop what appeared to be an oncoming tirade from the lead council. "I am here because you were told otherwise, and I was party to that. I easily imagine that you are angry that the Empire would take water that flows from the bounds of your village and would do so without asking. But, the Empire will have its way, regardless of what you or I have to say. I want to now urge you to request that the Empire and the town of Nemausus compensate you for using your water as they should compensate a farmer for taking his grain to feed the armies."

The lead council stepped forward. "I am Portius Gaius. I speak for the village. I do not think the Empire will compensate us for the water." The crowd murmured in assent. "The Empire does not care that a small village objects; they will do as they please. What is left for us?"

"You must try," Appius said. "At this moment, while Nemausus may be aware that you object, the Empire has not heard nor is even aware that there is a problem. Claudius is the proconsul for this region; he is *your* proconsul. I urge that you go directly to Claudius and make your request. He is in Lugdunum." Appius had conceived this approach in the middle of the night. He imagined that if the villagers approached the *Corporata*, the *Corporata* would use the difficulty of the villagers as a means to curtail the project effort. Although Claudius might finally dismiss the objections of the *Corporata*, the project could be slowed, perhaps stopped, until the issue was resolved. A direct approach to Claudius would bypass *Corporata* pranks.

the *Aedifex*: Building the Pont du Gard

"Do you have anything more to say?" The lead council glared at Appius, then at Marius and Pentius standing behind.

"Only this," Appius said, "Please do not do anything that you will regret. You must know that the Empire could crush you like a bug." He looked at the other council, Lucius, and his two partners. Appius then nodded to Marius and Pentius indicating they should leave. The crowd did not part to let them pass; the trio had to jostle their way through to get clear. Pentius and Marius were careful not to be overly physical, as Appius had requested, but they found making way to be difficult. Once they were beyond the crowd, Appius shook his head. "I suppose I really should not expect them to thank me for letting them know."

Marius looked around to see if anyone followed. None did, somewhat to his disappointment. "I wonder what they will do?" he said, tapping Appius on the shoulder.

"I wonder too," Appius mumbled.

Did he do the right thing? Would it have been better to have not told them? After all it was possible they would not have been discovered. What would Bernius say?

They arrived back at the camp before noon. It was still possible to make substantial progress in the remainder of the daylight hours. They ate lightly then set out to find the first section of the route that needed adjustment. It would be this portion from the Alzon to the ridge that would require the most work. Bernius calculated that he had assumed too much slope; therefore, they had to reroute the conduit higher along the line of hills in order to arrive at the ridge at a higher elevation. This meant that Marius and Pentius would have to clear a considerable amount of new path to be able create a line of sight. Once they reached the ridge, the conduit would be above ground—elevated—so they could use the line they had established before.

The crew worked hard for three weeks, clearing, sighting, and installing new stakes until they finally reached the turn at the ridge. They would leave the next day for Nemausus before returning to make adjustments to the route on the other side of the Vardo. Appius hungered for Antonia and was excited to see Sergius although he was pleased with the work they had accomplished. They had not encountered any difficulty from the villagers, nor even seen them. He slept well that night.

317

After they awakened the next morning, Marius gave a shout. Next to the chorobate, were piles of stakes, one pile of the tall stakes and another of the red-topped, short stakes.

Appius, distraught, hands on hips, looked at the piles of stakes in disbelief. The stakes they had just installed and those previously installed along the Alzon were probably all in the pile. Marius and Pentius were staring intensely at him. He turned and spoke. "I guess we have our answer." He cringed, thinking that he should not have confronted the village. After all, he and Bernius had agreed that he should not. The outcome had to be evidence that he was not capable of handling difficult situations. Appius shook his head. "Let us prepare to return to Nemausus. I do not know what we should do about this." Pentius and Marius did not know either, but inflicting punishment rather than walking home was their prevailing thought.

The crew returned to Nemausus. Antonia was delighted to see Appius, and he was sure that Sergius recognized him as he held him, happy to see his father. Appius did not seek Bernius the first night of his return. He wondered if any of the designers had arrived. He was eagerly anticipating start of design but was apprehensive about talking to Bernius, not eager to tell him that the Ucetians had destroyed weeks of their work. Perhaps if he had not gone to Ucetia, not told the villagers that their water would be stolen—perhaps others could have prevented the calamity. Would Bernius be upset? Or, *how* upset would he be?

Appius appeared in the doorway of Bernius's apartment. Bernius, busy making a sketch at a desk by the sole window, did not look up until Appius tapped on the opening, startling him.

"Oh, so," Bernius said, standing. He clutched Appius's shoulders and said, "You have returned and you look good. I could not help but worry that the Ucetians might... bother you. How did it go? Did you understand the changes to be made?"

Appius managed to smile. "I am well, Bernius, thank you for your worry. However, I must tell you that I have caused us great trouble. The Ucetians have pulled all our stakes, from the Alzon to the ridge. Much of our work is for naught."

Bernius winced. "No! But this was not your fault. How could you have prevented actions of the villagers—you were only three?"

318

the *Aedifex*: Building the Pont du Gard

"Bernius, when I arrived at the Alzon, I decided it would be best that I try to talk to the villagers. My reasons may have been foolish, but that was what I decided to do. Of course, they were hostile, even though I suggested that they might be compensated. They did not harm us, but they have done great damage to the project. I regret that I did not go about our work as you and I agreed."

Bernius said nothing, standing, gazing without focus. Then he said, now with a direct look, "Appius, there was always a danger that the Ucetians would do something. As I told you, I worried that there could be trouble. Yes, we agreed to minimize your exposure, but I must say that had I been able to be there, I would have also gone to talk to the villagers. I thought that trying to avoid them would be the best approach, but I am not so sure."

"But, Bernius, what do we do now?"

Bernius walked back to his table, beckoning Appius who was holding rolled-up drawings. "If you have been careful to mark the drawings to show our new route, if we can see where we will have to change the nature of our structures, we can still proceed with design. The information you collected was the task required. We have not lost as much as you might imagine."

Appius nodded, thinking through Bernius's reasoning. Then, he said, softly, "But what do we do about the villagers?"

Bernius pointed to the table, indicating that Appius should unroll the maps upon it, and looked at Appius. "Yes, that is a situation that I fear. It is not that we cannot be protected from the Ucetians. It is that the Empire's means of ensuring peace may not be delicate. That is why I was reluctant to bring up the incident in front of Claudius and the *Corporata*. Caligua, not Claudius, controls military support. If we ask for help, we are liable to witness great harm to the village. The general with legions in this province is General Artius Crassius, not known for reason and constraint, and he is a military man that Caligua favors."

"I wish the villagers had understood. We... both... tried to tell them. But, what must we do?"

"I think that we do nothing for now. As I have stated, we can proceed with our design without having to prowl in the Ucetia region. It could be a year before we must go back for additional information, and it will be even longer before work is started. Perhaps we can negotiate peace before the military is called to intercede. We must not tell the *Corporata* of our problem."

319

Appius nodded. "There are a number of reasons why they should not know." He reached for the maps. "I will show you how I have altered the route, but have the designers arrived?"

Bernius nodded, "Yes. They have. I have arranged for an office... it is a *Corporata* building. I am ready to challenge the designers with the task. I need a little time to see what you have done, and then we will have our session. I think you will be interested to hear how we will go about our work."

The design office was situated in a rude building, an annex to the offices of the Aqua *Corporata*, next to the building where Marcus had his office. Bernius and Appius walked into the enclosure, dusty and cobwebbed, a space sighing a sense of abandonment. Bernius shook his head. "We will need much more light than this. Designers often work in the dark but not so much as this. We must make some changes. I hope the *Corporata* will not mind that we cut holes in the wall. Can you arrange with our carpenter?"

Appius nodded.

"And, we should have the carpenter construct a covered working area outside the building. In fair weather, we will have abundant light."

Within one-half hour, three men, the designers, arrived at the building. They knew each other, fellow arrivals in an unfamiliar town. Appius was introduced to Gaius, Numerius, and Vibius. Bernius explained the strengths of each, in turn. Gaius was unbeatable on arches, Numerius solid on foundations and Vibius experienced in the underground structures and tunnels. Bernius handed them rags, and they wiped dust off the stools and tables that were mute furnishings of the forsaken structure.

Bernius made a semi-circular gesture in front of him indicating they should bring seating and gather around. "Our project is a magnificent and challenging one. The water will gradually descend from Ucetia, cross the magnificent gorge of the Vardo, and eventually travel 30 miles to transport water to Nemausus. To this date, we have devised and roughly staked a routing that will comply with the very shallow slope."

Appius cringed at the words "staked," reminding him of his difficult encounter.

Gaius asked, "How shallow?"

320

the *Aedifex*: Building the Pont du Gard

"Less than ½ inch in 100 feet. It will be of similar slope to Aqua Virgo although two or three times the distance. We must be very careful in our design to always consider that factor." Bernius looked at Vibius, nodding. "It will be you who are most concerned with that challenge. You must always be mindful of the terrain. You will probably have to vary the slope, slight as it is, in various sections in order to arrive at the minimum of height for the above-ground structures—so that we do not have so much above-ground structures to build."

Vibius pointed to maps Bernius had hung on the walls. "I see that you show the slope and the terrain. That will be a good start."

"Yes. And there is no reason to use a design different from what we have used on other aqueducts—our standard underground design. You, of course, will do an excellent job of maintaining the minimum trench depth." Bernius smiled.

Gaius shook his head. "Bernius, this gorge that the water must cross, it is... overwhelming. I cower at the thought of conceiving a structure as high."

"Yes, Gaius," Bernius nodded, "it is true that you have the greatest challenge. We must, perhaps, consult those with the experience of designing and building tall structures, those who have built a similar structure in the Empire. It is important that we bring focus to your effort."

"One of the first things," Gaius snapped his fingers, emphasizing his remark, "I would like to talk to local masons. From them I can determine the characteristics of local stone and determine the skill level of the masons in this region. That should be easy to arrange... yes?"

Bernius looked at Appius who nodded and said, "I will arrange it."

"Also, Gaius," Bernius smiled, "do not think you will have it easy and all the glory only working on the one magnificent structure. We will also need your advice on the lower above-ground structures, although your cronies," he looked at Vibius and Numerius, "will be able to assist in the detail that will be required."

The cronies nodded.

Bernius turned to Vibius. "Vibius, it appears that it may be advantageous to construct several tunnels. We will need to know the nature of the earth that will be encountered. As has been done in the past, we will first establish a route over the ground, the hills, under which the tunnel will be driven. We will do this when we are assured of our routing. Then, as you have done—or at least witnessed—in the past, vertical shafts will be dug to the level of the tunnel at intervals that we determine. Digging of the shafts will disclose the material through which we must pick and determine whether we will have to contend with groundwater. Of course, it may happen that the earth is too difficult or there is too much water to handle. If that is the situation, we might first try altering the tunnel direction, of course, digging more shafts, hoping to find a suitable condition. If we cannot tunnel, we have determined that we can route around these obstacles—hills—but it will not be as efficient. If the tunnel can proceed, the shafts will be used to maintain our alignment while we are digging the tunnels. After the aqueduct is put into service, the shafts will be used for access when maintenance is required."

Vibius nodded. This routine was familiar to him.

"So," Bernius clapped, looking at the designers, "after you have taken time to study the maps and our notations, we will walk the aqueduct route. Appius must finish rerouting from the crossing of the Vardo back to Nemausus. In a few days, he will return to the Vardo to continue that work. We will travel with him to the Vardo. He and his crew will then continue their re-routing, back down the aqueduct, while we follow the route from there to the source... well, not quite to the source." He looked at Appius.

Vibius asked, "Why not all the way to the source?"

Bernius scowled. "Hmmm. We have a... situation. The villagers are not happy that Nemausus will take their water. We want to avoid contact with them. And, recently, they have removed the stakes that Appius set from the source and for several miles along the hills."

The designers were silent but glanced at each other. Appius waited for Bernius to continue.

"This is a delicate situation... with the villagers. I must ask you to treat this information confidentially, for now. We hope to get the problem resolved without... harsh measures. But, for now we will avoid contact... at least I hope so. We will travel as far as the Alzon. From that location you can imagine the nature of the route to the springs. Do you understand?"

The designers nodded slowly. They were familiar with possible harsh measures inflicted by the Empire on non-compliant groups.

Gaius raised his hand to catch Bernius's attention. "How long do you think we will be at this task?"

Bernius was silent for a moment. "I have given that a little thought. Although some of the design may occur quickly, using the knowledge of structures we have built in the past, I see that with investigating the terrain and making revisions but especially considering the bridge over the Vardo, we may be finishing design two years from now.

The designers said nothing. They were not startled that the task should take two years. Appius, though, leaned forward, eyes wide, not having thought that it would be so long before they started construction. It would be wrong to assume he could have forecasted the difficulties they would encounter.

Appius had several more days before they would make the trip back to the Vardo. He talked to the carpenter about work at the design office. He found Pentius and Marius and let them know that they would be back to work in just a few days.

Most of his time, however, was spent with Antonia and Sergius. Appius was fascinated by his child. He pestered the infant with nudges, asked him questions, and held Sergius aloft so he could see the world. "I cannot wait for him to be able to talk and walk. I have so many things to show him."

Antonia smiled, hands on hips as she watched Appius with their child. Sergius bore an attentive expression, probably puzzled by the nudgings and questions and abrupt displays of scenery. However, Appius was certain that the child was rapt to his presence and impatient to have his father introduce him to the world.

CHAPTER 32

At the project office, now fitted with an outdoor overhang and the interior modified to provide more light, Bernius suggested to his designers (Gaius, Numerius, and Vibius) that they study the plans to give them an orientation. They had walked the intended route of the aqueduct so could somewhat relate the terrain to the requirements for the individual structures.

In the meantime, amidst answering questions and giving suggestions to the designers, sessions in which Appius absorbed every thought, Bernius started a new phase of the project, that of devising a schedule. Neither the *Corporata* nor Claudius had pressed them by questioning how long the project would take. At some point, they would be asked that question. Also, to manage the project, they needed to have a plan detailing the sequence and timing of activities.

One fine day at the office, Bernius beckoned Appius to join him at a table. "We are going to start another phase of our project, meaning we will have two phases going at the same time." Bernius pointed at the designers, huddled over sections of the aqueduct maps. "One of the phases is design—we are now designing the aqueduct. The second is *scheduling* of the project. Scheduling is a skill which you must also learn if you are to become an architect... at least one who would be taken seriously."

Appius was dubious. "By making a schedule... does that mean that we will imagine how the project will be constructed?"

"Yes. We will start by referring to our estimate. It is a great foundation for understanding the activities required to build the structure. You will notice that we arranged the estimate so that we could picture each of the activities. We did not just assign days of work to a blended mix of activities. The estimate will aid us in devising our schedule. In fact, we can use the activities, as described, as direct input to the schedule."

Appius grinned. "I think *we* did it that way because *you* have done this before and knew the estimate method would be beneficial."

Bernius laughed. "I will not deny that. But, you will see how useful it really can be. Let me show you." He grabbed the sheaf of the estimate papers, now stitched together to curtail losing a sheet or two. "We will first work with the big numbers—I mean the accumulation of hours for a number of activities involved in—let us say—building the tunnel." He flipped to the page where the tunnel activity was summarized. "Here, it shows there are 1500 mandays required to construct the tunnel section. Let us think. How many men would we expect to be able to work on the tunnel at one time. For now I am going to assume that 10 could. They, each, will work, say, 6 days out of every week. That means that in each week, we will accomplish 60 mandays. But, since this is a tunnel, we should also be able to work at night—it will make no difference. Therefore, we will have two shifts and in a week can accomplish double or 120 mandays. I can now calculate how long it will take to excavate the tunnel. My calculations show that it would take 12 or 13 weeks. Do you see what I am doing?"

"I do see, but is it possible to work 20 men? I am thinking that a tunnel is a close working space. Or, perhaps more could be used. I do not have a feel for the numbers you are choosing."

"Yes. You are exactly right. After we quickly calculate the rough time required for all the major activities and assuming the number of men that can be employed, we will have a bare understanding of the duration required for each of the major activities. We will keep that in mind. Then we will begin anew, analyzing the detailed activities that make up the larger ones. We, by using the imagination technique we used before, will be able to visualize a reasonable number of men that may be worked at one time. No doubt, the amount of men we assumed working on the tunnel, the one we just described, will be changed. And, it may be true that we can work 30 men for a time, then 10 for some time. As an example, it may be possible to be digging the tunnel and quarrying and preparing the tunnel cement and stones at the same time. The quarrying and making of cement will not be going on inside the tunnel."

"I think I will have to see you do this to understand. Now my mind is having a difficult time." Appius shrugged.

"You will see. It is somewhat like doing the estimate—one activity at a time. However, it is then made more complex but more useful as we re-arrange activities and assign more or fewer men to the activities. This method we are using will really drive us to *plan* the project. I will mention this now, but we will deal with it later. It is very important that we keep in mind the required sequence of the activities."

"Can you give me an example?" Appius frowned.

"Yes. We must first clear the land before we excavate a trench. The trench must be excavated before we can start placing the stones for the floor and walls. But, none of these is required to be completed before we start quarrying and dressing the stones. Those activities can go on before clearing or excavation or can take place at the same time. But sufficient stones must be available in time to start installing the stones in the tunnel. Yes?"

"Yes."

"So, we will complete timing calculations for the major activities. That will get us started. We will then have an idea of the size of the project, a rough idea of how many men will be required and how long the project will take."

"Bernius?"

"Yes."

"Where will we be able to get all the men that will be required? It seems like the work will require many."

"I do not know, Appius, I do not know. That is a thought of huge importance. Soon we will have to consider what is possible and by what means. But, we will know the requirements. We will have an idea of the consequences if we are able to obtain more men for the project or of the situation where we are unable to obtain enough workers on the project. We must advise our employers of the requirements. If they have any influence, they will use our information to obtain resources. For these matters, it is our job to inform and theirs to make decisions and to provide the resources."

Appius and Bernius were able to roughly calculate the duration required for the major activities during the remainder of the day.

Bernius pointed to the results. "We have identified the project feature that will take the longest time. It is not the bridge over the river Vardo, but, because there is a vast distance of underground conduit to be constructed, that is the single feature requiring the most time—16 years using an average of 200 men. But, that assumes that we start at the springs and work to the *Castellum*, the entire 30 miles. We know that we can shorten our duration dramatically by working sections, maybe many sections, simultaneously. As we are creating our schedule, we will keep this in mind. We now have a way to gage which activities need special attention."

"How about the bridge over the river Vardo? It does *not* seem that we will be able to work in more than one place. If we shorten the time required for the underground section, the bridge may then take the longest time."

Bernius smiled. "Yes, very good. That is a likely outcome. We will, no doubt have to give the bridge works much consideration. That is why I would like to visit our local quarry. I believe we need the quarryman's input before we continue with our design and our schedule. Will you make an arrangement for us," he swept the room with his hands to include the designers, "to talk with him?"

"I will leave now to go see the quarryman. I should be able to tell you tomorrow."

Bernius, Appius and the three designers walked to the quarry outside of town and were greeted by the quarryman in his dusty quarters, situated near the entrance of the rocky 'scape.' Dust seemed to effuse from his person as he moved about, puffs of beige released by his contact with objects in his path.

"Appius tells me, although I, of course, had heard, that an immense project will be built." The quarryman looked at the group, now assembled outside his quarters, shading their eyes from the sun. "The aqueduct, as I have heard described, will use much stone, but my small quarry," he swept the site with his hand, "is not situated well and is much too small for the needs."

"Quarryman," Bernius stepped forward, "you may have also heard that the aqueduct will cross the Vardo on a magnificent structure. Of course, we will build it of arches to minimize the amount of stone that will be used. We are just now beginning the design of the structure." He turned and put his hand on the shoulder of Gaius. "Gaius will be designing our arches. He will be most interested in what you might have to say about use of stone in the very tall structure spanning the Vardo. What can you tell us?"

The quarryman coughed, dipped his head, nodded, then looked at Gaius. "For a structure that is very tall, you should not use mortar joints. How tall *is* your structure?"

Gaius replied, "155 feet."

"Ah, yes, very tall." He raised his dusty eyebrows. "Our stone weighs about 163 lbs for a cubed foot. If your structure is 155 feet tall, you must stack 155 of the one-foot blocks, let us say, one atop the other to know the force that will be exerted on the lowest of the blocks."

Gaius, having recently studied the structure, had already made this calculation. "It is 25,000 pounds for a square foot. And, because the piers will carry more load than that only directly above them, the force at the piers will be substantially larger."

The quarryman nodded. "Yes, a significant force. Our stone is very strong, but mortar is not nearly so, perhaps having one-third the strength. It would be disastrous to have mortar in the structure; you could easily expect the mortar to crumble from the weight in the lower elevations. Your structure would settle, causing severe problems with the water conduit above and would possibly fail given some passage of time."

Bernius looked at Gaius. "Yes, we had presumed such but wanted to talk to an expert. What will be required of these blocks, fitted together without mortar?"

The quarryman grimaced. "They will have to be fashioned precisely to ensure good contact. It would not do to have voids between stones as the force from above would then be concentrated on the smaller surfaces that do have contact. All surfaces of the stone will have to be true to each other. Such craft requires lengthy time, skilled masons, and for that reason will be of great cost, especially for such a huge structure."

Bernius looked at Appius. "We included substantial time in our estimate for the production of these stones. But, we must determine if our assumptions have been sufficient." He addressed the quarryman. "Can you tell us how much time we should allow for the production of one stone? "

The quarryman turned and pointed to the quarry works behind him. "I can best tell you by showing you at the same time. Let us walk to where we are freeing large stones from the native rock."

The group made their way to a stepped cutout on the quarry face, scaling several ladders to do so. Two men were in process of chipping around the perimeters of a stone to be removed. The quarryman pointed. "The finished size of this stone will be 2 feet by 3 feet by 4 feet. We will remove a stone 4 inches larger than the finished sizes to allow for spalling when the stone is freed. As you can see, we are chiseling a trough at all the perimeters. The trough determines the lines along which the stone will fracture. Once we have chiseled the troughs, we will drive many wedges along their lengths, hammering them slightly in a sequence until the block fractures and can be removed. Of course, some blocks fracture so as not to be useful for the stone being fashioned. If that happens, we finish the stone to a smaller size, avoiding the fracture. What this means to you is that, you must allow for more stones to be freed than will actually be used. Unfortunately, that is part of the production."

Bernius looked at Appius. "We did not include that."

The quarryman continued. "You should also know," he pointed toward an area in his yard where many large stones were lying, "the stones should be freed for a year before they are chiseled to the finished sizes. Sometimes the stone will fracture a while after being freed. It would not be good to install a stone in the structure, which fractured after you had placed many stones upon it. You might find it very difficult to replace." He grinned.

Bernius drew in a great quantity of air. "This must be accounted for in our schedule. We must have a year of stone cutting and aging before we even start laying the first stone." He looked again at Appius who nodded.

"Let me now show you the finishing work." The quarryman walked to the edge of the quarry shelf in the direction of the ladder. "Let us go to where my masons are fashioning a stone that will be cut precisely, owing that it will be used in a decorative placement. It has the same requirements of the stones you will need. Note the hoist works beside the ladder, the means by which we transport the stones from this quarry level to the finishing yard."

They descended the ladders and walked to where two men were working with chisels. On the surfaces of the stone were markings made with the pigment of ochre, obtained from nearby *Rossello*. The quarryman pointed, "You see the wooden frames, the rectangles? The stones will be cut until the frames can be just slid over the surfaces. The other L-shaped frames are squares to assure that adjoining surfaces are true. The masons constantly try the fit, check for trueness, mark the stones and continue removing the excess very carefully. When they are very close to having finished the work, the stone is dragged over a flat surface to create a very smooth finish. This is done for all faces that will be in contact with other stones. By that means, even most of the tooling marks disappear. This is the stone that you will use in your structure." He crossed his arms.

Gaius shook his head. "How many hours would be accumulated in the production of one finished stone?"

The quarryman's eyes glinted. "I have cut many of these, and I am certain that each will require **70** hours—to remove the stone, transport it to storage, transport it to the finishing area and then to accomplish the finishing work."

The visitors were silent, absorbing and imagining the effort required for the river crossing.

"And, Quarryman, are there quantities of masons that are skilled such that they can produce a precisely finished stone?" Bernius asked, looking at the few masons in the quarry.

"Because Nemausus has lately built many fine structures, we are fortunate to have a number of masons who have the skill. But there are not nearly enough. However, the expert masons are capable of training others of less skill over a length of time. That is how it must be done in addition to attracting masons from other regions."

Gaius asked, "And if you were producing our stones, what would you require of us, your designers, to enable an efficient operation—at your quarry and for those who are placing the stones?"

The quarryman drew a deep breath, triggering his cough. "I know how to work one stone—we can work it to perfection. But, for the size of the project you imagine, I have not been a part, but I can be certain about this: you must design your structure so that many stones of the same size and shape can be used. If you design and produce stones using the same precision of *my* work, you will not be spending more time finishing or reworking the stones at your site. That you must do."

Gaius looked skyward, as if to imagine the great structure before him "I do understand what you mean, quarryman. I do understand."

Bernius put his hand on the quarryman's shoulder. "Thank you, sir. You have been a great help to us. We must talk to you again about locations for other quarries. And, we will likely see you producing stones for our project."

330

the *Aedifex*: Building the Pont du Gard

The quarryman nodded then shook his dusty head, overwhelmed by the thought of what must be done and doubtful of success.

They were back at the project office. Bernius gathered the group under the outdoor covering. They stood, elbows on the high table used for laying out large maps. Bernius, at one end of the table, spoke. "We have learned much from our quarry visit. Although we had thought the stone work needed to be carefully done, we did not consider the precision suggested by the quarryman, but his thoughts are rational, and we should use his methods in our design. One other very significant understanding is the required aging of the blocks. If we wait for all of our design to be done before we start quarrying stone, we will have a year delay in starting our bridge—or nearly so. And, as we expect the bridge will be a feature that will take much time, we should consider a means of eliminating this delay."

Gaius said, straightening up and lifting his arms off the table, "There is work to be done on the bridge foundations. This could be done while the blocks are curing."

Bernius nodded. "Yes. True. But, that will be a month at most. What I am suggesting is that we concentrate on the bridge design to the point that we are able to identify the size and shape of the stones to be used. We will all assist in this effort when reasonable to do so, leaving other design as secondary. When we have thus identified the stone requirements, we will start quarrying operations so that we may get a significant number of stones freed and aging before we are totally complete with the design."

"You mentioned we need to find other quarry sites nearer to the location where we cross the Vardo." Appius shook his head. "How will we do that?"

"As we were leaving the quarry, I told the quarryman we would be back to discuss that. We will contract the production of stones, so we should talk to those who are in that occupation. I do not know if our quarryman will be interested in such a volume of work, but I think we should start by talking to him. We will do so, soon."

Gaius spoke. "To be able to start, we must know the requirements at the bottom of the canyon, the features that will determine the foundations for the arches. There are rock formations on which we will install the foundations; we must know their locations and their extent. The distance between foundations, especially across the river channel, will determine the width and height of the arches. And, as everything else will be built on top of the first row of arches, their dimensions are a matter of first order."

Bernius nodded. "Yes, you are right. Several of us must go to the Vardo crossing and take the measurements and determine the scheme for the foundations. I suggest that you, Gaius, go with Appius and take our two able woodsmen who are familiar with the measuring work. While you are there, you may be able to conceive the arrangement of the arch foundations. If more study is needed to determine the final design, you will have the necessary information to allow you to do so."

Bernius turned to Appius. "Will you arrange with Marius and Pentius and gather provisions? I think you should leave within the next few days. You may use my horse to ride or to carry provisions. The chorobate will be needed and must be carted, of course."

Appius nodded. "I will make the arrangements."

"Good. While you are away, I will work on the schedule. I should have much of interest to show you when you return."

Appius searched the town for and found Pentius and Marius who were eager to begin the expedition. They offered to start walking the chorobate cart the next day so that they could find a way to get the chorobate to the bottom of the canyon before Appius and Gaius arrived. Appius smiled, exhilarated to be working with souls that were so enthusiastic for the work. He made the rounds to local shops to acquire provisions.

Having completed arrangements, he walked home in the late afternoon. He stopped as he entered the courtyard to watch Antonia with Sergius, his son. He was still bewildered by the attachment he felt toward the baby. Appius opened the gate and strode quietly toward them. Antonia looked up, a slight smile on her face. She understood what Appius was thinking and that understanding thrilled her. Sergius saw Appius and pumped his arms in anticipation as Antonia handed him to Appius.

"Hello, Sergius." Appius let the infant grab his finger. He then looked at Antonia. "Hello, my good wife."

the *Aedifex*: Building the Pont du Gard

Antonia crossed her arms. "I notice that Sergius gets your first attention. I am only the mother and then the wife. I remember when *I* would get your first greeting."

Appius smiled. "It was your wisdom that was responsible for producing this child. Would you have it otherwise?"

Antonia only smiled in return but tapped her foot. "Appius, how goes the aqueduct business? You have visited the quarry today. Are you ready to start building with the stones?"

"I know you are much more informed than to think that. We have learned much from the quarryman. We now understand how important the production of the stones will be. Bernius has decided" —Appius felt that requirements from Bernius moderated any ill will that Antonia might direct toward him for being away— "that we must survey the bottom of the canyon so that we can get started immediately with the design of the arches. Marius and Pentius will leave tomorrow. Gaius and I will leave the following day."

Antonia nodded. "I do not think such a task will take too long. What do you think?"

"I do not think it will take longer than a week."

"Yes, you do not want to be gone too long. Otherwise, you may miss seeing your baby son grow into a child. I think Sergius is valuable in assuring that you do not linger in the wilds."

"Indeed, Antonia, indeed. What have you prepared for dinner?"

"I have prepared nothing. We are eating out."

CHAPTER 33

I drove to Uzes, perhaps relying on nostalgia to ease my funk involving the circumstances with Lisele. No, I wasn't depressed—this was no long-term relationship, no strong emotional ties here. It was folly to think that sharing time in France with someone you were fond of... well... thought a lot of... actually... craving to know and share time with, someone whose essence burned in your brain.... Gasp. No, no. It was really for the best. Falling for someone who lived in France, someone who had no intention or desire to relocate to California, would be nuts. Not that I hadn't done other similar, nutty things in my past. When that happens, you just wade in and sort out the consequences later. Yes, Lisele's rejection was... really... a good thing. Yet, we could have been friends... anything wrong with having a good friend in France? Not one thing. Yes, *that* was the failing. The possibility that two people could have become very good friends, but due to ironic circumstance—didn't get there. A tragedy. Ha, ha. I was really making this into a major calamity. Oh, well, retired folks have to have something to do. I suppose researching the aqueduct wasn't enough. I took a deep breath.

I parked on the street, a half block walk to the town center. I liked the way Uzes was arranged. The traffic was routed around the central area, leaving the middle, the old town, with open areas and easy walking past shops, restaurants, and residences. At the center of the old town was the public fountain. I selected a restaurant—outdoor seating of course—with a grand view of the fountain. As I sat, waiting for my beer, I wondered if the fountain I was viewing was the original, surviving from Roman times. I could imagine village folks at the fountain, children splashing the waters, those with water jugs—filling, lingering and talking. Really, I wasn't that good at imagining ancient activity, but in this time and place I forced myself and it worked. I would have to check to see if the fountain dated to Roman times.

The beer was good and colder than the usual French serving; they even served it in a chilled glass. Recently, I had ordered a mixed drink nearby where they sneered at my request for ice. The cold beer, the warm afternoon, the gurgling fountain, people chatting pleasurably around me generated a euphoria that sometimes occurs. The sharp edges of the Lisele encounter softened to an amorphous memory. *Life is good.*

Before long, my practical nature overwhelmed the moment. What aspect of the aqueduct would next consume my time? There would certainly be no distractions due to Lisele... or Laurie. Dismissed! I felt that I had determined the reason the aqueduct was routed via the Pont du Gard location, a matter of the ridge across the depression. I had not spent much time considering other routes that were radically different than the one taken. Could the aqueduct have been initially routed to the west of Uzes? I could look at that; it would also give me an excuse to explore the rugged gorge of the Gard.

All written references seemed to marvel that the Romans were able to discover, engineer, and manage the slight slope of the aqueduct due to the minute elevation difference between Uzes and Nimes. I had convinced myself... I doubt if the professor would pay much attention... that the chorobate could not have done the job, but through my research and my own brain, I was unable to come up with an alternative. Reference material seemed insistent that the chorobate was the device of preference—puzzling, because it was fairly easy to convince oneself that it could *not* do the job. Perhaps archeologists placed little value on math to explain the secrets of the past. Yes, inadequacy of the chorobate was a big mystery and one I wanted to solve.

Then there was the matter of timing. Written references talked about Augustus and Agrippa, but I did not feel comfortable accepting that. Perhaps my thoughts about the city walls in Nimes were causing me to look beyond. How could I find out more? You would think that the local researchers would have already nailed the timing, using modern means of investigation. I must give the situation more thought. Then I remembered. The professor was to release a paper discussing timing. Well, perhaps that would be soon, but in the meantime, I thought that I would stay tuned to information that might be of interest as it might lead me to learn more about who had been involved in the building of the aqueduct. Yes, it is peculiar that on this aqueduct, contrasting with others, there is very little information as to who was involved in the construction.

But, what for now? I did not know how I would proceed to investigate the mysteries—timing, the identity of the builders and level—so I would explore the gorge. Oh, yes. I forgot that I was interested in the inscriptions I had found. Investigating them might be fun. I wasn't sure there was anything to discover, but some were very interesting, indeed. I would do that.

I did not order lunch. For some reason, the beer was enough. I headed back to Vers.

I spent several days cataloguing inscriptions, taking a considerable time on the Pont du Gard itself on which many inscriptions were present. Of course, I could not tell which were done at the time of construction or which were etched hundreds or thousands of years after that. I looked at the markings, trying to discover a key to the inscription dates via aging. No such key appeared. Yet, I investigated on, taking pictures, making sketches, identifying locations, and speculating.

At night, I would consider a few of the markings that were more complex and not readily understood. There were many displaying the mason's hammer and some of these were dated, but dated much later than the original work. Were any of the marks from the original masons, marking their sign and identification for history, proud to have been a part of such a magnificent structure, the highest in the Roman Empire? They were there. They had to be.

And, how about the architects and builders or the guy that was in charge? There must be some remains, a monument, or existing markings to commemorate their struggle with such a vast project. I knew they were there, somewhere. Unless time had erased the markings, they were there. From my investigations of the stones in the structure, looking at the joints on the foundation, for example, the markings would not have withered. Where on the structure... I mean structures... would it be most likely they would be hacked?

It was fun speculating the meaning of markings that were images. However, it became apparent to me it would be difficult to know what I was seeing.

One night as I was trying to sort markings I had observed earlier that day, the phone rang. I did not often get phone calls, so I jumped when the rather clamorous bell on this particular instrument overtook the moment. I, expecting that the caller was most likely a Frenchy answered *"Oui."* My *modus* was to explain later, in my most-used French phrase—"I don't speak French." However, my greeting was answered in English.

"Hello, Warner. It is Lisele."

My silence was conspicuous; at least it must have been from her viewpoint. She would imagine that I was trying to think of a smug rejoinder. However, it wasn't that at all. I was dumbfounded that she would be calling me, and I was flummoxed to gather a response that registered my surprise, expressed my pleasure, and sounded urbane, all in one. I instead managed, "Lisele," which accomplished none of my objectives but got me through the moment. I followed with, "I am a little surprised that you are calling."

"So am I, Monsieur Warner, but life has its mysteries and turn-arounds, and I am involved in this one."

I shook my head. She made no sense. "What do you mean?"

"Warner, it seems that I've had the misfortune to be led down my own primrose path. You told me that you hadn't spent the night with Laurie, and I did not believe you. I told you that I had overheard Laurie make the reservation. Later, I was talking with Maurice and mentioned the circumstance, probably with cynicism in my manner. I told him you had denied that you spent the night with her, which, in my mind completely dismissed you as a worthwhile character, someone I would not care to spend time with. Maurice said, 'But, Lisele, I don't think he did. I think he is telling the truth.'

"I must say I was stunned. It was hard for me to accept that Laurie would be creating this fabrication and you, whom I had *not* raised with care and ethical guidance from an infant, were the victim of her story. She still will not admit that it did not happen. You can imagine that I have been in difficulty, trying to determine what is best to do, but as it *should* happen, the best thing to do is to tell you that I was mistaken and that I apologize."

"Thank you, Lisele, that is very kind of you. I think it takes a strong person to do this. I might imagine that you would be one of those persons, but still... I'm surprised."

"Warner?"

"Yes."

"You asked me to dinner, and I turned you down. I would like to complete this turnaround by asking *you* to dinner. I hope you will accept; I would be very grateful."

I didn't hesitate. There was no intent on my part to be reserved or stand-offish, to punish her for doubting me. "I accept, of course, Lisele. When?"

"Are you free tomorrow evening?"

"Yes." Life was good again.

"I will pick you up at six. We are going into Nimes... because... as contrite as I might be, Warner, I remain unable to display such in public or flaunt my relationship with you in the face of public opinion. I hope you understand."

"I do."

"And Warner, I have to admit that some of what I am doing is not complete redress. I do really enjoy your company, and I am hoping we will be friends."

I was speechless. I fumbled for a response. Finally, I said—and I don't know what prompted me to ignore her sincerity and to bypass an affirmation—"Did you teach Laurie to drive?"

"What?" She was silent, then laughed. "No, Warner, that is another one of her characteristics that is beyond me. You'll find our trip, over the mountain to Nimes, boring and, I hope, tranquil."

I made a move to respond to her sincerity. "Lisele, I don't ever imagine my time with you would be boring. I am very excited."

A pause. "See you at six."

Her Peugeot crunched to a stop in my drive. I watched her pull up but did not want to bolt out of the house and get in her car. I wanted to see her lithe and graceful figure glide to my door. I watched, gratefully, through the window in the door then retreated around the corner, so I could answer the door as if I hadn't seen her. When she knocked, I walked to and opened the door.

She smiled. "Ready?"

I bypassed the urge to give her a hug. It didn't seem right—perhaps later. "Hi, Lisele. Yes, I'm ready."

"And, you don't mind if I drive?"

I laughed. "Are you kidding? To be driven around the region by a good-looking woman is the height of my ambition."

She didn't acknowledge my banter with a comment, but I could see that she was pleased. I stepped out the door, and we were off.

the *Aedifex*: Building the Pont du Gard

I am happy to report that the drive to Nimes was uneventful, at least compared to the thrill ride I'd had before. I actually enjoyed the scenery, the rugged canyon of the Gard as we crossed. We arrived in Nimes, a warm evening, and walked a considerable distance to the restaurant Lisele had chosen. We were seated. I did a mock wiping of my brow. "Wow, Lisele, that walk was enough exercise for me to claim a right to any meal. Nimes is tough."

She sat back in feigned surprise. "But, Warner, I thought you liked walking... or hiking."

"I do, I do. I just thought it would be fun to comment. Do you like to walk?"

Her eyebrow shot up—very French. "*Oui*, but of course. I have done much hiking. I take a few hikes around Vers, but I have gone several times to the Pyrenees. Have you been?"

I shook my head. "No, no. I didn't know... didn't know, I mean, that you liked hiking. What's in the Pyrenees? Should I go?"

"Oh, yes. You must. There is the Cirque de Gavarne, the Napoleon Bridge, Cauterets—the Pont de Espana and many more destinations. The Pyrenees are very young mountains and so, very rough and dramatic. They are beautiful."

Of course I imagined hiking there with Lisele, but I didn't blurt my thoughts. Not now. "I promise to hike the Pyrenees before I leave. They sound spectacular."

"They are, Warner." The flash in her eyes diminished however, as if a cloud, ripe with worrisome thoughts, had obscured the light.

As we were nearing the end of the meal, Lisele made final forays into her plate, then set down her fork, looked at me and smiled. "Warner, at our last meal you talked about the engineering mind. As I said, I was not aware that engineers had minds that were notable for their differences. They are just like people, aren't they?"

I laughed. "Lisele, I don't know. Perhaps the myth of the engineering mind exists more in the U.S. than elsewhere. The engineer is supposed to be concerned only with numbers and the physics, very practical yet unconcerned or uninterested in human relationships or culture—what we call left brained."

"You are correct. I have never heard of this idea. Perhaps it is that way with the American engineers. I don't think Maurice is like that."

339

I jerked my head in acknowledgement. "I agree. Maurice is not like that, but it is like a lot of things—the iconic idea is a lot more extreme than the actual version. The same is true with the Italians, or Poles, or the French, for that matter. But, let me give you an example of how engineers are regarded in the U.S." I made an imaginary square in the air. "A cartoon character is drawn, plastic pencil-holders in his pocket, a slide rule snapped to his belt; he is holding a diploma and wearing a graduation hat. His comment, "Four years ago I could not even spell 'engineer' and now I *are* one."

Lisele shook her head and laughed. "I must say. That is the perception?"

"Yes." I nodded emphatically. Engineers are thought to not care about English or other refinements."

"Do you have any other examples?"

"I do. I have one that points out the engineer's ardent quest for fixing things or solving a puzzle, oblivious to his surroundings. In this episode it seems there were three people assigned to be executed by guillotine. Take note, this could have occurred in France. One was a lawyer, another a doctor and the third, an engineer. The doctor was first. He put his head in the blocks and the rope was pulled. The blade did not fall. Therefore, by French law he was allowed to go free. The same happened with the lawyer. When it became the engineer's turn, as he was about to put his head in the block he looked up and said, "I think I see your problem."

Lisele gasped and laughed. "I think I am getting the idea. Engineers are really not part of the human race. They are driven by other demons."

"They are, indeed." I took a gulp of water and just stared at her with a silly grin. This caused her to laugh again.

Lisele regained her composure and was able to order crème brulet and coffee as a grand finish. "How is your aqueduct, Warner? Have you solved any mysteries?"

"I have, indeed. I walked a few of the critical routes and have determined why they took the route they did."

She pursed her lips. "Don't they just go from A to Z? I mean, yes, they must cross the big river, but I do not see the mystery. What is it?"

"I wanted to know why they crossed the Gard where they did. Why did they leave the hills at Vers and cross to the Gard canyon at that location? It was, I determined, because there was a ridge across the valley that they could use. I didn't read that anywhere, and the professor either could not or would not tell me."

She sat back between dessert bites and sipped her coffee. "So you found this out by walking the aqueduct."

"Yes." Her question gave me an idea. After her hiking comment, I had been trying to think of a way to get Lisele to go on a hike with me. "Lisele, would you be interested in taking a walk along the aqueduct? I think you would enjoy it—find it interesting. Or is this just my engineering mind thinking you might be interested."

"I'd love to. I've lived here all this time and really don't know what the aqueduct is all about. I was hoping you'd ask."

I nodded and smiled. Of course she was ahead of me. Perhaps I should get used to it. The evening ended in my driveway. Lisele did get out of the car and gave me a hug—a damned nice one.

On a cool summer morning, we began our walk along the aqueduct at Vers. I wondered if Lisele was still 'spooked' by not wanting the public to know that she was cavorting with me, but nothing was said. I explained to her that the aqueduct followed the line of hills from Uzes to a point above Vers then headed on the ridge across the valley to the Pont du Gard. From the fountain in the center of Vers we walked up the hill on streets and then onto the path that leads to the trail following the aqueduct. When we encountered the first evidence of the aqueduct, I told Lisele how the conduit was built. We then followed the trail until we were upon the series of arches I had seen earlier, still ghostly and dramatic in my thoughts.

Lisele stood on the path, sighting down the arches and reached for her water bottle. "Warner, I have never seen this—only the Pont du Gard. Of course I knew there was an aqueduct, but I never took the time to explore. I didn't even know there was more to see. This is fascinating."

A smug smile worked its way to my face. "Enchanting isn't it? The structure has been out here for two thousand years, waiting for us to appreciate the magnificent project that it was. I hope you can feel the same sense of awe that I have."

"I am awed. Show me more." She took a drink of water and replaced the bottle in her waist pack.

We walked the path until we encountered the highway in the gorge, climbed down and crossed it, then scrambled up the other side to rejoin the path that followed the structure. As we walked I pointed to the right and left. "See how we are on a high spot? The aqueduct followed this high spot and that is one reason the Pont du Gard crossing is near."

"There are other reasons?"

I turned as we were walking. "Yes, one of the other reasons is that after crossing the Gard, there is a path for the aqueduct on the other side. You'll see."

Immediately before we got to the Pont du Gard, we saw the remains of the diversion structure. I explained that it was possible to divert the water in the aqueduct to the river Gard, should they want.

Hands on hips, again, "Why should they want to do that?"

I liked being the authority, displaying the results of my research. "Let's say they wanted to perform maintenance on the water channel that crossed the bridge. In that instance, they would divert the water. In fact, after they built the structure, they discovered that the water piled up upon encountering the bridge, overflowing the sides. They had to add to the walls and, of course, had to divert the water to do it."

"Really? I guess the engineers must have been distracted by a guillotine or something. How did they let that happen?"

I smiled. "Engineers, although they would not give you this impression, are *not* know-it-alls. There are many tries, failures, and re-tries. Hopefully, we learn by our experience. But, you must remember—I think I told you—on this aqueduct, the slope is very slight. They were working with a situation they had not encountered on most aqueducts. It is a wonder to me that they were able to make this route work. There were probably other re-dos."

We walked across the bridge, the Pont du Gard. As we were doing so, I pointed to the many inscriptions that had been carved into the masonry. "I have an interest in the inscriptions. At the moment I can't distinguish between what might have been done at the time the project was built and what might have been added afterward—like graffiti."

the *Aedifex*: Building the Pont du Gard

Lisele traced the outline of a bulls head, chiseled into the stone. "And why are you interested in the inscriptions?"

I had been kneeling to look at a marking that was hard to see. I stood up and faced her. "Because... I am interested in these, because... they really do not know who was the architect or the builder of the aqueduct. It remains a mystery. There is speculation—an army general, or an architect from Rome, or a prominent local figure—but there is no factual background, only history indicating *how* they had done work on other projects. I have a strong desire to know who was responsible for the building of this structure. I want to know the person who made this work, planned the schedule, gave directions, dealt with the problems, overcame the obstacles. Who was it? What was he like? How did he get the assignment? I am driven to know him, but I fear that we will never find out. The accomplishment of this man is lost to history."

Lisele blinked but said nothing for a while. "Warner, I'm beginning to understand your fascination for this project. You identify with it. Your perspective is that you were the one responsible for its creation and execution. It is your crusade."

It was my turn to blink. Lisele had peeled my exterior and exposed my core, observing something that I, standing too close, had not comprehended. I was obsessed by the project, as if I really were responsible for its execution. I responded slowly. "Yes, Lisele, although I had not been aware of it, I am gripped by the spell."

"And what will you do if you don't find out about the builder?"

I nodded. "I'll have to be happy with imagining how *I* would do it."

Lisele smiled. "Do you have a good imagination? Are you able to fantasize?"

I looked at her and smiled. "Yes, Lisele, I do. I am able to fantasize the most exciting thoughts."

She smiled and didn't dignify my statement with a reply. Lisele turned back to the stone, pointing to an impression just barely visible. In fact it wouldn't have been visible had the sun not been grazing the stone as it now was.

I squinted to sharpen the image and moved so that I could see it more at a swiping angle. "I have not seen that before. I must make a note." I fished into my waist pack for paper and a pencil.

Thomas Hessler

The marking appeared to be three commingled letters, an 'APA' over what looked like a sawhorse... well, perhaps an arch. I had no idea of its meaning. "Good catch, Lisele."

She smirked. "I hope that in a small way I have enriched your experience, fed your obsession, enhanced your passion. It is what I do, you know." She laughed.

I looked up from my notepad. "Do you mind if I don't comment on that? It would be too revealing and, although I am certainly not a man of mystery, you don't need to know the depths of my passion... not now anyway." I laughed. "I think you see me too clearly. I will have to be more guarded."

"Now you are relapsing into your engineer mode. I like it more when your 'self' bubbles to the surface."

"I'll work on it." I said, "Come with me." I walked to a pier and pointed. "See that inscription?"

She looked. "You mean the one with three words, one atop the other?"

"Yes. The three Latin words are:

MENS
TOTUM
CORIUM

"Taken literally, they mean the skin has been measured. Scholars think this was an original inscription, by the builders, indicating that the structure has been carefully measured, carefully designed and carefully built. It is a message to the visitor, and I am fascinated, thinking that the person I am pursuing had his hands on, or at least had a part in, this very inscription."

Lisele stared for a while. "I think I am being captured by the same ghosts that are haunting you. I have a mystical feeling, looking at it, now that I know what it means and what it means to you."

I smiled then pointed to the far side of the structure. "Let's walk across then follow the trail on the other side. We will go through the tunnel and walk as far as the deep canyon—a good place to have our lunch, our *pique nique* as you say in French."

Lisele resumed walking. "*Oui*, a *pique nique*. You brought the sandwiches? I suppose you brought the wine."

"As a matter of fact, I did."

CHAPTER 34

Appius and Gaius were riding, side-by-side, after having made an early morning start to the Vardo canyon. In the afternoon, Appius, spotting the bridge crossing the Vardo, said, "Marius and Pentius were going to try to find an easy way to get to the bottom of the canyon. If they have done so, they should meet us at the bridge to direct us up one side of the river or the other."

Gaius nodded. "Before we are done, we must take measurements on both sides of the river. Do you think we will have to come back to the bridge to get to the other side?"

"I do not recollect any other locations where we might cross. I think so."

"Yes, it would seem that way."

After a few minutes Appius said, "Gaius, I have talked with Bernius about the arch. I do understand that the arch provides a means of reducing the amount of stones required, and allows the passage of water beneath but still provides structural support; it has advantages beyond that of a solid stone wall. But, Gaius, what is the principle of the arch? Why does it work?"

"Ah, yes, my line of work. The secret of the arch is sideways forces. I think that you can imagine that if you had an arch, and it was not braced on the sides, it would first move sideways as you pushed down on its center from above. Imagine the wedge-shaped blocks. A weight from above tends to drive the wedges down and, due to their shape, forces the adjacent blocks sideways. Here, let me demonstrate. We must dismount our horses."

Gaius led Appius to a flat rock and faced him from the other side. "Put your palms together with your fingers facing up, your forearms in an inverted 'V' and your elbows resting on the surface of the rock. If I push down on your fingertips your elbows will spread. If we could constrain your elbows from spreading, I will not be able to force your fingers down. So, we must constrain the sideways force of the arch to make it work."

They climbed back on the horses. Appius said, "Does that mean that when constructing the arch, it must be so constrained?"

"During construction, the arch stones are supported by wooden framework. Sideways support is not needed until the frame is removed. At that time, you had better be certain that your structure cannot move sideways or your arch stones will be on the ground or in the river or your structure will slump."

Appius nodded. "I shall be very interested to see so many arches built at one time. Removal of the framework must be an important moment."

"Yes, and a disastrous one if you have not been careful."

They arrived at the bridge but did not see Pentius or Marius. They looked up one side of the river then crossed the bridge and looked at the other side, trying to understand if they should make their way up the canyon or head up to the rim, and if so, on what side. Soon, a cartman, part of a caravan, walked to them.

He smiled. "I see it is you, Appius. Do you remember me from your trip nearly two years ago?"

Appius raised his hand. "Oh, yes. It is you—the cartman. You are taking your vegetables to the market?"

"Yes, I am. But I am here waiting for my cousin who comes from the north and who will join me in the trip to Nemausus. It so happens, I have a message for you. This morning, Pentius, who I understand is part of your crew, came from upriver, found me and asked if I would give you a message. He said to ride above the river on the south side to the vicinity of the crossing. He will meet you there."

Appius grinned. "Yes, Pentius. He is a stout lad. I thank you for the message, and I am happy to see you again."

The cartman shook his head. "Your stout lad tells me you will build a great aqueduct. I cannot imagine being involved in such things."

Appius shrugged. "Cartman, if you tire of transporting vegetables to market, you might try carting stones from the quarries to the work site."

"No, I will remain with my vegetables. They idea of carrying stones does not interest me."

Appius waved as he turned his horse. "Thank you. Perhaps I will see you again."

"Perhaps. Go well."

the *Aedifex*: Building the Pont du Gard

They rode up the south side of the river, occasionally looking over the edge into the canyon. About 600 feet before the intended aqueduct crossing, Appius spotted Pentius chopping a tree at the side of the path. They approached and Appius shouted, "Pentius, hello. Are you chopping that tree for a reason?"

"I did not like just standing here to wait. I had to do something. I am sure we will be able to use this tree—for something." He pointed to the canyon side. "You can lead the horses down there. I would not ride them; it is farther to fall from up on the horse."

Appius looked over the side, took a deep breath, and said, "Your advice is wise, Pentius. I will lead my horse."

They descended into the canyon with no mishap and were able to walk upriver. Appius spotted the location where they had fixed the crossing, noticeable by the disruption of the stream flow as it encountered a protruding rock. Marius was upstream, tying ropes to what appeared to be tree trunks in the water. They walked to his location and were able to see that a substantial raft had been built, the tree trunks lashed together with rope. Marius was running another rope from the raft to a stout pole hammered into the bank, 100 feet upstream at a bend in the river.

Marius walked back to them. "Hello, Appius." He nodded to Gaius. "I think you will like our arrangement. We felled some tress, de-limbed them and skidded them down into the canyon to make this raft. The rope, anchored upstream, will allow us to get on the raft and swing in the current. By means of working our paddle against the current, we can make the raft cross from one side to the other... I think." He laughed.

Appius shook his head. "You two did all this in the time you were here? An amazement."

"We couldn't just sit here." Pentius looked at Marius.

Appius laughed. "How do you think the horses will do on the voyage?"

"I think we should leave the horses where they are. They are not good sailors, and I do not want them soiling our ship." Marius slapped Pentius on the back.

Gaius walked back downstream to the intended crossing, stood on the bank and looked across to the rock protruding into the river. "I believe we should adjust the crossing line so that we are able to use that rock for a pier foundation for one of the

347

arches. At that, it will be a wide arch to span from the opposite shore to the rock."

Appius asked, "Is there a limit to how wide an arch can be?"

"Aches can be wider than this. But, you must know that the wider the arch, the taller it must be. And, for this structure, while a tall arch might be accommodated, it reduces our options above and may be more difficult to build. Tomorrow, we will take our measurements and check the foundation rock. If we are fortunate, it will be sound and will not show any fractures.

They spent three days at their task. The chorobate was used to establish the height of the protruding rock and other locations where arch pier foundations could be made. The distances, widths, and lengths were measured at the direction of Gaius. He walked up the slopes along the proposed line of the bridge, satisfied that rock would be found against which the arches could be restrained as the structure climbed the canyon. The raft was able to easily transport men, chorobate and provisions from one shore to another. When Pentius and Marius were not required to be doing something, they got on the raft and 'practiced' drifting it from shore to shore.

At the end of the third day, Gaius said to Appius, "We are done for now." We can go back to Nemausus, tomorrow."

Appius walked to the raft upon which Marius and Pentius were practicing their maneuvers. He shouted, "We leave tomorrow. We should beach our raft on high ground so that we may use it again."

The duo nodded and made for the near shore.

In Nemausus, two mornings later at the project office, Appius told Bernius of their expedition. Bernius was pleased with their work but intrigued with the idea of the raft, always amused at the antics, initiative and energy of the two woodsmen.

Bernius said, "I have been working on the schedule, looking at the detail of the activities to give us a better idea of the sequences and the requirements for workers. I also made adjustments to the schedule in the time prior to building the Vardo bridge to allow for the blocks to be aged. I think that while we are designing the bridge, we must also find quarry sites near the bridge, as the sites must be developed and roads built from the quarry to the bridge site. Let us go talk to the quarryman again about this."

"I am anxious to see what you have done on the schedule, but I will walk to the quarry and tell the quarryman that we will be there tomorrow. Did you devise a means to work on more of the underground construction at one time? It seems like that would cause a dramatic difference and must be done."

"No, I have not done that." Bernius shook his head. "You were not gone long enough. I spent my time on the detail of the different modes of construction. I will show you. Then you can be a part of devising a means of working several parts of the route at the same time... I think we can do that."

They sat in the quarryman's shack, trying not to stir the air. The quarryman, coughing, gave them old rags to sit on to avoid contact with the patina of dust that had accumulated uniformly in the office.

Bernius spoke. "On our prior visit, we mentioned that we must find quarries that are near the bridge. Can you help us with that?"

The quarryman shook his head. "I have no interest to be involved in another quarry nor in looking for one. However, this quarry is financed by Vernius Portius, a wealthy Nemausus man whom I am sure you have heard of, Appius. He would be interested in other quarries, and we have talked of your project. After Appius told me you would be here today to talk about a quarry near the Vardo, I contacted Vernius. He will be here soon to talk about this with you. I must tell you, he is a difficult man. Do not expect that he will assist you if it is not in his interest."

After a short time, a man arrived on horseback. He descended slowly, tied the horse, walked to the shack entrance and stood in the doorway, assessing the two visitors. "I am Vernius Portius. I am told you have an interest in quarry operations. How may I help you?"

The quarryman prepared a place for his employer to sit. Bernius looked at Appius and shrugged. "Vernius Portius, I am Bernius, an architect working for the proconsul Claudius and the *Aqua Corporata* of Nemausus." He nodded to Appius, "Appius Polonius, of your city, my assistant."

Vernius remained impassive.

349

Bernius continued. "I am sure you are aware that we have been commissioned to enable the building of a great aqueduct to service the city of Nemausus. Somewhat north of the city, upstream of the existing crossing of the Vardo, a bridge will be required. As the canyon is quite deep and wide where we will cross, many cut stones will be required to build the bridge. It would be difficult to transport stones from this quarry, nearly twenty miles to the site. Therefore, it will be more efficient to quarry stone nearer the site. We would like someone experienced in quarry operations to identify a site, or sites, which may be suitable. That is the help that we seek."

Vernius nodded. "I understand your interests. However, under what understanding would I spend sestertii and effort to find these sites? I will say that I am interested in your project—would like to have a contract to supply your stones. However, I am reluctant to spend the effort to find quarry sites only to have other parties use them in your supply. I think you can understand."

Bernius hesitated, then said, "Then what would you suggest, Vernius?"

"I suggest that when you are serious in your understanding of the stones you will require, you draft a description of your requirements and have those who are interested provide you a price for supplying the stones. Finding and developing the sites will be each contractor's task."

Bernius raised his hand to emphasize, "So, you would ask the supplier to make his own survey, to find a suitable site or sites and give us a price to supply stones?"

"Yes, and I would further suggest that you include the price of drayage of the stones, from the quarry to your bridge site. By that means, you will be able to determine your real cost considering also the distance the stones must be transported. Said another way, someone who responds to your pricing might have a very low price but from a quarry at a great distance. You will use up the advantage in the low price of the stones in transporting the stones to your site."

Bernius nodded. "I think your suggestion has considerable wisdom. I intend that we draft a requirement for our supply of stones. If it is not a great imposition, I ask that you review that draft so that we can ensure that those who are to provide a price are clear in their understanding. Can we expect that you will review this draft for us?"

"I would be pleased to do so. Although I am sure you will select the offer that is most advantageous to the project, I do understand that my effort will not be forgotten." Vernius smiled.

"Your suggestion has been invaluable." Bernius stood and addressed Vernius. "I do hope that your pricing will result in a successful contract with the project. Appius—any questions?"

Appius shook his head. "No. I marvel at the ability of a contractor to propose such an undertaking."

Bernius looked at Vernius Pontius and the quarryman. "Thank you for this most valuable input. We will contact you when we have a draft of our request."

As Bernius walked with Appius back to Nemausus along a tree-lined path, negotiating the deep furrows hewn by carts with heavy loads, he said, "The quarryman mentioned that Vernius was a difficult man, yet I found his suggestions to be quite reasonable."

"Yes, the idea that the supplier would take the responsibility to find a suitable quarry site, to develop the quarry, and to transport the stones to the site makes it simpler for us. If we were to say, 'use this site,' it is possible that the site would not be adequate. In that outcome, it would be very doubtful as to who must shoulder the blame and the additional costs that would surely result. What will you do now?"

"We will continue with our design. When it becomes known of the sizes, shapes, and number of blocks, we will be ready to ask those who are interested to provide pricing. However, I am thinking that it would be useful if we were to inform the suppliers of our *approximate* requirements now, before we know the final quantities and configuration so that they can start looking for sites."

Appius nodded as he walked alongside, "Yes. I do not know how long it will take experienced quarry operators to find and investigate possible sites, but, if it requires many months, your suggestion should be a useful means to shorten the amount of time needed to respond to our request for pricing. Will you do that?"

"Yes. See how our schedule is changing as we uncover more information?"

"I do see." Appius turned to Bernius. "I am overwhelmed, yet intrigued as to the considerations that are made on such a project. In looking at other projects of large scale, I did not have

351

44

erThomas Hessler

any concept of what it takes to accomplish that which I was seeing."

"Indeed, Appius, indeed."

Gaius worked for several weeks studying the measurements they had taken in the canyon of the Vardo. It was clear. One arch would have to span 80 feet so that its piers would rest on the rock outcroppings. From this width he calculated, based on his experience, the height of that widest arch and then the vertical distance of stones atop the arch, required to provide a continuous flat surface upon which the next level of arches would stand. The remainder of arches at the first level would not be as wide as the one spanning the river, but nearly so. Gaius said to Bernius and Appius, looking over his shoulder as he explained, "You will not be able to tell that the arches are not of uniform size by looking. The scene will be graceful and pleasing."

"I see that the arches you have atop the bottom arches, the second tier, are exactly aligned with those underneath." Bernius pointed to the sketch.

Gaius nodded. "Yes, the piers of the middle and bottom arches are in vertical alignment. In that way the forces are transmitted through the lower *piers*, minimizing the weight supported by the lower arches. The arch, although strong, cannot carry as much weight as the stacked rock of the piers."

"I have a question." Appius pointed to the rock outcropping into the river. "We have to assume that the rocks under the pier foundations are... solid, that they will not sink or fracture. What if that is not so?"

"If that were not so, it would be very difficult, indeed." Gaius looked at Appius, then at Bernius then turned to again look at the sketch. "I have spent much time looking at the outcroppings when we were in the canyon. If we experience a problem, we would have to find a solution. That is all I can say."

Bernius asked. "What now remains? Of course, you must plan the top row of arches to support the conduit and to reach the top of the canyon. It appears that those arches will be much shorter."

"Yes, much shorter and of much less width, perhaps three or four will be used to span the distance of each of the arches below. I will calculate the most useful arrangement."

352

the *Aedifex*: Building the Pont du Gard

Bernius looked at Appius. "Once he has done that, we may make assessments of the amount of stone required. We can advise those interested in quarry operations of our approximate requirements. They may start looking for quarry sites." He turned to look at Gaius. "Then, Gaius, what will you be doing?"

"I will then begin the very laborious task of designing the shapes and dimensions of the stones. The arches, in particular, take a long time, especially if they will be precisely fashioned in the quarry yard. I will spend much time with my design, my geometry, to ensure that all the many components of our bridge will fit together well to provide a sturdy structure and to minimize the corrections that would be made at the bridge site. It is in these tasks that I can use help from the rest of our team. We must work with precision and constantly check each other's work to see that we have not overlooked an error."

Bernius nodded toward Numerius and Vibius, looking at maps involving their work. "I will have Numerius and Vibius work with you. Appius and I will help from time to time, but for now, we need to work on the schedule. We have much to consider."

Gaius nodded. "I will devise a scheme for the upper tier of arches then I will need the help. I am pleased to be the designer on such a magnificent structure."

A few days after Appius and Bernius met with the quarry owner, Bernius showed Appius a written statement. "This is to be made public so that those interested in providing the stones for the structure can begin looking for sites. I describe the location of the bridge on the river Vardo, provide a description of the structure—three tiers of arches—and a description of what the vendor should provide. Simply, the vendor will provide stones, precisely cut and smoothed, to our worksite. It is intended that the vendor will locate a quarry or quarries near the site, free the stones, age them for a year and then cut them and finish them to the dimensions required. With this statement, the vendor is responsible for finding the quarry and transporting the stones as Vernius Portius has suggested. It also requires the vendor to be responsible for guessing how many stones quarried will be unsuitable for use in the project."

"You mean because they split or spall when being quarried or during the aging process?"

"Yes. Although they are responsible, we will, of course, see this result of this requirement in their price."

"I have a question. Does the requirement to transport the stones mean that the quarry vendor will be responsible for building the road from the quarry to the site?"

"That is a good question—one that I had not considered. I am inclined to require them to build the road. It would be an idea similar to that of requiring them to do the cartage; those that include the lowest transportation costs have a better chance of providing the low price and, of course, opportunity to include more profit in the price. Yes, the road should be part of the transportation costs."

"It is also possible that they could deliver the stones from a quarry upstream or even downstream, on the river. No road required."

"Hmmm. Yes. A good thought. Also, if the quarry operators could use the route along the aqueduct, we should receive a lower price, but it would mean we would be required to have that route cleared and excavated before they started transporting stones. I think I will suggest that option in our notice. The stone vendors need to know that information to select the most useful quarry location. We are taking a chance that we can actually provide the road at the time required, but we could change that condition if we have to, prior to the time we give them the final bidding information. Anything else?"

"Nothing else."

"Then let us visit Vernius tomorrow and get his advice on our notice. You will make the arrangement?"

Appius nodded. "Yes."

Appius and Bernius sat on benches in a peristyle open area, a fountain gurgling in the center—the house of Vernius Portius. It appeared that quarry operations could be profitable although Vernius was invested in other ventures besides the quarry.

Vernius read the notice that Bernius had drafted. "Yes, I find most of this to be acceptable. I think you should include one more provision, although I understand this is not the final document requesting prices. I think you should advise those who are interested that the final pricing will identify the cost to establish the quarry—or quarries. The successful vendor will be reimbursed costs for establishing the quarry, even before the first stone is delivered—perhaps on a monthly basis. Any viable quarry vendor understands that the intentions and the actions of the Empire can be... wispy. In other words, the quarry owners could spend a fortune developing a site and quarrying the first stones only to have the Empire decide to use the treasury money to wage war in Anatolia. Under my provisions, once the stone delivery begins, the Empire or *Corporata* will be given a credit spread amongst the first—let us say—10,000 stones, for the sestertii that have been paid for the development. Do you understand my method?"

Bernius nodded. "I do understand. Otherwise, it may be difficult to get vendors to risk their sestertii for such a time. I will include your suggestion." He reached for the notice and scribbled the suggestion upon it then looked up at Vernius. "I will go to the *Corporata* and inform them. A request for pricing has to be done by an agency to which the vendor will be contracted. To be honest, I do not think this responsibility—for financial responsibility on the project—has been established between the *Corporata* and the Empire. We might as well get that process started if it has not been done."

Vernius nodded, gave them a knowing look then stood. "I assume I will hear of your progress on that issue."

Bernius nodded, also standing, "Yes, and I hope that we will soon issue this notice."

As Bernius and Appius walked to the project office, Bernius said, "I am anticipating that the *Corporata* will not be pleased with what we are doing. They, no doubt, think that any substantial payment requirements are some time in the future, and I do not think they want to be named as the party responsible for payment. I expect we will see drama as a result of our 'notice.'"

Appius smiled. "Do not leave me at the office. I do not want to miss the encounter."

CHAPTER 35

Bernius and Appius sat on stone benches in the atrium of Nemus's house. Nemus was standing, reading the notice to be given to interested suppliers, those that would bid to supply stones for the bridge across the Vardo. After reading the brief statement, he turned to Bernius and Appius. "You would have the quarrymen look for quarry sites at this early date?" His question did not address the concern he disregarded for the moment—that of having to supply sestertii earlier than imagined.

"Yes, the stones must age a year before they are cut to the final dimensions—a year before they can be used to start the structure." Bernius looked up at Nemus. "We must start the activities that lead to production of the stone or else wait for a year with little progress on the bridge structure—the project feature that will take the longest time."

Nemus thought, *Better if we do not want to spend sestertii.* "What do you want of the *Corporata*? Why are you showing me this statement?"

Bernius shrugged. "When a contract is made, the supplier must contract with a responsible entity, one they can depend on for payment. At this time I am not aware of whether that entity is the *Corporata* or the Empire. When I issue the statement to the interested suppliers, I would like to advise them of the contracting entity. What do you have to say?"

"You are correct. There is no agreement between the *Corporata* and the Empire. Payments, so far, have been on a casual basis and paid by the *Corporata*. But we have not contracted with *you*, as an example. You are aware that the *Corporata* is obligated to a limit but beyond that, it is the Empire. What would you have us do?" Nemus scowled, letting his arm holding the statement fall to his side.

Bernius, who had diverted his gaze to the mosaics on display in the atrium, turned to Nemus. "It seems like you must make an arrangement with Claudius. That is what I am suggesting unless the *Corporata* wants to assume the responsibility. My thought is that you do not want the *total* responsibility."

Nemus nodded. "Of course, you are right. I will talk to the *Corporata*, and we will deal with Claudius. I will tell you what has been decided when we have come to an agreement. I do not see this as a simple matter. I hope you are patient."

Bernius smiled. "I am not so patient, Nemus, and I am not a novice in observing the pace at which understandings are reached between government entities. You can understand why I am talking to you now. We will leave the issue in your capable hands and wait... if we must... for the outcome."

Nemus nodded and summoned a servant to walk his visitors to the door.

While walking, as they turned from Nemus's property onto the road, Appius asked Bernius, "It could be months before an agreement is struck. Must we wait until they agree before issuing the statement?"

"No, I will issue it now. Those who would be interested in supplying the rock might be concerned that the responsible party has not been identified, but they will look for quarry sites. They will take the risk that a proper contracting entity will be formed by the time they have to sign a contract. The eventual contract will be of great value, and, if the supplier is diligent, has not made any errors in the estimate and his bid, does not suffer extreme bad fortune, and the paying entity does not default, he will earn a decent profit."

Appius shook his head. "Such men are mad. Any of the considerations you mentioned could go wrong. Why do they do it?"

"The temptation to be involved in great works is strong. Contracting large projects is truly the game of kings."

"Do you think Nemus thinks that you will wait for them to make an arrangement?"

"He might be assuming that. I rather think so. We should know shortly as I intend to advertise the statement immediately."

"How will you do that?"

"I will have the statement posted in Nemausus and other towns having a substantial commerce in the region. I will have the statement posted in Rome, and I will have a copy delivered to quarries that exist. Their operators or owners are possible, maybe probable, contenders."

Thomas Hessler

"Then, while the quarry suppliers are wandering the hills, we must determine the actual requirements, stone by stone."

"Yes."

Nemus was entertaining the *Corporata*. As expected, Titus was upset. "What happened to the two years of design costs that we were expecting before the heavy outflow required of building?" Titus set down his wine cup—pottery, because Nemus was not serving the *Corporata* using his collection of expensive glass goblets, having lost one in a prior fray.

"You heard the explanation about aging of the stones." Nemus shrugged. "I can only tell you that... except... I did think Bernius would wait until we had a contracting agreement with Claudius before he posted notice."

Titus stormed. "We are much closer to having to provide large outlays of funds, probably a year closer—would you say, Aulus?"

"That is my sense of it. Marcus?" Aulus squinted as if seeing the progress.

"The notice states that payment will be made as the quarry is developed and the stones are produced, before they are aged. I think we could be closer than one year." Marcus shook his head and took a drink.

After several moments of silence, Nemus spoke. "Nevertheless, we must talk to Claudius about contract arrangements. I am not sure it matters—if we run out of money, it will make no difference—but perhaps there are advantages to having the *Corporata* as the contracting agency. It seems this responsibility could wield great power. Imagine a number of contractors intent on pleasing us; that *could* be to our considerable benefit. The alternative is that all work be done under the authority of the Empire. That situation could be worse, the funds would be spent—our funds—and we would have no say."

Julius put his finger to his head. "Perhaps we should propose to Claudius that we, the *Corporata*, be the contracting entity, with funding backed up by the Empire. As you say, Nemus, it may not make a difference in the long run, but at least the perception would be that we had operational authority and the Empire the financial responsibility."

Marcus mused. "I like that. If we agree, we should go to Claudius and suggest that arrangement. But, if we are the

358

contracting party, we will be required to have staff to oversee and administer the project."

The others blinked. Aulus said, "Perhaps the Empire should be the overseer. Do we really want to deal with the contracts? I think not. There will be many problems. The contractors will look to us to provide solutions—often more sestertii. Rather than receive benefit from these dealings, we may, more likely, incur their wrath. Better that there only be an arrangement between the Empire and us that we provide the first 5000 sestertii, each month, as the limit of our responsibilities."

"That month will be sooner rather than later," growled Titus.

"I do understand the concern of Aulus," said Nemus, "and, although I thought there might be an advantage if we were the operating entity, I now think it better if we were at arm's length. Do you all agree?"

All agreed except Titus who agreed with nothing.

"I have not had an opportunity to show you what I have done on the schedule." Bernius sorted through several loose, large scraps of paper to find the one he sought. "While you were gone, I arranged the elements of each major activity into the sequences we discussed... remember... some operations must be finished, or at least started, before another can start."

"Yes, I remember you saying that." Appius turned the paper so he could see.

"We also talked about constructing the buried portion of the aqueduct in sections that may be all under construction at the same time, thus reducing the time required—16 years—if we were to start at the springs and work toward Nemausus. I am thinking that the separate sections would be—the run down the Alzon River, the run from the Alzon to the turn before the ridge, the ridge to the tunnels below the Vardo, and the long run from the tunnels to Nemausus. If we are working on those four major sections at one time, we will cut our 16 years to 5. There will be other underground work, not in those sections, but we will also construct that work in parallel. Do you understand?"

"Yes. But it seems very important that we be able to tell the workers how deep to excavate for the bottom of the conduit. If they are starting in the middle of the entire route at some location, how will they know how deep to dig without the knowing what is behind them? Is there a way to do that?"

"Here is my thought, Appius. Our maps and our calculations will provide our best understanding of the depth or height of the water conduit, even though we know there is still some error. At each section we will excavate the first 6 feet of earth. We will flood each section with a small depth of water to determine what is level. I have communicated with the architects in Rome. That method was used on the Aqua Virgo. If we can establish *level*, we will know the drop between the Ucetia springs and Nemausus precisely. We will be able to accurately slope the floor of the conduit to our calculated drop. The top 6 feet should be able to be excavated more quickly than the earth below, as we will run into less rock, and we will ensure that we have a robust crew removing the first 6 feet. I am thinking we should complete the excavation of the first 6 feet in *all* the sections before we continue the stair-step excavation down to the floor of the trench. What do you think?"

Appius wagged his head. "I am trying to picture the process as you have described it. You flood the excavated section with water, identify what is level, and then you must remove the water. Yes?"

"Yes. And that is sometimes difficult. We use as little water as possible as it may take considerable work just to get water *to* the excavation and then to remove it afterwards."

"There is also a problem with water leaking out?"

Bernius nodded. "Yes, that too. They sometimes had to find clay to apply to the sides or bottom of the excavation when the water escaped through a crack in the rock or through porous soil. The method is difficult, but provides a solution when great accuracy is required for a shallow slope."

"We do not have that work identified in our estimate." Appius pointed to the document.

"No. We will have to add it. It will be significant. I estimate that it will add 2500 mandays and 50,000 sestertii to the cost."

"That is significant. Is there no other way?"

"Not that has been used nor of which I can imagine. Perhaps you have an idea?" Bernius swiveled to look at Appius.

"I do have a thought. We need standing water to establish accurate level, correct?"

"Yes."

"But we do not need to fill the entire channel. The water could be in a trough cut into the bottom of the excavation. In that way we would have to handle less water." Appius pointed to a sketch of the channel.

Bernius nodded. "Yes, that would be an improvement. I believe that method may have been tried at the very end of the excavation at the Aqua Virgo. I wish I had paid more attention. I believe that when using that method, they were still plagued with leaks."

"Hmmm. What if instead of cutting a trench, we install short sections of clay pipe—I mean clay pipe with no top—so we can see the water level. If we had mastic to seal the ends of short sections of pipe, they would not leak. Even less water than the trench would be used. We would not have to find and seal leaks. In a trench, the floor is liable to be uneven; a trench to provide level might be difficult to construct. With the pipes, you could prop them off the floor to level them even with the water in the pipe. And the pipes could be used again and again."

"Let me think about this. It seems to me the pipes would also be useful for the aboveground construction if the slope of the ground is not great. Yes, the pipes are a useful idea, but where do we get clay pipes with no tops?"

"In Nemausus, the potter also makes clay pipes. I will talk to him. I am sure he can make them; my concern would be that they be strong enough to stand the rigors of transportation and handling."

Bernius nodded. "I think we should investigate. Yes, talk to the potter. We should also be able to do that for less than my estimate of 2500 mandays." He reached for another scrap of paper. "If we can be assured of an accurate means of establishing the bottom of the conduit, our construction by section will work; the entire construction time will be shortened. Using that approach, the bridge at the Vardo will then take the most time."

Bernius pointed to the diagram. "If you look at my plan, I have shown work activities as horizontal lines. On the diagram, work flows from left to right. In some sequences, one line begins where another ends, in a continuous string of activities. When you see this, it means one activity must be completed before the next one starts. An example, on the Vardo bridge, we have to prepare a rock foundation before we can start installing the first cut stones on top—the piers that support the arches. The piers follow the foundations and the arch section follows the piers. But, you will see that before the arch installation starts, we have to build the framework that supports the arch, and we need the piers installed to support the framework."

Appius nodded. "The sequence is foundations then piers then framework then arches."

"Yes. I call this the *essential* path. But, you will see that other activities are *not* on that path. They have to be done just in time to allow the essential activities to start, but they are not dependent on items along the essential path. The supplying of stones is an example. Production and delivery of the pier stones must be complete before the pier installation but do not have to wait for the foundations. The supply of the stones is done in parallel with the *essential* path."

"I see that your diagram is useful to understand if the parallel operations are being accomplished in time to support the essential operations."

"Yes. And, if we accumulate the time along the essential path, we can determine how long our structure will take to construct. On this essential path, the duration is five years."

"Five years to build the bridge... "

"Starting with the foundations—but that assumes that the stones are ready to install upon them when the foundations are complete. That is why we are starting the quarrying operations early so that we will have finished stones when we are ready to build."

"I see a number of activities are required to be completed before starting the foundations."

"Yes. We must be complete with the design of the first two tiers of arches, and we must have awarded a contract for the foundation work." Bernius looked at Appius. "There is another advantage of the essential path. What if the Empire told us to have the work completed six months earlier than our path indicates? We would first look at the activities on the essential path to find a way to shorten them. We could possibly do that by adding additional manpower, working longer, or providing additional lifting devices. Once we see what is possible to shorten the essential path, we adjust the parallel activities to suit, perhaps starting them earlier, perhaps applying more manpower to them. It is a way to control the work."

Appius sat back. "I see another value to diagramming the work."

"What is that?"

"Now that I have looked at your diagram, I understand how the work will progress. I understand how one activity relates to another. I could not do that by just seeing a list of the activities required."

"Good. You are now able to make decisions based on your understanding. If the work is behind schedule, do you work everybody longer hours or add men to *every* activity? No. You work on the ones that will do the most good. The diagram is a primary decision-making tool. In this way, the project does not just happen; it is managed."

Appius smiled, understanding that the 'tool' that Bernius had shown him was similar to acquiring a tool for physical work, an invaluable tool. He noted such in his daily log.

Bernius ate dinner with Appius and Antonia on many occasions. The couple provided the food; Bernius brought the wine and often news from Rome. Bernius enjoyed his evenings with the family; otherwise, he would be foraging on his own and entertained only by his lonely thoughts.

Appius hefted Sergius in his arms and once again introduced him to his 'uncle' Bernius. Sergius was delighted to meet Bernius and gurgled much about the status of Bernius's health and other issues of the day. Bernius participated in these ooglings, much to the delight of the child. On this date, he brought a wooden ring for Sergius to play with. Then, Appius was off with Sergius, pointing out birds, the moon, and trees visible from their yard.

Bernius walked to Antonia. She was standing, cutting vegetables. As she turned to look at Bernius, he said, "It would seem that Appius is very much captivated by Sergius. It is as if the two were playmates. I am sure Appius will have Sergius working with us in only a short time."

Antonia beamed. "It is as if Appius has been captured in a spell. The child is his delight. I am glad to see it."

"Sometimes I regret that I did not stay in one location and take a wife, or take a wife and bring her along. That could be me romping with Sergius."

Thomas Hessler

"Well, Bernius, it is interesting that you should say that. I am just about ready with our meal, so I will speak of my thoughts, later. Can you help me carry the vegetables to our table?"

"Yes. And I will pour more wine."

Later, with the toddler secured at the table, they ate cheese, bread and a goat stew. Antonia, nearly complete with her meal, looked up and said, "Bernius."

Bernius looked up abruptly. "Did I do something wrong, forget to pour your wine, commit odorous offenses? What is it?"

Antonia set down her bowl and smoothed her *tunic*. "Bernius, earlier you were talking about your interest in finding a wife."

Bernius held up his hand. "Antonia, I do not think I said that. I merely entertained the thought that I had not taken a wife."

Antonia shook her head and went on. "No matter. Perhaps it seemed to me that you regretted that you were not fortunate to have the advantages of a wife in your life." She looked at Appius.

Bernius considered thoughts ranging from advantage to disadvantage but smiled and said only, "Antonia, what is your point?"

Antonia, tapping her foot, said, "Bernius, one of my sisters—a very delightful person, I must say—has been suffering somewhat because her husband was a year ago killed by thieves. We, the multitude, help her and her children, but, of course, life is still difficult for her. Bernius?"

"Yes, Antonia?" Bernius was fidgeting with his knife and fork.

"Bernius, perhaps it would be interesting for you to meet Juliena. She is very bright, has exceptional abilities, and intensely admires men who design aqueducts." She laughed. "There are many of the local men who would like an opportunity to meet Juliena, but Juliena will listen to me. What do you say?"

Bernius, torn between the possible outcome in which he was no longer invited to dine and a situation in which he might have to feign an improbable story, said, "You think that I should meet this fascinating creature, obviously a pinnacle of womanhood, a divine spirit, and a maternal wonder." He delighted in using humor as a means of deflecting serious consideration. "Of course. How could I possibly say no?"

Antonia smiled. Appius looked between Antonia and Bernius. Bernius looked to Antonia for his next assignment.

Antonia said, "It is good. The gods would approve. Bernius—show up properly bathed and groomed two nights from now. I will invite Juliena and her three children so that you can appreciate the entire package. If you need to do more investigation to determine the nature of Juliena, that will be up to you. What do you say?"

Bernius shuddered inwardly at the thought of assuming the responsibility for other people but also calculated the advantages of acquiring children without having to go through the early stages. "It will be my delight, Antonia. And, you can be assured of the grooming and bathing tasks if Appius does not work me too hard."

"Good. It is done. Let us enjoy our wine." Antonia sat back, beaming, looking at Bernius.

Appius said nothing but was rather amused at the entertainment.

Gaius was standing next to Bernius's desk, a rolled sketch in his hands. Bernius looked up. Gaius said, "Bernius, I have finished devising the general concept of the bridge. Of course, I do not have the actual dimensions for the sides of the canyon at different elevations, but we will best determine them as we are building. We will extend the line of arches at each of the three elevations until we contact good foundations on either side."

"Let me see. Ah, yes, you have also shown a scheme for the conduit across the top. How did you determine the size of the water passage?"

"I considered the quantity of water provided by the springs and estimate that the water will take one day to travel from Ucetia to Nemausus. I then increased the size, based on that requirement by one-quarter."

"And the one-quarter takes care of...?"

"It is of a higher capacity because our knowledge in estimating flow is not precise. Also, for aqueducts that have been in service for a long time, minerals deposited on the walls restrict the flow. Our aqueduct will last longer if this condition is anticipated."

Bernius looked at the diagram of the water passage, nodding his head. "I believe this means you are ready to start detailing the dimensions and shapes of the stones that will be required. Have you given thought to this?"

"Yes. The stones at the arches will need to be precisely cut. Because the arches on the first two tiers are of different spans, we must detail the stones differently; that will take some time."

"What span is the largest arch?"

"The largest is the one that crosses the river—a little more than 80 feet; the next largest is 70 feet. They are of great span but not the greatest the Empire has built."

"I see from the sketch that the bridge is graceful, a structure capable of flying. Let us gather Numerius and Vibius. We will begin the detailing of the stones."

"Appius, we need to continue to improve the schedule. I would like you to take a large piece of paper—or several large pieces, probably—and draw a representation of the entire schedule. The schedule will be arranged in months from left to right, starting now and extending to the end of the project. At this time, we have assigned the number of men that will work on each activity and by using our estimate have determined how long that task would take. You will establish the lines representing the tasks to the same scale as the months. In other words, an activity—say excavating a tunnel—lasting 3 months would be scaled to represent 3 months—one of 4 months scaled to 4 months. Do you understand?"

"Yes, but I need to know where to draw those lines."

"I will show you." Bernius grabbed a scrap piece of paper. "We will first establish the lines along the essential path. That is the backbone of our schedule." He drew several lines connected in a series, a small triangle denoting the end of each line. "Other activities that feed into the essential activities will be arranged so that they will start *just in time* to finish before they are required for their dependent essential activity."

"But will not some feed-in activities continue to be required while the dependent activity is ongoing? For example, stones will still be quarried and finished as the bridge is being built."

"Yes, we will find a way to show that. But, let us say that we have done what I am suggesting. We can now look at each month and accumulate the mandays of all the activities occurring in that month and then for all the months. In that way we will be able to determine the number of men required at any time."

"I see. That would be very useful."

"Also, from the number of men required each month, we can calculate the funding requirements for each month."

"Such a display would cause the *Corporata* to choke."

"I am afraid you are right. But, let me get back to what we are doing. When we first do the layout, we will find that the manpower requirements will be erratic and that there will be peak requirements at various times. It would be best if the manpower for the project built up on a gradual basis, stayed at a given level then declined on a gradual basis. So! We will see what happens when we draft our first try. From that, if we want to smooth our manpower, we will rearrange activities that are *not* essential activities to occur earlier than we have shown if it will help us. When we are satisfied we have done what is reasonable, we will know when to start each of our many activities to try for the best result."

"This task will require much work, especially if we have to redraw the schedule many times."

"It is true. But you will find that you... and I... will become very familiar with the requirements of the project. Our effort in developing the schedule may be the greatest value, helping us to get an understanding of the requirements of the project. Oh, I must tell you something else. We will identify the months on the schedule... Maius, Quintilis and so. If we see that we are arranging an activity to be done in the wet and cold winter months, and it is an activity that would suffer much from foul weather and if we can move it to a milder part of the year without affecting the essential path, we will do so."

"What about things that do not go as our plan shows or that take longer than our estimate? Or, what if we cannot get the manpower that we calculate?"

"Yes, and probably all of that will happen. We must be able to adjust our schedule to accommodate those problems."

"Hmmm, Bernius, I am thinking. It seems like it is very laborious to redraw the schedule for each time we want to make a change or to rearrange the activities. If we acquired another building from the *Corporata*, we could remove all the furnishings and scribe your months on the floor and fashion sticks of various lengths to represent the duration of the activities. We could then create the schedule on the floor. If we want to make a change, we merely pick up the sticks and move them. When we are satisfied with our plan, based on what we know at that time, we can draw the schedule on paper so that others can see more easily. Will that work?"

Bernius smiled. "Appius, you have a gift for imagining a better way. It will serve you well. But, yes, I like your idea. Let us see if the *Corporata* will provide a building at least as lovely as this. You will talk to them?"

"Yes. This activity feels like it is the very heart of planning our project. I will go at once. I am anxious to start although I am overwhelmed as to what we must do."

"Oh, Appius, there is one scheduling concern that bothers me, and it has to do with natural phenomena, the seasons."

"You mean that in rainy seasons the work may be slowed?"

Bernius nodded. "There is that, but of even more concern is that the Vardo occasionally floods, sometimes severely. If we were to be in vulnerable activities at the time of flood, we could experience a disaster."

"What activities would be vulnerable—surely they would have to do with the bridge."

"Yes, although other structures could suffer—where we crossed smaller gullies or canyons. I am concerned that if we had only a few stones placed for the foundations, the force of the water could dislocate them or wash them away, even if they are of great weight. Even more catastrophic and more probable would be that the timbers supporting arches would be swept away. If our arches in the lower tier were only partially complete, their destruction would cause the entire arch structure to collapse."

"I understand what you are saying. We must give that serious thought."

"Indeed."

It was not easy for the quarrymen. They, of course, searched the terrain near the location of the Vardo Bridge. Often, parties of competitors, both intending to submit pricing, encountered each other as they searched the terrain for suitable quarry sites. Although their encounters were good-natured on the surface, each party was wary that the other party might be watching their activity to discover if they had missed a quarry site with suitable stone.

the *Aedifex*: Building the Pont du Gard

The terrain was difficult. Earth and shrubbery covered most of the rock, making it difficult to know if a quarry site lay underneath. Nevertheless, if they wanted to participate, they had to find a site or several sites. The outfit that did the best job of this, or, as is often the situation with bidding, the contractor or supplier willing to take the most risk and offer the lowest price would be awarded the work.

Vernius Portius was satisfied that he had a reasonable approach to establishing a quarry for the stone production required on the bridge. He sat on his horse on the banks of the Vardo, nearly one-half mile below the intended crossing. Staring across the river with him was Sextus Ventius, the leader of the crew that had been walking the terrain, looking for rock outcroppings, picking at loose earth if necessary, and mapping what they had found.

Vernius addressed Sextus. "I believe that the rock we see across the river will provide much of what is needed for the bridge. Fortunately, we can see the extent of the rock and must presume that it will continue as we quarry farther into the rock face. Unfortunately, all of our competitors can see it too. We cannot assume any pricing advantage in using this site. The distance to the bridge is not far, and it appears that it would be possible to transport the finished stones by use of a barge pulled upriver by capstans or donkeys.

Sextus asked, "Perhaps it would be easier to build a road?"

"Perhaps it would. But, as you can see, the terrain is difficult. We must study alternatives before we provide a price. However, we may have an advantage that other bidders have not discovered. The other site we discovered to the north and west appears useful and would be located along the route of the aqueduct. We will be able to use the road along the aqueduct for transport, and we will not have to build it. I do not think our competitors have found that site."

"We need to get pricing from carters for drayage from that site to the bridge."

"No, we will not. If we ask for their pricing, others will hear of our site from the carter's lips. We must calculate our drayage pricing based on *our* best knowledge and be confident that we can receive adequate pricing from the carters after we are awarded the contract. If we do not get pricing that is under our price, *we* will provide the carting. I must have your word and that of our crew that you will not speak of the other site. I believe that other bidders will worry that *this* river site," he pointed across the river, "will not be adequate to provide all the stone and will have to consider another site to be used, and the site they select will be more difficult than the other that we have found. That is our advantage."

Sextus nodded. "You have my word, and I assure you that those on the crew will not speak of what they have seen. We want you to be the successful bidder, thinking that we will be able to obtain worthwhile work with you."

"Yes, I understand that. But, often, men talk if they are induced to do so by immediate reward."

"It is so. However, I will know if this happens. I have means to make sure that it does not."

Bernius and Juliena circled each other like wrestlers watching to spot an advantage. They were in the early stages of a dinner in the courtyard of Appius and Antonia, the courtyard brimful of activity with three children bouncing here and there, bent on discovery and utilization of all that foreign territory had to offer. Juliena had to take time away from her assessment to tame her offspring, to no avail, of course.

The confines of the courtyard, the activity of the children, and the subtle tension involving the other circling wrestler unsettled Bernius. However, at his best, he was often uncomfortable with women if there was a possibility of a relationship. How should he handle this particular encounter?

It was true. Antonia had not misspoke. Juliena was an attractive woman and somewhat calm in the midst of the storm and rampage that swirled around her. She had a nice smile, directed at Bernius, actually. He was warmed by its implications— one human approaching another—inviting—accepting. He was tempted. Oh, yes, he was tempted to engage, find out more about this creature, imagining intimate rendezvous over wine as a result of his effort. But, once started, these situations were hard to stop.

He must soon encounter Juliena, as part of his agreed role, but he would maintain a 'distance' in order *not* to give the impression that he was... interested. Would he be able to be that clever? And, really, what nature of person was Juliena? Would he be able to talk to her at length, about other than town chatter? Ah, yes, that would be the outcome. She would not be able to talk of much other than that which went on about her. He could easily steel himself against interest in... future activity.

Bernius summoned inner strength and, after Juliena had once again established law and order amongst her children, he approached her and offered his opening gambit for a conversation. "So." He tried an engaging smile.

Juliena looked up at him, returning his smile. "So? You are making it difficult to respond. 'So' has so many possibilities that I am reluctant to pick one that I might favor. Would you like to reintroduce your statement... or was it a question?"

Bernius was momentarily flummoxed at Juliena's response, but impressed that she had made a fair assessment of his lack of approach. "I will have to admit, I was hoping you would ignore my inartful comment and start a real conversation. I will try again. Read any good books, lately?" Nothing like jumping to the crux of his investigation. He was sure his notion of a vacuous existence would soon be validated.

Juliena's eyes bugged and she stepped back. "Books? What happened to 'are you having a nice summer' or 'your children are good looking,' neglecting, of course, that they are not well behaved. You ask me about books?"

Bernius laughed. "I am not a gifted conversationalist, especially when it involves talking with striking women. So—and I hobble with *that word*, again—in just a short time you have learned something about me. It is my turn to learn something about you." He took a drink of wine, giving Juliena a direct look, thinking he had spoken cleverly.

"I will answer your question. No, I have not recently read any good books."

Just as he thought.

"In this town, not much more than a village in some respects, it is not easy to acquire books, especially good books. Perhaps with your connections to Rome, you might be able to start a few books on their way. Or, perhaps you have some that you would be willing to share."

Quite unexpected, actually, putting one on the back of one's heels. A response would be appropriate. "I do have a number of books with me, some that I consider to be good. What do you like? I was not prepared for your response."

"I like Greek plays and accounts of history, and I like poetry. I do not care for technical accounts although I have looked through Appius's book by Vitruvius and find interesting passages. I may actually read it in my desperation. So—my turn now—you did not expect that I would read. If you have spent much time with Antonia, you must know that we were poured into the same mold, nurtured in the same nest. We are women to be reckoned with."

"You are indeed." Bernius imagined that he had just fallen in a pit, a deep one with steep sides. It was going to be difficult to escape. "I will be most happy to have you look at my books. As far as reckoning with you, I note that I am clay in the hands of Antonia. She is much too clever for me. Might I expect the same treatment from you?"

"Of course. Do you have the courage?"

"I think it might be worth a try."

Antonia, reluctant to break up what appeared to be a rapt conversation, nevertheless put a hand on the shoulder of each. "Juliena, please gather your children. We are ready to eat." She looked at Bernius. It was not a questioning look, more of one that indicated superior wisdom.

Appius stood, hands on hips, overlooking the floor on which were arranged hundreds of sticks, all parallel, running left to right. He turned to Bernius who was scanning the floor. "I think painting the sticks a distinctive color for each type of operation and the essential path is useful. I can visualize how the project will progress. See the colors for excavation, stone production and, stonework on the underground sections? Very useful."

Bernius nodded. "Yes. Excellent work. It is perhaps as good as we can do for now. Our situation will change; we will discover new requirements and new difficulties requiring adjustments, but we have incorporated our best thoughts for now."

"You have arranged to have roads built in the vicinity of the bridge for transportation of stones if that is to be required. What if it is not?"

Bernius shrugged. "It will not be of much effect. The road building will not then be crucial to execution of the essential path. We can accommodate the road as it best works out in the sequence."

"And what of the manpower? You have accumulated the requirements for each month for many separate assessments. We have made many adjustments. How many men will be needed and at what time?"

Bernius reached to a nearby desk for a pile of papers, thumbed through them and extracted the latest. "My accumulations show that one month after we have secured a supplier for the bridge stones, we will start work. After a year of stone production and aging, we will gradually increase the number of men over the time of the first year so that at the end of the year we will have 500 men working. Then, in the following six months, increase to 1000 men and continue at that level for four years, then decrease again over the next two years."

Appius held up his fingers. "I counted seven years."

"Yes. There are still instances where we could shorten the time, but it would require more men. At this time, I do not even know if we can depend on the 1000. If not, the work will have to be spread out."

"I noticed that you have planned to start clearing for the path soon, also in two months. Did you do that to make our woodsmen happy?"

"No." Bernius laughed. "Although I would do a lot to make them happy, that is not the reason. I have started clearing because it *can* be started and is an easy way to start increasing the number of men involved. Great skill and training is not required. Also, an earlier start—excavating the first level in the underground runs so that we can establish level—will be most useful. It is of much importance to establish level earlier rather than later. For that reason, we will also start that excavation soon after the clearing begins. You can see that on our schedule."

"Yes, I do see that. Now, to get us started, we must get pricing from suppliers and contractors. Are we able to do that?"

Bernius nodded. "The designers are completing their detail of the blocks required for the bridge. For clearing, we have mapped the path that will be used. We can get pricing from contractors for clearing and for excavation. All we lack, at the moment, is an agreement between the *Corporata* and Claudius—or the Empire. They have been communicating, but I have heard nothing."

"The *Corporata* will not be pleased that we are soon to require heavy funds."

"No. I think they know only about the stone production contract."

"I have been thinking. Who will oversee the work? It is true that we have been assigned the design, but it is not clear to me if we are to direct the construction. What do you know?"

"You are correct. That direction is not clear." Bernius wagged his head. "Assignment of an overseer may depend on the entity that is agreed to as the contracting party. In the past, the overseer could be a military engineer, the architect, or at times a citizen who was rewarded with the task... or punished if that is the outcome. If we are to manage the project, the schedule we have developed will be of great help, but there will be other things to consider."

"If someone else is the overseer, will they use our schedule?"

"If they are wise, they will. If they want to appear to be great intuitive leaders, not subject to the thoughts and wisdom of others, they may not. However, they would be fools not to involve us. It would be a question as to how they would do this."

"Our fate should be known soon?"

"Good or bad, it should be so."

CHAPTER 36

Two months had passed since the *Corporata* meeting. Bernius sat at a table amidst the fallen leaves of drawings, sketches, charts, lists and calculations. He sifted through the collection, anointing several for special attention; those he clutched. He looked up at Appius and the designers assembled in front of his table; they expectantly awaited a declaration. He smiled. "We are ready. We can advise the potential stone suppliers of our requirements. I understand there are five who have been trampling the ground in the vicinity of the river crossing."

"What will we provide for them?" Appius peeled back the top sketch for a glimpse of those underneath.

"Every bidder will get a sketch of the entire structure showing the system we have arranged to identify each block. Of course, *they* will not be building the structure, but the sketch will enable them to understand the sequence in which the stones will be needed. Although there will be many stones with identical dimensions and shapes, they will be able to identify how many of each shape and size will be required and at what time. We will ask them to chisel an inscription on each stone, using our identification system; this will allow our installers to identify the stones at the site."

Appius frowned. "There must be more we must tell them."

"Yes, much more." Bernius nodded. "We will make sure they understand that the stones must be aged, and we have to identify timing for the arrival of each stone. The stones must be finished accurately; we will have a representative at the quarry to measure and approve each stone before it is transported. We will tell them of provisions for payment and penalties for failure to provide acceptable stones in time. We will advise them that they may use the road along the conduit for transportation of the stones."

Numerius said, "That means that we must have the road from their quarry location to the bridge completed in a little more than a year from now."

Thomas Hessler

"Yes. If we allow the bidders one month to calculate their pricing, three months to mobilize their workers and equipment and to remove the outer layers of earth before quarrying, the quarrying, aging the stone, and then finishing, we have about 17 months to complete the road." Bernius glanced at Appius. "If the road becomes a requirement, we must make sure that our schedule allows for that."

Appius nodded. They had already discussed this.

Bernius continued. "Now—the design of the remainder of the aqueduct." Bernius looked at Numerius. "You mentioned the road. Because the road is constructed from surplus earth removed in excavation for the underground structure, we must soon produce the requirements for the underground aqueduct in the vicinity of the river crossing, assuming that the stone suppliers will find a quarry near the site. When we are finished with those details, we must go out for bid for an excavation contract so that our road will be constructed by the time the stone suppliers are ready to transport. If we are not on time, the Vardo installation will be delayed."

Appius asked, "What about the clearing of brush and trees from the route? It must be done prior to the excavation." Appius felt the heady exhilaration, the ability to display knowledge he had acquired. He belonged to the fraternity of builders.

"We will also be immediately asking for pricing on the clearing, so that it can begin a month before the excavation. I am preparing a notice."

Appius laughed. "I think our woodsmen, Marius and Pentius, could do this by themselves. Maybe they would need assistants to sharpen their axes to avoid downtime. I can hear it, a constant ringing of the axes."

"And others to drag off the fallen trees. I agree." Bernius smiled and swept a path with his arm.

"Will you have the clearing contractor also remove the stumps?" Appius shrugged.

"No, I think stump removal works better as part of the excavation. And, you remember, we calculated it that way in the estimate." He paused. "So, we are busy... still busy that is. Any questions at this time?" Bernius looked at each, in turn.

There were none. The designers turned and walked to their tables. Many months of effort awaited them.

376

the *Aedifex*: Building the Pont du Gard

After the finish of the day's work, Bernius and Appius trudged to their homes. Bernius shook his head. "Although I did not mention this to the designers, we have a problem that must be quickly resolved. The *Corporata* and Claudius have *not* come to agreement on contract arrangements. We do *not* know who will be the responsible agency. The situation is difficult because the *Corporata* is bent towards delaying start of operations, anything to forestall the coming torrent of sestertii they must release. I am thinking we would *not* be able to urge the *Corporata* to resolve the issue, especially if they knew we were intending imminent start of stone work, clearing and excavation."

"Claudius?"

"Yes. I am convinced we should approach Claudius. He is likely to make something happen, perhaps by edict. He is now in Lugdunum. After we post the notices of our requests for bid, I will travel to see him. I should be back in time to talk to suppliers and contractors that might have questions about what they are to provide. If I have not returned, you can talk to them."

Appius was concerned that he might not have enough background to answer questions from the contractors, answers that might make huge differences in price or foster complaints on the part of the bidders if he were to mislead them. He bleated softly, "Me?"

"Yes, of course. And just what is it that you do not know about the work?"

Appius was silent. It was a struggle for him to understand that he had to accept responsibility for decisions and direction given that would have significant impact or consequences. He stuck his chin out and answered, "Yes, I will use my knowledge and best judgment." He looked at Bernius. "I suppose this is all on the road to becoming the... an... architect."

"Yes, Appius, yes. Are you still keeping a log of what you hear, do, and observe—events that have to do with the project?"

"Yes, and I have been copying some of my prior notes and my log onto vellum, as you suggested. Why?"

"At some time it may be important for you to remember what you said, what others said and what you saw. Your log is a powerful bulwark against hearsay. Those who would fabricate incidents that would favor their own situation are often refuted by the written word."

"I will remain dedicated."

They walked in silence for several minutes. Bernius, without looking at Appius, said, "Who is this Juliena?"

Appius turned to look at Bernius and smiled. "Oh, you ask about Juliena. Well, you have met Juliena. I am thinking you already learned much from that encounter. Is there a particular question I can answer?" Appius felt—for the first time in his association with Bernius—superior positioning.

Bernius walked for several more strides. "Juliena is not what I had expected when Antonia suggested a... 'meeting.' I thought she would be easy to dismiss. I would have used excuses such as 'too busy,' 'too much the bachelor,' 'not a family man.' Now, I find that I am trying to cultivate excuses to see her—talk to her. I loaned her several books under the provision that she *must* discuss them with me after she had read them. No, I do not have a specific question for you. I suppose I only wanted to talk about this, probably because it is such a surprise to me. I need to say the words aloud."

"I have not heard Juliena say anything. I do think Antonia is amused over the situation. She knows about the book exchange, and I think she has exercised her intuitive skills to divine that she has kindled a flame. Other than that, she says nothing. I really think she might want—be waiting—to hear what you have to say. It is certain that she has heard Juliena talk. Now that you have talked to me, is there a message you would like me to pass along?"

Bernius grimaced. "I am not skilled at this. My instinct is to appear indifferent. But, thinking about Juliena—her nature and skill at understanding one's thoughts—I think it would be dishonest and have the putrid smell of playing a game. I am compelled to be forthright."

"And that forthright statement would be...?"

Bernius took a deep breath. "That I am... much... attracted to Juliena, that I seek her company, that I find that I want to continue the encounters."

"Any thoughts about the... her... children?" Appius tried not to smile.

"Oh! That sounds like a question that Antonia pressed you to ask. I do not think you are as detached from this situation as you might let me think."

Appius chuckled. "The ways of women are clever. They are very good at manipulating men. I am no exception. But, can you give me an answer?"

"An answer. The children. At the moment I am oblivious to the children and to any long-term consequences involving them. Perhaps you understand what I am saying—that we blindly surge ahead not reckoning the possible outcomes. I would not care if you were to tell Antonia that. It is the most honest thing I could say."

"You know that you will one day have to answer a more precise question on the subject, and it is more likely to be sooner than later."

"Yes, I will have to give thought to the question and my answer. As I said, I am not skilled in these maneuvers."

"I can give you no help on this, Bernius. I can only speak of the delight I am experiencing with my own son... Sergius. I could wish that you, as my close friend, would experience that same joy."

Bernius nodded, deep in thought, and they walked on.

Bernius posted announcements for the stone supply contract, a clearing contract, and an excavation contract at the Nemausus city wall, a location designated for this purpose. Of course, posting the notices in Nemausus would not immediately come to the attention of all the prospective suppliers and contractors, but word would reach the stone suppliers that had made the effort to prowl the vicinity in the past few months. He would also post the notices in Lugdunum and make provisions to have the notices posted in Rome. He had no doubt the notices would reach those who were interested.

He sat slumped on his horse, at a walk now because he was tired of the rough ride while trotting. He was lazily following the cart path from Nemausus to Lugdunum. The *Via Domitia* did not pass through Lugdunum; therefore, the trail was not as well traveled. Bernius had much time to think. How long would he be involved in the Nimes project? He could easily spend six or seven more years. That was the situation with building aqueducts. One was rooted to the project, once involved. But he had doubts. It seemed like the project had more than the usual problems. Yes, the elevation drop was part of that, but, really, it was the *Corporata*, the entity—the agency that *should* have been championing the aqueduct. Instead, they were the counter-force, the resistance. The project was an extension of the Empire, but given the highly variable tastes of the Roman *imperators*, could the project last? One could not predict such. He would have to take the project forward, one step at a time.

He wondered how Claudius would react to his concerns. Almost with the same intensity, he wondered how the *Corporata* would view his trip to Claudius—going around them, as it were. Yet, to let the project stagnate would be abhorrent to his nature. He had to take this action, even if it was... political.

Claudius received Bernius in a flamboyant mood, full of grandiose statements about involvement and the glory of the Empire. They sat in the cool of the overhang on the deck of the home in which Claudius was raised, each with a cup of wine. "So, Bernius, I expect that you have made good progress. What of my elegant bridge, a magnificent structure, one that will speak to the competence of empire?" He made a wide sweep with his free hand.

"Excellency, I note your appreciation of the Vardo bridge. I have brought a sketch for you to see... to keep, actually. We have completed much of the design on the structure." He unrolled the sketch. "Behold!"

Claudius smoothed the sketch, pressing it to lie flat. He sat back. "It is colossal. Magnificent. Soaring. Artful. You will start its building?"

"That is what I need to talk to you about. Yes, we are ready to begin fashioning the stones." He explained the requirement for aging. "We are also ready to begin other operations such as clearing and excavation."

Claudius raised his eyebrows, smiled, and took a sip of wine.

Bernius also took a sip of wine. "Yet—unless I misunderstand—there is no agreement between the *Corporata* and the Empire. And, I must tell you—I did wait for the *Corporata* to get this resolved although they are my employer. Is there an understanding of which I am not aware?"

Claudius frowned. "There is no understanding. You are correct. There are only endless messages transmitted to and from. Until now, I have only been annoyed, have not given direction, and not taken strong action. I see now the situation must be resolved." He sat back, twirled his wine goblet and looked at dark clouds forming on the horizon. "I do not think the *Corporata* will take responsibility for the project, nor if they were to expand their reach—the city of Nemausus. Their whining messages have listed reason after reason why they cannot do this—be the final guarantor. And, in reality, they would not be able to make payment for all the costs while the project is being built. Nevertheless, their messages have been couched to evoke endless discussion, containing more questions than propositions or statements. I will confirm the prior agreement with them—that of the payment schedule, and establish the Empire as the contracting party. Your suppliers and contractors will contract with the Empire, through me."

Bernius nodded. "Then, sir, *you* will be able to establish those who would oversee the work. It is time. I respectfully ask, how will the project, the actual work, be managed?"

Claudius tilted his head back, looking at Bernius down the length of his nose, a slight smile upon his lips. "You, Bernius—of course—you. As long as I am involved... by you."

Bernius nodded—a courtly nod, accepting the responsibility. "Thank you for your confidence, Excellency. I will strive to fashion a structure that will be one of which you will be proud to have inspired... truly."

Bernius, however, harbored a concern for the phrase Claudius had used—"as long as I am involved." Perhaps Claudius suspected that his involvement would end. Perhaps he suspected the Empire could easily thwart the assignment he had just executed. If so, Bernius knew there was nothing he could do to avoid such dire possibilities except refuse the assignment. That he would not do. "I am most pleased to serve your Excellency." He held out his wine glass.

Claudius held his wine glass aloft. "I look forward to the day we will hoist our glasses, turn and behold the magnificent structure."

They commemorated the forecast with a sip.

Claudius mused. "I wonder if the *Corporata* will agonize over losing control of the project? They could have had it otherwise if, instead of sniveling, they showed courage. Yet, it is better this way. They will not be able to exercise any means of delay. It is ironic. They will have to pay your wages, yet they will

381

not be able to exert great influence. Ha! Ha, ha, ha, ha, ha. The outcome is just, but you can be sure *they* will not think so."

Bernius smiled. "I shall return to Nemausus so we can start spending their sestertii. I assume that you will prepare a message for them, explaining—directing—what you have said."

"Yes. It will be done tomorrow."

"Good. I will advise the suppliers and contractors that their payment will be backed by the nearly unlimited resources of the Empire, a concept that should beckon their confidence."

Claudius nodded and smiled. In his thoughts, however, he was grateful that those who had confidence in the Empire did not know the depths of its fickle nature.

Titus was insane. His rage resounded upon the peristyle walls, competed with the breeze, made reasonable men cringe, curdled the mead. The *Corporata*, not surprised by this behavior, nevertheless wished the tirade would soon blow away, expend itself, spent and panting, drowsy from its excess.

At last, Titus was through ranting. Marcus raised his eyebrows and said to Nemus, "Perhaps I am not so upset as Titus, but it is a surprise to us all. We—or I, at least—did not expect that work would be upon us so swiftly, that we would soon be draining our resources."

Nemus nodded. "It is apparent by the message from Claudius that he will no longer discuss arrangements with us. He must have tired of our intent to... clarify... the understanding." He looked to Titus who was still seething, speechless for the moment.

Julius spoke. "It was Bernius. I heard that Bernius traveled to Lugdunum to see Claudius. The direction we got from Claudius resulted from that trip. No doubt! Bernius went around us." Julius swept his hands in a circular motion. His seething ran a close second to that of Titus.

Nemus nodded, looked at Marcus and Aulus, remaining calm in contrast to the fury of their partners. He spoke. "I am not surprised. When we deliberately used the question of contract responsibility as a means of delay, I knew it could not last for long. But I did not expect Bernius to bring this about. Perhaps I should have. He would not have expected us to resolve the issues quickly." Nemus seemed to be talking to Marcus and Aulus only, perhaps knowing that a reasoned viewpoint would not be accepted by Julius and Titus.

Aulus, ever the calculator, said, "I believe that we will be expected to start making heavy payments possibly starting at the end of two months, but for certain at the end of three. The three contracts are to be bid in one month; the successful bidders will have one month to mobilize their forces and equipment before they start work. The quarry and clearing work can start immediately thereafter, the excavation as soon as the clearing has progressed for only a short distance."

The three looked at Julius and Titus. What were they thinking? What would they do? Was Julius now balking, too? Getting payments from them would not require an actual receipt of their sestertii. The amount would be deducted from their proceeds from the water works. Although it would be efficient, it would not be pleasant.

Nemus urged, softly, "Titus, Julius—did you hear what Aulus said? We will be required to make heavy payments in two or three months?"

"I heard, I heard!" Titus, now recovered from his fit, straightened his back and shouted again, pointing—at nothing in particular, "We cannot idly stand by and allow the Empire to drain our coffers. Are we done? Why do we not just funnel our proceeds directly to Rome? Do we have no say?" He looked at Julius for support.

Julius only shook his head.

Nemus said, "Are you not aware that the Empire *could* take all that we have? That if they thought it necessary to preserve the Empire, they would not hesitate to take the property of the rich? It is true with every civilization. Until you are *imperator*, you must be aware of that which can be done to you... and, even then, you must constantly look over your shoulder."

Nemus, of course, had history on his side but did not know how prophetic he was.

Titus puffed up, fists clenched at his sides. "I will not quit here. I will continue to resist. I only hope that the other members of the *Corporata* will support me." He looked first at Nemus, Marcus and Aulus, but finding no assurances, looked to Julius for support.

Julius, in the penumbra of Titus's stare, nodded after a telltale moment.

Titus fell silent, unclenching his fists. He was as puzzled as the *Corporata* in imagining what he might do.

CHAPTER 37

I was delighted with the renewal of the Lisele/Warner partnership, using my imagination to generate reasons to share time with her. I came up with several. We would explore the remarkable gorge of the Gard upstream of the Pont du Gard, hiking whatever trails might be wrought for the exploration of that rugged canyon. Also, although I had done a fair job of sifting through the piles of rubble at several of the aboveground structures, I hadn't really concentrated on the inscriptions. Perhaps there were none at the other structures, and many of the structures no longer existed. But, I should check. And, I wanted to take another trip to the *Castellum*, in Nimes, inscription snooping, probably a pathetic quest to spot evidence of the ancient project manager.

I should have had the good sense not to suggest all these opportunities to Lisele at one time, but once I got started I couldn't stop. I phoned her and stated my agenda. "So, Lisele, what do you think?"

"I am breathless imagining all those ventures challenged in a short time. These activities on your agenda...I mean...you want me to go along?"

I relaxed. "Yes. That's what I mean. And, I don't have a priority. Why don't we walk the gorge? I'll take a break from the aqueduct—a short break."

Lisele said, "I have walked the gorge, but not for some time. I think you will find it magnificent. I of course would be glad to be your guide. Catch me if you can. When do you want to do this?"

I was eager. "Tomorrow."

She laughed. "Okay, okay, Warner. I will gather my gear and see if I can find my trail maps. You will pick me up—when?"

"I'll pick you up at eight in the morning. We can have breakfast first."

"I can be ready." She laughed, again. "I will see you at eight."

Thomas Hessler

In the meantime, I continued the investigation of thoughts and ideas that had been adrift in my brain. In my preoccupation to understand the means by which the Romans were able to establish an accurate level line, a question modern archeologists, engineers, historians, and translators had not solved, I ran into a mystery within a mystery. The translation of Vitruvius I owned was published in 1914. In this translation, Vitruvius says, "the bed of the channel shall have not less than the gradient of ¼ inch in 100 feet. A paper done under the American Society for Civil Engineers, in 1922, acknowledged the same value. Yet, references abound to the presumption that Vitruvius had indicated a required 6 inches fall per 100 feet. This is madness. Why hadn't the researchers resolved the difference? The 6-inch reference had to be wrong. Most of the Roman aqueducts had a fall of 3 inches per 100 feet, and the aqueduct Aqua Virgo, in Rome, had a fall of ¼ inch. Vitruvius surely knew of this. How did the 6-inch recommendation come about? Pliny the Elder agreed with the ¼ inch number, but he wrote his *Natural History*, perhaps over 40 years later than Vitruvius. It must be that translation of first century Latin is complicated. I mean, can't someone just go look at the original writing and see if it says ¼ inch or 6 inches? It must be there, stated in plain Latin. It made me crazy, but nothing a beer couldn't cure. Sigh.

Perhaps Vitruvius wrote 1/2 *inch* per 100 feet and it was interpreted as ½ *foot*, instead. They must have had some confidence to build Aqua Virgo and he, presumably, watched them do it. But, maybe there were lessons learned in the operation, after the building. Maybe they had to settle with less flow than they had anticipated at ¼ inch per 100. It's for sure they didn't have the means to calculate what the flow would be. At least I don't think so. So, perhaps because Aqua Virgo could have used a little more slope, Vitruvius bumped up his recommendation from ¼ to ½ inch and the bleary eyed interpreters got mixed up between feet and inches. Finding no explanation, I settled on that hypothesis for the time being. I know—I could have asked the Professor in Marseille. Ha, ha. I'd rather live in ignorance.

But, realizing the Romans had constructed the Aqua Virgo with only a slight slope, prior to the building of the Nimes Aqueduct, meant that somehow they were able to accurately determine level. How did they do it—flood the channel as they went along? I mean, that was not *totally* unreasonable. I had read something suggesting that possibility. It would mean that they could only work in one direction—from the source to the castellum, gradually letting the waters flood the   channel to the end of the most recently excavated section, taking a measurement—making adjustments. But, that all supposes that they knew the nature of the drop before they started, before Agrippa, who financed the whole thing, started spending his sestertii. Imagine, he built the aqueduct so he could enjoy a cold, refreshing bath. Good boy, Agrippa. Think big. "I'll just build my own aqueduct." To his wife, "Are the Acilius's coming over for dinner and a swim tonight?" "No, dear. They do not like cold baths. They said they were busy tonight."

All well and good, but I'm left with this friggin' mystery. Sometimes one beer is not enough. I would have thought we, the historical community, 'we,' the curious world, 'we' would have investigated this more thoroughly. Everybody writing about the Pont du Gard is amazed that the Romans were able to construct the slope so accurately but don't have a notion on how they did it. The chorobate? Absurd.

One note of interest. In my review of the ancient instruction manuals—Vitruvius, for example—I had learned that the term engineer—for those who would design aqueducts and such—was not in use. These ancient engineers were referred to as architects.

After breakfast Lisele and I drove to the brim of the gorge. One hikes the gorge mostly along the top, as it is rough going, often impossible to hike in the depths. At least I assumed so.

We walked along the rim, Lisele in her charming and somewhat revealing hiking shorts, our waist packs loaded with water bottles and snacks; we sauntered to enjoy the view.

The day was warming, and the river, evidenced by a not-so-faint rumble, flowed as a silver-white ribbon hell-bent to exit the canyon. Large boulders were dodged, chutes were carved, and mist generated as the torrent crashed against the rocks, the aftermath of the inevitable meeting of the irresistible force and the immovable object. I could see rainbows in the mist as the sun pierced its veil. Still, the water looked inviting, especially the mists. "Tempting, isn't it," I said.

Lisele leaned over the edge of the canyon wall and looked down. "Let's go down. I think it can be done."

I looked over. Good grief. It was a handhold, toehold, root-grabbing, boulder-scooting type of descent, one not tried by those that have a difficult time with the tango. "Lisele, you're kidding."

"No, I am not. Over here, Warner."

She had spotted a bare trail, only slightly less hazardous than just jumping from the edge. It really wasn't a trail. There was only slim evidence that people had taken this route. She was on her way. What could I do?

Working our way down the canyon wall required use of your hands, to slow your descent—barely gripping a too-steep surface as you slide on your belly down a boulder. The river hissed below, ordinarily a threat, but I would have loved to fear only the river as the end point of a fall. I shook my head and tried not to think about the many ways I could suffer a mishap.

There were spots where we had to help each other—footholds, a cupped hand for a last step that didn't exist, holding the other's hand so a soft landing was managed to the next, lower, level. Yes, a real team effort. We were dirty, sweaty—well, I was—and exhausted. There was dirt under my fingernails, scrapes on my legs and arms and dried blood on my calf where a jagged rock had interfered with my descent.

When we reached the vicinity of the mist, nearly on the bottom, we stood, arms outstretched, and let the mist run over our faces, clothes, arms and legs. We laughed hysterically.

I enjoyed the moment, one of those times when you feel you have defeated the mountain; you survived, you proved yourself—happy that you did it. Yet, my laughter turned a tinge hysterical. "Lisele, we have to go back up."

She walked over and gave me a misty hug, then a kiss. The cool moisture trickled down her face and mini drops sparkled in her hair. The kiss was soothing in a way that I couldn't have imagined. Perhaps I would never climb back up. We would eke out a cool existence here in the bottom of the canyon.

Lisele nodded, indicating she had heard my comment—about climbing back out—over the growl of the water. She spoke into my ear. "Do not worry, Warner. You know it is often easier to climb up than to climb down. I am sure of it."

I wasn't sure of it. We disengaged and took a sober look at the canyonside. *We came down that?*

the *Aedifex*: Building the Pont du Gard

We struggled to the top. Lisele was right about climbing up. At least you can see where you are going when reaching up, rather than stepping blindly into thin air as you make your way down. As we stood panting and exhausted at the top, no mists to cool us, we laughed again.

I said, taking a look askance, "Lisele, I think you may be a hazard to my health."

She laughed. "Oh, Warner, I am just getting you in shape for the Pyrenees."

Good god, what is it with the women in this family? If it wasn't Laurie trying to smear me across the highway, it was Lisele bouncing me off the rocks. Yet, I was able to return a smile, though manufactured with great effort. "Let's go have a beer." The car seemed to be at a great distance.

It took me days to recover, damping somewhat the enthusiasm for the activities I had imagined, that of taking up more than my share of Lisele's time. Yes, I had survived the canyon challenge, a gritty adventure, and not one damn photo.

I called Renat. He was pleased to hear from me and looked forward to having lunch. I told him I would be accompanied by a charming lady from the neighborhood.

"Oh, the fast driver," he said.

I forgot, he was one girl behind. "No, no, Renat—not that one. She had too much energy for me, and way too young. This lady, Lisele, is more my age."

"I suppose she is old enough to be the young one's mother. Ha, ha. You always hear that."

I paused, mentally shaking my head, "It just so happens," I couldn't believe I was saying this, "she *is* her mother."

The statement propelled poor Renat into a paroxysm of laughing. He stopped only to utter, "What are you doing up there, Warner. I don't think you should be left alone, unsupervised." He continued laughing.

I let him wind down and said only, "Yes?"

Renat blew his nose, then said, "And what date and time might I expect you and...."

I took a deep breath, trying to play the part of 'these displays don't bother me,' and was able to annunciate, quite clearly, "It's Lisele. And, how about the day after tomorrow? At

389

noon, say. Renat, we're going to the *Castellum* again. Okay with you?"

Renat, trying to behave, now said, "That is fine, my friend. I have taken a multitude of visitors to see the *Castellum* in a very few years. I consider it similar to showing off a rare piece of art. I never tire of it."

"Good. See you Thursday, Renat."

Lisele and I drove to Nimes, found parking three blocks away from the *Castellum* and walked to the site. Renat was not yet there. We stood on the sidewalk against the low railing separating the modern day public from evidence of their ancient past. The *Castellum* was in a void between buildings. It had been discovered in 1844, and I presumed that Nimes had built around it, wisely preserving it for my visit.

I leaned sideways against the railing as if I owned it and nodded at the ancient structure. "Here it is, Lisele, the end of the aqueduct's journey, the terminus of all the effort it took to get it here."

Lisele didn't answer immediately, but gazed for a while, trying to understand its nature. "Where did the water come in?"

"Through that square aperture you see on the side facing us. Those round holes you see were for the pipes that distributed water into the city."

She nodded. "I am surprised there is no temple, no statues, no plaque of dedication. Did not the Romans go in for ceremony and dedication?"

"Yes, they did. In fact you may have seen the temple they constructed at the original springs, La Fountaine they now call it. It is a curiosity that we don't see something remaining here, but it could have been built nearby and later dismantled by people looking for trendy garden ornaments."

Lisele scowled. "Is there nothing on the remaining stones, no inscriptions, dates or hieroglyphics?"

"I don't think so... well, I really don't know. I haven't looked."

She looked at me, "Yes?"

I glanced in both directions, up and down the sidewalk; there was no one approaching or watching. I vaulted—well, more like clumsily worked my legs over the railing in a slow-motion, hand-assisted western roll. I was in forbidden territory, but hey, if they really wanted to keep us out, they would have installed a more robust fence and signs saying so. The railing was just to keep most of the people out. As I walked toward the structure I looked back. Lisele was over the railing and following me.

I reached the edge of the remaining structure, about 70 feet from the railing and stood, arms akimbo. From here I could see the drains in the bottom, pipes used to flush the ancient city's waste systems. Seeing the openings was worth the hop in itself. I slowly gazed around the circular perimeter as Lisele joined me. There was a stone walkway around the *Castellum*, like the deck around a swimming pool. I stepped upon it and started walking around. The *Castellum* actually seemed like a small pond, too small, lacking as the recipient of such a great volume of water, perhaps in contrast to the effort and magnitude of the rest of the aqueduct. I would have imagined it to be larger. But, somebody must have calc'd it.

I could not see any inscriptions. Perhaps this structure was just a very utilitarian work, like a modern steel water tank on a hill—not worthy of much ceremony or inscription. Well, they painted water tanks to look like a tee'd golf ball. Nevertheless, I kept a keen eye on the stone as I strolled. Lisele followed me around, also looking intently.

As I walked over the water intake aperture and beyond, I heard Lisele say, in a whisper, "Warner!"

I turned around. She was pointing to the vertical ashlar wall above the slab covering the intake aperture. The wall where she pointed was at the end of the arch that covered the incoming conduit, the outline of the arch visible in the wall. The stones of the wall were rough hewn, so it was difficult to spot an irregularity. I walked to her side but she nudged me out of the way.

"You are blocking the sunlight," she said.

I walked to her other side and squinted, trying to see what she was seeing.

"There it is," she said, "The same inscription we saw at the Pont du Gard—the APA. and the figure of an arch. What do you think?"

What did I think? There had to be a connection; it was too much the same thing. But, it could be anything—a mason who had worked on both, graffiti, a symbol of the organization that maintained the aqueduct, a territorial marking, so to speak. Then I noticed the stone below. Scratched into it, bold chisel marks at

391

one time, I suppose, was what looked like a pipe below which was attached—a rectangle. What was it? It was difficult to see. I finally answered. "I don't know what it is, Lisele. It could be anything. It is curious, though," I pointed to the stone above, "that we have managed to see the same inscription in two places. We were just lucky to see the one at the Pont du Gard. You wouldn't have seen it if the sun hadn't been grazing the stone at that particular time of day. Interesting. I wonder if we would find others—at any of what remains of the other structures."

"I think this is exciting. We are doing our own archeology. Perhaps you should ask your professor about this." Her eyes had a mischievous glint as she looked up at me. "But," she pointed to the lower stone, "What is this pipe on a stand? Maybe it symbolizes the aqueduct or maybe it is more like the pipes that take away the water from this pond."

I traced the etched lines. "Yes. I don't know what it is, but I will take a picture." I fished my camera from my waist pack and made different shots from various angles and tried several exposure values. "I don't know if the inscriptions will show. I must go back to the Pont du Gard and do the same—and take more photos if we find anything similar on the other structures."

Lisele looked smug. "So, I have helped you on your research. Does that mean you will buy me lunch... and maybe a glass of wine?"

I stood back, taking care not to fall into the dry reservoir. "Of course, Lisele, a reward for your good work. I only regret that our... your... discovery will only add to my mystery—another piece of the puzzle. I don't know how it fits."

We heard a shout. It was Renat on the 'legal' side of the railing, yelling at us. "What are you doing, defacing our monument? I should call the authorities." He stood with arms locked.

I knew it was Renat and that he was kidding, but Lisele didn't know him and looked at me with concern. She should have been suspicious that he yelled in English and not French. I decided to keep the blather going. "Just mind your own business, sir. We are finished with our graffiti and will soon be on your side of the railing—but, call the authorities if that is your idea of fun."

We walked to the railing. I still had my camera in my hand. I held it out to Renat. "Sir, would you mind taking our picture with the *Castellum* in the background? I would like to show my friends at home that I am having a wonderful time in France."

Lisele, eyes wide, looked puzzled. "Warner, perhaps we should...."

"Lisele, meet Renat." I laughed at her expression as I revealed the deception.

She slowly stuck out her hand. "You are both villainous and should be locked up. I should have known."

Renat guided us toward a restaurant. The *Castellum* was actually nestled amongst buildings that belonged to the university, so we had to walk a distance before we found a restaurant that Renat judged suitable.

After we were seated in the garden setting, potted flowers in abundance, Renat addressed Lisele. "So, Lisele, has this mad American been traipsing you up and down the aqueduct. He *is* mad you know. He is likely to wear you out, climbing up and down one structure or another."

I raised my finger. "Renat, I'm *so* glad you brought that up. It is not I who is wearing down Madame, it is she who is in the process of wearing me down and is also exposing me to grave dangers." I sat back and crossed my arms.

Lisele shrugged. "He is exaggerating, you know."

I looked at Renat. "Renat, have you ever descended into the gorge of the Gardon? Wait a moment. 'Descending' does not quite describe it. I mean clawing, hanging, dropping, scraping, and sliding your way to the bottom. This one," I pointed, "led me in your so-called 'descent' of the canyon."

Renat started laughing again. I thought it might be one of his uncontrolled versions, but he shook his head and said, "Warner, you are always barely surviving these helter-skelter adventures of yours. Lisele, I'm so glad you are around to provide entertainment for my friend."

Our wine had been delivered. Renat raised his glass, tilted it in Lisele's direction, nodded, and said, "To you."

We each took a sip. Renat asked Lisele a few questions about her past. I listened and heard new background even though I'd heard most of the story before. Renat explained that he and I had worked together, some number of years ago, and he took credit for enticing me to visit the region. Addressing Lisele, he said, "You can blame me."

393

He then turned to me. "Warner, it has been some time since you talked to me—your last visit to Nimes to see the *Castellum*, actually. What do you know... what have you found out about the aqueduct?"

I rearranged my salad—our meal had arrived. I was collecting my thoughts. My most recent experiences propelled my response. "Renat, while I have discovered interesting aspects of the project, I have encountered a parallel chain of mysteries that neither the researchers nor I have been able to solve. At the suggestion of a local Vers resident, an engineer actually, I visited a professor in Marseille to ask him questions." Note that I did not look in Lisele's direction as I said this. "I asked him about timing, asked about why they located the Pont du Gard where they did, asked him about construction techniques, about the means of establishing the gradient and about who built the structure. Of these, he could only hint that he had new information about the timing, the era in which it was built. I think he agrees that it had to be later than prevailing information would indicate—in the reign of Claudius, perhaps, rather than under Augustus. I have also found in my research severe discrepancies in the amount of water flow, the accuracy of the instrument used to establish level and the recommended minimum gradient for adequate flow, information extracted from the ancient writings. So, Renat, I have actually uncovered more mysteries rather than resolving them." Renat smiled, all-knowing.

I continued. "But, Renat, and you perhaps can appreciate this, I am compelled to think of this project as if I were the project manager. I have found that I can't just read bits and pieces about how this magnificent structure was built. I now want to imagine the project as if it were my own. How would I have gone about it if I were in charge?"

Renat raised his eyebrows. "You have done this?"

"No." I sat back in my chair, away from the salad I had neglected during my harangue. "At just this moment, as I was explaining all this to you, I realized that I must do this. I suppose I won't be satisfied until I think my way through it."

Renat looked at me, then at Lisele. "You must include me in your thinking... discuss your thoughts with me. It is something I would like to do. That is, if you tire of telling Lisele about your vision, or, rather, she tires of hearing about it."

Lisele brightened. "I actually have been interested in Warner's expedition... more than I would have thought. It's like a lot of things—you get exposed, and you develop an interest." She touched Renat's hand. "This is not to say Warner need not discuss with you. I think he should."

I was silent. Prior to this lunch I was thinking that I should take a deep breath and call it an 'adventure.' I would acknowledge that I had learned a great deal, had some interesting if perilous times and dedicate myself to keeping up with any new information that developed. Yet, that scenario was not satisfying. I now understood that I might be satisfied only if I could imagine that *I* had constructed the project, that *I* was the project manager. I smiled, puzzling my lunch partners. It would also provide an excuse to spend more time, in France, with Lisele.

CHAPTER 38

"Appius, there is a situation that I have neglected." Bernius stood in front of Appius's desk in the office. "My prior experience with aqueducts has been in the vicinity of Rome. Food and shelter were always available to the workers within walking distance of their work. Here, and I just realized this, our workers will be remote from villages of any size. Only those near Nemausus, and perhaps Ucetia, will have provisions."

Appius frowned. "I had not given any thought to that either. Marius and Pentius foraged to find farmers with produce they could buy, but only for the short time we were out there."

Bernius paced, hands behind him. "Now, imagine that there will be vast numbers of workers out in the wilds for over five years. In time, the workers would build shelters and the present inhabitants, mostly farmers, would find that they had new markets for everything from olives to women. But, at first it will be chaos and there may be problems if the workers start ravaging the crops, not to mention the women."

"If you have been thinking about the problem, I am sure you have ideas on what to do." Appius smiled and leaned back.

Bernius turned toward Appius, hands remaining locked behind him. "Yes. Here are my thoughts. We could contact the farmers and let them know what is intended, that there will be hundreds of men in their vicinity, and because we know the conduit route and where the work will be situated, suggest locations where they might establish markets. If they see the advantage, they will prepare, they will talk amongst themselves; perhaps they will be clever enough to plant other crops that will provide a variety."

"It is possible that people of commerce will also bring products to those markets—clothes, furnishings... wine."

"Yes, and if you continue with that thought, other men of commerce may realize that shelter is needed. They can build simple structures that the workers can either rent or buy. We could contract to have this done, but I think that it will happen without our involvement... eventually. We can make this happen more smoothly if we plant the idea now."

the *Aedifex*: Building the Pont du Gard

"We will post the idea—here in Nemausus?"

"Yes. We will post the concept and provide information on the route and suggested shelter locations. However, for the food supply—for the markets—I think we need to visit the farmers, although many of them do transport their crops to Nemausus and would eventually hear of the concept."

Appius shook his head. "Even those from as far away as Ucetia. The Ucetian farmers and merchants travel to Nemausus. It is too bad that the citizens of Ucetia have created problems for us. They may have difficulty in sharing in the commerce that will occur within their sight."

"Yes, like it or not, the region will change forever. Many of the workers will settle permanently along the way. The Ucetians' village will grow even without their cooperation. But, Appius, as we talk about Ucetia and consider the entire route of the work, we know that there will be a time of adjustment. Both locals and the arriving workers will jostle to accommodate the intrusion and the opportunities. If we are still concerned with the Ucetians and we think about the possibilities for trouble caused by the workers, we might need forces to assure there are no major problems."

"You mean... military?" Appius raised his eyebrows to emphasize his amazement.

"Here is my thought. If we were to utilize a small squad of military, the workers and Ucetians would be more likely to behave. We could employ the military on a constant patrol, moving from one end of the work to the other. Their intermittent presence might be enough to keep peace."

"You were worried about getting the military involved."

Bernius nodded. "Yes, but with just a small contingent, I believe we still maintain control. At least that is what I am thinking."

"I see that something... some provision should be made. Will you talk to the General Crassius about the squad of soldiers?"

"No, I will first talk to Claudius. He will want to work his political way through that cobweb."

"Ayyyee. It would be much simpler if we just had to deal with building the structure."

"If only it were so." Bernius grimaced as he walked back to his desk. He shuffled his documents absentmindedly.

Bids on the quarry work were first to be taken. The bidders were required to have their sealed pricing documents delivered to the office prior to the bid opening on a Monday at high noon. The bidders, trusting no one, all delivered their bids just prior to the time of opening and loitered about waiting for the bids to be opened. Five bids were received.

Bernius opened the bids in the order received. The first three bids opened were quarrymen from other locations in Gaul. After the three bids were read, Vernius Portius smiled, indicating to all that his price would beat those that had just been announced. The smile, of course, was disconcerting to the low bidder of the three that had been opened. The next bid to be opened *was* that of Vernius Portius. His pricing was a respectful amount lower than his nearest competitor, low enough to be significant, yet not so low that he 'left a lot of sestertii on the table' as they would say.

Vernius Portius crossed his arms defying the remaining bid to be lower than the price he had whittled to a competitive nub, yet a price that would still provide him with a decent return. He was taking some risk. Yes, that was always the situation, but he had calculated that if his worst fears came true, he would still break even. In that situation, he would not make the money that should be his, considering the risk and effort, but he would not lose his fortune either. If he did a good job, and the gods saw no reason to smite him, he should reap a bountiful profit. He knew that utilization of the second quarry was salient in creating his advantage.

The remaining bid was opened. The smile disappeared from the face of Vernius Portius as the pricing was read; the price was well below his. Vernius turned his head to see who had submitted the bid. A wealthy goods merchant from Nemausus was crowing and flapping his wings. He looked at Vernius—a definite smirk on his face. As the terms of the bid were read, it was apparent that the bidder relied solely on the quarry at the river. He did not have a second quarry. He would not require the use of roads along the aqueduct. Vernius was stunned. How would a goods merchant know enough to put together pricing for operations of which he was unfamiliar? It did not make sense.

Bernius announced that the goods merchant, Quantus Tarius, was the low bidder and would be awarded the contract. Mobilizing of equipment and forces would be expected to start immediately. The physical work on the great structure was starting.

Bernius and Appius, somewhat surprised at the outcome, would, nevertheless, hold a celebration at the quarry site to commemorate start of the vast project. It was soon heard that the winner, Quantus Tarius, was a close friend of Titus, although a friend who had *not* overspent *his* sestertii. Quantus had submitted a bid in the form required and had resources substantial enough to be considered a serious bidder. However, his lack of experience in this work worried Bernius. A week later, he and Appius visited Vernius Portius at Vernius's home.

Vernius, somewhat surprised at the visit, scowled but beckoned them to enter leading them to his atrium. After they were seated, Vernius said, without first resorting to inconsequential talk, "Perhaps you have questions about the low bidder—a successful goods merchant, it is true, but not one skilled in the operations of creating useful stones. Is that the reason for this visit?"

Bernius accepted a cup of water from a servant, nodded, and said, "We have our concerns. What do you know?"

"I know that Quantus is not a total fool. He sought help to prepare his estimates from a quarryman nearby Rome. It seems that Quantus's friend, Titus Domitius, knew of the quarryman, who, from my knowledge, is able enough to calculate the operations required and the cost thereof. I know this man from Rome. He created the estimate and was compensated for that effort. He has no further interest in the venture. Apparently, he calculated the cost, but, above that, Quantus included only a scant amount for contingency against unknowns and only a small profit—this in order to be the low bidder. But, there is another factor. Titus has a friend who has access to Caligua. Titus has convinced Quantus that with his influence in the *Corporata* and influence in Rome, the contracting arrangement will not fail. Titus will, of course, share in the sestertii that flow to Quantus and in any windfall the venture might receive. Any difficulties encountered will be generously considered."

Bernius shook his head, "But, as far as running the operation...?"

"Quantus will have to find someone. He cannot do it. Perhaps one of the other bidders will provide supervision for a price. You should be wary. On this very important contract, your first, you have a potential for disaster."

Bernius stood. "Thank you, Vernius. It would seem that your pricing, including your scheme to use a second quarry, was the responsible price. I would have preferred to award the contract to you but cannot do so. I have seen this happen before. The outcome is nearly always difficult."

Vernius led them to the door. "Yes, that is so. But there is little you can do about a foolish bidder if it appears they have the resources. Your problem."

Bernius paused, turning before he walked down the stairs to the portico. "Yes, our problem, and we will soon know its depths."

Bernius walked in step with Appius. "Ayyye. Now you see that in constructing the aqueduct—as if that was not difficult enough—we have to deal with an overlay of politics and favors. Not a grand beginning, and... there will be more."

"Perhaps you can deal with the politics, and I will handle the more simple aspects—the construction."

"If I were to craft the arrangement, it would be the other way around. But, seriously, we must be vigilant to observe progress—or lack of it. Which reminds me, we must hire additional people to be on site—our representatives—our 'eyes and ears.' Let us see if we can find someone who has experience on quarries to become our employee. They will also have to be willing to live near the Vardo crossing. You will look for such a person?"

"Yes. Will we pay that person the amount we have included in our estimate?"

"We will see if we can pay somewhat lower, but yes, the price in the estimate should be reasonable."

"I will begin a search."

The designers made swift progress on the remainder of their work. The route of the conduit now clearly defined which sections were underground—trenched, on low elevated structures or, in several instances, in a tunnel.

Vibius summoned Bernius to his table. "Two items, Bernius. We now have enough information to investigate our tunnel situation. See," he pointed to a section of the route about 2 miles beyond the Vardo crossing, "we will start the tunnel at this location before the hill and exit here—on the other side. Of course, it will be useful if the tunnel were to follow a straight path. However, we must determine what is underground—see if there is difficult earth or water problems that will prevent us from maintaining a straight run."

"You are saying it is time to dig exploratory shafts."

"Yes."

"Good. I will prepare a contract to be bid. Because we do not know how many shafts we will eventually dig and because we do not know the material that the contractor will encounter, we will do as we will on the excavation contracts—we will pay in accord with the number of feet excavated in earth of differing nature. The contractors will price each type. I will soon post a bid for this."

Vibius held up his hand. "The other item, Bernius."

"Ah, yes. You said you had two. What else?"

"See this run of the underground conduit about 5 miles before Nemausus?" He traced the line with his finger. "In this area it floods. We heard of this from the locals then we investigated. We could see evidence of the pooled water. This does not happen every year but perhaps once in every ten years."

Bernius looked at Vibius and nodded. He understood. "If the area floods, the standing water will find its way into the aqueduct. Have you thought of a means to prevent this?"

Vibius smiled. "I would not just bring the problem to you. Would not the world's best designer of underground aqueducts have a solution, not just a problem?"

Bernius laughed. "Of course. That is why you are here."

"This is what I am thinking, Bernius. We must excavate a second trench alongside the trench we dig for the aqueduct. This will be an open trench. When there is a flood condition, it will drain the water to the Vistre River." He pointed to the river.

"Well done, Vibius. Keep going. However, we must now budget for the excavation of that addition. I wonder if the contractor for that section of the aqueduct would dig the second trench using the unit pricing submitted for the conduit."

"If not, you will have to seek additional pricing?"

"Yes... and on a competitive basis. The low bidding contractor may think he has a competitive advantage as he is already in the area. The trench does not have to be dug until later.

401

It might be to our advantage to wait. I will need to think about this."

Vibius pointed to a document showing the route of the aqueduct, pointing to several locations along its path. "I must now get on with the tasks of designing the diversion structures and the *Castellum*. After that, we will probably have to wait for results from digging our tunnel exploratory shafts."

"On you go."

Within three weeks, other contracts were bid, those of clearing and excavation. The bidders were competent, had done similar work, and had sufficient funds to reinforce their expenditures. The contracts were bid as separate sections of the work. As it turned out, one outfit was the low bidder on all the clearing contracts, yet there were four separate contractors that were successful on each of the excavation bids. All the bidders had walked the route of the aqueduct following the narrow path used to stake the route, even though the Ucetians had removed the stakes in some areas.

Each contract stipulated start dates and completion dates. Clearing and excavation on the run from the River Alzon to the ridge was scheduled to start first. Bernius reasoned that the excavation on the section down the Alzon from Ucetia could start later as excavation would be simpler. Although starting later, the contractor should be able to excavate to the depth of 6 feet in time to perform the precision level work required for the *entire* length of the aqueduct. Bernius was also somewhat reluctant to immediately start work under the nose of the Ucetians. He must first make an arrangement with Claudius to establish the military control.

"Appius, we need to make changes to our schedule and to our estimate." Bernius beckoned Appius.

"But I have just redrawn the schedule. Do we have a change so soon?"

"This is not much of a change. We need merely to free the road work from the tight constraint we imposed. The successful quarry contractor will not require the use of our road."

"Oh. That will be easy to fix. I will do that now. But you said that there would be a change to the estimate."

the *Aedifex*: Building the Pont du Gard

"There is, but not for the road. It seems... Vibius told me... that we must dig a secondary trench along the conduit in the River Vistre region to avoid flood intrusion into the conduit. This will add considerable cost, and we must forecast it. On the schedule we will add excavation of the trench, but that activity does not affect the essential path. In fact, it could be done after the project is completed—but soon after. I would like you to develop the estimate. You can get the information from Vibius."

Appius nodded, looking over to Vibius. "I will do so."

"But, Appius, that is not of the highest priority. As you are well aware, we have no stakes in the route from the Alzon to the ridge. The *clearing* contractor says he can easily follow the narrow path we cleared when we sighted with the chorobate. However, the *excavation* contractor... and I think rightfully so... says, without stakes, he will be required to dig his trench somewhere in a cleared swath that is 80 feet wide. He insists that we provide staking for the alignment of the conduit. He says it would be difficult to move the trench over once dug but found not to be in the correct location. Ha, ha."

Appius laughed. "Very funny. But it does sound like we must establish new stakes. What about problems with the Ucetians?"

"Here is my plan. We will let the clearing people remove the growth on the route away from the Alzon for several weeks, clearing a substantial length of the route. Then, starting at the beginning of that section, we will establish new stakes for as far as has been cleared. The excavation contractor can start digging to the depth of 6 feet and will never catch the clearing contractor. At the time the excavator needs us to do more staking, the clearing contractor will be much farther along, and we can go out again. In the meantime, before you set the first new stakes, I will visit Claudius and make arrangements to establish our roving military patrol. Your stakes will be safe... or should be."

"I notice that you said 'your stakes.' My guess is that you want me to lead the party to do the staking."

Bernius cocked his head. "Oh, yes. Did I not mention that?" He chuckled. "Yes, please make arrangements to do so. You will have at least three weeks before the clearing contractor is mobilized and progresses to some distance."

"I wonder if Marius and Pentius will work for the clearing contractor. I have not heard." Appius shrugged.

"Perhaps. It is likely. However, they will not need to do any clearing for you. You will have a very easy 80-foot swath to wander through. You could almost do the work by yourself." Bernius smiled.

"It is true; progress will be much easier. But, I am accustomed to those two and entertained by them. I would always pick them first, trees to fall or no."

"I am not sure they would take on work that is so easy. We will have to find a way to make the work more difficult for them." Bernius laughed.

"Perhaps they could remove stumps as we go along."

Bernius, once again, trotted his horse to Lugdunum to talk with Claudius. As he rode, his mind churned the upcoming discussion regarding a military presence. He was concerned over possible usurpation of control which often happened away from Rome. However, the discussion with Claudius was not the only reason for the journey. In his satchel were contracts signed by the excavation and clearing contractors. The contract for the stone quarry work had been previously delivered by messenger and signed by Claudius.

"Your Excellency." Bernius raised his arm in salute of the proconsul. "I am here to report that work is under way on the quarry, and I have contracts for clearing work and underground excavation for your approval and signature."

Claudius nodded in acknowledgement and indicated that Bernius should sit. It was a blustery day, and the duo met in a room outfitted as Claudius's office. "I am pleased to know that work has started on the quarry. Are they to the point of cutting stones from the quarry face yet?"

"No, much uncovering of earth must be done before the first stones will be struck. Hoists must be erected, ramps hacked, and loose rock removed. However, on the clearing contract, although you have not signed the contract—it is in front of you— the clearing contractor *has* started. It did not take special equipment to mobilize, and the contractor was able to find a number of men who were willing to work and to live in the woods and have past experience in doing so. In a short time, we will start the excavation, behind them—the contracts that are on your desk."

Claudius nodded. "I will want to read them. I may not be able to find any problems, but I can gain an understanding of how the work will be done. However, you could have had messengers deliver these contracts, also. Although I am pleased to talk to you about the project, you must be here for additional reasons."

"For an additional reason." Bernie held up a finger. "In a short time, we will have a considerable number of men working along the route. We have contacted farmers and suppliers to let them know that men with regular monthly pay will require food and other essentials. We do not want the men to be looting the countryside. It is likely that a concentration of men will breed trouble, but I think we can reduce this possibility by employing a squad of perhaps... six... military men who would wander the route along the worker encampments. They would continually patrol the route. Their presence should curtail most thoughts involving 'might means right.' I am asking you to arrange such a troupe."

Claudius shook his head. "I was hoping, possibly in naïve fashion, that we would not have to involve the military. We *do* have sufficient military in the region, and I am thinking that it would not be difficult to provide military support as you require. However, as you know, the general in this region—General Crassius—is not under my command. He reports directly to Caligua and is somewhat favored by him. The general has already suggested to Caligua that he and his men supervise the building of the aqueduct. I have been—so far—able to snub any thoughts of that. If the military were to be in charge, we would have access to their resources. That is true. However, we would lose control of the project, and *I* want to have control. The military will run it haphazardly. It will sink into the muck pots."

"Is there another way?"

"Not that I know, unless you want to depend on the goodness of your fellow man."

"I already know that does not work."

"Something I have missed?"

"Oh... no, no." He shook his head to dismiss the thought of the Ucetians as if Claudius could see the image. "No, I have had the opportunity to observe those left without structure. Chaos is often the result." He straightened. "So, perhaps keeping a small squad will not let the camel's nose under the tent."

"I am wary. But, we must make this initial arrangement. If the military were to be called in to solve a problem, they would use

405

that problem *prima facie* to justify a larger force. I will try to finesse the requirement when I speak to General Crassius. I will ask for a squad only of the six men. I think you can plan on having the troupe on site within two weeks. I will get word to you. And, they should report... where and to whom?"

"If you will get word to them to meet us at the existing bridge crossing of the River Vardo, we will orient them from there."

"I will make the arrangements and advise that they are to take orders directly from you. Of course, their pay will be levied on the financial back of the *Corporata*. Their wages and the funding of the new contracts should be exhilarating for our men of Nemausus. Ha, ha. Is there anything else?"

"If you could advise General Crassius that Appius is second in command and that the troops are also subject to his orders. He may be on the route more often than I."

"I will do so. It sounds as if you place much responsibility on Appius. You know that I was impressed with his resourcefulness in the early stages of our effort. He must be serving you well."

"He is indeed. He continues to be resourceful, is eager to be involved, and his mind soaks up knowledge like a sponge from Kalymnos. You are a good judge of human attributes and capabilities."

"Thank you. So, anything else?"

"No. Nothing else, thank you, but if you were to offer a cup of wine to a traveler with mostly dust in his throat, the traveler would feel well compensated."

"It shall be done." He clapped his hands.

CHAPTER 39

In two weeks, Appius set out for the Alzon valley. Bernius would ride with him until they met the military. Appius had not searched for Pentius and Marius as he would only be setting stakes along several hundred feet of the route, and he would not be using the chorobate, marking the route based on the prior map they had made. He would need someone to hold a line and to help him measure for a short time. He could find someone on the clearing crew to help. His trip was timed to meet the *centurion* in charge of the military squad and the centurion's men, scheduled to arrive at the existing Vardo crossing at the same time. Bernius, as first in line of command, would travel to this meeting along with Appius and then return to Nemausus.

Bernius spoke as they slowed. "I forgot to tell you. When Claudius asked if any stones had been produced at the quarry, I told him 'no,' that there was much work to do before they could access suitable stone." Bernius urged his horse forward, to trot more nearly to the side of Appius. "In truth, I am somewhat worried that the contractor is not getting much accomplished, but I did not want to say that to Claudius."

"The man we hired to be our representative—our 'eyes and ears' at the quarry—Spurius Vitellus Varro—reports they are making reasonable progress, although they have encountered obstacles they had not foreseen." Appius turned in his saddle to face Bernius.

"You mean obstacles like 'hard work?' I have my doubts. I think that when you visit the quarry site, you should take time to observe progress and see how they are managing the work—ask questions as to their plans for the next week or so. It will be good for you to have your own impression."

"I will do so. My task at the Alzon will take less than a day."

They approached the river crossing. Bernius stood in his stirrups. "I can see the military; they are watching our arrival. No doubt they are thrilled about taking orders from civilians. Let us take stock of their attitude."

Bernius and Appius rode up to the *centurion*, the only one of his squad on horseback. Bernius raised his hand, careful not to have the gesture appear as a military salute. *"Centurion?"*

The *centurion*, astride his horse, took time to assess the two civilians, deliberately, insolently, before he responded. "Yes, I am *Centurion* Flavius Darius. These men will be under my command. And you are...?"

"Bernius, the manager of the project and," he nodded, "Appius, my assistant. Appius will lead you along the route of the aqueduct that is currently in progress."

"We are to take orders from your... assistant. That is not a question, it is my understanding."

"Yes." Bernius looked to the squad of men behind the *centurion*. "I see that you have brought supplies." A second horse was pulling a cart. "We expect that soon we will have means of securing food and goods, but, at this time, it is good to be prepared." Bernius smiled.

"If we run short of food, we will be able to... find some." The *centurion* did not smile.

Bernius knew that the military were sometimes known to commandeer their supplies from local, unwilling tenants. "We have provided funds for you to secure supplies from the locals. We presume that is the manner you will practice. You are here to prevent trouble, not to incite it."

The *centurion* nodded slightly, but smirked. "And, if I understand our mission, it is to ensure there is no trouble along the route and to punish those that would cause such. If we act strongly, others will not think too long on similar actions."

Bernius stared intently at *Centurion* Flavius Darius. "It is our thought that your impressive presence will discourage any activity. Hopefully we will not witness any trouble. However, we would expect you would weed out unruly participants."

Centurion Flavius Darius returned the stare. "I will depend on my experience as will the men," he nodded toward the squad, "to ensure there are no problems. Now, if we have understood each other, let us be off to start our mission."

"As you will. Appius will be on his way in a moment. Appius, a word before you leave."

Bernius led Appius a discrete distance away. "I may regret that we have done this. I have assessed the military attitude and found it... arrogant. I would have you continue to assess the *centurion's* nature as you spend more time together."

"Yes. It is obvious that the *centurion* intends to do things his way. I will observe and talk to you of this when I return."

"Yes... when you return. And... we will talk of the quarry operation. As you can see, these are the nuances of project management. It is not all schedules, contracts, estimates, and design. Unfortunately, we must deal with people, politicians, and now the military. Be on your way."

Appius joined the *centurion* who explained, "You and I will ride ahead; the men will follow. After you have shown me the route and the work sites, I will return to guide the men. It is my intent to remain with the men for a week or so, but the *decanus*, one of the men, will be in charge. After that, I am only one day's hard ride away. Let us be off. We will follow this trail?"

"Yes, for some distance."

He waved to the men and pointed to the trail. They shouldered their gear, got the horse and cart moving, and started walking.

As they rode, Appius said, "I understand your plan—that of leaving the squad. One of the sites we will observe will be the quarry. A good number of workers will be encamped there and more to follow. When your troupe regularly visits that location, I ask that you draft a report to be transported to us in Nemausus. In that way you can advise us of the situation as seen from your eyes."

"A report? A written report? None of my men can write, and I see no need for such. If there are problems, we will find a way to let you know."

"Your leader can state his report to our representative at the quarry. He can write. He will draft your report and have it sent to us, along with *his* report."

"It is not necessary."

Appius shook his head. He did not think it would be useful to accept the *centurion's* way. "I must insist, *Centurion*."

The *centurion* reined his horse to a stop. "And, if I refuse?"

"We are paying for this service. If you will not take our direction, we will dismiss you." Appius thought this rather bold, but it seemed to satisfy the situation.

The *centurion* glared at him but said nothing. He urged his horse forward, again.

Appius took a breath and strapped the horse forward to a trot, passing the *centurion*. The encounter angered him. He would welcome a reason to dismiss the arrogant bastard.

Appius rode quickly to the ridge that would support the aqueduct on its way to the Vardo. He then turned north. As he did so, he shouted a curt, "This is the aqueduct route," pointing backward and then forward as they rode. An hour later, Appius turned his horse to the west as they encountered the line of hills. "The aqueduct turns here," he shouted. "We will return on this route; you will have a second look if you are not able to remember the landmarks."

The *centurion* straightened his back, but trotting behind Appius, turned in his saddle and searched for useful indications of the change in direction.

They rode on until they encountered the clearing crew, now hundreds of feet from their starting point on the Alzon. As Appius approached, he thought he saw... yes... it was Pentius and Marius. They had gone to work for the contractor. They did not spot him until the horse was nearly in range of their axes. They looked up, frowned then identified the rider. They threw down their axes and nearly pulled Appius from the saddle. On the ground, a round of back thumping took place with all the whoops that such a reunion deserved.

Marius looked beyond the horse and saw the *centurion*, still mounted, doing his best to look disgusted. "Who did you bring?" He straightened, the mirth draining from his face.

Appius nodded. "*Centurion* Flavius. He and his six men will regularly patrol our works. They are to make sure peace happens."

"You mean the Ucetians? You know, me and Pentius could take care of that." He pointed at Pentius who nodded agreement.

The *centurion*, listening, moved closer.

Appius ignored him. "I have work to do, only a few hours. Do you think your crew leader will let you help me? The *centurion* and I will then ride to the river crossing. He hopes to intercept his men, walking the route, at that location."

Pentius laughed. "The contractor had better let us help you. We do the work of four men, and he knows it. Yes, we can be certain."

the *Aedifex*: Building the Pont du Gard

"Then let us start. I have only to use our maps and a measuring line. We will walk to the start of this run and set new stakes."

Pentius asked, "Is the military really here because of the Ucetians?"

"Not entirely, but we should not have to worry about the Ucetians taking our stakes." He looked back at the *centurion* then to the duo. "Please get word to me if the military are not operating as you think they should. I do not favor them much... at the moment."

Pentius and Marius looked at each other and nodded.

Appius pointed to the *centurion*. "I will let him know what I am doing, talk a minute with your crew chief, then we will walk to the turning point on the Alzon."

As they finished the restaking, Marius said, "You know, Appius, even though the Ucetians removed the stakes, as we walk the path we cleared before, we see the stake impressions in the ground. We did not bother to re-mark them in this distance we have cleared, so far, but we could. Should we?"

Appius brightened. "Yes, that might be of great help. It should keep us from making mistakes, although I will still check against our maps as we stake on ahead. I will return at some time when you have cleared farther along. Now that we have restaked, the excavation crews can start this section. You should see them here tomorrow."

"Great." Pentius said. "We have been hewing cut timber in our spare time. Several of those on our crew pay us to do that and then they construct a crude hut. Sometimes we help them with that, too. The excavation crew will provide us more of that work."

Appius smiled. "This evening, I hope to be able to use one of your other ventures, the raft on the Vardo. I am thinking it is still available."

Marius laughed. "Yes, it is. On our way here, we walked to the crossing. We tried out the raft. You will find that it is in good shape."

"I will go now. I will look forward to the next visit. When I am not babysitting the military, we can have a meal together, and you can tell me how it is going."

411

Appius found the *centurion* resting about twenty paces from the work site. "Let us ride quickly, *Centurion*. We will try to meet your men then cross the Vardo to see the quarry site and the eventual location for the great bridge. If we hurry, we can do most of that in the daylight."

"How do you expect to cross the Vardo? We must go all the way back to existing bridge. You have not planned this trip well."

"Ah, *Centurion*, but you do not know everything. If you pay attention, you will find that there are other useful things that do not appear in your manuals. It seems that you only *think* that you know everything." Appius dug his heels into the flank of the horse. The horse, always allowing only a trace of accommodation for Appius, turned his head and whinnied to show his displeasure. The *centurion*, however, was silent.

They encountered the military squad 2 miles from the existing bridge, not too far from the route towards the intended crossing of the Vardo. The *centurion* pointed at the route along the ridge and advised the men he would join them in a few hours. Appius then led him to the canyon of the Vardo.

Appius pointed. "Our river crossing will be here."

The *centurion* looked at him as if Appius was deliberately trying to mislead him. "You are going to build a bridge across this canyon?"

"Yes."

The *centurion* shook his head but made no reply.

Appius pointed downstream to operations in progress at the quarry. "That is the quarry—where our work is taking place. They will be working there nearly a year before the bridge construction starts." Appius dismounted and tied his horse. "We will walk down into the canyon and cross to the other side."

"You are crazy. What are we going to do... swim?"

"No. There is a raft. We built it and used it before when we were surveying the canyon."

"I will not do such a thing. Go if you must."

"As it suits you. I did not think you would be so fearful." Appius pointed. "You know where the quarry site is. That is on your surveillance route, the location where your men will submit the report." Appius walked down a crude trail into the canyon.

the *Aedifex*: Building the Pont du Gard

The *centurion* yelled down. "At the clearing site near the Alzon, your men mentioned problems with the Ucetians. What was it?"

Appius stopped and turned. "They pulled up our stakes and left them in a pile. That is why we are restaking."

"What did you do about it?"

"Nothing."

"As I thought." He turned his horse and headed away.

Appius found the raft, dragged it to the river, re-attached the ropes to the shore anchor, found the steering oar and launched into the river. As before, the current, deflected by his oar, efficiently moved him to the other bank. He happened to glance to the top of the canyon. The *centurion* was watching him.

The quarry was a short walk downstream from the raft location. It took Appius nearly a half hour by the time he stored the raft and made his way. As he approached the quarry site, he looked up at the cliff face. Some loose earth had been removed. A rock shelf was being cleared from which the work would start. A hoist was being assembled at the base. But did they not receive a report that the hoist was built, the ramps constructed, and the crew nearly ready to start freeing the large stones that would eventually be lodged in the piers? There must be a mistake.

A crude shack had been built in a location that would, one day, be the work yard below the cliff. In the area were lean-tos and a fire pit, the workers' encampment.

Appius supposed that the man they had hired, Varro, their 'eyes and ears,' could be found in the shack. He was right. However, Varro was asleep and quite startled to be woken and more startled to see that it was Appius who stood before him. This was not going to be pleasant.

Appius regarded him for a while, then said, "Would you tell me what has been done here and... more important... tell me what is *going* to be done here?"

The 'eyes and ears' stood and stretched, avoiding Appius's eyes. He walked to the shack entrance and pointed outside to the quarry face. "You can see all that you need see from here. The hoist is nearly assembled, and the last of the earth is about to be removed from the rock that will be taken first. You can see ropes anchored above, the means of accessing the rock."

"I am puzzled. Your last report, nearly two weeks ago, said that the hoist had been assembled and that the ramps were nearly complete. I see no indication that what you stated was so at that time. What say you?"

"Yes... well... the report takes several days to get to you. I thought the hoist and the ramps might be finished by the time you read the report. You can understand that?"

Appius felt a surge of anger. "Let us both understand *this*. Your reports are to state what has been accomplished... not what you think will be accomplished. Do we both understand *that*?"

Vitellus nodded. "Yes."

"And, is there a reason the contractor has not made more progress?"

He shrugged. "Ah, it has been difficult to get men. And, there are always problems one runs into that were not thought about—like having to remove bad rock from the face, rock that would not be suitable. You would not want that rock in the structure, would you?"

"Of course not. But did the contractor not know he had to do that?"

"It was not that he did not know. He just was not prepared, at first, to do so. He should do better now."

"I see. The other notion that bothers me is that you recommended payment to the contractor that included work that had not been done. We paid it. I must hear from you that you will take payment recommendations more seriously."

"I will do so."

Appius turned. "I am on my way back to Nemausus. I will eagerly anticipate reading your next report. And please advise the contractor that we must free some stones soon to begin the aging. We are already behind schedule." He walked out of the shack.

"I will do so," Vitellus Varro muttered.

Appius encamped at the quarry rather than at the existing crossing as he had intended. In the remaining daylight, he climbed to the top of the quarry to better assess the status of the work. *I hope they understand the next payment will be less than they think, having paid them already for work they are accomplishing now.* Appius spotted a man who appeared to be directing the other workers. *I wonder if that is the crew supervisor?* He walked to the man who stood at the edge of the cliff, directly over the quarry operations.

"I am Appius Petronius. I assume you are the contractor's man on site."

"Yes, Appius Petronius. I am. I know who you are. Quantus Tarius mentioned your name."

"I have a question. Can you tell me when you will free the first stone that will be used in the structure, starting the year of aging?"

"The first stone should be freed in two, perhaps three, weeks, but there are always problems to encounter."

"I am not sure if that is an answer or a guess. What will you do next week?"

"The same as we are doing this week except that the hoist will probably be completed."

"And the ramps?"

"Well, maybe not completed until the following week."

"And then you will be able to start with the first stone?"

"Yes, hopefully."

"I say that your progress is only slight, your schedule built on 'hope.' It appears you need more men and perhaps better supervision."

The contractor's man, not so dull that he missed the barb, said, "You will have to talk to the contractor about more men; he is reluctant to send them or cannot find them. As to the supervision, I cannot comment."

"You are wise at that. Now it is my turn to hope. I hope you will have advanced much further by the next time I visit."

"And when will that be?"

"In two weeks. I will be here to see that you have started work on freeing the first stones. You will tell our representative that you are ready."

"Yes. I will be sure to do that."

"It has been nice meeting you."

Appius returned to his household, lavishing attention on Sergius and commenting on the glow he observed about Antonia. Antonia sat him at a table in the courtyard, still comfortable in early fall at this time of day.

Thomas Hessler

Antonia, after she had poured her man a cup of wine and placed a plate of bread on the table, said, "I am anxious to hear about your trip."

"Ayyy," Appius said. "The trip had to be done. There is no question that strong guidance is needed. You cannot just turn the work over to the individuals and trust that things will be done as you imagine."

"You sound frustrated. What happened?"

"As I told you, we engaged the military as a means of reducing trouble with future large encampments of men—also somewhat because of the Ucetian situation. The military, especially this arrogant *centurion*, may be the *cause* of more trouble. We are not on good terms. I am expecting a dismal outcome."

"You and the *centurion* are not getting on well. Is that it?"

"Yes, and the quarry work is miserably behind. The contractor's man does not appear to be aggressively approaching the work. And our representative is meager and perhaps useless."

"It seems like managing large projects does not just amount to pointing at the work and standing there, hands on hips, until the work is complete." Antonia's eyes sparkled, hoping Appius could accept some humor to help him through.

"Ha, ha. Well, I was not so naïve as to assume that, but I must admit that I did not think I would be so embroiled. But, Antonia, there are some rewards. Our clearing is going well. I saw Marius and Pentius, and their enthusiasm always rubs off on me. They helped me with my staking. And, the excavation behind the clearing should be starting today—as we have planned it. I will focus on the good in order to adjust to the bad."

"Here, my husband, have another cup of wine. Its soothing nature should also help." She poured. "Did you know that Bernius is paying attention to Juliena?"

"No... well, he has talked to me once—saying that he finds her bright and attractive." Appius thought it best not to reveal that Bernius was several grades more enthused than that.

"It seems... I hear... that Bernius is creating many opportunities to visit Juliena under the notion that he finds it noble to keep her supplied with good reading. Ha. Of course he does not need such a reason."

"That is interesting. I would expect Bernius to proceed slowly, to not suggest that he has found a gem right here in Nemausus... and there is the three children situation, also."

"Has he mentioned anything about the 'three children' situation?" Antonia said brightly, focusing on Appius's eyes to make sure she acquired the entire message.

"No," said Appius. "I do not know what he thinks of that."

Antonia thought otherwise. "If he says anything, I would be most interested to know."

"I will tell you, of course." Appius reached for the bread, avoiding her eyes.

CHAPTER 40

"No, the remainder of the time spent with *Centurion* Flavius did not increase my confidence. I think that he will work more against us than provide us with help." Appius sat with Bernius under the outdoor covering of the office.

"At least we should not have to worry about the Ucetians. Did you tell Flavius about them?"

"Yes, although only briefly. He sneered when he heard that we had taken no action. I asked him... no, I told him... to submit a report each time the squad visited the quarry site. He was not pleased. We can expect that the report will be terse and probably incomplete. We must depend on the words of others to know what is really happening. Pentius and Marius agreed they would let us know if unusual military action was about."

Bernius nodded. "I fear one day we will sorely regret the military presence. Now—about the quarry—you confirm that they are not making good progress and that our representative recommended payment for work that they had not performed."

"Yes. It was evident. They need more manpower—perhaps the contractor is deliberately controlling this—and the contractor's man at the site relies on hope. Our essential path operations are stagnating; we have already lost time."

"Yes. It is true. Here is what we must do. We will pay close attention to the reports from our Vitellus Varro in the next two weeks then visit the site to make an assessment. Also, today, I will advise the contractor, Quantus Tarius, that he is severely behind, that we demand that the first blocks will be freed in two weeks and that we must be assured that he has the means and resources to maintain the schedule as we have described in the contract. We will advise that if he cannot do that, we will replace him, collecting damages from sestertii that might be owed him."

Appius asked, "Will you deliver that message?"

"Yes, and I will remain in his presence for his response. I would like you to be there as well. I would like to hear your impression of his attitude and his remarks."

"Yes. I will be most interested in doing so."

the *Aedifex*: Building the Pont du Gard

Quantus Tarius scowled as he read the letter. Bernius had a copy of the letter and requested that Quantus Tarius sign it to acknowledge that he had been put *on notice*. Quantus Tarius did so with an exaggerated flourish, nearly throwing the document back at Bernius.

Bernius rolled the letter and stuck it in his tunic. "What do you intend to do to ensure that you have a going operation? We have visited the site and do not see activity suitable to provide stone for this grand project."

"I will make no promises. We have encountered... difficulties... and are diligently working to overcome them. Your man at the site has not been upset with our progress. Does that mean anything to you?"

Bernius, understanding that Vitellius Varro, their own man, was their liability, said, "Our man has bent to your favor, even advanced payment for work you have not done. That is why I have given you this letter, to make it clear to you that your progress is not satisfactory and that if you do not make a serious effort, you will be dismissed."

"Oh, do not be too sure of that. You are not the last word on what will be done on this project. I have... acquaintances... within the Empire who will ensure that I am treated... fairly."

"Then, that is your response? You will not make an effort to improve your operation?"

"I do not have a response for you. I will take your letter under advisement. You will have to observe what you will and take what action you will at what time you will. Now, I will dismiss *you*." He pointed to his door.

Bernius gave him a stern look, turned and beckoned Appius to follow.

Outside, Bernius shook his head as they walked back to the office. "He will not make the effort—I do not think. We must consider action we must take to replace him."

"We have to adjust our schedule for his delay."

"Yes. And, we will also be further delayed if we have to replace him."

"We are not in a good situation. Do you think that he will get help from the Empire?"

"Yes, it is likely, although I do not know how much leverage could be put upon us. Claudius has much say. It would almost require a direct order from Caligua for action to be taken that will threaten us."

"Then we must do what we think will be best for the project, as if we were free of political constraint."

"Yes. We must be stalwart to resist strong reaction to such things. Also, we have to act quickly on this matter. It seems clear to me that the longer we retain Quantus Tarius, the further behind we will slip and the less control we will have on the entire project."

Appius nodded. "I see that." He walked a few more paces. "How is Juliena?"

Bernius looked sideways at him. "Ha!"

The *Corporata* was discussing funds that they must provide for the ever-growing monthly progress of the work. Bernius and Appius were present to answer questions.

Nemus read the list aloud. "Five hundred sestertii for the quarry operations, 1500 sestertii for the clearing contract, 1000 sestertii for the excavation, and 400 sestertii for administrative expenses. And, I see that we are being charged for support of military operations—700 sestertii for this month. We do have questions. First, do we not already pay for the military by the taxes the Empire extracts from the city? Why do we pay again?"

Bernius shrugged. "The answer is that—if the military is dedicated to one thing or another, they are no longer free to carry on the mission for which they are charged—that of protecting the region. Hence, any entity requiring forces, not a subject of the mission, is charged for the service."

Julius scowled. "Is not this military troupe protecting against insurrection of a government entity?"

"Not as defined by their mission. The argument is that if any entity should elect to employ a force to keep the local peace, it would be paid for by the entity."

"Absurd. And what calamity do you fear that will be prevented by this troupe?"

"We will have a substantial number of men in the camps. It is likely that under such circumstance problems will appear. The military is on hand to minimize those problems."

Titus, adopting an insolent look, arms crossed, said, "Does not one of the possible problems involve difficulties with the Ucetians, something you have said little about, something that you neglected to tell Claudius when he was making the decision of which route to take?"

Several of the *Corporata* had not heard about the Ucetians. They looked from Titus to Bernius.

Bernius answered the question calmly. "We have had problems with the Ucetians. No damage to humans has occurred. We had to... have to... restake part of our route. We do think the military presence will prevent further problems."

Titus continued. "Ucetians are in Nemausus from time to time. I hear that they often ask questions about plans for the work. I would not be surprised if the problems with them are not over."

"I hope they are. But, we will have to be vigilant. Are there other questions?"

Aulus asked, "Are you satisfied with the progress?

Bernius knew that Aulus did not ask an innocent question. "We are pleased with progress of the clearing contractor. They are doing better than expected. The excavation has just started, so it is early to make a judgment although they seem to know what they are about. However, we are... disappointed... with the quarry contractor. He has not made good progress; he is behind; he has delayed the project, already. Our man on the site paid him too much in the first month. We have adjusted his payment for this month to account for this. In addition, we have put him on notice that if he does not have a going operation in two weeks, we will replace him."

The *Corporata*, as one, turned to look at Titus; they were aware of his connection with Quantus Tarius. Titus blushed uncharacteristically then adopted his hard-shelled demeanor, standing and thrusting out his chin and chest. "This contractor has worked hard to get the project started. There were difficulties, and I am assured... confident ... that he will prove that he has a robust operation in the next month. As far as the overpayment, that is the fault of the man in your employ. Do not blame the contractor for your incompetency."

Bernius, standing the while, straightened and said, "I shall be most happy if the contractor does improve his operations, but I am not confident that he will. As for our man on the project, Titus is right; that is our responsibility. I do not expect such overpayment will occur again. Anything else?"

Nemus shrugged. "We will provide the sestertii to the accounts. We ask that you be available, each month, to identify the work performed and answer questions prior to our approval of these transactions." He looked at writing he had scribbled. "Our limit is 5000 sestertii per month. We are already nearly at that limit. I assume that the requirement will soon exceed the 5000 sestertii."

"Yes—this next month. We must contract to dig exploratory shafts for the tunnel. The excavation payment for next month will be more substantial, and we will be initiating additional contracts soon. Your limit is upon you."

"Upon us like a plague," Titus muttered.

"If that is all, we will leave you." Bernius raised his eyebrows.

No one had further questions or comments.

"Why do you think our 'eyes and ears' allowed the contractor to be overpaid?" Appius asked Bernius as they trudged back to their office.

"I can only be suspicious." Bernius turned to Appius. "If there was a surplus of sestertii flowing to the contractor, perhaps the contractor's friend, Titus, would have... access."

"If that were so, then our man would likely be a party to the scheme."

"Yes. We must be aware. We will visit the site soon, in addition to scrutinizing the reports. Also, we must employ a representative on the clearing and excavation. That must be done this next week. He, if we do a better job of selection, will also be able to let us know what the military is doing."

"We are busy."

"We are, and the project is only two months along. That reminds me. At some time, sooner rather than later, it will not be useful to manage the work from Nemausus. We are at the far end of the work. When we have bid and awarded most of the contracts, we should relocate somewhere near the mid of the work, perhaps near the crossing of the Vardo. One day soon, we should find a location and contract for building of an office and our residences."

"You mean, our families... er... my family would live there—no markets, no relatives, no fountain?" He was thinking of Antonia's reaction.

"Perhaps by the time we move there, you will have your markets and fountain... and your shelter. Your relatives will be at a convenient and advantageous one-day's walk away." He smiled. "What will Antonia say?"

"I do not know. I think the idea will be a shock, although she has the ability to think beyond. Will you take Juliena and her family?"

"Appius—for shame. You are a shameless shill for Antonia and her... very attractive, very bright sister. I have no plans. You can make that report." He smiled to acknowledge that he knew Appius was the 'eyes and ears' of the multitude when it came to matters Bernius/Juliena.

"Antonia would be happier if she had a favorite sister at hand."

"Yes, well that would be an excellent reason, I suppose, but not necessarily from my viewpoint." He quickened his step. "We must work on our schedule to see how we might adjust to recover the time we have lost and to plan our actions in the highly probable instance in which we dismiss Quantus Tarius."

Appius concluded that the conversation involving Bernius/Juliena was over for the time being.

Appius and Bernius read the reports from their quarry representative. They traveled to the site on a surprise visit after receiving the second of the next two weekly reports. The report turned out not to exaggerate the progress as deliberately and dramatically as the prior ones. The contractor had finished the hoist, and it was rigged into its stance against the face of the quarry. However, the ramps were still not finished (in the report the ramps were *nearly* finished), and it looked as if it would be some time before the first block could be freed. The weekly report stated that five additional men had been employed. Bernius and Appius were able to determine that such was true. Their own representative treated them as if they were enemy. The duo headed back to Nemausus.

As they rode from the quarry, Bernius said, "They have not produced the first stone in two weeks, as we require. It is highly unlikely they will produce the first stone in the next week. During this time, we should talk to the second bidder, Vernius Portius, to see if he is willing to take over the contract and under what terms. It will be best to be prepared, to know what we must do, rather than muddle around after we have terminated the contract."

"I wonder if he suspects that Quantus Tarius will fail."

Thomas Hessler

"I am sure he is paying attention. He is an astute businessman and feels stung because an incompetent was able to snare the contract. He will know we are coming and will ask for terms that will be to his advantage. And, frankly, I do not blame him. We are skewered by the sanctity of the bidding process, and now the project must pay the price."

"What do you mean 'sanctity of the bidding process'?"

"I mean that if you take bids, you cannot select someone other than the low bidder just because you favor them or think they might do a better job. If you were to make a practice of doing that, you would not attract many responsible bidders—if they thought that the process is subject to favoritism; the effort to make a bid would not be worth the while. If the responsible and canny bidders opt out, it leaves more room for the... less competent ones... to submit higher pricing. So you get a sense of what I am talking about?"

"Yes. It might seem favorable to pick the contractor you want, but you corrupt the bidding concept."

"Indeed. There are many facets to bidding. Incompetent *owners* often corrupt the process as much as incompetent contractors. This is a contentious business."

"I am beginning to see that."

Vernius Portius rewarded Bernius with a sardonic grin. "I am not surprised," he said. "I have been paying attention to Quantus Tarius and his operation. His lack of experience has shown up as timidity in his approach."

Bernius was visiting Vernius, once again. The conversation would remain undisclosed.

"What do you mean?" Bernius really did understand the situation, but wanted to hear it described by the knowledgeable contractor.

"He is feeling his way through the work rather than attacking it. He has a small number of people working so that he is not so exposed if he makes a mistake. He has to try every new operation before he is comfortable."

Bernius shrugged. "I suppose he might get comfortable with his operation and thereafter make reasonable progress."

"Yes, that might be true." Vernius tilted his head. "But, any difficulties in his operation will not be easily solved. Whether or not you have the patience is a matter in which you must judge."

the *Aedifex*: Building the Pont du Gard

"Truly, I have seen enough." Bernius stood and paced. "I feel that it is likely we will replace Quantus—void his contract—and I would like you to tell me under what terms you would take over the work—as the second bidder and a contractor that is qualified."

Vernius shook his head. "Of course I have given this thought. I would require payment for mobilization although you have paid Quantus to do so. But, it will cost me to establish an operation, even if you have paid the other contractor for such."

"I hate paying for the same item twice, but I do understand your requirement. What else?"

"Quantus has made mistakes in his approach to accessing the required stone. I will have to make corrections. My original price for the pre-work was less than that of Quantus but due to the corrections my price will now exceed his by several thousand sestertii. That must be accommodated."

Bernius nodded, understanding that Vernius was negotiating additional money into his contract, a consequence of the non-competitive situation, somewhat expected. "Of course we may subtract the work Quantus has done from your payment, work that will benefit you."

"Yes. Of course."

"If that is all, I agree with your request."

"That is all."

"We will have to wait another week or so. It should be soon apparent that Quantus will fail." Bernius nodded and walked to the door.

One week later, Bernius walked into the office, reading as he walked. "I do not believe it."

Appius looked up, puzzled. "What is it?"

The report from the quarry says that the contractor has produced the first block. It is now aging in the yard."

"That *is* a surprise."

"Yes. We must go see for ourselves. We leave tomorrow morning."

Early the next morning they were on the trail to the quarry. Bernius said, "I have not asked. Did you talk to Antonia about living on the project?"

"She is not happy, yet it was clear that she had been thinking about the possibility. I have some talking and negotiating to do before she is willing."

425

"I suppose she asked about *my* intentions."

"Yes, she did say that she could be much more content, away from Nemausus, if, for instance, Bernius might take a wife meaning that *family* would be nearby."

Bernius laughed. "That is hardly subtle."

"Too true. I will leave it up to you to provide reasons to bolster my ability to persuade Antonia, or not."

"It is good to have those choices. But, on the same subject, we should consider a location and a concept of what we want to build—for our residence and for the headquarters. Let us do that in the next month. Then, when it is convenient, we will get some builders to work."

Appius nodded.

The quarry works was ahead. As they rode through the yard, they did not spot the first aging block, one of the large blocks that would nestle on the native rock foundations. They rode to the shack where Vitellius Varro resided, dismounted, and walked into the shack. Vitellius Varro, disturbed as usual with visitors, especially *these* visitors, made as if he had been busy drafting reports.

Bernius said, without preamble, greeting, or acknowledgement, "Where is the first block? We did not see it as we rode through the yard."

Vitellius Varro jerked his head up and said, "Oh! Well, it is quite easy. Come with me." He led them outside and into the yard about 100 feet away and pointed to a block of stone about 2 feet by 1 foot by 3 feet.

"What is this?" Bernius stormed.

Sotto voce, Varro said, "This is the first stone, as you requested." He did not look at them but pointed to the stone.

"This is not one of the first stones specified. It is about one-quarter the size of a foundation stone. What is this?"

"Why I believe it is an arch stone. Surely it is of use."

Bernius erupted. "You fool. You have reported to work for the last time. We have no need of your efforts. Gather your belongings and depart. We will pay you through today, in Nemausus." Bernius gestured toward the quarry. "Appius, let us look at the works. As I suspected, they are far from being able to free the first foundation stones, but we will make note of their exact status as of today. I will also tell the contractor's man that we are terminating the contract. They can keep working or wait until Quantus Tarius tells them to stop."

While Vitellius Varro gathered his belongings, destroying several current reports in the process, Bernius and Appius made their way up the quarry face, using ladders in a few instances and climbing steep steps hacked into the rocks.

From a viewpoint to the side of the quarry face they stopped and looked. Bernius said, "It is as I thought. They are still weeks away from creating a face from which to take the large blocks and having a ramp to move them to position where the hoist can remove them from the face. I will talk to the contractor's man."

They walked to the face works where several men were working on the ramp. Bernius approached the supervisor. "You are weeks from freeing a large stone."

The man looked at Bernius, knowing the intent of the statement, but pausing before he answered. "Yes."

"I will ride back to Nemausus and tell Quantus Tarius that his contract has been terminated because he has not made sufficient progress. I will replace his contract with that of Vernius Portius. You and your men may keep working, and I assure you that you will be paid for the work you have done and will continue to do. Whether you keep on working is, of course, your choice. What say you?"

"We have talked about it—the men and I. We would like to continue working. Of course it is up to Vernius Portius if he chooses to keep us employed. So, I will tell the men and they will choose, but I think they will remain upon the assurances of your good word. They are not bad workers. It is just that Quantus Tarius would not provide the number of men needed to accomplish the preliminary work. I hope Vernius Portius will choose to keep us on."

Bernius nodded. "You have my word. I will tell you that I have told *our* representative to leave. He is of no use. I am thinking that within a week, Vernius Portius and the two of us," he nodded to Appius, "will be here to assess the situation before Vernius takes over. At that time you can tell me how much time you have spent. We will get the sestertii to you."

"I understand." The contractor's man nodded. "So, you are dismissing your representative. I must tell you this. He bragged to us that he was also being paid by Quantus Tarius and

427

told us that he was helping us out by reporting our work favorably. It angered me. The best thing he could have done for us would be to say we needed more help. Now we are part of a cloud of ill will in which we are blamed for lack of skill and hard work. I am happy he is gone. I will be happier, of course, if Vernius Portius continues with us."

Bernius, lips compressed in anger, said, "Thank you for telling us that. I will do my best to help you with Vernius. We will probably see you within the week." He turned, beckoned to Appius, and they descended to yard level. "This episode just demonstrates the requirement to keep a close eye on the work. It also demonstrates the necessity of having reliable people. Is it not disgusting that our representative was getting paid by Quantus Tarius?"

Appius, as he was mounting his horse, answered, "It is disgusting and altogether more clear now. But—not a good start here."

"Fortunately, Quantus Tarius has not ruined anything. It is not as if he had placed stones incorrectly in the construction. We can at least continue with the work he has done, late as it might be." Bernius turned his horse to home.

"Yes. I am anticipating an exciting time in Nemausus the next few days. I wonder what Quantus Tarius thought we would do?"

"I think he expects that he is protected by those in high places. We shall have to see what happens. We could encounter some difficulties originating from 'on high.' Yet, we must do what e think is best and not subject ourselves to the politics."

CHAPTER 41

Appius held Sergius on his lap, alternately feeding the boy and himself. Antonia watched them. A wave of warmth engulfed her, an automatic response of a mother watching her husband, her protector and provider, lavish loving attention on the life she had produced.

"So, Appius, you must make a big change to the quarry operations. Is it difficult to have this problem when you are just getting started?"

"Yes... well, I have not been a part of a project like this before, but I suppose it would be naïve to think one would experience no problems. Yet, the quarrying of the stone is so important, we must *do* something. Perhaps it is best the problem showed earlier rather than later."

"Titus will be upset."

"Yes, of course, and maybe not just because his friend has been dismissed... the contract terminated. There may have been an arrangement whereby the progress at the quarry was inflated, generating payment in excess of what it should be—the excess going to Titus. I do not know that for a fact, but it is one possibility."

"Have you been accosted by Titus or the *Corporata*—since you told Quantus Tarius?"

"No, but Bernius and I are to make our monthly report, in person, to the *Corporata* tomorrow. I am sure we will have to stand in the fierce wind generated by the wrath of Titus."

"Can Titus do anything—I mean through Quantus Tarius and his friends in Rome?"

"I do not know. Perhaps he can. If someone in Rome tried to exert influence, I do not know if Claudius could or would intercede. Unless somehow constrained, I think he would support our actions. He thinks a great deal of Bernius."

"Hmmm. So does Juliena." Antonia stretched her shoulders and brightened. "Has Bernius mentioned... or can you tell if... he might want to... *consider* Juliena?" She ended the rambling question with a smile.

"Yes, we have talked about the subject."

"Oh," she smiled, "what did he say?"

"He did not leave me with any thoughts one way or another. We were talking about the need to live closer to the work. I told him that you would be more favorable to doing so if you had family nearby. You see, I sometimes support the projects you are working on."

"Appius, you must not think I am trying to influence Bernius into taking Juliena as a wife. That would be wrong—could lead to a mistake. No, I am just interested."

"Oh! Well then, I promise to keep you informed." He smiled, looked down at Sergius then lifted him to look at Antonia. "See—that is your mother, your merely interested mother. Smile Antonia."

Bernius, with Appius at his side, made his monthly report to the *Corporata*. That is, he started to make his report, but Titus abruptly stood and held up his hand.

Titus stormed. "I do not wish to sit here and listen to a list of expenditures when we have more difficult considerations to discuss." Titus looked at the other *Corporata* for support then refocused on Bernius. "Of course we know that you have terminated the contract of Quantus Tarius just when he was getting started and have now given favorable treatment to Vernius Portius, treatment I must add that will cost the project and the *Corporata* sestertii that need not be spent. We cannot allow this foolish and reckless waste of our funds. If you do not reverse your actions, we will petition for your removal." Again he looked to the *Corporata*. Julius nodded but the rest remained passive. Because he could not speak for all, he pressed Bernius to defense. "What say you?"

Bernius looked at Titus, then at the rest of the *Corporata*. "The contractor was not abiding by his contract and was warned that it would be terminated if he did not act reasonably to establish a going operation. He did not do so; we gave him even more time than in our warning. We then acted to prevent substantial delay. Yes, there will be additional costs, but Quantus Tarius is responsible for most of them, and his payment will suffer as a result."

Titus, still standing, bellowed, "The contractor, in good faith, provided additional men—as you requested, and produced the first quarried stone—as you requested. He has not been treated fairly." Titus was red in the face but not yet frothing.

the *Aedifex*: Building the Pont du Gard

Bernius, a calm contrast to the tirade, said, "The addition of just a few men spoke to his lack of understanding of the manpower required and probably to his lack of ability to find capable craftsmen. The block he produced was an arch stone, not required for possibly two years. It was not one of the pier stones that will rise from the foundations, the first stones he was supposed to produce. If he does not understand that, then it is further proof that he is not capable of managing the contract."

"Fi! You have dismissed him only because you favored Vernius Portius. I am thinking you were paid by Vernius Portius to do this and then salted his fortune with additional money that *we* must provide."

Bernius could not suggest that Titus may have been responsible for diverting funds to his own use, a temptation hard to resist. "He was not performing, Titus. Even his own man said that more help was needed."

"That was only an excuse. Perhaps they had enough men but only needed to work harder."

"That, sir, is also the responsibility of the contractor." Bernius looked at the others. "I intend to proceed with the replacement of the contract. I will continue with my report."

Titus smashed his wine cup, shattering a pottery product this time. There he sat, arms across his chest. "You will be reprimanded for your actions and punished. I promise. I will see that you are removed."

Bernius shook his head. "I will continue my report in the time I have left."

Nemus spoke. "Bernius, apparently we must accommodate Vernius Portius as he takes over the contract. You have just spoken of that. I ask that you advise us of the conditions that you have agreed to."

"Yes, of course." Bernius, reached for a document. "We agreed to pay the second bidder's—Vernius Portius's—price for mobilizing. That will include getting his tools and equipment to the site and making arrangements. Unfortunately that cost was already paid to Quantus Tarius and will be a duplicate. In addition, we must pay for cost to finish the ramps, cost for completing the removal of earth and the building of the road to the bridge site. Some payment for these items has been paid to Quantus Tarius but was for work he had not accomplished. Any overpayment will be subtracted from the final payment to Quantus. Note that we will

431

have to expedite a road from a second quarry site to the bridge, a provision of Vernius Pentius's bid."

Nemus said. "The terms do not seem unreasonable."

Bernius nodded then finished reporting the list of funds to be distributed. "The clearing contractor has been making good progress, has completed a total of 860 feet and will be paid for completing 500 feet this month for a payment of 3300 sestertii. The excavation contract is paid depending on the type of excavation that is encountered. To date, he has excavated to the depth of 6 feet for 352 feet in earth with tree stumps and a moderate rock situation for a payment of 4600 sestertii. The total to be paid this month is 7900 sestertii, with no payment made to Quantus, plus an additional 2000 sestertii for supervision, designers and the military.

Bernius continued. "As to operations in the immediate future, we will bid and award more contracts—one to dig shafts for the tunnel operations. I will soon travel to visit the sites where clearing and excavation is ongoing and will visit the springs to make a final determination of the elevation of the conduit at its starting point so that the next excavation contract can start."

Marcus asked, "Do you expect further trouble from the Ucetians at the springs? Will you take the military with you?"

"No, I do not expect trouble. I will only be there a short time—an hour at the most, something I can do by myself.. However," he nodded at Appius, "following that, we will have Appius re-stake the route down the Alzon so that clearing and excavation may be started. At that point, I intend to make use of the military to ensure that we have no problems."

The Corporata approved payments as Bernius requested. The Empire, through Claudius, would provide the amount over 5000 sestertii. Titus appeared not to be paying attention. Payments meant nothing to him. It was clear, however, that he was listening.

A new man was found and employed at the quarry as the representative of the project: Servius Rufius. He was aware of the breach of faith committed by the man he was replacing and was able to convince Bernius and Appius that his only compensation would be from the project. A week later, his report indicated that 15 additional men had shown up on the site—employed by Vernius Portius. Most of the prior men had remained working. With the crew strength at the present level, it was believed that the first foundation stone would be freed and in storage at the yard in two weeks.

The project office was also receiving reports from the military. The reports were mostly concerned with observations of possible trouble but seemed to exaggerate the possibilities to portend more than deserved. However, there was usually a passing reference to progress made by the clearing and excavation contractors.

Bernius was reading the report from the military. He beckoned Appius to join him at his desk. When Appius approached, he said, "We should start the chorobate on its way to the springs. After I establish our starting elevation, we will need it—or you will—to establish our route, having not restaked that stretch on our prior episode."

Appius nodded. "I will find two men who will take the chorobate. Perhaps two of the contractor's men, starting on the new excavation or clearing at the springs, will be able and willing to do so as they walk to the site."

"Here is what I am thinking." Bernius pointed to the map. "I will ride to the springs and make my notations to calculate where to start digging and the elevation to which we must excavate to provide the useful beginning of the aqueduct. While I am determining those items, you will locate the military and advise them we will need them to establish a presence near the springs to ensure that the Ucetians know of their existence. Of course, we will want the military to provide actual protection. I think you and I should meet somewhere along the route that is convenient after I have done my work at the springs. You can tell me about your meeting with the military."

"I hope the soldier that the *centurion* put in charge is more easily dealt with than the *centurion* himself." Appius grimaced.

"Let us hope so. It is difficult to think he would allow someone as arrogant as he to serve as his underling. But... we do not know."

"Bernius?" Appius looked puzzled. "What will you establish at the springs? The start location and the elevation—what does that mean?"

"We do not want to start our excavation closely adjacent to the spring's flow but at a distance away so that we do not flood our excavation; we will leave earth as a barrier. I will imagine a means

433

by which we later divert the spring flow from its present path so that water will not be present while we build the inlet works to the conduit. We can then build in the dry.

"The elevation I establish will ensure that the bed of the springs is above the top of the water passage. We want to make sure the springs will fill it. I made this calculation before and made notation on our map; I have to make an adjustment now that we have decided the size and geometry of the conduit. The other task is to identify a suitable location for a nearby diversion structure. If we want to divert water away from the conduit for maintenance or repair, it will be done at this structure. We will also limit and control the flow of the water at this point by releasing part of the flow to the Alzon by use of boards in the slots. Does all that make sense?"

"Yes. I will find a few men to take the chorobate and make arrangements to be away for some time. I am anxious to see the excavation. I have not seen it for four weeks, and even if they have encountered hard rock, I should be able to see progress."

Bernius laughed. "I would hope so."

Bernius and Appius rode together until they reached the road to the quarry at the existing Vardo River crossing.

Appius said, "As we do not know where the military is, at the moment, I will start here and work my way along the route, going first to the quarry. At some point I should intercept them. After doing so, I will ride to join you at the springs or at the excavation trench. I should find the chorobate in that vicinity."

As Bernius continued down the path, he looked back and said, "I will see you either at the end of this day, or possibly tomorrow."

Appius did not find the military at the quarry but took time to observe the activity on the face and to talk to Servius Rufius, the new representative.

Appius said, "I see much more activity. What is your opinion?"

Servius walked Appius outside the shack and pointed. "You can see the number of the men working on the ramp, the item to be completed before we can transport the first foundation stone to the yard. They will be finished in the next few days, and the contractor has already begun to chisel around the first foundation stone to be removed. That should happen well before the two weeks that was promised. It is clear that with the additional men and with better direction, the work is progressing efficiently."

"And, the men that were working before...?"

"Yes, they continued working. But the supervisor was replaced by one of Vernius's own men. The new supervisor has more experience, but the prior one is useful and is working as a lead on the ramp crew. You made a change for the best."

"Good. When were the military last here?"

Servius hesitated. "Two days ago. I do not get along well with the *decanus*. He is gruff, and you would think he was in charge of *my* work. I am pleased when they have gone."

"I am looking for them, and I should find them along the trail. I want to say that I thought the first report you sent us was well done. Thank you. Please continue."

Servius smiled and nodded. Appius walked to his horse and was off. He could not take the horse on the raft, so he had to ride back to the river crossing.

Riding from the river crossing to the aqueduct route, Appius spotted the military approaching him, their cart not able to avoid all the path's bumps and depressions. He halted as they met.

The soldier with rank, the *decanus,* stepped forward, took off his cap, dusted it by slapping it across his arm, looked up, and said, "You are?"

Appius thought the manner surly but chose to ignore it for the moment. "I am Appius."

"What is your business, Appius?" He snapped the cap back on his head.

Appius considered that he might respond that he was admiring the flowers along the way, but then thought that would be sinking to the level of the *decanus*. "I am actually looking for you. I need to give you direction."

The *decanus* gave him a hard look. It must have occurred to him that Appius was of a position to give him direction, perhaps remembering that he was to take direction not only from Bernius, but of Appius, too. It was absurd, taking direction from civilians. "Yes, what can I do for you?" He spat.

"The project will soon be starting operations along the Alzon. We need you to start patrolling along that route. In fact, we will be starting operations there in two days. I request that you turn around and make your presence known along the Alzon, especially in sight of the village of Ucetia."

The *decanus* said nothing for a moment, then, "We have heard that the Ucetians have caused trouble in the past. Perhaps we should walk through the village."

"No, do not do that. For now, your presence at the spring will be of most use. The Ucetians will know that you are there."

"If you were a military man, you would exhibit more strength. That is the way to keep problems at a minimum."

"You will do as I have stated?"

The *decanus* nodded, spat again, turned, and walked to address his men.

Appius walked his horse past the soldiers and the cart. The *decanus* turned his back to Appius as he rode by.

Appius mused that his life situation had changed. He could not have imagined giving orders to the military two years ago. Although the exchange was not pleasant, he felt exhilarated by the notion that he could exert that authority, although he was really exerting the will of Bernius.

He rode on until he encountered the clearing crew, now 1200 feet along the route from the Alzon. He talked to the supervisor about the work and was pleased to see they were making decent progress with few unexpected problems. As he was talking, Pentius and Marius approached, axes over their shoulders.

They hailed him, Pentius speaking, "Appius, we saw Bernius ride by earlier. He is on to the springs to make observations."

Marius shook his head. "We offered to go with him, but he said his task would only take an hour or so and he could make better time on his horse, get his work done, and be back. He intends to spend the night here. You?"

Appius had dismounted to greet the duo. "Yes. I will ride to meet Bernius and then be back here tonight. Bernius probably told you that I will be re-staking the route down the Alzon. Did our chorobate go by?"

Marius nodded. "Yes—yesterday. The workers hauled it as far as the excavation. Pentius and I wonder if you would like us to assist in the staking. We have... made arrangements with our supervisor."

"I had that in mind, also. I am happy to have your help." He remounted the horse. "I will find Bernius, talk to him about the starting location, and we will return for the evening meal." He waved and rode off.

Appius soon encountered the excavation work, as he neared the Alzon. As he rode upon the scene, he could see the linear pile of earth to the right side of the cleared path. Men with baskets of earth were climbing out of the trench, baskets strapped over their backs as they labored up the sloped sides. They emptied their load at the terminus of the ever-lengthening triangular pile, walked back down the sides of the trench and disappeared. As he got closer, he could see men in the trench working at the leading edge of the excavation, hacking at roots and stumps, tossing them behind for the muckers, then attacking the earth that lay beyond. Several men were struggling with a large stone that had been unearthed. It was unable to fit in a basket, much less be carried by one man. The stone was levered and barred to a ramp that had been created for the easing in such an operation. They proceeded to walk the stone up the ramp. *Hmmm,* he mused. *Perhaps the contractor assumed more of these problems than we when we made the estimate. That could account for the higher prices we received. The contractors may have been more astute.*

He talked briefly to the supervisor then rode on. It would not be too long before the excavators would need more stakes set, but he noted that Pentius and Marius had marked the holes of the prior stakes, as they had promised. His restaking should be easy.

Appius trotted to the Alzon, along the cleared path above the trench—now excavated to 6 feet. He used the gait of his horse for measurement to determine a length of 750 feet. He had expected to see Bernius returning by this time but, knowing the vagaries of any chore, assumed that Bernius had run into difficulties.

Appius reached the springs and saw where Bernius had driven several stakes but did not see Bernius. He raised his head, spotted the rooftops of the village, and wondered if Bernius had, for some reason, ridden to the village, perhaps to make another appeal for the villagers to talk to Claudius. But he spotted Bernius's horse, the reins wrapped on a branch. As he approached the horse whinnied, dissatisfied with being so constrained. Bernius must be nearby. Appius rode into the shrubbery. Bernius was probably looking for signs of high or low water that might give a more precise indication of any fluctuation of the spring. He rode about 150 feet from the springs and startled some crows into the

437

air. A chill ran through him. When he looked to the crows' launch point he saw... something... on the ground... something not of a forest nature. He rode closer. It was Bernius lying face down. Appius was numbed. Had Bernius drunk too much wine? It was true, he drank much wine, but never as much as to put him down and... not while he was working.

Appius rode to within several feet. He remained in the saddle. He knew. He could now see the blood on the back of Bernius's head, clotted in the curly dark hair. He shook his head and slumped forward in the saddle. He knew. Finally, he dismounted, walked to the prone figure, kneeled, and gently turned him over. He could already feel the chill. Mercifully, Bernius's eyes were closed. Appius sat, cradled Bernius's head in his lap, and sobbed.

In time he became aware that it was darkening, the evening soon to be upon him. He gently laid Bernius's head to the ground, walked to his horse, retrieved a blanket and leather thongs from his satchel, wrapped Bernius within and cinched the thongs. He retrieved Bernius's horse and, with much difficulty, was able to lift and lay Bernius across the saddle and secure him. He grabbed the reins of Bernius's horse, climbed into his saddle, and started a slow reverent walk down the Alzon, glancing at the Ucetia rooftops, now just a silhouette against the fallen sun. *It cannot be!*

Bernius is... was... my best friend. Appius shook his head to ward off a threatening emotional breakdown. *He is the creator of the project, its brains and its motive power. All is lost. I cannot think of a worse calamity. What will I tell Antonia? Juliena? Poor thing—another man in her life taken from her. I cannot imagine what will now happen. I must get word to Claudius.*

It was well into the evening when Appius arrived at the far end of the excavation. The men were completing their dinner, a small fire keeping the chill at bay. As he approached, the men could see in the flickering light that he was leading another horse, with something large draped across the saddle. They knew, stopped conversation then stood as Appius approached. They said nothing.

Appius spoke in a hoarse whisper. "It is Bernius. They have killed him."

The men looked up to Appius, expecting him to tell them more. However, Appius chucked his horse and moved on; the other horse followed. As Appius went by, one man asked—"The Ucetians?"

Appius, now with his back to them, nodded and said, "I am afraid so."

The men looked at one another.

Appius rode on until he reached the clearing crew camp. He could see the fires well ahead of him. Before he got to the encampment, two men approached then stopped fifty feet in front of Appius. He rode up to them.

"Bernius?" Marius said, looking back at the other horse.

Appius nodded.

Pentius pointed, "How did...?"

"He was killed. A blow to the back of his head."

Marius and Pentius looked at each other. "The Ucetians," said Marius. "We will take care of that problem... now." He turned to walk back to camp.

"Wait... no!" Appius raised his voice with effort, straining against the emotions racking him.

The men, both now heading back to the camp to retrieve their axes, stopped. "We must do something," yelled Pentius.

"Yes, you are right. We must do something—but I do not want to lose you two. We will put the military to use. I would rather lose them."

Appius spent the night at the clearing camp. He talked to Marius and Pentius. "I have a thought and need your help. Tomorrow, we will take Bernius to the Vardo, to the site of the bridge. I would bury him in view of the bridge that I swear will rise from the canyon. Will you help me?"

Both men put a hand on his shoulders, nearly causing another emotional episode. Marius said, "You can be sure that we will be with you. We will place Bernius so that he can watch the bridge being built. He will be with us."

Appius nodded. "That is what I had in mind. In truth, I do not know what is going to happen. The Ucetians may have been thinking that if they took out Bernius, the project would falter. I hope they are not right. I must talk to the military tomorrow, also."

"I would like to go to Ucetia with the military. I want to make the Ucetians suffer for taking our friend." Pentius shook his fist.

"I understand what you want to do. So do I, although I find it hard to believe that they would carry out this act of violence. Are they total fools, or was it one hothead who took it upon himself to defy the might of the Empire? Stupid."

Marius took a deep breath. "We will go with you. Settling Bernius is more important, but I will always seethe that I did not get my hands on Bernius's killer or killers."

The next morning, Appius set out with Marius and Pentius with Bernius strapped across the back of the second horse. At a mile along the route, they encountered the military. The troupe stopped, and the *decanus,* riding the horse, rode forward.

"And what is this?" He nodded toward the trailing horse, crossing his arms over his chest.

Appius felt irritation rising in response but was able to remain calm. "On the horse is the body of Bernius. He was killed yesterday while he was taking measurements at the spring."

"Killed, meaning killed by somebody?" The man punctuated his remark by compressing his lips.

Appius nodded. "It is so. He was hit on the back of the head in the forest."

"The Ucetians, the ones of which you spoke, yesterday?"

"It must be so." Appius paused, not easily assuming responsibility. "Therefore, you must go to the village and investigate, find those responsible, bind them and bring them to Nemausus. We must make it clear to the Ucetians that they have made a big mistake and that no more trouble will be tolerated. I am sure your presence will stop further lawlessness."

The *decanus* uncrossed his arms and rested his hands on his hips. "Of that I do agree with you. We will surely make it clear to the villagers that no more trouble will be tolerated." He dismounted.

"As I mentioned, we will soon be starting the clearing and the excavation at the springs—perhaps tomorrow or the next day. We must have some of your men present, at least in the beginning. After we know more about the situation, we can discuss what should be done on a regular basis." Appius, while staring at the *decanus*, did his best to assume the aura of one in charge.

the *Aedifex*: Building the Pont du Gard

The *decanus* said nothing but returned Appius's stare. There was something in the stare, insolent in its middle, portent on the edges. He walked to the burden on the horse, pulled at the blanket until the head of Bernius was exposed. He took a look at the evidence on the back of the head and yanked Bernius's head up by the hair to get a look at his face. He smirked and did not bother to rewrap the blanket but stood there staring.

Marius and Pentius had been abreast of Appius but now walked to the horse, shoved the *decanus* out of the way, angered by his lack of respect. They rewrapped the blanket and made it secure. The *decanus* walked back to his men.

Marius and Pentius rejoined Appius. He nodded in the direction they were heading, and they continued toward the Vardo, walking past the soldiers, now turned and trudging towards the Alzon.

Marius spoke after they passed the military. "You might wish that you had sent us to Ucetia rather than the military."

Appius nodded. "I do not trust this man or his centurion—Flavius Darius. To be truthful, I do not know what is best to be done now. I must let Claudius know. He is the only person who will ensure that the project goes forward—that we have a capable leader. Who will we get as a replacement for Bernius—someone from Rome? None of the designers are capable as leaders as good as they are at their work. It will have to be someone that Claudius knows. I must get to him soon."

He said nothing for several moments then looked at the two men. "After we bury Bernius, I will quickly ride back to the springs and set stakes, enough for the clearing contractor to work for several weeks, the excavator to follow. I will do that today. If there is any daylight remaining, I will ride toward Lugdunum. I must get there quickly so that the project can be stabilized as soon as possible."

Appius, Marius, and Pentius stopped at the rim of the Vardo canyon. Pentius looked up at Appius. "Where?"

Appius pointed. "On the opposite bank. He will have a good view from there."

Marius nodded. "We will have to cross the river on the raft."

441

They eased down the side of the canyon to the raft, tethered the horses, and loaded Bernius onto the raft, rode the current, and landed on the other side.

"I think about 300 feet downstream—there is a good view and the location should be undisturbed by building operations."

Pentius and Marius carried the bundle while Appius shouldered digging tools. Downstream, Appius looked around, looked back up the canyon, pointed to a spot between two trees, and said, "Here."

Pentius and Marius dug. At a fair depth, Pentius looked up. Appius nodded. Pentius climbed out and all helped to ease Bernius into his grave.

The men made ready to backfill the dirt. Appius said, "Wait." He rummaged in his satchel and retrieved a jug of wine. He held it out, looking at it. "I got this from the supplies Bernius was carrying. It is a very good wine. You know how much Bernius liked his wine. We will leave it with Bernius in case he needs to ease his way into the next world."

The men smiled. Pentius wiped a tear. Appius lowered himself into the grave and tucked the jug under the blanket. He climbed out and nodded.

After the earth was replaced, they marked the spot by encircling it with three large stones. "I will return with a proper monument at some time. We will do a proper ceremony."

Marius shook his head. "We must be there."

CHAPTER 42

I called Lisele. "Let's go for a walk."

Lisele, not puzzled for long, absent my announcement that I was the caller—she did not get many calls in English—said, "Oh... Warner. Hello, but... a walk? It seems to me like you had a lot to say about danger to your life, extreme exhaustion, and rough treatment the last time we... walked. Either you are trying to inflict severe situations upon yourself, or you have forgotten the experience, owing to your advanced age. How can I possibly contribute further to your undoing?"

"Lisele, it is your fault... the undoing I mean. I would scale the canyon, hang on to tree roots, skin my knees, and drive myself to exhaustion to have another kiss with you in the mists. No, I am very aware of what I am doing. Besides, our walk should have none of the difficult elements. I only want to walk the aqueduct remains to see if we can find other inscriptions. Or, if I am to be totally honest, I am using that as another excuse to spend time with you."

Lisele was silent for a moment. When she spoke, it was hesitantly. "Okay. Yes, Warner, let us go for a walk along your aqueduct. I don't know how many more opportunities I will have to take a walk with you. At some time you will have done all you can with the aqueduct and must return to your home. Any kisses will be just a memory."

It was my turn to be silent. It was painful to have to consider reality and even more painful to have to discuss the consequences with Lisele. "I have the same... fear. I have been telling myself that I should heed the advice of Buddha—'Do not dwell in the past, do not dream of the future, concentrate the mind on the present moment.' I'm sure Buddha hadn't met you. Perhaps he would change his mind."

"Buddha didn't have property, friends and relatives ten thousand miles away—no silver planes to fly, taxes to pay, or alimony. It was easier for him to say that. But, for today, let *us* live for the moment. We'll sort out the rest, later. When would you like to go for your walk?"

Thomas Hessler

"Tomorrow. Let us do our walk tomorrow. And, I do like your devil-may-care attitude. I'll do my homework, decide where we are to investigate and pick you up at 8 a.m. Does that work?"

"Yes, Warner, that works very well—for the moment. 'Devil may care' of me, yes? I will even prepare a picnic. Will you bring the wine?"

"Yes, the wine—or maybe the beer. Do you drink beer?"

"Yes. I will drink the beer—cold, I suppose. I'll see you at eight."

I was propelling myself down the path with Lisele. I knew at some time I'd have to face the consequences. But could I really have expected I would have better sense? It could only result in some sort of dramatic outcome, and it did.

We started at Vers, walking toward the Pont du Gard. We left the path and walked both sides of the standing arches, weaving in and around the openings, skirting fallen stones and climbing on the structures where it was necessary. We carefully inspected the structures for the APA sign. Remembering that we would have not seen the original inscription on the Pont du Gard had Lisele not seen it in a glance from the side, we used that technique as part of our method. We walked the path to the diversion structure, just before the Pont du Gard, then back to Vers. Alas, our hard work did not produce any further inscriptions.

On our expedition, however, I again paused at the rubble piles and kicked over a few stones. In a few piles I saw some of the half-round clay pipe remnants I had seen before. I pointed them out to Lisele. "See these? I am not sure how they were used. I thought at first they were broken, but I looked closely and they were made that way... as a half of a pipe... the bottom half I presume. I wonder if they used them to drain water away from the structure while they were building it."

Lisele said, "Do you think that is how they used them?"

"I don't know. It makes little sense. A pipe such as this will let debris in and is not as strong as a whole pipe."

Lisele laughed. "Well, at least you could see if water was flowing in the pipe."

"True, but I see little use for that."

"You and Laurie could go ask the professor." Lisele giggled, then laughed.

444

"Very funny. You won't leave that alone, but I'm happy to be the object of your entertainment and even happier that you're able to laugh at the situation. By the way, how is it going with you and Laurie?"

Lisele wagged her head and grimaced. "Between you and me, I can laugh about what happened, but not with Laurie. While we are polite with each other, it wasn't long ago that she called me a whore, assuming that I had slept with you."

"Oooh! What did you say?"

"I told her that I had not, that just because that was the way she operated, she couldn't assume that everybody acted that way."

I smiled.

"Oh, so now I am providing entertainment for you. What are you thinking?"

I shrugged. "I wonder what you will say to her if... if it should ever happen... that... you... we... do... sleep together."

Lisele gave me a fixed stare that seemed to last forever.

I asked, "What?"

She shook her head. "I haven't decided."

I didn't need to ask 'decided what?' I knew what she meant. I defused the moment. "Otherwise, you are able to have a conversation with Laurie? She isn't just going through cold motions, feigning cordiality?"

"Yes, otherwise it is somewhat normal, at least lately. She even asks what you are doing, about your investigation. I guess you did inspire some interest in your time with her."

I nodded. "Let's walk back to Vers, get my car, and drive to Uzes. After we look at the structures at the springs, we can go back to town and have lunch. Yes?"

She nodded. We turned and walked back down the trail.

At Uzes, we walked in and about the diversion structure in the green valley, really the only feature that was more or less intact near the springs. We saw one inscription, a faint remainder, that seemed similar to the APA we had spotted before, but I think we were forcing the idea.

I shrugged. "Let's have lunch."

Lisele smiled. "We cannot say that we found what we were looking for, but we can say that we did investigate. Our lunch is a reward for trying."

"Yes, I would be nagged by the thought that I should have looked had we not done this. Let's go."

We had a pleasant picnic—on tables in the Fountaine Eure park below Uzes—a table in the shade, a slight breeze to remove the stifle. The beer was thirst quenching, as beer is known to be. As I looked through the trees in the park toward the source, the springs, I thought of Lisele's remark about the clay pipes. I don't know how the idea came to me from my subconscious, but it startled me, and I guess it showed.

Lisele's eyes bugged. "What?"

I held up my finger to punctuate the moment. "I was thinking about what you said."

"What, about sleeping together?"

I laughed. "No, no—although that thought will surely get much of my attention." I shook my head. "No, I was thinking about what you said about the pipes—that you can 'see the water.' That may be the point... the only one I can think of. It is possible that they used the pipes to establish their level."

"Warner, I don't understand what you mean."

I splayed my hands. "I remember reading a researcher's comment. He was wondering how they determined the level on the Aqua Virgo and suggested that as they excavated, they let the water into the trench and were able to determine a level measurement from the water surface. But, that would have been difficult—they would then have to contain the water then remove it to continue their dig. What if, instead...?" I shook my finger again, "they used the half-round pipes. They would let a small amount of water into the pipes, observe their level, mark it on the side of the trench, remove the pipes and install them again after they had excavated some of the next section. *Voila.* Lisele you are remarkable."

Lisele didn't comprehend all that I was saying, but, nevertheless, enjoyed the moment. "Warner, you are the one that makes the connection. I just... *say* these things."

"Yes, but your observations are fresh and jolt me to think beyond... beyond the usual. We, a synergistic 'we,' may have made an important discovery—well, it isn't really a discovery, it is a hypothesis."

"A hypothesis? It is more of a guess."

the *Aedifex*: Building the Pont du Gard

"Yes, well, I suppose a hypothesis is a guess but possibly supported by background and circumstance... and maybe a little intuition."

She smiled. "I have never contributed to a hypothesis before. What will we do with it?"

"A hypothesis is useful. While it may not be correct, it may represent the best thinking to date. If the scientific world were dealing with it, some would try to prove it true and some would try to prove it false. If it is shown to be false, the hypothesis is replaced by a new one—a new thought. That is how science progresses."

"But, again, what will we do with *our* hypothesis. It seems as if it is doomed to just rattle around in our brains."

"That's a very good question. I came over here to discover how this project was built. I discovered a number of mysteries and have worked to solve them and have some good ideas... at least I think so. But, what do I do with them? I'm not part of the scientific community, not part of academia. I write no papers, and ivory-tower professors don't want to listen to me."

"Perhaps you shouldn't think that all the academics are like Professor Durand. Perhaps you should talk to others. Warner, you've put in serious effort, and your thoughts might be valuable. There must be others to talk to."

She was right. I should or could seek out and talk to others. The thought that someone in the research business might listen to me was inspiring, but what could be done with my suggestions? They couldn't be proved. My mind slid off the exciting thought of gaining traction in the research world, something that was improbable, to the thought of sleeping with Lisele, something that was... possible. I smiled.

She observed my deliberation. "You are thinking about what I said?"

"Yes, Lisele, yes."

That night, I thought about my experience, my research of the aqueduct. It was true; I had learned a great deal, encountered some mysteries, and perhaps stumbled upon some answers. I had not found written material that provided the answer. It was difficult to believe that I, just a visitor more interested than most, could be working at the leading edge of the available knowledge. Should I try to find an academic who might be gracious enough to listen to me? Somehow, I didn't have the enthusiasm even though I may have imagined something useful in furthering the understanding of ancient technology and practices.

I would like to really understand how the aqueduct was put together. A few days prior, I had convinced myself I would be satisfied if I thought my way through the project. In other words, I would imagine how I would have built the project. So, I had appointed myself the project manager and started imagining my way through, making notes as I went along. It was pleasant, sitting in the warm afternoon on my deck, letting my thoughts roam the history that had existed around me. That thought was intriguing. The ancient events had actually happened near and around my very location those millennia ago. It was just an accident of time that kept me from seeing them happen. But, imagining my way through wasn't as easy as I thought.

My vision of the actual circumstances wasn't working well. Yes, I might come up with a sense of how they went about conceiving, designing and building the project, but it didn't work as a means of satisfying my yearning to know what really had happened. I was agitated. I hadn't talked to Maurice in a while so called and arranged to meet with him for lunch. Of course, he was happy to do so.

We met in the little enclosed courtyard near the mayor's office. We sat at a small table, chairs and table wobbling on the rough stones of the courtyard. We pulled the table closer to the building to take advantage of its shade.

Maurice was buoyant, elbows on the table, hands framing his head. "So, Warner, your adventure continues. I am thinking you have many things to tell me. I hear that you are continuing to investigate, have encountered mysteries and have your own thoughts—even though our local academics were not too helpful. Sorry about that."

I smiled. "Yes, Maurice, I continue to trudge through the background, what there is of it. But, I don't think I have much to tell you. Apparently, you must be able to follow my activities closely just by listening to the local chatter."

"Oh, but no, Warner. When did the local chatter ever provide information that was correct? I must hear it from you."

Over a pre-meal beer, I told Warner of my latest encounters with inscriptions, troubles with leveling devices, and conflicting information about advice from ancient architects—

Vitruvius. "I must say, Maurice, I have uncovered as much doubtful information as that which is verified and reasonable. I am surprised at that."

He grinned and raised his glass. "Then, Warner, you must stay much longer and help us solve the mysteries. I look forward to the pleasure of your continued presence." He took a swallow.

So did I.

With a mischievous look, he said, "I imagine Lisele would be interested in a plan like that, as well."

Aha. So the 'town chatter' also involves what is going on there, I thought.

"Maurice, I have a question. When I was in engineering school, the instructors were anxious to expose us to and have us practice what they called 'the engineering method of problem solution.' Did you... here in France... did they also teach that approach?"

"Hmmm. You are stressing the mind of this poor, old fellow. I'm reaching, reaching... ah, yes there it is. Yes, now that you mention it. We did drills... we were given problems in which we applied such a method. Why do you ask?"

I laughed. "I've been having a running discussion with Lisele about the engineering mind. I may have mentioned it to you. But as I was trying to solve the aqueduct builder's problem with 'level,' I remembered the problem-solving process. I tried to identify the steps but could only remember vaguely. But it so happened that in one of the books I brought I had made notes, the steps to take. I was curious if you had been schooled likewise."

"The answer is, yes. And, you know, Warner, it actually became second nature after a while, starting in school and into useful pursuits afterward."

"That's interesting." I sat back. "To find out it is somewhat universal, I mean. I think we use it... second nature, like you say... as part of our modus. I remember taking business courses in which we had to work on what they called 'cases.' The instructor commented that I seemed to go to the problem and the answer quicker than most. Actually, I think it was just the engineering problem-solving training."

"So, but there is the opposite side of the coin. Some engineers don't make good managers."

449

"Yes, that's true. I've always said that 'things' are easier to deal with than people. I think some engineers would naturally like to avoid people problems."

"That is because your so-called 'engineering method of problem solution' doesn't work with people. Ha!" Maurice brightened.

I shook my finger. "Exactly. Don't try it. However, I will say this. I had more success when I used engineers for project managers than when using business grads. I'm not sure the method was the reason, but it could be."

"So. What are the steps? Refresh me. And, how did you use them in your attempt to solve the level problem?" Maurice sat back, taking his beer glass with him.

I took a scrap of paper from my shirt pocket upon which I'd written the steps. You'd think I would be able to remember. "Okay, Maurice, see if these sound familiar." I read from my notes:

1. Establish what you want to accomplish. This means, maybe, stating the problem in a different way.
2. Figure out what you now know and write it down.
3. Identify the bits in between that you don't know, can't know, or are missing. Make reasonable assumptions about those bits. Identify how you would get the needed information.
4. Use the analytical tools (physical principles, past experience, equations, sampling) that you can to fill in or describe the unknowns in a way that they provide needed information. Taken together, do they contribute to a solution?
5. Take a look at your results, and put them in context. Do they make sense? Is this a reasonable answer? If not, cycle back. Re-examine your assumptions. Check your arithmetic. Rethink whether or not those were the correct tools to use.
6. If it makes sense to do so, validate your results with data.

"So, if this revelation," he spread his arms to symbolize a religious significance, "came to you while you were thinking about the Romans and about 'level,' how did you use it? For instance, what is the problem? What do you need to know?"

"I think that defining the problem is perhaps the most important step. Many people charge into problem solving without doing so. In the instance I stated, how were the Romans able to establish level so precisely—meaning 1/4 inch in 100 feet, let's say?"

"I don't see anything wrong with that. Now, what do you know?" Maurice was asking the right questions.

"I know they had the chorobate. They used a weighted line to level the chorobate. I know that the use of the chorobate, as suggested, was not accurate enough. I know that the final product was installed with acceptable accuracy. I know that they constructed the Aqua Virgo in Rome, requiring the same shallow slope, before they constructed the Nimes aqueduct. "

"You know that use of a weighted string *does* give you a line that is perpendicular to level." Maurice made an imaginary vertical line with his hand.

I slowly responded. "Yes, that is correct. But, given the geometry of the chorobate, there is no reliable way to establish an accurate level line from the weighted string. That is how the chorobate was supposed to work but the error involved in the process would render it useless for precision work."

I thought for a moment. "Now for 'what I don't know.' I have *not* seen any references to a device that provides the accuracy required. There is no physical evidence in the structures that indicates level measurements. At this point, I am stymied."

"Warner, I think you left something out of the 'things that you know.' What *is* the most reliable means of establishing level, and maybe, I have to say, the best available means to those in the ancient world?"

I thought for a moment then smiled. "I can think of only one. It is the means by which they probably calibrated the chorobate and is the actual subject matter of the whole exercise. Water level, standing water, is perhaps the only way they could establish level. Any device they came up with would have to first be adjusted to level water. How's that?"

"Just right. You will have to admit it should be included in the list of 'things you know.'"

451

"Yes."

"Then any device you build or method you use as a solution would have to be based on water level."

"Perhaps so."

"Then what is missing is the device or method, based on water, that was used." He took a drink of beer. "Now, using your own method, I think we are on your step 4, we know that the method has to be based on water. Any ideas?"

"I have read—the Aqua Virgo—a suggestion that they flooded the excavation with water from the source. They marked the level. From that mark they could measure the drop they wanted at that point."

"Okay. I see a bit of a problem in that they must have been able to know that they had a drop in the first place before they started excavating."

"Yes. I agree with that."

"But, jumping to step five—does it make sense they would do this? Is flooding the excavation with water a reasonable approach?"

"It seems like a big nuisance to me. At some point they would have been looking at filling and draining over ten miles of excavation. It doesn't seem reasonable at all."

Maurice tilted his head and scowled. "Does anything else come to mind, using water as your reference, any device that might be utilized?"

"Well," I think I played this rather well, "in modern day, craftsmen use a length of clear plastic tubing, filling it with water so that when the two ends are upright, water at both ends will be at the same level. This method even works around corners. Of course, plastic tubing was not available to them, but perhaps they used a similar method. Maybe they manufactured lengths of clay pipe, lengths that were half-round, open at the top, joined and filled for the length of the section in which they were working."

Maurice shook his head. He knew he had been had. "How long have you been thinking this, Warner? And must I jump to your step six to see if you can validate your results with data?"

"Yes, Maurice, jump to step six. This is exciting. I have found remnants of half-round clay pipes. I can't help but think that I have found the solution."

the *Aedifex*: Building the Pont du Gard

"Yes, Warner, you may have. Congratulations. But, I must point out that you didn't solve the problem using the engineering method."

I smiled.

"You encountered the substantiating data, step six, then circled back to step five. So much for your method."

"Maurice, you are absolutely right, proving that it is better to have a mind that works without supervision rather than to use a cookbook. I'll take answers 'out of the blue' any day."

"Me too. Actually I'll entertain any functioning of the brain these days. It isn't always something I can depend upon. But, seriously, Warner, you have a wonderful idea. You should be proud to have uncovered the concept, as if you had found it scratched on an ancient parchment."

"If only we could find such an ancient parchment, Maurice. If only we could."

Several nights later, while sitting at the rustic kitchen table, I looked at the photos I had taken at the *Castellum*. After another hard look at the inscriptions, I noticed something a bit odd. I pulled the light closer. You would think it would have been more noticeable at the site, but the aged mortar joints had assumed the color of the stone, or perhaps the other way around, disguising an anomaly. Perhaps the camera film was more sensitive than the eye to differences in color. I don't know. I was looking at the stones that were used to create the wall from the deck up to the top of the arch, the end of the tunnel over the spot where the aqueduct dumped into the *Castellum*. We had discovered the inscriptions in that wall. All of the other stone blocks in the ashlar wall were staggered except for the five or six stones surrounding the inscriptions. The vertical joints around it were aligned rather than staggered. This configuration was hard to notice, as the stones in that area were somewhat irregular as necessary to fill in the arch. But as I looked at the rest of the wall, now that I was paying attention, it was unmistakable. And, the inscriptions, the APA with the arch symbol were at a very significant location, the end of the aqueduct, the end of the road, so to speak. What did it mean? And, within the square pattern of stones was also the inscription that looked like a roll-up window shade, with part of the shade hanging down, or as Lisele said, a pipe on a stand. That inscription must be significant too. I thought, *what else could it be?* I

453

supposed that it could be a roll of parchment, partially unrolled. *Oh, my God!*

CHAPTER 43

After they rafted back across the Vardo, Appius left Marius and Pentius to walk as he rode, trotting and galloping back to the clearing camp. He was told that the military had gone through on their way to Ucetia. The chorobate had been taken on to the springs by men who would be starting work at that location. Appius would use these men to help him place new stakes. He trotted on, passing the excavation heading and the start of the windrowed pile of earth. Within an hour he reached the springs. He spotted the chorobate, several of the clearing crew and the soldiers. The *decanus* and the horse were not there.

Appius dismounted and walked to the clearing crew. "I must talk to the military, then I will use your help to set stakes."

The men nodded.

Appius turned and strode to the small gathering of the military. "Where is the *decanus?*"

One of the soldiers responded. "He is riding to Lugdunum."

"Lugdunum?" Appius was puzzled. "Is he taking prisoners there?"

"There are no prisoners." The soldier thrust his chin forward.

"No prisoners? You did not go into the village? What has happened?"

"Oh, we went into the village. We... talked... to some of the residents... several actually, even one of the council. They would admit nothing about the killing. They said they knew nothing about it."

"So you left?"

"Yes, we left, but we took disciplinary measures before doing so."

"What does that mean?"

"We left them with the understanding that it was not wise to defy the Empire." He looked at his comrades and smiled. "Perhaps we should accompany you to the village, and you may see for yourself."

Appius nodded. He looked in the direction of the village and spotted a plume of smoke. A chill coursed through him. *Oh no!* "Let us go."

Appius and the soldiers climbed the hill from the valley into the village. As they approached the fountain square, former vendor stalls smoldered, the former shelves, tables, and partitions reduced to a charred pile. Villagers sifting through the remains, pouring water here and there, fled at the sight of the military, leaving the fountain area abandoned. On the stones of the fountain, Appius saw fresh stains and pools of blood. Lying on the steps of the fountain were two men, the bodies not yet removed.

Appius was furious. He turned to the soldiers, glaring, questioning.

The soldier who had spoken before said, "I do not think these people will bother you again."

Appius, barely able to prevent himself from yelling, said, forcing a whisper, "How many did you kill?"

"How many?" The soldier looked at his companions. "I think it was about seven. Does that seem so?"

One soldier spoke. "I counted as we retrieved the lances. It was seven." He was proud to display evidence of his presence of mind, one who could keep his head in the tumult and clamor.

Appius could no longer look. He turned away. "You will need to protect those that are starting work at the springs. Make sure you do so. Otherwise, leave these people alone. Do you understand?"

The spokesman nodded. "We will receive further direction after the *decanus* talks to the centurion—Flavius Darius and General Artius Crassius. We must take our orders from them. For now, we will protect your workers."

Appius returned to the springs and talked to the clearing crew. "Did you know they sacked the village?"

The crew chief nodded. "Yes, as we were arriving here, the soldiers were returning to the valley. The *decanus* bragged that he had stemmed the trouble and that we could now work safely. We saw the smoke from the village. After the *decanus* left, his men told us more. What will happen now?"

"I will take time, but very little time, to set stakes so that you will know where the clearing must take place. I will leave instructions with you and show you where the excavation must start. I would like you to show them to the excavation contractor so that he can start his work. I will tell the contractor the same if I see him on my way to Lugdunum. Let us hurry. I need to be on my way soon. I must talk to Claudius."

Appius started toward Lugdunum in two hours. His thoughts were in turmoil as he continually urged his horse to go faster, hoping to cover as much distance as possible before dark. Lugdunum was over 100 miles away, and he wanted to be there by the next morning—possible but difficult, as he would have to cover much of the distance in the dark, slowing to a walk to avoid stumbling. The *decanus* must have started at least four hours prior, but it was questionable if he would travel at night, questionable if he would goad his horse to higher speeds. Was it important to talk to Claudius before the *decanus* talked to the general? There was no question that it would be better if Claudius were informed before the General talked to him. That seemed certain, and it was that thought that propelled him. He hoped that he did not encounter the *decanus* asleep along the way. He would kill the man.

After darkness, he rode on, now at a walk. The horse could be trusted to pick his way, so Appius had more time to think. What would become of the project? It seemed like it would drift for some time before Claudius could get an able manager to the site. What would it be like to work with someone other than Bernius? Would the new supervisor take the same interest? Would he care about teaching him? He was fortunate to have been tutored under Bernius; he had learned a great deal. Another sob worked its way through his system.

How he would miss Bernius. He ached with the thought; a feeling of loneliness soaked him, imagining that his time devoted to the project would now be shallow, not rich, not exhilarating. Much of his effort had been to please Bernius. Would dedication to the project consume his energies and fire his resourcefulness from now on? Bernius would want it so. The thought had promise, something for him to grasp, a principle to apply. Yes, that would be the thought that would drive him, provide his energy, boost his efforts. The project would be his dedication to Bernius. He gave a gentle kick to the flanks of the horse.

At dawn he was still hours away from Lugdunum but thought he could see smoke from early morning fires rising as he rode the path along the river. In the light, he could travel faster, more than twice as fast as the slow walk during the night. He had not spotted the *decanus,* thankfully. What if Claudius was not in Lugdunum? He would not think of it.

Two hours later, he was searching for the house of Claudius. The town residents were able to guide him to his destination but did not know if he was at home. He climbed a hill to a wooded area overlooking the river and to the west of it. He spotted the impressive residence, atop the hill, a gate beyond which a sloping path curled to the portico. There were guards at the gate. Would they admit him? If they did not, he would find another way.

He dismounted twenty feet from the guards and walked his horse to them, observing their attentive glare and somewhat threatening stances. One stepped forward and demanded, "What is your business?"

"I am here to see his Excellency, Tiberius Claudius."

"He is not here."

Appius considered it possible that the guard made that comment to any stranger, testing their resolve, discouraging those that had a disruptive or harmful intent. He would test them. "I think you are mistaken. Claudius has sent for me. If you will ask him and give him my name, you will see that I am admitted." But, it might be true that Claudius was not at home.

The guard glared at him, assessing his unkempt state and lack of impressive traveling gear. The horse was nice, though. "What is your name?"

"Appius Petronius."

The guard sneered then turned to the other guard. "See if the proconsul left word for Appius Petronius."

While the one guard trudged up the hill, Appius tended to his horse. Perhaps Claudius was not at home, but it seemed like the guard would be direct if he were not. The guard watched him closely. Shortly, the other guard came tromping back down the hill.

"Appius Petronius is to be received at the portico." He pointed up the hill.

Appius mounted and rode past the intense scrutiny of the guards. At the portico he was met by a servant and taken to the atrium. He asked the servant, "Claudius is here?"

A curt "Yes!" was the response.

He was seated and soon Claudius walked swiftly into the room, a frown on his face, perhaps more a look of concern.

"Appius. You are here without Bernius. I can only think that there is a problem." As Appius rose, Claudius touched him on the shoulder.

Appius hesitated. It was hard for him to say it. "Bernius is dead—killed by the Ucetians."

Claudius showed genuine shock and dismay. "No."

Appius nodded, lowering his gaze to the floor. "It is so. He was taking measurements at the spring, as we would soon start the excavation from there. He was hit on the back of the head."

"The military...?"

"Bernius was only to spend an hour or so at the task. He did not think he needed protection."

Claudius shook his head, prolonging the shaking to augment his display of distress.

Appius raised his gaze to look into the brooding eyes of Claudius. "That is not all. When the military arrived, they went to the village, set fires, and killed seven citizens."

"Killed—under whose authority? You did not...."

"No. Not by my authority. The *decanus* did so on his own authority or perhaps authority bestowed upon him by the centurion—Flavius Darius—under General Artius Crassius."

"But, the Ucetians are Roman citizens and were due a trial."

"It may be so, but I have seen the dead and the destruction. The deed was done."

"Did anybody admit to the killing of Bernius?"

"The soldiers I talked to did not say so."

"You mean the *decanus*?"

"No. The *decanus* was not there. After the incident, he rode here—to Lugdunum—to report to his centurion and to the general, I suppose. I rode all night so that you could hear what happened before you are confronted. I did not see the *decanus* along the way."

Claudius touched him on the shoulder, again. "It is good you rode here with haste. I do not trust General Crassius. He could and would... will... use this incident to his advantage. I know that his wish is to take command of the project. He has spoken of it. I must find an able replacement... it will have to be from Rome. I wish you had more experience. I have great expectations for you, but supervising a project with so many political difficulties and with a difficult project to build... I believe it would be an assignment that both of us would regret."

Appius nodded. "I think the same. But, I will, at the best of my ability, assist as I can to continue the project to completion. I would do that for Bernius."

Claudius nodded. "I understand." He paused. "I must go see General Crassius. I will register my complaint first. I should catch him unawares, as he will not know that you have ridden in the night to inform me. Perhaps that advantage will keep him from taking actions he might favor. This is my region; however, he has the ear of Caligua and might even act as if he had Caligua's approval. I do not know what to expect."

"I will return to Nemausus and do what I can to give the appearance of stability. I will let it be known that you will soon send supervision from Rome. Will you get a message to me as soon as you have made arrangements?"

Claudius nodded. "I will do so. My dedication to this project... and to Bernius... is at least as strong as yours. You can expect I will do what is in my power. I will make it clear to the military that they will take their orders from those of you supervising the project.

"Now," Claudius continued, "you must have a meal and rest before you start toward Nemausus." He clapped his hand and a servant appeared. Claudius gave the instructions then said to Appius, "I will leave to visit our most difficult general. I presume I will not see you before you leave. Be careful. You do not *really* know who killed Bernius and why; they may have the same thoughts for you." He touched Appius on the shoulder again, turned, and walked to his rooms.

Appius rode toward Nemausus, feeling strength from his rest and nourishment and confidence from his effort to inform Claudius. What would be the result? His immediate task was to show leadership, dispel the perception of chaos. Contractors, the *Corporata*, and others needed to be assured. He must also tell Antonia who would then tell... Juliena. Were there strong feelings between her and Bernius? It seemed so, although he would not have heard it from Bernius. What other matters must go on? There were other contracts to be bid and awarded. He had followed Bernius through the process. Could he do likewise?

460

Perhaps, but when difficulties emerged, Bernius had known what to do. Experience and good judgment were vital.

Claudius's comment intruded on his thoughts. "You do not really know who killed Bernius." What if it were not the Ucetians? It was likely that it was the Ucetians but Claudius was right. They really did not know. If it was someone else, the acts of the military were even more hideous.

Nemausus was nearly 100 miles from Lugdunum. Again he would cover as much distance as possible before nightfall and ride on rather than rest. Antonia would not be expecting him. Had she already heard about Bernius? Probably not.

Appius arrived in Nemausus in the early morning, just before dawn. By the time he stabled and fed the horse, daylight was about. He was sure he had experienced moments of sleep in the saddle but two days with little sleep numbed him. He was tired, but he had chores to do.

Antonia was startled when he appeared; he dropped his saddle pack at the door. "Appius? You are here. I thought..."

She obviously did not know. Appius held up his hand. "Bernius has been killed, he...."

Composure drained from Antonia. She clutched her arms at her chest. "Oh, no, no...."

Appius reached for her and she gratefully accepted the embrace, sobbing against his chest. He gave her time—until she looked up at him to explain. He brushed tears away from her eyes. "He was at the springs. We believe the Ucetians... ," he paused, not sure, "killed him as an angry attempt to stop the work... or for revenge—I do not know."

"It is horrible. You...?"

He shook his head. "I am not in danger." *Was it true?* "The military sacked the town, killed some citizens. The Ucetians will cause no further trouble."

"Juliena. Oh, no! I have to tell her—she had much hope...."

Appius nodded. "I am sorry—sorry for her and Bernius, sorry for you and me. We have lost a good friend and my dedicated mentor."

After Antonia pressed her head against him for a while, Appius held her away. "I must tell the *Corporata*, must tell the designers, must tell the contractors before rampant word is about. I have been to Claudius, and he will take action—military and

461

political—and will speed an able supervisor to Nemausus—probably from Rome."

"You rode to Lugdunum—then to here?"

"Yes, in less than two days. I am tired, but I must go—to tell them and answer their questions. I will return to rest—soon, I hope."

Appius told the designers, Nemus, Vernius Portius, and the clearing contractor, assuring them that Claudius would ensure payments and would provide an able supervisor. There were questions. He answered them to the extent of his knowledge, embellishing when necessary to create an atmosphere of confidence. All were stunned but made no statements as to their intent. Finally, after mid-day, he was able to trudge home and drop on the bed, not having energy left to remove his clothes and shoes. He slept the remainder of the afternoon and through the night.

Next morning, he arose, still groggy. He ate, walked to the office, and talked to the designers in an effort to understand how far they had progressed on their tasks and to hear their problems. He sat at his desk, sometimes staring at nothing. He forced himself to create a list of items, which must be done soon—in the next few weeks—perhaps in the time it would take for a new supervisor to arrive from Rome. He would do his best to continue progress and to create a perception that control was being maintained. He reviewed the schedule to identify the activities that needed his attention; he would address each one separately, noting what needed to be done to accomplish them.

At noon, a messenger walked through the door, looked around, and said, "Appius Petronius?"

Appius rose and walked to him. "Yes?"

"I have a message from his Excellency, Claudius." He handed it to Appius.

Appius read: *I have met with General Artius Crassius and told him I condemned the action of the military at Ucetia, that I would secure leadership for the project, and that it would be clear that his military would act only at the direction of the project leadership. General Crassius told me not to bother, as he, with the consent of Caligua, would now be in control of the project. I do not know if Caligua has given this direction, but for the moment it may not matter. The general is mobilizing his forces to assume control.*

the *Aedifex*: Building the Pont du Gard

I am disgusted by this action, but my only recourse to insurrection is to thwart it with the military. He is the military, so until I can make my argument to Caligua, the project and I are subject to his action. I regret this circumstance—for the project, for you, and for me. I will do what I can.

Signed Claudius Tiberius, Proconsul, Narbonensis Region, Empire of Rome.

Appius stared at the document, shook his head then looked up at the messenger and nodded a dismissal.

The messenger stated his customary, "Is there a message to be returned?"

Appius shook his head. "No."

Appius told the designers what he had read. They had experienced projects under control of the military. Some had gone well; some had not. Appius wondered what he should now tell the *Corporata* and the contractors. He pondered the situation the remainder of the afternoon, absent-mindedly considering the tasks he had identified.

In late afternoon, someone appeared in the doorway. It was a military man. It was the centurion, Flavius Darius.

CHAPTER 44

The centurion, Flavius, stood at the office doorway, hands on his hips, head tilted back arrogantly. Appius got the impression that he expected those in the room to salute or kneel. Flavius took off his hat, handed it to an aide and looked around the room. "This will not be adequate. I will need to find other quarters."

Appius bristled. "Adequate for what? Are you establishing an office from which you will give orders to butcher innocent villagers?"

The centurion straightened, nearly coming to attention. "Are you talking about the same villagers that killed your co-worker? Surely those people are not innocent. Would you have me send them flowers instead?"

"Are the people you killed those that are responsible?"

Flavius laughed. "You would not last long, given the task of preserving the Empire. It is always best to act swiftly. You must admit that you expect no further problems."

Appius walked until he was directly in front of Flavius. "I am sure your military mind cannot make the distinction between those that should be punished and punishment for show, a show to demonstrate the toughness of a particular military leader. Exhibitions like the one in Ucetia are the mark of amateurs, I have observed, not of successful military leaders. That is why Roman citizens are protected by the law. That is why Roman citizens must be tried and found guilty in the courts before they are executed. You, sir, have acted beyond the concepts of the Empire and have violated your own military law."

Flavius, red in the face, said, "We will see who establishes law and who must comply. If you have not been informed or do not have the facility to understand, *I* will be supervising the aqueduct construction. *I* will return in the afternoon to receive a briefing from you as to the status. *I* will issue any further direction. You will be working for *me*. Is that clear?"

Appius gave Flavius a hard stare. "Much is clear to me, centurion, foremost being that you are second-grade military talent."

Flavius turned and walked from the room. "This afternoon, Appius Petronius."

Appius looked at the designers. "From your experience, would you say that this is a project that will fare well or not well under military supervision?"

Murmurs were his only response.

Nevertheless, Appius spent the morning reviewing the project's current status and considering the near-term actions required. He would put the centurion to the test. What was bluster and what was the nature of the man who would be giving him orders? The exercise was worthwhile; Appius needed to consider action that *he* must take. He would not be able to benefit from the artful prodding of Bernius.

In mid-afternoon, a soldier appeared in the office and walked to the table where Appius was sitting. "You are to report to the centurion, Flavius Darius, in the building to the east," he pointed. The aide assumed the authority of his commander—all the more irritating and humiliating that even the lower ranks would impart the aura of authority.

Appius would not give the man the satisfaction of acknowledging what appeared to be a direct command. The two stared at each other until the soldier turned and walked from the building.

Appius, deliberately slow to gather his documents, sat, thinking. *The centurion has occupied the building where we have arranged the sticks that define our schedule. No!*

Now Appius was in a hurry to observe what he knew must be true. He walked to the adjacent building and through the door. He could see the centurion, sitting at a table in the back of the room. Several aides stood to the side, smirking as they watched him enter. The floor was bare. "What have you done with the sticks?" He pointed to the floor, the scribed date lines still visible.

"Oh, the sticks? Some careless person had not swept the floor. I had the floor swept of them, and they are now burning, out in back."

Of course Flavius knew they were not just random sticks, but Appius would not give him the satisfaction of an emotional display. Only an arrogant bastard, to satisfy his own ego, would destroy a valuable tool of the project, a project for which the fool was now responsible. Yet Appius must remember that he must

465

persist with this idiot to ensure that the project got built—in spite of the centurion—for the sake of Bernius.

Appius stood in silence, documents under his arm. He had not brought the schedule. It was the key to understanding the project, and Appius was not going to share.

The centurion tired of waiting for a response. "What have you got for me?"

Appius remained standing and spoke quickly. "We must bid and award a contract to excavate shafts for the tunnels. We must start the contractors to work on the two excavation contracts that have not started. We must establish staff to observe and report on work at all locations. We must buy clay pipe for the purpose of leveling. In two weeks, the *Corporata* must be advised of amounts to be paid to the contractors and of upcoming requirements and progress."

The centurion nodded. "And the office here? What are the designers doing?"

Appius took note. He had not completely overwhelmed Flavius. Flavius had the presence of mind to ask about other facets of the project. "They will continue to work on the tunnel design as information is received from the shaft excavation, continue design of the elevated structures, the diversion structures, the *Castellum*, and continue devising the numbering system that will be used to identify the many stones that will be installed in the bridge."

"And you, what will you be doing for the glory of the project—and for me, of course."

Appius closed his eyes. It was apparent that Flavius knew what statements would upset him and was eager to use them. He must not react to this provocation. Flavius was probably looking for an instance to demonstrate that he was in charge. He would punish Appius for insubordination. "I will regularly visit the ongoing work sites, aid in starting the new work, and assist the designers if I can. At the same time, I will prepare documents to be used in the bidding of future work."

"And, that future work is...?"

"Primary is the installation of the stones on the Vardo bridge to begin in nine months. In addition, we must prepare and bid contracts for the building of other elevated structures, for the building of the underground structure in the trenches we are now excavating, and for the cement that will be used in their building."

"And how is it that you know what contracts should be let and when?"

"We established a schedule, the sticks you swept from the floor." Appius said it without drama or implication.

"I see. I am sure it was a worthwhile exercise. However, you will not have to consult the sticks from now on. I will tell you when the activities are to take place."

"And how will you determine that?"

"The construction of the project is obvious. However, leave the list you are reading from for my reference. I will tell you if there are additional requirements to which you must attend."

"The list has other notes that were not part of our discussion. Surely you do not want or need other than a list." Appius had suspected this would happen. He had noted on the document—'the centurion appears inadequate for the responsibility he is assuming.'

The centurion smiled. "Your list will be adequate even with the spurious notes; perhaps they will be illuminating." Flavius thought it would be interesting if the notes contained Appius's personal observations. It was difficult to tell who was the most astute in perceiving the attributes of the other. "That will be all for now... oh, except for one task you must do... that of preparing the payments and progress report that I will present to the *Corporata* in two weeks."

Appius nodded and walked from the building. The centurion's last request was to be expected. Flavius may be arrogant, but he, it seemed, was not a *total* fool. Appius wondered if Flavius was concerned that the slaughtered Ucetians, Roman citizens, had not had the benefit of a trial. He could not tell from the recent discussions. It seemed not.

Two days later Appius returned to the office after his mid-day meal and saw Bernius's horse hitched at the side of the building. Puzzled, he could only think that either Marius or Pentius had ridden in, as they were the last to have care of the horse. He walked inside and was surprised to see neither Marius nor Pentius but a man dressed in rough clothing talking to the designers. As Appius walked in, the man looked at him and disengaged from the designers to confront him.

He said, "I am Decimus Nautius, a co-worker with Pentius and Marius—I have their horse."

Appius nodded. "Why are you here, Decimus Nautius? Is something wrong with Marius or Pentius?" He feared that a further calamity had occurred and braced for bad news.

"No, they are well. They wanted me to tell you what I saw at the time your Bernius was killed."

Appius, anxious to hear more, said, "Go on."

"I work on the same crew as Pentius and Marius—clearing. On the day Bernius was killed, I was away in the woods, looking for a new location for the crew to spend the nights. I was seeking a spot with rocks—for sitting and for use at the fires—and was quite some distance from the route we were clearing. Coming toward me—he didn't see me—was a man on horseback. I thought it unusual that he did not ride the easier, cleared route or the regular path from Ucetia to Nemausus. I waited. When he was nearly upon me, I walked to him, as I was curious"

Appius asked, "Did you recognize him?"

"No."

Appius, harboring a distant thought that the military might have been involved, said, "Was he in military uniform?"

"No. He appeared ordinary, not in working clothes," he looked down at his soiled tunic, "nor in clothes more elegantly fashioned than yours."

"Go on, then."

"I yelled to him as he approached. He seemed surprised... maybe shocked to see me, slowing his horse to a walk. He tilted his head down as if I would not get a good look if he did that. He nodded. I said, 'Do you not know there is a path you could ride that would be of more ease than crashing your way through the brambles?'"

Appius shrugged. "What did he say?'

"He said that he did not know that and asked the way. I pointed toward the trail. He was in a hurry but turned his horse in the direction of the trail and rode off. I walked to a hillock where I could watch his progress. At the other side of a thicket—I presume he thought he was out of my sight—he again turned to ride away from the path."

"And you say that this was after Bernius was killed?"

"Yes. It had to be. Perhaps about the time that you rode through our clearing operation."

Appius took time for thought. "You are right. Marius and Pentius are right. That *is* highly unusual. An ordinary traveler from

Ucetia would follow the path that the Ucetians would take to get to the river crossing. Very unusual. It would seem that he was avoiding being seen. What time of day was this?"

"It was mid-afternoon. I asked Marius and Pentius. Bernius had ridden through, on his way to the springs, three hours before."

"I see."

Decimus Nautius straightened somewhat, proud that he could be of importance. "That is all I can tell you. I must return to the work after I visit the market to bring back supplies."

"Decimus Nautius, thank you for making the trip. Your input is valuable. It seems we have other thoughts to consider; it is possible that someone besides the Ucetians killed Bernius. It may be very difficult to know who else might have been involved, but now that we have other possibilities to consider, we may be attentive to the situation and listen for implications."

Decimus Nautius nodded to Appius, nodded to the listening designers then left the building.

Appius was distraught, remembering the pain of losing Bernius and asking 'why?' He walked out of the building to help generate clear thoughts. Who, other than the Ucetians, would want to kill Bernius? Immediately Titus and Quantus Tarius came to mind. Titus would think that killing Bernius might scuttle the project, stop his sestertii from bleeding into the aqueduct. And Quantus—well, both of them—upset that Bernius had terminated their contract—had ample reason to take mortal action. How would he confront them?

Another thought bloomed, unprovoked. *Could it have been the military?* The killing of Bernius and the subsequent project takeover had happened so quickly. Little time was allowed for the situation to fester, for investigation of the guilty, and for usurping the control of Claudius. Of course the military would not be foolish enough to send a man in uniform to take Bernius. An accomplice? It would not be that difficult. Sestertii or blackmail or a threat to him or the man's family would be sufficient. Yes, the military was at least as likely to have been responsible. In truth, Appius wanted the military to be responsible, another reason to focus hatred and contempt upon the centurion, Flavius Darius. He looked at the building that now officed someone he thought evil enough to take the life of his friend in order to stoke his own glory.

Before long, Decimus Nautius came galloping back into the waterworks yard, brought the horse up abruptly, and dismounted. He walked briskly inside to find Appius. It happened that Flavius was also inside, peering over the shoulders of the designers, hands locked behind his back. Appius did not engage Flavius, but stared at him with a smoldering contempt. At the moment Decimus Nautius burst in, all looked up at the breathless man, who was momentarily flummoxed to see the centurion.

He approached Appius and spoke between gasps, "I saw the man in the market."

The comment caught Flavius's attention, but he stayed where he was, listening.

Decimus Nautius looked at Flavius, but continued. "I nearly rode back here at that time, but I had the thought that he might be more easily found if I followed him. Perhaps he would walk to his dwelling. And—that is what he did."

Appius involuntarily looked toward Flavius, thinking he might see the picture of guilt. He did not see guilt, but Flavius walked to them.

"What is this?" he demanded.

Appius considered ignoring Flavius, but then thought he might like to observe his reaction. "Decimus Nautius spotted a man circumventing the clearing work shortly after the killing of Bernius, a possible accomplice of those who were responsible."

His head snapped up. "The Ucetians were responsible," Flavius blurted.

Appius had momentarily forgotten that a suggestion that any party other than the Ucetians would reflect poorly on the military. If the military was responsible for the killing of Bernius, they were doubly damned. He addressed Flavius with an intense stare and said, "Of course you would be quick to deny the foul deed was done by other than the Ucetians. Especially if you—the military—were the ones responsible."

Flavius was stunned, then furious. "You dare say that the military is responsible? You dare say that we contrived this?"

Appius was pleased he had gotten a reaction, neglecting that any entity so accused might react the same. "Is it so?" It was his turn to be pompous.

"It is *not* so," Flavius thundered. He addressed Decimus Nautius. "Take me to the dwelling of this man. We shall soon understand that I—the military—had nothing to do with the killing." He pointed toward the door. "Take us."

Appius, Flavius, and Decimus Nautius exited the building. Flavius walked quickly to his building to collect four subordinates. "Come," he said to them. "We have a mission. Be quick."

As they walked, Appius considered the situation. The man would be confronted and made to talk. Was there any doubt that he would say whatever the military wanted him to say? They had their ways. Flavius would manage the outcome. It was too important to Flavius that anyone but the Ucetians be held responsible. If the soldiers took the man away to be questioned and Flavius then reported the results—his version—there would be little that could be done. He must be present to hear the man... 'questioned.' He glanced sideways to Flavius, trying to read his manner. The centurion—not so cocky, not so arrogant—returned the stare although he was careful to express confidence.

The man was at home. Decimus Nautius confirmed that he was the person he had encountered. The man was fearful and backed into a corner of his squalid room. Appius reasoned—an innocent would be puzzled.

Flavius looked around, easily convincing himself this was not the place to question the man. He motioned for his men to seize the man and said, "We must find a suitable location to ask questions." He looked at Appius and Decimus Nautius. "You must stay. We will inform you of the results." He turned.

"No!" Appius yelled. "I will not. I will be present to hear this man questioned."

The centurion nodded toward Appius. Two of the soldiers surrounding the man broke off to restrain Appius. "See that he does not get free," barked Flavius. "I will return to tell him the truth."

"Why do you not tell me now?" spit Appius. "Your 'truth' will be what you want it to be."

The centurion did not reply but turned and led the group out of the dwelling. The centurion and one soldier, with knife drawn, led the man from the building. The man was barely able to walk, stumbling with fear. Two soldiers restrained Appius.

Decimus Nautius looked at Appius and shrugged. "I must return to my work. Night will soon be upon me." He walked from the dwelling.

After some time, the centurion returned and nodded toward Appius. "You may release him now," he said to his men. He looked at Appius. "The man knows nothing. He was in the woods looking for bay trees and did not want anyone to know what he was about. You can go back to your office."

Appius thought he would be told something similar, but tried another tack. "And will the man say the same to me?" He looked at Flavius for a reaction.

Flavius spread his hands. "It is unfortunate that a man who was innocent was so frightened. It seems he has caused his own death. I should have, perhaps, treated his capture more gently. I must be more careful in the future."

Appius slumped. Although he thought it might be difficult to get the truth from the man, if he lived, it was nevertheless a possibility—a hope. Now the centurion would get away with his deceit. Yet, Appius now had more information. At some time, he might discover a means to the truth. His fondest wish was to have the opportunity to 'question' Flavius. He let that thought help keep himself under control. As he walked from the dwelling, he turned to Flavius. "Whether the military or someone else was responsible—someone besides the Ucetians—either way you are damned."

Flavius crossed his arms and looked at his men.

Appius walked to his home, spent his habitual one-on-one with Sergius then poured wine for Antonia and himself. There was a clatter at the gate. Appius looked out to see Decimus Nautius walk in. Appius, wine jug in one hand, cups in the other, watched curiously as he approached. What could he want? He was supposed to be on his way to the clearing camp. Appius walked out into the courtyard.

Decimus Nautius approached him and spoke. "I could not abandon the situation as it was. I think too much of Marius and Pentius to have just ridden away."

Appius shrugged. "The centurion did as I thought. He reported that the man was looking for an unusual tree and had nothing to do with Bernius. Unfortunately, the man died."

"No, that is not what happened. I followed the centurion and his men—without them seeing, of course. They walked to the edge of town and found an abandoned shelter. It so happened that the shelter was partially cut into the side of a hill. I was able to stand on the hill at the side of the residence and listen through an opening."

"You heard them questioning the man?"

"Yes. I did not know what they were doing to him, but he cried out in pain. He did not last long before he revealed what he did. He said that he had been paid to kill Bernius—had been told that Bernius would be alone at the springs."

"Who paid him and told him about Bernius?"

Decimus Nautius shook his head. "I do not know them but repeated the names to myself so that I could remember them. There are two that he mentioned—Titus Domitius and Quantus Tarius." He looked to see if Appius showed recognition.

Appius jerked his head back. "So, it was *them*. Yes, of course I know Titus and Quantus. This is of great importance." He shook his head, thinking. "And, did they kill the man?"

"I believe that they did. I heard the man cry out and then heard from him no more. The soldiers left the building and two of them were dragging and carrying the man."

"They disposed of him somewhere?"

"I do not know. When it appeared they were leaving, I moved from my location to a thicket of brush so that I would not be spotted."

"You have performed a great service. I shall somehow find a way to reward your initiative. For now, you have my sincere regard, and I would have you tell Marius and Pentius the same. But, for now, please keep what you know to the three of you. It may take time for the situation to resolve. Do you still intend to ride back tonight?"

"No. It is too late. I will ride in the morning."

"Then stay and have dinner with us. You may sleep in the courtyard or at our office." He thought for a moment. "It is better you sleep here. I would not want the military to know you are still around. The horse?"

"Thank you. I will be happy to share your meal and have a protected spot to sleep. The horse is at your gate. I should perhaps move him to a less obvious location."

"Yes. Take the horse to the stables; they know him and regularly care for him. The cost will be covered, and he will not be noticed by those we would be concerned with."

Decimus Nautius nodded and left.

473

Appius, after filling his cup and Antonia's, walked into the house and handed the cup to her.

"Who was that?"

"That was a messenger bearing evil. I will tell you."

"He did not look evil."

"No, the man is not evil; he is just the messenger. What he told me will cause problems for many people."

She gave him a direct look. "I hope you are not one of them."

"Antonia, it would be impossible to avoid. You will understand."

CHAPTER 45

Appius did not sleep thinking of what he must or should do with the information. If he confronted Flavius directly, Flavius would, of course, deny the account, letting no time lapse before he gave the word to his men to see that Decimus Nautius encountered a mortal 'accident.' He must protect Decimus Nautius. As for Titus and Quantus, an accusation would go nowhere without more substantial background. He came to the conclusion that he must use the information subtly. He knew the situation, knew the truth, and knew the weaknesses of the individuals. The involved people did not know he knew. That was an advantage. Perhaps he could apply pressure at the weak points and let the individuals yield as a result. It would have to be that way. He allowed his mind to work on the possibilities.

In the meantime, he must keep the project moving and expanding. There were bid requirements and contracts to draft, new work to be started—the remaining trench excavation contracts and the tunnel shaft excavation—and it was time for him to make a trip to the sites of the ongoing work. He would note the rate of progress and use that information to predict how long it would take to accomplish the various activities. Now that Vernius Portius was the contractor for the quarry and stone production, the trench work must be timed to provide a road from the secondary quarry site, and a road must be constructed along the section where many of the elevated structures would be built—from the turn at the hills to the bridge over the River Vardo. He would include building of the road in the contract involving construction of the elevated structures.

He did not see much of the centurion in the days following the interrogation. Perhaps the centurion was avoiding him. Good. He detested orders from the man. He would go about his business, the business of constructing the great aqueduct. What actions would Flavius take? It was certain, Flavius would exert his authority at some time in some way. Appius would have to accommodate direction from Flavius as it occurred.

Appius drafted the bid requirements and the resulting contracts for the remaining trench excavation contracts and the tunnel shafts, then posted the bid notices at the town board and sent messages to Lugdunum and Rome to enable similar postings. The word would spread from those locations.

His trip to the work sites would be immediately prior to the status meeting with the *Corporata*. Progress must be noted so that the contractors would receive correct payment for the work they had done—but no more. Bernius had cautioned him to ensure that the contractors not be overpaid. If they should fail, the project would have to pay someone else to accomplish work that had not been done but already paid for.

Appius did not advise Flavius that he would be away. To do so would give the impression that he needed permission to make the trip or acknowledge that he was subordinate to the centurion. The designer, Vibius traveled with him to the tunnel location to assist in staking the locations for the tunnel shafts. Vibius then returned to Nemausus while Appius rode on.

Appius had also arranged for the contractors of the two remaining but unstarted excavation works to meet him at their starting locations. Appius made certain they understood the requirements and the path they were to take. The clearing contractor was also present at one of the meetings, as, on one of the routes, he would start clearing a week prior to the start of excavation. All understood what was expected and the timing. Appius advised the excavation contractors that he would return after they had completed excavation of the first 6 feet of depth to establish level and thus the gradient line for the ultimate bottom of the trench. He remembered—he must soon make arrangements to produce the clay pipe.

As he rode between locations, he had ample time to consider the means by which he would reveal the treachery by Titus and Quantus... well, and that of Flavius. He could not be sure of the outcome, but thought he had a fair chance of revealing the truth without jeopardizing Decimus Nautius. Imagining the outcome, even though it was not a certainty, generated a smile. Perhaps it was a fantasy. He encouraged his horse to a faster pace.

He reached the forward progress of the first section of the clearing work and noted the location on his map. From memory, he knew they were progressing somewhat faster than had been estimated. There should be sufficient time to build the quarryman's road—at least the clearing people would not hold up the excavator. He pulled Marius and Pentius aside and expressed his gratitude for initiating the ride of Decimus Nautius to Nemausus.

"Have you nailed Titus and Quantus to a cross, yet?" Pentius asked, looking around to make sure he was not being overheard. He spotted Decimus Nautius looking, but Decimus Nautius remained where he stood, having been warned by Marius and Pentius not to give the appearance of conspiracy. The military were often watching.

"No. That has not happened," Appius responded. "But I will be creating trouble for them soon. I will get word to you or you will hear of it."

Marius said, "There are now more military men present. They ask questions and advise the supervisors to do this or that. It is not really advice. They would like to think they are directing the work; however, the advice often is of little value or reason. They are a nuisance."

Appius shook his head. "I cannot do much about that for now. Perhaps, though, I will find a way to make the military behave, but that will take time. They are able to do what they want for now."

Pentius raised an eyebrow, "The Ucetians?"

Appius did not respond. He nodded slightly. Marius and Pentius deserved some satisfaction, even if it was only by implication, that their effort might help right an injustice.

Appius rode on to the leading edge of the initial trench excavation. The workers had made progress, but the going was tough as a result of much stone encountered even in the first 6 feet depth. They were in a heavily forested area, and working out the stumps and roots also slowed them. The contract, however, provided for different pricing depending on the nature of the work encountered—higher payment per foot for more difficult stretches. In that way, the contractor did not have to be overly protective, anticipating *the worst* when he bid the contract. Appius noted the work accomplished under the various pricing structures and got agreement from the contractor's supervisor. Soon there would be a man on their forces to assess this condition—unless the centurion had other ideas.

He rode along the partially excavated ditch to the Alzon and turned to ride north along the river. He shook his head at the remembrance—now two years ago—of his first walk up the river in search of the springs. It was incredible that his earlier effort had led to this colossal project. He encountered the clearing operation along the Alzon, talked briefly to the supervisor, noted the extent of progress, then rode up river to view the excavation work. In this stretch, the excavator would often be required to cut only an L-shaped excavation into the sloping hillside. The hill would provide support for *one* side of the aqueduct while the other side, with no supporting earth, would have to be supported by masonry. Less earth would have to be removed, especially for the first 6 feet. Again, the contract provided for pricing of this manner of excavation.

However, in the segment just downstream of the springs, the trench was of the ordinary ditch construction. Appius talked to the supervisor for the excavation contractor, in this case the contractor himself, and got agreement for the upcoming payment.

He sat on his horse, looking at the woods where Bernius was killed. Without much thought, he rode to the clearing where he had found him. It was odd. The location took on more than ordinary significance, as if the trees had observed the atrocity and forever held their silence, brooding. The essence of the foul act was about. He slouched in the saddle. His head sagged to his chest.

He coaxed the horse to turn, rode out of the woods, back down the river then along the trench and the cleared section until he came to the clearing camp. He would spend the night there and return to Nemausus the following day. The meeting with the *Corporata* would occur two days following his return, and the centurion would want to be updated on the work. Flavius would spiel his report to the *Corporata,* but it would be inevitable that Appius would have to answer questions. Flavius and the *Corporata* would not be pleased at what else he would have to say.

Flavius required Appius to brief him in the military office. Appius stoically reported the progress of each contractor and the resulting payment. He also showed Flavius the calculation whereby Quantus Tarius, the original quarry contractor, would receive *no* further payment due to additional money the *Corporata* would have to pay to his replacement, a payment for which the aqueduct owners would receive no value. The additional sestertii to Vernius was deducted from payment that would otherwise be due Quantus. Appius might have been overly aggressive in his determination; however, that harsh treatment would assist in his strategy. The centurion noted the calculation, although puzzled as to its meaning. Appius then told Flavius about the work recently started and the activities in progress leading to bid and award of additional contacts. The briefing would comprise the centurion's report.

The centurion looked up from the notations, "You made a tour of the work sites?"

"Yes." Appius thought this would be interesting.

"I do not remember your mentioning you would do that." Flavius stood more erect, a military characteristic that implied superiority.

"It is one of my regular duties."

"Next time you will advise me beforehand, and I will accompany you."

"Good. At least you will not be somewhere else slaughtering innocent villagers."

The centurion raged red. "You are not to speak of such again. If you do so, I will have you punished for insubordination."

"And someday I will see you punished for illegal killing of Roman citizens unless, of course, you kill me to silence my accusations." Perhaps he should not have said that.

"I was clearly within my responsibility. You had better be careful. Now go." He pointed to the door. "You will appear with me at the *Corporata* meeting."

Appius was not sure that continued needling of the centurion about the atrocity would yield useful results. Perhaps he did it more as a satisfaction to himself. He shivered involuntarily. Tomorrow *something* would happen. Appius thought he should be careful, as there was no question that he could be inflicting his own harm. He *could* play a less disruptive role, be a willing and useful subordinate but knew he could not respect himself if he did so.

Flavius had arrived at Nemus's villa before Appius. When Appius entered the atrium, Flavius was standing by himself, puffed up, in a commanding military posture. His aide stood to the side of the room. Appius observed the *Corporata* jawing amongst themselves, occasionally pressing wine goblets to their lips, and making expressive movements with their hands.

Nemus saw Appius arrive and involuntarily looked at Flavius. No wine was offered to either of the non-*Corporata* guests. Appius remembered less contentious days. He was somewhat apprehensive of the trouble he would cause. A cup of wine would have been helpful.

After Appius joined the centurion at the table, the *Corporata* focused their attention on the two men. Nemus felt it his duty to make an opening remark. "We have lost the use of Bernius due to the tragedy at the hands of the Ucetians. Perhaps, as you update us, Centurion, you will tell us how the project is to be managed."

Appius looked at Titus as Nemus made his statement. Titus tilted his head back, slightly, as if to indicate—'the circumstance regarding Bernius is accepted to be true.' At least that is what it seemed to Appius.

Flavius shifted his gaze from Nemus, acknowledging that Nemus was through talking. He looked intently at each of the *Corporata*. "I am in charge. The military is now executing this project—as it should have from the beginning. Perhaps Bernius was useful in creating the design but severely inadequate in being able to bring about the construction. It is a shame that the Ucetians chose to take his life, but at least you can be satisfied that the project will now be executed with military efficiency and precision."

The *Corporata* showed no expressions. They did not show assent to the centurion's remark about efficiency and precision.

Flavius reached for the notations given him by Appius and read from them. "The clearing contractor has progressed 1400 feet beyond the Alzon and from the springs—160 feet down the Alzon; the contractor is due 4620 sestertii. *Excavation* has progressed 946 feet beyond the Alzon through several difficult sections of earth. Payment to that subcontractor, including stump removal, is 7840 sestertii. The second excavation contractor started at the springs and has excavated 110 feet. He is due 1544 sestertii, including stump removal."

Marcus, not caring much for the centurion, probed the depth of his understanding. "Flavius, you mean that the excavation contractors have progressed over 1100 feet. If they have finished that excavation, will a contractor soon start behind him to build the underground works?"

Flavius stood there, imperceptibly straightening his posture as if military bearing would see him through. He thought hard to remember if Appius had talked of this, could not remember then struggled to create an answer. He glanced at Appius then his notes before saying, "We will talk later of the upcoming contracts," and pointed at the next item on his list. "The quarry contractor...."

Marcus persisted. "Just a moment, Flavius, I do not think you answered my question. Is the trench ready for the building of the structure?"

Flavius fumed and turned red. Finally he turned to Appius.

Appius, conscious that he had not actually received a verbal request from Flavius, reveled in the discomfort of the centurion. He stepped forward, looked at Marcus, and spoke. "The plan is to excavate the entire length of the underground section of the aqueduct first to a depth of 6 feet. At that time we will determine level and from that a more precise slope of the aqueduct. From that determination we will locate the bottom of the trench to be excavated at any point in the aqueduct. After that time, the remainder of the earth will be removed after which the installation of the structure may start."

Marcus nodded. "I see. In that way you will not mistakenly dig too deep nor too shallow and especially not install the underground structure at the wrong elevation."

"That is exactly correct," Appius replied. He knew that Marcus was already aware of the concept but welcomed the chance to demonstrate that the centurion was operating by bluster without a grasp of the project.

Marcus looked at Flavius. "Were you not aware of this approach?"

Flavius remained silent and defiant.

Appius said, "He could have been aware; however, his first action in the execution of this project was to destroy the schedule."

"Enough!" erupted Flavius. "We will continue with the funding requirements."

But Marcus was not to be put off. "You mean you are now operating without a schedule?"

Appius shook his head. "Fortunately I had made a copy of that which Flavius destroyed."

Flavius looked at Appius, rage threatening to set him afire, humiliated to the core.

Appius took note. He must hide the schedule.

Marcus, now satisfied with the disclosure, said, "Yes, and what of the quarry contractor?" He yielded the floor.

Flavius snorted three lungsful, then continued, barking his statements. "The quarry contractor has completed the preliminary work to expose the valued stone and has now produced twenty-three stones. For his mobilization and progress of the work, he is due 1800 sestertii."

Titus rose, raised a hand, and said, "And what about payment to Quantus? He is due some for the work he did in the past month." He splayed both hands.

Flavius looked closely at his notes. "Quantus would have earned 1300 sestertii; however, that amount was deducted from the payment due him to account for overpayment in the prior month...," he pointed to his notation, "and for the cost of mobilization by the new contractor. Quantus will receive no payment."

Titus erupted. He walked to face Flavius and blustered in his face, shaking his fist. "You appear not to know what is going on, yet you are able to perceive that one contractor should be sacrificed for the benefit of another. I demand that you reinstate payment for Quantus."

Appius noted, *this is going well, perhaps better than I could have hoped.*

Flavius looked at Appius, upset that he had not questioned Appius as to the reasons for the accounting—the deductions from Quantus. In the meantime, Titus, his purple face inches from that of Flavius, was demanding. Flavius must show that he was tough. "The deduction will stand. Quantus gets nothing."

Titus backed off and pointed at the centurion. "You are worse than Bernius. At least Bernius knew what he was doing. But, as with Bernius, we are not without means. We shall see about you. We shall have you replaced." Titus spoke his words with such force he was spitting. He put his hands on his hips and jutted his chin.

Appius knew it was time. Titus had given him a reasonable opening. He turned to Titus who was still gazing menacingly at Flavius. "Titus Domitius, you said that—as with Bernius—you had your 'means.' What was the intent of your statement? What 'means' did you employ against Bernius?" Appius did his best to maintain a neutral composure.

Titus turned slowly to look at Appius, raised his hand to point at Appius but stopped. A cautious thought seeped into his pool of rage. "Of course, I meant that we could have appealed to

Rome. Even though Bernius was protected by Claudius, we are not without influence." He looked satisfied and relieved that his explanation had a semblance of reason.

"And by we, do you mean you and Quantus?" Appius continued in a neutral tone.

Titus did not answer. It must have occurred to him that to say 'yes' was perhaps too indicative of complicity. "I do not believe I have to explain that to you," he looked around to the *Corporata* and swept his hand to include them.

Here we go, thought Appius. "Oh, Titus, I thought that you possibly meant that you... and Quantus... used your own *means* to get rid of Bernius."

Titus was stunned. Flavius braced then looked at Appius. Titus turned around to the *Corporata* again to gauge their impressions then looked back at Appius. He said, "I... we... did not have to do anything. The Ucetians 'removed' Bernius without our hand." He looked at Flavius who nodded.

Appius stepped forward. "I believe that is not so. I understand" he nodded toward the *Corporata*, "that you and Quantus paid to have Bernius killed." Appius focused his attention on the *Corporata*, beyond Titus's back, making sure that Titus noticed this.

Titus wheeled around, looking at the *Corporata* to identify the subject of Appius's gaze. He looked back at Appius again. "You have no proof of that!"

Appius shrugged. "Proof—perhaps not. But there are those who know the truth." He glanced to Julius then shifted his gaze away.

Titus switched his gaze between Julius and Appius. "But Julius knows nothing. I've told him nothing."

Julius shook his head but portrayed a look of concern, understanding that something foul was implied, understanding that such *could* have occurred, and he was being swept into the maw.

Titus knew he had not chosen his words carefully. The *Corporata* were all looking at him. He was aware that the man he had hired to kill Bernius was missing, but the man could have taken his sestertii and fled. Or... could he be in the hands of the military? It was impossible to understand who knew what.

Appius let those present continue with their thoughts, hoping that Titus, the *Corporata*, and the centurion all had time to

483

contemplate the situation. It would seem that Flavius would *not* want to volunteer that he had questioned a man who was suspected of killing Bernius, and would *not* want to reveal that he told Appius that the man did not admit to such under torture. Flavius would be concerned that Titus or a member of the *Corporata*—Julius—might reveal Titus's involvement. Such an outcome would imply that he was participating in the conspiracy.

Finally, Appius looked at Titus and said, "Are you aware that the man you hired to kill Bernius was held and questioned by the military?" He nodded to Flavius.

"No!" Titus looked at Flavius. His worst fears betrayed him. *They know.* He looked around to see shocked looks on the faces of the *Corporata*. He stood, frozen, thinking that he would hear an indictment—details of his involvement.

The centurion was conflicted. Appius had deliberately misstated the results of the interrogation—at least the version he had *told* Appius. Yet, Titus had acted as if he had been discovered. Flavius could not let the current perception persist. Addressing the *Corporata*, he said, "It is true. We questioned the accused man. He admitted no responsibility for the murder of Bernius. Appius was told that." He glared at Appius. "It was the Ucetians."

Appius pointed to Flavius. "The centurion is not telling you the truth in order to mislead you. Titus had Bernius killed—you can tell from his manner." Appius pointed to Titus then looked at the *Corporata*. "This means that the Ucetians did not kill Bernius. Yet, Flavius and his men slaughtered the Ucetians, villagers who were innocent of the deed. That means Flavius executed Roman citizens without a trial. He stands here, also guilty of a crime. That is why he is misleading you."

Appius's statements were convincing. The *Corporata* were numb, unable to react. They looked from Appius to Flavius to Titus. Something had to happen. Titus, knowing that he had implied complicity, and not trusting that he could reasonably portray innocence, walked from the room.

Flavius grimaced upon seeing Titus walk then pointed to Appius. "This is nonsense. Appius knows nothing. I am relieving him from any further responsibility for the project. Leave," he commanded.

Appius rolled the documents at hand and took several steps toward the exit then turned to the *Corporata*. "I expect that you will have Titus and Quantus apprehended. At some point I can provide evidence of their direct involvement. I also suggest you advise, through your court system to the courts of Rome, that the military has acted beyond their bounds—the Ucetians. The Empire must not let rogue operations persist, else the Empire will crumble."

Appius walked from the Nemus's villa. He understood that he had placed himself in jeopardy by stating that he could supply direct evidence. The centurion, or perhaps Titus, would not let that happen.

CHAPTER 46

As Appius walked from Nemus's villa, he worried. Perhaps he had gone too far. But, then, would the centurion, now accused publicly of illegal slaughter, compound his error? It would not be the first time that an oppressor removed any and all possible threats. What should he do? He no longer had employment. He would have to flee with his family as they were in danger, too. Yes! He must.

But, there was something he should do at this moment. The centurion was still at the meeting with the *Corporata*, presumably. He must go to the office and retrieve his schedule and other documents of value. Otherwise, they would end up in the hands of the centurion.

He entered the office, nodded to the designers, and walked to his desk where he arranged loose documents and the schedule into a roll. On his way out, he addressed the designers. "Flavius has discharged me from service. I cannot tell you what will now happen."

The designers all had questioning looks; however, Appius turned and walked from the building. As he exited, the aide that had attended the *Corporata* meeting was just approaching. "You must not take anything from the office," he said.

Appius paid no heed and kept walking. The soldier moved to confront him, pushing Appius in the chest to arrest his movement. "Hand me the documents," he said.

"I will not." Appius walked around the soldier.

The soldier drew his knife and reached around to the front of Appius and sliced him on the hand in which he was carrying the documents. This enraged Appius, already in a high state of anxiety. He involuntarily dropped the documents and reached down as if to pick them up. The soldier stopped, expecting Appius to tend to his cut and to back off. This would allow the soldier to retrieve the documents. Instead, Appius picked up a stone from the ground, wheeled as he straightened and threw the stone at the soldier's face, an easy target at five feet. The stone's impact caused the soldier to drop the knife; he clasped his hands to his face and his broken nose as he dealt with intolerable pain. Appius picked up the knife and the documents and ran. Trouble would soon be about.

He must get his family out before the military mobilized. He ran to his home. "Antonia! Gather Sergius and some belongings. We must leave. I am going to get the horse and I will return soon. Be ready. We are in danger."

"But...?"

"I have no time to explain now." He ran out of the courtyard and on to the stables, threw a saddle on his horse, nodded to the stablemaster, and left, galloping to his house. As he walked into his courtyard, he saw several soldiers surrounding Antonia, Sergius in her arms. Appius could not run—could not flee when his family was threatened.

One of the military, not the aide with the troubled nose, nodded toward Appius. Two of the soldiers rushed forward and surrounded him. He recognized them from the interrogation incident. "You will wait here. The centurion will soon arrive."

After some time, Flavius walked in. He looked at Appius and Antonia and noticed the documents on the ground, bloodstained from the wound Appius had received. He walked up to Appius. "You rightly assumed you are in trouble, and it appears you are about to flee." He did not wait for Appius to reply. "Here is what will happen. You will return to work with your documents. You will continue to work under my direction and to my satisfaction. You will not engage in insubordination. I know you will do as I ask." He nodded in the direction of Antonia and Sergius.

Appius, his shoulders slumped, looked at the ground.

The centurion applied the point of his knife under Appius's chin and lifted until Appius was looking at him. The centurion said, "Do you understand?"

Appius said, "Yes."

Flavius looked at his men. "We can go now." He turned back to Appius. "Bring your documents and return to work." He wheeled and walked through the gate.

Appius walked to Antonia, still in fright. Sergius, in her arms, seemed unaffected by the situation. Appius hugged Antonia. "I am sorry. This is my fault. I could not let the killers of Bernius go unscathed. This is the result. I should have found another way."

Antonia glanced at Sergius then looked up at her husband. "Appius, we do not always act in a way that is approved by others.

I might be guilty of doing something similar. I will not judge you harshly."

Appius thought she meant that if she were in the same situation, she might have acted similarly. He was relieved that she was not upset at him and accepted her statement. "Thank you, my dear wife. I will not put you... ," he looked down at Sergius, "and my son... in danger." However, he thought, *one might think that the centurion would extract further revenge at some time.*

Flavius was no fool. He was in charge but knew he needed Appius. Therefore, it was important that Appius continue to draft contracts and administer the upcoming work. Discussion of method and schedule was always contentious between the two. Flavius ruled by bluster, making sure that Appius knew who was in charge, holding to a course of action even when Appius pointed out the folly of doing so. Appius never missed an opportunity to identify mistaken thinking and constantly pointed out that Flavius was inadequate to manage the project. Perhaps Appius should not be so contentious.

The schedule was always a focus of this struggle of wills. Flavius demanded, "Why have you not bid contracts for the underground structure work that follows the excavation?"

"Are you not aware that the structure work will not start for a long time?" Appius pointed to the activities on the schedule, avoiding the bloodstains. "Had you been listening, I explained before that we are excavating only the first 6 feet for the entire length of the aqueduct. We will establish level—and the resulting gradient—then excavate to the full depth. After that, the structure work can start—possibly in two years."

Flavius did not bother to look at the schedule. He puffed, "That is nonsense. You will instruct the excavation contractors—all four of them—to immediately begin digging to the full depth. In that way we will start the underground structure work in months rather than years. I will report to General Artius Crassius of this improvement. We will save those years."

Appius looked at Flavius. "Does it bother you that you may be installing stones and cement and finished aqueduct that won't work—that may either be too shallow or too deep—that the water will not flow—that the work you do may have to be redone or abandoned?"

the *Aedifex*: Building the Pont du Gard

Flavius responded. "I see. So, the route and elevations that you have set are not accurate. Why did you not take care to do so?"

"I have explained to you before. The devices that we have on hand are not accurate enough to establish our slope. At the 6 foot depth we will establish accurate level readings for the entire route allowing us to slope the aqueduct to assure that the water will flow." Appius shook his head. Would his explanations be of use to someone not wanting to acknowledge other's thoughts and methods?

"And how will you be able to be accurate now when you could not do so before?"

"Again, I have explained this. We will use water to establish level rather than an instrument that is subject to error. From level, determined by the water, we will establish the slope and thus the depth to dig and to construct the conduit." Appius threw up his hands in exasperation.

Flavius crossed his arms. "Nevertheless, my direction is to excavate for a short distance, flood the excavation, establish the level, then dig to the full depth." Flavius was proud that he had thought his way through the problem.

"Oh, yes. Let us say you establish the level for 300 feet. At the 300 foot distance, how much deeper should the aqueduct be than at the start?"

"Why it shall be what you have calculated from your prior surveys."

"I have told you the prior were not of sufficient accuracy. It is with the entire length verified that we can be sure of the required slope and thus the depths."

"Fi, you talk in circles. You have not convinced me. We will do as I have suggested. Prepare the contracts for the structure work, establish the levels after the first 200 feet of each excavation contract and then have the excavators dig to full depth."

Appius said nothing. How would he feel if there were significant errors in the work? Would having Flavius humiliated be more important than to have taken part in a colossal project that was successful? It was not clear. He felt he should do his part to see the project completed as a tribute to Bernius and, he knew, as a satisfaction to himself. Finally, he said, "I will prepare a document listing your instructions so that I will be clear as to what I am to do."

"Yes. That is a good idea." Flavius nodded.

"You will sign it?"

"Yes, of course I will. I will one day use it as an example of the foresight with which I managed the project."

"I must mention that if the structure work is to start soon, we must also bid and award contracts for the production of cement and other materials that will be part of the structure."

"You should have been doing that already—obviously—instead of proceeding by your foolish schedule."

"Our foolish schedule had us bidding and starting those contracts while we were performing the first phase—that of excavating the first 6 feet and establishing the workable gradient."

"Yes, well you have a new schedule now."

Appius continued to prepare several of the remaining contracts, going over them many times to include provisions he had forgotten, removing errors, and rewriting the wording to make the requirements clearer. He struggled to remember what Bernius had told him, referred to contracts Bernius had written, and in a few instances created provisions that made sense to him. There was no one he could consult. He spent no time on the underground structure contracts—those that Flavius had directed him to initiate—and did not modify the schedule to reflect what he considered the lunacy of Flavius's direction. But he knew—nevertheless—at some time he must change the schedule, otherwise the project would truly be out of control.

The *Corporata* released funds for payment of 5000 sestertii per their requirement. Three weeks after the *Corporata* meeting, however, the supplementary payment by the Empire had *not* been received. The contractors who had started work on earlier contracts had been paid, but the last contracts to start—the two new excavation contracts, and the tunnel vertical shaft work—had not received payment. Those contractors had now been working seven weeks, paying for labor and purchases with their funds, without compensation from the Empire.

Appius was reluctant to tour the project as he knew he would encounter disgruntled contractors. *I will be changing the order of operations if I execute the orders of Flavius. The contractors will have to provide additional men now, rather than later, to start the deeper excavation. And, if we must establish our level by means of water, they will have to take on the added*

490

expense of flooding the channel because I do not have the clay pipe on hand. This is chaos. And I must hear their complaints because they have not been paid.

He rode first to the location of the tunnel exploratory shafts. The work was slow by nature, as they now were digging in solid rock. Only four men could work at the bottom of the shaft, freeing the rock and loading baskets that were lifted by men with a hoist, dumped, and returned. Nevertheless, at this time they had dug three shafts to a depth of 40 feet. As he expected, the contractor asked when he would receive payment. Appius said, "The military is applying to Rome for the transfer of funds, but such has not yet happened. When the funds are in Nemausus, they will be delivered to you that day."

The contractor, not a patient man, said, "I am paying these workers from my own funds. I am aware that I am usually required to do this for at least a month, but not two months. I cannot continue work without being paid."

Appius nodded, "I understand. I will do everything I can."

The experience was similar with the two new trench excavation contractors. They would not work much longer without payment. Appius, noting that each had progressed over 200 feet, discussed means by which they would get water into the excavation and prepare for the operation to establish level. There were no close water sources. "What about the clay pipes that were to be used?" they asked.

Appius shrugged. "The clay pipes have not been produced. They were to have been used later. You will have to either flood the entire trench or excavate a narrow trench at the bottom of your excavation."

As Appius left, the contractors were shaking their heads and threatening that the means of establishing level and the requirement to start digging at full depth were outside of the contract they had bid. The Empire would have to pay for additional costs. It was difficult to be firm when the contractors had not been paid, and all were quick to point this out.

Appius explained this same requirement to the two excavation contractors nearer the Alzon, the two that had started earlier. They were as upset as the others at having to do the unanticipated more difficult leveling procedure. At least they were not suffering from lack of payment. They recoiled, however, when

Appius told them that at the direction of Flavius, they would have to add additional personnel to start digging deeper.

The clearing contractor was unaffected by payment, water-level maneuvers, and onerous additional digging requirements. In fact, they were doing quite well, propelled by the mighty axes of Marius and Pentius.

Appius briefed Pentius and Marius on the outcome of the meeting at the *Corporata*. The duo promised that if Titus and Quantus were not apprehended and punished, they would exact justice themselves. *Did they mean what they said?* Appius told them to advise Decimus Nautius that his name had *not* been mentioned as a witness to the interrogation of the killer, but Appius did say that he told the *Corporata* he had proof that Titus and Quantus were involved.

Appius looked at each of the trench excavation operations and tried to visualize a means of using water as a leveling mechanism. He pondered—*at the 6-foot depth, the trench is about eleven feet wide; the bottom is uneven. If a 200-foot section is filled to a depth to provide a continual water surface, it looks like the water will have to be about a foot deep. Getting that amount of water to the ditch will be a difficult task. Draining it might be easy in some instances and not so in others*. He noted that the roughness of the bottom of the excavation also made excavation of a narrow trench difficult. Either means would require additional work for the contractors, work they had not been asked to do under the contract. *They will ask for additional payment—no doubt.* It was incredible how much difficulty was created by supervisors who proceeded with bluster rather than acting with reason.

I'll try to see how soon the clay manufacturer in Nemausus can produce the half-round sections.

Appius rode back to Nemausus. He told the contractors he would return in a week to advise them of the payment situation and to discuss the means of establishing level. Hopefully, he could tell them to only use the procedure on a short section, that they would soon have use of the clay pipes.

Upon his return, he was curious to see if Titus and Quantus had been apprehended or questioned by any authorities. They had not. The centurion had topmost authority from the Empire and, of course, it was doubtful that Flavius would be interested in public exposure of their crime. It would cause trouble for him. And, Titus had influence in Rome. It did not seem that the killers of Bernius would suffer for their crime.

Yet, Appius knew the situation gave him leverage over Flavius, trumped, however, by the threat to his family. They could be harmed, and Flavius could get away with it. Appius could not help but be angered and depressed at such oppression. He must wade through this, act reasonably and wait for opportunity. Well, he had created his own opportunity to expose Titus in the *Corporata* meeting. A lot of good it had done him. He had exposed the truth to other people, though, some of whom might be considered good public citizens.

The clay pipe manufacturer agreed to begin working on the half-round clay pipes, telling Appius that it would be two weeks before he could produce the first 100 feet. Appius thought, *I do not think Flavius will allow another two weeks to lapse before his directions are enacted. I do not like doing this, but I must talk to the centurion.*

Standing at the centurion's desk, Appius explained the situation. "The excavation contractors were to dig their sections to a depth of 6 feet. After all had done so, we would establish level and gradient for the entire aqueduct, modify our slope calculations and dimensions then start digging to the required and known depth. That is what is written in their contracts."

Flavius shrugged. "There is nothing to keep them from starting to dig the next 6 foot depth. Why have you been so foolish as to work only on the topmost 6 feet?"

"The intent was to use the available manpower to complete the first 6 feet as fast as possible. Also, due to the known errors in our measuring equipment, it is possible that a modification could be required, even in the second 6 foot depth."

"It makes little sense to me." The centurion shook his head.

"This seemed to be the most prudent way to determine the requirements."

"It seems obvious to me that the work can be completed sooner if they start the excavation now and do not wait to complete the first 6 feet. I directed you to have that begun. Why are you here?" Flavius pointed at Appius.

"I am here to advise you that the contractors were not expecting to add additional men at this time. The clay pipes are not yet ready because they were not required to be used until later. More difficult means will have to be used. The contractors will request additional payments to accomplish the work in this way. Also, with the second depth excavated, it will be more difficult to use even the clay pipe method."

"Yes, and...?"

"I am asking that you allow me to acquire the clay pipes—a period of two to three weeks—before we begin the level measurements. I am asking that you allow me to delay the start of the digging of the next 6 feet until we have done the level measurements and allow an extended start of the deeper excavations." Appius hated to have to ask permission.

"As to the level measuring—I do not care." Flavius shrugged. "You find a way to get it done. If it costs the contractors additional expense, they will have to convince me that they are due it. If I am not convinced, they will not be paid the additional. However, on starting the additional digging, I insist that it be started now. What do I have to do to make this happen? It has already been two weeks." He pointed in the direction of Appius's home.

Appius said nothing. He glared at the centurion then mumbled, "I will advise them." Then he remembered. "What can you tell me about the payment for those contractors who have not yet received it?"

Flavius showed no concern. "I have made the request, and I am waiting for Rome to respond. Perhaps Caligua has more important payments to be made. The contractors will have to be patient." He shrugged.

"The contractors have said that they will not work much longer without payment. You are aware that they have to pay their men even if they have not been paid by the Empire."

"Yes, well the men might have to wait for their pay also."

Appius wheeled and walked from the building. He shook his head. *I will take his statement—that he did not care how the measuring got done—to allow time to utilize the clay pipes. However, I must advise the contractors that they are to acquire additional crew to start digging the next layer. No telling how Flavius might threaten me, or Antonia, or... Sergius, if he wants to have his way. Looks like I will have to take another trip to visit the work. The project is out of control. It is happening rather than being managed.*

One month later.

Antonia looked at Appius, slumped on his stool. "Work is making you dismal. Talk to me. Perhaps if you tell me the difficulties, your manner will be eased."

Appius shook his head. "The project is suffering. The centurion has made it difficult for those trying to get the work accomplished. He directed that the contractors employ additional men to start digging below the original first pass, yet the Empire has not paid several of the contractors the amount due them over a month ago. Now, as of the last *Corporata* meeting, there are 13,000 sestertii the Empire must pay in addition to the 5000 sestertii payment by the *Corporata*. Last month's *Corporata* funds were allocated to *only* the quarry and the clearing contractors. The excavation contractors received nothing. They are not only refusing to employ the additional men, they are threatening to stop work altogether."

"Do you blame them?"

"No, I do not."

Antonia put a hand on Appius's shoulder. "If the project were still under the hand of Claudius, would the Empire be paying?"

Appius shook his head. "I believe Claudius would ensure payment. He would not be creating turmoil by upsetting the planned flow of the project."

Antonia smiled. "Is anything happening that is good?"

Appius took a deep breath, giving himself time to collect his thoughts. "The quarry contractor is competent and able to proceed without being subject to the ranting proclamations of Flavius. The same situation exists with the clearing contractor. And, I was able to obtain sections of clay pipe from the potter; we were successful in establishing level lines using that method—my idea. Although, with only one section of pipe available, we had to transport the pipe from location to location. That will not have to be done the next time we do our level-marking operation."

"What does the centurion say?"

"He puffs up and tells me to ensure that the contractors follow his direction. I do not know what he will do if the contractors refuse to do more work."

"Does he threaten you—or us?"

"He does not directly mention a threat. However, by one means or another, he reminds me. It is difficult. I am torn between telling him he is a fool and that of keeping my mouth shut to avoid mad action he might take against us. Each time I tell him that it is impossible or difficult to do what he asks, I cringe to think that he might show me that he is serious—that his commands are to be followed without question or delay."

"That worries me too."

Appius looked at Antonia, knowing she would feel the sorrow of a further concern. "I despair because Titus and Quantus are walking about after it is obvious they had Bernius killed. At the *Corporata* meetings, Titus maintains an air of impudence, which is infuriating to me and it frustrates me that he... they... are able to go about with no consequence. The centurion knows that this causes me great distress and takes pleasure in knowing so."

"But the *Corporata*...?"

"They are helpless. They seem to resent having Titus in their midst but are powerless to take action against him for the crime. I think they are frustrated, also."

Antonia sighed. "Ayyye, why is our life so hard? What must one do?"

Appius shook his head. "I do not know what is best to do."

One week later, Appius stood before the centurion. "I have talked to the contractors. Of course they complained about lack of payment. Again they threatened to stop work."

"Have they also refused to put on additional men?"

"They have told me that additional men are not immediately available. It will take time." Appius and the contractors had agreed to this positioning rather than make a direct refusal.

"I have a solution for that." Flavius stood.

Appius said nothing, waiting.

"I can have 200 slaves here in one month—from northern Africa. They can provide additional forces for the excavation contractors and perform all the contractor's work should they decide to abandon the work."

Several thoughts competed for attention in Appius's mind. *Would the contracts be abandoned? Who would supervise the slaves? Who would have the skills to understand the work? How would the slaves be cared for—fed, and housed?* Appius frowned. "Slaves?"

"Yes. I am sure that you have heard of this practice. We have ample stock available. Why should we not use them?"

Appius considered that the aqueduct provided opportunities for local commerce and employment; the region would prosper. The use of slaves would severely reduce those opportunities. Perhaps the centurion would have *most* of the work done by slaves, replacing the contractors who must stop work because of lack of payment. Was this Flavius's ultimate aim? Had he intended this?

"They would be supervised by...?"

"Our military, of course."

"Is that what you mean to do?"

"Yes, in fact I have already given the order to send the slaves. They will be transported by galley, rowed by galley slaves. Ha, ha. Our slaves will have the satisfaction of having other slaves row for them. Ha, ha."

"Is the lack of payment by the Empire deliberate? Is that the means and the reasoning for replacing the contractors workers and bringing slaves?"

"I do not have to answer your questions. Perhaps you should pay attention and learn how to run a project. Your amateur approach would have been ruinous."

"We weren't doing badly until you showed up."

Flavius laughed. "Oh, yes. Your project manager was murdered, and your first quarry contractor failed to perform. Oh, yes—very well. Ha, ha."

"You forgot to add that villagers in the proximity were needlessly slaughtered, the military took control, and they do not know the first thing about building an aqueduct."

Flavius erupted. "You are not to speak thus. What do I have to do to make you understand?"

"You need to do nothing. I understand without you having to tell me."

Flavius was not sure he was hearing words that assented to his power and control. "Do not antagonize me. Nothing good will come of it for you."

Appius turned and walked from the building. *Flavius's statement is correct. I will get nothing from angering him and pointing out his errors and bad deeds. He has the power to hurt my family and will act as he wants on the project. Well—I was able to get our level measurement done; he thought it of no consequence. I must not cause harm to my family, but it is so difficult to have to listen to and operate under his arrogance.*

Slaves. Somehow I did not think we would have to do that. Flavius must have had that idea in mind for a while. Get rid of the contractors and bring on the slaves, supervised by his military, surely executing the project in his way. I must get back to my schedule. But, what good is it? I may find that what we are doing makes no sense, yet... if I told that to Flavius, he would wave me away. What am I doing? What is my value? When the slaves arrive, what influence will I have? Flavius will never let me give instructions to the military overseeing them. The project is going on without me.

CHAPTER 47

I stared at the photo of the *Castellum*, thinking of the implications of a cache. There were too many particulars to be ignored. Yes, they all involved items I had stumbled upon, but doesn't it often occur that someone happens to be in the right place at the right time, is exposed to the same images, thoughts, and circumstance as others but in the right sequence and timing? Of course, a mind that can make the connections is a factor. I gave myself credit for that.

I was at the kitchen table. A reading lamp was arranged for my ease in inspecting clues appearing on ancient artifacts. I leaned back, hands locked behind my head, the bare light bulb in the overhead defocused as I let my mind wander. What were the value-added thoughts that led me to believe I had possibly discovered a cache of ancient documents, documents which perhaps would aid me to understand how the great structure was built? I craved for that information, wanting it to be there, wanting something to tell me the story. Could I think that I had a possible *find*?

What were the crucial thoughts that led to my conclusion? First, on the Pont du Gard, we found the APA with the arch underneath. Could be anything. Finding the same mark at the *Castellum* could be a coincidence, could be the work of a mad inscriber, eager to etch his mark on several significant structures and possibly in notable locations. It is probable that no one in modern times had the good fortune to encounter and notice both markings. That was significant in the path that led to my hypothesis. Then, at the *Castellum*, the interpretation of the cylinder as rolled parchment, partially unrolled, was a stretch. Or was it? Actually, it was the parallel thought that the irregularly laid stones might be a cache that triggered the thought of the parchment. We hadn't guessed a reasonable meaning before. That is probably where most people left off. And, it was only in looking at the photo that I noticed the irregular installation of the stones. Yes, we had been fortunate to witness this chain of clues. I had to tell Lisele.

"Bonjour."

"Lisele, this is Warner."

"Oh, hello, Warner. And what are you doing, today?"

"I am very excited. I must show you something. You will be impressed that you may have contributed to a great discovery. Can I come over?"

"Well, yes you *could*, but Laurie is here at the moment, and I should not dismiss my rare time with her to pay attention to you, if you understand what I am saying."

"Oh. Yes, yes. Well, why don't you let me know when you are available? What I have to tell you has been a secret for two thousand years. I suppose a few hours will make little difference."

"Warner, what can you be talking about? You've certainly stirred my interest. I will call you when I am able to share in your discovery. It should be soon—this morning."

"Okay." I hung up.

I tried to keep busy for several hours. Finally the phone rattled rather than rang—it had its own disposition, calling me to attention. Lisele said that she would be over to see me. Soon, I heard the crunch of gravel in the drive, and Lisele was at the door.

After a quick hug and kiss, she said, "So, Mr. Warner, what is so mysterious, this ancient secret that you want to share with me? I rushed over here at great speed, tires squealing, pedestrians scattering, dogs chasing, in great anticipation. Now, what is it?" She put hands on hips.

"Lisele, come with me." I took her hand and walked her to the kitchen table. I picked up the picture of the *Castellum* and pointed. "See this stone? It is the one with the APA and the arch. The stone beneath has the inscription that you say is a pipe on a stand."

"Yes—I see—of course."

"But, look at this. Do you see that the stones around the inscriptions are placed differently than the others in the wall? They are aligned vertically when the others are staggered."

"Yes. Why do you care?"

"Because, my friend, Lisele, I think the stones are arranged in that way because a cache exists behind their outline." I paused to let Lisele look. She scowled, but then I said. "And, if that were to be, what might your 'pipe on a stand' represent?"

Lisele scowled again, then her face brightened. "Oh, I see. The cache is the location of valves that turn on and off the water

500

that is entering the pipes." She beamed, encouraged that she had possibly solved the mystery.

I shook my head, but smiled. "I should be most disappointed to find out that your suggestion is so. No, Lisele, I have a more exciting thought. What if there is a cache and it holds ancient documents? Could it be that your 'pipe on a stand' is really a partially unrolled scroll?"

She looked at me. I could tell by the slight smile that she willed that I had guessed correctly. She knew what that would mean to me and hoped that my thought was more truth than fantasy, hoped because at that moment I could tell that she would be delighted if I was delighted.

Yet, she teased me. "Warner, you have been dreaming of this adventure too much, perhaps drinking too much wine. I think your mind would have made a delicious stew of whatever ingredients we might have come across. Poor boy."

I shook my head—impatient now. "You think I am creating my own fantasy? Surely you can see the connections. You think I am making too much of this?"

Lisele turned toward me, put her hands on my shoulders and gave me a kiss. I recognized the characteristics of one person comforting another. Perhaps she really did think I had forged my own excitement.

"Warner, I think you really do have something here." Her hands remained on my shoulders. She moved one hand from my shoulders to point to the photo. "Now what?"

I hadn't managed to consider 'now what.' You would have thought I would have done so in the time I was waiting for Lisele. I smiled. Was she testing the depth of my conviction? Was I willing to take my 'discovery' to others, others having the authority to remove stones from an ancient, historical structure? I understood that I must. "I think I will go to Renat. He may be able to find someone who might be persuaded."

Lisele spoke softly. "Very good, Warner, very good. You know that you must pursue this. If you don't, you will regret it forever. I will be your cheerleader."

"You feel as strongly about this as I do?"

"Perhaps it means more to you, Warner, but I love the thought. Imagine your exhilaration if you are able to remove the stones and discover the ancient history describing the building of the aqueduct. Can you, can I imagine a more magical moment?"

"The moment would be awesome and humbling. I can only imagine another moment that might be as magical."

"Yes, Warner?"

"Renat, this is Warner."

Renat made the seamless transition to English. "Yes, Warner. Two times in a little over a week I get to talk to you. What is up?"

"Renat, I think I have discovered something, a something that I think you will find interesting. And, I need your help."

"But, what is it, Warner? Of course I will help."

"I must show you what I have found, first. I am hoping you will validate my suspicions. If you think that I have discovered something worthwhile, then I will ask for your help. I don't want you to be part of a foolish exercise if you are not convinced."

"Okay, okay, Warner. You will come to my house? I will have lunch for you. Today, is it?"

"Yes, today, Renat. I am bursting to show you. I will be there in an hour."

I readied for the visit and made the drive to Nimes, deliberately taking the longer route over the Nimes-Uzes road. I liked the drive, notwithstanding the terror I had experienced at Laurie's hands, and I wanted to put space between my conversation with Renat and a face-to-face encounter. Maybe the desire for space really masked a concern that I was entertaining a folly. Oh, well, the mountain route wasn't much longer.

Renat opened the door; the house sat well back on a tree-shrouded street, a pleasing setting, barely noticed by me in my determination. Before Renat served me lunch—cucumber sandwiches and a glass of Nostura Azuro beer—he made me explain my mission. I told him. I showed him.

He looked up after investigating the photo and the sketch I had made of the inscriptions. "Yes, Warner, I may be able to help you. Of course, you want to remove the stones. I do not know, personally, the curator of the antiquities, but I have a friend who is on a committee that takes responsibility for protecting and providing public access to the structures—you know, the Nimes Coliseum, the Tour Magne, the Maison Caree, La Fountaine and... The *Castellum*. You must convince Monsieur Grambeaux and perhaps the committee that the wall should be partially dismantled to access our ancient past. Do you think you can do that?"

"I have only my enthusiasm and the items I have shown you. Perhaps it will be enough. What do you think?"

"I will be very enthused to be your interpreter. I do, however, have my doubts that they will consider your request."

"Even if it means they might discover more about the magnificent structure that was... is... so important to the history of their city?"

"Yes. I do not see that it is so bad to remove a few stones. But, it does not help that you are an American and may have discovered something that has been right under their Gallic noses."

I nodded then shook my head. "Renat, I must try."

Renat maneuvered me to Dr. Grambeaux's office. Grambeaux was a man too heavy for his suit and with the breezy air of an effected art aficionado. I found it hard to warm up to him, a condition also limited by not being able to converse with him in French. As Renat was making our pitch, I could see that he was exasperated. He turned to me several times but did not say anything, just taking my temperature as if I were following the conversation. Finally, there was silence. Grambeaux stood up. Renat and I stood as well; it was perfectly clear that we were being sent on our way. Renat retrieved the photos from Grambeaux's desk. Grambeaux made a move to stop him but reconsidered. We shook his hand and left the room.

In the wide hallway of the museum arcade, Renat and I walked for some time before he spoke, the footfalls a staccato tattoo on the stones amplified by the otherwise pervasive silence. "It is as I thought. He doesn't like it that you have uncovered this possibility. He said that he could not possibly consider 'destroying' a monument dating from antiquity on the whim of a visitor to the area. He will not allow it. The committee would not allow it. I asked him if the investigation would be more highly considered if a local doctor of antiquities were to make a similar request. He said—of course they would give respectful consideration, but the answer would most likely be the same. I do not think he really means that."

"Thank you for trying, Renat. I think you were correct in your assumption. Grambeaux did not look at me once during the exchange—as if I didn't exist. He didn't even look at me when we shook hands to leave.

"What will you do now?"

"I suppose we might find a local academic who would get more consideration, but, judging Grambeaux, I think he would scuttle the effort for a while, anyway, knowing that I was the genesis. I'll go home and think about it."

"Warner, someday somebody will take action on your suggestion. When I hear of such a thing, I will let you know. I'm sure you'd like to know if there was a treasure, and if so, the contents and meaning."

I was very discouraged. It is not easy to arrive at the brink, anticipating the view, only to be turned away. Oh, yes, I could try to find a local archeologist, anthropologist, historian, a specialist in antiquities or of the Roman Empire or the Aqueduct, someone who would front my cause, but I had no enthusiasm to do so. Perhaps I was uncertain, afraid to pull another person, especially a person with background, into my foolish adventure. Maybe I was afraid my idea would be pronounced... 'absurd.' The word and its ringing echo haunted me.

Lost archeological opportunity was not the only element of my funk. I seems that I had now traversed the mysteries of the aqueduct, plowed the obscure information, as viewed through the lens of an engineer/constructor, to a reasonable depth. It was time to call 'game over.' If I were to assess the success of my investigation, if I stood back and considered only that, I would award myself a B plus... maybe an A minus. Okay, not so bad. However, the winding down of my adventure and the obstacle erected at the brink of my discovery were compounded with the thought that I must return home, must leave Lisele behind—'over there' somewhere. Should I have known better? Would I be better off to have been prudent enough to keep her at 'arm's length?' That's ridiculous. You must go with life's opportunities.

How would Lisele react? I knew enough—had read the body language, had seen the looks. She would be as distressed as I. But she had better sense. Why had she allowed herself to be drawn into this exhilarating fall ending in an abrupt—cancel that— *prolonged* impact? I agonized for several days. It was time to talk.

I phoned Lisele. I had already told her of the failed mission at the hands of the Director of Antiquities. I had tried to give the impression that it was 'just one of those things,' a 'road bump in life's journey.' She had been able to plumb the depths of my disappointment, however, soothing me, praising me, trying to resurrect the fading spirit. Now I must talk of leaving. It was hard to exude the gaiety of life.

I tried, using a somewhat breezy approach. "Hi, Lisele, your amateur archeologist, here—or does that translate to 'ancient friend?'" Too breezy? Yeah, well....

"Perhaps your translation *is* a little zany, but at least *'amateur' friend* does not make it through the translation. How are you, Warner?" I noticed a trace of concern around the edges.

"I'm okay—really." In just a few moments I knew I would feel worse, after I mentioned that it was time to pack my bags, get on the silver plane, time to turn and wave at her as I paced the concourse. "I think we need to do something celebratory." Was I putting off the inevitable, defusing the bomb, saving the surprise for a rainy day?

"I have been thinking exactly the same thing. We should do something celebratory, a raucous testimony to the success of your adventure."

"You want to have a testimonial dinner?"

"No, no. What I have been thinking—do you remember when I talked about hiking in the Pyrenees?"

"You think I should go hiking in the Pyrenees?"

"Not you—not *just* you—*we* go hiking in the Pyrenees."

I was silent for a moment, thinking about the several implications of her statement. "You mean... we travel together." Adrenalin rushed.

"Of course, silly. Oh, well, it really isn't an 'of course.' I have given this thought, and I can tell that you are surprised. Yes, this will be unpleasant between me and Laurie, and countless local tongues will wag. I don't care."

"Is tomorrow too early? I can't tell you what this would mean to me."

"Ha, ha, I hoped you would think that. But, Warner, I'm not finished. After the Pyrenees, since you have a great interest in the ancient world, let's go on to the ancient ruins of Troy, of Pompeii, of Rome."

"Turkey and Italy?"

"Yes. Can you do it? Will you do it?"

I tried not to react like a slobbering puppy. It was my good fortune she couldn't see my tail wagging. "Lisele, I don't know what to say... I can't imagine... I hadn't thought.... "

"Oh, perhaps you cannot do this." She sounded a little hurt. "Perhaps you must now go home, take care of your house, see your friends.... "

"No, no. Of course I will go with you. I'll let my house burn down if it must, let my friends drop me from their Christmas card list. Yes, I will go."

"Oh... good! I am so happy. We must make plans. Will you come to my house for dinner? We must prepare for our trip, I'm thinking, over shellfish crepes. Yes?"

"Yes, Lisele, I'll be there."

We rang off. Of course my mind exhausted itself in contemplation of the phrase—"prepare for our trip."

CHAPTER 48

Appius dismally trudged home in despair. He had been rendered inconsequential to the project, entrapped by the might of the Empire and by threats to his family. The project was wheeling out of control, exercised by a madman who had no care for the thoughts that had gone into the planning and scheduling. Appius had imagined personal involvement, deep immersion in the day-to-day running of the project—keeping track of progress, anticipating next week's or month's needs, solving problems. Now he was nothing but a lackey, kept around because he filled in niches that the centurion found useful. Appius felt that this was *his* project, but try as he might, he could not influence the actions that made it an accomplishment to be proud of.

Slaves! Animals doing drudgery with no sense of participation, mindful only of the numbing fetters that were their life. No pride of accomplishment, no understanding of what was being done. And what if... what if Flavius was successful in getting the project built with slaves, at less cost than would have been obtained with contracting? It was too much to accept.

Appius entered their house. He walked to Sergius and put his hand on the year-old infant's head as Sergius shook his fists in delight at the sight of his father. Having no enthusiasm for engaging Sergius, Appius walked to Antonia and gave her a routine pat and kiss.

Antonia could not help but notice. She looked up at him to see his closed eyes. The energy and enthusiasm were gone. This was not good. She had hoped he would have more zest at this time—on this night—on which she must navigate with precision and perception. Perhaps... perhaps after he had a cup of wine, he would see the world through more accommodating eyes. She poured the wine, handed Appius the cup, and pointed at Sergius. "You had better pay attention to your son, or he will not forgive you."

Appius shook his head, realizing that he was ignoring something that was highly important to him—the joy in his son's heart. Instinct overcame depression and lethargy. He brightened, stooped, and picked up his son.

507

Appius heard Sergius screech to have his fondest wish come true. Sergius smiled at Appius and screeched again. Can the aqueduct matter? This is the essence of life.

Antonia noted Appius's transformation with satisfaction. She let the two get the most from the engagement—a warm scene. Then she shuddered, thinking of what she must do. Now would have to be the time.

Sergius was now content to rest his head on Appius. Appius had his hand upon the infant's back.

"Appius." Antonia stood with her hands locked in front of her.

Appius looked up. "Yes."

Antonia hesitated. "Juliena is pregnant."

Appius stared at her trying to gain perspective—re-order his thoughts. Finally, he said, "Bernius?"

"Yes, Bernius." Antonia smiled and nodded.

"We have a gift from Bernius, a being who will survive him? I can only think that this is something to be happy about. I will treasure the child."

"Yes, I feel the same way, but it is about that which I must talk to you. Juliena is already struggling to care for her existing children. There are other options, but... would you consider being father to the child of Bernius?" She was hopeful that Appius would accept the suggestion with ease.

Appius stared at her. "But, of course. I would consider no greater honor than to raise Bernius's child, a duty that I would gladly take on in gratitude—and friendship." He nodded his head, absentmindedly patting the head of Sergius. "But, Antonia.... "

Antonia anticipated his question and gave him a direct look.

"We will have other children of our own. Will that make a difference? Are we doing the right thing?"

I must, I must, Antonia thought. She took a deep breath. "Appius, my dear husband, I think we cannot have more children."

Appius looked confused. "Not have more children? Why not? You did not suffer a problem during birth—did you? Or... *did* you and you have not told me about it?" He looked at her with distress and concern.

"No." She straightened her shoulders. "I do not think I have any problem. I think that you may not be able to father... a... child."

"Not father a child?" He pulled Sergius from his chest and held him up. "What about this? What about Sergius? How can there be a problem?"

Antonia held his eyes with hers, but her look softened. "You are not the father of Sergius." She did not know how Appius would react. As well as she knew Appius, she did not know what would happen next.

"I do not hear what you are saying," Appius said in a whisper, not wanting to believe what Antonia had said.

Antonia replied. "After we had been married three years, I became convinced that we were not going to be successful in having a child. All of my sisters conceive easily, so I suspected it was not me. I ached to have a baby for you and so I found a way."

"Found a way? Found a way? With another man?" He looked at Sergius then thrust him to Antonia.

Antonia clasped the baby and turned him toward her. "Yes."

"Who is this? I will kill him." He demanded. "Who is this?"

"It would be better if you did not know."

"I will not *rest* until I know."

"Appius, I will tell you, but you must know this first. I forced this man to take me. He had little choice. I had knowledge that if revealed would ruin his life, and I used that knowledge. He was not a willing father."

"How could you have knowledge that would be so powerful? I do not believe this."

"One of my sisters knows that this man takes care of other women. If he were exposed, his wife, whose fortune he depends upon, would cast him out. He would be ruined."

"He will be ruined at my hand. He should have resisted. At least he would have survived the consequences."

"I promised I would never tell you. But I find that I cannot live with this. I cannot deceive you further. And with Juliena, and the possibility of raising Bernius's child, it seemed that it was important that I tell you."

"Who is it? I must know." Appius raged. His pulse throbbed in his neck.

Antonia shook her head. "It is Marcus. I told him what I demanded the second time he delivered the payment. He did not want to do this. He thinks highly of you."

509

"It does not matter. I cannot let him live." He slapped Antonia, turned, retrieved his cloak then walked from the house.

Antonia, reeling from the hit, yelled after him. "Appius, please do not.... "

He must get away. He ran to the stables, saddled his horse, and rode out of town at a gallop. Beyond the city limits, he slowed, head hung, letting the horse set the pace. Every so often he would rage, shaking his fists at the sky, the sky putting on the day's last and most vibrant display, a tribute to the actors on its stage.

On he rode. He knew where he was going without thinking of it. How could his life have deteriorated so rapidly and completely? The project was beyond his control or influence, run by a tyrant; he was inconsequential. Bernius had been killed, and the killers walked about. Worst of all he had been deceived by... Antonia. It was too much—too much to be able to try to understand or accept or accommodate. What was left for him?

By the time he reached the bridge at the Vardo, it was dark, yet he rode the path up the south side of the river, along the canyon, then down into the canyon to a spot well above the river. He watered the horse, tied it where there was grass, and took a wine jug from the saddlebags. He walked to the three stones and sat, his back against one of them. Bernius was his solace, now, as he was in the past. He drank directly from the jug.

How could she? How could Antonia deceive him— humiliate him? He must cast her out, her and that child of Marcus. He would not look upon the face of the child again—ever. And Marcus—of course he could have refused. He was actually probably quite willing, as he always did favor Antonia. He must kill Marcus. Why not? He would have to leave, be on the run—hide. But what difference? There was nothing left for him in Nemausus.

He would be a soldier... no... not a soldier, one who abused the power of the Empire, abused the citizens. He would find something, maybe another large project. But, he could not stay in Nemausus—not in shame.

The wine eased his mind beyond the realm of a dismissed past, instead exploring and imagining an adventurous future. He would put all this behind him, bury the refuse that now depressed him, use the knowledge he had gained and go on.

He slept; he dreamt. Bernius walked to him, carrying something, then handed it to him, giving Appius a beseeching look.

Bernius then turned and walked away. Appius looked down; he held a child; it was Sergius.

Appius suddenly awoke; it was the middle of the night. He was lying on his side amongst the three stones and the toppled wine jug. The dream was still vivid. He was chilled. With great effort he stood up and walked to the saddlebags, extracted a blanket, then returned to the stones and once again sat with his back against a stone. He gazed at the location where the aqueduct bridge would be built, evident even in the dark.

Bernius. What would *he* do? Was the dream meaningful? Like many dreams, it was a mixture of thoughts, of concepts, of meanings, not necessarily of any substance or importance. Yet, he could not dismiss the intensity, could not dismiss Bernius in the dream any more than he could or would dismiss him in real life. What would Bernius do?

Would Bernius abandon Antonia and Sergius, kill Marcus, and flee? Appius tried to create that imagery in his mind, but it did not work. He shook his head causing his temples to throb, a legacy of wine consumed. No, that would not be Bernius. Bernius would not give up the project, kill recklessly, abandon Antonia and... Sergius. He pictured the recent image of Sergius reaching up for him, shaking his fists, screeching to be in the arms of his father. He had hit Antonia. He lowered his head and wept.

He awoke again, his neck and back aching from resting his head on his knees. The first light of morning was showing, reflected on the rippled surface of the river in the distance. What must he do? He now abhorred the idea of abandoning and killing and running. Bernius would be disgusted with him. He considered each of the turmoils in his life. Was it possible—probable—that Antonia was right—he could not father children? He dismissed the thought. But, if that were so, what *should* Antonia have done? If she had not willed Marcus... they would not have Sergius. Would it have been better if she had not? Of course she could not have asked Appius for permission. Absurd. No!

He could not give them up. He would raise Sergius as his own. Marcus would never again be mentioned, and they would happily raise the child of Bernius. They would go on.

Could he dismiss the thought of Marcus and Antonia... he shook his head. *It will be my burden, perhaps just punishment for hitting Antonia.* That thought seemed to help.

511

And, what about the project? Bernius would be patient. Bernius would find a way to show the centurion better ways. Bernius would work slowly and deliberately, if he must, to create reason from chaos and bluster. Could Appius dismiss the asinine directions and statements from Flavius, not yielding to personal attacks and threats to his family? It would not be easy. He must have his own plan, his own strategy and guidelines. Perhaps, when... if... the project was one day completed, his influence would have made a difference. That might be his satisfaction—not what he had imagined, but he would have to think otherwise.

He stood and stretched, now feeling warmth from the rising sun, walked to the horse, and saddled him. Astride the horse, he rode back to the three rocks, looked down and said, "Thank you, Bernius."

Appius rode slowly at first, going over his thoughts. Then, he nudged the horse to greater speed, galloping across the river bridge finally settling into a fast trot. He thought he now had the conviction of direction. He would work it all out. But, a thought struck him. He grimaced at the implication—would Antonia forgive him?

CHAPTER 49

Appius fretted as he rode back to Nemausus. Why had he hit Antonia? Would it ever be the same between them, again? No. Given the recent events, it could not. The question was—would they be able to trust each other and have a loving relationship? This episode would always be with them; it could never be struck, never be whisked from memory. Would he even have the opportunity to try to rationalize or defend or justify his outrage? Antonia may not have him, and he would have to watch Sergius grow up from afar. He supposed he could find another woman; yes, that was possible. He might even be happy with someone else. But, the thought of being without Antonia, watching her walk to the market, leading the toddling Sergius by the hand, sank him to an emotional low. It sapped his energy, nearly disabling him. *What would she do?* He felt dread; she would turn him away.

Antonia heard him unlatch the gate. She stood in the doorway, dried tears on her cheeks, hair not combed, red welt showing where the blow had struck her face. Why was he here? Would he tell her to leave, to go live with her sisters, to be a woman trying to get along without the support of a man? Had he killed Marcus and was returning to inform her? If he had done that, there was no hope for them. He would either be imprisoned or on the run. She braced herself for the next onslaught.

Appius walked toward the door, his face expressionless, until he stood before her and gazed into her eyes. He could not detect her attitude or resolution. Knowing Antonia, she may have already determined that she would have a life without him, already considered how she would be able to survive and punish him for his attack, keeping Sergius from him, treating him like a leper, sneering at him when he was in her sight. But, he had to try. He took a deep breath. "Will you forgive me?" he asked.

Antonia did not respond for a few moments, closing her eyes. *Oh, yes, I can forgive him. I only hope he has not done something rash, something that neither of us cannot undo.* Antonia held out her arms.

Appius walked slowly to her and encircled her with his arms, noting that she was sobbing. Appius wept too. They would heal this injury—get beyond the hurt. He could sense that Antonia would work to the same end. "Let us go inside," he said.

Appius, having a general sense of the work that he must accomplish, continued drafting provisions for upcoming contracts. He did not have experience or knowledge of contracts involving masonry construction. So, as Bernius had done, prior to the bidding the quarry work, Appius talked to masonry contractors to get help in the contract wording and requirements. The contractors were willing to do so in order *not* to end up with a poorly written contract, one on which less capable contractors might make errors in the bid process and inadvertently end up with the work. However, the contractors stated they would *not* bid if it was true and the situation persisted that the Empire would not provide funds.

Within the next two weeks, the contractor who had been the first to start excavation, Publius Acilius, appeared in the office. He looked stern as he entered the building, observing the designers at their work as he stood in the entrance. Then, spotting Appius, he approached and stood before him.

Appius watched Publius approach, anticipating the intent of the visit. "Hello, Publius Acilius. What brings you here?" He knew better than to ask how things were going.

"I came to tell you that if we do not receive payments due us in a week's time, we will stop work. We cannot continue." He shook with tension.

Appius nodded. "I understand your situation and understand why you must do so. I will tell the centurion... in fact, you may tell him yourself if you like."

Publius Acilius bared his teeth. "I *will* do so. Then, it is correct—he commands and arranges for payment?"

"Yes."

"Then let us talk to this man." He pointed toward the door.

Appius stood, walked past Publius, out the door and toward the building the centurion and his aides occupied.

As they entered the military building, Flavius was walking about. Appius wondered how he spent his time. It was certainly not in studying the needs and complexities of the project.

Flavius watched them approach, arms across his chest. "What is this?"

"Publius Acilius is the excavation contractor on the segment from the Alzon—east. He would like to talk to you." Appius managed a neutral expression although he was thinking that Flavius would now hear a complaint resulting from a dire situation that he, the centurion, had caused.

Flavius tilted his head to the side. "Speak."

"I have told Appius Petronius that if we have not received payment within a week, we will cease work. I cannot make any further payments to those I owe, and I cannot keep accumulating debts." He punctuated his remark with a downward jerk of his head.

"You will stop work in a week?"

"Yes."

"Good. That is rather fortunate as the slaves will be arriving about that time. They can take over your work, and we will lose little time, not to mention that we will save money by not having to pay your inflated prices."

Publius was stunned into silence for several moments, then with stumbling words, "But they do not have the skills. We have a contract. You cannot...."

Flavius smiled. "My men have been watching the operations of all the excavation contractors for some time. We have observed your skilled crews at work and can instruct and utilize similar techniques. We will probably improve performance, as we will be able to extract longer hours and coax more effort. Yes, I would say that your quitting the contract is our good fortune."

Publius looked at Appius noting his eyes were closed. He then looked back at Flavius—still smiling. He slowly turned and walked from the building. Appius could not look at Flavius, feeling helpless in the face of this absurdity and not wanting to *see* the gloat matching that which he *heard* in Flavius's voice. He followed Publius out the door.

They walked in silence back to Appius's office. Upon reaching the building, Publius Acilius said, "There is nothing to be gained by me in continuing to work my men. I will only accumulate more debt. I will cease work immediately." He looked at Appius who only nodded. He then strode briskly to his horse, angrily leapt up, and rode off at a gallop.

Appius shook his head in disgust. *The project deteriorates more with each day.*

In two days, word from the work sites confirmed that Publius Acilius had, indeed, stopped his work. However, it was also understood that the other underground excavation contractors had also quit working their contracts, as had the tunnel shaft excavator. The clearing and quarry contractors continued their work because they had been receiving payments via funds from the *Corporata*.

Appius did not know how Flavius viewed these circumstances, and he did not ask. He anticipated that, if asked, he would hear Flavius reply that all of this was more good fortune. He did take a ride to observe the status of the stalled work. Of course, not only had the men disappeared but so had the tools—the hammers, wedges, pry bars, shovels, carts, ropes, sheaves, buckets, and saws. Appius wondered if Flavius would suppose that the replacement slaves could work with their bare hands.

Appius had sent word to Flavius that he was making the trip, but Flavius had chosen not to accompany him. Of course, Appius recorded what he observed in precise detail, in his log, as was his practice. Flavius did not require a report.

It was three more weeks before the slaves arrived. Appius hoped that the delay caused Flavius to squirm somewhat. He fantasized Flavius reporting to General Crassius, making excuses for lack of progress, but painting a bright picture of slaves toiling at no pay under warm skies. Understandably, Appius heard no feedback that such an encounter had actually occurred.

The arriving slaves, accompanied by their military overseers, were encamped at the existing Vardo bridge. Appius rode to the site, curious as to what he would see. He observed several groups, each of distinct racial characteristics, grouped because it was easier to control men who understood a common language. He was able to learn by talking to random soldiers he encountered that the captives were from the lands of Thrace, Judaea, and Ethiopia.

Flavius had, of course, ridden to greet them also. Appius spotted him conferring with the military overseers. The slaves were fed, watered, and sheltered for several days before they were walked to the work sites, again distributed more or less in accord with their common characteristics. Appius, curious as to how the military would transition the captives to useful work, remained in the field, camping and eating with Marius and Pentius.

On the fourth day, Appius observed initial activity of the slaves on two of the excavation sites. That night after dinner around the fire, he told Marius and Pentius what he had seen. "I wondered if the military had thought about tools and provisions." He shook his head. "As to provisions, it seems that the military are accustomed to looting the countryside. They did a fine job of that, angering and frightening local farmers and marketeers. I talked to several of each, confounded that their livelihoods had been stripped and obliterated."

Marius spoke. "I suppose the plundering will make it more difficult for us. Perhaps we should stock up to avoid going hungry ourselves. The slaves may end up better fed than we."

"Ayyy, I do not know what to tell you, Marius. I cannot imagine how the situation will evolve." Appius fed more wood into the fire as he spoke.

Pentius asked, "How was the work started? Are the workers able to make progress?"

"It is pitiful," Appius shook his head. "It was apparent that the military thought the contractors would leave tools and equipment behind. They were baffled when they discovered that there were no means beyond the use of human hands. The only work they could accomplish was to have the men roll rocks away from the work face and find downed tree limbs to use as pry bars. As I said—pitiful."

"I suppose the military are now also looting the farms of work implements in addition to taking the crops. Soon the farmers will have nothing. They might as well join the slaves. At least they will be fed." Marius managed a rueful smile.

Appius said, "I am sure you are right. I expect I will see some tools tomorrow. I only wish I could needle the centurion for failing to think about this. Perhaps, someday, if I am patient."

Marius shook his head. "I would not rely on that. It is similar to having to accept that Titus and Quantus can roam free after having had Bernius killed. You end up enduring that which gnaws at your gut. Justice only happens in stories."

Appius lowered his head and nodded.

Appius stayed for several more days, curious to see if order and reasonable work progress would result. The slaves had only been recently captured and were not accustomed to hard physical labor, but progress suffered more from lack of experienced supervision. At first there were too many men assigned to carry the loosened earth and rocks away—then, after an adjustment, not enough. Supervision did not allow those clearing tree roots to advance far enough ahead of those loosening the earth; they stumbled over each other in close proximity. Appius shook his head, but he knew that the operation would become more efficient. It was difficult for him to accept that the project would once again bump along and perhaps proceed more quickly as the slaves became hardened to the work and the supervisors extracted gritty effort, only limited by the amount of daylight.

At present, there were too many men working the underground excavation. Flavius would soon be in a hurry to spread the work, using additional labor to begin digging the next levels. What would be the natural outcome of proceeding thus? It was time for Appius to modify the schedule to reflect current conditions. However, given the fluid and irrational circumstances, it would be difficult to chart expected outcomes.

As he rode slowly back to Nemausus, Appius shook his head to help clear his mind. The excavation work would not suffer much more than the three-week hiatus. However, if the masonry contractors were wary of nonpayment, the project would have difficulty in attracting additional qualified bidders. If no contractor would bid on performing the underground and aboveground masonry work or on the production of cement and stones, that work would not start. But, by the original schedule, except for the Vardo bridge construction, those activities were not intended to start for over a year. What would happen? He must work with the schedule to see what they might encounter.

The centurion insisted they now bid the masonry construction and cement production contracts. The masonry work on the excavated sections required four separate contracts, matching the segments of excavation. A single contract was let to build the *elevated* structures—mainly before and after the bridge crossing the Vardo and a separate contract would be let for the building of the great bridge itself. All of the bids were due at the same time on the same day.

There were few bidders present at the bid openings and only a few bids received for all the contracts. The centurion scowled when it became apparent to him that the turnout was dismal. "You must have been unclear in your bid notices," he thundered at Appius.

"You read the bid notices, Flavius—all of them. Did you think they were unclear?" Appius tried to keep sarcasm out of his voice.

Flavius did not reply. "Let us open the bids," he said to the small group.

Appius broke the seal on each of the bids. There were separate bids on several of the underground segments and one on the cement production. However, no bids were received on the elevated structures or for the Vardo bridge. Appius said, to no one in particular, "It does not look like we have coverage, and in each of the bids the contractor requires the Empire to pay an amount for each month in advance."

Flavius blinked. Could he have thought that he would receive bids, regardless of the fact that he had not paid the existing excavation contractors? With hands on hips, he roared, "What is this? Why have I not received an adequate bidding response—and, the bids received require payment aforehand?" He stared at the bidders. "This is not acceptable."

One of the contractors addressed Flavius. "How could you expect bidders to work for the Empire and suffer as have the excavation contractors? We are not stupid. You do not pay the contractors, driving them to quit work then you bring in slaves to take over their contracts. Do you think us mad? The only way I offered to take this risk is if the Empire paid for the work in advance."

Appius could not help but enjoy the centurion's humiliation. "What will you do, Flavius? I must also mention to you that the bids are highly priced compared to our estimates. The contractors must have anticipated foul treatment at the hands of the Empire." Appius mused that he was being subtle by not saying "... foul treatment in your hands."

Flavius ignored him but addressed the group. "We will take the bids under advisement, but I do not expect we will award contracts under these conditions. We may well build the entire aqueduct with slaves. They do *not* require to be paid in advance." He turned and strode from the gathering.

Appius nodded to the contractors, shook his head then departed also. He wondered what Flavius would do. The masonry work required higher levels of skill than did the excavation, a situation where the expertise and experience of the contractors was clearly needed. Could he build the great bridge with slaves? Perhaps there were military men, who could be acquired, having such background. Appius would adhere to his commitment not to cause problems—he would not needle the centurion—but it would be interesting to see what would happen. In the meantime, there would be less pressure to excavate to full depth as there were no masonry contractors waiting to get started—a reprieve, for now. How would he handle this circumstance on his schedule? Would Flavius now try to get funding from the Empire in earnest? Was there a problem in getting funding? Claudius had moved to Rome, having been usurped in his own region by General Crassius, therefore Appius did not have access to imperial information that might have otherwise been available.

Flavius muddled. He had deliberately not paid the excavation contractors, forcing them to quit, thus providing the excuse to bring the slaves. Now he had to decide whether to bring in more slaves or actually procure funding from Rome to pay contractors. If he were to seek funding from the Empire, he would request such through General Crassius. In fact, Crassius had recently sent a message asking if Flavius would do so. Flavius had not responded because he sensed that he had more control over slaves supervised by military than having to acknowledge contract requirements when dealing with contractors. He could squeeze the *Corporata* further, but there was a limit. At some time, he would need more, but he did not know how to frame his request.

Appius regularly visited the sites. The quarry contractor continued to efficiently produce stones suitable for the bridge construction. The yard where the stones were being aged was impressive as one looked down from the quarry face—a sea of rectangular stones neatly patterned in the order required to suit their imminent precision sculpturing and subsequent delivery to the work site. In four months, cutting of the stones could begin. Appius noted from his schedule that work on the bridge foundations should be starting soon in order to be ready to accept those first blocks of stone as they were produced. He wondered if Flavius was aware that this important activity could not start soon because they did not have a contract or even a successful bid for the work. Should he mention this to Flavius? Yes, he should.

The excavation by slaves was progressing. The military had acquired more tools, other than those 'obtained' from the local farmers. Now, lack of equipment did not slow the work. The slaves had become accustomed to hard labor and, with the numbers available, excavation to the assumed full-depth, in stair-step stages, had started. Each time Appius looked at the excavation to full depth he involuntarily shuddered, knowing that the chance of error increased as more was completed. The problem would not be severe if ultimately they had to excavate deeper. However, if they excavated too deep now, they would have to refill the trench to establish the aqueduct structure at the required elevation. More serious troubles would occur if the masonry structure were started. A significant error would require the work to be dismantled. He was thankful that those contracts were at an impasse.

The military had organized means of provisioning for the slaves. From the farmers, stipulated portions of crops were required to be 'donated' to the project, an additional tax due the Empire as a *quid pro quo* for receiving benefit of the great project. The farmers noted dryly that there were no plans to provide water to *them* from the source. Of course, the farmers found ways to keep the 'observed' quantities of their produce and livestock at a minimum and were better at this than were the 'observing' skills of the military. However, the farmers had been paid for supplying worker provisions prior to the military takeover. They were, naturally, seething over this change in circumstance, not appreciating that they should be grateful to contribute to the 'glory of the Empire.'

Appius was aware of this; he talked to the locals regularly—except for those from Ucetia, of course. The Ucetians had become reclusive—fearful of the military. Other locals, reluctant to talk to Appius at first, eventually understood that supervision of the project had been ripped from him. They were happy to share misery with him.

Appius questioned Flavius to see if he was aware that preparation of the bridge foundations should be starting soon. Appius, judging from the facial expressions of Flavius when he asked, was certain that consideration of the impending requirement had not occurred to him.

Nevertheless, Flavius responded. "I have thought of a suitable means to contract the Vardo bridge work. I will require the *Corporata* to make additional payments to fund the work on the great bridge."

Appius wondered—*why not funding by the Empire? What is the problem? The Empire does not have to pay much to support the slaves. Has Flavius requested payment and been denied?* "You are going to request *Corporata* payment beyond the monthly 5000 sestertii?"

"Yes. Initially, the amount will not be substantial." Flavius shrugged.

"Do you intend that the *Empire* will make funds available for the project—at some time?"

"Yes."

Appius shook his head but did not speak his thoughts. He instead pried for more details. "Then you will re-bid the contract for the bridge construction."

"Yes." Flavius nodded. "I will advise the contractors that payments will be made by the *Corporata*, and good faith will be shown by paying mobilization costs in advance."

It seemed to Appius—*Flavius must have given thought to this. He cannot be making this up as we go along.* Appius thought to ask another question. "On prior contracts, it was agreed that the Empire was ultimately responsible for the contract. Claudius signed for the Empire. What arrangement is in place now?"

"I will sign for the Empire." Flavius expanded his chest appropriately.

"When Claudius signed for the Empire, it was presumed that he could make Empire funds available. Are you assuming that capability?" Appius tried to maintain a look that did not indicate a taunt.

Flavius was slow to respond. "Enough of your questions. I am in charge of this project. You are asking about provisions that do not concern you. Do you have anything of importance to discuss?"

"Only the question about timing of the new bid for the building of the bridge."

the *Aedifex*: Building the Pont du Gard

"Immediately. You are to draft a revised invitation to bid, stating the funding provisions I have mentioned, then take the bids immediately."

"I will have you read the funding provisions to make sure they are as you intend."

"Yes," and with a dismissive wave, added, "We are done."

Appius returned to his home to find that Antonia was not there. He was momentarily concerned. Although Antonia often went about with Sergius to the market, to visit her sisters, or on other tasks that required her to be out, she was not usually away at the time he arrived home. *What could it be? Perhaps...*

He was right. In a few hours Antonia came through the door, Sergius gurgling at her hip. "It has happened. Juliena has given birth to a boy—our new son." She looked down to Sergius, somewhat in apology, somewhat in glee.

Appius was silent, then smiled. "When can I see young Bernius—that is what we will call him—yes?"

"Let us do that tomorrow morning. We will give them both time to rest—and, yes, I think we should call him Bernius Caelius and perhaps Bernius Caelius Filius—son of...."

"That will be it, then." Appius took Sergius who was totally oblivious to have recently acquired a brother. For now, he was the most important being in his father's life. Appius thought, *I wonder how it will be, raising someone else's son...* well.

Antonia, now gesturing with both hands, said, "We shall have a cup of wine to celebrate the return of Bernius." She poured the cups and fitted one to Appius's free hand. "I could not help but think when I looked at the infant that he had the soul of our lost friend and mentor. I will have a hard time thinking otherwise."

"I shall think that, too." He raised his cup and took a sip.

Sergius looked on, interested in the liquid that Appius seemed to enjoy.

"How long before young Bernius joins our household?"

"Juliena will nurse him for several months and then we will have him."

"Will it be hard for Juliena to give up the baby?"

"Of course, and not just because of the natural attraction of the mother for the baby. She also is aware that she will be giving up the soul of Bernius. Yes, this will be difficult for her, but she knows it is for the best."

Appius nodded and smiled at Sergius, now grabbing at his father's nose.

Flavius stood before the *Corporata*. He did not now command Appius to attend the monthly meetings, thinking it best to provide evasive answers—or none at all—if questions surfaced beyond his understanding. It was better than trying to counter difficulties that Appius made obvious, even though Appius might do this subtly.

Appius would have had a difficult time at the meetings. It was best that he did not attend. Titus attended and walked free, presumably untouchable for his part in the death of Bernius— infuriating and frustrating. And, Marcus would be there in presumed innocence. Although Appius was committed to not give any impression that he knew Marcus had fathered Sergius, it would be difficult to interact without showing anguish and dislike.

Flavius presented the accounting for the month's progress, noting that for the quarry and clearing contracts and for payment of the enhanced military forces, the 5000 sestertii amount was exceeded. He straightened as he announced, "I will expect the *Corporata* to pay the additional amount, but that is not all. Although we are extracting provisions for the slaves from local farmers and merchants, there remain costs that must be paid and should be considered as part of the military oversight. The *Corporata* will pay those costs. Also, we will bid... re-bid... the construction of the Vardo bridge. The *Corporata* will be assessed an additional amount for that contractor's work, and we will pay that contractor in advance."

Titus blurted, "What?" Titus, although not as vehement as in the past due to his presumed crafting of the murder of Bernius, nevertheless enjoyed insulation from severe criticism at the hands of the *Corporata*. It was obvious that he had the favor of those in Rome as he was able to live as if there were no consequence to his actions.

Flavius, expecting a reaction, shrugged his shoulders. "You have a question?"

Titus looked to the other members, hoping that someone else would take on the burden.

Nemus did. "Flavius Darius, what has happened to our agreement? Our understanding with Claudius, Proconsul of the

Narbonensis Region, was that we would pay no more than 5000 sestertii each month."

Flavius feigned indifference. "As you say, that agreement was with Claudius. He is no longer in the region but in Rome, *not* attending to matters that are about—including this project. I am in charge of this project and have advised you that I will extract the additional payments."

Marcus asked, "Will you seek no payment from the Empire?"

"Oh, yes. It is clear that at some payment amount, the *Corporata* would not be able to fund in total. But, for now, I think my requirement is reasonable."

"Is it reasonable that you will double our contribution, leaving us little for our waterworks effort?" Marcus shook his head. He looked at Titus. "Titus, with your influence in Rome, perhaps you can arrange payments from the Empire." It was clear that the request suggested a taunt.

Titus sat with his arms crossed, his face flushed as he slumped on his stool. He said nothing, only shaking his head.

"This is an outrage," Nemus said, "You cannot tax us out of existence." He said this, although all knew he was powerless to enforce his statement.

Flavius looked at each of the *Corporata* then said, "In a few days we will re-bid the bridge construction. I will assess an amount from the *Corporata now* to be sure we are able to make the advance payment. Are there any further items or provisions that we must discuss?"

No one responded.

"Then we are done." He walked from the room.

After the meeting, Flavius, more to demonstrate that he was in charge rather than as a courtesy, told Appius of the arrangement with the *Corporata*. Appius had drafted the second bidding notice for the Vardo bridge and was submitting it for Flavius's approval. Flavius, after reading the notice, said, "Yes, let us get on with the bidding."

Appius walked back to his office, thinking: *The Corporata is in great difficulty with payments. Bernius's killers walk around freely. We have abandoned the rightful contracts for excavation and replaced the contractors with slaves—looting the countryside and the farmers in order to feed them. We are proceeding with the excavation as if we knew the proper depths. The supervisor is a power-hungry lunatic.*

He walked into his office. The designers were excited about some matter, talking actively amongst themselves. They turned to Appius with expectant looks on their faces. "Have you heard?" Vitruvius asked.

"Heard what? I have been in the office of the centurion."

"They do not know, yet?" Gaius expressed his amazement.

Appius shrugged. "They said nothing. What are you talking about?"

The designers looked at each other, then Numerius blurted. "I have just returned from the town center. A messenger has just arrived bringing news that Caligua has been assassinated."

"What?"

"Yes, and as we understand, by his guards and at the urging of his own sisters."

CHAPTER 50

Claudius Caesar Augustus Germanicus (Claudius) had been born sickly and walked with a limp. His mother was known to utter statements in which Claudius was the object of ridicule. His poor physical condition probably allowed him to live through the blood purges under Tiberius and his successor, the mad Caligua. Claudius's family denied him public office; however, Caligua, for expedient reasons, appointed Claudius co-consul for one year at the time Caligua became *Imperator*. It became apparent that Caligua was mad, so Agrippina and Livilla, Caligua's sisters, plotted to murder him but failed and were exiled. However, a subsequent assassination attempt by his guards succeeded. The Praetorian Guard made Claudius consul because he was the last male member of the royal family, the Claudians.

Appius was stunned. What would happen with Claudius as *Imperator* and without the influence of Caligua? One could only hope for significant change.

Antonia had similar thoughts as she discussed the situation with Appius. "What will happen, Appius?"

"I can be hopeful that much will be changed." Appius looked at Antonia. A tight-lipped smile expressed the hope he stated. "Tell me what you think might change."

Antonia tilted her head, as if to slide all her thoughts to one side so she could corral them. "First, I think that Titus and Quantus should be very concerned that they might be tried for the murder of Bernius. And, if that is a possibility, then your 'friend,' the centurion, is in trouble, along with his men, for executing the villagers."

"All that is possible and I hope will become reality. Also, because Claudius was insistent on and was responsible for initiating the aqueduct project, I would expect him to retrieve control from General Crassius and end this inept management by pompous rule. The image of my fantasy would be to see the centurion and his staff ride away from Nemausus."

"In chains, walking away, would be an even better image."

"Truly, and I have thought of that."

Antonia tilted her head back—she was able to ponder best in that stance. "I wonder if Flavius is concerned. If he is not, he should be."

Appius smiled. "I will be entertained in the near future by observing his manner and whether he tempers his actions with a similar thought in mind."

"Oh... and Appius," Antonia asked this as if it were mere curiosity, not a matter of immense importance to Appius, "who do you think will then manage the project?"

Appius looked at Antonia. "I cannot second-guess Claudius, but I know that you know—I thirst to be the one."

Antonia smiled. "I wish that it would be so."

Appius found several reasons to appear in the presence of Flavius. One such included revision of the contract terms for the re-bid of the Vardo bridge, a task he was now prolonging, hoping that it would not have to be bid under the terms of Flavius. He did not get to behold the image of a slouching cur, as he had hoped, but Flavius gave him a long look upon their first encounter after Claudius had replaced Caligua. Flavius then averted his eyes. Appius read *distress* behind the deliberately rigid stare, and possible acknowledgement that the centurion was considering that he might have been too smug in his oppression.

Appius was torn, not knowing how to proceed. *If I now resist the orders of the centurion, Flavius can still punish me. He remains in charge of the military. Yet, it must only be a matter of time. Claudius will surely remedy this insanity. I will keep my head, not antagonize the centurion but do what I can to slow the execution of those practices that are of doubtful use for the project.*

But, what will happen to Flavius? What is he thinking? Flavius must also know that Claudius will act to regain control of the region and the project, not allowing him to continue in his present circumstance, not to mention the worry that he may now be required to account for the atrocity at Ucetia. What would Flavius be thinking he could do to protect himself? It would be good to let this question simmer in his mind, for a while. He would observe Flavius, thinking that what he saw might provide answers.

In the meantime, others were also concerned about the demise of Caligua—those who had enjoyed his favor and were protected from possible legal processes involving their actions.

Titus and Quantus Tarius met in the overly ornate and pretentious atrium of Titus's home.

Titus spoke, his eyebrows scrunched in consternation. "I worry that we will now have to answer questions by the authorities. They have been reluctant to challenge us so far in fear of a heavy hand from Rome."

"Have you encountered any threats or even implications?" Quantus took a sip of wine.

"Not directly." Titus shook his head. "However, the *Corporata* treat me like a leper. They talk amongst themselves. I do not know if they will take action, but it is clear they detest having to deal with me. Their manner was so cold I did not go to the last meeting. But, I detect that they expect a change will occur, and they will somehow have me removed."

"Do you think they will make a complaint to the court?"

"I think their action would be more concerned with removing me from the *Aqua Corporata*. I would be more concerned with Appius, using what influence he might to avenge the killing of his friend."

"So, we are more threatened by Appius."

"I would think so."

"Perhaps we can think of a way to reduce that possibility."

Titus did not reply but responded with a slight nod.

Appius strained to continue compliance with orders from the centurion. *Nearly a month has passed since Claudius became Imperator, and nothing has changed. Flavius, wary at first, is now acting as if he will continue—that nothing will happen. I can tell from his manner that he has regained his confidence. What if Claudius is too concerned with other matters to intercede? It cannot be. What can I do?*

Appius shook his head as he spoke to Antonia. "Flavius still orders me about, and Titus and Quantus walk the streets unscathed. Perhaps I placed too much hope in the change of leaders."

"Yes, I must admit that I had hoped for a dawn of reason, that a messenger from Rome would appear with notification of abrupt replacements and direction. We have heard nothing—not even rumors." Antonia rose from her stool, walking restlessly around the room. "We still live under the fear of Flavius, and I am never without fear that I will see the military in our courtyard again."

"I wish I could do something—talk to Claudius."

"Perhaps you *should* talk to Claudius."

"You mean... go to Rome?"

"Claudius would see you."

Appius reflected for a moment. "I think so. The project was important to him, and he must be outraged at General Crassius for usurping his control of the region."

"It would seem so, but why has nothing happened?"

"It can only be that he is busy with other matters. You may be right, Antonia. We might get Claudius to act now if I can get him to spend a few moments to consider what he must... or might... do."

"Then you will go?"

He nodded. "I will go. I think I should get word to him that I am coming, so I will not have to convince those that protect him that I have valuable reason to see him. But, I do not know how to do this."

"It would be best if no person in Nemausus knew you were going. But, you will be away; you will not be at your office. What will explain your absence? They will ask me."

Appius hesitated but then nodded, "I agree. There are several parties that do not want Claudius to make changes. I must think of a way."

"One more thing, Appius."

"Yes."

"It is time for us to bring the infant Bernius into our home. Juliena said, and I agreed, that the longer he is with her, the more difficult it will be."

"Let us not do that until I have returned from Rome."

"What are you thinking?"

Appius met with Nemus at night because he did not want others to speculate as to his intent.

Nemus, somewhat wary of a visit by Appius, asked, "Appius Petronius, what is it that prompts you to talk to me?" Candles, dimly lighting the atrium, projected flickering images of sculptures, furniture, Appius, and Nemus onto the walls.

"It seems to me that you—the *Corporata*—are suffering at the hand of Flavius and from the past regime of Caligua. I—and perhaps, you—expected that we would have seen a change by now, that Claudius would, once again, rule our region with a firm hand. Yet, nothing has happened. Nothing has changed. I believe we should do something to get the attention of Claudius amongst all those matters to which he must now attend."

"Go on—I am listening. I am thinking that you have a suggestion."

"I do. I intend to travel to Rome—to talk to Claudius. I believe that if I can speak to him for only a short time, prompting action from him that will end speculation and dealing with the nonsense that Flavius slathers upon the project. He can stop the thoughtless plunder of the countryside and curtail the severe depletion of your coffers. I intend to propose to Claudius that General Crassius be replaced, Flavius and his men be removed, and—of this, I wanted your assent—that the payment provisions return to that which you—the *Corporata* and he—agreed. He will surely ask me if I have talked to you about this, and I want to be able to tell him that I had. What say you?"

"Of course, we—I can speak for the *Corporata*—would support your proposal. Who would you intend to manage the project—to replace Flavius?"

Appius nodded, thinking that Nemus suspected what he would propose. "Regarding Crassius, I may not have to suggest his removal; Claudius may already have reconciled that thought. The region still needs a military, but Claudius would surely station a general that agrees with him. I will propose to Claudius that *I* run the project." Appius waited for Nemus to respond, certain that he heard the words echo in the atrium. He braced for a reaction.

"You are young and inexperienced for such a responsibility."

Appius cringed. *Will Nemus not support me in this?*

Nemus continued. "Yet, you were well schooled by Bernius. You have continued with crafting the contracts and managing the contractors—ably—in spite of the difficult conditions applied by Flavius. You, with guidance from Bernius, devised a well-conceived plan for the entire project. I have always appreciated your creative activity." He looked up from his musing to look at Appius. "I am talking aloud as I think this through." He shook his head. "You, as the leader, would be remarkably better to work with than Flavius. Yes, I will support you as the one to administer the project."

Appius sighed with relief. *That obstacle passed, now I must....* "I thank you for your confidence. Now, I ask that you aid me in my quest. Will you send a message to Claudius advising that I will soon be in Rome to talk to him, that you have discussed the project and regional situation with me and that you are in agreement with my proposal?"

Nemus was silent. "I must first advise the *Corporata*. I think problems may result from doing so."

"Titus?"

"Yes. We know that Titus is understandably frightened that the new regime may prosecute him for what appears to be *his* foul deed. He clearly understands he no longer has the protection of those that surrounded Caligua. I do not know what he will do."

Appius stared at Nemus. "I also intend to suggest to Claudius that Titus and Quantus be tried for the crime and that Flavius and the decanus, and probably General Crassius, account for their actions at Ucetia."

"If Titus were found guilty, it would save the *Corporata* the painful exercise of removing him from our organization. I have not thought through the other consequences."

"What will you do?"

"I may meet with the members, individually—but not with Titus. He has not attended our last two meetings, so I have some justification, flimsy though it might be. This I will do, unless I change my mind. After meeting with them, I will send a message. I will get word to you."

"Thank you, Nemus. I rely on your good judgment."

"Be wary, Appius. You will ride alone?"

"Yes. I will be traveling the Via Dometia then Via Aurelia. I should have companions coming and going on the highway."

"Of course, nevertheless.... "

Appius nodded, stood, and departed.

The shadows continued to flicker on the walls of the atrium, reminding Nemus, as he remained sitting, that life was as dependent on circumstance as the movement of the shadows depend on the vagaries of the candle flame that projected them.

Appius received a message from Nemus informing him that he had talked to the *Corporata*, and he had assent to that which Appius had proposed; a message would be sent to Claudius.

the *Aedifex*: Building the Pont du Gard

It was time for Appius to make his journey. He advised Flavius that he would be absent for a time, visiting an ailing father in the vicinity of Lugdunum.

As a precaution, Antonia and Sergius would stay with Juliena for the time—no telling who might want to use them to enforce a threat. Their stay would also enable a transition to wean young Bernius from his birth mother.

Titus spoke to Quantus. "I have heard through discreet sources—from the *Corporata*—that Appius Petronius travels to Rome for an audience with Claudius. It is significant that Nemus did not talk to me, but to all the others."

"That is indeed troubling. What will Appius discuss with Claudius?"

"Appius is concerned with the project and will discuss future arrangements. But, Appius will advise Claudius that he will instigate proceedings against us for the death of Bernius."

"Hah, they have no proof."

"It is unlikely that the military will testify that Servius Arrius, under torture, admitted he killed Bernius. However, Appius has stated that he has proof that such occurred."

"What proof could he have? He was not there. Of that, we are assured. Perhaps he is bluffing."

"Perhaps he is, but he intends to punish us, and he says he has proof of our deed. Need I say more?"

Quantus said nothing for a few moments, then, "You need *not* say more. We must do something, but will *we* be the first to be suspected? As we have discovered, hiring others to perform our... task... is of doubtful discretion."

"Yes. That is true. But, I have been thinking; we have an ally, as difficult as they might be... or have been. The military has an interest to maintain that Bernius's death did not occur other than at the hands of the Ucetians. They are triple damned if it is exposed that the Ucetians did not do the deed and that they, the military, discovered this from the killer, did not reveal the fact and disposed of the man—those incriminations on top of slaying the Ucetians without a trial."

"So, the military have an interest in preventing our trial. What do you suggest?"

"The military do not know that Appius travels to talk to Claudius. I am sure that if they did, they would know what Appius

533

is about. If I were to tell them about the journey, they may act on their own. That *is* a possibility. However, I can increase the chances that they will act if I tell Flavius we will say that the military was complicit in the killing of Bernius—to gain control."

Quantus was thoughtful. "I can see how that idea might be believed. Yet, the current thought does not support that idea. Court opinion would consider *our* statement versus *their* denial."

"The military have created local difficulties. They are not favored, and they have disposed of the only person who could state otherwise, although the man would not have necessarily known if the military was involved." Titus shrugged.

"That is true. But, what is to be believed in court? I do think Flavius will surely see that Appius, talking directly to Claudius, is an extreme threat. We must do something."

"Ayyy—I think you are right. If we do nothing, we will surely suffer consequences."

Quantus asked, "You will talk to Flavius?"

"Yes. Tomorrow."

Appius prepared for his journey. Antonia, leaving with Sergius, timed her transfer to Juliena's house to coincide with Appius's departure. Those who did not know otherwise could assume that Antonia was traveling *with* Appius. Along with the necessities of travel, Appius included a clean, unfrayed tunic. He did not have a toga in which to appear before Claudius. Claudius had seen him in no other than the tunic, but now Claudius was *Imperator*, living in extravagance and civility.

In darkness, in front of Juliena's home, Antonia said goodbye to Appius. "My husband, please do be careful. As we have discussed, there are those who will not favor your visit to Claudius. Even if they do not know, they can speculate as to your intentions."

"Yes, Antonia. I will be wary. And, for you... and Sergius... please do not venture from the house. I know that a month is a long time to be stowed with Juliena's children, but it is only one month out of our lives, and after that we will enjoy the benefits of enduring this difficult time."

"I know and will use that thought to keep from wandering from the house if I get delirious from the surroundings. I know you will not waste a moment to retrieve us once you are back in Nemausus."

"Of that you can be certain." He smiled at Antonia, still holding her, reluctant to depart.

"Until I see your face at the gate, then...." Antonia closed her eyes, gave a final squeeze then let go.

Appius had a plan, somewhat different than what might have been expected. He would travel fast and far the first day to thwart anybody who might set out to harm him. He would ride at night to cover a greater distance than might be presumed. He had to believe that even if his plans had not been directly divulged, someone might be concerned that he was off to other locations... not Lugdunum.

He covered a substantial distance in the dark, a sufficient distance from Nemausus, then rested until daylight. In the saddle the next morning, he maintained a quick pace. Day's end would see him over one hundred miles from Nemausus.

Titus arranged to meet with Flavius the day after he had met with Quantus. They agreed to meet on a walk, away from town, in the direction of the quarry. Flavius's aides followed at a distance.

Flavius turned. "And what is it that you would discuss with me? If you are to plead relief for the *Corporata*, do not bother. We will turn around now."

"No, it is not that. I will speak to a matter of which we are both concerned. Appius goes to Rome, not Lugdunum. Appius will not talk to his father but to Claudius."

Flavius snorted a deep breath. "I was suspicious of his trip. But, what of it? Why should we be concerned?"

"Ha. I am sure you can guess. Appius will talk to Claudius about regaining control of the project, dismissing the military—of that it is certain. But, he will also ensure that Claudius will not interfere with court action involving the death of Bernius and the slaughter of the Ucetians. Do I have to explain why all that is important to you?"

"No, you do not have to explain. But, I would like to know why you are talking to me. Why did you want this meeting?"

Titus walked for several paces, then said, "You have the... resources... at the moment, at least, to keep Appius from his mischief. I... we... do not. I am hoping that you will understand that Appius talking to Claudius is a vile threat to your career and even—your freedom. I am hoping you will do something."

"If we prevent Appius from getting to Rome, Claudius will eventually make a change. It is only a matter of time."

"But, making a change is much less dramatic than a prompt initiation of *court action*—an action that might be subject, over time, to fading of the memory and possibly be forgotten if it is not promoted by Appius, bent on revenge."

Flavius said nothing for a while. Then, he looked down at the beseeching, upturned face of Titus. "Is Appius traveling the Via Dometia and the Via Aurelia? Do you know?"

"It would seem... and... yes, I have heard so."

The centurion stopped, turned and signaled for his aides to approach. When they joined Flavius and Titus, he said, "See if you can find Appius—at home or at his office—or at any location you can detect from talking to those who might know. Apprehend him and bring him to me. If you find that he has started his journey to Rome, assemble three men with horses and ride at great speed to apprehend him. Once you have done so, send word to me. Do not return him to Nemausus. Questions?"

The ranking aide asked, "He will be traveling the Via Dometia and Via Aurelia?"

"As we understand."

"We will proceed with haste." He beckoned the others to follow.

Flavius and Titus now walked toward town. Titus said, "I am comforted to know that you understand that actions unfavorable to me are also a problem for you."

Flavius did not reply.

The centurion's soldiers quickly found that no one was at the home of Appius. Neighbors did not know where he and the family had gone, even after they had endured rough handling. They *did not* know. A team of four soldiers, soon after, quickly rode from town, along the Via Dometia, riding swiftly in the direction of Rome. They questioned travelers along the way, determined to find that a horse-bound traveler of Appius's description had passed by—'not that long ago.' On they pressed, sparing the horses little in their quest. After over a day of riding, they must surely overtake Appius.

the *Aedifex*: Building the Pont du Gard

But, Appius had not traveled the Via Dometia or the Via Aurelia as he had stated to Nemus. Utilizing maps, he had planned a route that would take him to Rome, although along cart paths and secondary roads that were not so direct and efficient as the Via Dometia. After all, '*all* roads lead to Rome,' do they not?

Appius had many thoughts as he rode. *Am I on a fool's mission? Will Claudius even see me? A message from Nemus might or might not get to Claudius, and Claudius might be busy with other matters or not want to deal with a citizen of such low station.* Could he still persist and somehow gain audience? He had to try.

CHAPTER 51

Lisele and I hiked several days in the Pyrenees—the Cirque de Gavarne, the Napoleon Bridge, the Cauterets, and the Pont de Espana. When not hiking the stunning sights, we stayed in a small mountain village, so small it had neither restaurants nor markets. I think the word is quaint. I was in awe of the impressive range of mountains and dramatic scenery, rivaling even the rugged Sierra in California over which I had rambled.

After the Pyrenees expedition, we flew from Nice to Istanbul to start a traipse through vestiges of the ancient world. I was fascinated with Istanbul—the Blue Mosque, the Grand Bazaar, the Hippodrome, and the underground cistern. The trip to Troy, down the Dardanelles to Çanakkale intrigued me also. As we toured Troy, I learned that a German, who had made a fortune in the California gold rush, discovered Troy. Actually, he went looking for and found it. Before, Troy was only mentioned in Homer's Iliad and the Odyssey. Travel sometimes resets your understanding of the world. If you had asked me before, I would have said Troy was in Greece. It seems Turkey is a cornucopia of sites that were prominent in the ancient and biblical world. I am convinced I want to go back for a long look at Turkey.

Pompeii was very impressive—the extent, the sophistication, the restoration. It is substantially more re-conditioned than Troy. Pompeii helped fill in my understanding of Roman living conditions, commercial activity, and government that existed until it was buried by Vesuvius in 79 AD. As I walked the streets, I shook my head, looking up at Vesuvius, awed that the volcano could have buried the whole works in ash.

But, I also ended up fascinated by Ostia Antica, the ancient port city of Rome. You felt like you were walking onto an archeological site that had recently been discovered. Few people were roaming, many of the sites had not been fully uncovered, and you were free to walk over, around, amongst. One of the interesting aspects of the site is that the port city was the home of maritime corporations, a significant component of the city life. There was also an impressive theater, a school of architecture and a water supply system to hold my interest. Claudius also was influential in the building of this city. It was at Ostia Antica when it occurred to me that at each one of the ruins I had visited, all on coastal locations, the sea level had been substantially higher two millennia ago. At Troy and Ostia Antica, they had to move the port to the lower elevation. At Pompeii, you are made aware that the water was *up there* when the city was covered. Now you see that it is *down there*.

Oh, but I haven't mentioned the most significant outcome of the trip—more fascinating than the ancient civilizations, more intriguing than the structures and the glory and beauty of Rome and southern Italy. I have to report that my relationship with Lisele had surged to a fully bloomed romance—not a budding romance but blooming—gloriously. I knew then that I could not go back to the U.S. without her—could not leave her in France. Something would have to be done. I can report that she felt the same way. She must have known. To arrange the trip, as she did, she must have suspected that we would become close. I told you she was brighter than I.

So, I was back in my rented house in Vers. We were not co-habiting... yet. Maybe she had sensitivity remaining with regard to Laurie—she mentioned it once but didn't elaborate. It was okay. It was perhaps good to have space after a very intense four weeks. The space did not change my perspective. Lisele was going to be a permanent part of my life.

As I was going through my mail, three evenings after I got back, reading a few letters from friends and relatives at home, mentally cataloging those I must answer, the telephone rang—the sound of the Harkness Tower Bells gargling. It was Renat. He asked about my trip, with some impatience, I thought, but showed delight that Lisele and I had ratcheted our romance to a more significant notch.

Then he blurted, "Warner, you must come to Nimes."

"Why?"

"Tomorrow they are to remove your stones—you know, the ones at the *Castellum*—the ones that you suspected...."

"Were fronting for a cache."

"Yes."

"How is that happening—I mean why?"

"While you were gone, they used electronic equipment to scan through the stone. They received a signal that indicates a metallic presence. I found out through my friend on the Antiquities

Committee. He told *me* because he knew of my... our... interest. You will be here tomorrow?"

"Yes, Renat, I can be there and I will. Shall I pick you up?"

"Yes, thank you. I would not miss this. It is very exciting, you know."

"I do know. I have to admit, I'm excited yet a bit disgusted, too. I, of course, think I should have had a more direct involvement in this. But, I *am* excited. Yes, I'll be there. I'll pick you up at eight."

I called Lisele. She was happy for me and somewhat excited herself, although not as excited as I would have imagined. She would not be able to go to Nimes the next morning.

In Nimes, I picked up Renat, and we drove to a street near the *Castellum* and found a parking place. As we walked towards the *Castellum*, we spotted a throng of people standing at the fence, on the sidewalk. As much as I regretted it, I would have to stand *outside* the fence.

Inside the fence, a small air compressor was chugging, emitting a blue haze; preparations were being made. A tarp was arranged to catch the cement fragments and dust; a table was arranged to receive and catalog the blocks as removed. Wood framing material, saws, hammers, drills, cold chisels, nitrogen cylinders with attachments were also nearby, at the ready. I assumed they would gently use the air chipping equipment but would revert to hand chipping if there was a possibility of damage to the stones, especially to those with the inscriptions. The wood framing would be used to prop up the stones as the 'cache' stones were being removed. The nitrogen would be used in the event that any removed documents were in immediate need of oxygen deprivation to ensure that they did not deteriorate before the eyes of the examiners.

At the *Castellum*, several people near the table were busy making sketches and photographs. Others were standing, waiting, their presence an honorary bestowal, no doubt. I recognized M. Grambeaux, arms behind his back, looking very officious and important, although not doing anything else but that. Then, I saw... wasn't really prepared to see... Professor Durand. What? Why was he there? If there were one more way to grind my irritation to the nub, it would be his presence. The betrayal was complete. Not only was I being bypassed in this grand maneuver, no notice, no consideration, no acknowledgement, but I was also being further taunted by the presence of the knowledgeable, self-important, Professor Durand, the one who had dismissed me from his office for asking impertinent questions. I was crushed. I identified the two men to Renat. He had already spotted Grambeaux, but he did not know Professor Durand.

Renat looked at me. "It is a sad day for French-American relations, it seems."

I worked my way to the fence to make sure I was... visible. I was certain both Grambeaux and Durand spotted me, taking a while to recollect then turning quickly as if to dismiss me, once again. I was placated somewhat at their discomfort.

A workman started the removal with the small air operated chipper; however, it must not have been going well; they resorted to use of a hammer and small stone chisels. The picture was—one man at work with the hammer and chisel and five men in a semi-circle, in a half crouch, watching him.

It went very slowly. Many of the crowd wandered away. Some returned with coffee and a pastry. We stayed, reluctant to leave, then realized it was going to be a while before anything would... or wouldn't... be discovered. Finally, we resorted to the coffee, pastry, and bathroom-break ritual.

It took a long time to get the first stone removed. The cement groove was about 5 inches deep, and the going was slow with the small chisels. However, once the first was removed, it was easier. The chipping was stopped after a few blocks had been removed, and Grambeaux was selected to shine a flashlight, to have a look about inside the void. Some people are better at this than others—it seems. Grambeaux took a good look but shook his head. Four others looked also, just in case. Each one shook his head as they passed the flashlight on. Grambeaux nodded to the mason who then continued to remove several more stones after which time the flashlight ceremony began anew. This time, Grambeaux aimed the light, looked, jerked his head back, and turned around. He spoke to his colleagues who applauded. He then turned to the awaiting fence sitters and shouted, "We see something." I noticed that he avoided my eyes.

The other four men repeated the process, each one nodding their heads as they confirmed that Grambeaux was not hallucinating. Really, having four backups was just a courtesy. Grambeaux may have been short sighted when it came to dealing with Americans, but he clearly was able to see the something that had rested, we presumed for an age—several ages—behind the masonry.

Renat looked at me and shook his head.

The group continued to watch the sole worker as he carefully removed more stones and propped up those adjacent. Grambeaux took a look, we thought, to determine if there was enough clear space to remove the object. The man with the chisel was not capable of determining this.

Finally, Grambeaux indicated, by pointing, that a support spanning all the removed stones should be fashioned. The multi-talented mason was able to measure and cut the framing, working around the learned assembly as each took their turn shining the flashlight, reaching in, and making valuable assessments. That something significant was at hand was apparent, though. They were excited and impatient at what seemed like slow progress on the part of the craftsman. As he neared the end of the support installation, the mason made taps here and then taps there at wedges, seemingly more to tease those waiting nervously behind him than to make necessary final adjustments. Apparently, he tired of that ruse, stood up, spread his hands, turned to them, and said... we could hear... *"Voila!"*

Five men again took turns with the flashlight, all nodding as they relinquished it for the next. As they took their turns, several of them reached in to touch the object, but then backed off, and dusted off their shirtsleeves. Then the craftsman got the nod, letting him know that he should reach in and remove the... object. The craftsman was not as fussy about dirt on his sleeves. He reached in with both hands and struggled to slide the object to the entrance. He tipped it and turned it so that it could be removed through the aperture. There it was. The learned talent graciously stepped aside so the loyal fence throng could see. There was an audible gasp and excited chatter. Flash cameras blinked. The object was removed and lifted to the table. Renat and I could see it because the learned ones were on the far side of the table. The object appeared to be—and probably was—a ten-inch diameter pipe—lead pipe, I supposed—with flat ends sealed with lead—a cylinder about 28 inches long.

Grambeaux inspected one end closely, fetched a rag and wiped the dust. After allowing his colleagues a look... even the mason got a look... he turned to the crowd and announced—"An inscription. It appears to be Latin."

The crowd applauded. I brought my hands up to applaud, an automatic reaction, but my hands froze, my mind confused as to what emotion should be prevailing. Renat did applaud, but looked at me and nodded as he did so.

At discovery central, the cylinder was encircled with burlap; the mason/carpenter was instructed to contrive a wooden carrying case.

I had in mind to wait by the fence as Grambeaux and Durand made their victory hurdle, but somehow I was too disgusted at them to make a scene. What did I expect I would get out of that? They had seen me. Renat and I walked off along with the titillated crowd.

Renat said, as we walked, "Warner, you can be proud knowing that you provided the intelligence that made the discovery. Perhaps you can imagine the situation somewhat as a spy would—doing the difficult work but knowing you can't be publicly thanked."

"Oh, that's good, Renat. I'll keep that in mind." I looked over to him and smiled. After all, he was just trying to help me along a bit. "I must say though, more than receiving public acknowledgement, I am interested to find out what is inside. I hope the results will be public information. If not, I may use some clandestine maneuvers to find out. I wonder how long it will take them."

"It won't take long to unseal the container. After that, under nitrogen, I suppose, they will carefully examine the contents. Hopefully, it will not be an assembly of cheap artifacts. Hopefully, the scroll inscription chiseled into the blocks is intended to indicate a cache of documents. If it is, with multi-spectral imaging technology to assist in viewing what is written, followed by translation of the first-century Latin, and then making a further analysis of what is described... well, it will probably take months. I will talk to my friend on the Antiquities Committee and let you know. He will tell me."

"Thank you, Renat. As I am sure you know, I'm most interested."

"As am I. For now, my good friend, Warner, let me buy you a meal and a... maybe... several glasses of wine. You need to relax."

"You are very right, Renat. Lead the way. I'm long overdue."

I called Lisele and told her what had happened, about Grambeaux and Durand, about the cylinder and the crowd. She voiced the proper excitement and acknowledged my achievement, but then she was silent.

"Lisele?"

"Warner, I have to tell you something."

"What?"

"This is my fault, some of it anyway."

"What do you mean—'your fault'?"

"Warner, I told Laurie about your idea—about your idea that there might be a cache and about the inscription and the APA. When you told me, yesterday—that the cache was going to be opened—I feared that Durand might be involved. I asked Laurie. She admitted that she had told Durand, that she had called him and told him. We are not speaking."

"She did it to distress me."

"And me. How could I raise such a vengeful person? Warner, I am so sorry."

I gave myself a few moments. The outrage stung, but I had to assuage Lisele's state of mind. I was, after all, in love with the woman. "Look at it this way, Lisele. If Laurie hadn't gone to Durand, I might not now have experienced the excitement of seeing my 'find' and would not now be anticipating hearing of the treasure of history that might be contained. In some ways, Laurie has helped me. Maybe it will be my vengeance to thank her for taking the action that she presumed would distress me."

"I hope that is how you truly feel. I feel bad—that I played a part in a betrayal. I should have known better, but I was excited for you and wanted to share with my daughter. I would not have thought she would be so sinister—with you—with me. I don't know what it will take for me to forgive her. I don't want to be around her. Can I stay with you, tonight?"

"Of course, Lisele, if you are not worried of what Laurie will think." I laughed. "Come over now."

"It's good to hear you laugh about this, Warner. It gives me confidence that you are not upset. Yes, a good sense of humor trumps all—religion, attitude, charity. I will be there quickly.'

the *Aedifex*: Building the Pont du Gard

I couldn't help but think of the "unswerving punctuality of chance" as Thomas Wolfe described it in "Look Homeward Angel." Or, in other words, how fate contrives its strange outcomes through the vagaries of human activity.

I would be anxious—too anxious—to find what the cylinder contained. My hope was that therein was the story of the building of the great aqueduct and a glimpse of the person who was in charge of its construction.

CHAPTER 52

Rome was a hard five-days, ride from Nemausus. Appius avoided the Via Dometia and the Via Aurelia for the first two days. On the second day, he intersected the Via Aurelia and was tempted to take it to Rome but continued to avoid it, instead taking the secondary roads between villages. Wrong turns and less direct routes cost him a day; he arrived at the outskirts of Rome on the sixth day.

It was evening. He was aware of the glow from the lights of Rome and inhaled its compounded odors before he could see the greatest city in civilization. He was somewhat tense trying to imagine how he would fare in the big city, not knowing its ways and hazards, so he took the opportunity to spend the night at a roadhouse, just outside the city. It would be best if he cleaned up at the available bath, not knowing how to go about this in Rome. He had harbored a fear of navigating his way to Claudius, in the *palatium* on the Palentine, but had kept those thoughts in background. Now, it was real. He must actually find his way through the protection of the Praetorian Guards to the *Imperator*. He shook his head, not knowing what to anticipate.

Rome was glorious. Never had Appius seen such an accumulation of grandeur. Yes, there were collections of hovels—the poor are a part of every setting—but the expanse of the Forum and the overwhelming magnificence of the nearby Coliseum were thrilling. He walked his horse slowly as he viewed the Forum, stopping to view the Senate, the temple of the Vestal Virgins, and the Basilica Julia.

He took a deep breath as he looked up the hill to the Palentine. Should he ask someone for directions to the palace? They would think him a fool. Perhaps he would be able to identify the location by the evidence of the protection provided.

The palace location *was* obvious. Uniformed Praetorian Guards stood, in deliberate military manner at posts, not blocking the path to the entrance but surely protecting it. How could he manage this? He was so inadequate for this mission, naïve to think he could somehow find a means to talk to the *Imperator* of the

Great Roman Empire? His tunic, clean and new as it was, seemed entirely unsuitable for what he was about.

There was a hitch to tie the horse. He had stowed his gear at the roadhouse and would retrieve it as he returned. How long would he allow for them to ignore him before he left in shame and frustration?

Off to the side of the guards and the path to the entrance portico, there was a throng of people, some dressed as plainly as he, others more elegantly outfitted in togas. He guessed they must be waiting for access to the palace. This would not be easy.

He involuntarily shivered as he approached the guards and was met by one assigned the duty of challenging him, as he expected. "What is your business?"

Appius thought it would be best to show confidence. "I am to see the *Imperator*, Claudius. I have a matter that he would discuss with me involving the aqueduct in Nemausus."

"The *Imperator* sent for you?"

Appius knew he would be asked. "I have previously talked to Claudius about the aqueduct he has directed to be built. My visit has been preceded by a message from Nemus Amatia, *aedile* of Nemasus, regarding contracts to which Claudius has been a part. His direction is needed."

The guard, not easily persuaded, said, "I do not believe you answered my questions. Has Claudius asked to see you?"

"No."

"Wait over there." He gestured toward the standing throng. The inquisitor walked between stationed guards, into the palace, then returned in a short while.

Appius stood watching, now amongst the others. As the guard returned, he did not glance in the direction of Appius, merely resumed the position he had maintained prior to their exchange.

Hours passed. Many of those waiting endured the time in conversation. Appius knew no one but after a while tried to engage others, similarly dressed. They responded, but did not appear willing to continue conversation. Only seldom did a *lictor* emerge from the palace entrance to summon a person or a group to enter. As evening approached, the collection wandered off. It was apparent: palace business was done for the day. He asked one of those leaving, "You will return tomorrow?"

The petitioner looked at him, shaking his head in consternation. "I must."

Appius did not know what to do. Well, yes he did. He must also return tomorrow. But how would he even know if a message had been given to Claudius or in what form. He would have no way of knowing. What was his choice but to wait?

He took the opportunity to walk Rome by night, gazing at the magnificent structures, the Circus Maximus, the Coliseum, and the many features of the Forum. It was easy to find prepared food and, by asking, Appius found a suitable room to rent after observing several that were unsuitable—filthy, or poorly situated next to open sewers or in rough neighborhoods. He found a stable for the horse. Not knowing how long he would be staying, possibly for some time, he rode back to the roadhouse, gathered the remainder of his gear then rode back into the city.

He endured another day outside the palace receiving no indication that he would be given audience. He thought, quite right, that if he asked the 'greeter,' he would be told that the request had been made to the attendant of Claudius. In frustration, he started asking those around him—would they be told if access to the *Imperator* was denied? He got varied responses but nothing more positive than "sometimes." Others only shook their heads.

He could not endure this for long. Yet, the effort of the trip and the thought of returning to Nemausus with no result prevailed in fortifying his attitude and gave him the mental strength to remain.

He continued to make attempts at conversation and on the third day was successful in finding someone who wished to talk, a citizen of Rome who needed Claudius—the Empire—to intercede in a dispute he had with the local aediles. From him, Appius heard more details of the death of Caligua, of the excesses of Caligua—the depths of disgust to which he had sunk his subjects—and, to the surprise to all, the elevation of Claudius to *Imperator*. The man was impressed that Appius had spoken to Claudius one on one and thereafter became even more helpful and engaging. Yet, the lictors came, made their beckon to entities of the expectant crowd then disappeared back into the cherished *domus*, leaving a throng of the disheartened.

In the middle of the fifth day, a lictor appeared and shouted "Appius Petronius." Appius was slow to react, not understanding that he was being summoned. He shook his head to dismiss his stupor then approached the lictor, cringing in anticipation of rejection, having observed, over the days, for some, the denial of an audience. The *lictor*, after treating Appius to a sneer, said, "the *Imperator* Claudius, will see you." He turned and walked through the entrance. Appius followed, joy erupting within.

He was led to a room where several others sat, waiting their turn. At a door, four more guards were stationed. He sat for two hours and was finally beckoned into the room.

Appius was humbled by the treasures strewn in Claudius's office, by the *Imperator*'s bench, and by the attire of Claudius. *What am I doing here?* His breath came in short gasps. Yet, Claudius stood as he approached and held out his hands.

"I have been thinking about you, Appius Petronius, and of your situation in Gaul. You must forgive me for not taking action, but, as you might imagine, I have been busy with the trivialities of Empire. I thank you for making the journey; our discussion will give me the opportunity to *discuss* the details of changes which must occur rather than try to communicate by messenger. Here... sit. Tell me."

Appius momentarily forgot what he would tell Claudius, then forced himself to remember his list, one that he had reviewed many times, modifying and improving it for simplicity and reasonableness. Claudius started asking questions and the rest followed easily.

After Appius completed, Claudius leaned back and thought for a while. He spoke, slowly at first. "Crassius is on his way out. I have given the order that he be replaced—removed, actually. He disgraced me in my own region. Imagine his dismay and terror when he heard that I was made *Imperator*. Ha, ha. He will be banished even though I need generals to enforce our slaught upon Britain. But, I say to you, I will replace him with a general who will maintain the military in a secondary position as goes the aqueduct. And, while we are talking the military, I will not only support trial of the military for slaughtering the Ucetians, I will insist on prosecution. To the extent that Crassius and Flavius are involved, they will be punished."

Appius straightened. "It would be my fondest dream to see Flavius pay for his arrogance."

"Yes, well any personal revenge will have to be extracted at the pleasure of the court. On to the aqueduct arrangements. Yes, of course I will return to the agreement that was made—from this moment on. I will leave, as is, the additional payments made by the *Corporata*. It will be good if they understand the differences that result between *imperators*. I will immediately instruct that funds be made available in Nemausus for past and near future requirements. The funds will be kept by the local court but administered by you for payment."

Claudius continued. "The message from Nemus was very complimentary of you. He apparently has great faith in your abilities. I do, too. I therefore appoint you as overseer. The project will now thrive—or not—at your hand. Please update me monthly on your progress and concerns."

"I am humbled, your Excellency. I shall try to make you proud."

"The slaves."

Appius looked up from his humbled expression. "Yes?"

"You may make them freedmen, if you like. Do you have further use of them?"

"Yes. They are now work hardened and are adept at their tasks. It also seems that we will encounter a shortage of manpower. My thought was to pay them a stipend for past work, one that would allow return passage home—to remain if they liked or return with their families to work the project. They will be as freedmen, however, and not... yet... Roman citizens."

"I think that is reasonable. I shall instruct it."

"And, your Excellency, a matter for which I am passionate. I seek your approval to prosecute Titus and Quantus for the murder of Bernius. I have a witness to a confession extracted by Flavius— from the man who killed Bernius. He stated that he killed Bernius at their request."

"Yes, you have my approval. I will not obstruct it." He paused for a moment. "It seems that it would be favorable to first conduct that investigation and trial prior to the trial of the military. I am sure you would not mind if Flavius and his men be held until such has occurred."

"No, your Excellency. I think your idea is appropriate."

"Do we have any further business? I will transcribe all we have discussed into a proclamation. You can expect that it will arrive in Nemasus even prior to your own return. Have you seen enough of Rome or will you remain to explore more of its mysteries, oddities, and grand style?"

"As to your first question, I think we are done. I would only add that I will expedite the construction so that you may dedicate the work as the one who envisioned the project and, of course, as *Imperator*. Will you do so—travel to Nemausus?"

"Yes, but perhaps you should hurry. The life of an *imperator* in Rome is fragile and may vanish as if a vapor."

"I hope that you remain as *Imperator* well after the dedication, your Excellency, but I will expedite the project, nevertheless. As to the answer to your second question, I have wandered the streets of Rome at night and have seen many sights. Of course I could stay longer and experience the sophistication— the best of what our civilization has to offer—but I am anxious to return home—return to my family and return to building the aqueduct."

"I have one thought. You might gain considerable benefit by talking to our people who have been involved in the building of aqueducts. If you can remain a day or two more, I will advise them of your visit and your station."

Appius, anxious as he was to begin his return trip, knew he must take the time. "Yes, of course. I would be enthused to talk to them. I should have thought of that."

"I will advise them. Go to the Domus Aquius tomorrow, and you will be received." Claudius stood up and again extended his arms. "Now go and finish the aqueduct. I am anxious to see the first water appear in Nemausus."

Appius bowed. "Thank you, your Excellency. I could not have wished for more." He turned and walked from the chamber.

Appius made his return trip to Nemausus and, although buoyant from his discussion with Claudius, nevertheless traveled the more obscure route in return. It might happen that the proclamation would arrive in Nemausus simultaneous with or before his arrival, but those who had not gotten the word could kill him, no matter. He anticipated with relish the humiliating removal of Flavius, the horror of Titus when charged with murder, no longer under protection of the Empire. Yes, his trip to Rome was necessary and expedient and satisfying. But, he had created his own challenge. He must now build the aqueduct. Was he capable? It was overwhelming.

As he rode, he pondered—how would he enter Nemausus? It was somewhat confusing. The military remained the only force,

551

and he could surely be apprehended, a paradox, incongruous to the situation. Who would enforce a proclamation that required the military to stand down? Must he wait for a new general to appear on the scene? He wished he had had the presence of mind to have thought of that circumstance and discuss it with Claudius. What must he do?

The constant gait of the horse created a rhythm for his thoughts. What would be the result when the proclamation was read? The populace would certainly understand. The *Corporata* would understand and comply. Would Titus run? What would Flavius do? Would it be reasonable that he would stay at his post, knowing that he had been replaced, knowing that he would stand trial? If Flavius encountered Appius, dare Flavius act insanely or out of revenge? Although such acts could only make his situation worse, the actions of Flavius could not be predicted. Appius concluded that he must first determine that the proclamation had arrived, consider its wording, and take covert time to observe what happened as a result. Nothing was simple.

Appius arrived at night. He camped outside Nemausus, but he ached to enter the city to see if the proclamation had arrived as Claudius had pledged. It would be posted on the board near the Templum Agrippa, the site of all proclamations, local or empirical. In the early dark hours, he walked to the Templum, to the posting boards. Using a lit taper, he scanned several attached documents but could not see a Claudian proclamation. He was discouraged. His shoulders slumped in exasperation, but he did take comfort that he had been cautious.

He walked to the *Corporata* yard, to his office, looking most carefully, but not approaching, the building Flavius had commandeered. There was no indication of any change. But, what could he expect?

He next walked past his house—nothing to observe except that the outdoor plants appeared to have been watered and weeded. On he walked to Juliena's house. Should he wake them, let Antonia know he had safely returned? At least there were no military present about the home. He had not expected there would be, but it was prudent to know. He took a deep breath. He would remain incognito for another day—gather more information, observe action in the same locations, perhaps give the proclamation another day to arrive. He took a deep breath then walked from the city to his camp and a fitful sleep.

In the morning Appius dressed to escape recognition, walked to town directly to the home of Juliena. Of course Antonia was not to be spotted outside so he strode to the door and gently knocked. Juliena opened the door, smiled and said, "We have been expecting you."

Appius, shocked, said, "Expecting me—why so?"

"Yesterday a proclamation from Claudius was read twice— once at noon, when it arrived, and then again, just before dusk."

"But I looked at the postings last night—after midnight. There was no proclamation posted."

Juliena shrugged. "Perhaps they were copying it, overnight, as they sometimes do. They were probably not expecting persons to read it at midnight." She opened the door wider. "Come in. I will get Antonia. I think she wants to see you."

Juliena left and Antonia soon appeared, smiling and arms outstretched. "Oh, Appius, I worried so."

"But I am back. You must know I met with Claudius from the proclamation."

"Yes, oh yes. Hearing it, I knew that you had arrived in Rome safely, and furthermore, were successful with Claudius. When we heard that, we expected to see you soon, but I was still concerned about your return trip. The proclamation will anger some and terrify others. When that happens, one can expect anything."

"Yes. I have the same concern. But, tell me, what did the proclamation say?"

Antonia, with her hands on Appius's shoulders, looked up as if consulting the spot where her memory resided. "General Crassius has been removed; a new general will soon be named and will tour the cities of the region. Flavius is dismissed from duty and you—you, Appius—are named to supervise the building of the aqueduct. The disposition of the slaves will be in your hands."

"Was there no more mention of Flavius?"

"Oh, yes. He and General Crassius are to report to Rome."

"But, no mention of a military trial?"

"No."

553

"Claudius told me he *will* try the military for the execution of the Ucetians. Perhaps that will be a surprise for them when they get to Rome."

"They may expect such."

"Yes, they may, especially because Flavius knows I promoted the actions of Claudius."

"Perhaps you should be careful."

Appius nodded. He reached for her hands and held them in front of him. "I have much to do. Stay with Juliena for the time being until we know that it is safe. Before I go, though, I would like to see Sergius."

"I will bring him. He will bubble with excitement. Would you also like to see your other son?"

Appius was momentarily baffled. He then held up his hand and smiled. "Bernius."

"Yes. We have been getting acquainted, but go easy on Juliena. It is not easy for her."

"I shall. Now, bring my sons."

Appius walked to his office. As he entered, the designers looked up in unison, looked at each other then said, "Appius!"

"Yes." He set down his satchel and turned back to them. "You have heard the proclamation?"

They nodded. "Yes," said Gaius, "we have been eagerly awaiting your return and have not had a visit from Flavius for several days. We are anxious to hear what will happen."

Appius leaned against a high table. "We will reform the project to abide by the schedule we originally crafted, but taking into account the events that have occurred. I ask you, what is the status of your work? Gaius?"

"I am nearly complete. I have only to adjust the bridge structure based on the actual shape of the canyon walls. That we will do as we go along."

"Vibius?"

"The tunnel vertical shafts are complete. We have detected nothing in the shafts that would discourage us from taking a tunnel route that would intersect them. I have already created the structure we will use and the means of navigating while we are in the midst of their excavation. The remainder of my work will be to be to consider what we encounter in the horizontal excavation and adjust the elevation of the tunnel if we must. And, my work on the underground conduit will also depend on what we discover and modify after we do the final level measurements. While you were gone, I visited the four excavation sections and noted the nature of stone encountered and the condition of the earth. All is well, but, as I have mentioned before, we must make provision for the swampy area near Nemausus."

"And, you Numerius, what have you been doing?"

"Ah yes, the aboveground structures. I have devised the schemes we will use—single-tiered on most but double-tiered arches on deeper gullies and canyons. As with the underground structures, I await the final outcome of the level measurements."

"So," Appius looked at the three, "you are nearly complete in your design tasks. I will continue to need your help to assist me. I would have you inspect the construction of that on which you had design responsibility. I will need your help to draft contracts for the work that has yet to be bid, and I will have other tasks that will not relate to your expressed field but for which you are fully qualified. We are the team that will be responsible for building this magnificent project. We will acquire more people to help us, of course. Are all of you able to remain here and see your project completed?"

Gaius said, "I have no other obligations. The assignment you described is that which I would favor."

Appius nodded and smiled.

Vibius said, "I have a wife and son in Rome. I have not seen them in six months and would opt to be with them whenever that is possible. If I know that my work here will be continuous, I will bring them here."

"The project will help you." At this statement, Appius had a brief thought questioning the extent of his own power. Fortunately, the thought soon evaporated.

"Thank you, Appius. I hoped that such would happen."

Appius looked at Numerius. "And you, Numerius, what will you do?"

Numerius brightened. "Before I came to Nemausus, I was like Gaius—with no obligations. However, I have managed to meet Arboretia and would like to continue to cultivate her favor. I shall be glad to stay here—oh, yes, and because I am also anxious to have a part in the project."

Appius smiled and said, "It is good. It is as I had hoped, and I am delighted. But, if you will excuse me, I have other tasks which I must now confront." He pointed in the direction of the military.

Appius knew he was being incautious but was driven by anger resulting from the humiliation he had suffered, arrogance observed, and ignorance empowered. That he had the favor of Claudius also bloated his confidence. It would be prudent if he waited until Flavius left for Rome as the proclamation commanded, but that would not do. The sight of the departing centurion would be satisfying, but would lack the depth of retribution he sought.

Appius entered the military building. He saw Flavius at the back of the room, who, upon seeing Appius, raised his arms, hands locked behind his head. The aides, slouching against the walls, straightened as he walked in, looked uncertainly at Flavius then back to Appius.

Appius walked up to Flavius and kicked over the low table onto him. "Remove you and your men from this building. You remain here against the orders of the *Imperator* and are occupying property which you do not have the right to use."

Flavius stood up against the overturned desk, righting it with his knee. The aides grabbed for knives in their belts and hurried toward Appius. Appius swept his hand to indicate they should back off. Flavius exploded. "You do not have.... " But, he looked uncertain. He looked at his men who were ready to take whatever action commanded, but he said nothing more.

Appius pointed. "I said, leave. Now! Gather your belongings and go. Appius saw Flavius's eyebrows forced downwards in the intense expression of hatred, the hatred that Appius longed to see. He reveled at the sight. He could not retreat; he could not stop. "And what do you say to that, centurion?"

"I have nothing to say to you."

"I have more to say to *you*. On your way to Rome, you must travel to your sites and tell your men to stand down and await further orders. Do you understand that?"

"I will not do that."

"I am ordering you to do so."

"It is of no matter to me."

"Then go. Go!" Appius turned and walked between the threatening aides, challenging them with his eyes as he passed.

Outside, Appius quaked with latent anger and emotion. He shook his head, not believing what he had done. What would happen? It was unlikely that Flavius would tell his men to stand down. But, would Flavius leave? It was possible, but Flavius would be resistant to obey Appius's order, and Flavius was still the only force in the region. Still, it had been worthwhile to see Flavius's anger, tormenting him to accept that he was now unable to legally defy Appius. Would Flavius retaliate after he had thought over the situation? Appius thought not.

Appius walked slowly toward his office. He must think about his next actions. He must decide what changes should be made and must visit the construction sites and the contractors to confirm his authority and to reestablish progress along a path that would reflect reason rather than bluster. Oh, yes—he had to manage the slave situation.

CHAPTER 53
The month of Quintilis

Appius was not sure how to handle the transition. At the moment, slaves were providing the labor for the excavation contracts. The original contractors were gone, presumably drinking wine and in quest of other contracts; their forces were looking for or had found other work. The slaves were being supervised by a military that was no longer in charge. Military control under a new, more pliant general had not yet been announced; therefore, supervision remained uncertain. Also, the military had fed the slaves and presumably provided other requirements. What would happen if he went to the sites and told the slaves they were free to go or stay? It did not take long for Appius to realize *he* must resolve the situation.

Before he traveled to the sites, he visited the excavation contractors that had quit their contracts. Fortunately, three were available in Nemausus. For the other, he was required to take a day's journey to Lugdunum. The contractors had heard of Claudius's proclamation, of course, and wondered what would happen.

The contractors were willing, even eager, to return to their work; however, there was the matter of prior payments due. No, they would not begin work again on word from Appius that he was making arrangements for payment from the Empire and that Claudius had promised that sestertii would be deposited with the courts in Nemausus. Appius acknowledged his understanding, but told them to expect that they would be paid within two weeks and to prepare to return to work—he hoped.

The contractors were certain that most of their men would reappear—but not all. Appius advised them that they could hire the freed slaves—those that wanted to stay— and, *if* the contractors wished to do so, they should notify Appius in one week of the numbers of freedmen they might require. Appius also advised that clearing was substantially ahead of their excavation work and asked that they consider working at a faster pace. The contractors were willing to do so if additional manpower was available—meaning the slaves. After all, they would be making sestertii at a faster pace and would complete the work earlier. The contract involving exploratory shafts for the tunnel work was complete. Although the contractor had not been paid for the work he had accomplished, the slaves had completed the work.

Appius had much to do—drafting new contracts, and arranging for payments, but, as a first priority, he must visit the sites, determine the status and handle the slave situation. It was probable that some slaves would remain. He must negotiate a way to provide for them, as they would have no means to do this themselves. He enlisted Gaius and Vibius to visit the farmers who had been plundered by the military. They might, nevertheless, be interested in, once again, being *paid* for providing their crops. The marketeers were another possible source, and they would also be consulted. But, any of the actions he took required sestertii on hand. *Claudius, please send the sestertii.* Appius did not think that he could depend on the *Corporata* to make a bridge loan.

Appius continued to ponder as he rode towards the nearest work site. He could expect pandemonium if the military departed and the slaves were left with no provisions. Gaius and Vibius had departed a day prior; perhaps they had found a provisioner who would furnish basic food without ready payment. Or was that a dream?

Somewhat to the surprise of Appius, the military were still at the work site. Flavius, true to his word, had *not* traveled to the sites to advise his men that they were no longer in charge of the work. So, even the military were quite anxious to hear what would happen. There had been no official announcement to the slaves that they would be freed; however, as it often is with jailors and their keep, the soldiers had whispered the volatile news to the captives.

Appius sat on his horse before the soldiers, their *decanus* to the fore. Appius eyed the men, considering their expressions and attitudes before he spoke. "You may have heard. The military is no longer in charge of the project. Centurion Flavius has been relieved of duty, and Claudius has appointed me to supervise the project. A general will be selected to replace General Crassius; however, I would presume that you are to operate under your standing orders until directed otherwise." He looked at the *decanus.* "Is it so?"

The *decanus* nodded. "As on the battlefield when we lose an officer, we soldier-on with the latest orders until the situation becomes unreasonable, or we are relieved of those orders by the next... military... higher in command. We are in a similar situation, although we *could* think that it is now unreasonable to continue the mission as ordered."

Appius nodded. "I would tend to agree with you. I cannot order you to do one thing or another. I will... officially... advise the slaves that they will be freedmen; however, they will not yet have achieved that status until they go to Nemausus and receive the documents that will certify that they are so. They remain slaves at the moment. I will make that clear." He looked at the *decanus*. "I request that you remain at your posts, for now, and continue to supervise the work, also providing for the slaves. If you do so, I must advise that the farmers and merchants will hereafter be paid to provide the supplies. My men are talking to them in this area, as we speak. I anticipate they will be willing to supply provisions for another week or two, with the agreement they will be paid in lieu of having the goods taken. What say you?"

"We have already discussed the matter. We will stay. We are the military and paid through the military channels. If we desert this post, we will no longer deserve payment nor the supplies that sustain us. To disband and then be at the mercy of the new general would be stupid. It is true; you cannot give us orders. However, tell us what you want us to do, and you can be fairly certain we will do as you ask. I am sure you are aware that the provisions we depend upon, our food, are acquired by the same means as for the slaves.

Appius faced the slaves, overseen by the soldiers. They appeared anxious and attentive in contrast to the bleary, distracted look one noticed as they slogged through their captive day in a life without rewards, future, or hope. It was apparent they had heard. Appius focused on several of the faces before him, understanding that there was potential for these men to meld into the population, providing worthy but unyoked contribution. He spoke. "I have talked with the *Imperator*, Claudius, and he has agreed." He paused to have the words translated by one of the soldiers adept at doing so. The listeners were alert to the message; several nodded. "You will be freed from your captivity. You will be of a status in Roman society known as freedmen." He, again, waited for the translation, hearing the familiar word 'freedmen.' He continued. "As freedmen, you may return to your homelands or remain here or go anywhere within the Empire, if you choose. If you wish to continue at this work—to be paid for your efforts, at wages equal to the Roman citizens working beside you—it is likely we can find assignments for you." Appius saw several dip their heads forward, humbled by the news. Some looked at others to divine notions of leaving or staying. "If you wish to stay and work, you must advise us that you will do so. Regardless, you must travel to Nemausus to receive your freedman documents and to collect a stipend the *Imperator* has agreed to give you for past work performed. At that time you can advise if you wish to continue working on the aqueduct." He paused. "As freedmen, you are not citizens of the Roman Empire. But, it is possible for you to eventually attain that status. You will learn what you must do to do so."

The slaves had not known of the stipend. Many had been wondering how they could manage to return home. Now, there was a possibility the stipend would resolve that problem. Appius let them buzz amongst themselves for a while, and then regained their attention. "The contractors will return. If you choose to remain and work, you will likely work for them. For the present, we are arranging provisions for food, but you will now be required to pay for that food from the stipend." He paused for the translation and to let the thought digest. "I would expect that actions I have stated will happen within the next two weeks. In the meantime, the soldiers will supervise the work. You will find that the soldiers will now *request* that you do something rather than *order* you to do something." Appius looked at the *decanus* then back to the former slaves. "You may leave at any time, but you must make your walk to Nemausus within the next two weeks. Am I understood?"

After the translation, there were nods amongst the throng. After years of captivity and abuse, none were so bold as to ask a question.

Appius nodded to them. "I am done, then. I wish you a decent life and, if you wish, to eventually become a citizen of the Roman Empire."

The slaves, accustomed to commands from the military, stood—waiting. The military, at the moment not understanding their new role, were also slow to act. However, the *decanus*, perceiving the situation gave orders for the soldiers and former slaves alike to return to the work. Uncertain instructions were given, but the group dissembled and noisily headed off, all engaged in conversation with their walking comrades. Appius determined that it would be prudent for him to return and observe the circumstance after a few days.

The provisions situation had not been resolved. However, there was several days' food stored at the site. Gaius and Vibius found Appius and told him they were successful in finding a few farmers and marketeers willing to supply provisions under the promise that they would now be paid.

Appius traveled to the three remaining sites and repeated the procedures and instructions. After his last pronouncement and after ensuring that there was at least a crude understanding of the supply lines, he headed back to Nemausus but stopped at the first site to see what was occurring. The work was continuing, more or less as it had been with the exception that fifteen of the slaves had immediately secured food for their travel and set off for Nemausus to receive their freedman documents and their stipend. The *decanus* said that these men were anxious to return to their homeland and probably would not return to the work. Appius hoped that sestertii from the Empire had arrived and realized he had not instructed the court as to the amount and means of distribution of the stipend. He rushed back.

He found that the sestertii from the Empire *had* arrived. He made a calculation of the days worked by the slaves and allocated half of a non-slave's wage for the time, thinking that they had been supplied food and other provisions at no cost. They should be happy to receive anything. Of the slaves arriving first in Nemausus, most said that they would not return to work, but twenty said they would attempt to return with their families. They were very appreciative of their good fortune. They were required to wear a felt hat denoting their status as freedmen.

Flavius had departed while Appius was away, depriving Appius the sight of an excruciating and humiliating exit. Appius realized that he had missed the event he had so longed for but took a deep breath and knew it was time to put Flavius and all that frustration behind him and bend to the serious task of returning the project to equilibrium.

Appius addressed the *Corporata, sans* Titus. Titus remained a member but chose not to attend because he detected a cool contempt to his presence. It was doubtful that he could or would participate in matters of consequence, his fortune now in tatters.

"I am certain you are aware that the arrangement, originally struck between the *Corporata* and Claudius, has been reinstated. Funds have been deposited with the court and will be distributed by my direction, under the watchful eye of the regional court. You do not have to be concerned about further excess drains of your fortunes nor will you have to raise rates on water you now sell. Funds you are expending, even those extracted under Flavius, will buy you an interest in the water that will someday be delivered to our town. While you might have thought that the project would not continue... before... perhaps you now have confidence that it will. It seems that you should plan for distribution of the resource—the water, its return to you for your investment, and determine how you will deal with the Empire.

Individually, the *Corporata* members could not help but think of the rapid assumption of authority bestowed on Appius. It was not long ago that he was merely of secondary importance, necessary and useful but not of much stature. Yet, his audience with Claudius and his anointment by the Imperial touch as the one to manage the project, gave him status that could not be denied. They could not help but notice the transition. Yes, what he had said was true and his suggestion meaningful.

Nemus spoke. "Yes, Appius Petronius, we are grateful to return to a situation that is at least more reasonable and dependable. We thank you for your effort. I think you will find that the *Corporata* members," he looked at the others, "will be of a more cooperative posture as you execute the project. We request that you continue to brief us, at least on a monthly basis, and advise of any difficulties that might threaten. Besides giving thought to the future water distribution, what do you ask of us?"

Appius shook his head. "At this time, I do not have a request, but such will likely occur."

Marcus asked, "We understand you will move the office and your staff to the vicinity of the bridge to be built across the Vardo. Will that make coordination more difficult?"

Appius, clenching his fists at his side, paused to consider Marcus. It was difficult for him to maintain a neutral composure in the presence of the man who had lain with his wife, who had fathered his child, a task he, Appius, could not accomplish. He felt his temperature rise yet he forced himself to consider only the question. "Some tasks will be more difficult. It is true. But the location near the bridge is central to all of the construction, close to the work needing the most attention. I will establish a functionary in Nemausus who will act on our behalf, initiating purchases and making other arrangements. You may contact him to get word to me, and at times I will get word to him that is to be passed to you. You can be assured that messages will be transmitted daily."

Marcus nodded, perhaps taking too long to assess Appius's reaction before he did so.

Appius reached for a document. "If there are no other comments or questions, I shall read the list of this month's expenditures and requirements."

There were none; he proceeded.

Reestablishing of the contractors, arranging for their back pay, arranging procedures for the freedmen, and for the inception of the Vardo bridge construction contract, preparing a briefing for the *Corporata*, and hiring of staff to be the representative of the project supervision took all of Appius's time.

He was anxious to re-assess the schedule and make modifications as a result of the analysis. Gaius and Vibius had not yet returned, continuing to make arrangements with farmers and suppliers for provisions. Appius remembered that he must reserve some of the allotment from the Empire to pay the farmers. At some time he would consider a stipend for the farmers, partial compensation for what was taken from them.

Because Numerius remained in the office, he got the assignment: convert the building Flavius had occupied, clear the furniture, and re-establish the stick schedule from the paper schedule Appius had maintained. Appius now focused on scheduling, careful to include Numerius in his thoughts and actions.

The schedule would allow Appius to grasp the situation based on current conditions. Once that was done, Appius would consider various alternatives to visualize the outcome, including work that could be expedited and contracts that should soon be let. He already knew that it was vital that the contract for building the bridge across the Vardo be bid and awarded immediately so that the foundation work could be started in order to accept the stones that would soon be available.

the *Aedifex*: Building the Pont du Gard

A comparison with the original schedule showed that the trench excavation and the subsequent masonry construction of the underground work were not well timed. The bridge would finish years prior. Appius tried several possible courses of action, rearranging the activities as represented by the sticks, to see the outcome of doing such. After several similar exercises, he determined that accelerating the underground work would be an activity that would result in less lost time and provide a coordinated end to the project. He made changes to reflect this thinking. However, the bridge foundation work needed immediate attention in order to place a maximum number of stones during the times between flood seasons on the Vardo.

Fortunately, Flavius had not done anything further on the Vardo bridge bid. Appius was able to modify the contract wording to state that the contractor would be paid for his mobilization effort followed by progress payments on a monthly basis; the Empire would be ultimately responsible for payment. If one were a contractor, one would need to know the circumstances, the latest events, the change of leadership, the proclamation from Claudius to feel comfort in now risking one's effort and sestertii. Fortunately, all the interested contractors *did* know.

Appius, as he and Numerius reviewed the schedule, said, "Numerius, I have a scheduling concern that has not been fully addressed. Bernius mentioned that we must be wary of executing vulnerable activities during times the Vardo might flood. One of those activities, placing foundation stones, is of immediate concern."

"Can you tell me...."

"I think you can understand that the flow of water could exert considerable force against an object in its path. And, if the object is under water, that object is made lighter by the bouyancy effect of the water... Archimedes, you know."

"No, I do not know."

"Well, as Bernius explained to me, objects that are lighter than water tend to float. Even objects that are heavier become lighter when immersed. That means that our stones would be lighter and would have less resistance to movement if they were under water."

"I see. But does the shape of the piers not help the situation?"

565

"Yes, but with an extreme flood, the shapes that divert the flow will not be enough. Bernius and I climbed the walls of the canyon and saw that there are signs that the river has flooded to 50 feet above the normal flow."

"That is incredible. What must we do?"

Appius shrugged. "I am thinking that we must install enough stones to ensure that our piers will be above a flood stage; their weight, especially those *above* water, will help keep the lower stones in place. We must do this before the time of year when such might occur."

"And that time is...?"

"Autumn. I remember floods, and they occurred at that time. But I have talked to others, farmers in this area who are older. They say that in their memories and from stories told by their elders, extreme storms occur in the autumn."

"We must favor that condition in our schedule?"

"Yes. And we must address such in the contract with the bridge contractors. We must also include the same thought when constructing the lower arches, a situation that might be even more hazardous than when constructing the piers. Bernius was concerned that if we were incomplete with our arches, with some or most still dependent on the temporary wood supports, a flood destroying those supports would result in failure of the entire structure."

"How will you handle this with the contractors?"

"I would like to make them responsible for damage in the event of a flood. In that way, they will be diligent to make sufficient progress to avoid a calamity and not construct in periods of time when the work has a higher chance of being destroyed."

"I will ponder our schedule to see what activities are now occurring in the autumn and see what we must do to avoid the calamities."

"Yes." Appius nodded. "I think it is by the schedule that we have a tool to plan this work. But, I am thinking, we can only *reduce* the possibilities; we will still have substantial risk. It is now *Quintilis* and the flood season is upon us. After three months of the flood season, we have nine months to install many stones on the lowest piers. That is why I am anxious to get the bridge work awarded so that placement of the pier stones may be started immediately when safe."

the *Aedifex*: Building the Pont du Gard

. Appius became worried that the quarry would not be able to supply stones quickly enough to accommodate the contractor's expected rapid placement during the non-flood season. Therefore, before the contractors bid the bridge, the quarry contract was modified to accelerate his production to exceed the requirements of the original contract. Appius acknowledged that the acceleration was beyond the original contract and agreed to pay additional costs. The quarry contractor was now able to take advantage of the second quarry location he had surveyed and had intended to develop—his plan from the start. However, the Empire would now help him with that development. The Empire would also have to quickly establish a road upon which the stones would be transported from the new quarry.

Appius had also convinced the excavation contractors to accelerate their work. Once the contractors considered their situation and Appius's suggestion, they hired most of the available freedmen. Of course, the fact that the contractors had again started their work meant that they had now been paid for work done in the past but for which Flavius had stiffed them.

The quarry contractor, in the meantime, was waiting until the first stones removed, the ones that would be used for the bottom pier foundation stones, had aged for the required year. In fact, though, he started chiseling on the stones one month before the specified year had elapsed. This was at his risk, but he did this for a number of reasons. He wanted to take his time on hewing the first stones to the final dimensions. He had quarried an additional number of stones of the size required for the first stones because it was possible that some stones might fracture before the year was up. If so, alternatives would be needed else the project would be delayed by a year, waiting for a replacement stone to age. After the initial courses of stones were laid, the stones above would be of a more consistent size and, because many would be produced, failure of several would not be a problem.

Two weeks after the precision crafting of the stones started, the quarry contractor had worked the first large foundations stones to the required dimensions. The entire stone block process had developed into a production run. From atop the quarry bluff, Appius observed the process. Below him, on rockfaces still native to the hillside, he could see several men hacking troughs into the stone, outlining the next blocks to be cut. Other men at adjacent blocks were using hammers to drive wedges into the rock in the bottoms of the troughs, previously cut. Appius could hear the ring of steel upon steel as hammers hit the wedges, the different weights and sizes of the devices producing an array of pitches at varying cadences. A quarry symphony.

Adjacent to the wedge drivers, he spotted a stone recently freed from the quarry face, having fractured along the intended lines from the multiple driven wedges. Several men were applying prybars under one edge, lifting while another worker inserted a wooden roller under the bottom lip.

One hundred feet away, other men were edging a block, on rollers, toward a sloped ramp. The men moved the stone by leveraging it along with long steel bars. When on the inclined ramp, the block would be restrained by ropes as gravity tugged it along on wooden rollers repeatedly applied under the fore edge. At the end of the ramp, atop a descending vertical face of the quarry, riggers were attaching binders to a stone that would be swung away from the face and lowered to the horizontal stone surface below, to land upon other rollers, so that it could be positioned in the yard now containing hundreds of stones, tombstone silent in their aging, a mosaic of patience—a result of the first year's production.

At the far edge of the aging stones, men with chisels delicately applied hammer strokes to work the stones to their final dimensions, reaching for a wooden gauge that would tightly surround a precisely cut stone. Most often the gauge showed that the stone had not yet reached the finished size; they continuing the chiseling. On stones more advanced in the cutting, men with small rocks held in their hands, abraded the stones, constantly applying the gauges until it barely fit the face being measured.

From his view, it seemed to Appius that the original quarry face was melting, the stones flowing from their ancient location in the hillside, along the steps of the quarry, down the face, through the yard, pausing then flowing onto carts transporting the stones to the bridge location, the flow then reassembling in military formation to emerge as the bridge.

The quarry contractor had hewn a cart road from the rock rather than attempt to move the stones on the river. Appius walked his horse along the haul road to the bridge foundations where a number of stones now awaited their imminent placement. Men were in process of assembling a large hoist, binding husky poles fashioned from the trunks of pines cut nearby in the clearing operation. The poles, bound with rope, would allow the stones to be lifted from a cart and swung over the prepared foundation.

CHAPTER 54

General Servius Ovidius appeared in Nemausus with his aides. The general temporarily occupied the basilica. He was evidence of Claudius's proclamation, establishing a new general as the leader of the military presence in the Narbonensis region. The general sent for Appius, rather than calling on him, establishing the importance of his position and perceptually diminishing the authority of Appius.

Appius was anxious to gauge the character and intentions of the man, notwithstanding that Claudius said he would select someone who would support his own views and, importantly, support Appius in the building of the aqueduct and not presume the supervision of such.

Appius was led to the temporary office of the general—he would later establish his headquarters in Narbo. The general did not rise in greeting as Appius approached, nor did he look up. Appius tensed, remembering recent arrogant handling from the military, anticipating that he might distressfully be in dispute with this man and his regime.

Appius stood before General Ovidius for a moment before the general acknowledged him, taking a long moment to assess Appius. The general seemed to be determining if the description in his briefing matched the man who now stood before him. He nodded his head and spoke. "Appius Petronius."

"Yes, General Servius Ovidius." Appius thought he would learn more if he let the general make the opening statement.

The general smiled; was it a sardonic smile? "Our *Imperator*, Claudius, for whom I have the greatest respect, says that you will supervise the construction of the aqueduct and that I will provide support. I do not know you and do not know your capabilities, but I have sworn to do as he says. Perhaps you can describe your concept of support—support that you might expect from the military."

Appius realized that his statements might have great importance. He involuntarily took a deep breath and squared his shoulders. "I am sure you know that your men remained at the worksites to supervise the freedmen who chose to remain. I thank them for providing this valuable service. The contractors have returned and will be responsible for supervising their work. I hope for a smooth transition." Appius paused to get affirmation from the general.

"I am proud that our men acted reasonably. I accept your gratitude. What else?"

Appius continued. "Prior to the takeover by General Crassius," Appius could not avoid a jab at the military for the agony he had endured, "we asked the military to provide a presence along the construction route. I ask that you re-establish that support and do so in a manner that does not cause abrasions with the contractors, workers, farmers, or merchants. I expect the military to pay for their provisions rather than plunder the locals."

General Ovidius again smiled. "We can surely pay for our provisions, understanding that we will be reimbursed by the *Corporata* or the Empire for the support that we provide."

"Of course. I am happy that is clear. If my staff encounters trouble with individuals or groups, we would rely on your men to help quell such disturbances. There is always the question of whether the military should act on their own. I expect and hope it will be obvious when they should do so. For certain, any acts of retribution should *not* be initiated by the military, and only with my instruction.

General Ovidius gave a hard stare but nodded. "Anything else?"

"Yes. Your men will be in constant contact with the work and the surrounding situations. I asked before if I could receive a weekly report on their observations or actions taken. This report was never done in a helpful manner. I think there would be value in such. Can you assist me?"

"I can. I understand what you want and the value of doing so. I will discuss this with my men, and you will be advised as to how we will do this."

"Thank you, General. That is all I have to say, for now. How will I communicate with you if need be?"

"I will have an officer in charge of the men involved with your project. He is also the overseer of security for Nemausus and the surrounding area. He will call on you regularly and you may contact him if, as you say, need be."

"I think we have a working arrangement. I thank you for your cooperation and hope that our joint efforts will result in a project the Empire can behold with pride."

"I hope you are right, Appius Petronius."

The contractors bidding the bridge construction had ample time to consider and prepare their estimates because the initial bid had been rejected followed by the waiting time to re-establish the contract requirements. Therefore, Appius allowed only two more weeks to submit bids. On bid day, he was pleased to have five substantial contractors submit prices to build the inspiring structure. It was not unusual that several of the contractors wanted to build the bridge as a monument to their own glory. That they should, if they were prudent, also make significant sestertii was noteworthy further enticement. There were many excited people at the bid opening, including Appius and his office crew.

Bid openings are as exciting as any other game of chance. The envelopes are opened in no particular order save the whim of the person opening the envelopes or perhaps in order received. When the first number is read, the other contractors know if they are higher or lower than that number. If they are higher, they are immediately disappointed. If they are lower, they involuntarily hold their breath. The contractor whose bid has been opened knows nothing except in observing the reactions of others. As the remaining prices are revealed, some contractors understand they have been outbid; some are still in the running, still holding their breath. The opening continues, chance touching some on the shoulder, punching others in the gut. At last the final price is revealed. The last bidder already knows by now whether he has won or lost; however, the low bidder, up to that time, is frantic, searching the eyes of the last bidder to see if he can divine *the answer*. If the last contractor knows he has won, he will do his best not to spoil the fun. The crowd becomes quiet; the final number is read followed by great whoops and shouts by the contractor and his cohorts who ended up low. There are more tense moments as the bid openers scan the bid to see if the apparent low bidder has noted any contingencies, provisions that might disqualify them if serious.

In the winning bid, there were no contingencies; in the documents of the other contractors were complaints about responsibility for damage due to flooding. The winning contractor, from Lugdunum, however, made no mention. He prevailed and was grudgingly congratulated by a few of his more charitable competitors. "Let me know if you cannot handle it."

Appius was interested and somewhat surprised. He expected that the added wording in the contract—holding the contractor responsible if the works were destroyed by flood—would have been challenged in the bid. The day after the bid, as the contract was being signed, he asked the successful bidder, "Contractor, what did you think of the provision in which you are held responsible should a flood destroy the works?"

The contractor looked up from the document he was reading. "I was happy to see that you added the wording. Only contractors with competence would take that challenge, leaving those of less ability to bid higher or not at all. The way I see it, if we are diligent and a flood still destroys the works, the contractor will *not* have the funds to recover. The Empire will have to provide funds to clean up the catastrophe and re-do the work. If we have done our best, the Empire is likely to continue our employment—having us complete this work knowing that we have performed satisfactorily. I am happy to take that gamble. If, in the contract, on the other hand, the Empire was stated to be responsible—not the contractor—you are correct, the contractor would not be motivated to expedite the work, knowing that however dismally he performs, the Empire will pay for his miserable progress and for him to do the re-work."

"I like the way you think, contractor. I now expect great performance from you."

"I hope you will say the same in five years."

It was now time for Appius to move the project office to the vicinity of the bridge. The significant work on the bridge would then be near, as would the operation of the quarries. The office would be nearly in the middle of the length of the aqueduct.

Living in the new location was not without conveniences. By this time, due to the significant number of men working the quarry and underground excavation to either side, the vicinity had become a locus, expedient for markets, services, and gatherings. Enterprising souls had built a bathhouse, using wood fuel from the clearing operations to feed fires, heating the water. These enterprising souls did quite well.

Yet, Antonia would be a long day's walk from Nemausus and her sisters, from shops having more breadth of supply, and from medical care. She was reluctant to move her household to the new location but could not think of a persuasive argument and did not want the family to be separated from Appius.

Three months prior to their move, Appius started construction of their home and an office building to house his growing staff. Antonia was comforted because Vibius retrieved his wife and family from Rome and Numerius had married the woman from Nemausus, all to be housed at the site near the bridge construction, the site called *Versus Pontis*. For his home, Appius acquired a sizable plot between the bridge site and the nearby springs of *Versus Pontis*, those that he and Bernius had discovered while determining the aqueduct route. In the beginning it would be a somewhat crude existence, but in time there would be more. Antonia's life was easier because Appius, at the direction of Claudius, was now receiving pay equal to that of a general. They could afford help, sharing their *aquarius, hortulanus,* and other help with the families of Appius's staff.

Prior to the move, Appius had worked hard to bid and award the remaining contracts—cement production, tunnel excavation, tunnel construction, construction of the masonry structure that would be built in the trenches now being excavated. The bid for the aboveground structures would have to await the results of the leveling operation and the subsequent adjustments. There were other remaining contracts to be bid and awarded, but all that could be done from his new office. With the exception of the aboveground structures, the project was now being worked the full length.

The bridge contractor started working the foundations. In addition to the hands-on work, his mobilization included the establishment of shelter and food preparation areas for the workers. Appius, astride his horse, looked down from the canyon rim and saw the shelters.

Groups of men were at work on the flat expanses of rock, rock that would provide the foundations for the lowermost stones to be placed. There were seven locations subject to the flow of the Vardo and of those, three would be at the lowest elevation. It was important that the tops of the first stones placed at each location be level and of an elevation to coincide with stones at the other piers. Elevations at the native rock had been measured and the heights of the first stones designed with that requirement in mind. Now, the native rock beneath the piers must be chiseled, hacked, broken, and carried off to result in a level surface, at the cherished elevation. The pier foundation in the middle of the three lowest was chosen as "boss" or the point from which the others would be measured or adjusted. Appius's improved chorobate was situated at this location, and the foundation levels on either side, across the river channels, were determined. Numerius, designer of the foundations, was on the site nearly continually to check the methods and progress of the contractor and to answer questions that resulted. Because they could not establish a measurement as precise as that obtained by stringing the clay pipes, it was known that actual comparison of the heights of the piers would not be able to be gauged precisely until the structure had been built to the top of the arch, 72 feet above the lowest foundation, allowing a continuous run of the leveling pipe.

Great care was taken for the preparation of the foundation. The chorobate was placed at each of the foundation locations—sighted to the other foundations, across the water—the sight taken again under different light using several people known to have good eyesight—until it was agreed that the measurements were acceptable.

The end of the month of *Quintilis*

The extreme storm and flood season of three months was considered to start the first of the next month, *Sextilis*. To expedite his work, the bridge contractor considered use of additional personnel; the contractors had been advised in the bid solicitation that it was possible that some former slaves would be available for employment. The number was known at this time as more than two weeks had passed since Appius advised the slaves they should process through the Nemausus court. Of the original 200 slaves, seven had died; some had left for their prior homes although a handful said they would return with their families. In the region, 120 remained, mostly employed by the trench contractors and 32 freedmen remained available to be hired by other contractors.

End of *Sextilis*

"What work will you continue during this flood season?" Appius stood with the bridge contractor watching men chipping at a stone foundation next to the river.

The contractor turned to face Appius. "We have been working on the foundations for nearly three weeks, and I think that we will take another month to complete our foundation preparation. At that time we will be two months into the flood season. If a flood should occur, it will be of no great consequence except, perhaps, to clear the work area of debris. We will place no stones during the flood season, but at the top of the canyon we will prepare our lifting devices so that they may be taken to the streambed and assembled quickly. Therefore, at the beginning of *Novembris*, we will start immediately to place stones, racing to stack as many as possible before next flood season in nine months."

"I understand and think your plan is reasonable. Have you given much thought to the following phase in which you will be starting the arches? It seems like there is even more difficulty to place all the arch stones before the danger of flood." Appius shrugged.

The contractor nodded. "Yes, I have given that some thought—something I wanted to talk to you about. It is true, the lower tier arch structure is extremely vulnerable if we have not completed the arches on the full length of the tier, and we still rely on the wood supports. However, I have an idea. Would you have your designers consider modifying the pier structure so that a ledge protrudes just above the start of the arch? Instead of supporting the wood structures from the ground, or even the riverbed, we will use the pier structure itself to support the wood. If we do that, we will not be susceptible to timber columns being exposed to a flood but will rely on the more stable rock of the piers."

Appius wagged his head. "I suppose such a change is possible."

"Will you do it?"

"I will discuss your idea with the designers. While it is true that you are responsible, I think we could and should decrease risks of damage using your idea." Appius smiled.

"If you will let me talk to your designers, I will tell them of my thoughts. We will also need a small ledge below the one I mentioned—to support the stones which will protrude."

576

"Yes, please talk to them. I will tell them you have talked to me. If we make this change, we must also have these special stones available from the quarry—aged and of the correct size. We must see if that is possible."

"Yes, and while we are talking about the quarry operations, please do not let the quarryman get behind in his deliveries." The contractor shook his head. "A slow production of stones while I am using my resources to place stones quickly would be an embarrassment. If we should be slow to receive stones, I would not then be responsible for damage from a flood."

"This I understand, and I will ensure that the quarry contractor is diligent in his production. In fact, I have already made provisions to do so, at the expense of the Empire, I might add."

"It is good."

"You will soon be in our office?"

"Yes." The contractor walked to the foundation site to talk to his supervisor.

Novembris

It was time for the first stone to be placed. The lowest foundation surface had been checked and rechecked. The first stone to be placed had been checked and rechecked. During the pier foundation preparation and while waiting to place the first stones, the contractor prepared timber poles and lines for hoisting devices at each of the seven pier foundations on the lower tier of arches. The first of such devices was now erected and ready for use.

The bridge contractor found Appius and said, "Appius Petronius, we are ready to place the first stone, and I want you to participate."

"I am excited to be part of a ceremony. Do you expect me to power the hoist?"

The contractor laughed. "No, we have several of your able ex-slaves to do that. You will merely help guide the stone into place as it is lowered. So will I. It is important that the first stone be placed with as much dignity and ceremony as possible. All will go well, thereafter."

"Is that so?"

"I wish that were true, but I do not want to ignore fate nor displease the gods. You are ready?"

"Yes. Let the bridge be built." Appius smiled and thought of Bernius.

The first stone was hoisted and placed with the ceremonial guidance of Appius and the contractor; crucial operations were performed by other men who actually knew what they were doing.

After the stone had been carefully set into position and measurements taken, Appius walked to his saddlebags and retrieved a jug of wine from which all present took a sip. Appius was pleased and so was the contractor. It never hurts to have all those upon whom you depend feel they are part of a larger entity. The contractor proposed a toast to Appius, adding to his *nomen* from that time forward, the *cognomen* Aedifex—the builder, creator, architect. Behold Appius Petronius Aedifex. The men all repeated the *tria nomena* several times, and he was known as such from that time on. Appius mused, remembering when he told Bernius he wanted to become an *architectus*. He shook his head in amazement to think that he had gone beyond even that lofty goal.

The contractor said, "Now, stand back, Appius Petronius Aedifex, so that you will not be in the way of our rapid placement of stones. We must compete with the river."

Although the floods occurred only occasionally, one could not depend on one year or another for mild weather. What would Bernius have said about the probabilities in this situation?

Appius initiated the prosecution of Titus and Quantus. Any number of citizens could apply to the courts with the complaint; however, the task fell to Appius or at least he was the person who was most intent on revenge for the killing of his friend. The *Corporata* preferred to have others initiate action so that removing Titus from the *Corporata* would appear as a consequence of his conviction, not an action initiated by them. A *quaestor* was appointed, who, in turn, appointed two citizens to join in an investigation of the accusation. As the accuser, Appius brought in Decimus Nautius to testify; he stated he had heard Flavius and his men question the man who, albeit under duress, admitted that Titus and Quantus had paid him to kill Bernius. Members of the *Corporata* were called to testify, to recount the statements and actions of Titus in the *Corporata* meeting, actions that implied guilt. In his complaint, Appius identified the motives Titus and Quantus harbored for killing Bernius—termination of their quarry contract and eliminating Bernius with the hope that the project could not survive without him. The court agreed that there was enough substantiation to bring the two to trial, and a trial date had been set. Titus and Quantus were still free to go about.

The trial was scheduled to occur two months later. The *quaestor* and his appointees, now the *quaestora paricida* (originally applied to killing of a father but extended to killing of any free man) would hear the trial. There was little additional information to be investigated or presented, but Titus and Quantus could now present their defense. The punishment for murder in the Roman Empire had in the past incorporated several means including, for the wealthy—confiscation of their estate, various means of execution, or banishment to lands remote from the Empire. At this time, the method called *culleum* had become popular in which the convicted was sewn into a bag made of oxen skin and dumped at sea, the convicted in the company of a snake or other obnoxious animal. Where a sea was not present, the executioners did without, somewhat prolonging the ordeal, we assume.

One week before the trial, Titus and Quantus disappeared and upon search of their premises, it was evident that any valuables that could be carried away had been carried away. Their wives, as the closest relatives, had also disappeared. Neighbors, friends, and relatives claimed no knowledge of the disappearance. It was dryly noted that the duo probably preferred life on the run to terrifying last moments in a leather sack.

Appius insisted that the trial be held *in absentia* so that guilt could be established, providing basis for the trial of Flavius and those who were tainted in his orbit. The court convened, having no trouble coming to a conviction of the two, their guilt more indelible by their disappearance. The court also dealt with the disposition of their estates and, not wanting the value to descend upon relatives who might be of a plot to re-distribute portions to the convicted. Instead the value to the region was bequeathed after creditors were paid. For Quantus, the remaining value was substantial. For Titus, reeling from debts, some value remained, but not what one would expect from a man of his position. It was ironic that the estate he intended to save by the killing of Bernius was lost by that very action.

Appius requested the *quaestora paricida* to send a message to the court of Claudius. They would have as a matter of course, but Appius was anxious to get the word to Flavius, now sequestered in Rome. If he could only be there to observe Flavius's reaction when he got the news.

CHAPTER 55
Novembris **of the same year**

The excavation contractor who had started first—on the segment from the Alzon, working to the east—would soon complete excavation to the depth of 6 feet for the entire length of his segment—the first phase. Two months prior to completing this excavation, Appius had Vibius—employing Marius and Pentius—established accurate level lines using the clay pipe scheme. The other underground segments would undergo this same procedure. Once 'level' for the entire aqueduct was established, the slope of the aqueduct could be determined, defining the final excavated depth at any location along the trench. The level lines would also define the bottom of the *conduit* through the underground sections, atop the elevated structures, through the tunnels, and across the Vardo bridge. Therefore, establishing level along the entire run was a significant milestone, and Appius chafed to have it completed.

Working with a little over 100 feet of half-round clay pipe, level for a 100-foot length of excavation was determined. Marius and Pentius arrived at the site with a cart loaded with approximately 30 four-foot lengths. Of course, the bottom of the 6-foot excavation was as uneven as any hand-hacked excavation of earth. In 100 feet, one could easily expect variations of a foot or more.

They first distributed the pipe along the length. Then starting at one end, using varying sizes of scrap wood, they propped the pipe, inserting the end of one pipe section into the bell shape beginning of the next section. The leveling was first done by eyesight, understanding that adjustments would be necessary. The bell shaped ends had received a liberal dose of a tar to prevent water from escaping the trough.

When the entire length had been propped and the ends sealed, water was poured into the trough. At this time it would be apparent that some pipe sections were too low or too high. Marius and Pentius, after a partial filling of the trough, set out to raise or lower the pipes by replacing props with wood of greater or less thickness. They did not have to be precise. As long as water would be present in every section, the continuous water level would provide the needed accuracy.

The first time they did this, the procedure took them an entire morning. Thereafter, the process went faster as the learning-curve became effective. Once the water behaved, the level line was measured from its surface and marked on the floor of the excavation. If they were not in a section of rock, a stake was driven into the earth and marked.

When complete with a 100-foot section, one end was unstoppered and the water drained into buckets; the clay pipes were separated and moved ahead to the next 100 feet. Marius and Pentius worked hard to keep improving the process and the time that it took, dazzling Vibius as they worked. In a short while, they were able to make ten set-ups in a day.

Within six months, all of the underground segments of the aqueduct had been excavated to the 6-foot depth. The crew establishing level, continuing to the other underground sections, completed their work soon after the 6-foot excavation was completed on the last section.

Now that level had been established for the entire route, Appius huddled with Vibius, reviewing diagrams showing the current bottom of the 6-foot trench in relation to level. They were now able to calculate the differences resulting from the use of the less accurate, although improved, chorobate and the more accurate clay pipe method.

Level for the segments of the aqueduct where the structure would be built *above* the terrain could not easily be established by the clay pipes. When the structure was to run above the ground or over canyons and gullies, there was no well-behaved bottom of an excavated ditch to lay clay pipes. Vibius, with the useful but noisy crew of Marius and Pentius, used the improved chorobate for these relatively short runs. From notes by Bernius, Appius determined that the error would not cause difficulties when not shooting more than 100 feet, a situation they could easily handle.

The Vardo bridge canyon was more of a problem. A clay pipe could not be run down the canyon sides; and supports to cross the river would be out of the question. Therefore, they made careful chorobate shots from both sides of the canyon a number of times to determine the relative elevations on either side. Appius determined that in 400 feet, they could have an error of several inches, but again they could adjust without problem. Appius was wistful that he could no longer work in the wilds with Marius and Pentius.

Appius had Vibius assemble the aqueduct profile documents to display a continuous run of the aqueduct; the diagrams ran the entire length of the office wall. Required conduit elevation could now be established for any point along the aqueduct. However, due to errors, some existing excavations would have to undergo substantial corrections or else the constructed conduit would be too shallow at some locations and too deep in others. They were now constricted by the route they had chosen, so they could not, without a significant amount of additional work, move the route up or down the hill to help correct the problem. Therefore, Appius and Vibius decided that they could slightly modify the desired slope in section to section, some being of steeper descent than planned, and some being flatter, to reduce the more radical differences. On the diagrams, they made a number of trial adjustments, noting the results after each try, until they optimized the situation. Satisfied, Vibius could now establish markings on the side of the trench, below which the contractor must excavate to the calculated depth. Appius felt a sense of accomplishment, again marveling that significant improvements could result if one just had the tools and the method.

The underground excavation contractors had continued work, starting on the next 6-foot depth. Any adjustments to their work would occur at the third 6-foot level. When, finally, the bottom line of the aqueduct had been determined, excavation of that third level could start behind the second, in stair-step fashion. And, once the *final* depth had been excavated for a short distance, construction of the underground structure, the conduit and all the cement and masonry construction involved would be able to start.

Appius's revised schedule had anticipated the date that the conduit masonry construction *could* start, so bidding and awarding of the contracts had occurred preceding the available start date.

Additionally, they now knew the requirements for the slope and the dimensions for the *aboveground* structures and those contracts could also be bid and awarded. Soon, the project would be under construction from one end to the other, employing contractors and men from the region and those more distant. Some ex-slaves, now freedmen, had encouraged other countrymen to make the journey, to earn attractive wages for a time, the considerable time that it would take to construct the aqueduct. The buildup of manpower was evident.

The landscape around the home of Appius and Antonia became more populated. Workers, contractors, marketeers, clothiers, cobblers, entertainers, artists, woodworkers, wine merchants, along with those who ran stables, eateries, transportation and message services, often with their families, established homes which, in the beginning, appeared crude and primitive, but over time took on multiple patinas of organization, decoration and convenience. A village appeared generating all those attributes defining such, including a loose arrangement of leaders, patronized by the village for self-interest, protection and justice.

Appius, although the most senior in terms of Empire, was not a village leader, although he was often consulted in order to tap his superior knowledge of the overall circumstances and the future. Yes, Appius was highly regarded and respected. He was honored due to his effort with Claudius to re-establish the project as a part of the local economy rather than to be executed by a phalanx of slaves laboring for the Empire under the military. Also, he was popularly considered to provide apt leadership and reasoned resolutions to the myriad of problems that surfaced daily, nearly always understanding the practical basis.

Antonia, Sergius, and Bernius basked in this aura disarming somewhat the complaint that Antonia might have harbored—that of being shucked from the comfort of family, market and neighborhood—not that Appius did not have to hear about this circumstance from time to time. His rejoinder, that she return to Nemausus, for Appius to see her and for Appius to play with his sons when convenient, was always a possible solution but never one that she favored. Life, in many ways was easier for her due to Appius's elevated status and wages. Hired staff created and cultivated a garden, broomed the grounds, fetched water from the springs, protected them, and occasionally watched the boys, Sergius and Bernius, while Antonia visited families who had lodged into houses that had evolved into homes as time went on, building a community as surely as the project around them took place as a useful structure.

the *Aedifex*: Building the Pont du Gard

Yes, Sergius and Bernius. Appius would have hated to be away, not to experience every nuance of their fascination and understanding. Sometimes when he arrived home, thinking of the crushing problems of the project, defiant in their resolution, a transition occurred, difficulties evaporated, as Sergius walked to hug his legs and Bernius whooped to get attention.

Maius, the next year

Appius was impressed and captivated with the flow of construction, for example his vision in which the stones flowed from the quarry face to the *Pontis Vardo*. Construction of the underground structures had its own flow. For each of the four underground segments under construction, he rode from the least completed location to that furthest along. Currently, 'furthest along' meant complete.

On a typical inspection he would start his ride, riding and viewing miles of trench dug to only the 6-foot level—stretches in which there was no current construction. Further along, his first vision of activity was of men unloading buckets of earth upon the ever-growing windrow to the far side of the cleared path while other men coaxed boulders to the base of the piled earth with steel bars. As he rode closer, he could look over the brim of the deeper trench, seeing men with picks facing him, prying earth and stone from the advancing edge, now 12 feet below the surface. Boulders, pried loose from the face, often bounced or rolled down to the trench bottom. Beyond the men with the picks, others bent to fill buckets, working around those with bars who were moving the larger stones toward the ramp. The men with buckets trudged up the ramp, past the men rolling stones, until they reached the top of the ramp then crossed the trail to the base of the windrow. At the trench, beyond, Appius could see several hundred feet of the 12-foot excavation and in the distance a taller and wider expanse of piled earth, indicating the advancement of the trench excavated to the third level.

As Appius rode on, the bottom of the trench would be free of workers at the 12-foot depth until he reached the final downward stair-step excavation, an operation similar to that prior but experiencing more difficulty. While digging the final 6 feet, more large rocks were encountered, and often solid rock faces, not individual boulders. Men worked to loosen and separate the solid rock, sometimes resorting to practices similar to that used in the quarry. In these sections, the earth now had to be hauled, scooted, rolled, or winched 19 feet to the surface in order to join the growing pile of earth.

Along the trail, Appius saw men with hammers and chisels working on many of the larger stones deposited alongside, creating usable blocks, rough hewn, for the masonry walls being constructed farther along the trench.

The trench now seemed to stretch endlessly before Appius. On the trail he passed carts pulled by horses, mules, and oxen, trundling their heavy loads of hewn stones to the construction that lay ahead, or returning toward him, empty, for the next load. Appius waved to them and sometimes stopped and talked. It was always interesting to hear viewpoints of the workers and the details of their particular situation. Cart wheels squeaked and men shouted to each other, trading jeers, jesting, and complaining.

He encountered the rubble gatherers. They did not have to range as far as the stonecutters and were usually closer the initial masonry operation, that of laying the rubble in the bottom of the trench. Appius rode alongside the rubble carts to the point where in a noisy rumble, the stones were merely dumped over the side of the trench to piles on the bottom. The individual stones were plucked and somewhat artfully placed across the bottom to provide the first course of the structure.

Riding beyond several hundred feet of placed rubble, he arrived at a location where a more extensive operation was in process. Above the trench, men were stirring a mixture of cement, sand, small stones, and water in a mixing trough they had created using hewn wood for the sides, braced by stones around the perimeter. The operation was carried on in batch mode in that the materials were dumped into the trough and then mixed. Here, also, was exuberant yelling, the batchmaster directing more sand or more water, urging those bringing the materials to move along. Men filled their buckets with the mixture, walked down ramps to the bottom of the excavation, and deposited the contents on top of the rubble and between wooden forms, which created a 5-foot wide higher section in the middle. This surface would be the bottom of the conduit. As he watched atop his horse, Appius perceived the line of men with buckets causing the cement mixture to 'flow' down the ramp and onto the floor.

To sustain the batching operation, men on the trail were arriving with buckets of ingredients for the next batch. The cement, stored at sheltered locations along the conduit, arrived in carts. It was a line of ants, doggedly transporting their booty along one line, returning on another.

Along all stretches of the excavation, men were prospecting the piled, excavated earth, looking for small stones to be used in the concrete mix. Some locations yielded more of this material than others, so groups of men were clustered in the 'richer' deposits, throwing shovels or buckets-full of rocks onto a series of screens sorting rock of the desired size. They continually moved their operation, creating random piles of the aggregate. Sand was more rarely found; therefore, it had to be transported longer distances. And water, difficult to transport, was usually miles from the mixing location, so it was always transported in buckets aboard a cart, the carters urging their teams carefully over the uneven ground to avoid spillage. These carters were the most ill tempered of all, continually cursing their stock and their lot.

After riding past several hundred feet of curing concrete, Appius encountered piles of the roughly hewn stones placed on the trail above the trench. He could see men loading the cut stones onto small carts then edging the carts down the ramp towards the start of the masonry wall construction built atop the concrete. The men removed stones from the cart, stacked them, then returned up the ramp while men working with the masons, continually carried single stones to them.

At the trail, above the work, in an operation similar to the concrete mixing operation for the floor, smaller batches of mortar were being mixed and carried by bucket to the masons at the emerging walls. The masons, working with string lines, slathered the mortar against the concrete floor, pasted a trowel of mortar against the face of the prior stone, grabbed an awaiting stone and expertly placed it, swelling the mortar below and to the side of the stone. Two men, one in advance of the other, placed the initial stones, the bottom course of the walls, approximately 5-feet apart. Behind them the wall arose in stair-step formation as the masons worked from the inside. It was a narrow space between the walls, never enough room for masons, stacked stones, and those that were carrying the materials.

Appius saw the completed walls ahead of him, and farther along, men applying the red-colored cement lining to the insides, the lining that would provide a smoother surface for water flow and provide a seal to prevent leakage. On the trail above, for the lining, was another mixing station with the attendant piles of cement, sand, and pottery shards, unloaded by the men who brought them, and mixed by two men. After the mixing, another line of men with buckets transported the mixture to the masons applying the lining. The lining application was far distant from the next phase of work—that of building the wood supports for the conduit arch. The spacing allowed the lining to have sufficient curing time before the hazards generated by the rambunctious carpenters could destroy it.

As Appius rode further, he could see stacks of wood on the trail, along with more rough-cut stone. Men slid the timbers down the slope to carpenters waiting below, who, with saws, adzes, wedges, augers, and hammers, fashioned the wooden arch upon which stones would be placed. Not too far behind the form installation, masons were laying stones with mortar against the wood forms, creating the top of the conduit, the arch that would support the earth fill above.

Four-hundred feet farther along, men were pulling wood out of the conduit wall, wood disassembled from arch forms that had supported the stones until the mortar set with sufficient strength. A month was allowed for this curing, resulting in a stretch of newly constructed arch well ahead of the sufficiently cured section. The prior arch forms were used again for new form installation. Of course, Marius and Pentius found additional work involving the production of wood for the forms, not the more precise and slower building of the forms but the more rough and tumble shaping of fallen trees into usable timber. Appius always found time to locate them and arrange to eat his midday meal or dinner with them, and often to share their campfire overnight.

Beyond the arch stone section under cure, Appius could see men collecting earth from the windrowed pile and moving it across the trail to the edge of the trench, where it was dumped. Men working atop and alongside the arch then spread the earth over the arch and to the other side. For every 6 inches of spread earth, men with a concrete foot on the end of a wooden stick, tamped the earth in a continual up-down motion, the multiple thuds symphonically mingling amongst the sounds of the squeaky cart wheels, grunts of the men, and the sounds of earth and rock tumbling over the sides.

Appius rode beyond the activity. The trench had disappeared. Raw earth was now level with the trail and a depleted windrow remained at the side of the trail, amounting to the empty space inside the conduit. Appius forced a mental image of the process—from the 6-foot excavation to the completed work, imagining it being performed at a higher speed, a growing thing, earth flowing out of the trench then back in as rubble, sand, masonry, and backfill.

The bridge contractor was placing stones at an impressive rate often worrying Appius and the quarry contractor that slow production of finished stones would delay the installation. The designers had accepted the modification of the piers suggested by the contractor, allowing the temporary wood frames for the arch to be supported by the structure itself rather than from the ground. The quarry contractor was able to accommodate production of these stones—a size and shape not identified in the bid. The stones would be incorporated in the upper levels of the piers near the start of the arch.

The project office, situated at the top of the canyon, overlooked the work at the Vardo. From the office it was possible to see the multiple activities stirring, all minuscule yet all contributing to the slow but consistent growth of the structure. From day to day it was difficult to sense the accomplishment. Yet, if one were away for a week, one could tell the difference.

Appius craved time to stand and watch. From his vista he could see carts arriving from the quarry, depositing the precisely chiseled blocks in areas strategic to their ultimate placement. A man with documents checked each stone for the proper designation and dimensions as it arrived and was slid from the cart. Appius defocused his view, imagining the ant-like flow of stone from the quarry into the canyon and upward onto the structure. Given enough time and ants, the structure would one day be complete.

Quintilis
Flood season now approached. The bridge contractor worked his men seven days per week, rather than the usual six. The hoists were lifting stones to the piers, nearing the limit of their reach. Further heights of placement would have to be accomplished by a different arrangement in which the timbers

supporting the pulleys would be atop the structure, not from timbers anchored to the ground.

Motive power for lifting was provided by men walking in a vertical circular treadmill, lifting stones weighing as much as 6 tons using mechanical advantage of the treadmill, drum, and pulley system. The cut stones awaiting placement were at such locations that when they were lifted from the ground, they swung under the pulley blocks and were lifted above the structure and laterally to the final location above stones placed prior then lowered to the final precise location.

Finished stones, shaped to divert the water, were being placed at the upstream face of the piers. Appius and the contractor were aware that the river had flooded even above the top of the piers--over 50 feet above the normal river surface. The contractor lashed additional timbers to those being used on the hoist yielding a higher reach to place more stones atop--additional weight--as a precaution. These rough-cut stones were temporary and would have to be removed later.

Appius stood on the rim of the canyon, impressed with the structure that was taking shape. The piers stood as a tribute to the effort that had been expended. It was exhilarating.

Appius spotting the contractor watching his men, walked down the side of the canyon to join him on the canyon floor. "Contractor, I have to say that you are expending every measure possible to avoid a disaster. I am very pleased with your work."

"Thank you, Appius—Aedifex. Although I am not doing so to please you, I am happy that you can understand we have made a considerable effort. Will you be disappointed if we do not experience a flood?"

Appius laughed. "No—well, I have to admit that your extreme effort will seem to have been wasted if we only experience a normal rainy season. But, if one thinks about having to restart the work should the stones be dislocated... it is easier to accept that we will be grateful not to put the work to a test."

"We will soon know."

Appius thought the contractor an extraordinary man, an excellent supervisor, a person with vision—the ability to imagine consequences. "Contractor, what is your situation? Do you have a family? Are they here at Versus Pontis?"

The contractor turned from observing his crew, shading his eyes as he looked toward Appius and into the sun. "I had a wife and family. We lived in Rome and, because my wife was the daughter of a wealthy corn factor, we lived quite well. However, my passion was not for living a life of wealth and ease; I prefer the challenges of the work. So, although my wife's fortune was used to finance my early construction operations, she tired of my continual absences as I began to work beyond the confines of Rome. We found it best to part. My former wife and two sons live in Rome. I live elsewhere, recently Lugdunom."

Appius nodded. "Would you join me and my family for dinner? Perhaps you are tired of buying your meal from the vendors. And, I would be pleased to have a man such as you at my table, all the more significant in the completion of this first phase of work."

The contractor smiled. "Indeed... I would. You are correct. I would enjoy eating with your family. I understand you also have two sons."

"Yes. They are growing fast. It seems like they will soon be building large projects. It takes a lot of energy for me to keep up with them at the end of the day. You will see. Can you join us tonight?"

"Yes, of course."

Appius strode to his home mid-day, finding Antonia tending to the boys. "Antonia, I have invited a guest for dinner."

"Is that so? Someone visiting from Rome, one of your staff...?"

"No, it is the contractor building the bridge. He is a very capable fellow, worthy of conversation, and perhaps worthy as a friend."

"Do you think it is a good idea to have close relations with a contractor?"

"Your point is well taken. I have given that some thought. Do you think a business relationship is strengthened or weakened because of a friendship?"

"I see. Yes, perhaps there could be an advantage. One might think twice before skewering their friend—even in a business sense."

"That is what I have thought, also. It is true; there is a possibility of good or evil. In this situation, I choose to err on the side of a friendly relationship."

"What is the contractor's name?"

Thomas Hessler

"It is funny. I call him 'contractor' from habit. He is the one that named me 'the *Aedifex*.' But, his name is Publius Acilius."

"I will have a fitting dinner prepared. I will see you both at the meal."

Sergius and Bernius, trying for their father's attention during this time, gave up their facial antics and rushed to embrace his legs.

* * *

"Antonia, I would like you to meet the man I call 'contractor,' out of respect, of course. But perhaps you will call him Publius Acilius. Publius Acilius, my good wife, Antonia."

Publius, accustomed to Rome repartee, said, "Antonia, my pleasure. If I had a wife such as this, Appius, I would not spend so much time at work."

Antonia beamed. "Thank you for that, Publius Acilius. To me it does seem that Appius spends too much time on the project. I have to ponder your remark."

At dinner, between episodes of caring for the boys, the adults shared descriptions of their past—their history.

Antonia tilted her head as she asked, "So, Publius Acilius, you were raised in Rome, by—it seems—parents who saw to your education. Were they wealthy?"

"They were not of vast wealth, not of such that they would qualify as *equestrians*, but my father made a good living, also as a contractor. It appears that I not only inherited his blood but his interest and fascination in building. However, my wife—that is, my ex-wife—is from a family of much greater wealth—her father a corn factor, as I explained to Appius. I could have taken a path to politics, if I chose, but I chose *not*. I would rather deal with the vagaries of stones, workmen—even floods—rather than the deception, treachery, and frustration of politics."

Antonia said, "And now you are dealing with the floods—Appius tells me. Are you afraid of the risks that the Vardo might thrust upon you?"

Appius and Publius exchanged glances. "I am not afraid. My risks are calculated, but, of course, the outcome is not certain. Most of the time I am successful at this. Sometimes, fate punishes me. Consider my approach to some other person's approach in which maximum safety is assured."

Antonia smiled and glanced at Appius. "My husband understands what you are saying. If he had not taken chances, had not acted rather than waited, he would not be... the *Aedifex*."

"Yes, such is life. I hope that the risks I am taking on this project will not result in catastrophe." Publius Acilius smiled.

Appius nodded.

"But, if so, I will recover, as I did when my wife and I decided to part."

Antonia displayed her brightest smile. "Perhaps you would like to meet my sister."

Sextilis

Publius Acilius kept his crews working well into flood season. In addition to continuing to pile stones atop the piers, with difficulty at this stage, he was fashioning timber members that would comprise the arch supports. As it was the rainy season, floods or no, the work was often miserable, a slog in the mud, or at a standstill due to thunderstorms that occurred with antagonizing frequency.

The quarry had produced the stones required for the support of the arches and the contractor installed them. When the protruding stones were in place on two piers and the pier built above, the crew lifted and pinned the hewn arch-support timbers for one arch into position. Between the two piers, at a lofty 70 feet above the riverbed, carpenters precariously straddled beams and stringers of the form while reaching for additional timbers lifted by the hoist; they positioned and secured them as part of the first arch form installation. Underneath, men were fashioning wood with saws, axes, planes, hammers, chisels, and augers. A growing pile of chips and cut ends were evidence of the work that had been done for the truss. The large timbers, hewn of select wood, were squared, the ends augered to accept pins that would connect the timbers. The span of the supports was considerable, the largest over 80 feet; the truss design, using the strength of the triangular arrangement, provided nearly mystical strength.

The contractor explained, "I am taking a risk, but not a huge one by installing a truss. I wanted to see how our temporary support system would work. In fact, we have discovered changes we can make to improve the installation and removal of the others.

It was worth the effort although we had to work between thunderstorms."

Appius gazed at the timber arch-support structure, resting between the piers. He could now imagine arches in a graceful parade across the canyon.

CHAPTER 56

Lisele was at my house most of the time, preferring my company to that of her daughter. I'm not sure they spoke at all. Lisele could not forgive Laurie for deliberately trying to make life miserable for me—truly a difficult situation for Lisele. Laurie will never forgive me, I suppose, for not taking advantage of the enticing opportunity she provided, a girl so attractive—yet rejected and her mother chosen instead—quite understandable for Laurie, actually.

I continued my stay in France because of Lisele, obviously, but I also wanted to be in proximity when the results of the *Castellum* document review were made known. Renat fed me snippets of information every so often, resulting from his contact with his friend on the Antiquities Committee. To date, they had been able to transcribe the written content and most of the graphical information in the documents. Now, an array of experts was interpreting the first century Latin, the charts, and the drawings. Although I was seriously miffed about the way I had been treated, I must admit I thirsted to find out what the documents revealed.

One autumn afternoon I was in the kitchen, my leisure location of choice given that the weather had turned cool. I heard a knock. Lisele went to the door. I could hear a subdued conversation.

Lisele walked into the kitchen and put her hands on my shoulders. "There is somebody here to see you. He is in the front room." Uncertainty showed in her eyes, and I was puzzled, not able to guess the reason.

I nodded and walked into the front room. Lisele followed me, knowing she would have to provide translation. Standing there with a briefcase and a rolled document in hand was Professor Durand. I was flabbergasted. "What?" I said.

Durand smiled slightly at me but shook his head and spoke to Lisele. She translated his words. "I knew this would be a shock. I could have called first, but I wanted to show up and see how you reacted. A bit perverse, perhaps."

Rage engulfed me. "You taunt me, reject my interest, and steal my ideas... " Lisele repeated in French, perhaps adding even more vitriol than I, as I looked with disgust upon Durand.

Durand held up his hand. "I know... I knew this would be your reaction, and I think you have a right to express your anger, but please hear what I have to say before you throw me out." He looked at Lisele, then at me.

I remained impassive for a moment then nodded. *What could this asshole possibly say in his defense? Is that what this was all about? And, why?*

Durand looked at me and spoke. "We have transcribed and translated the documents. I, and my associates, have scrutinized the charts and drawings. There is a great wealth of information contained... a treasure actually... not just a glimpse or a hint, but an *account* describing how the aqueduct was conceived and built. Herein... " he opened his briefcase and extracted a sheaf of papers, "is a history, a log, answering several of the questions you asked and telling a story of difficulties encountered and resourcefulness used in building the aqueduct. It is marvelous. There is a daily log, starting from the time the aqueduct was conceived. As I say, a treasure."

I let the implications sink in, watching Durand as Lisele spoke the English version to me.

He smiled, watching me as Lisele talked, then continued. He held out the sheaf of papers. "These are for you." He handed them to me. "I have made you a copy of the translations annotated with our best understanding of what was written."

I grasped them.

He then handed me the rolled documents. "These are *copies* of a schedule and diagrams obviously used for the building of the structure. Of course we cannot show you the original schedule—it is too fragile—and, enigmatically, it is smeared with blood. No telling what calamity occurred to cause that. Ha, ha. You will find that the methodology in building the structure is somewhat sophisticated. We were all very surprised."

I took the rolled documents and remained holding the sheaf of papers. All my anger had subsided, and I was overwhelmed by having the means to resolve my appetite—quench this fire that burned within me. I could now *live* the project that had captured my imagination. Those thoughts were consuming me, but I said nothing, staring at the documents.

Durand waited until I glanced up, looking me in the eye. "We... I particularly... are grateful for what you have done. I will write a paper—co-authored by a number of associates—describing what we have learned. I will be proud—and I am asking your permission—to include your name and describe the work you have done to produce this grand result. I hope you will accept my offer and my apology." He looked to Lisele then back to me to assess my reaction.

I took a deep breath. The word 'apology' brought several ugly incidents to mind, but my thoughts quickly slid to the present. The professor had overcome his distaste for my impudence, my rash interest in a treasure that was clearly the province of the French. Here he was, apologizing and offering me recognition to make amends. I had to admire what he was doing. Only a jerk would enact spite and revenge. I said, although it was not easy, "Thank you, Professor. I will be happy to have recognition in your work and will be thrilled to read the product now in my hands." I smiled, perhaps weakly.

At that instant, Durand held out his hand and beamed.

We shook hands.

"Perhaps we could celebrate with a glass of wine." He pulled a bottle from his briefcase.

Perhaps we could, and we did. We made light conversation as we drank, doing our best to communicate in the inconvenient world of multiple languages. I couldn't help think as we were talking and enjoying the wine, that this was surely an unintended circumstance for Laurie. How would this visit by Durand affect the relationship between Lisele and Laurie? But, the thought uppermost in my mind, one that continually intruded, was—I can't wait for this celebration to be over so I can start reading.

CHAPTER 57

Septembris

Messages regularly reached Nemausus from Rome. Rome was inclined to establish close and frequent communications with its outposts and, therefore, sent regular missives to which they expected a reply. As one might expect, most of these communications involved tax matters, the collection, allocation, and the sending of. However, the Romans could see beyond the collection of sestertii and actually took time and expended energy to send along newsy bits and pieces, perhaps with some arrogance, thinking that everybody wanted to know what was going on in Rome, but also using a stratagem considering that—an informed empire was an empire that complied. Another concept that prevailed at the time, mostly amongst the far-flung empire inhabitants was—familiarity breeds contempt.

Appius heard that Flavius and General Crassius had gone on trial, the trial judges selected from senators because a general was involved. Confusion reigned as to the whereabouts of the *decanus* at whose hands the Ucetians had been punished. Apparently the military was not able to locate him as witness and the man with primary responsibility for the slaughter. However, through the wiles of the Senate, General Crassius was 'persuaded' to find the men who had participated in the atrocity at the command of the *decanus*.

At court, in testimony, and in the mind of the judges, no clear link was established between the general and the incident. However, his actions following the incident, usurping the power of the proconsul who now, embarrassingly, was at the very pinnacle of the Roman Empire, was damning. The general's hands-off treatment of his men over the incident, no doubt contributed to his sentence of exile, a virtual death sentence as he would have to abide in lands naturally hostile to the concept of Roman hegemony and not appreciative of the skills of even *ex*-Roman generals who had a glorious past plundering the resources of those he conquered.

For Flavius, however, the court presumed that strict instruction of conduct must be given to subordinates—the *decanus*—performing duty amongst Roman citizens. They, therefore, found Flavius sufficiently guilty to receive harsh sentence. At the core of the matter was intent to impress the citizenry that law protected Roman citizens and that the Empire was serious in the application—citizens are not to be put to death without a trial. That Flavius also did nothing to reprimand his men for their action added considerable weight and gravity to the accusations, compounded by results of the Nemausus trial—the Ucetians were not responsible. As to Flavius's direct actions in the incident, the lack thereof became forgotten when one knew all the circumstances. The judges sentenced him to a life in chains at hard labor, also a virtual death sentence as one did not last long under the whip, exhaustion, and ill treatment that was the practice. Better that the Ucetians had their way with him.

Even Appius winced at the sentence, shaking off the thought, although his fondest dream had been to see Flavius in chains. It would not be worth a trip to Rome just to taunt the former centurion, but perhaps someone traveling to Rome could visit and describe the miserable circumstances of the prisoner.

The Ucetians were still wary of the military, and Appius instructed the military to stay away from the village and the operations near the springs. However, due to the burgeoning commerce in the region, the demand for food and services, the Ucetians began venturing beyond their village and beyond involvement only within the village. They gradually became a part of the supply chain that fed the growing needs of the aqueduct construction though they did not forget what had happened. Appius worked with the Empire and the Corporata to include compensation to Ucetia for the water that would eventually course in the veins of the aqueduct.

Octobris

To the amazement of Appius, Publius Acilius continued construction although the danger of floods had not passed. The quarry had been producing the arch stones for some time and the contractor proceeded to install a few stones above one arch, upon the frame that had been installed. He also installed a second then a third set of arch supports.

Appius, remembering Publius's statement regarding the ultimate responsibility of the Empire, was concerned that Publius was putting Empire sestertii at risk. He approached Publius. "Contractor, are you not concerned that you are exposing yourself to great expense should the river flood and carry your trusses away? The trusses could even cause the destruction of their supporting piers if the river should flow against them and they should be dislodged."

Publius shook his head. "We have been through two of the three months of flood season and have only a month to go; therefore, my exposure is reduced. It is true, catastrophe could still strike, but I think the chances are slight that a flood would be of such magnitude that the piers would be overtopped and even less so, if that happened, to cause destruction. I am more concerned with our next phase—that of building the first arches. Should we not have all the arch stones in place and the intermediate stones filled in, between arches and the stones in place above the topmost part of the arches, we will not have achieved the full strength of the structure and, therefore, would still need to have the trusses in place. To me, we would be at severe risk. That is why I am taking this smaller risk now, to avoid a situation of more consequence."

Appius took a deep breath. "I understand your reasoning. You have my full support. I hope that the fates and the gods are not working against you... us."

"We will soon know."

The thunderstorms often produced heavy rainfall, often at one-inch per hour. If the storms were short, the consequences would be minimal, although the river would always rise a foot or so in response. The Vardo, starting at an elevation of nearly 5000 feet, ran a length of 70 miles before reaching the bridge. It was susceptible of collecting vast amounts of water over the length, supplemented by the many tributaries of seeps, brooks, creeks, and streams—a dangerous river.

It rained heavily starting one afternoon. Unlike most of the thunderstorms, lasting an hour, possibly two, this heavy rainfall continued. It was raining hard when Appius went to bed, a concern that allowed only fitful sleep. In the middle of the night, he awoke; it was still raining hard. He leaped from the bed, startling Antonia.

"What is the matter? Are you worried about the storm?"

"Yes. I must see. I fear that we may have trouble."

He dressed and walked first to the home of Publius Acilius, rapping on the door. There was no response—not to his surprise. He continued his walk to the bridge, shaking his head at the appearance of flowing water in every gully, creek, and crevice. *This is not good.*

the *Aedifex*: Building the Pont du Gard

At the edge of the canyon, he could see the river, already in spate, up beyond the foundation stones, 12 feet... or was it 16 feet... up the piers. At higher ground, on the canyon wall, he spotted someone... it must be the contractor... standing, watching. Appius struggled down the canyon, fighting the mud and water tracing spiderweb paths across the slope. He slipped several times, cursing, righting himself, and slogging on. He finally reached the side of the contractor who had been watching his difficult approach. He looked at the face of Publius Acilius to determine his concern. "Contractor, do you fear the worst?"

"I think the river will continue to rise, and it is still raining. I am not able to predict what will happen. But, yes, I am fearful of the situation, and I am happy to have company."

"There is nothing we can do."

"No. We must only wait and watch."

The rain stopped, dwindling to a light drizzle, well before the dawn. However, it was certain that the river would continue to rise as the slug of water from upstream feeds, continued, building as it neared the bridge. The lifting devices in the riverbed had disappeared, swept downstream by the torrent. Two remained but were sure to be lost as the river continued to rise. There had been no time to assemble a crew to save them. Publius Acilius smiled wryly as the water reached the base of the wooden arch supports.

Appius could not help but think, *the loss of the lifting devices will surely be borne by the contractor. I hope that is the worst that happens, but...* shaking his head... *I am fearful there is more.* He did not say this to the contractor.

Appius and Publius had been joined by others of the contractor's crew. The crew members knew there was nothing they could do, but they had a close regard for the work they had performed and were drawn to the site as mourners are drawn to a funeral, although it was true, some were there for the spectacle. They silently nodded to Publius Acilius and Appius as they reached the observation site, an acknowledgement of all that mattered between a contractor and his men. Soon, it seemed, their viewing ground would also be inundated.

Appius noted, "One of your arch supports has the stones placed atop. I wonder if they will anchor the wood."

Publius nodded. "The weight of the stones is considerable. We will see." He shook his head.

Appius could not help but think that he might have been mistaken to allow the contractor to proceed with the arch supports. Of course, nobody could have predicted this storm, but those who criticize are always gifted with more clarity afterwards than those who have taken the risk. He decided he would defend the contractor's actions no matter the result. Somehow this thought gave him strength to witness the growing possibilities of destruction. Would this episode mean the end of his career?

At dawn, the water reached the top of the piers—the top of the stones that were arranged to divert the water—38 feet above the foundation. The wood trusses were submerged to a depth of 6 feet. The wooden form with stones atop seemed immobile, and one of the other trusses, wedged into place against the adjacent stones, was not showing signs of stress. However, the third support, newly assembled, had not been wedged and was clearly being lifted, floated by the rising water. Suddenly it moved downstream only to rack and be bound by the pier stones on either side. Would it hold and be saved? No! In fifteen minutes the rising river forced the truss free from captivity by the piers. Slowly at first, it floated through the opening between the piers, bashing the stones several times until it finally cleared the piers, racing hell-bent with the current. The viewers were stunned into silence, at once understanding the display of force by the rampaging river and the loss of effort and sestertii that must surely befall the contractor. Many—most—furtively glanced at Publius then at Appius to gauge their reactions.

In a short while they were watching the truss that had been wedged into place, the timbers groaning as they withstood the stresses imposed by the force of water striking them directly. A wedge popped from its pocket, then another as the upward and horizontal force of the water pried the truss from its position. Soon, the truss lifted as a whole and drifted downstream as had the prior support. All turned to watch its progress. The observers had been forced to scramble higher on the riverbank to avoid being washed away.

The support with the arch stones atop held although its timbers groaned as they bent to resist the flow then occasionally made a snapping sound as they resumed their intended position when an occasional eddy permitted. It was possible that the structure would remain intact; the river ceased to rise and would perhaps now abate. It peaked at a height of nearly 50 feet above the foundation.

After the river subsided, the contractor and his crew struggled through the mud at the base of the piers, prying mud from stones that had been waiting to be lifted atop the structure. Some had been displaced by the force of the river and men with shovels were digging through the silt, mud, and trapped vegetation wherever a suspicious lump appeared.

Appius at first watched from a dry spot higher on the bank but soon slogged through the mud to talk to Publius Acilius. "What can you tell me, contractor?" He smiled at the man, bending to examine an unearthed stone.

Publius straightened to look at Appius, saw his smile, and took a deep breath. "I think we will somehow find most of the stones—at least the ones that weren't swept into the present channel of the river. Because the stones are inscribed with their identification, we will soon be able to tell you which are missing. The quarryman can replace them. We have found both trusses, one within eyesight and the other a mile further downstream. They ran aground as the river made a turn. Some of the timbers suffered damage and many of the pins connecting them are bent beyond use. It will be difficult to disassemble the truss and move the timbers to a path where they can be returned, but we will do so. Two of the piers must be rebuilt at the tops where the truss dislocated the stones as they smashed against them on their departure."

"The lifting devices?"

"We were at the height limit of the gin pole arrangement of the devices we were using. We would soon have had to rebuild the hoist supports atop the piers. It is true we would have used the timbers of the devices that were swept away. They will have to be replaced, but at least we will not have to duplicate the building of the pulley supports. Of course the circular treadmills, all seven of them have been destroyed and swept away. They will have to be swiftly rebuilt so that we may place the remaining arch supports although we will only have to build six for the six arches."

"Beyond this flood season, you were to be intent on placing the arch stones. Are you severely impacted?"

"Yes. We will lose cherished time in the race for completion of the arches before next flood season. We will use all of the men, working as many hours as we dare, to assemble the new lifting devices. I believe we will be lifting arch supports again in two weeks—in one location, at least, followed soon by lifting at the other arch locations. We have lost, probably, the equivalent of one month's placement of stones."

"And the next flood season looms in nine months."

"A catastrophe if we are not completed with arch stone placement and we experience a flood as we have just seen."

"But, I think it not likely that we would have two such floods, one year apart."

"Let us hope you are right. But, do you want to depend on that?" He smiled.

"No. We must work as if the gods will smite us again. I must ask. Do you have funds to recover the stones and timbers, to rebuild the lifting devices, to correct work that was once in place and paid for?"

"I have the funds. However, if the Empire were late in their payments, I would be seriously crippled. Please make sure that does not happen."

Appius nodded. "I will do so. I hope I can find other ways to help. It would be to our advantage that you do not suffer for funds or resources. It is clear to me that destruction of the nearly complete first tier of arches would be our calamity also. I will help if I can."

Publius Acilius was correct, or nearly so. In less than two weeks he had built one new lifting device, the first with the hoisting blocks and pulleys atop the piers. The giant wheel in which the men trod their circular path was located in the streambed, still at risk of high water although the time had passed for the season most considered as treacherous. Now, the crews were spinning the stones upward in airy flights to the top of the arch form. The contractor chose to provide the reassembled device at the form that had escaped damage. In that way, he—the crews—could gain experience in further placement of the arch stones, experience that could be applied to the other five arches. Also, he was immediately able to start stacking stones, whereas on the other arches, he would be first lifting timbers to build the form.

The next two lifting devices were built in 1-1/2 weeks as the men became more experienced in their assembly and avoided errors made on the first. On the remainder, even that duration was shortened. As soon as each lifting device was completed, it was used to place the timbers, already shaped, sawed to length, and augered for the connections, and stacked in their order of lifting. Men often rode up with the load as flying was much easier than climbing.

Now, it took little time to build the arch frame—five days—and the form construction crew nagged those building the lifting devices to a faster pace, not wanting to have to wait for them. Quickly, after the form was placed, the stone hoisting crews assembled, and arch stones flew to the location where they were to remain for the millennia. All arches were under construction in less than two months after the flood abated. Seven months remained before the threat of floods was once again upon them.

The motive power for the hoists was an elaborate contraption; the contractor used seven such for the piers on the lower tier of arches. The distinctive element consisted of a large wheel, 12 feet in diameter, mounted vertically. Sturdy wooden yokes, 8 feet high, supported the shaft. Spokes protruded from the shafts to the rims, maintaining the integrity of the wheel. The outer rim consisted of continuous wood planking with cleats spaced 2 feet apart on the inside, wide enough for two men to walk side by side as that is exactly what they did, walking one-quarter the way up the circular slope—an endless circular treadmill to power the hoist. The shaft protruded from the side of one yoke and was fitted with a drum around which the hoisting rope was wound. The taut end led to the array of blocks and pulleys overhead. A rope tender pulled on the free end of the rope line as it came off the drum. He maintained a tight wrap on the drum ensuring that the line did not tangle or slip as the stones were being raised or lowered. When the hook on the end of the line was being lowered for another load, the tender let the line slack so that it would slide on the drum, lowering the hoisting hook. The men in the treadmill did not have to walk to the other side to lower the hook.

Appius was fascinated, not having seen such a device before. He had watched the initial assembly—every day shaking his head, not entirely believing that the device could work. Upon the first use, the men on the treadmill were not coordinated causing tense moments when the load was lifted then lowered into place.

605

When the six arch hoists were in operation, Appius was exhilarated to see the stones flying up to their landing atop the wooden arch supports. It was often that most of them were doing so at the same time, cages spinning, men with tag lines attached to the loads to deftly assist in guiding the stones to a useful landing. While the stone was being received atop the structure, men on the ground were preparing the next stone for a lift, cradling it with ropes as it rested upon wooden dunnage, allowing the ropes to pass beneath the stone. When the hook returned, the next stone was ready for lifting. Meanwhile, atop the structure, men were prying the arch stones across the top of the wood form or across the tops of previously placed stones using rollers. One crew moved the stones to position but a crew of masons performed the final adjustments, delicately chipping here and there to achieve a precise fit, using hammers and chisels where necessary.

As one can easily imagine, six crews lifting nearly identical loads naturally generated competition, which quite often was organized so that all crews were given a signal to start at the same moment; compensation or handicapping was made for the different heights involved. The men in the wheel walked faster, nearly running, necessarily higher on the rim of the wheel. All crewmembers and any spectators in the vicinity yelled and shouted as the stones flew to their destinations. Atop, the stones were landed, the hook and cradles swiftly stripped from the stone and returned to the ground where the next stone awaited. The *win* occurred when the hook was reset in the cradle, ready for the next lift.

Crews kept their hoisting equipment in good working order. They made arrangements to employ heavier but faster wheel men and adept rigging crews. The contractor, Publius Acilius, was favored by this competition, of course, and did his utmost to maintain fair competition, understanding that the crews were composed of *his* employees—*his* selections. If a crew knew of men, not yet employed, that could churn or rig faster, and identified such to Publius, he was naturally happy to hire them. It was up to the crew to mollify those that had been displaced, creating a hierarchy of skill and rewards, similarly arranged. Publius established booty of sestertii for the winning crews from time to time. When the idea surfaced that a similar contest might be interesting—booty for the most stones lifted in a day, it was suspected that the idea had been planted by Publius. Nevertheless, the competition charged on.

The contests were of great interest for several months, but eventually the interest lagged except upon special occasions. The outcome of the contests, however, resulted in a reward system in which crews were paid additional sestertii for a superior quantity of stones placed during each month's time.

Publius was pleased. The stones were placed faster than he had estimated, thereby providing him additional sestertii after he paid his men—even after paying the rewards. This margin allowed him to offset the outflow of sestertii he had suffered to replace equipment and to repair the piers. Of utmost significance, production was maximized, a condition necessary to complete the first tier of arches prior to the coming flood season. However, Publius was working his crews more hours than he had intended for each day, knowing that when longer hours were worked, the production rate suffered. Yet, he could not falter.

CHAPTER 58
Lunius the following year

"Why is it necessary to have all the arches completed?" Antonia brought Appius a cup of wine after he had romped with the boys. It was summer, yet he did not get home until after dark. The contractor worked long hours to maximize his production and Appius thought it necessary that he also be on site if the contractor was working.

"A good question, Antonia." He took a sip of wine to wash an imagined layer of dust from his throat. "It is not just a matter of perhaps losing only the arch that is incomplete. We must leave all of the arch supports in until the structure is fitted with stone from one side to the other and the stones are tight to the canyon wall. The reason for this requirement is—once the forms are removed, the arch does not fall because it is held in place by restriction to its sideways movement. Each arch out there is depending on an adjacent arch to keep it from moving to the side, the entire structure, then, dependent on the walls of the canyon to resist the movement. Can you imagine that—the entire structure held in place by the walls of the canyon?"

"Yes. I have a feeling for what you are saying. My thought was that you could just leave the arch forms in place if you are not finished and you experience a flood. But, then I thought, you lost forms in the last flood. You could not depend on them."

"That is true. We lost forms, but not the one with stones atop. Perhaps if all the arches had stones atop, the water would not destroy the forms. However, if we should lose just one form on an uncompleted arch, it is fairly certain we would lose the entire structure. That is the reason the contractor is working each day as long as there is light and the reason I am there with him, not chasing the boys nor caressing your beautiful brown hair."

"And, after you finish this tier of arches...?"

"After we finish...this tier...we should no longer worry about the ravages of the river. We will not have to work as hard nor worry so much about a disaster due to a flood."

"It has been some time since I have seen the bridge. Soon I will take the boys, and we will walk to the side of the canyon. What is it like?"

"It is wondrous to me. I see the arches completed, the crews installing additional stones above to create the platform for the next level. I look at what has been built, and I can now imagine the completed tier of arches. I am anxious to see them without the wood forms. It will be beautiful."

"I am most anxious to see it. But, I ask, why is it necessary for you to be there at all times when the contractor is working?"

"There is work for our staff to do. When we are fitting the stones from the structure to the rock walls of the canyon, we must measure the distance required so that the quarryman can fabricate the stone to fit. Also, we must constantly check to see that the quarry is fashioning the stones that will soon be required—for hoisting into position. It would be a disaster if the hoisting crews were stopped because the stones were not available. We—me and my staff, as the coordinator of all contracts—would be remiss, if a shortage should occur, even though the quarryman has a schedule that details his requirements. But, in truth, not all the additional time is spent on the bridge. With contracts from one end of the aqueduct to the other, we are constantly dealing with their payments, questions, problems and squabbles. We scarcely have time to handle it all, even given the long hours we are working."

"Do you think about the questions, problems, and squabbles when you are here?"

"Nearly constantly."

Quintilis

Much work can be done in seven months by determined men. Two of the arches had been completed, the four remaining were in stair-step modes of completion. The crews, working steadily and swiftly, were fatigued from six months of long hours at hard work. It was evident that more work could not be obtained by additional urging of the men now somewhat cantankerous as a result of their toil.

Appius stood next to Publius at the top of the canyon. "You have spare manpower now that you have completed two arches, yet it seems that they cannot be used to speed the remainder."

Publius nodded. "It is true. The work is limited by the ability to hoist the stones, and we are doing so as fast as can be done. We are replacing tired men with those that are spare, usually after they have worked half their day. In that way we *can* use the spare men."

"You could increase the speed of the work if you moved the lifting mechanisms that have completed their work."

"Yes, I have thought of that. I have been reluctant because I have paid the men more sestertii to work the longer hours. It will cost me many sestertii to move the devices, and we will have to dismantle them and then reassemble them when we begin the second tier."

"Will you not remove the devices so that they will not be carried away by the flood—then reassemble them to start the next work?"

"Yes, that is true."

"So the additional work performed would be re-building them and removing them before this flood season."

"Yes."

"Although it is true that you are responsible for damage by a flood, I believe it would be in the best interests of the Empire to expedite the remaining work. I will have the Empire pay for the additional re-assembly of the hoists at the remaining arch locations if you will pay for their additional disassembly. I am thinking that you will more quickly take them down than assemble them. What say you?"

"I will do so. To be honest, I was going to do that without your offer. It made too much sense."

"Then we have an agreement?"

"Yes. I am starting immediately. I thank you for having the foresight to compel me to do what should be done." Publius smiled.

Appius also smiled. "We both understand that the quality of our lives depend on a satisfactory outcome—the results of good decisions—as it should be."

"As it should."

Antonia said, "It seems you favor the bridge contractor. I mean—you always speak highly of him. Why is that?"

Appius accepted bread recently baked, pungent and warm. "It is true. Publius Acilius is always thinking ahead—of tomorrow, or next week, or next month. Will he need more men? Will he need to modify his lifting devices? If he needs new timbers, when should he start the crews hewing the wood and augering the holes so that the timbers are ready when the crews need them? He expects a good day's work from each man, yet he is fair and understands their difficulties, strengths, and weaknesses. The men respect him and most perform well for him. We are fortunate to have him for the bridge contractor."

"I mentioned to him that he should meet Juliena. Has he ever talked about that?"

"No. I think our bridge contractor is much too busy to think about spending time with a woman."

"Perhaps when he has finished this tier of arches."

Sextilis

They were three weeks into the season known for flooding. Five of the arches had been completed. The horizontal stones above the arches were in place on four of them, and rubble infill was being placed on the fifth, prior to placing the horizontal stones that would support the second tier of arches. The sixth arch, with two hoists flying the stones atop the forms, was filling in gradually. Appius and Publius worried constantly that a significant flood would be upon them before the last arch was completed. Every thunderstorm was endured with suspicion, fear permeating their thoughts as they silently speculated that this would be the storm that would continue, increasing in intensity until it equaled or surpassed that of the prior year. They silently acknowledged relief as each diminished, not daring to speak of such, knowing that the next storm could leave them awash.

Yet, the arch was being filled, even though the crews had to work around thunderstorms lasting several hours. When it was storming, the men hunkered under the shelter of completed arches.

Publius wanted to remove the formwork from the completed arches prior to completion of the last arch. However, he understood that sideways forces would be created by removal of the supports. He suspected and worried that extensive force might be imposed on the uncompleted arch, it being vulnerable to displacement of stones due to the sideways movement. He and Appius agreed, it would be best if the stone structure were totally self-supporting, complete, all forces constrained by the immovable rock walls of the canyon. If some of the stones were still dependent on the wood supports, the tier of arches would not develop its ultimate strength and would, therefore, be susceptible to destruction by a flood.

Nevertheless, one day, after a thunderstorm lasting longer than most, Publius appeared in front of Appius in his office. "I am going to start removing trusses. In my opinion we are sufficiently built on the sixth arch and any sideways force will be resisted."

Appius knew the answer to his own question but asked anyway. "How can you be sure?"

Publius shrugged. "Of course, I cannot be sure. You know that. It is a judgment I am making. However, we will carefully observe the stones on the last arch as we remove the other forms. Any displacement will be considered. If it appears too severe or threatening, we will stop the form removal."

"When will you start, Publius?"

"I started an hour ago." He smiled.

Appius stood. "I must see this removal for myself. I noticed that you have removed the hoists that are no longer being used to lift stones on the completed arches. They are out of danger of being swept away. This means that you will remove the arch supports using overhead hoists, as you explained before."

"Yes, our wheels will be able to be used above, on the second tier. And soon, if the gods and the river do not thwart us, we will have forms that may be used again, without having to retrieve them from a mile downstream."

"Let us go see this."

"Yes. To do so, we may walk across the top of the first tier—from one side to the other. It is significant that we can do so."

"Indeed. I have already made that walk, although I had to scramble over stones. It reminded me of my excursions when first looking for a water source, five years ago. I made my way along canyon walls by holding onto roots, using my fingernails to keep from slipping off the rocks."

"I do not know that history. You must tell me sometime."

"That I will do. Let us go."

They arrived atop the farthest arch. A hoist had been erected over each side, and lines over the edge were being connected to the top timbers of the form, the first to be removed.

the *Aedifex*: Building the Pont du Gard

Publius looked over both sides, plucked the lines to ensure they were taut, then nodded. Men let themselves down atop the frame, sliding down the ropes. When situated, by straddling a convenient connecting timber, heavy hammers were lowered along with some sturdy pins of various lengths. One man held a pin while another swung the hammer, having to swing with significant force to start the connecting pin from its position in the augered holes.

While the pins were being driven, Appius told Publius about his earlier adventures locating water sources—the difficulty with the Ucetians, wandering the canyons, and the decisions of Claudius.

"You have much time and effort dedicated to this project already. You must feel strongly about it—want to see it built— want to see the water flow."

"Yes. It is my passion."

Publius smiled. "I will do my best for you."

The crew signaled to Publius indicating the pins had been removed. The timbers were not yet loose, being squeezed between remaining timbers by the weight of the stones. However, the contractor had anticipated that removal of the first timber would be difficult. Publius explained to Appius. "I had the men fashion wedges to hold this timber in place. Now, when the wedges are driven out, the timber will be released. See, the men drive them out now."

As the wedges were removed, Appius could hear the form creak and groan as forces were relieved and weight was transferred to the remaining timbers.

The men, holding on to the trusses, yelled and nodded. The freed uppermost timbers were hoisted to the deck above.

Publius said to Appius. "Let us go to the incomplete arch to see if any movement has been noted. I have asked the men to watch the joints for any sign of movement."

They walked across the top of the first tier to the nearest arch where the men were expecting Publius. "We saw nothing move," he was told, "except, perhaps, at the canyon wall. A man thought he felt the gap narrow."

Publius nodded to Appius. "I think all is well. We will continue the form removal. And, when we place the last stone on this arch, I will have food and drink for all who wish to help us celebrate. I think it of great importance for *you* to be there. I will wait to place the last stone until you are available."

613

"In the same manner that the first pier stone was placed. It seems a long time ago."

"That is because it has not been easy. We have been through much."

"I look forward to your ceremony. It will mean that the gods did not smite us again."

"Ayye. I did not want to mention that."

One might wish for only minimal problems from the rains, but we are subject to the vagaries of weather and the seemingly random nature of events. Appius knew this as did Publius and so they could not be assured that it would only be a rare possibility— two severe floods within a year. Yet, with every day the last arch was more complete—less susceptible to damage.

Publius had removed all but the last arch support; the arch lacked the top horizontal layer of stone. The horizontal layer, while not providing support, kept the arch stones in place and assisted in transmitting forces sideways to the canyon wall. Substantial movement or dislocation had not been noticed—yet. Publius had been supplementing the hoisting of stones by now rolling stones across the platform of arches that were complete.

In mid *Septembris* a storm started gently but built to the strength of 1-inch per hour. Publius worked his men for as long as he dared, for as long as work could be achieved. He then decided to disassemble his two remaining wheeled hoists on the side of the riverbed. The river had risen so that only 3 feet of freeboard remained at the hoists. The men, barely able to move in the lashing rain, nevertheless slogged, dragged, and pried away at the devices until they lay as scattered pieces on the bank. Then, rather than try to wield the pieces up the canyon wall, Publius hoisted them to the top of the arch, using the mechanism he had used to remove the arch form timbers on the other five arches.

At this time, it might have been possible to continue moving stones across the top of the arch; however, two men were swept from the platform, tumbling over the side into the torrent below. Men searched, hoping to find that they had survived by struggling out, perhaps in a slow eddy. However, 3 hours of searching in the hard rain and shrieking winds failed to locate them. Publius stopped the work.

The last form remained in place. It was doubtful the river could dislodge it with the weight of many stones atop. Yet, it was the structure's weakest link because it still supported the stones, not allowing forces to be transmitted sideways to the canyon wall. If the river should reach the same height as last year, the entire structure would have to withstand the force of the river. It is not good to have one weak side, a location where the forces in structure are not continuous.

Publius approached Appius, hunkered in the shelter of a rock overhang, watching the rise of the river. Yelling, he said, "I am going to free the form. If we can remove one timber, the entire rock structure will be as one piece."

"*You* are going to do this?"

"I have seven men who will go with me. They are willing. It will not be easy. It will be dangerous, but I am going because I cannot ask my men to do something I would not do."

Appius looked at him and nodded. "I will go with you."

"It is not necessary...."

Appius shook his head and pointed to the structure. "We must go."

Atop the structure, the hoist that had lifted the man-wheels was in position. Four men were completing the work of assembling another hoist on the other side, fighting the wind to do so, barely able to see in the rain.

Publius conferred with the crew then he and another man used ropes to climb down to the truss. They attached slings to the topmost members of the wooden structure. A pair of men did likewise on the other side. Publius signaled; tension was applied to the lifting ropes by means of a windlass at the hoist.

Now the driving pins and hammers were lowered, the wind blowing them sideways on their lines until they were grabbed and retrieved by the men, who then set about knocking the connecting pins from the timbers. During the operation, pins and one hammer were dropped—the tools made slippery by the rain and the men's grips weakened by fatigue.

The pins were driven out with great difficulty. Publius and his helper were exhausted, trying to secure themselves on the timbers and apply gruesome swings to drive pins made tight by the load and even tighter by the swelling wood. They finally completed the task. Now it was time to drive out the wedges.

Appius judged that the men did not have much remaining strength. He questioned whether they could drive the wedges. He descended the rope to the truss, scrambling to find a position of safety below the arch.

Publius watched his arrival in amazement. "You cannot...."

Appius, his mouth a scant 6 inches from the ear of Publius in order to be heard, said, "I do not ask my contractors to do what I would not."

They exchanged hard stares then Appius said, "Let us continue."

A man from the deck above had also joined the crew on the other side—to help them. Publius and his man were unable to swing the hammer to drive out the wedges. Appius did this, assisted by the others.

The topmost timbers were now loose. The crew remaining above raised them, the timbers guided by those who had freed them. They then clambered to the deck. As Publius helped Appius onto the deck, he looked at him. "I will never forget."

Appius smiled. "Neither will I. I have just one request."

"Yes?"

"Do not tell Antonia."

Publius laughed and said, "Let us get out of the rain."

After 8 hours, the rain stopped. The river had risen to the top of the piers, still under the tops of the arches. However, due to accumulating upstream flows, the river would rise further.

Because the storm had stopped, Publius now resumed rolling stones across the top of the nearly complete first tier—the stones to be part of the horizontal layer atop the sixth arch, adding to the weight and increasing the grip of the structure to the side of the canyon. The river continued to rise but nearly all the stones had been placed by the time the floodwaters crested just below the top of the arches. Prior to the cresting, all—the contractor, Appius, and his men—were nervously anticipating signs that the structure might fail. However, the structure silently faced and endured the onslaught, making no sounds of resistance although the thunder of the rampaging water masked more subtle murmurs.

The river height dropped. It was clear the structure had survived. It was time for celebration.

It was a fine fall day, curiously free of thunderstorms. Publius Acilius was happy that his investment in time and sestertii survived and that the work in place would remain as the base for one of the world's impressive structures. He provided a feast atop the completed first tier of arches. Any person could attend—wives, children, friends, workmen from other contracts, quarrymen, material suppliers, food hawkers, beverage suppliers, and slackers. Some of the food and beverage providers supplied additional treats along with the food and wine supplied by Publius. At times, the entire structure was covered with celebrants, small boys throwing rocks in the water, young men walking the unguarded edge of the structure, fortified although not yet disabled by too much wine.

Antonia stood next to her husband, a slight smile on her face. "I have not had an appreciation for the number of lives you affect until I observe a scene such as this. It must be exhilarating to be responsible, to guide all these people, each with a small task to do, every day, all of which sums to a magnificent structure such as this. No wonder the work is still upon you when you are finally home at night."

"Yes. All you say is true. Perhaps we will worry less now we have completed the first tier and it has survived the floods. I and the contractor, Publius Acilius are greatly relieved."

"Speaking of Publius, he now approaches." Antonia held out her hand to the contractor.

Publius made a mock bow to Antonia. "I am glad you are here to celebrate your husband's hard work." He nodded to Appius.

"I think you are the one who has worked hard and braved the storm. At least Appius did not have to work in the rain and wind."

Appius nodded, grimacing at Publius. "Yes, that is true."

"Appius was just saying that you are both relieved and the work will be easier. Is that true?" Antonia was chiding the contractor and anticipated his answer.

Publius struck an orator's pose, one hand on his hip, the other outreached, as if to sanctify his words. "The work may not be easier, but at least it is not fraught with perils."

Antonia smiled and said, "Will you now have to wait to continue work until after the storm season? Perhaps you will have some free time—to travel to Nemausus, for example."

"Is Nemausus where your sister...?"

"Juliena." Antonia filled in this forgotten name.

"... where Juliena lives? But—no, we will continue work. Tomorrow we will be rolling stones across the deck, stones for the piers in the second tier of arches. I again find no time to travel... to Nemausus."

"No need. Juliena will be here to visit me. I shall have you meet her when that happens. You need not travel."

The contractor smiled. "I thank you for being so thoughtful of my welfare. I will anxiously await your word."

"I think you are mocking me, but you will think different, so mock me all you want." Antonia feigned a pout; they all laughed.

Appius shrugged, "Then you will continue to work. I expected you to."

"Yes, of course—between thunderstorms. We have a bridge to build." He pointed out along the structure.

Appius straightened as if to shoulder the additional tasks forthcoming. "Indeed."

CHAPTER 59
Three years into building of the aqueduct

    Stonemasons were exalted amongst those working the aqueduct. Yes, there were other men with greater technical prowess—those that established level, using diagrams to determine the depths and line of the aqueduct as it pierced the landscape. But, of those with their hands on the work, the stonemasons and carpenters prevailed as the most skilled. There had been a number of masons in the region before the aqueduct construction, building homes, government structures, walls, roads, and temples. Work of that nature was still required, so, for the aqueduct, willing and able young men were apprenticed to available, experienced masons. They learned the trade by watching and doing. The contractors, knowing that the skill was vital and that their work could not proceed or could be stifled due to lack of the craft, hired experienced masons to teach the trade in practical schools at the site. Once one became a mason, one embraced the status deserving of the respect it garnered.

    Masons were required at the quarries to precisely cut the blocks intended for the Vardo bridge; on the bridge they placed and shaped the stones as necessary to account for the vagaries of construction. They created the rough-cut stones along the underground and aboveground portions of the aqueduct for placement into the walls and arches of those structures, and installed those stones to line and grade using mortar. Other work was considered to require little training, skill, or patience.

    Partly because of the aura of status—masons preferring to socialize with other masons—and partly because of associations created through the schools and even less structured training, the masons formed, loosely at first, a cohesiveness that was evident. The rough-cutting masons were aware that the masons cutting the stones precisely earned a higher wage and noddingly accepted that it was rightfully so. Masons also maintained an awareness of wages paid to other masons on the project doing similar work and were able to pry higher wages from contractors who were not at equilibrium. The contractors always needed more masons or better masons or faster masons so parity was easily obtained. Yes, some masons were dismissed because they were slow or careless, falling back into labor that was less skilled. The loose association of masons took a dim view of this downgrade although they might grudgingly agree with the assessment, but many, the many on the lower tiers of the skill, speed, and quality rungs, feared that they could also suffer dismissal.

It was from these fears and aspirations that a guild was formed, first interfacing with the contractors to apply reasonable standards and not to dismiss workers on arbitrary grounds. The contractors, eager to keep the masons from unrest, did not object to the lowest common denominator standards. For the masons, success at this maneuver increased the perception of power amongst the guild leaders, quick to trumpet their achievement.

It was not remarkable that it occurred to many of the masons that they could surely have the power to extort higher wages. The guild leaders, by now chosen as representatives on a structured basis, met and determined that all in the treasured guild should receive wages one-third higher than that at present. The representatives presented this proposition to their respective contractors. The contractors had some latitude in dealing with wages but because they had bid the work competitively were forced to use what was considered the prevailing wages in their estimates. Paying the additional sestertii requested would erase any profit and in most contracts result in a losing venture for the contractor. The contractors refused the wage increase. All of them.

The guild leaders had anticipated this reaction but had not made any threats associated with the original request. Now, however, the contractors were advised that while the masons would continue to show up for work, the contractors could expect output to recede to a level that matched what they now considered to be their low pay. The contractors asserted that they would not be blackmailed by these tactics but were severely worried about their ability to prevail. They again refused to capitulate.

The guild leaders, anticipating that this attitude would also exist amongst the contractors, proceeded with nearly universal cooperation from their members. The work slowed substantially, not only slowing the output from the masons, but for all the other labor supplying, carting, servicing them, and depending upon them.

The contractors, at first, tried getting rid of the most flagrant slow walkers. The guild leaders did not say anything to the contractors, did not threaten them, but it was evident that when this means was used, the work slowed even further. The contractors, feeling powerless to prevent their ultimate demise, requested a meeting with Appius. The guild, quite capable of understanding that the contractors could not financially support their demand, imagined that the Empire would relent and enable the contractors to pay higher wages by a universal increase of payments to the contractors. The guild was convinced they had handled the situation adeptly. Even non-masons were hopeful, as higher wages to the masons might ultimately mean higher wages for them.

The contractors stood in a group outside the project office, some ranting, some listening to determine if their experience was the same as the others. Appius walked out of the building, Vibius two paces behind him, a quiver of pens and scraps of paper clutched in his hands. The contractors fell silent. Appius assessed the attitudes of the contractors from their looks, aware that they were angry and frustrated. Was he capable of resolving the issue or would the project slip into chaos—more chaos?

Appius spoke first. "I am aware of the situation you contractors face on this project. Many of you have spent hours entertaining me with the history of the mason movement. Now, the situation threatens the completion of the project, and I suppose you think that I or those funding the project can solve the problem. I must remind you that management and handling of labor is your requirement—your responsibility. So, what would you have me do? What do you want to discuss with me?"

The group, although seasoned contractors, were momentarily stunned by the admonition. Finally, the quarryman, Vernius Portius, for whom Appius had much respect, spoke. "What you say is true. Responsibility for the labor is our requirement." Vernius gave a hard look to those who appeared annoyed at his statement. He looked back to Appius and continued. "Perhaps we could or should have prevented formation of a guild, using goons and punishment to discourage the association of men who by their strength of numbers can have their way on this project. But I say that in contemplating a project of this size, one that requires the extent of this region's resources, and beyond, you have created a situation in which this manner of coercion can occur. Yes, you can

621

turn your back and tell us to solve the problem, but in the end, we will—all of us—have to tell you 'no!' We will not work without reward. We will *not* work at a loss, creating a continual and growing drain on our own holdings. It seems that your options are to help us or to once again bring in slaves, train them as masons, feed them as you will and supervise them with stifling military overseers in order to prevent them from assuming the same power." He looked around to see nodding assent from the others. "What say you?"

Appius paused before replying. He had not considered the aspect of responsibility created by overloading the region with the work of one project. In the quick moments he considered the comment, he felt there was some justification, but he had not thought it through. However, it was clear that if he continued to deny responsibility, rely on the contractors to solve the problem, he might lose the project once again. The suggestion of slaves caused a cold tremor. "Vernius, I am not sure I agree with all that you have said; however, you have at least a glimmer of argument. It is true, the *Corporata* and the Empire have Draconian options that might see the project completed but at the expense of the workmen of the region and with it the economy and social structure. I detested the slave work under military control before, and I do not care to consider slaves as an option.

"However, the use of slaves *is* an option, one that might ultimately be used. Perhaps, if you contractors can be as united as the masons, we might resolve this situation. Are all of you willing to say that you will quit your contracts rather than accede to the demands of the guild?"

It appeared a few contractors were about to reject the concept, but under the hard glare of others, finally nodded.

"I hear no objections," Appius continued, "so here is what I intend to do. I will send a message to Claudius explaining the situation and the consequent actions of you contractors if nothing is done. I will suggest two alternatives to Claudius. One will involve dismissal of all contractors and to bring in nearly one thousand slaves, all to be supervised by the military. A second option suggests paying contractors an additional amount to cover the escalated wages of the masons. I expect that neither of these options will appeal to Claudius; however, we can tell the masons what has been suggested. The thought of replacing the workers with slave labor should sober their fantasies even if they believe

the *Aedifex*: Building the Pont du Gard

the thought is anathema to Claudius. In sending this message, my office would *not* be seen to be caving in to demands but suggesting options that would continue the project. And, the decision rightfully resides with the Empire, the ultimate project funder. Perhaps the slave concept is one that will bring equilibrium to the power situation, even if that power resides with the Empire and not with you contractors. Do you understand what I am saying?"

One of the contractors said, "What happens in the meantime? I am assuming we *will* tell the guild about the suggested options sent to Claudius."

Appius nodded. "Yes. I suggest you tell them that they continue to work at their original pace and their current wage until we hear from Claudius. If they refuse to do so, or if any pockets of them refuse to do so, then you contractors should all suspend work. I suggest you council before you decide to do so, to make sure the circumstances are valid. I cannot tell you to do this, only advise. I shudder at the thought of work stoppage, but it sounds like we are headed in that direction if the problem is not reasonably resolved."

Vernius Portius said, "Then do so. Send your message. I say to my fellow contractors—be sensible regarding the thought of stopping work—to do so is a severe upheaval to all of us and should not be done on a whim. I hope that Claudius will be swift in his resolution, but to be truthful, I do not think Claudius will be coerced into paying additional sestertii. The slave threat may be real."

Appius looked at the men. "I will send the message today and urge a quick response. Please keep me advised as to the attitude of your workers and any action you might take or even consider. We are done?"

The contractors nodded, but frowns, curled lips, and grimaces signaled their disposition. They were not happy or hopeful.

Appius sent the message, the Rome courier dispatched two days earlier than scheduled. Appius confided to Vibius, "I agree with Vernius. I do not think Claudius will consent to either option, but I cannot imagine that he will allow the project to be scuttled. Perhaps we have only extended the project for a week or so, less if the masons will not work at their prior pace."

623

"I think that the thought of slave labor might have an impact on the mason's attitude," said Vibius. "Perhaps that thought will soften their resolve and frighten them into thinking that they may lose the work entirely."

"Yes, you are right. I did not want to make that direct threat, one that would be sure to anger the workers. We might win assent, but lose any cooperation. And, as the work gets closer to completion, the slave threat lessens. Instead, our message to Claudius is more a plea for resolution, but noting the possible options. We will surely hear how it is perceived."

"Yes, and probably soon," Vibius smiled.

The contractors reported that the masons were somewhat stymied upon hearing the suggestion of slave labor, the heady feeling of power having overwhelmed their ability to consider the options of Empire. However, the pace of the work improved although not quite back to that prior, as the masons extracted a grudging but slim toll, one that would not cause severe action but was nonetheless perceptible. Peace reigned momentarily.

One week later, Appius read the return message from Claudius, amused at the clever turn that Claudius had provided. He proposed that the contractors could be paid an additional amount to cover the increased costs of the masons, but that the increased costs would be levied against the citizens of Nemausus and any other future users of the aqueduct water over a five-year term. Claudius urged Appius to calculate the amount required for the wage increase and to determine the estimated amount that each citizen or family unit would pay.

Many of the workers were from outside the region and would return to their homes when the work was complete. They did not care if the locals had to pay a levy. However, most of the workers either currently lived in Nemausus or had family in Nemausus and many, settling in the area, would be subject to paying the levy for future water use. At the least, the citizens of Nemausus knew that the masons were a source of their potential financial discomfort and were not taciturn in displaying their disgust of the masons, an attitude forcing the masons to only reluctantly make obvious visits to town. The good folk of Nemausus recognized greed and were quick to condemn those that would live more grandly at their expense. The masons had descended to the level of a scourge to the region, angry that they should be cast as such, but angrier that there was justification in Claudius's direction.

Yet, they refused to publicly give up their demand. The contractors taunted the guild, asking them how much they would have the citizenry pay. The project continued to waver uncertainly. Neither contractor nor labor knew how to return to stability. Both contractors and guild leaders understood that Claudius would not simply send more money to resolve the issue. Appius felt the tension constantly and decided he would try to resolve the uncertainty, understanding that each side must think that there was something to be gained. He met with each group separately, proposing that there would be no wage increase; however, the masons and contractors would agree on a reasonable output per day, a pace that the contractors could not require them to exceed. In return, the contractors could remove those they considered to be slackers or incompetent without concern for reprisal from the guild. Neither camp was happy with the concept, but the other options were unthinkable. The contractors and guild met and agreed. In truth, not much changed. The contractors drove the masons to produce the agreed quantities under nearly all circumstances while the masons slowed if their brothers were dismissed. Neither, however, wanted to start the fracas anew. However, a means of resolving other issues had been established. The guild and the contractors occasionally met to resolve them, with the sword of Claudius above their heads.

In the five years since the excavation had started on the underground runs, the work on one underground section had been completed and the trench backfilled. The others would finish within a year. The upper arches were being installed on the Vardo bridge, the second level of arch completed and the wood forms removed.

The tunnels had been hacked quickly, in less than a year. The internal floor and walls had followed, the laborious process of hauling materials half the length, causing construction of the walls and floor to be tedious. Nevertheless, the tunnels had been done for years.

Once the level calculations and adjustments had been made, the aboveground structures began. Foundations were excavated into the sides of gullies, across low terrain, and on tops of ridges, followed by installation of foundation stones. Most of the stones for the aboveground structures were rough hewn, some obtained from sources nearby but many of the stones were from the river quarry, unsuitable for the precision stones of the Vardo bridge, and many from the quarry at the end of the east-west run, developed by the quarry contractor. Upon the road that was built and maintained by the underground and aboveground contractors, carts constantly squeaked their way, filled with the rough-cut stones, to their point of installation, the carts returning spryly to pick up another load, carters hailing others trudging in the opposite direction.

As with the Pontis Vardo, arch forms of wood were required on the aboveground structures. There were enough carpenters on the entire project to form a guild of more skilled workers, such as with the masons, but the carpenters tended to be a more independent lot and resisted those that tried to organize, dismissing the concept of unity and the power it provided. In fact, the carpenters admired themselves for their independent traits, needling the masons as 'of the mindless masses,' highly regarding their own ability to negotiate for themselves based on their skill and output. In many instances, the contractors were willing to increase the pay for those who exhibited such. Marius and Pentius were at the top of that heap.

A significant number of the more skilled masons envied the carpenters for this circumstance, understanding that they might be worthy and capable of the same advantage. A number of masons quit hacking the stones and became carpenters to enhance their earning power. Such men were skilled and hard working and had no trouble rising to the top levels of their new craft. However, with the masons, there were many who were not skilled, and not as inclined to hard work. They prevailed.

Appius continued to make practical and frequent use of his schedule. He would note the progress of the different structures and operations over time and use the resulting rates to predict completion of separate facets of the work, and in the broader view, the entire project. He could now predict that the project would complete in less than a year. It was time to plan for operations that would place the aqueduct into practical use. One did not just turn the water loose and yell, "here she comes." There was a substantial amount of work to be done flushing the residue from construction, checking for leaks, and regulating flow.

He had help. Vibius and Numerius had participated in devising these operations on prior aqueduct projects. At the request of Appius, Claudius sent an architect familiar with such start-up programs, a man Appius had met in the latter days of his trip to Rome when he visited the Domus Aquius. They devised a scheme.

The *Castellum* in Nemausus and the intake structure at Ucetia were the last structures to be built. The intake structure at Ucetia was dependent on completion of the conduit leading away from it and the completion of the regulating structure 500 feet downstream which would allow water to flow in the first stretch of the aqueduct but to be diverted rather than continue and cause problems at unfinished works downstream. These structures were nearing completion and could be put into use.

The flushing operations were devised to start at the springs and work section by section to the terminus at the *Castellum*. The section farthest upstream would be flushed and the residue diverted and removed before introducing water into the next section. In that way, residue would not be flushed and accumulated for the entire aqueduct length, a practice that would cause blockage and difficult removal problems downstream.

There were three diversion structures: one was 500 feet downstream from the springs; the second was immediately prior to the Pontis Vardo, and the third after the low area 7 miles prior to Nemausus. Of course, the *Castellum* provided the final point of deposition and clean up. In addition to the diversions, removable slabs provided access to underground sections at reasonable locations. As each section was completed prior to the flush, the contractors were required to sweep their conduits, broom clean, and the refuse removed. The manual removal of loose mortar, stone chips, dust, clothing, food, and human waste eliminated a substantial amount of undesirable material; nevertheless, there would be a significant amount of dust and other particles that would still be borne by the water, rendering it undesirable for bathing, cooking and drinking for some time. Hence the flush.

At the first diversion structure, water from the springs could be routed to the Alzon River. The first run was not lengthy, so a relatively short duration was planned for its flush—two days. The water in the conduit would be allowed to flow for a day, after which samples would be taken in a wooden bucket. If the water in the buckets, sitting overnight, showed little residue on the bottom for a number of such samples, the section was deemed to be satisfactorily cleaned. Water would be slowly introduced into the next section by sequentially removing timbers from the slots in the weir. The first rush of water picked up much residue. The water level would initially be kept low in the conduit so as to not deposit this residue upon the walls above. When the water quality collected at the downstream diversion improved, additional timbers would be removed from the weir, allowing ever-higher water level and flows. The operation would be repeated for each run of the length, in turn.

Therefore, a celebration of the first clean water to arrive in Nemausus would be anticlimactic, but it just wouldn't do to celebrate a muddy surge into the *Castellum*. Ceremonies are often secondary to substance, and it was true for this aqueduct as well. The ceremony would celebrate the first gush of *clean* water into the *Castellum*. The water's journey from the springs at Ucetia, thirty miles to the *Castellum* in Nemausus, would take over a day, an observation made while flushing the last run into the *Castellum*. Appius, constantly concerned with the slight slope of the aqueduct, knew that the water would flow, would eventually reach Nemausus. But the question was—how fast would it flow? How much water would the aqueduct provide to the city on a daily basis?

Claudius was advised several months ahead of time in order to witness the *aqua triumphe*. Fortunately, he could manage to be in Nemausus close to the intended time. Knowing this made Appius somewhat tense, understanding that any major problems would have to be handled in a hurry. Leaks would not be a concern that would delay the ceremony.

Appius, one year ahead of time, carefully laid out the flushing sequence and timing, keyed to the completion of the various elements of the aqueduct. An efficient flushing sequence, however, did not match the finish of the segments, so he spent time and effort working with several of the contractors to achieve earlier completion dates. Acceleration occurred by urging the contractors to work longer days and to hire more workers. However, Appius had to be careful not to give the impression that additional sestertii could be expected for this accelerated effort. He knew the thought swirled in the minds of the contractors. His best argument was—the sooner they finished the less they would have to spend on supervision and other costs related to time rather than labor.

Appius was successful at this effort. Almost all contract operations were nearly completed when the flushing for their sections started. Those downstream, not quite complete, suffered from their own desire—not to hold up the water as the flushing operation worked its way toward them. By now, they all were prideful of their part in this astonishing structure, and it would be shameful, not worth bearing the humorous barbs and insults, if one were to be late.

Appius personally observed the flushing of each section, noting only to himself that the water did, indeed, flow. As the flushing for each section completed, he observed the clarity of the water, marveled at it, and remained to see water released into the next section. He would return in four or five days to witness the next operation. When they had flushed across the *Pontis Vardo* they noticed that, as a result of their level adjustments, the water upstream from the bridge raced at a faster pace but slowed upon reaching the shallower slope across the bridge. The force of the onrushing water, encountering slower moving water, caused water to slosh over the tops of the conduit. This was a major problem, derisorily visible to all. A correction, possibly raising the walls of the conduit at the bridge, would have to be executed in the future.

Claudius was in town. Water had been flushed into the *Castellum* but was not yet running clean. Well, it would surely do so within the next few days. Appius was thankful that the final operations had gone as well as they had, but here was the *Imperator*—waiting. Appius brought his family to Nemausus, as did many of those working along the route. Nemausus was crowded and excited. Appius was busy and anxious.

Appius returned to the quarters in the *Corporata* yard but found little to do in the office. He did not wait for a subordinate to advise him of the status of the residue in the sampling buckets from the *Castellum*. He was there at first light to see for himself. On the morning of Claudius's third day in town, the water showed little residue. It was time.

Appius's plan for first 'clean water' arrival at the *Castellum* was to divert the entire flow at the diversion structure upstream of

Nemausus. You could not just stop the flow of the water at any desired location by building a temporary wall, let us say. The water along the aqueduct upstream would continue to flow, could not be stopped, but, if restricted by a barrier, water would be forced to escape the conduit from every access hole and opening available, possibly exploding through the walls of the masonry. The flow was, instead, diverted. Appius calculated that the final duration of flow from the nearby upstream diversion to the *Castellum* would take approximately from sun-up until noon. Therefore, Appius gave the order to remove the diversion and send the water on to Nemausus at sun-up the next morning, anticipating a ceremony approximately at midday, but allowing the remainder of the day for the event to happen if the water was slower than he had calculated. Not all understood the gymnastics of the operation, but Claudius smiled when Appius advised him.

The *Castellum* was installed in an undeveloped area to the north of Nemausus. Nearby, residue from the construction, piles of earth and rocks remained, yet to be used and spread by the populace. The bottom of the *Castellum* was damp from its recent scrubbing after the final residue from the flushing had been removed. The drains in the bottom of the structure had seen their first use, carrying the initial muddy gushes through the new waste system, eventually joining the existing city waste system.

It was well after midday and the throng standing upon the deck of flat stones surrounding the *Castellum* pool was restless, talking amongst themselves, shuffling their feet, and occasionally looking to the aqueduct's entrance aperture, imagining a possible rush of water. On the circular stone apron stood Claudius and several of his *lictors*, protected by several Praetorian guards. Also, standing on the apron were Appius, Antonia, the six-year old Sergius, and his younger brother Bernius, the boys carefully walking the inner edge of the circle, lying down on the stone apron or pestering their father. Antonia remembered that it had been five years ago—wondering if she would ever wear a *stola* in public; she smiled, understanding that hard work brought its rewards.

They were flanked by the remaining *Corporata*, contractors, suppliers, other town leaders from Nemausus, and representatives from Rome, Narbo, and Lugdunum. The bridge contractor Publius Acilius was nearby, standing with Juliena and her three children.

Beyond the stone circle, a larger crowd in a holiday mood also talked, shuffled, and glanced at the structure. Food and drink vendors prowled amidst the many workers who, if you heard them tell it, had nearly single-handedly built the aqueduct. With them were their families and interested ordinary citizenry. Two such were Pentius and Marius, pounding each other on the back to celebrate their participation, one chiding the other for slacking. They were not too far from those who stood on the apron and were spotted by Appius as he corralled his sons. He yelled at the duo while he held each of his sons by the hand. "Marius, Pentius— you had to be here. Will you join us on the apron, or would you rather be closer to the food and drink?"

Marius looked at Pentius and shrugged. "Yes, we will join you. Why not? If it had not been for us, this project would have never been built." This was worth a cackle from both, after which they joined the privileged circle.

Appius ushered them toward Claudius, past the hard looks of the Praetorians and caught Claudius's attention. "Your Excellency, I would like you to meet Marius and Pentius who were with me and our late friend Bernius from the very start. I think you will find, if you ask them, that this project could not have been built without them."

Marius and Pentius again thumped each other, possibly in a more reserved manner, but did manage a slight bow, muttering, "Your Excellency."

Claudius smiled. There were clowns in his life also, and he appreciated their light-heartedness. It was obvious the pair worked hard, and Claudius knew Appius would not present them if they were not of great value. Claudius actually made a slight bow and said, "Then it is to you two I am indebted."

Pentius smiled. "Please, your Excellency, find us another aqueduct to build. We would not like the boredom of ordinary work."

Claudius nodded. "Stay close to Appius. If such should occur, he will be among the first to know."

Marius and Pentius bowed again and moved to take their place on the surround.

Appius, nearly an hour earlier, had received word that the water flowed under the city wall. It was time. He directed Antonia, the boys and others nearby to closely watch for the first water. Immediately before it appeared, it seemed like all sensed the imminent appearance although no sound accompanied the occurrence. Perhaps it was the slight compression of air forced from the end of the enclosed conduit that was noticeable. Nevertheless, the first wave of water, about 4 inches high, rather unceremoniously rushed in to wet the floor of the *Castellum*, not pausing to note the time, nor taking a moment to acknowledge the end of its journey. A great whoop sprang from the crowd, many raising both arms in exuberance. Appius kissed Antonia, hugged the two boys, thumped Marius and Pentius, congratulated the *Corporata*, even Marcus, then walked to Claudius and extended his hand. "Your Excellency, today is a tribute to your foresight and perseverance. I salute you." Appius saluted Claudius, then turned and saluted the crowd.

Claudius, by his side, smiled and said, "You did it, Appius. I did not know if you could. Sometimes the best men cannot overcome the vast problems of empire and nature. And I, of course, was not sure I would survive to this day. Thank you for advancing the progress—one never knows. I salute you." He did, an action observed by the crowd and to which they responded with a tumultuous cheer. It had to be Appius's finest moment, yet in that moment he thought of Bernius and the three rocks that marked his site, the wine jug clutched to his chest.

Claudius, with the *Corporata* behind him, dedicated the aqueduct to the citizens, praising them and freedmen alike for the effort that was surely symbolic of the greatness of the Roman Empire, not to mention its leaders, of course. Claudius raised his hands to the acclaim of the crowd then held his hand toward Appius, beckoning him to speak—"Appius Petronius Aedifex."

Appius gazed over the attentive crowd, receptive to the glory heaped upon him. Appius spoke. "I want to acknowledge those whose effort made the project a reality. Often, I would stand on a hill and imagine the stone flowing from the landscape into the structures that make up this project. But, as remarkable as that concept was to me, I marvel at the effort that created the flow. I thus salute all those who provided the muscle and energy to craft, what to me seems most remarkable." He paused for a few moments to acknowledge the cheers, the return salutes and then let the cheers die to a murmur. "All aqueducts have a name and I suggest that it is most fitting that this aqueduct be named for the leader that had the vision, the perseverance and the fortitude to ensure that it was built. I do not have the authority to do so, but I suggest that our aqueduct be named *Aqua Claudius*."

The crowd erupted again, chanting "*Aqua Claudius, Aqua Claudius*."

Claudius took this well and quipped, "How could I proclaim otherwise?"

After the crowd silenced, Appius spoke. "This aqueduct is remarkable for the great bridge crossing the Vardo. It is my personal wish that we honor my friend Bernius, who now lies downstream of the completed structure, admiring it, I am sure, from his grand viewpoint. If it were not for Bernius, it may have been impossible for this project to be built. I regret he could not see the results of his efforts, but I would like to suggest that our magnificent bridge be named *Potis Bernius Caelius*."

The crowd, in a buoyant and accepting mood, chanted "*Pontis Bernius, Pontis Bernius*."

Appius looked at Claudius to assess his approval. Claudius nodded, but Appius detected what might have been remorse, remembering that it seemed to be Claudius's vision of the great bridge that inspired his selection of the Ucetian source. Well, he would see to it that Claudius's name would be magnificent on the commemorative stone at the bridge location.

Appius held up both arms to the crowd, then turned and beheld the filling pool, the water starting to enter the ten-inch lead pipes that would distribute it to fountains, bath houses, and gardens. The water was cool and clear, its value immediately apparent.

Claudius, at his side, pointed to an opening above the conduit entrance. "It seems that your stonemasons have not finished their work—revenge, I am sure, because they were not able to force higher wages."

"No, your Excellency. That opening is there at my direction. Tomorrow, I will bring copies of the diagrams used to build the structure and a copy of the log that I have scribed daily since I started looking for the water source. The copies will be sealed in a lead cylinder then cemented in the recess in back of the opening. The diagrams will bear the title *Aqua Claudius*, if you have no objection, and the bridge will be *Pontis Bernius Caelius*. I, and the others involved with this project, will one day be long gone. I will rely on these sealed documents to tell our story, perhaps one hundred years from now. What do you think?"

Claudius turned, "It is with actions like this that future generations will understand what we have accomplished. It is good. I wonder, though, will our efforts seem small compared to what might be accomplished with the advance of civilization?"

Appius pondered. "I cannot answer that. I only know that at this moment, we have done a remarkable thing. I only hope that the world will somehow remember."

CHAPTER 60

Lisele and I decided that our life, in the near term, would involve living for episodes in France, intertwined with stays in the U.S. Lisele anticipated the opportunity to spend time in California, and the visit would allow me to handle situations requiring careful monitoring and attention—house painting, renter eviction, and assessing status of relatives and friends.

But, for the present, I had to remain in Vers, not to be dislodged until I absorbed the translations and interpretations from the documents found in the cache at the *Castellum*. The treasure of information provided the understanding I craved, but more so, association with the builder of the project, ultimately leaving me with a sense of participation—well, as best could be expected given the two millennia dislocation.

The log generated by Appius was enormous, eight years worth, with details of design concepts, construction methods, decisions to be made—and the options thereof, attitudes, problems, and their resolution, personal matters, descriptions of others including never-before revealed glimpses of Claudius, and, if one were willing to spend the effort, a timeline depicting progress of the work.

The translation from first century Latin to French was an achievement in itself, as there were only a sparse number of academics that could accomplish such. The resulting document, written in French was absolutely of no value to me, so the task befell Lisele to translate the work and read to me as a parent to a child. While Lisele read the log, day-by-day, I was engrossed and involved to the point that I easily imagined that I was the project manager. I was Appius.

And, the experience was not lost on Lisele. She became immersed in the story as completely as she had when reading Hugo's *Les Miserable*.

After the log had been read, I scrutinized the project diagrams at the kitchen table, a cup of coffee at hand in the morning, a beer in late afternoon. I could study the diagrams without much help from Lisele.

635

One afternoon, I set down the package, feeling satisfied at what I had gleaned, sat back, stretched, took a swig of beer, latched my hands behind my head, and smiled, thinking—*so, Appius, glad to get to know you. Thanks for having the foresight to cache your documents. I'm astounded that you had the discipline to create and include your log. I wish many of our modern day constructors were as diligent. Your log has allowed me to live your project.*

I closed my eyes. *I can only imagine what you look like, but I see you at your desk, or riding along the aqueduct viewing the progress, hiking through the canyons, talking to the contractors, standing beside Claudius with your family. You have given me a gift I could not have anticipated.* I smiled. *I wish that I could bring you forward in time so that you could see the marvels, two thousand years has wrought. Yet, I marvel at what you were able to accomplish and your resourcefulness. My contentment could only be more extreme if I could talk to you.*

I grabbed my beer glass, nodded, took another swallow, and tipped an imaginary salute to the ceiling.

At the moment, I was exhilarated with the journey and wanted to share. I yearned to talk about my experience with Maurice and Renat. They shared part of the adventure, pondered some of the mysteries, accompanied me on my investigations, and listened patiently to my theories. I owed them and they would enhance my appreciation. The natural extension to this thought was to concoct a get-together, a discussion lubricated by beer and wine, followed by a dinner to celebrate the completion of the aqueduct. Well, it was to be celebrated, wasn't it? At least I felt that connection. My friends and Lisele would have no trouble with a celebratory concept and would contribute to the entertainment. I talked to Lisele who bubbled with the idea. Because she had read, translated, and spoken the log of Appius to me, she had shared the moments, had been exhilarated by the progress and the triumphs, disheartened by the setbacks, and surely felt the magnitude of what had been accomplished. It would be a grand event.

Renat and Maurice had not met. I shook my head at this realization, thinking how long I'd been in the area with two friends only twenty miles apart. It was entertaining, as if they had shared a past. I suppose one could have expected the outcome as both had suffered careers in engineering and construction, and both had a sense of humor; both knew me, and of my Diogenesic search for the aqueduct story. There was much ammunition for them to use in taunting me, or to actually discuss. With Lisele as referee, we were a raucous bunch. Yet, Renat and Maurice were truly interested in hearing what I had to say.

I began by briefly telling... hold that... I began by making sure they had a robust portion of wine or beer. After their outlook became tranquil, I launched into a brief summary of the timing, significant events, personalities, and the choosing of the route, only to get the session started.

Renat, after I took a breath, looked thoughtful and said, "So, this Appius was not a general, not a practiced architect, in fact had little knowledge of how to build a rock garden, much less an aqueduct of world proportions, a gem of the Roman Empire. Yet, it appears that he endured, overcame his inexperience, and persevered to see the water flow. Yet, he was young. I wonder if he had concerns, worrying that he might stumble—might be overwhelmed by circumstance."

I said to Renat, "Yes, his story is somewhat remarkable, although you've heard it a number of times—someone who is at the bottom of the heap rises to the pinnacle of excellence. Appius started as a very subordinate maintenance worker on the existing Nimes... Nemausus... water system. He was given the assignment to walk the terrain to find other sources. Through a series of circumstances, his ingenuity, and because the intended architect/builder was killed, he was available, knowledgeable and involved. He got the job."

Maurice nodded after a gulp of beer. "Did he worry that he might not be capable, that he might be thwarted by any number of those who might be upset or revengeful or... anything?"

I smiled. "Yes, Appius wrote about self-doubt several times. Early in the project, when he was still subordinate, he worried that he might not have the talent to be an architect. He worried about having to interface with Claudius as a mere subject, rash in thinking he could be of some importance to the higher reaches of empire. And, when he was finally put in command of the project, although he yearned to be the builder, he knew that the contractors all had more experience than he, and worried that there would be insurmountable problems, and he with no one nearby to consult. Yes, he worried, but it brought to mind my own career. With every promotion to greater responsibility, I worried that I might not be capable. I cringed thinking that I would have to face the labor unions, or protect my company from loss or from shabby dealing at the hands of the owners. Yet, for me, as I suppose it was for Appius, I grew into the job, pulled the cloak of responsibility around me, and did my best to carry on. In time, I found that I was handling problems routinely, problems that would have caused me to cower only a year or two before."

Both Renat and Maurice nodded in understanding—a shared experience, a facet of life revealed. Lisele looked at each of us, attempting to comprehend the journey of which our careers consisted.

Maurice asked, "Warner, you spent a number of hours imagining how the builders established the slope of the aqueduct with such precision... not just you, but most who have given the concept much thought. Did you get your answer?"

"Ah, yes," I said, "two of the greatest treasures revealed by Appius. There were two improvements which helped, actually, and if I read the log correctly and Appius isn't just blowing wind into his own sails, he was resourceful and inventive, creating a means of ensuring they didn't build a calamity."

Renat raised his wine glass. "Hail, Appius. What did he do?"

I looked at both men and smiled at Lisele because she had heard me carp about the gurus who claimed that the chorobate was used to establish level on the project. But, Renat and Maurice had heard me ramble on about it too. "As you all know, a relatively simple geometrical diagram convinces one that the chorobate, as is ordinarily described, could not have provided the needed accuracy. Appius suggested an improvement, essentially making a large spirit level out of the device, using water to establish level against a sloped gradient, increasing the accuracy of the device many fold, not unlike our modern spirit level. Use of the improved chorobate gave them more confidence—actually convinced them that there *was* a fall from the springs to Nimes. That helped, but Appius later conceived the use of the half-round clay pipes to finally achieve the accuracy needed. I eventually guessed what they were up to, with the help of Lisele." I glanced at her and enjoyed her reaction at having played a part. "But, you can't imagine my exuberance when Lisele read the passage where Appius revealed his idea. I whooped and shouted scaring Lisele, who shrank back at my actions. It was a delight I'll never forget."

Maurice quipped, "Well, you can't go wrong with water. It is the medium that knows when it is level... or not... or when it is on a slope. Elementary, really." He laughed.

Renat grinned. "It's true—water knows."

We all laughed.

"However," I said, "Apparently it did not all go smoothly. They were not able to use the clay pipe system until they made the first excavation cut, having already routed the aqueduct using the best method they had, the improved chorobate."

"Why is it that they needed to wait until they made the first cut?" Renat's eyebrows puzzled their way toward his nose.

I answered. "They needed a somewhat level surface on which to lay the pipes. Even though, on the excavation floor, they still had to prop the pipes here and there until they were level, the method was infinitely superior to having to manage hill and dale, swale, gully, and ridge. I think you can see what I mean."

Renat nodded thoughtfully. "Yes, yes, I do."

I continued. "Because the route was established before they could use the more accurate system of clay pipes, errors occurred. On some sections the route they followed was too steep; on others, too shallow. When they finally were able to establish an accurate level, determine the accurate amount of total drop, rather than re-route, they adjusted the slope, making the best of the situation. We know that the conduit has varying slopes in the separate sections. It so happened at the Pont du Gard, the section immediately prior was too steep. As a result, the water piled up—so to speak—when it encountered the flatter slope at the bridge. Water spilled over the side."

"Aha," blurted Maurice, "That is the reason they added to the conduit walls at the bridge—so it wouldn't slosh over. I wonder if Appius was embarrassed."

"Appius's log ended after the first water ceremony. We didn't get to hear about the fix, although the water cascade was mentioned, no question about his consternation." I looked at Lisele.

Renat said. "He had nothing to be embarrassed about. He accomplished, with primitive tools and methods, that which would be difficult even with today's equipment." He paused and grinned. "Nevertheless, I can see him standing, hands on hips below the

Pont du Gard, watching a waterfall cascade over the side, telling other observers, 'It is supposed to work like that.' Ha, ha."

Renat, Maurice, and I all smiled, we having been in similar situations and having muttered the same inapt comment. I gave them a moment to savor the irony.

"Did they have other big problems to overcome? I mean, how about their labor? It seems like a project of this size would sap the resources of the region—and beyond." Renat shrugged his shoulders.

"They did indeed have their problems with labor. Early in the project, the military took over and instituted the use of slaves and sent the contractors home—most of them."

Renat winced. "Ooohh. Really? I've always wondered if slaves were used in the construction. Was it mostly built with slaves?"

I shook my head. "No, the military was dismissed when Claudius became Emperor and Appius took over. With the help of Claudius, they freed the slaves although many of them continued to work the project; the contractors were reinstated. But, that wasn't the end of the labor situation. The masons united to demand higher wages. In that situation, Claudius, more cagey than we might have assumed, found a way to make them relent by using public opinion against the masons—actually, Claudius told the citizenry they would end up paying for the higher wages in their water bills."

"Ha, nothing changes. It is the same way today; we just don't realize it." Maurice grinned and reached for another bottle of beer.

We all laughed and shook our heads.

"One visible, remaining indication of the mason's solidarity, if you call it that, is the prevalence of the mason's common inscription, the outline of the mason's hammer."

"You can see them everywhere on the Pont du Gard," Maurice noted.

"Yes, exactly so, although some were inscribed over time, masons through the millennia are showing support for the guild that formed during the construction."

"Oh, Maurice," I said, pointing my finger to the south, "you'll be interested in this. In Appius's log, he described the location of the grounds he used for his home... oh, I didn't tell you, he moved the office, staff and family to Vers during most of the construction."

"Really? I guess it makes sense, being near the Pont du Gard and somewhat in the center of the entire aqueduct." Maurice was nodding his head. "Well, what of it?"

"Yes, as I was saying—Appius gave us a good description of the location of his property, south of the Vers springs, along a line that ran from the springs to the Pont du Gard." I stopped and smiled, letting that sink in with Maurice. Lisele already knew.

Maurice imagined the location, considered what I told him. "No! The estate? It seems impossible that the grounds would be intact after two millennia. How did that happen?"

"I don't know Maurice. It was you who told me that the estate has been maintained, all these years, but nobody seems to know who is responsible. Perhaps that is a mystery *you* might want to solve."

Maurice shook his head. "I'm sure there is a reasonable explanation."

I laughed. "I thought you would enjoy that, and since you are the collector and distributor of lore, ancient and current in the area, you are free to tell the locals your version."

Maurice showed a mischievous smile. Yes, he would have fun with this.

"Here's more local lore for you, Maurice. Appius tells us about encounters with wild boars when he lived here in Vers. It seems that some things don't change much. Lisele was tickled with that thought, as it helps us to understand that our relation to the past is not as remote as we might think."

Renat held up a finger, "Like being able to see the spring at Uzes, the same spring that was the source of their water."

"Yes," Maurice nodded. "But the boar story is a closer touch. I will be happy to pass that on. I may even embellish it, a bit."

"That reminds me," I said. "Appius made the comment that he thought his story, his documents, would be of interest one-hundred years from the time he cached them. I'm sure the thought that they wouldn't appear for two thousand years would have overwhelmed him, much as it does me."

Lisele stood and disappeared into the kitchen. There were sounds of liquids poured, pans scraped, and ovens opened. She appeared at the table, bowed and said, "We have dinner."

"Good," Maurice said. "The beer has given me an appetite. I intend to continue our discussion. I intend to get more lore from you, stories to entertain my friends."

As I responded, we all stood. "Of course, Maurice, there are endless facets that you'll find useful. I only hope that when I hear my story repeated, I'll still recognize a bit of truth."

We all laughed and adjourned to the kitchen to help Lisele stock the table.

We had celebrated. I had shared the experience with my friends. Yet, something else nagged me. I could not explain why, but I craved to see Appius's actual log, the source document. It had something to do with seeing and being in the presence of the ancient document, the document I knew Appius had put his hand to—two thousand years ago. I remembered standing next to a drawing by Leonardo de Vinci at the Smithsonian, knowing that the great master, the genius, had actually laid hands on that very work. It was not cognitive, but something you felt—an emotion. I contacted Professor Durand, via Lisele, to arrange a viewing. There was a bit of confusion as Lisele explained that she was Laurie's mother. It would have been better to have not said anything.

On the phone, I heard Lisele ask the question. There was a pause. Lisele shrugged her shoulders at me. After a moment, she listened, nodded then told me. "It is an unusual request. The documents are protected under an atmosphere of nitrogen, but some pages—significant entries—have been placed under glass, and although stored in a facility that is much like a warehouse, it should be possible to retrieve the display for you to see." Lisele paused, then smiled. "Professor Durand said that after he thought for a while, the request did not seem too troublesome considering that you are responsible for its present existence."

We drove to Nimes. The warehouse was operated by the *Curator of Antiquities—Narbonne region.* They had retrieved the glass panel, nubs on the side for periodic injections of nitrogen, and it was resting on a large table in a well-lit room, a room accustomed to occupants hell-bent on intense scrutiny of ancient works. There were several men whom I did not know, standing in back of the table, smiling. They introduced themselves, shook hands over the table then pointed to the display. Lisele stood at my side.

the *Aedifex*: Building the Pont du Gard

I viewed the log, scribed in ancient writing. I was struck. It was like the moment in the Smithsonian, like a haj to Mecca but with more emotional impact. Appius wrote this.

Then I saw...

APPIUS PETRONIUS AEDIFEX

his signature on one of the pages displayed, presumably the last entry he made. I imagined Appius signing his name on the very piece of paper, standing back and taking a deep breath. I was overwhelmed and emotional, surprising Lisele and bringing delighted smiles to the faces of the observers behind the table. I didn't need to say anything. In fact I couldn't. They understood the depth of meaning and attachment this moment had for me. Perhaps, that the emotion was from an American, overwhelmed by a connection to their heritage, generated some of their delight.

The documents swam before my eyes, now unreadable. I nodded to the men, then to Lisele and we left.

It seemed appropriate after my contact with Appius. Actually it was Lisele's idea, she being more adept at making significant emotional connections. After our trip to Nimes, we drove to the Pont du Gard and walked the paths to the east side of the river, downstream of the structure and to the hut that sells wine, beer and snacks. Around the hut on the spacious deck area were a number of tables and chairs. Others were sitting here and there, several near the river wall, relaxing with a glass of wine, overlooking the Gard, anticipating a beautiful sunset in the warm evening, the Pont du Gard in silhouette. We were there for the same reason, enjoying the display but surely to experience more meaning and significance than the others.

We bought our wine at the hut, opting for the best they had—to emphasize the significance—and headed for tables near the wall, the best viewpoint from the wine garden. Around us were Brits, Yanks, Aussies, the French—of course—and representatives from many other lands, I'm sure. These days, you can't tell by looking.

As we sat and I looked at the Pont du Gard, then the river, something occurred to me. I got up and started walking around, stopping to look at various landmarks, then adjusting my viewpoint by moving again. I must have looked like a fool. Finally I stopped and beckoned Lisele to join me at another table. Although puzzled, she dutifully picked up both wine glasses, her white wine, my red, and walked to where I was rooted.

"What is it, Warner?"

I smiled. "Something occurred to me when we sat, and I looked at the surroundings. Appius gave us a description in detail of the location where they buried his friend Bernius Caelius. Because Appius actually named the structure *Pontis Bernius Caelius*, I thought it fitting that we sit atop his ancient resting place and celebrate the magnificence of the structure he inspired."

After we sat, Lisele nodded, smiled, and held forth her wine glass to me, then turned toward the Pont du Gard, pointing the glass to the structure and said, "To the *Pontis Bernius Caelius*, to Bernius and his friend Appius."

I faced the structure, tipped my glass to it then took a sip. "I wonder what Bernius would think—us saluting him over wine, two thousand years later."

Indeed.

Finis

AUTHOR'S NOTES

My fascination with the Pont du Gard began nearly as described in the first chapter. Upon first sighting, twenty years ago, I was truly shocked that such a magnificent structure existed—still existed, nearly complete. In one moment I experienced the past, understood that a magnificent people existed, two millennia, gone, with the ability to create awesome facilities, and here was the *prima facie* evidence, not to be challenged. I was snapped back to Roman times, at once appreciating the capability, imagination, foresight and effort that existed.

At that time I had recently read Ken Follett's *Pillars of the Earth*. In that spirit of accomplishment and history, I vowed to write a historical novel—building the Pont du Gard.

I spent many hours researching the available information, reading a significant number of fiction and non-fiction works, hoping for glimpses that might aid in my understanding of Roman times and hoping, every so often, for a clue revealing their methods for constructing large projects. I was somewhat surprised to discover many inconsistencies and inaccuracies in the information. Some of it was obvious, but some took additional effort to confirm. Recent theories place the building of the aqueduct somewhat later than the reign of Augustus Caesar, yet references to its building in the Augustan era still abound—Agrippa playing a star role. It appears that the project was built later, probably under the reign of Claudius. That situation works well for several reasons, and, knowing that Claudius had a strong penchant for building great works, it is a good bet. Other inconsistencies abound in matters such as the amount of water carried by the conduit, and, although written material often refers to the chorobate as the leveling device used on the project, a simple math exercise indicates that it could not have been reliable for the work on the Nimes aqueduct. I spent time in my back yard working with a makeshift chorobate. The use of a peephole sight improves the process substantially. Even so, I found it difficult to be accurate within an inch at 100 feet. The neighbors wondered what I was doing. So, the ancient means of accurate level measurement remains a mystery, unless, of course, they used the methods identified in the story.

If the reader should be intrigued to visit the aqueduct and the Pont du Gard, I believe they will find the experience worthwhile if not exhilarating. The museum at the site is well done, with many exhibits arranged to explain devices, terrain, quarry locations, slope and route. In the vicinity of the Pont du Gard, in either direction, you will find trails that parallel the ancient aqueduct, allowing you to see and access remains of the aboveground structures. At the springs near Uzes, the water from the ancient springs, still flows prior to joining the Alzon; the area is a great place for a picnic, and, as in the story, Uzes dining is a delightful experience. In Nimes, the Castellum is a very dramatic encounter, nestled amongst buildings, a survivor of the encroaching civilization.

In the story, Appius, Bernius and crew stop several times at a spa with bubbling water in their search for and investigation of the western water source. That spa is known in modern times as the Perrier source. During my two trips to the area, I did not visit Perrier nor hike to the western springs that Appius found. The springs exist on the topographic maps but otherwise only in my imagination. If anyone should have the time and gumption to visit and locate the springs—they look like they are in a remote area—please fill me in on your adventure.

I am sorry to say, no cache of daily logs or ancient construction documents have been found. Most of the actual history of the works is still shrouded in mystery. However, because a written history does not exist, I have been able to use my imagination to create the story, a great opportunity for me. I hope you have been able to supplement my imagination with yours as you glimpsed how it was, two-thousand years ago, building this inspiring structure.

Thomas Hessler

f

Suggested Reading

Vitruvius: The Ten Books on Architecture (Translation by Morris Hicky Morgan, Harvard Press, 1914), General Publishing Company, 1960, Toronto

Pompeii: A Novel, Robert Harris, Random House

Conspirata, Robert Harris, Simon & Schuster (Cicero)

Imperium: A novel of ancient Rome, Robert Harris, Simon & Schuster (Cicero)

Natural History: A Selection, Penguin Classics (Gaius Plinius Secundus—Pliny the Elder), translated by John F. Healy,

The First Man in Rome, Colleen McCullough, First Avon Books, 1991

Augustus: The Life of Rome's First Emperor, Anthony Everett, Random House

The Pont du Gard. Water and the Roman Town, Paris, 1992 Fabre, G., Luc-Fiches, J., Leveau, P. & Louis Paillet, J.,

Rome, M. Rostovtzeff, Oxford University Press, 1960

ABOUT THE AUTHOR

Thomas Hessler was of fortunate circumstance to write this story. Background in the engineering and construction of large projects is necessary to appreciate and understand the challenges faced and operations required of the Romans in undertaking large civil projects. Yes, there are many out there, capable of understanding such. However, of those with that understanding, if you ask those that are writers to step forward, you have whittled the number down to a few. The capstone of this circumstance is to be fascinated by the works of the Romans and reverence for the Pont du Gard. Thomas feels privileged to take on one more project—writing this story.

Thomas spent much of his career involved in large project construction—the conceptual process, funding, design, bidding, construction and initial operation—the estimating, scheduling, contract negotiations, cost control and labor management. That all this occurred in the twentieth century is notable, but Thomas was able to apply that understanding to means available to the Romans.

Thomas has served as a consultant, evaluating construction operations for the cities of Los Angeles and San Francisco. He has been an adjunct professor, instructing in the construction management program for California State University, Sacramento.

Thomas writes from his home in Carmichael, California, finding time to do so amongst other activities of jazz piano, hiking, and researching foreign lands for topics of fascination. *The Aedifex: Building the Pont du Gard* is his second published novel, following *the Caucasus: a Novel* published in 2011. Contact Thomas at txhessler@comcast.net.

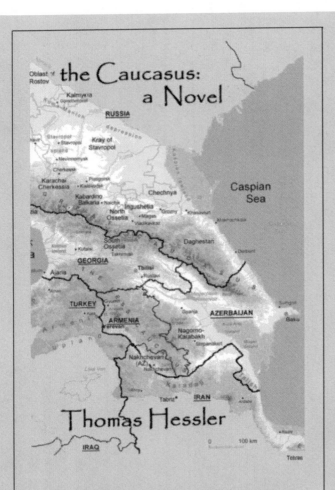

the Caucasus:
a Novel

Thomas Hessler

Read "the Caucasus: a Novel" by Thomas Hessler, published in 2011.
The Iranians finally develop a deliverable nuclear weapon and are hell-bent
on causing turmoil in the region a problem which the USA National Security
Advisor and Administration must handle.

"The Caucasus" received 24 of 25 points in the 2012 Writer's Digest
competition. "The Caucasus is available via Amazon and Kindle.

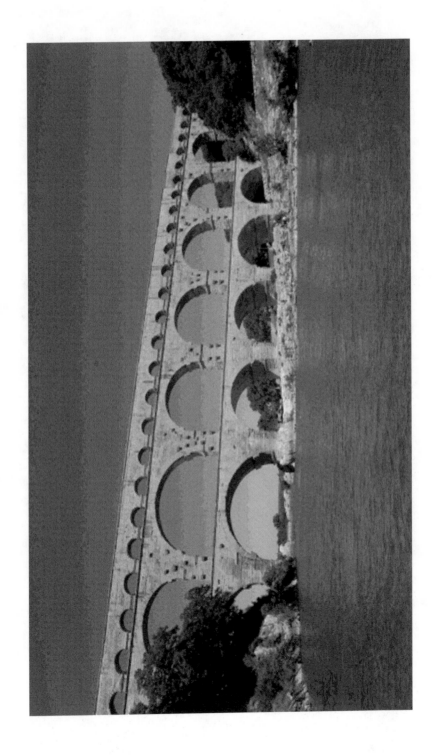

Castellum--Nimes

Photo by Jacqueline Conway

Aqueduct remains near Vers

Photo by Jacqueline Conway

Underground Section at Uzes Diversion Structure

Made in the USA
Columbia, SC
02 November 2023

25396843R00372